BARBARA ERSKINE

The Warrior's Princess

HARPER

Harper
An imprint of HarperCollins*Publishers*
77–85 Fulham Palace Road,
Hammersmith, London W6 8JB

www.harpercollins.co.uk

This paperback edition 2009
1

First published in Great Britain by
HarperCollins*Publishers* 2008

A catalogue record for this book is
available from the British Library

ISBN: 978 0 00 717429 4

Set in Meridien by Palimpsest Book Production Limited,
Grangemouth, Stirlingshire

Printed and bound in Great Britain by
Clays Ltd, St Ives plc

For Liz Graham and for Brian Taylor
In memory of happy conversations much missed

Prologue

In her dream Jess was standing on the track near the wood. In front of her the gnarled, ancient oaks and taller, stately ash stood in a solid silhouette against the moonlit sky. Behind her, her sister's white-painted stone-built farmhouse lay sleeping in the warm silence of the summer night, bathed in moonlight, pots of lavender and rosemary mingling their sweet fragrance with that of the wild mountain thyme in the still air.

'Where are you?' The child's voice was clear in the silence, coming from deep within the trees. 'Are we still playing the game?'

In answer the leaves of the trees rustled in the gentle breeze.

'Hello?' Jess took a step towards the wood. From where she was standing she couldn't see the track which led into its depths.

There was no reply.

Jess moved closer to the trees. 'Are you there?' A slight chill played across her skin and she felt herself shiver.

Behind her the house was silent. The windows dark. She had been aware, seconds before, that there were people there, asleep. Her sister. Her sister's friends. Her own friends. Now she knew in the calm logic of her dream that the house was empty. The curtainless windows were blankly staring eyes and the hearth was cold.

'Where are you?' The child's voice was closer now. She could hear the fear in it.

'I'm here.' Jess ran a few steps closer to the wood. 'Follow my voice. I'm here. On the track!'

She could hear the wind in the valley now, its gentle murmur growing louder as the branches of the trees began to move. The sound was coming closer, the whisper turning into a roar. She could feel the cold on her face. Then in her hair. Across the broad valley moonshadows raced across the dark swell of the hills.

'Come to me, sweetheart. You don't want to be caught in the storm. You'll be safe here with me. We'll go and hide in the house!'

She was shouting now as loudly as she could, hurling the words towards the thrashing branches.

Then she saw her in the moonlight as the black clouds raced up the valley towards her. A girl with pale, flaxen hair, a long dress, colourless in the whirling shadows, her feet bare, her arms outstretched in desperation, her eyes huge in her frightened face.

'Come on, sweetheart! I'm here!' Jess was running towards her. She was only feet away now. In a second she would be able to reach the child, to draw her into her arms to safety.

The moon vanished for a second. When it reappeared the squall had passed. The night was silent. The girl was no longer there.

'Jess?' The voice behind her was her sister's. 'Jess! Come inside. You shouldn't be out in the dark alone.'

In her sleep Jess turned over and reached for her pillow. Tears were trickling down her cheeks. Already the dream was gone.

1

The curtains were open. There were voices in her head. A lost child, crying; two children. Three ...

For a while Jess lay completely still staring, puzzled, at the narrow beam of sunlight as it moved slowly across the painting on the wall. Her painting. Her picture of the woods behind her sister's house with the leaves touched to fire by the first frosts of autumn. There were magentas there and crimsons she did not remember seeing before, though she herself had painted it. Extraordinary, beautiful details; nuances of shadow that without that spotlight she had never fully appreciated. Why? Why hadn't she studied it properly like this before? Why had she not looked at it in its full glory?

And where were the children?

Moving her head to glance out of the window a dizzying wave of nausea overwhelmed her. She groaned, the picture and the dream forgotten. Outside the window she could hear the roar of traffic in the distance as it surged up towards the lights at the High Street crossroads, briefly stopped and surged on again. When she dared to open her eyes again the sunlight had moved on and the picture was once more in its accustomed shadow.

Raising herself with difficulty she squinted at her bedside clock. 'Shit!' It was midday. No wonder everything in the room looked different. With a groan she swung her legs over the side of the bed, her head spinning. How much had she had to drink the night before? Levering herself upright she caught sight of herself in the mirror and stared, appalled. Her blonde, shoulder-length hair was straggly, her eyes, normally a clear blue-grey, were bloodshot and slightly swollen. Her gaze moved on down her body and she froze with horror. The pretty new blouse she had worn to the party was torn almost in two; her bra had been dragged down below her breasts; her skirt had been pulled up around her waist. Looking down at herself disbelievingly she ran a finger over the livid bruise on her thigh, the raw scratch across her belly. There were more bruises on her arms.

'Oh God! What's happened to me?'

The words hung soundlessly in the room as she stared back at her reflection. Staggering slightly, she made her way to the door of the bedroom and clinging to the frame, she peered through. There on the coffee table in the living room were two wine glasses, stained with the dregs of red wine. The empty bottle was lying under the table. Whoever had been in the flat with her the night before, there was no one there now; nor in the kitchen, nor in the bathroom. The front door was closed. With shaking hands she examined the locks. No one had broken in. Whoever had been in here with her had not forced an entry. She must have asked them in.

She had been at the end of term party at school, that much she could recall vaguely. Beyond that, nothing. What had she had to drink while she was there? Where had she gone after the disco? Who had she been with? She could remember nothing.

The end of term disco had been in full swing when she had arrived. The sixth form college sports hall was a whirl of spinning lights and the noise astronomic. She stood in the double doorway, open to the humid air of the summer night, reluctant to step inside. She wanted to clap her hands to her ears, she wanted to turn and run, anything but plunge into the heavy mass of perspiring bodies with the overpowering smell of cheap scent, aftershave, stale tobacco, weed, sweat and booze. They hadn't managed to frisk all the kids then. But what was the point. They were selling drink inside the hall and half of them were legally allowed to drink anyway.

'Hi, Jess!' A figure emerged out of the heaving darkness. Dan Nicolson, her head of department, stepped out onto the tarmacked parking area outside the hall and gave her a weary grin. 'I'm getting too old for this!' His lurid T-shirt belied his words; this was the one night of the year he let himself be seen at the college without more formal attire.

She laughed. 'I've always been too old for it, Dan. Since the day I was born. You're looking very cool.' His short mouse-coloured hair had been brushed to stand upright, his brown eyes were hidden by a pair of designer shades. 'I hear you've drawn the short straw. You've got to stay to the bitter end?'

'And tear the copulating kids apart!' He glanced heavenwards. 'Unless I can persuade someone else to do it. Can I get you a drink?' He pushed the glasses up onto the top of his head.

She nodded. The wave of noise coming out of the doors was too loud to fight. What it was like inside she could imagine all too well, but she had promised she would come and she had promised someone a dance. Ashley. Ash was her most promising pupil, the most promising for years. Destined to get Grade A in every subject he was taking, this young Jamaican was someone in whom she had invested a huge amount of time and effort and she could see him even now in the distance with his mixing desks on the stage, cranking up the volume. All she had to do was make sure he had seen her there, wave, raise her thumb in acknowledgement, shrug to show that there was no need to dance, something that was anyway all but impossible in that wall to wall crowd, then she could slip away.

As Dan disappeared towards the bar somewhere in the depths of the hall, another colleague appeared at her side. 'Hi, Jess!' Will Matthews grimaced at the noise. 'We'll be in trouble for this with the neighbours.' He gestured towards the doors of the hall with a half-empty bottle of lager.

She and this tall, good-looking blonde-haired man had been an item for most of the three years she had taught English literature at North Woodley Sixth Form College in south London. Most, but not now. Will was senior master in the history department. He also coached basket ball, squash and athletics. In an open-necked blue shirt, jeans and a heavily engraved and studded leather belt he was, she noticed, the target of several pairs of lustful eyes amongst his teenage girl pupils.

She and Will had been a perfect couple in so many ways, but there had always been something between them that was not quite right. Will's ambition, perhaps; his assumption, engendered courtesy of an adoring mother and two younger sisters, that he was irresistible, his tendency to assume that his work, his career, his opinions all took precedence over hers, his probably unintentionally patronising attitude to the study of literature as a career and to her undoubted talent as a water colourist. That had all rankled with her and when he had asked her to move in with him she had realised that on top of all those irritations, she couldn't bear to lose her independence, however much they loved each other. That had started them on the slippery slope towards the break up.

There wasn't another woman, at least she had never heard that there was anyone. It was purely his refusal to compromise and acknowledge her autonomy that had finally come between them, ended their relationship over the course of two or three short weeks and left her angry and uncomprehending and Will unhappy and bitter. After their acrimonious parting they had avoided each other completely, hard to do within the college, but still perfectly possible if they both worked at it. Which they had done. Until now.

'Come on, Jess. What about a dance for old times' sake?' He grinned at her winningly.

She frowned. 'I don't think so, Will.'

'Oh, come on. To show there are no hard feelings? End of term. Good results, please God! Then you need never see me again!'

She raised an eyebrow. 'Why? Are you leaving?'

He laughed. 'You wish! No, but I promise I shall avoid you next term like the plague itself.'

She fought the urge to smile back. That smile of his had always been her downfall. It was too charming; too persuasive; too attractive by far. She had to fight it. 'Let's go on avoiding each other now, Will, shall we? Excuse me. I need to say hello to Ash.' Not letting him see the longing inside her, the temptation which was still so strong, she gave him a strained, apologetic shrug and turned away. Taking a last breath of fresh air she plunged into the seething mass of dancing bodies, leaving Will staring after her.

As soon as he saw her Ashley stood back from his music mixing, nodded to his younger brother Max, on stage beside him, to take over and leaped down from the stage. 'Come and dance, Jess!' He was laughing, his handsome face running with perspiration, his bright shirt soaked, his hands reaching for hers, pulling her fists up into the air, then releasing her, positioned and ready for the dance as he gyrated, hips swivelling in front of her. She shouldn't laugh. She should reprimand him for calling her Jess, but what was the point? School was over in every real sense. Exams were finished. The night was hot and enticing and all these young people were enjoying themselves. Surely she could let her hair down too. She danced with Ashley, she danced with several other pupils, and she danced with Brian Barker, the Head of the college, and finally, she was at last unbent enough to dance with Will – it had seemed too much effort to refuse. She drank Dan's fruit punch. Then some more with a shot of staff-only extra-bite! She danced with Dan again and then with Ashley one last time. It was in the early hours that the disco broke up at last after a second visit from the police.

Ashley had been waiting for her outside the hall.

After that she remembered nothing. Making herself a cup of coffee with shaking hands, she sipped it slowly. Who would she have asked in to share a glass of wine so late at night? There had been no other relationship after Will. She fancied no one, especially not any of her colleagues at school. Not now. She was not the type to ask a casual acquaintance to come back with her and fall into bed with him. And no one, absolutely no one she knew would have hurt her and left her in this state.

Cudgelling her brain as she sipped more coffee, she remembered Ash leaping from the bonnet of a car onto its roof and declaiming, his fists raised to the stars. Shakespeare. He was quoting Shakespeare, this boy she had so carefully nurtured in her class, this boy who led his own team of street actors and who had a secret dream to go to RADA, a dream to be an actor on a West End stage, to defy his background, his absent father, his drug-taking brothers, to confirm his mother's quiet determination to believe in him. He had yelled the speech to the world and then, laughing, had jumped down and swept a courtly bow in front of her. 'Let me walk you home, Jess!' She could hear his voice now, resounding in her ears.

Then nothing.

Her memories from that point were gone. Her flat was a half-hour walk from the school but she didn't remember crossing the main road still with its heavy traffic long after midnight; nor walking down the busy street, half the shops still open to the hot July night air. Nor turning down into the terraced square with its tiny precious oasis of dusty bushes and trees in the centre behind the protective spiked railings with a raft of tossed litter inside them. Nor opening the front door, nor climbing the stairs, and unlocking the door into her flat and going in and presumably offering her escort another drink.

No, not Ashley. Please let it not have been Ashley.

It had to have been Ashley. People had warned her. They had said he could be violent. They had said he had become too familiar, too physical around her. But she had ignored them. She knew best. She had seen his potential and nothing was going to stand in the way of her ambition for him.

If it was Ashley, was it her fault? Had she encouraged him to make love to her? 'No!' The word came out as an agonised whisper. 'No, I wouldn't have. I couldn't have.' Gingerly she fingered the bruises on her arms. Whoever had done this to her had forced himself on her and had held her down. That wasn't love, it was rape.

She stood for a long time under the shower, aware that she should not be doing this; that if she had been raped, she should call the police; that she should preserve whatever evidence lurked inside her body, but knowing at the same time, as she scrubbed herself raw, that she could never bring herself to go through the awfulness of the police process. One of her students had had to do it once and she had gone with the girl to the cold impersonal room where the teenager had been questioned and examined and eventually disbelieved. Jess shuddered at the memory. She would never put herself through that. Never. She could feel herself slowly beginning to burn with anger. However much she had been made to drink, even if she had been drugged to make her acquiesce and then forget, she would find out who had done this to her and she would make sure he paid for it.

Sitting on the edge of the sofa, huddled in her bathrobe, she could feel herself starting to shake again as in her head she went over and over the facts that she could remember. Had she asked Ash in? She had danced with him several times, after all. She had had another drink. Then another. Who had given them to her? She couldn't remember. Obviously she had drunk too much but had they been laced with something? Had she, in whatever state she was in, agreed to sex? Enjoyed it? Her hands were clammy. She could feel a wave of nausea building somewhere under her ribcage. The room was starting to spin again.

She became aware suddenly of the sound of steps on the

8

staircase outside running up towards her flat. Scrambling to her feet she ran to the front door, rammed the bolt across and slotted the chain into its keep then slowly, shaking with the kind of fear she had never in her life experienced before, she slid to the floor, tears pouring down her face as she leaned backwards against the wall, hugging the white towelling robe around her. Outside, the footsteps ran on up past her door without stopping and the sound disappeared somewhere on the upper floors.

In the end she fell asleep where she was, on the floor, her back against the wall.

When she woke it was to the sound of knocking. The door handle turned. Holding her breath she looked up at it, her stomach churning.

'Jess, are you there?' It was Will's voice. 'Jess, are you OK? Look, I wanted to apologise for last night. I behaved like an idiot. I'm sorry.' There was a long pause, then she heard a deep sigh. 'Jess? Are you there? What's wrong?' There was another pause. Then an angry exclamation. 'I'll see you on Monday for clearing up, OK, Jess?' She heard him turn away from the door, then his footsteps as he ran down the stairs and the bang of the street door behind him. Then silence.

He had behaved like an idiot.

How had he behaved like an idiot?

Surely it could not have been Will. They had quarrelled in the past, even before that last break up. They had done more than quarrel. They had fought. But he wouldn't force her against her wishes. Would he?

Could he have followed her and Ash home? If he had he could have let himself in. She was certain he still had a key in spite of his insistence that he had returned it to her. They had danced last night in the end. More than once. She could remember that. She'd felt his arms around her for a moment with such loving familiarity, felt herself relax into them. It was Will who, after a few minutes, had drawn away and moved alone to the music leaving her to dance by herself.

With a weary sigh she closed her eyes.

Much later she heard Mrs Lal from the ground floor flat open her door and go out, her slippers slapping on the steps. She was going to the corner shop; no need for proper shoes then. In spite of her misery Jess gave a fond smile. Sometimes the old lady would call up and see if Jess would like her to fetch a Sunday paper or some milk, but not today. Today there was silence; perhaps she had heard Will rattling her door and thought Jess must be out.

Climbing stiffly to her feet, she went over to the window and looked down. Mrs Lal was walking slowly down the road, a blue cardigan pulled over her sari, her grey hair clamped into an untidy bun. As Jess watched she saw the old lady hesitate and slow down suddenly and cross over the road. Jess frowned, wondering why. Then she saw them. Two black youths loitering by the gate into the square. She watched them for a moment, her throat growing dry. One of them was Ash. The other his elder brother, Zac. They stood staring at poor Mrs Lal, obviously enjoying her discomfort. She saw Zac call out and the old lady moved more quickly, hurrying away from them towards the shop. Perhaps she should go down and chase them away. What were they doing here anyway? The boys lived on the Constable Estate on the far side of the school. Almost as though he was conscious she was watching him she saw Ash move suddenly. He stepped out into the road where she could see him more easily and perhaps he could see her, and she saw him sketch once more the elaborate theatrical courtly bow in her direction. She saw Zac laugh and aim a half-hearted kick at his brother's head, before Ash blew a kiss towards her house and both boys turned away, loping non-chalantly towards the Underground station and the busy High Street.

Jess backed away from the window. He couldn't have seen her. It was much too far away. And he didn't know where she lived. Correction: he wasn't supposed to know where she lived. She felt herself grow ice-cold. He had done it. It was Ash and he was mocking her. Oh God, what was she to do? He was telling her what he had done; gloating; knowing she could never nail him for it. Daring her to try. That was why he bowed. Her best student. She had thought she'd won his trust and respect and this was how he had repaid her.

She phoned Brian Barker with her resignation on Monday morning. She told him she was ill; too stressed to teach any

10

more. She cut off his protests by switching off her phone. Then she went to the doctor who confirmed that her memory loss could well be the effect of some kind of drug. She had gone for the morning after pill. She had not thought of the HIV test, the other tests the doctor insisted on; the doctor's worried glance as she examined her. 'If you don't know who it was, Jess,' she said gently, 'you cannot take chances. The bruises, the muscle stiffness. You obviously weren't a willing participant in this. You are right, you were raped and you should go to the police.' On that point Jess had not changed her mind. She spent the rest of the day huddled in a miasma of depression and self-pity.

The doorbell rang at just after five. This time she opened it. It was Dan. After a moment's hesitation at the sight of her white face, he strode past her straight into the sitting room, taking a seat in the armchair near the window. 'So, what's this I hear about you resigning? You can't! The school needs you. I need you in my department. Besides, you have to give a term's notice.'

'I told Brian I was ill,' she said after a moment's pause.

'And are you?' He was scrutinising her face carefully.

She shrugged. 'No. Yes. I have my reasons, Dan. I'm sorry to let you down.' She met his gaze defiantly, then at last looked away. She had perched uncomfortably on the edge of the chair opposite him.

'You are my best literature teacher. You've done wonders. You're part of the team, Jess,' he said carefully. 'Can't you tell me why you want to go?' He narrowed his eyes, still studying her.

She shook her head. 'I'm sorry.' She shivered in spite of the warmth of the afternoon drifting in through the window with the roar of distant traffic from the High Street.

'Come on. I need a reason. What can be so bad? Is it Will? I saw him pestering you at the dance.'

She shrugged.

'Jess?' He moved forward and reached out to put a hand on her knee as she sat across from him.

She flinched at his touch and he frowned, sitting back. 'What's wrong?'

She shook her head.

'It was Will, wasn't it? He did something to upset you.' He stood

11

up and took a few paces across the floor and back again. 'Did he hurt you?'

She shook her head. She couldn't tell him. She couldn't tell anyone what had happened.

'It was Will, wasn't it?' Dan repeated. 'I've never trusted that arrogant bastard!'

'He's got nothing to do with it, Dan.' She was shredding a tissue.

'You were quarrelling with him at the disco. I saw you.'

'Not seriously.'

'It looked pretty serious to me.' He narrowed his eyes. There was a moment of silence. 'Why did you and Will break up?'

'That's none of your business, Dan. I don't want to talk about this.'

'He looked pretty pissed off when you left after the disco. He could have followed you and Ashley home.' There was another long moment of silence. 'It was Ashley! Ashley did something!' Dan said softly at last. 'The little bastard! What happened, Jess?'

'Nothing.' She clenched her fists. 'Leave it, Dan.'

There was another pause. She was picturing Ash, by the railings near the gate to the square. The bow. The arrogant way he had looked up at the window of her flat. The blown kiss. She tried to force the image out of her head, but it refused to go. She had danced with him. She liked him; she had encouraged him. Perhaps she had given him the wrong idea. She sighed miserably. He was a lad with so much potential, set to get top grades. If she accused him and she was wrong and it wasn't him a police enquiry would destroy him anyway. It would never go away.

'So, you've made up your mind.' Dan gave up asking questions. 'You are definitely going to leave?' He was watching her so closely she felt he was reading her mind. She nodded.

He continued to look at her for several seconds in silence. 'OK. I'll make it right with Brian.' He seemed to have decided not to argue with her any more. 'Don't worry, you'll get a brilliant reference, I'll see to that, if that's what you want. Looking on the bright side, you'll probably get a fantastic position in some private girls' school. Just right for you.' He gave a small sharp laugh and she frowned at the sudden bitterness of his tone. 'Take the summer off, Jess,' he went on. 'Forget all about whatever it was that has upset you so much and start again in the autumn!' Leaning forward, he patted her knee again. 'Whatever it was, Jess, get over it. Don't think about it. Put it all behind you.'

2

Stephanie Kendal was seated at the work table, painting designs onto a tray of small ornate mugs ready for the final glaze. Glancing up at the window, she frowned. The sunlight had gone from the garden. Long shadows were advancing across the grass towards the studio where she sat listening to the radio. Leaning forward she turned it off. In the sudden silence she could hear a thrush singing in the distance through the open door. Slightly shorter, slightly plumper and slightly older than her sister, Jessica, there was a definite family likeness in the two women, inherited from their mother. From Aurelia Kendal they also took their love of literature, their artistic talent, their charm and their unconventionality. As a reaction against their mother's decision to live as a hermit in a small cottage in the wilds of the Basses-Pyrénées when she was not bestriding the world in her capacity as travel writer and journalist, both her daughters had gravitated to inner London after graduation and teacher's training college. Jess was still there. Steph had caved in, turned her back on the bright lights and spent her latest divorce settlement on this Welsh dream, a small mountain farmhouse not very far from the place where her mother had once lived before she had decided to swap the hills of Wales for the mountains of France.

But she wasn't sure any more if she had done the right thing.

Setting down her brush she reached for a paint rag and wiped her fingers, frowning a little as she did so. The sound had been so small she had barely heard it over the music on the radio. A click, no more, from the far side of the studio.

She scanned the shelves of pottery, the bags of clay, the jars of glaze, the tins of paint on the table by the wall. The rough stones of the old byre were white-washed, the medieval window slits glazed, the crook beams high above her head brushed, with here and there an ornate iron hook from which were suspended the light fittings and a glass mobile which jingled faintly in the draught, a gift from one of her many admirers. There it was again. A click, followed by a rattle. A bird or an animal must have come in through the open door while she was working and be poking around on the shelves. Quietly she pushed back her tall stool and stood up.

Several minutes of careful searching produced no clue as to the source of the noise but she was feeling more and more uneasy. She could sense something or someone there. Watching her. She could feel the stare of eyes on the back of her neck.

'Hello?' Her voice even to herself sounded nervous.

Going to the door she stared out. The byre sat at right angles to the house with its white-washed walls and roof of old Welsh slate, joined to the kitchen by a newly built passageway. The door at which she was standing led directly outside into the L-shaped former farmyard where her car sat surrounded by terracotta pots of lavender and rosemary. She frowned. The total isolation of this old mountain farmhouse had been one of its attractions when she bought the place and mostly she adored the quietness, though admittedly the peace was often short-lived as a succession of friends came through her doors. But lately, when she was on her own, something had begun to unsettle her. This feeling that she was being watched. That someone or something was in the house with her. Not a human being. She could deal with that, she reckoned. No, it was something more subtle. More sinister. It wasn't the noises, although she found herself listening constantly, aware of them even over the sound of the radio. No, it was something else.

She turned back into the studio and caught her breath. Just for a fraction of a second a shadow had moved near the back table. She blinked and it was gone. Or had never been there at all.

Outside she heard a crow calling as it flew across the valley, its shadow a swift flick across the warm stones of the yard. That was what she had seen. The shadow of a bird. Relieved, she turned to go back into the house just as in the kitchen the phone began to ring.

'Steph, it's Kim.' The bubbly voice seemed to fill the place with sunshine. 'Have you thought about my invitation? Come to Rome, Steph. Please. You can work here! Whatever you like. I'm rattling round in this apartment on my own. All my friends have gone away for the summer, it's weeks before I'm leaving for the Lakes and I need you!'

Steph glanced uncomfortably over her shoulder at the door which led to the studio. When Kim had first issued her invitation she had hesitated. Rome in summer would be unbearably hot and noisy. Kim, widowed after less than ten years of marriage to her wonderful, too-good-to-be-true, adoring older man and ensconced in her beautiful flat in a palazzo, no less, and with his considerable fortune all to herself, just could not be as desolate as she made out. But then again perhaps she was and perhaps the lure of Rome was too exciting to ignore. After all, what had Steph to lose? At most a week or so's production of her pots. Less, if she and Kim no longer got on as they had in the old days when they were all at college together. Half an hour later she had switched on her computer, booked her flight and was already rifling through her cupboard for her case.

Jess smiled ruefully as her sister's voice rattled on until finally there was a pause.

'Jess? Are you there? Aren't you pleased for me? You knew Kim and I had kept in touch, didn't you.' Already there was a lilt of Wales in Steph's voice.

'That's fantastic, Steph. Only . . .' Jess grimaced. 'Only, I was going to ask if I could come to Ty Bran to stay for a bit over the summer. I'm fed up with London and a bit desperate for a break. I want to go somewhere no one can find me. I want some peace to do some painting. Maybe rethink my lifestyle. I'm considering a career change. See if I can hack it as a painter.' No point in telling her the real reason, spoiling Steph's day; no point in making her feel she should cancel her holiday.

'But that's brilliant!' Steph's excitement dulled her usually perceptive reading of her sister's moods. 'Come here and welcome. In fact I'd be really pleased to have someone look after the place. My pot plants will need watering. If you come, that's perfect! You can have some peace to do all the painting and thinking you want!'

Putting down the phone Jess sat for a moment staring towards the window. Was she doing the right thing? She was allowing someone to chase her out of the job she loved; out of the flat she adored, out of the city she had come to enjoy and she was allowing him to think he had got off Scot free. He had got off Scot free. There would be no police. No identification. No repercussions for him at all.

As the sunlight shone in through the window, focusing on her pale green patterned rug, illuminating in minute detail each small criss-crossed shape of the design, she heard the downstairs door bang and footsteps on the stairs. She held her breath. Slowly the steps grew closer, steady, loud, masculine. She swallowed, sweat breaking out between her shoulder blades. Had she locked her front door? Surely she had. She had become obsessive about it. She sat, unable to move, her eyes fixed on the door handle, hearing the sound reverberate round the flat. The steps reached the landing outside and she heard them stop. For a moment there was total silence, then slowly the steps began again, walking up towards the next flight. Only then did she realise that she had stopped breathing altogether. She was shaking from head to foot. Jumping to her feet, she went out into the hallway and checked the chain on the door. It was safely in place, as was the bolt and the dead-lock. It was then, as usual, that her fear was replaced by anger. He had done this to her! No one ... no one had the right to terrorise her like this, to make her feel vulnerable, threatened, in her own home! It was outrageous. She hated the man who had done this to her, and she hated herself for having been made a victim. She would not be a victim. Somehow she had to regain her confidence.

It was better outside. She felt safe on the bustling, noisy street and in the crowded shops and sitting over a latte at a table outside one of the little pavement cafés, watching the pigeons plodding fearlessly amongst the feet of passers by, dodging between the wheels of buggies and bicycles. The pub across the road was festooned with banners, shredded by the winter wind and still hanging there months later. *Two meals for the price of one. Watch today's match here.*

Crowds of people waited in front of her to cross the road, constrained by the railing which stopped them spilling into the traffic. The lights changed, they flowed across; behind them another group built up again. Above her head, a tattered silver balloon hung like a dead bird in the branches of a tree, flapping amongst

17

the leaves. At the end of the road the traffic whirled on an endless choreographed dance around the mini roundabout. She sipped her coffee, reluctant to move. The noise was unstoppable; deafening. Engines; music; the cooing of pigeons on the ledges of the buildings high above her head; people talking and laughing and shouting and swearing; the warning siren of a reversing lorry; mobiles ringing every few seconds, their insistent ring tones an endless selfish cacophony against escalating raucous yells.

Here, she used to feel safe; at home. Suddenly she hated it all. What she wanted was silence.

Methodically she began packing up, sorting out the paperwork, loosening her ties to school and friends. Only for the summer, she explained. Just going away to be on my own for a bit. Taking the chance to do some painting. She didn't say where she was going. Made it sound mysterious. Fun. Lonely. It wasn't going to be for ever. She loved the flat. She didn't want to sell it. She just needed space. Somewhere safe. Somewhere he couldn't find her.

When the phone rang as she came in through the front door she answered it unsuspectingly, expecting it to be the headmaster's secretary, Jane, with yet more red tape to sort out. 'Hello?' She was juggling handset, handbag, shopping, unloading her stuff on the table, the front door still open behind her.

'How are you, Jess? Recovered yet?' The voice was muffled; deep. She didn't recognise it.

'Who's that?' Her carrier bags had fallen to the floor. Turning she walked the two strides to the door and slammed it shut, reaching for the chain to ram into its slot. 'Will, is that you?' He had rung two or three times and she had refused to speak to him.

There was no reply. For several seconds the line stayed open; she could sense him, whoever he was, there, listening. Then he hung up.

Her hand was slippery with sweat as she put down the receiver. She sat down at the table, her head in her hands, trying to steady her breathing. Ring the police. She should ring the police now. But how could she? She had made her decision not to tell anyone and she was going to stick with it. Abruptly she sat up and reaching for the handset again dialled 1471, her hands shaking. The caller had withheld his number.

Half an hour later the phone rang again. She stood staring down at it for several seconds before she answered.

'Jess? I wanted to check you'd received all the bumph from the Head's secretary.' It was Dan. He was calling from school. When she didn't answer immediately his voice sharpened. 'Jess, what is it? What's happened?'

'I've been having calls, Dan. When I answer there is no one there. This time he asked how I was. Then he hung up.'

'Did you recognise his voice?'

'No.'

'So it wasn't Will?'

'No, I don't think so. I don't know. You didn't say anything to Will about where I'm going, did you, Dan?' Dan was the only person she had told; after all, he had known Steph as long as he had known her. They had all been at college together.

'You made me promise not to.'

'And I meant it.' Jess bit her lip.

'If it wasn't Will,' he said slowly, 'it could have been Ash.'

She breathed deeply for a moment. 'No. Yes. I don't know.'

'Ash is an actor. He is quite capable of disguising his voice, Jess. OK, so he shouldn't know your phone number. Anyone could find it though. He could have looked while he was in your flat.' There was a pause. 'He was in your flat, wasn't he, Jess?' When she didn't reply he went on. 'Or he could have looked it up in Jane's office here. I know the kids aren't supposed ever to get in here, but they do.'

She nodded numbly.

'Do you want me to come over?'

'No. No, Dan. Don't worry. I'm OK.'

'Well, you know where I am if you need me. When are you going?'

'In a day or two. As soon as I've sorted all the paperwork.'

'All right, take care. I'll ring you tomorrow, OK?'

Her case was lying open on her bed. She was folding the last of her clothes into it when the phone rang again. She paused for a moment, her heart thumping then she leaned across to her bedside table to pick it up. There was no one there.

'Hello?' She started to shake. 'Who is it? You may as well tell me! Ash, is it you?' There was no answer. 'Hello!' She shook the receiver. 'Hello! Who is there?'

There was a quiet laugh the other end of the line. Male voice. Deep. Anonymous.

She dropped the receiver back on its base with a whimper of fear. The bastard was enjoying this. Well, she wasn't going to give him the satisfaction. She glanced at her watch. She could leave tonight. Now. There was nothing to keep her here a moment longer. She had even found a tenant for a few weeks to look after the flat. And if she left now she could catch up with Steph before she left for Rome. She would be safe in Wales. No one would find her there. She glanced at her mobile. He hadn't rung her on that so far. Hopefully he didn't know that number which was another reason to think it wasn't Will. Will knew her mobile number; he knew Steph's address – he had even been to Ty Bran. He knew everything there was to know about her. It couldn't be Will who was tormenting her. If it was, she was lost. He would guess at once where she had gone.

Dan was the weak link in her plan. The only person who knew where she was really going. He answered at the third ring.

'Dan, if anyone asks, tell them I'm going to Italy to spend the summer with Steph and Kim, OK?'

She smiled grimly as she heard Dan laugh. After all, it might even be true. If Kim didn't mind maybe she would follow Steph there. And just in case, it would do no harm to throw her passport into her bag.

Closing her case she stood it by the front door. The contents of the fridge went into a cardboard box and a cool bag; the papers scattered across her desk into her briefcase with her laptop, and beside that her two beleaguered house plants with her artists' materials and sketchbooks too long abandoned for lack of time, already in another cardboard box.

Cautiously she opened the door and peered out onto the landing. She had already dropped off a spare key with Mrs Lal who had promised to keep an eye on the flat for her until the tenant arrived. Her car was parked two streets away. Picking her keys up off the kitchen counter she ran down the stairs. It was early yet and the streets were still bathed in sunshine as people made their way home from work. She could hear music echoing above the sound of traffic and smell the smoky spiciness of cooking meat from the tandoori restaurant near the tube station.

Someone, probably Mrs Lal, had left the street door on the

latch. She hesitated, looking left and right along the street, then pulled it to, leaving it unlocked for the old lady as she hurried round the square to find her car. It was hemmed in tightly as usual and the roof had been liberally splattered with bird droppings from the plane tree under which she had parked it. With careful manoeuvring she managed to extricate it and drive back to her flat leaving it double-parked outside. The street door was still open. Frowning, she glanced up and down the road. She couldn't see Mrs Lal or any of the upstairs people. There was a gang of boys hanging around on the corner, some builders packing ladders and paint pots into a van; two African girls in bright dresses were giggling at them; beyond them she could see a couple of women in black headscarves. No one was near her door; no one who would have been into her house. Pushing the door open carefully, she looked into the hallway. All was quiet. She ran up, taking the stairs two at a time and stopped on the first floor landing which was in deep shadow, the lightbulb broken yet again.

'Hello?' she called out nervously. 'Is there anyone there?'

There was no reply.

With a shaking hand she groped in her pocket for her keys. Before she tried to slot the first into the lock her door swung open. Holding her breath she looked in. Her bags and boxes were still standing in a line where she had left them. The flat was silent but something had changed. Someone had been there; she could sense it. Smell it. She sniffed. Aftershave. And sweat.

'Will?' It wasn't the brand he used, but he was the only person she knew of with a key. Unless she had left the door open. But she hadn't. She knew she hadn't. Had she? 'Will, are you there?' she enquired shakily – she was poised, ready to run.

There was no reply.

Cautiously she peered into the living room. There was a large bouquet of flowers lying on the coffee table.

Her heart seemed to stop beating. Frozen, like a rabbit in the headlights, she stared round the room.

'Will?' Her voice was trembling.

There was no sound. Even in her panic she could feel the emptiness of the flat.

'Will?' Her mouth dry, she tiptoed to her bedroom door. There was no one there. The neatly made bed, the tidy surfaces, the half-drawn curtains were all as she had left them. She turned and went to glance into the kitchen and bathroom. Both were empty. No one appeared to have been in there. Her boxes by the door had not been touched as far as she could see. Whoever had been into the flat in the short time she had been away, had gone. Pushing the front door closed she took a deep breath and went back to the flowers. There was a card tucked in amongst the pink and blue petals of the shop-bought chrysanthemums in their swathes of pink Cellophane and ribbon. With shaking hands she pulled it out and opened it.

> *We two, that with so many thousand sighs*
> *Did buy each other, must poorly sell ourselves*
> *With the rude brevity and discharge of one.*
> *Injurious time now with a robber's haste*
> *Crams his rich thievery up, he knows not how.*
> *As many farewells as be stars in heaven,*
> *With distinct breath and consign'd kisses to them,*
> *He fumbles up into a loose adieu,*
> *And scants us with a single famish'd kiss,*
> *Distanced with the salt of broken tears.*

> *Thanks for everything, cheers,*
>
> *Ash.*

Underneath he had scrawled, *Your door was open. Sorry to miss you. A x*

Ash had been in her flat. Not Will. Ash, quoting from *Troilus and Cressida*. He must have been watching, waiting for her to go out so he could sneak in. She closed her eyes with a shudder.

It took ten minutes to load the car, racing up and down the flights of stairs with her boxes and cases, constantly scanning the pavements. At last everything was in. She went back to the flat one last time and glanced round to check she hadn't forgotten anything. Just the flowers. With a grimace of disgust she picked them up and rammed them head first into the waste bin. She threw the card in after them, ran out of the flat, double-locked the door behind her and headed into the car.

Slamming down the door locks, she sank down behind the

wheel taking deep breaths to try and calm her panic. 'All over. He's not here. He won't know where I'm going. I'll be safe.' She was whispering the words out loud as she rammed the key into the ignition and turned it.

3

As the old Ford Ka bumped up the track towards the house Jess peered through the windscreen at her sister's small sprawling farm-stead nestling against the wooded hillside and felt a sudden wave of intense happiness and relief. The feeling wavered a little as she turned into the courtyard and switched off the engine. Where was Steph's car? The house was empty. She was too late. Steph had already gone – why else would the front door be closed? She had never seen it closed before in all the time Steph had lived there, even in winter.

Climbing out, stiff after the long drive, she stared round. Fighting off a wave of sudden loneliness she went to look for the key. It was in its usual hiding place, cocooned in cobwebs, a sign of how seldom it had been used, under a terracotta pot in the porch. As she bent to pick it up an indignant swallow swooped out of the nest tucked into the shadows above her head, leaving a row of sullen babies, half-fledged and bursting out of the nest leaning out, glaring down at her.

She pushed the key into the lock and turning it with difficulty, opened the door and went in. The house was eerily silent.

Her sister was a sociable woman. In the past when Jess had visited, the place had always been full of people – artists and writers fleeing the town, ex boyfriends and husbands who all appeared to be on astonishingly good terms with her sister, fellow teachers from the west London art college where Steph had taught for ten years before retiring to her pottery, people she had picked up on her travels, animals who followed her home, together with waifs and strays their mother had met on her research trips and blithely redirected to her daughter in Wales. As Jess unloaded the car and cautiously began to explore the house which would be her kingdom for the summer, she was expecting at any moment to see a sleepy face peering at her from one of the bedrooms, a stray cat, a motherless lamb, a homeless artist. There was no one. The house was neat and tidy and empty. On the kitchen table there was a note with a box of nougat.

Sorry I'm not here to welcome you. Enjoy the peace. Stay as long as you like. I _mean_ *it. Wine in fridge. See you some time.* S xxx

She chose the largest of the spare rooms to make her own. It had a double bed with a patchwork quilt, an antique pine chest and an old French armoire with a beautiful if threadbare Afghan rug on the polished oak boards, plenty of space for her books and its own quaint old bathroom set in what must have once been another bedroom behind the huge chimney breast. Carefully she put the smaller of her plants, an exuberant Flaming Katy in full scarlet flower, on the windowsill. The other plant, a mother-in-law's tongue given her by Will, which had barely escaped with its life after their break up, when she had still been throwing things about, she put in the bathroom, a room large enough for an antique dressing table and an ancient creaking settle covered by an exotic crimson shawl, and yet another bookcase beside the free-standing bath.

She wandered round the rest of the house, the sitting room with its open hearth swept and filled with dried flowers, the dining room with its refectory table, so often crammed with talking, arguing, noisy people. Steph's cooking was adventurous and not always terribly successful – she was frequently rescued from her culinary crises by more talented visitors who didn't seem to mind standing in at the last minute as chef. Jess smiled fondly at the memory. She wandered on into the large old-fashioned kitchen which was unnaturally tidy, overlooking the courtyard, and then through the passage with its small pointed windows, built to blend with the medieval lines of the lovely old byre which Steph had converted as her studio. Standing in the doorway she looked round at the unused materials on their shelves, the newly made pots carefully packed in boxes, the craftsman pieces which Steph sold through galleries in Radnor and Hereford and Hay, the piles of broken crocks. She hated the studio like this. Empty, like the house, the kiln cold, the soul somehow gone out of the place without her sister there. She stood for several moments, listening to the distant songs of the birds and she shivered. Walking back into the passage she turned the key in the lock and leaving the studio to its own devices she went back into the kitchen.

Maybe it hadn't been such a good idea to come after all, with Steph not being here.

Why hadn't Steph said at once, come with me. Come to Rome. Come to the sunshine. Jess glared at the plants crowded onto the windowsill behind the sink. 'It's all your fault,' she said out loud. 'I'm plant sitting and it's not what I had in mind at all!'

She frowned. What she had in mind was to paint. To forget London and what had happened to her there. To look forward and not back. The thought cheered her. Suddenly she could hardly wait to open her sketchbook, to feel again the reassuring grip of a pen or brush in her hand. She wanted to capture everything. Trees. The silhouette of the hills. The warm soft outlines of the stone walls; the colours of the flowers, the incredible structure of the petals of the orchid on the kitchen windowsill. It was going to be OK.

That night her dream returned. She was standing outside the front door, staring across the yard towards the open gate and the wood behind it. The branches of the trees were moving uneasily and she could sense a storm drifting along the broad river valley below the fields. The voice when it came was thin and wavering.

Can we stop playing this game now. I'm frightened.

It was coming from somewhere in the wood, almost drowned out by the sound of raindrops pattering down onto the leaves.

'Where are you?' Jess ran towards the gate. 'Come in. It's going to pour. Come here, sweetheart. You'll be safe here.'

The rain was growing heavier. She could feel it soaking into her jacket, drenching her hair. Her fingers were slippery on the top of the gate as she peered into the darkness. 'Where are you?'

A flash of lightning lit up the track and in the distance she caught sight of the child, her pale hair hanging in ropes across her shoulders, her little face pleading as the darkness closed in once more.

'Wait. I'm coming! Wait there.' Jess started to run down the track, her feet slipping in the mud as the first crash of thunder echoed around the hills.

With a start her eyes opened and she lay looking up at the

ceiling. For a second the dream lingered, then it was gone as she became aware of the drumming of rain on the slates above her head and on the flagstones in the courtyard outside the window. The rain was real. As was the thunder. As another rumble echoed round the house she sat up and reached for the light switch.

In the kitchen she found herself staring out of the window into the darkness. There had been a child in her dream. A lost child. She shivered. It would be awful to be outside on a night like this. She was about to reach for the kettle when she heard a crash from behind the door which led into the passage to Steph's studio. With a shiver she hugged her bathrobe round her. She ought to go and see what it was. Perhaps a tile had been dislodged by the wind or the rain or a window had blown open. If she left it something might be damaged. Her sudden fear was irrational. That was London fear. She was safe here. There was no one threatening her in this cosy haven. There was nothing to be afraid of except possibly her sister's wrath if some precious piece of work got broken. Making her way to the door she paused, her hand on the latch, her ear pressed to the wooden panels. The rain was rattling on the roof, splattering out of a gutter somewhere onto the stones below in the yard. Slowly she reached for the key and turned it. It was several seconds before she could make herself pull open the door. The passage was in darkness. She could feel a damp chilly draught on her face. Somewhere a window must have blown open. Taking a deep breath she ran the few steps along the passage to the studio door, unlocked it and groped for the light switches. The sudden flood of cold light from high in the old beams revealed at once a box of finished figures which had been packed ready for delivery, lying on the floor. The box had splintered and broken open and the figures inside were smashed into a thousand pieces.

'No!'

Jess ran to them and crouching down, touched the shards of delicate broken pottery with gentle fingers. She looked up, gazing round. No windows seemed to be open. The studio was ice cold but there was no draught now, nothing which could have knocked the box off the table where it had been standing. Biting her lip sadly she stood up. Perhaps an animal had got into the studio. A cat or a bird. She stared round again, more carefully this time, listening, but the sound of the rain drowned out any other noises there might be. She could feel herself growing more and more nervous as she forced herself to walk slowly round the entire building, staring onto the shelves, peering into the shadows behind the kiln, trying the outside door into the yard to make sure it was securely bolted, standing on tiptoe to scan the higher shelves of tins and bottles, running her finger over the pale terracotta clay dust on the table. There was no one there. No sign of any intruder. Nothing else seemed to have been disturbed. Pausing at last she turned full circle, staring round one last time. Outside the windows the lightning flickered. The rain was easing off. Conscious suddenly of the absolute silence in the studio she hastened over to the door, gave one last look round, flicked off the lights and pulling the door closed behind her, locked it.

Back in the warmth of the kitchen she found she was shivering violently. Pulling down the bright flowered blinds, she blocked out the blackness of the night behind the windows. She was reaching for the kettle when a voice whispered from right behind her,

Can we stop playing now?

Jess froze. The voice from her dream was in the room with her.

It's cold and wet out here. Let me in.

No, she wasn't in the room. She was outside the door. Jess ran to the door into the yard and put her hand on the bolt, then she hesitated. 'Hello?' she called. She listened. There was no reply. 'Are you there?' Slowly she turned the key. There was no chain on the door like the one she had in London. Steph would have laughed at such an idea out here in her country idyll. Nerving herself with a deep breath Jess pulled the door open a crack and peered out. The night was still wet and full of wind and rain. She could hear the thrash of tree branches, the slap of leaves against a wall, the drip of water into an overflowing butt. Groping on the wall near her she reached for the switch to the outside light. The courtyard was deserted, the windscreen of her car plastered with ash leaves torn from the trees on the track, a puddle reflecting the light shattered by raindrops. A broken slate lay on the ground near the door. She looked round, scanning the darkness for several seconds. There was no one out there. How could there be? Slamming the door shut again quickly she locked it once more, hugging her robe around her against the cold. The child had been part of her dream, nothing more.

Back upstairs in her room she climbed into bed leaving the light on, and lay miserably back on the pillows. She had never felt more alone. It seemed like hours before her eyes closed and she drifted off into an uneasy sleep. In seconds she had plunged back into the dream.

'Hurry, children!' Eigon, the eldest daughter of King Caradoc, could hear the panic in her mother's voice. It terrified her. Her mother was never frightened; Cerys was a courageous, calm, beautiful woman, idolised by her husband and her three children, respected by her husband's people, loved by her servants.

The messengers, trembling with fear and exhaustion, had scrambled up the steep side of the hill fort from the broad river valley below bringing with them the news they already dreaded. There had been a terrible defeat. The screams of battle, the shriek of horses, the gleam of fires had reached them from the distance as they had watched from the palisades and waited and prayed. Up to now she had been strong; always sure of her husband, Caradoc's, victory. He was a warrior. He was the idol of his people.

His rise from being the younger son of the king of the Catuvellauni to that of leader of all the remaining opposition to the Roman invaders had been swift and spectacular. His prowess as a general and the death of his elder brothers had catapulted him to kingship first of his own people, then as the head of the confederation of the tribes of the west who were still holding out against the Roman yoke. Up to this moment he had seemed invincible. He was going to lead them to victory and throw the Romans out of the land. Always he had succeeded. He was the greatest king the British tribes had ever seen.

White with shock, Cerys listened to the messenger's stammered report. The battlefield, in the gentle curve of the arm of the great River Sabrina had seen bloodshed that night on a scale never before experienced by the men under Caradoc's command. The Romans had won the day, the king, her husband, had fled into the night and a cohort of Roman veterans had left the field of death and the stripping of the dead and turned towards the hill fort where Caradoc's wife and children were awaiting his return.

Ordering everyone left in the fort to flee, Cerys seized Eigon's hand and slipped between the great oak gates, followed by two of her women, Alys, the children's nurse and Blodeyn, one of her ladies. Between them they half carried, half dragged Eigon's younger sister, Gwladys and their baby brother, Togo. Wrapped in cloaks, with nothing but what they stood up in, the women ran down the hillside, panting, slipping and sliding in the darkness.

'This way!' Cerys veered sideways towards the deeper safety of the trees which covered the western flank of the hill and filled the valley at its foot. 'They won't find us here.' She breathed a prayer to the goddess of these woods that it might be true.

A summer storm had blown up out of nowhere. The wind was rising. The sound was like the thunder of waves crashing on the beach as the three women and three children ran into the shifting roaring shelter of the thrashing leaves. Almost at once they had to stop, snared by brambles.

'Which way?' Alys was trying to see through the darkness. She glanced over her shoulder. The enemy was already at the gates of the fort. The sudden flare of flames from the burning stockade was out of sight now. Over the moaning of the trees they could no longer hear the shouts of the soldiers.

'Mam!' Eigon clung to her mother's cloak.

Cerys looked down. Stooping, she dropped a kiss on her daughter's dark head. 'Be brave, sweetheart!'

'Is Papa dead?'

The child felt her mother's hand tighten for a moment on her arm as Cerys fought back her tears. 'No, I'm sure he is alive. He has to be.'

'But he wouldn't run away. He wouldn't leave us alone! So, where is he?' Eigon clung more tightly.

'I don't know. He's hiding, like us. Waiting for the Romans to go away.' Once again Cerys glanced over her shoulder. 'Come on. We need to go deeper into the forest.'

'Mam?' Togo was whimpering, near to tears. At five years old he was the youngest, named for Caradoc's elder brother, killed two years before by the invaders. Gwladys was seven, Eigon nearly ten. Eigon and Togo had the dark hair, pale colouring and clear grey eyes of their Silurian mother; Gwladys was fair with her father's piercing blue eyes.

'It's all right. Come on, children. We'll find somewhere to hide. We'll be fine.' Cerys could no longer keep the fear out of her voice. Blindly she plunged on and the others followed as best they could.

They were climbing again now, up through the woodland which cloaked the steep hillside as behind them the orange glow flared gradually brighter into the sky, reflecting off the clouds. The Romans had reached the fort itself now and fired every building within the palisade. 'Let us pray that everyone else escaped,' murmured Cerys. 'Those soldiers will give no quarter.'

They moved on, more slowly now, pushing their way through dense tangled undergrowth. The two younger children were crying with fear and exhaustion and Eigon was still clinging to her mother when Cerys fell with a cry of pain as her foot slipped over the edge of a foxhole in a muddy bank and her ankle turned sharply over.

'Mam?' Eigon tried to drag her mother to her feet in desperation. They were all glancing behind them.

'Wait!' Blodeyn helped the fallen woman to sit up. 'I'll find you a stick to lean on.'

'I'll manage somehow!' Cerys was struggling to stand. 'We can't stay here.' She spoke through clenched teeth. 'We have to find somewhere to hide. But not yet. We can't stop yet!'

They found shelter at last in a stone-built hut on the far edge of the woodland. The roof had partially collapsed and the warm darkness smelled of dry bracken and hay and sheep dung, but it was out of the roar of the wind. Exhausted, the women and children collapsed onto the ground, desperately trying to regain their breath. It was pitch dark in the hut but for the time being they felt safe.

Pushing the three children down into the comparative warmth of the hay, Alys crawled towards Cerys, feeling her way in the darkness. 'Let me have your foot. I'll see if it's broken.'

Eigon heard her mother's gasp of pain minutes later as the woman's questing fingers probed the swollen flesh above her shoe. 'It's just a sprain. I'll tear a strip from my tunic and bind it for you.' The ripping sound as Alys wrenched at the linen hem stopped Cerys's protest in its tracks. 'When it's morning, I'll find some shepherd's purse and dog's mercury to make a poultice to bind round it to bring down the swelling,' Alys went on. Her voice was strong. It comforted them all.

They fell asleep at last as rain began to seep into what remained of the rotten roof thatch, too exhausted to feel cold or hunger, the two girls huddling under their mother's cloak, the little boy curled up in Alys's arms.

It was Eigon who heard the horses. Her eyes flew open. She could see the torchlight, the reflection of the flames flickering on the wet wall near her. 'Mam!' she screamed. 'We must run!'

Four riders had stopped in full view, some twenty paces from the hut. Cerys stared at them, appalled, then turned towards the huddled children. 'Go! Run! Time to play hide and seek, children. Into the trees now. Don't come out till I call you!' She was bundling the three sleepy children towards the hole in the tumbled down back wall before Alys and Blodeyn had begun to sit up.

Two of the men were dismounting, one holding his torch high above his head so smoke and flame streamed past his face, illuminating the detail of his helmet, the cheek pieces framing the mud-stained, tanned face, the bedraggled crest of red fur. The light had not yet reached into the depths of the hut. When it did all he could see was the three frightened women as they rose to their feet, brushing straw from their clothes. The children had gone.

Eigon ran deep into the darkness, clutching her brother and sister by the hand. Her brother let out a wail of fear. She dragged his arm. 'Be quiet! Here, Glads, hold my hand. We have to hide!' They slid down a slope and lay panting in the muddy shelter of a sheep scrape beneath a clump of hazels. Eigon closed her eyes and waited. The rain had started again. In the distance she heard a rumble of thunder. Miserably she drew her brother and sister into her arms. 'We're playing hide and seek,' she repeated more to herself than to them, 'must wait till we're called. We're playing hide and seek. Must keep quiet.'

They waited for a long time. The rain was heavier now. All three children were shaking with cold. At last she could bear it no longer. She sat up. 'Wait here,' she told them. 'Don't dare to move till Mam says it's safe to come out, do you hear me! I'm going to see what is happening.'

It was hard to retrace her steps in the dark but after several false starts and detours she recognised the darker shape of the hut against the dark hillside beyond the forest's edge; from where she stood, hiding behind a tree, she couldn't see any horses. Soaked to the skin and shivering violently she crept onto the track and made her way closer to the hut.

'Mam?'

There was no reply.

'Mam, where are you? Are we still playing the game?' She

tiptoed closer and peered in. The hut was empty. 'Mam?' She turned round, staring out into the darkness. 'Mam?' Her voice was a trembling whisper.

Somewhere close by a horse whinnied in answer and she froze. The sound came from a stand of trees behind the tumbled stone wall. She crept towards it and then she saw them. The men had thrust one of the torches into a crack in the stone. The hissing flickering light showed her mother, lying on the ground, her gown pushed up above her hips as one of the soldiers lay across her. He was holding her wrists above her head, forcing himself again and again into her unconscious body. Her face was cut, one eye swollen. Nearby Alys was kicking and screaming as two of the soldiers took turns to hold her down. Of Blodeyn, there was no sign.

'Mam?' Eigon's whisper was soundless with horror. 'Mam, are we still playing hide and seek?' She had not seen the man behind her.

'Well, well, what have we here? Another little Brit!' Two hands had seized her and she was swung off her feet into the circle of the torchlight and tossed onto the ground beside her mother.

The child's desperate endless scream woke Jess. She lay staring up at the ceiling, the sound of Eigon's voice reverberating round and round the room. Outside it was barely light. She could hear the raw joy of the dawn chorus echoing from the woods beyond the gate below her bedroom window. She was shaking with fear and her bed sheets were soaked in sweat as she sat up.

She had been dreaming about a rape. Not hers. Someone else's. A horrible vicious murderous rape. The rape of a child. With a sob she staggered to her feet and ran to the bathroom where she was violently sick. The outrage of what she had witnessed was everywhere. She couldn't get it out of her head. The men's faces. The smell of lust. The cruel jeering. The casual way one of them drew a dagger and pulled it across Alys's neck as desperately she tried to throw herself between him and the child, leaving her slumped on the ground like a broken doll, her head half-severed from her body. And the child, the girl whose screams filled Jess's ears. One of them had held her down, another of them hitting her mother so hard as she tried to crawl to help her daughter that the woman fell back in a huddle at the base of the wall and stopped moving. It was the third man who had viciously raped the child.

Again and again Jess splashed her face with cold water, shuddering. It was the most graphic dream she had ever had. She had been there. She had watched, unable to help, paralysed by fear, as the men tossed the child's body aside like a rag doll, turned away to find their horses and rode off.

'Sweetheart? Are you all right?'

Had she really spoken out loud in the dream? She wasn't sure. Had she reached out to cradle the child in her arms? She wasn't sure of that either.

With a groan she turned on the shower and stood under the cleansing water feeling it beating down on the top of her head until she was numb all over. Only then did she turn it off and reach for her bathrobe.

She was halfway down the stairs when the image flashed through her consciousness. A man's arm across her body, holding her down. She was in the bedroom of her flat; she couldn't see anything but the pillow half across her face and she could hear music. One of her own CDs. Soft. Reassuring, and then an arm, across her breasts pushing her back onto the bed.

That was all. The memory had gone as soon as it had begun to form. She stood still, clinging to the handrail. That wasn't part of the dream about the child. That was her flat, her bed. The doctor had said her memory might start to return; she had said there might be flashbacks, nightmares, as the longterm effects of whatever drug he had used on her began to wear off.

Unsteadily Jess made her way down to the kitchen. On automatic pilot now, she plugged in the kettle and assembled mug and coffee pot. Her hand was shaking as she measured the coffee into the pot. Outside the window the yard was already bathed in sunshine. The geraniums in the tub next to the studio door were almost luminous as the light caught their petals. The rough stones of the wall threw a pattern of irregular shadows where the original byre met the more modern infill. She frowned. She could recognise the shape of the older stones. Sunlight. Torchlight. The kind of torch that trailed flames and tarry smoke. This was the

scene of her dream. Slamming down the mug, she opened the
door and walked out into the yard. The air was soft and fragrant,
mountain air with the scents of grass and wild thyme and gorse
and sheep. Walking across the still-damp flags to the wall in her
bare feet she ran her hand over the sun-warmed stones. With the
sun at this angle it was easy to see where the new wall had taken
over the old, transforming the ruined byre into a modern studio
workshop. Unlocking the door she walked in and stared round.
The huge room was very silent.

'Hello?' Jess approached the work table. There was no one
there, of course. A bumble bee flew in through the open door,
did a couple of quick circuits and flew out again. 'Hello? Are you
here?' She wasn't sure who she was expecting to answer. The
little girl of her dream, perhaps, because this building had been
at some time in the past the scene of the rape she had witnessed
in her sleep. Of that she was certain.

The phone rang as she walked back in through the front door.

'Jess, you OK?' It was Steph. 'I got no answer from your flat
so I guessed you were already at Ty Bran. Oh, Jess! I can't tell
you how wonderful it is here! I am having such a fantastic time!'

Jess turned to look out of the window at the sun-drenched
yard. 'Me too.' She gave a wry grimace. 'So, do I gather you've
got some gorgeous man out there you haven't mentioned?'

There was a snort from the other end of the line. 'I've told you
before, Jess, I've given up on men. I love them at arm's length,
but that's all from now on. They make for far too many complications if you let them get too close.' There was a slight pause.
'Are you sure you're OK? You're not lonely? If you need anything,
don't forget you can go and ask Megan Price. She would love to
see you and she'll look after you.'

'Steph –'

Jess always found it hard to get a word in edgeways with her
sister. It was probably trying for so many years that had made her
such a good teacher. Quiet persistence was the name of the game.
'Steph, listen, I want to ask you something. Is this place haunted?'

There was a moment's silence the other end of the line. At last
she had Steph's attention. 'Why?' Steph's cautious response in
Rome was almost drowned by a volley of hooting in the street
outside the apartment window behind her. Jess heard it and smiled
wistfully. 'I just wondered.'

'I –' Steph hesitated. 'To be honest I have suspected there might be something odd there once or twice. Just noises. The feeling sometimes that I was being watched. I haven't seen anything.' There was a pause. 'You're not scared up there on your own are you?' She sounded worried.

Jess grimaced. 'No, of course not. As you say, noises. It's probably because I'm not used to rural silence after London, that's all.'

There was a chuckle the other end of the phone. 'My dear, if you think London is noisy, try Rome! Listen.'

Jess guessed the telephone was being held out of the open window the other end. A muffled unspecified roar punctuated by the staccato wail of a car alarm confirmed her guess.

'Listen, Jess. Kim's come back with our *panini* and the *giornali*. I've got to go.' Steph was on the end of the line again. 'I'll call you again in a few days, OK?'

'Wait, Steph!'

But it was too late. Steph had hung up. 'Let me have your number, in case I need to get in touch . . .' Jess finished the sentence softly to herself as she put down the phone. All her life Steph had been doing this to her. Talking so hard and so fast Jess had either forgotten what she was going to say or she had given up trying. She gave a wry grin. Well, at least they communicated which was more than many sisters did. And there was always Steph's mobile.

4

The Prices were her sister's nearest neighbours. She remembered their warmth and friendliness from her previous visits and even the thought of going to see them cheered her up enormously. She glanced round the kitchen. The house felt welcoming and warm. There was no trace of anything spooky here now.

The spookiness, she reasoned to herself firmly, was tied up with the dream and the dream was tied up to what had happened to her. Rape was not something she was going to shrug off and forget just like that. The experience had wounded her in a way she would probably never completely recover from. But she was here in the peace and quiet of this beautiful countryside to do just that, she was a strong woman. She would get over it. Dan's words. Get over it.

The walk down the lane and up across the fields to Cwm-nant, the Prices' farm in the next valley, was a long one but she enjoyed it. She had done it several times before with Steph. Meg and Ken Price ran a sheep farm but had still found time to help Steph when she had first moved in, to welcome her whenever she looked in and to treat her as family. Jess was pretty sure of a pot of tea and some gossip in the farmhouse kitchen. Unused to country walking, she was exhausted by the time she climbed over the last fence and dropped down into their lane, noting the fields were empty. The sheep must be up on the hills for the summer. She walked into the yard and greeted the two collies who ran up to her.

The back door of the farmhouse was opened by a tall, broad-shouldered man with dark hair, a neatly trimmed beard and light blue eyes. He must have been in his early forties. Dressed in jeans and an open-necked shirt he filled the doorway with his bulk as he clicked his fingers at the dogs milling round her heels. They slunk away across the yard towards the kennel.

Jess's heart sank at the sight of the stranger. 'Are Meg and Ken in?' It hadn't occurred to her to ring first. Steph never did.

He shook his head. 'They're on holiday.' His voice was deep and mellow but not particularly friendly. Her disappointment must however have been obvious for he raised an eyebrow. 'As I'm sure you've guessed, I'm their son, Rhodri. Can I help?'

She shook her head. 'Not really. I just thought I'd call in to say hello.' She gave him a tentative smile.

He glanced over her shoulder towards the gate. 'Just passing, were you?'

The lack of a car and the fact that the lane dead-ended at the farm made that unlikely. She stuck out her hand. 'I'm Jess Kendal.' He ignored the hand and she dropped it, suddenly embarrassed. She hadn't even realised the Prices had a son. She didn't think Meg or Steph had ever mentioned him. 'My sister is a neighbour,' she ploughed on. 'Across the fields. Ty Bran?' She waited for a sign of recognition as she waved an arm vaguely in the direction of the ridge above the field beyond the lane. It looked deceptively close in the warm sunshine. 'I'm staying there for a bit while Steph is away. I just thought I would come over to say hello to Meg, that's all. I didn't mean to disturb you.'

'You haven't. Not so far.' He frowned.

She smiled uncomfortably. This was not the man in whom to confide her fear of ghosts or her fear of anything for that matter. Nor, clearly, was he going to offer her the hoped for cup of tea. Or even a civil smile. 'I'll be on my way.' She hesitated, not quite sure how to terminate the conversation. She needn't have worried. He was already shutting the door. 'Rude bastard!' She addressed the dogs with feeling as they reappeared, tails wagging as soon as the door was safely closed. 'I hope he's feeding you properly.'

The walk back seemed endless. Far more of it was uphill on the return journey and it was strenuous. She was breathless and thirsty by the time she reached Ty Bran and was diving into the fridge for a glass of cold juice when she noticed a large black 4 x 4 turning in at the gate. It drew up beside her Ka, the door opened and Rhodri Price climbed out. She saw him stand for a minute, glancing round the yard.

'Shit!' He was not someone she had been expecting to see again so soon.

He approached the open door of the house with what might have been a sheepish grin as he caught sight of her watching. 'I think I may owe you an apology.'

She stood her ground in the doorway, glass of orange still in her hand. 'Why?'

'I was rude.'

'Were you? I thought that must be your normal manner.' She could feel herself bristling.

He shrugged. 'Touché! It probably is, if I'm honest. I'm not very keen on fans tracking me down when I'm off duty, and I assumed you were one of them. My mother says it was unforgivable of me. She rang just after you left and she put me right. Forgive me.' He was wearing a contrite expression completely at odds with his squared shoulders and confident, upright bearing.

'I don't see why you should be rude to your fans, if they have taken the trouble to track you down in the middle of nowhere,' she retorted. 'Who are these fans? Are you a popstar or something?'

It was strangely satisfying to see him stare at her, genuinely shocked. 'You don't know who I am?'

'No.' She met his gaze and held it. 'Should I?' She had taken a huge dislike to this man with his smug arrogance and she was, she realised with sudden shock, feeling quite intimidated by him. Both emotions were unusual for her. Through most of her life she had found herself inclined to give people the benefit of the doubt; liking them until they gave her a good reason not to. But then he had done just that, hadn't he! He had made her walk all the way back across the fields without her cup of tea! She took a deep breath and stood a little straighter. She was not going to make it easy for him.

'It was nice of you to come over but there was no need, I assure you. I shouldn't have intruded on your privacy.' Stepping back into the stone-flagged passage, she gently pushed the door closed in his face. She listened intently, her ear to the solid oak. She could hear nothing. He didn't move for several seconds, then he turned on his heel and walked back to his car. In a moment he had backed out of the gate and disappeared down the lane.

'Oh God! I shouldn't have done that!' She bit her lip. As she walked into the kitchen she found she was giggling out loud.

'Pompous prick! Who the hell does he think he is? How can such nice people as the Prices have such an awful son!'

The dining room was the perfect place to put all her sketchbooks and paints and set up her easel. The line of north-facing windows looked out across the valley towards the distant hillsides, on the far side of the house from the courtyard and Steph's studio – nothing would persuade her to settle down in there. As she laid out her brushes and began to paint, the sun was setting in a haze of crimson cloud streaked with gold. Her mobile rang from her handbag as she watched, brush in hand. Reaching for it automatically she glanced down at the number. Will. She cut off the call. There were four other missed calls, she saw. All from Will. With a grimace she threw the phone back into her bag and went back to the window. She stood there for several minutes watching as the shadows lengthened across the valley filling the deep fissures in the hillside with velvet blackness. It was almost a shock to turn her back on the view at last to find the room had grown dark behind her, too dark to paint. Thoughtfully she went back into the kitchen, turning on all the lights on the way. The courtyard was lost in darkness now as well. And beyond it the woods. She needed to distract herself from those woods; she had no desire to think about her nightmare. None at all. Make soup. Cooking was something she enjoyed and while she was doing it she would listen to some music. She had spotted a pile of CDs on the dresser next to Steph's sound system. She grinned fondly. Sound system was altogether too grand a name for this old CD player and speakers which appeared to be liberally smeared with flour and clay and paint and other nameless substances. She glanced at the CDs and her mouth fell open in astonishment. The first two sported pictures of Rhodri Price. She stood, one in each hand, staring at the handsome arrogant face, the wild hair, the dramatic stance. In one he wore evening dress, in the other an open-necked shirt. In the first he had obviously been photographed in a concert hall, in the other, the more informal, he was standing on the wild hillside. 'Oh my God! He's the opera singer.' She bit her lip. Of course she had heard of him. Who hadn't? Alone as she was, she closed her eyes in embarrassment. It was no excuse that this was not her kind of music. She was not particularly keen on opera but she loved orchestral music and instruments like the harpsichord and this man sang all kinds of music. He gave recitals. He sang at football matches, he was often on TV. He was a celebrity!

Still smiling ruefully to herself, she slid the disk into the machine and his voice filled the room, singing in Welsh, a wild wonderful folk song backed by the rippling cadences of a harp. It was spellbinding. She stood and listened for several minutes before at last turning back to her cooking. She found onions and potatoes in the boxes she had brought with her and listened as she began to dice them and threw them into a heavy iron pan. His voice soared over the sizzling of the oil and she found herself standing still again, mesmerised, a knife in one hand, onion in the other as song succeeded song, some sad, some exultant, some wistful, all lyrical. She brushed her eyes with the back of her wrist. Onions always made her cry.

Standing at her bedroom window much later she could see the moon sailing clear of the wood. It was incredibly beautiful out there; something else to try and capture on paper. She frowned. There was a figure on the track, standing motionless in a silvery patch of moonlight. She bit her lip. Was it the child? No, the child was part of her dream. Holding her breath she pushed the window open and leaned out. The figure didn't move. It was a girl, she could see that clearly. A girl, standing with her back to the house, gazing into the trees, a girl with dark hair this time, not blonde. Eigon. Jess held her breath. The moonlight on the path cast silver-edged shadows before it; the long shadows of the trees. The figure threw no shadow. A band of cloud was racing down the valley now; she glanced up at the moon. In a second it would be obscured. She knew before it happened that when the path was again floodlit by the clear cold light the girl would have gone.

Almost as soon as her head touched the pillow Jess began to dream again. It was as though Eigon was waiting for her, a small lonely figure, her hair ebony in the moonlight, revealed in all its long tangles as the sun rose over the stone walls of the old byre where she was lying half-naked amongst the nettles.

When Eigon awoke the sky was blue and the birds were singing and she was looking up into the eyes of yet another Roman.

41

Only one of the men had raped the child. The others had sated their lust on the women. When finally they had ridden away just before dawn both Eigon and her mother were unconscious; Alys and Blodeyn were dead. There was no sign of Togo or Gwladys.

'What's happened here?' The Roman dismounted from his horse and bent to examine the women. Eigon saw him shake his head as he glanced at Alys. No one could have survived that vicious knife slash to the throat. It had almost severed the woman's head from her body. With a cursory glance at the naked twisted body which was Blodeyn, he laid a hand, gently, on Cerys's forehead. She groaned. He glanced over his shoulder to the men behind him. 'I think we've found the missing family. Look, this woman is no peasant. See her hands? She is either Caratacus's wife, or one of his family.' He used the Roman version of Eigon's father's name. He took Cerys's hand in his own and held it for a few seconds, examining her nails. Her eyes flickered open for a moment, then closed again. He could see the marks where her arm rings had been wrenched from her; her necklet too had gone, leaving a telltale bruise on the side of her throat. The woman had worn jewellery; what was left of her gown had been fine linen, beautifully stitched and embroidered. He turned to Eigon. His eyes moved slowly over the child's naked, pale body, noting the blood, the bruises, the obscenely splayed legs and his mouth tightened. 'Bring something to cover them,' he commanded curtly. 'Look for the other children. There were three, I understand; bury these two women with honour, then bring these two back to the camp. Gently!' He shouted the last word up at his second in command who nodded gravely, at last sliding down from his own horse.

'And find out who committed this outrage,' the officer went on, his voice deceptively quiet. 'Whoever they were, they will pay with their lives.'

When Eigon woke she was lying on a low bed in a tent. Her mother was gently sponging her body with warm water. Behind her a lamp burned, throwing shadows round the walls. She could smell lavender.

'Mam?' Her eyes filled with tears.

'Quietly, sweetheart. Everything is going to be all right.' Cerys managed an exhausted smile. She had been given hot water and clothes and food, though she had eaten little, watching over her daughter as the child lay, a small alabaster figure on the bed, moaning now and then as slowly the shroud of dreams lifted and consciousness began to return.

A figure appeared at the door of the tent behind her. It was the officer who had brought her back. His name she now knew was Justinus. 'Queen Cerys?'

There had been no point in denying who she was. Dozens of men and women from the fort had been captured together with hundreds of her husband's warriors. Some of them would be bound to confirm her name in exchange for a promise to save their lives. The others were dead. Thousands, he had told her. Putting down the sponge she carefully pulled the sheet up round her daughter's small body as he stood looking down at her. 'How is she?'

Cerys stood up wearily. The child's eyes had closed again. 'The gods have blessed her with sleep for the time being.'

'And she hasn't spoken at all?'

Cerys shook her head.

'We need to find your other children, lady. For their own safety. They are alone out there on the hills.' Justinus glanced towards the entrance to the tent and shook his head slightly. 'Better my men find them than ...' He didn't have to finish the sentence. Both of them looked down at Eigon's sleeping face. There was a short silence. 'I have spoken to our commander, Publius Ostorius Scapula,' he said quietly. 'There is as yet no sign of your husband.'

She closed her eyes with a murmured prayer of gratitude to the gods. If he had escaped the battlefield he would return to rescue her.

'He might have been slain, lady,' he said gently. He had read her thoughts immediately. 'There are still bodies to be recovered from the battlefield.'

'I think his capture or his killing would have been shouted from the highest summit of the hills,' she said sharply. She straightened her shoulders painfully. 'My husband is a king and the saviour of his people; the greatest warrior in Britain. If he had fallen, we would know it.'

He raised an eyebrow. 'You are probably right to say that.' He sighed. 'Scapula wishes to speak with you, lady. I told him you are injured.' He glanced at the bruises on her face and at her throat and on her arms, and the strapping on her ankle, showing beneath the mantle and cloak in which she was huddled. 'He has ordered me to bring you to him when you are well enough.'

'Thank you for giving me that respite at least.' She bowed her head. So far she had been treated with courtesy, even consideration, but that she was a prisoner was beyond doubt. Two men stood outside the entrance to the tent, their spears crossed over the doorway. They had snapped to attention as the praefectus had entered, but crossed them again behind him.

'If there is anything you need for yourself or the child, tell one of the guards,' he went on. Then he bowed. He left her sitting at Eigon's bedside, her hand over the child's pale cold fist as it lay on the bedcover.

When Eigon woke again at last the lamp had burned low; the oil was sputtering in the bowl and the tent was almost dark. She stared round. 'Mam?'

'Here, sweetheart.'

'Where is Alys?'

Cerys bit her lip. 'She isn't here, Eigon. I'm sorry.'

'And Togo and Glads?' The child's voice suddenly slid higher with anxiety.

Cerys shook her head. 'I don't know where they are.' She sighed. Was the officer right? They would be better off with her? Better that than to risk being raped and murdered on the cold hillside, surely; but if they were with her they risked, what? What would the Romans do to her and her children? Imprisonment? Ransom? Death? She shook her head violently. Caradoc would rescue her. He would find a way of saving her. Her duty was to keep the children with her, safely.

'Where were they, Eigon? You came to find us, but the children weren't with you.'

Her daughter shook her head. 'I told them to hide. I told them we were playing hide and seek like you said. I told them not to come out till I went back for them.' The child's eyes filled with tears. 'Why did those men hurt me, Mam?'

'They were soldiers, Eigon. Ignorant, vicious men. You must try and forget what happened. The gods will punish them for what they did.' Cerys closed her eyes for a few seconds, unable to look at her daughter's anguished little face. When she opened them she took a deep breath. 'Eigon. We have to find Togo and Gwladys. Do you remember where you left them?'

The child shook her head again. 'It was dark. The wind was roaring in the trees. I couldn't see anything. We hid in a ditch where the wind couldn't get to us. It was warmer there.' Tears began to run down her cheeks. 'Are they all right?'

'I don't know.' Cerys felt the words catch in her throat.

'It wasn't hide and seek, was it?'

'No, sweetheart. It wasn't . . .'

Hide and seek!

The words echoed through the bedroom as Jess sat up abruptly, suddenly wide awake. The moon had moved on and the room was dark. She stared round, frightened. 'She's telling me her story. Eigon wants me to know what happened. She knows I understand because it happened to me.' Climbing out of bed Jess stood for a moment in the darkness trying to steady her breathing. Padding barefoot to the window she looked out. The night was dark now. She couldn't see anything or anyone outside.

The luminous dial on her bedside clock told her it was just after three. Switching on the light she stared down at her pillows for several seconds before turning her back on them and heading for the stairs.

In the kitchen she switched on the kettle, then she went to the door and unlocked it. Pulling it open almost defiantly she stood looking out into the courtyard. The night was balmy; a gentle breeze touched her face. It was very quiet. Even the trees were motionless. Still barefoot she stepped outside and glanced up. The sky was bright with a myriad stars. She caught her breath. One could never see the night sky in London properly. This was spectacular and she was not going to lock herself inside, frightened by a dream. She had vowed not to be a victim. She was not going to be terrorised by a ghost any more than she was going to be terrorised by the man who had raped her. To walk to the gate was the first proof that she was succeeding. The flags were warm under her feet as she walked away from the open door.

'Eigon?' She whispered the name out loud. 'Eigon? Glads? Are you there?' Her voice was louder this time. With a shriek of alarm a blackbird flew out of the bush by the gate and disappeared into the darkness. Her heart hammering, she stopped. It was only a bird. Nothing to be afraid of. In fact, if there had been anyone there lurking in the shadows the bird would have long gone. She forced herself to walk on. Two more steps. Then one. She put out her hands to the gate and grasped the top rail. 'Eigon?'

She could just make out the line of the track outside the gate. In one direction it led towards the wood, in the other back down between high banks which eventually followed the contour of the hillside to the road in the valley bottom. Faraway in the distance she could make out two or three lights which showed a village tucked away in a fold of the hills. Nearer to her, to the east, the silhouette of the hillside blocked out the stars. She studied it. How strange that she had not realised it at once. That was the site of the fort in her dream. The fort which she had seen in flames as the women and children fled the vengeful Roman force. She could see the distinctive tiered shape of its summit now, outlined against the blazing heavens.

'Eigon?' she called out one last time. There was no reply and turning her back on the trees she retraced her steps towards the house. Inside she closed the door and bolted it. Only then did she acknowledge just how frightened she had been.

5

'Hi Steph, how are you?'

Steph answered her mobile as she walked out of the palazzo next morning on her way to buy some food for Kim's dinner party that evening. Kim was already entrenched in the kitchen, and last-minute guests had meant last-minute supplies.

'Who is that?' Pausing, Steph turned, pulling her dark glasses down over her eyes. The heat was like a furnace, reflecting off the pavements of the piazza, the traffic roaring noisily round the corner past her. Behind her the palazzo was a classic elegant Renaissance building, the faded terracotta façade peeling now and in places cracked and crumbling, the formal, perfectly symmetrical windows topped by swags and curls of exquisite stone carving. At the centre the huge old door was studded and barred in iron, a small pass door almost invisible in the ancient wood. Kim's husband, Stefano, had been born and brought up in the huge high-ceilinged shabby apartment in this ancient palazzo, an apartment bought by his father specifically so his family could be a part of this Bohemian artistic quarter of the city.

Turning to face it she stared up at the walls as the voice spoke in her ear. 'It's Will, Steph. Please, don't hang up. I need to talk to you.'

She raised an eyebrow. 'Why?' She began walking again, her hand tightening on the phone as she turned into a narrow alleyway. It was quieter here and she could hear him more easily.

'I've been trying to contact Jess. You know she's left school? She resigned without giving anyone a reason. She's not answering her mobile and I'm pretty sure she's not at the flat any more. I'm worried about her.'

'What makes you think I would know where she was?' Steph turned into the Via dei Capellari. She was heading towards the market in the Campo de' Fiori.

'That's a stupid question. Of course you'd know. You two always tell each other everything. Is she there with you?'

'No, she isn't. I'm in Rome, Will. I don't know where she is.' She stopped again, staring sightlessly into the window of a small picture framer. It was cooler in the shade of this long narrow street. Near her two men had brought their chairs outside, slotting them between two huge terracotta pots of camellias. They were sipping iced beer, drops of condensation running down between their fingers and dripping onto their T-shirts. 'Dan said he thought she might have come to stay with you.' Will sighed. 'Oh well. Do you at least know why she resigned?'

'No.' Steph began to walk on slowly. She had always liked Will, been sad when he and Jess split up, but if Jess was not telling anyone where she was, there had to be a reason. 'Will, there's no point in asking me. If Jess wants you to know where she is, she would tell you. I haven't seen her for ages.' That at least was true. 'I'm here for the summer, so I don't expect to either.'

There was a long silence. 'Do you think she's gone to stay with your mother in France?' He sounded crestfallen.

Steph shrugged. She wasn't sure if Jess had told Aurelia where she was; and she wasn't sure her mother would keep it a secret if she had. Aurelia too had been one of Will's greatest fans. 'Will, are you there? I don't think she's in France,' she said firmly. 'Mummy would have said. I spoke to her only a day or so ago and she was just leaving for a trip to India.' She crossed her fingers. Another lie, but only a small one. Aurelia had in fact just returned. As she tucked her mobile back into her bag she frowned. Why was Jess being so secretive? Something was going on. She would ring her tonight and find out exactly what it was

Dan phoned Ty Bran as Jess was eating a bowl of cereal. 'I'm in Hay. I wondered if you would like to drive over and join me for lunch.'

She rescued the slice of toast that had leaped from the toaster, juggling it with her bowl of muesli. The door was wide open and the blackbird had forgiven her enough for her nocturnal intrusion on its sleeping place to sit on the top of the studio roof, singing gloriously into the sunshine. Her depression had gone; the peace of this place was working its magic at last. After the noise and dirt of London it was balm to her soul.

'You're in Hay?' She frowned. 'What are you doing there?'

'Shopping for books. What else?'

'But you never told me you were coming over this side of the country.'

'Didn't I?' He laughed.

'No, you didn't. Are Natalie and the kids with you?'

'Not this time. Bookshops bore them, sadly. I'm on my way to join them in Shropshire in a couple of days. They've gone up to stay with Nat's parents. Oh come on, Jess. It wouldn't take you much more than an hour to get here.'

Jess glanced over her shoulder at the open door. She was, she realised, already surprisingly reluctant to leave this peaceful place in spite of its uneasy echoes. On the other hand she needed to do some shopping and perhaps a change of scene would do no harm.

They met in the bar at The Kilvert at twelve thirty. There were no outside tables left by the time she got there so they settled for a table inside by the window.

'So, are you feeling better about things now?' He put a glass of wine down in front of her, sat down across the table and studied her face for a moment. 'You look tired.'

She grimaced. 'I've been having some rather spectacular nightmares.' It was a relief to have someone to confide in but she hadn't intended to come out with it quite so bluntly or so soon.

'What about?' He looked away and took a gulp from his pint.

'A little girl.' She paused, wondering if she should go into any detail. 'Two little girls. Steph's house seems to be haunted by them.' She glanced up to gauge his reaction.

'Haunted? Really?' He was looking down into his glass. He seemed amused. He pushed the bar menu across the table towards her, still without meeting her gaze. 'Would you like to choose something? So, what form does this haunting take?'

She shrugged. 'As I said, nightmares and I think I may have seen them.'

'Wow.' He was still looking at the menu. 'Has Steph seen them too?'

'She says she suspected there was a ghost.'

'And so what happens in your nightmare?' His brown eyes were twinkling as he finally looked up at her.

'One of them is raped.'

She saw the shock on his face as he put down the menu and turned to stare out of the doorway where the sunlight was beating down on the umbrellas over the crowded tables around the front door. 'Raped?' he echoed.

She nodded. 'By Roman soldiers.'

'That must be a scary dream.' He still wasn't looking at her.

'It was.' Suddenly she was regretting telling him.

There was a long silence. They both went back to perusing the menu. Abruptly Dan stood up. 'I'd better order. Have you decided yet?'

When he returned to the table he had brought her another glass of wine. 'Has Will been in touch?'

'He's phoned my mobile a few times.'

'And?'

'And nothing.'

There was a pause. When she didn't elaborate he went on. 'And Ashley? Has he phoned you too?'

She sighed. 'Ash broke into my flat just before I left. He brought me some flowers to say thanks for teaching him.'

'Broke in?' Dan echoed. 'What do you mean, broke in?'

'I found the flowers on my coffee table. I suppose I could have left the door open but I don't think so.'

'You weren't there?'

'No.'

'And he'd gone when you came back?'

She nodded. 'I was only gone about ten minutes, Dan. He must have been watching for me. It scared me.'

'But you're safe now.'

She nodded. 'Do you know what he is going to do this summer while he's waiting for his results?'

He shook his head. 'He's convinced they will be good. He's a cocky lad, our Ash. He thinks the drama schools will be queuing up for him.'

'And he doesn't even need A levels to apply for those.'

'No.'

They both glanced up as their food arrived. 'It would be a shame to spoil his chances. It would destroy them if he ended up with a prison record,' Dan said quietly as he picked up his knife and fork. He looked up at her at last. 'Don't think about him, Jess. Or

Will, for that matter. Forget about them. Enjoy your summer.' He took a mouthful of food. 'So, what are you planning to get up to in that old farmhouse of Steph's?'

'I'm painting.' Jess was looking down at her plate.

'On your own?'

She nodded.

'And you're happy with that?'

'I'm fine with that, Dan. I like being on my own.'

'With a ghost?'

She gave an uncomfortable smile. 'They are not frightening ghosts. Just little girls.'

There was a pause as he picked up a bread roll and tore it into pieces. 'I've had an idea, Jess. Feel free to say no, but I was going to find a B and B tonight and then go on up to Shrewsbury tomorrow. Why don't I come back with you? It's on my way. I passed a super-looking deli as I came here just now. We could pick up something there for supper. We could comb one or two more bookshops to feed my addiction this afternoon, then you can lead the way back to Ty Bran and introduce me to your spectral children. What do you think? There must be plenty of room.'

'I don't know, Dan –'

It was tempting. Much as she enjoyed her own company the thought of the dark track towards the woods once the sun had gone down, the empty rooms, the strange noises in the studio were intimidating. Besides it would seem churlish to refuse him.

It was just after six thirty when she turned into the courtyard at Ty Bran and pulled up by the studio. Dan drew in beside her and switched off his engine.

For a moment he remained still. 'Steph was so lucky to find this place! Did you say it's near where your mother used to live?' He climbed out and stood looking round. 'My God, it's isolated, but it is so pretty.'

'Isn't it.' Jess turned back to the car to haul out her purchases. Bread, cold meat, paté, cheeses and salad and an early edition of Omar Khayyám illustrated with Edmund Dulac's magical colour plates. She went to open the door of the house as Dan unpacked his own trophies: several books, four bottles of wine, a four-pack of lager, some scrumpy and a box of very expensive chocolates.

He followed her into the kitchen and dropped the heavy box of drinks onto the table with a groan.

'There, we can see what mood takes us – or drink the lot and fall totally blotto to the floor. Oh, wow, Jess. This is so lovely.' He wandered through the open door to the dining room and stood staring out across the garden towards the hedge and the view to the north. Then he turned and glanced down at her sketchbooks, laid out on the table. 'Are these yours? I had no idea you were so good!' He turned several of the pages.

'Flattery will get you nowhere beyond the right to work the corkscrew,' she called through the door from the hall. 'Here. Let's open the wine.'

She went back into the kitchen in front of him and stopped dead. The contents of her basket and two of the bottles of wine lay on the floor. The bottles had broken.

They both stood for a moment looking down at the mess.

'Oh, Dan, no!' she cried. 'How did that happen?'

Dan glanced round. 'I can't think. I put the box on the middle of the table. They couldn't have just fallen out. Bugger! You haven't got a cat here, have you, by any chance?'

She shook her head. 'Since when have cats been able to pick up bottles?'

He shrugged. 'In which case, it wasn't the cat! Not to worry. There are two bottles left and at least the food was wrapped up. Not too much harm done. You wait there, I'll clear it up.'

'No. No, I'll do it.' She went to the sink and fumbled under it for the brush and pan and some dishcloths. 'What happened, Dan? I don't understand.' She was suddenly feeling panicky. 'It was all there. On the table. It wasn't on the edge or anything. Oh God!' She was looking round in sudden panic. 'Is there someone else here?'

'No, there's no one here. It's just one of those things. Wait.' He grabbed an intact bottle of wine and reached for the corkscrew which she had left lying on the draining board. 'Let's have a glass each first. Then we'll clear up. Then we'll be ready for something to eat. Don't worry about it, Jess. No harm done.'

They had finished their meal and were strolling on the back lawn later, carrying their mugs of coffee when Jess heard the sound of a car engine from the courtyard. 'Who on earth is that?' She turned back towards the house.

Getting no reply when he knocked at the open front door, Rhodri had wandered straight in and seeing them from the window came out. He seemed taken aback to see her with Dan.

'I'm sorry to intrude. My mother hasn't given me a moment's peace since she heard you were here on your own. She told me to bring you some food from the freezer.' He was carrying a basket. 'If I'd known you were with someone I wouldn't have bothered you.' There was irritation in his voice.

Jess made the introductions reluctantly. His arrival had spoiled the mood of the evening. 'It's very kind of your mother, Rhodri. Will you thank her.' She took the basket from him firmly. 'Would you like a glass of wine?'

Somewhat to her surprise he nodded. As Dan went to fetch a glass she smiled at him coldly. 'Are these homemade things from Megan?' she said politely. 'That is so nice of her –' She broke off as a crash sounded from the kitchen.

Dan appeared in the doorway, his hand wrapped in a tea towel. 'Sorry, folks. The glass slipped. We seem to be having a bad time, don't we!' He handed Rhodri his drink and strolled over towards the hedge, his hand still wrapped in the towel. The others followed him. 'Look at that view,' he said at last. 'It's sensational, isn't it.' Beyond the hedge the ground dropped away towards the valley bottom. The sun was beginning to set now in a pearly haze which rimmed the northern hills with gold.

'It'll rain tomorrow.' Rhodri was staring across the hedge. 'You're a painter, Mum tells me.' He glanced down at Jess.

'Only an amateur.' She couldn't keep the frostiness out of her voice. He sounded patronising and bored and even the fact that he was a head taller than her and therefore was looking down on her irritated her hugely.

'But a damn good one,' Dan put in amiably. 'This place is inspirational, isn't it. I reckon if I lived here I would finally write my novel.'

'What novel?' Jess said, amused. 'Is that before or after you get your headship?'

He grinned. 'After, probably. But before I get to be Minister of Education!'

Rhodri gave a snort of laughter. 'Well, my friend, while you

53

plan out your future I regret I shall have to leave you. Thank you for the drink, Jess.'

He turned and headed back towards the house. In the doorway he paused. 'Are you sure it was only a wine glass you broke?' he called back over his shoulder.

The floor of the dining room was covered in glass. The three of them stood gazing down at it. Dan shook his head. 'I don't understand. I picked it all up. That's how I cut myself. It was in the kitchen. Oh God!' He broke off as he caught sight of the table. 'Oh Jess –'

Her book of drawings was covered in red liquid. The pages were crumpled and one of the pictures had been scribbled all over. Jess reached for the light switch. 'Who would do that?' she whispered. 'Dan –?'

'No! Not me. I swear it! How could you even think it?'

'Is it wine?' Rhodri leaned over the table and touched the picture with a fingertip. 'It's sticky. Oh my God, it's blood!' Shocked, he stood back. 'It was you!' he accused Dan. 'You're the one bleeding all over the place!'

'I told you it wasn't!' Dan replied angrily. 'I would say if it was me, for goodness' sake! I never went near the pictures.' He strode over to the door. 'Someone else has been in here. Look, the front door is open.'

'That was me,' Rhodri said. 'Steph always leaves it open. I'm afraid I didn't think.' He took several steps out into the hall, looking round. 'But who would do such a thing?' There was real anger in his voice. 'And why?' He strode out into the courtyard. 'There's no one out here!'

Jess shook her head miserably. 'Well, the drawings weren't that special, I suppose. Nothing I can't do again.'

'That's hardly the point!' Dan said sternly. 'Should we call the police?'

'No.' Jess shook her head. 'They have long gone, whoever they were. Or at least –' She broke off, glancing back towards the staircase.

'I'll go.' Rhodri strode back inside and stood with his hand on the newel post, looking up. They all listened. Taking the steps two at a time he vanished across the landing. They heard doors opening and closing and his heavy tread across the floorboards. 'There's no one up here.' His voice floated down to them. Reappearing he ran down. 'I don't think anything's been touched up there. You've left some gold bangles on your dressing table, Jess. They wouldn't still be there if anyone had gone upstairs. I suppose it must have been some deranged kid who popped in for some quick vandalism. It sounds unlikely but can you think of anything better?' He shrugged. 'You sometimes get strangers walking or biking on the tracks up through the woods.'

Jess glanced at Rhodri thoughtfully. It felt oddly unsettling suddenly to think of him peering round her bedroom. She pushed the thought aside. 'But why? Why do that? Why spoil my pictures?' She realised she had started to shake. She turned back into the dining room and stood looking down at the table. The sky outside had blushed deep red with the sunset and filled the room with a warm glow. Only the pool of electric light on the table was harsh. Reaching out to the blood stains she dabbed them gently. The blood was already dry.

'I really do have to go,' Rhodri called from the hall. 'I'm so sorry this has happened. If there is anything I can do ...'

'You've done enough by leaving the door open,' Dan retorted curtly.

'Dan!' Jess was indignant.

'No, he's right. And I am sorry.' Rhodri moved towards the front door. 'Look, I'll leave you now, but if you need anything from the farm you know where I am.'

Dan grimaced as the door slammed behind him. 'Tosser!'

'It wasn't his fault,' Jess retorted sternly.

Dan sighed. 'No, it wasn't.' He gestured at the sketchbook. 'What do you want to do with this, shall I chuck it out?'

'No!' She spread her hands over it protectively. 'No, leave it!'

'At least let me clear up the glass.' He glanced up at her. 'No? OK, I'll tell you what. Let's have another drink before we go to bed.'

Jess froze. She stood for a moment unable to move then at last she looked up. 'Dan –'

He glanced up enquiringly, eyebrow raised and she looked away, embarrassed. He hadn't meant it like that. Of course he hadn't. She smiled uncomfortably. 'No more for me, thanks. I think I'll go up now. I'm a bit tired ...' Refusing to catch his eye as he moved towards her, obviously intending to give her a goodnight kiss, she stepped back sharply. 'Goodnight, Dan. Can you turn all the lights off for me.' In seconds she had dodged round the table towards the stairs, leaving him looking after her with a puzzled frown.

Hours later she woke with a start. The latch on the door had clicked up. She stared across the room in the dark, her heart hammering. The house was totally silent.

'Dan?' She whispered the name soundlessly. But there was no further noise. Quietly she slipped out of bed and tiptoed across to the door, pressing her ear against the oak panels. There was no movement from the other side as she ran her fingers gently over the small brass bolt she had found there. Without wasting time to wonder why Steph had thought fit to put bolts on her bedroom doors she had been almost ashamed to find herself drawing it closed against Dan. She did not have to ask herself why she had been overwhelmed by this sudden feeling of revulsion at the thought of anyone coming to her bedroom, or why she had even for a second suspected Dan would suddenly be interested in her that way. He was, after all, a married man she had known for years as a friend. There had never been anything between them. It was an instinct; self-preservation. An automatic response to violation and fear.

She tensed at the sound of a slight creak from the landing and almost unconsciously she ran her fingers over the bolt again, pressing it in place, reassuring herself that it held, her cheek pressed against the warm wood of the door.

She stood there for a long time, aware of the silence which had settled over the house. Outside the starlight was slowly veiled by the drifting mist. In the darkness raindrops began to fall.

Jerking awake with a start she realised she had fallen asleep on her feet, leaning against the door. The house was quiet. The drumming rain on the studio roof outside her window was a steady background to the inner silence. With a groan she stumbled away from the door towards her bed and threw herself down on it. Within seconds she was asleep again.

The woods were dark and filled with the noise of the wind. Rain drummed on the leaves and somewhere nearby a fox gave a sharp angry bark. Gwladys lay huddled against her little brother, trembling.

'Togo?'

He didn't reply

'Togo? I'm scared.'

She could see nothing; the ground was cold and hard and the roots of the trees hanging round them dug into her. 'I don't like playing this game. I want Mam.' She began to rock backwards and forwards, humming to herself. 'Where's Eigon? Why doesn't she come? She'd sing to us.' She was near to tears. 'I'm hungry. Are you hungry, Togo?'

Still he didn't answer. She put out a hand to him. He was warm and solid, fast asleep in his own little world of dreams. Suddenly making up her mind she crawled away from him and stood up. Away from the shelter of the overhanging ditch the wind was very strong. The noise it made was frightening. No one would hear her if she called. She turned round, confused. Which way should she go? Where were the others?

'Eigon? I don't like this game. Can we stop playing now?' Making up her mind, she set out down the track, her back to the wind, her pale hair blowing round her head, her eyes fixed on the bushes in front of her. 'Eigon? Mam? Where are you?' In seconds she was completely lost.

Behind her Togo woke suddenly in the darkness. He put out his little hand for his sister and found himself alone. Frightened, he began to cry.

Jess woke up late to the sound of the steadily beating rain. Pulling on jeans and a sweater after a hasty shower she ran down to find Dan's holdall standing by the front door. She glanced into the kitchen. There was a pot of coffee on the table and it was set for two but there was no sign of him.

'Dan?'

'I'm in here.' His voice came from the dining room. 'Come and look at this, Jess.'

Reluctantly she walked over to the doorway and glanced in. He was staring down at the table. 'It's gone,' he said softly. 'All gone.'

'What has?' She moved towards him.

'The damage. The scribbles. The blood. Look.'

He stood back, gesturing at the sketchbook in front of him. His face was white.

She glanced down and gasped out loud. He was right. The sketchbook was completely undamaged. Hardly daring to touch it she reached out and turned the pages. They were all the same. Her drawings and paintings were pristine.

'I don't understand.' She picked up the book and riffled through it. 'What's happened?'

'You tell me.'

She turned and stared round the dining room. Nothing had been touched. Everything was as neat and tidy as it had been before Rhodri arrived.

'We can't have dreamed it, can we?' She met his gaze at last.

Dan shrugged. 'All three of us?' He shivered. 'Let's go into the kitchen. I made coffee before I came in here.'

She followed him. 'We can't all have imagined what happened, Dan.'

'No?' He grabbed the coffee pot. 'Look in the bin.'

With a quick glance at him she peered in. 'What am I looking at?'

'Nothing. That's the point. Where is the broken glass?'

'Oh Dan!' She dropped the lid and went to sit down at the table, ramming her sleeves up to her elbows, then running her fingers through her hair. Two intact bottles of wine stood side by side on the draining board.

He pushed a mug of coffee towards her. 'It looks as though we all suffered some kind of hallucination,' he said thoughtfully. 'I don't see how or why, but there is no other explanation. If we had all eaten the same thing I could put it down to magic mushrooms or something, but Rhodri didn't eat with us.'

'And your hand. Where you cut it? Is the cut still there?' She reached out and touched his wrist.

He stretched out his right hand and turned it up to face her. There was no mark.

'Oh God!' She gave an involuntary shudder. 'What on earth has happened to us?'

'I'm afraid I am not going to be able to hang around to find out.' He glanced up at her again. 'I have to leave pretty soon, Jess. I've got a long drive ahead. Shall I ring up your mate Rhodri and get him to come over? You shouldn't be on your own to sort this out, but I don't know how my being here can help. Whatever it was it's over now.' He gave a small sharp bark of laughter. 'Next time I see you we'll joke about this!' Gulping back his coffee, he stood up.

For a moment she hadn't moved. She was still staring at his hand. Then she shook her head. 'Don't worry about me, Dan. I'll give Rhodri a ring later and tell him what has happened.'

She followed him out to his car and watched as he loaded his bag and his books. In minutes she was waving him out of sight as he headed down towards the lane, his car bumping over the ruts. Strangely she felt nothing but relief at his departure. Had he got up in the night and tested her door handle, she wondered? Probably not. She frowned suddenly. He hadn't offered to kiss her goodbye.

Walking back inside she went into the kitchen and straight to the sink. Without knowing why she turned on the tap and slowly rinsed her hands and face, then she reached for a towel.

Have the nasty men gone?

The voice was very close behind her. With a cry of fright she span round.

Can we stop playing now?

'Jesus!' She took a deep breath. 'Where are you?'

There was no reply.

'Eigon? Glads? Was it one of you who did that?' She was suddenly angry. 'Did you scribble over my drawings?' She scanned the room. 'Did you break all that glass?'

Outside the blackbird began to whistle from the roof of the studio. The rain had stopped and a stray ray of sunlight reflected off the wet paving stones. 'Did you hear me?' Jess called out again. She was suddenly every inch the schoolmistress. 'I want to see you. Now!' She held her breath, looking round. There was no sound. 'I mean it!'

Was that a gurgle of laughter? She ran to the window and stared out, scanning the courtyard. The house was full of sound. The creak of roof timbers, the rustle of leaves, the drip of rain down the gutters, birds, the baaing of sheep from the hillside on the far side of the track. 'Eigon?' Jess used the child's name without thinking, just as her mother, Cerys, had used it. 'Come here. I want to speak to you.'

59

But there was no response, as she had known there wouldn't be. She shook her head. Wandering back into the dining room she looked down at the table, half afraid that the sketchbook would once more be damaged. It wasn't. It lay there untouched.

'Shit!' She went to the phone, overcoming her reluctance to contact Rhodri again. After about twenty rings the answer service picked up. 'Rhodri? I'm sorry to disturb you, but can you come back here as soon as you can, there is something I need to show you.' She paused. 'Dan has gone. I'm on my own.'

Pulling the car into a gateway at the bottom of the lane, Dan turned off the engine and rested his forehead against the rim of the steering wheel. He was sweating hard. Fumbling blindly for the door handle he stumbled out into the long grass and nettles, dotted with campion, which fringed the trackway into the field and stood leaning on the gate waiting for the wave of nausea to pass. Then he turned and looked at the car.

It was empty. But someone had been in there, sitting behind him. Almost as soon as he had turned into the lane and pulled away from Ty Bran he had felt it. He could sense a presence. A solid threatening presence. A man. An angry, hate-filled man.

He had slammed on the brakes, staring into the mirror. Then he had turned, scanning the back seat. Nothing. Of course there was no one there. He accelerated away again, fast, over the roughly metalled lane, bumping the car over potholes and ridges, skidding over patches of red oozing mud which had leaked onto the road from the steep banks, growing more and more afraid until he had spotted the gateway, somewhere to pull up and throw himself out of reach of the malign shadow that was sharing his car.

Slowly the palpitations slowed. He wiped his face on his sleeve and turned, leaning on the gate, to stare at the vehicle. It sat there in the sunlight, the windows bright with reflections, the door hanging open as he had left it when he jumped out. Pushing himself away from the gate he forced himself to walk over and pull open the rear door. Leaning down, he peered in. Nothing. Cautiously he reached in, clawing at the empty air over the seat with his fingers as though to prove to himself the space was unoccupied. The film of sweat was drying on his face. He shivered, suddenly chilled. Somewhere in the distance he could hear the wild yapping cry of a buzzard, then near it, aggressive and primitive, the deep throaty croak of a raven. He peered up at the sky. It was up there. He could see it. The raven, a black silhouette against the blue, had set its sights on the buzzard. It was flying fast, on the attack, harrying, bullying, its call a sinister throbbing counterpoint to the alarmed yelp of the larger bird. Both birds angled their wings and swooped away over the fields and in a second they were out of sight over the shoulder of the hill.

Dan found he was breathing fast, as though he had been running. He swallowed hard, slamming the back door shut. Imagination. That was all. That damned haunted house and Jess with all her hysterical stories. They had got to him. He moved his head uncomfortably, his neck suddenly very stiff. For a moment he felt quite dizzy. He blinked. Something on the door had caught his eye. A smear of red. He held out his right hand and stared at it. A deep scar showed across his palm where he had cut it on the glass the night before. The cut that had disappeared. It was oozing blood. He shook his head. This was not happening! He straightened his back and squared his shoulders, furious with himself and with Jess. The sooner he got out of this god-forsaken place the better.

'So, what do you want to show me?'

Rhodri turned in at the gate just after twelve. He stood looking down at her with a quizzical expression, half irritation, half amusement as he held out a bottle of white wine. She took it with a cautious grin. 'The wine situation is not quite so dire as it was yesterday. Come and see.'

He followed her into the dining room and stood beside her, staring down at her sketchbook. 'I don't understand.'

'Neither did we. None of it happened. The pictures weren't spoiled. The glass wasn't broken. The wine bottles are full. Dan wasn't cut.' She glanced at Rhodri sideways. He was frowning as he looked down at the sketchbook. Almost nervously he reached out and turned the page. 'This is some kind of joke, yes?'

'No!'

'That boyfriend of yours –'

'Not my boyfriend. A colleague.'

'Well, your colleague. He was trying to scare you, wasn't he?

Thought if you were frightened enough you would jump into bed with him.'

'No!' Jess turned on him furiously. 'That is complete crap!'

'So, you're telling me he doesn't fancy you?' He favoured her with a look which made her feel first hot then cold as her mouth dropped open with indignation.

'No, he doesn't. At least . . .' She paused. 'No, of course he doesn't. He's a married man!'

'Since when has that stopped people? Two of you here alone, no one for miles. Pretty house, lots of wine, no one here to interrupt, till I blunder in! You both made it pretty clear you did not want company.'

'No, Rhodri. You've got it all wrong.' She stared down at the sketchbook again. 'How could anyone fake all that?'

'Easy. Another sketchbook – so badly damaged you couldn't tell. Lots of glass and spilled wine which could be cleaned up in the night. No real cut on his hand, just Kensington Gore.'

'Kensington Gore?' Jess was staring at him, bewildered.

'Fake blood, darling!'

Her mouth dropped open. 'No. You're wrong,' she repeated angrily. 'Quite wrong!'

'Am I? Maybe.' He smiled. 'Blame my profession. I have a taste for melodrama. But I'm a damn good judge of character. I wouldn't trust that guy further than I could throw him.'

'He's my friend.' She drew herself upright. 'You have no business to say things like that!'

'OK!' He raised his hands in mock surrender. 'Forget I said anything. The great thing is that no harm was done and if you gave in to his comforting advances, then I apologise.'

'He didn't make any advances!' Jess broke off abruptly. Suddenly she was remembering Dan's ambiguous goodnight, the way he had stepped forward to kiss her, the bedroom door latch, the creak on the landing. She shivered. No. That was rubbish. Dan didn't fancy her. He never had.

Seeing Rhodri's raised eyebrow she went on, 'Whatever else he might have done he couldn't have faked my sketchbook. That was ruined last night. You saw it. It was covered in blood. It's the same book.'

He shrugged. 'Then I can't explain how he did it. The man's a miracle worker!'

She glared at him, shaking her head. 'There is another possibility,' she said tentatively. 'Do you know if this house is haunted?'

Rhodri roared with laughter. 'Ah, so it was the ghost!'

'Maybe.'

When she didn't smile he sobered rapidly. He studied her face, his head on one side. 'Your sister thinks it is. She told my mother about it.'

'What did she say?'

'There's a child here. A naughty child. She breaks things in the studio.'

Jess felt her stomach lurch. For a moment she said nothing.

Rhodri looked at her thoughtfully. 'I think that is a cue for a drink if ever there was one.'

Jess watched as he vanished into the kitchen and with a confidence born of long association reached down two glasses from the cupboard, found a corkscrew and set about opening his bottle. He returned and handed her a glass. 'This whole valley is haunted. I was brought up with the legends of these hills. Down there,' he gestured towards the window, 'in the valley bottom where the river runs, is the site of an ancient battle, so the story goes. And up on the hill behind us, there is an Iron Age fort. The place is full of ghosts of fallen warriors and anguished gods. Stories like that are told over centuries and improve with the telling, but there must be some truth behind them. Round here they claim it is the location of the last stand of Caratacus against the Romans. He was the Welsh hero who rallied the tribes.'

'And the child in this house was his daughter,' Jess said, half to herself.

Rhodri looked sceptical. 'That's a huge deduction! But come to think of it, why not.' He took a swig from his glass. 'It would be surprising if there weren't ghosts round here. The Welsh borders are full of them. A thousand battles, two thousand years of strife. Mist and magic round every corner. It is a blessed place.' He grinned.

Jess found herself smiling back almost against her will. When he wasn't being aggressive he had a nice face. 'Unless you happen to be living on top of a hot spot!'

'Nicely put. You know what this house is called. Ty Bran. That means, Ravens House. And down there they call it the Valley of Ravens. It fits the story. Ravens come to a battlefield to pick the bodies of the dead clean. The battle goddess, is a raven goddess.'

Jess shivered. 'It's hardly surprising memories of something like that haunt a place.'

He hesitated. 'Well, don't let it put you off. It's all in the past.'

'Is it, though?' She smiled sadly.

'Yes.' He looked at her with a frown. 'Yes, it is.' He drained his glass and put it down. 'Look, I've got to go. My agent is coming over. He won't stay long though. He doesn't like to be out of the metropolis after dark! The ghosts are too much for him as well. Ring me if it all gets too much for you, girl, and I'll take you down to the pub later. Distract you with a bevvy and a meal.' He headed for the door. 'Believe me, you're better on your own up here. That chap was no good for you.'

She opened her mouth to argue but he was already halfway across the yard and climbing back into his car.

'Cheeky bastard!' she muttered as he began to back out of the gate. But for some reason he had made her feel better.

6

That afternoon she walked up the track and into the wood, splashing through glittering puddles, listening to the chatter of the leaves in the light wind, feeling the dappled sunlight on her face. The track wound its way upwards through stands of ash and oak, every now and then coming near enough to the edge of the trees for her to be able to rest and gaze across the broad river valley towards the north. From here she could just see the river, a strip of glittering blue, fringed with willows, winding its way across the water meadows. In the distance she could hear sheep calling, and the wild yelping cry of a buzzard, soaring out across the hills. It was blessedly peaceful and very hard to imagine a battle taking place anywhere nearby.

She was out of breath by the time she reached a stand of older trees, ancient lichen-covered oaks, near the top of the hill, and beside them a venerable yew. Falling away to the south the ground was steep, almost terraced, with knotted roots and tangled brambles hugging the contours down towards a rocky stream far below. As she stood trying to regain her breath she saw a fox, trotting across a clearing only metres away from her. Intent on its own affairs it never saw her, vanishing almost at once into a thicket.

Sitting down on a mossy log at the foot of one of the trees she leaned back against the trunk, content to rest for a few minutes in the sunlight, suddenly aware that in the distance a dog was barking.

The praefectus sent ten men out to the spot where Cerys and Eigon had been found. They spent a day searching the woods for the two children without success. Dogs were brought in and the whole area combed again; then Eigon was brought with her mother to the track near the tumbled byre. The child was crying as Cerys led her forward into the trees, followed by the legionaries. The men looked grave. They knew there was nowhere else to search. Every foxhole and badger sett, with all their miles of passages, the *nant* flowing over its rocky bed, the ditches and hollows under the roots of the trees had been scoured now by men or dogs. There was nowhere else to look. Before them the trees thrashed in yet another storm, leaves flying in a whirl into the mud, obscuring any tracks not already overlaid by the heavy tramp of the nailed sandals of the soldiers.

'Just try, sweetheart. Did you run up or down the hill, can you remember? Did you cross the stream?' Cerys held her daughter's hand tightly, trying desperately not to show her fear.

'We played a game. Hide and seek. I told them not to come out.'

'That was right. That was what I told you to do.' Cerys's voice was shaking. 'But now we need to call them.'

Already it was growing dark again. The heavy sky hid any trace of the sunset as the rain clouds streamed in across the land from the west.

Two of the men approached their officer and saluted. 'We're not going to find them, sir. We've been over every inch of ground. They must have wandered off or someone or something must have got them.'

'No!' Cerys's wail of despair echoed through the trees. Dropping Eigon's hand she grabbed the arm of the praefectus. 'Please, you can't stop looking. You can't!'

He looked down at her thoughtfully. The woman was right. It was not so much the plight of the children which motivated him, but the thought of what the commander would say if any of Caratacus's family were mislaid. Hostages were vital at the best of times and these particular hostages, more vital than most. The bargaining power implicit in their capture was enormous. He turned to the men. 'Widen the search. Continue through the night if necessary. Bring another fifty men.'

Justinus personally escorted Cerys and her daughter back to the encampment and left them at the entrance to their tent. As Eigon disappeared inside, her tear-streaked face wan with exhaustion, the praefectus put a restraining hand on her mother's arm.

'Could you identify the men who assaulted you?' he asked.

Cerys shook her head. 'I lost consciousness. I don't remember –'

'And the child?'

Cerys shook her head miserably. 'How can I even ask her?'

'If you want them punished you will ask her.' He looked down at her grimly. 'Consider, madam, whether those same men could have found your son and your other daughter.'

Cerys let out a small moan of distress. She turned back towards him but already he had saluted and turned away, tramping off through the mud into the darkness towards the long lines of tents. The guards at her own had already stepped forward, crossing their spears across the entrance to imprison her. Inside, in the gentle light of the single oil lamp on the empty clothes trunk which served as a table she could see the woman who had been assigned to wait on them gently rubbing Eigon's hair with a towel.

'Sweetheart!' Waving the woman away, Cerys knelt in front of the child and took hold of her firmly by the arms. 'I want you to tell me something. The man who hurt you so badly,' she paused, staring into her daughter's eyes, 'would you know him again?'

She saw the eyes widen, the terror at the violent return of the memory, a moment of total paralysis as the fear returned and then the slow reluctant nod.

'How would you recognise him?'

'He had eyes like a wolf; the colour of your sunshine beads.'

Amber.

'He had a tattoo high up on his arm. But not a beautiful pattern like our warriors. It was hard and rough. A picture of a Roman sword with writing on.'

Sinking down on her knees Cerys breathed deeply, releasing the child and clenching her fists in the folds of her skirt until her knuckles were white. 'Would you know him if you saw him?'

The little girl nodded. 'His face is a picture inside my head. And his arm too. I looked at it hard while he –' there was a sudden painful pause. 'While he was hurting me. I will never forget his arm . . .'

'His arm!' Jess's eyes flew open. The arm, across her throat, pushing her back, holding her down on the bed, she could see it suddenly as clearly as she could see her own hand, clenched on her knees. And the arm though it was tanned, and covered in fine dark hairs, was without any doubt at all the arm of a white man. It was not Ash!

67

She was still leaning against the tree. The sun was still shining. Above her the buzzard was calling, a lonely wild wail high amongst the clouds, and suddenly she was shaking violently. The bastard! He was holding her down on her bed. His face was there, above her, all she had to do was open her eyes to see his face. But she couldn't see his face. The memory had gone.

'Shit!' She lowered her forehead onto her knees. Will. It had to have been Will.

Raising her face to the sun, she stared out between the trees into the misty blue distances.

She couldn't bear it to be Will.

But if not Will, who?

Dan?

It was a long time before she stood up and headed slowly back along the track towards home.

She went straight to the telephone to call Dan. She could at least ask him if he had faked the wrecking of the dining room. As a joke as Rhodri had suggested. Some joke.

The message light on the phone was flashing. It was Rhodri. 'Jess? I've just noticed in the *Radio Times*, there is a play on Radio 4 tonight. About Cartimandua. Have you ever heard of her? Listen to it. I think it might interest you. Eight o'clock.'

'No, I haven't heard of her! Who the hell is Cartimandua!' Jess murmured as she punched in Dan's number. The phone rang and rang. Neither Dan nor his message service picked up and she hung up with a sigh.

The house was very quiet, the quietness almost eerie as though someone was there, listening. She walked over to the door and peered out into the hall, then walked slowly through the house, holding her breath. There was no one there, no sign that anyone had been in while she was out.

As the sun began to go down she bolted the front door, and removing Steph's dried flowers, lit a fire of old apple logs in the living room. Making herself a supper of scrambled eggs on toast she sat on the floor in the long summer twilight to listen to the radio as she watched the flicker of flames on the old soot-stained stone of the fireplace.

Cartimandua was, it appeared, an Iron Age, Celtic queen, a contemporary of Caratacus and of Boudica, but in contrast to her sister queen, she was an ally of Rome. Pushing aside her plate and picking up her glass of wine Jess leaned back against the sofa and listened enthralled as the play unfolded. Caradoc. The name echoed through the room as the evening faded into darkness round her. Caradoc was the name the Celts gave him. Caratacus was the Roman version. This was the man whose army had been defeated here in the valley below her sister's house. And now she knew what had happened to him. He had fled after the battle, having no choice but to abandon his wife and children and make his way almost alone and badly wounded, into the mountains, fleeing north and then east towards the lands of the Brigantes, the vast tribal confederation which was ruled by his kinswoman, Queen Cartimandua. There, he was sure he would find safety and help. He found neither. She took him prisoner, and feeling herself irrevocably bound by a treaty she had made with the Emperor Claudius when he had invaded the country seven years before, offered Caradoc, as a captive, back to his enemies.

'What a cow!' Jess threw more logs onto the fire and poured herself another glass of wine. 'So, what happened to him after that?'

The play did not reveal the answer. It followed the course of the queen's life and loves; once Caratacus had been dragged away in chains by his Roman escort he was not mentioned again. She wondered if Cartimandua had given him another thought.

Jess sat for a long time after the play finished, gazing into the flames, listening to the crackle of burning logs. Had Caratacus been reunited with his wife and children? Was he killed? Were they all killed? She did not know.

But she had a strong feeling that Eigon and Glads would tell her.

In her dreams, or as they rampaged round the house in their rage and fear, the ghost children who had been Caratacus's daughters would tell her the story whether she wanted to hear it or not. Jess shivered. She had no choice. A link had been forged between her and Eigon through the experience of rape and betrayal; as long as she stayed in the house she would have to listen to Eigon's story.

Is Papa there?

The voice was thin and reedy, terrified, echoing against the sound of the wind and rain against the window. Jess lay still, clutching the sheet to her chin, staring up at the ceiling. It was two thirty a.m. She had just checked the clock again. Closing her eyes against the bedside light she turned over, humping the sheet over her shoulder against the glare, yet not daring to turn it off.

Have we finished playing the game? Papa will know where Togo and Glads are. He knows everything.

There was a click from the door. Jess turned over, staring at it in terror. Slowly it swung open. Beyond it the landing was pitch dark.

Clutching her pillow to her breasts, she sat up. Someone was walking towards her across the room. She couldn't see them or hear them, she just sensed it. 'Go away!' she cried. Her voice wavered uncertainly. 'Please go away. I can't help you. I don't know where they are. I don't know where your father is!'

The presence stopped. It was listening. Jess clenched her fists into the cotton of the pillowslip. 'Look, I would help you if I could. Your father went to the Queen of the Brigantes for help. I know that much. He was hurt, but he wasn't killed in the battle.'

The silence in the room grew intense. It had a thick palpable quality; it was hard to breathe. Jess could feel her lungs straining; her mouth was dry, her eyes gritty. 'Please, Eigon. Go away. I can't help you. I would if I could. I know how you feel –' She paused. 'I understand.' The feeling of invasion, of pain, deep within her soul, the anguish of a woman who has been raped and violated and left for dead. And this child wasn't even a woman when she had been attacked by those men; she was barely more than a baby. Of course she understood!

'Sweetheart, I know how hard it is. But it will get better.' She shivered. How could she say that, utter platitudes to an invisible thought form standing in the middle of her bedroom floor when she didn't even know if the child had survived; or her father, her mother, her brother and sister. All might have been dead within days or weeks of the battle. One thing was for sure. They were all dead now.

'I'm asleep,' she said suddenly to herself. 'None of this is happening. This is a dream. I am asleep and there is no one here. I am all alone. Soon it will be time to get up and have breakfast in the sunshine and I will wonder what I was worrying about. In fact, I won't remember anything about this. Nothing at all.'

70

The child was gone. Staring round the room she could sense it. There was no one there. The house was empty again; in the garden the moonlight was slowly spreading through the wood. In seconds it would have reached the window of her bedroom and thrown a silver gleam across her floor and her fear would go. Leaning back she began to breathe more easily again. Within minutes she was asleep.

She was sitting in front of a cup of black coffee next morning in the kitchen, still wearing her nightshirt, her feet bare, her hair tousled, when the phone rang. It was Rhodri. 'Are you listening to the radio? Turn it on. Now. Speak to you afterwards!'

Her head was splitting; the amnesia she had promised herself in the moonlight had not happened. With a groan she stood up and went to turn on the radio.

'Viv Lloyd Rees and Pat Hebden's drama documentary *Queen of the North* was aired last night to huge acclaim,' the announcer's voice floated out across the kitchen. 'They are here in the studio with me to talk about their play and the research that went into it and to share with us the quite extraordinary experiences which they endured as they unearthed their heroine's story.'

Jess sat down and reached for her coffee mug as the two women told their tale. Somehow, by digging into the past, they had awoken it. Even now, so it seemed, embarrassed to talk about what had happened to them, they described the terrifying events which had occurred as they probed the story of Cartimandua, events which had led eventually to disaster and even death.

Jess listened to the programme with increasing horror and fascination until the discordant eerily Celtic echoes of the closing music broke the mood. Wearily she rose and went to turn off the radio, then she picked up the phone. 'How did you know it was coming on?' she said as Rhodri answered.

'They said so last night. After the play. Didn't you hear them? What did you think?'

She could hear music playing in the background, powerful orchestral music, and she wished suddenly that she was there in the Prices' warm kitchen. 'I thought it was terrifying. Do you believe what they were saying? I can't think how they could have gone on to write a play about her. I'd have been afraid I would go on raising the dead with every word I wrote.' She paused. 'Is that what I've done, Rhodri? Woken the ghosts here?' She had forgotten her initial hostility to this man. He understood.

'I don't know about you particularly,' he said thoughtfully, 'after all Steph has noticed things too. Although you do seem to have woken them up a bit!'

Jess bit her lip. Of course. He didn't know what it was that she and Eigon had in common; the reason the child who was the daughter of Caratacus had come to her to share her tears. And, perhaps, to ask for help. She froze. Is that what she was doing? Asking for help . . .

'It's interesting, isn't it, perhaps you should see if they've got a website?' Rhodri went on cheerfully. 'As long as you're not scared! What a bit of luck I spotted that entry in the *Radio Times* yesterday – I was looking for one of my concerts – as it happens they are putting it on tonight.'

Jess gave a wan smile. 'I'll listen to it –' She broke off as she caught sight of the reflection from a car windscreen as it flashed across the wall. 'Sorry, Rhodri. Someone has come. I'll call you later.'

Will's red MG sports car had pulled into the yard. Already he had opened the door and was climbing out, pulling off his sunglasses, looking round. 'Jess?' He strode towards the open front door. 'Jess, are you there?' Moments later he was standing in the kitchen looking at her. 'There you are! My God you've become elusive, Jess.' He stepped towards her, then registering the panic on her face as she stepped behind the kitchen table defensively, he stopped. 'What's wrong? Sorry. Did I give you a fright? I thought you'd seen me from the window.' He threw his shades down on the table. 'Is there any coffee left in that pot? It's still a hell of a drive from London, isn't it? Do you remember, when we used to do it together and get here at dawn, before Steph was even up?' He pulled out a chair and sat down at the table, studying her face. 'What's wrong, Jess? What is this all about?'

Jess bit her lip. She sat down opposite him. 'You know what it's about, Will. And you know I would never want to see you again. So, why come?'

'I've come because you wouldn't return my calls, Jess. I had to know why. I thought we had parted on reasonably good terms after the party; I'd thought we could be civilised. I thought we'd enjoyed dancing together. Then I find you have resigned from school and run away and no one will tell me where you've gone, and I was worried about you. If Dan hadn't rung yesterday –'

'*Dan* told you where I was?'

'He's worried, too, Jess.'

'I'll bet he is. Did he know you were going to jump in the car and come straight here?' She was fighting a wave of hysteria.

'I don't know –'

'Did it not occur to you to ring and see if it was convenient? To find out if I wanted to see you again?'

'I didn't think –'

'No, you didn't think!'

'If you would let me get a word in edgeways. I didn't think you would want to see me. That's why I came unannounced. I thought that way at least I would be able to see you face to face! I know we are finished, Jess, but at least give me credit for wanting to know you are all right.'

'All right! Did you really think I would be all right after what you did?'

'Oh, for God's sake. Haven't we got beyond that?'

They were both shouting now, their voices harsh and angry.

Can we stop playing now?

The words echoed round the kitchen.

Jess gasped.

'Look, Jess,' Will continued, jumping into the moment of silence before she could reply. 'I am sorry we split up. You will never know how sorry. And I still care about you. How can someone stop caring after all that time?' He didn't appear to have heard the child's voice. 'I wanted to make sure you were all right. Clearly you are, so I will leave.' He stood up. Then after a moment's hesitation he sat down again. 'Look, please, can we start this conversation again? You and I have muddled through since we broke up. We have managed to be civil in school; I thought we might become friends again, at least. I don't know what I have done to cause this fury suddenly. Explain it to me.'

'You don't know? You thought what you did was OK?' Her voice was shaking.

'No. It wasn't. I behaved badly. I was an arrogant bastard. And I'm sorry. You'll never know how sorry.'

'So you thought you would show me how much you still love

73

me?' Her voice sharpened. 'You've got a very strange way of showing it. Get out, Will.' Suddenly she was near to tears.

'Jess –'

'Get out!' Her voice rose to a scream.

Please. Can we stop playing now.

The little girl was close to her, whispering in her ear. Jess put her hands to her ears and shook her head. 'Go away!' She was speaking to the child.

'Jess –'

'You go too, Will! Now. I never want to see you again!'

'But, please –'

'Go!' Her voice was still dangerously near to a scream. 'Get out! I came here to get away from you. I left school to get away from you. I thought it was Ash, but it wasn't, was it. You let me think that! You would have let him take the blame, wouldn't you, ruined the boy's life to save your own beastly skin! You're a coward as well as a pervert and a vicious bastard, and you'll never know how nearly I went to the police. I could still go, you know!'

'Jess –'

'Get out, Will!' Her voice dropped to a whisper. 'Get out now.'

He stood up and without a word went to the door. For a moment she was too paralysed to move, then running to the window she watched as he climbed into the car, revved the engine and shot backwards out of the gate. He drove off without looking back. Only when he was out of sight did she finally burst into tears.

It was a long time before she stopped crying. Only then did she go to the phone and dial Dan's number. He picked up on the third ring.

'Dan! How could you! Why in God's name did you tell him where I was?'

'Hold on.' There was a moment's silence. She heard muffled voices, then a door banged. Then Dan came on the line again. 'What are you talking about, Jess?'

'You know damn well what I'm talking about. You told Will where I was.'

'He already knew, Jess. Well, it wasn't hard for him to guess, was it.'

'But you rang him. You rang him and told him.'

'No. He rang me.'

She paused, confused. Will must have lied to her about that

too. 'Then you needn't have confirmed it. You could have put him off. You could have told him to leave me alone.'

There was an amused chuckle at the other end of the line. 'You credit me with more influence than I have with him, Jess. I don't think I could have dissuaded him. He was obviously determined to find you. I take it he has spoken to you?'

'He's been here.'

There was a short pause. 'I see. What happened?'

'We had an argument. I told him to go away.'

'And he did, presumably.'

'Yes.'

'So, no harm done, then.'

'No harm done except that you betrayed me.' She paused. 'I've been trying to ring you, Dan. I've been thinking about what happened to my sketchbook. Was it you who messed up the house? Was that your idea of a joke? Did you break all that glass and spill the wine?'

'Whoa! Hang on! What are we talking about now? You know I didn't. How could I have done that? Why would I have done that? Get a grip, Jess.'

'It was a joke, though, wasn't it. What was it, you said? Mass hallucination? You took me for a complete fool, didn't you! And now you compound it by sending Will here. What are you trying to do to me, Dan?'

'I'm not trying to do anything, Jess!' Dan was indignant. 'Pull yourself together, love.'

'Don't patronise me!'

'I'm not patronising you.' His tone was exaggeratedly calm. 'I'm trying to make you see sense. You seem to have lost all perspective. Why are you like this? You've changed into an hysterical lightweight. There could be all sorts of explanations for what happened. Have you considered for instance that perhaps a bird might have flown in and knocked over the wine bottles and the glasses. Perhaps it cut itself.'

'And then miraculously got better?' Her voice was icy. 'No, Dan, it wasn't a bird. A lot of awful things have been happening recently. Nothing to do with birds. Your hand, for instance. How did that so suddenly heal itself?'

There was another pause, then he gave another exaggerated sigh. 'Poor old Will. Is all this because of what happened in London,

Jess? For God's sake, it wasn't that bad; anyone would think a bit of rough sex and the odd slap was the end of the world. Talk about overreacting. You've cast him as the villain of the piece and he doesn't stand a chance. No wonder he's angry.' There was a long moment of silence. 'Jess, are you still there?'

'How did you know what happened in London?' Jess asked tautly. 'I never told you what happened, Dan.'

'Of course you did. Not in so many words perhaps, but it was easy to guess. You decided in your own mind that you didn't like it; that it was rape or something and it has turned your head! You've become completely unstable.'

Jess could feel herself growing cold. For a moment she couldn't even speak, then at last she found the words. 'Who said anything about rape?'

He hesitated. 'Well, rape may not have been mentioned, but it wasn't very hard to work out what you thought had happened. A bit of non consensual sex! You decided to think of it as rape, didn't you? You worked yourself up into a tizz over it because you were so drunk you couldn't remember anything about it and then you decided to play the drama queen.'

There was a moment of total silence as once again she visualised the arm that had held her down. The tanned skin, the fine dark hairs.

It wasn't Will. It couldn't have been Will. Will was fair-haired.

'It was you, wasn't it,' she said slowly. 'You raped me! You've been so busy implicating Ash and Will that I never saw it. I never even guessed. But it was your arm that held me down. Your face in my nightmares.' Her voice had dropped to a whisper. 'I've been so stupid. I trusted you. You unutterable bastard!'

'Don't be so silly!'

'No, Dan. I can remember everything suddenly. You followed Ash and me home. You sent Ash away when we got to the front door and you came up to the flat. We had some wine –'

'No, Jess.'

'Why? What was it you gave me? Did you come prepared? You went to a school dance with date rape drugs in your pocket!' She paused, her hands sweating as they clutched the telephone. The receiver was slipping from her grasp. 'Just what were you planning, Dan? Was it me you wanted, or didn't it matter? Would anyone have done? One of the girls, perhaps? A child!'

'Jess, you're mad!'

'No. I'm just beginning to see. Does Natalie know about your little hobby, Dan? I know the headmaster doesn't. But he should, shouldn't he!'

'Jess, you're insane!'

'No. I've just realised what a fool I've been. There were signs everywhere, weren't there. You watch the girls. You touch them. I've seen you!'

'Jess, I warn you. This is slander —' His voice was suddenly harsh with anger.

'No, Dan. This is the truth!'

'Jess, you've got this all wrong. Look, I'm coming over!'

'Don't bother. It's too late.'

'I don't think so. I'm coming now. Look, I can explain. You don't understand. You've misunderstood everything! You are so wrong!'

'I'm not wrong, Dan. I'm going to the police.' Suddenly she was completely calm.

When Dan spoke at last it was in a shocked whisper. 'You go to the police, Jess, and it will destroy me. And Nat and the kids. Surely you don't want that.' She could hear the panic in his voice. 'You have misunderstood the situation. I never meant to frighten you. I thought you were willing. You were willing. You should have seen yourself. You were so drunk.' He gave a snort of derision. 'You weren't drugged. That's your imagination. It was just the drink. Ash had been giving you all sorts of things. The kids had loads of booze in there. Most of them were unconscious by the end. For God's sake, Jess. You can't tell anyone. It would wreck my career.' He paused. 'No one would believe you anyway. After all you haven't told anyone, have you.' He gave a small harsh laugh at her silence. 'I thought not. Look, I'm on my way. I'll make it up to you. I can explain. Wait there!'

'I don't think so. I'm going to be anywhere but here when you arrive, Dan,' she retorted. Her words reverberated into the silence. 'Dan, are you there?' Had he hung up? She could hear the line still open.

At the end of the field, where the phone cable ran through the corner of the wood, a tree branch had snapped. It caught on the wire, swung for a few seconds and fell. The line was severed.

'Dan? Dan, did you hear me? Don't you dare come here!' Jess slammed down the phone. Her hands were shaking.

Can we stop playing now?

The voice was louder than before. It was Glads.

Jess looked round wildly. She wasn't going to sit there and wait for Dan to arrive and try and persuade her to forget what had happened. Not when he was as angry as that. She had to go. What was there to keep her here anyway? Just her sister's bloody plants. Well, they could look after themselves for a bit.

It took less than half an hour to pack everything into the car. How far away was Shrewsbury? How long would it take Dan to get there? She had to be away before he came. Racing round one last time she locked the house and ran out to the car.

It wouldn't start.

'Don't do this to me!' She slammed the palms of her hands against the steering wheel and tried the ignition again. Still nothing. The battery was flat. She must have left the lights on when she went out last. Shit. Shit. Shit! She tried to steady her breathing. After all, what could Dan do? He was angry and threatening. He could shout at her. Swear. What else? Supposing he got violent? He could beat the daylights out of her. Or rape her again. Or try to kill her. Her mind was racing out of control. He was right. He had so much to lose. Was that a car in the lane? Horrified she paused, listening. He couldn't have got here already, surely. She swallowed, paralysed with fear, trying to calm herself as she realised the sound she could hear came from a tractor, somewhere in the valley bottom, the sound carrying on the still air. She pumped the clutch up and down a couple of times and tried again. Nothing. The engine was dead.

'God, what am I going to do?'

She climbed out and ran in to the phone. It was dead and her mobile battery was flat.

Rhodri was sitting at the piano when she arrived. She could hear him singing from the gate and she paused for a moment to listen, stunned by the power and beauty of his voice. He stopped at the sound of the dogs barking and came to the door to meet her. 'Ah, it's you. How goes the ghost hunt?'

Making her way across the fields to find him had been her only option without a car. 'Can I come in?' She was half afraid she would turn and see Dan running over the field after her.

78

Rhodri frowned. 'Sure.' He stood back and ushered her into the kitchen. Through the open door into Megan's sitting room Jess saw the grand piano, the lid raised, the notebook and pencil lying on the piano stool, the piles of music. He had been working. 'So, what's happened? You look upset.'

'Upset!' Jess realised suddenly what she must look like. Exhausted, out of breath, her hair tangled and wild, her shoes covered in mud. She struggled to compose herself, then abandoned the attempt. Her eyes were full of tears when she faced him. 'I'm sorry to interrupt but I need your help! The phone is broken and my mobile won't work.'

'OK. Sit down.' He turned away and reached for the kettle, just as his mother would have done. Behind them the two dogs were sitting in the doorway.

The few moments he took to fill the kettle were enough for her to get a grip on herself. 'The car wouldn't start. I had to get away. You were right about Dan. He's not quite the friend I thought.'

'And you're running away from him?' He looked incredulous.

She nodded miserably. 'Stupidly I rang him and accused him. He said he was coming straight back. I packed the car. I planned to be gone long before he arrived then it wouldn't start and I couldn't contact anyone and I was –' She paused, biting her lip, furious with herself for being so feeble.

'You were scared?' Rhodri raised an eyebrow. He slid the kettle onto the Raeburn, then he took the seat opposite her, clearing a gap in the piles of letters and notebooks on the table so he could lean forward on his elbows and study her face. 'Well, he's not going to find you if you are here, is he. So, why don't you tell me the whole story. Why on earth are you frightened of him? You were both very close last time I saw you. This must be about more than a stupid practical joke.'

'It is.' She paused, fighting off the urge to confide the whole story. 'We . . . we didn't get on at the college where we teach,' she compromised. God, she wasn't going to forgive herself in a hurry for appearing such a weak fool in front of this man. What must he think of her! 'That was why I resigned. I thought we were friends. But I made a mistake. I told him I knew about something he had done and he got angry. Vindictive.' She forced a watery smile. 'I'm sorry to involve you, it's just that he was so furious when I said I knew it was him and he said he was coming

79

straight over and, you're right, I was scared. I just didn't want to see him again.'

'I'm not surprised.' Rhodri levered himself to his feet and went to make the tea. 'I'll drive you back when we've had this. Sort out your car and wait for lover boy. I am bigger than him, don't forget!' He glanced over his shoulder with a wink.

In spite of herself, Jess laughed, suddenly very aware of his broad shoulders and muscular frame in the open-necked shirt and jeans. She looked away hurriedly. 'You are indeed.'

'Then I can respectfully suggest he goes away and leaves you alone.' He pushed a mug of tea towards her. 'Poor Jess. And you came up here to have some peace. Ghosts and arrogant opera singers and now vengeful teachers. What a combination!'

'I don't know what I would have done if you hadn't been here.'

'You would have thought of something.' He grinned. 'I'm just off to sing in a charity gala in Milan so you were lucky I was still here at all.'

She took a sip from the mug, astonished at how disappointed she felt that he was leaving. 'I am sorry to involve you in all this.'

'No sweat.' He noticed the dogs suddenly and clicked his fingers at them. They slunk away into the yard. 'Pity I can't lend you those two to look after you. That would scare the bugger off. But they wouldn't stay. Their job is here.'

'And they do it very well.'

'Working dogs, see. That's why they can't come in. Not that there are any sheep around at the moment. That's why Mum and Dad can get away for a few days. Dave, our shepherd, is keeping an eye on them on the hill. He'll be in charge once I've gone.'

Jess smiled. 'The dogs come in when your mum is here. I've seen her let them in.'

Rhodri snorted. 'I bet Dad doesn't know that.' He stood up. 'OK. Are you ready?'

As the big 4 x 4 bucked and strained up the steep pot-holed lane to the house, Jess found she was clenching her fists apprehensively, but there was no sign of Dan's car when they arrived. Rhodri pulled in and they climbed out. 'Right, let's have a look. Keys?' He put out his hand.

Looking nervously over her shoulder Jess handed him the car keys and waited while he unlocked it and levered himself into the driver's seat. She couldn't believe she had done this. She had

run away to find a man to save her, she had picked the most arrogant man she could find, arrogant even by his own admission,
and now she was letting him sort everything out. Her credentials
as an independent woman were completely shot.

The car started first go.

She stared at it uncomprehending. 'But it was dead. The battery
was flat. I'm sure it was.'

Rhodri touched his foot to the accelerator. 'Sounds like she's
fine. Nice little car.' He glanced up at her, his eyes twinkling.
'Perhaps you flooded the engine.'

'It was dead. Completely dead. Not even a light when I turned
the key!' Jess said furiously. 'No, this is not a stupid woman driver.
I know how to start a car!' Her panic had turned to fury.

Rhodri climbed out, leaving the engine running. 'Let her run
for a bit in case the battery was a bit flat. I never said you were
a stupid woman driver, did I?'

'No, but you thought it!'

'No. I didn't.' He strode towards the house. 'Now, let's have a
look inside and make sure everything is OK, then we'll sit and
wait for your friendly colleague to show up.'

Two hours passed and there was still no sign of him. Rhodri
made them an omelette and they drank a glass of wine, but Jess
could barely manage a mouthful. She was becoming more and
more uncomfortable and embarrassed.

'I doubt if he's coming after all,' Rhodri said eventually. 'Look,
I'm sorry, but I do have to go,' he grinned affably, 'I've things to
do before I leave.'

'Of course. I'm so sorry.' Jess leaped to her feet. 'And I am so
grateful for you coming to sort me out. I'm an idiot!'

He gave a tolerant grin. 'Not totally. You had got yourself in a
bit of a state. Never mind. I suggest you lock yourself in and get
a good night's sleep, then tomorrow you can make some calm
decisions about what to do. Don't let him chase you out of this
house, Jess. It's too nice a place. Just remember to lock that front
door. Don't leave it open for all and sundry to walk in.' He leaned
across before she could dodge back and kissed her on the cheek.
'My parents will be back in a couple of days. You'll have a bit
more support then. OK? And for goodness' sake remember to
charge up your mobile and report that phone out of order!' He
strode towards the front door.

Jess watched as he backed his car out of the yard. She stood for several minutes after he had disappeared down the lane, listening to the chorus of birds from the wood, then she stepped back inside and firmly closed the door. She wasn't going to stay and lock herself in. She was leaving now.

7

Steph put the phone down and turned back into the kitchen where Kim was frying onions and tomatoes. She was frowning. 'I've been trying all evening but there is still no reply from either phone.'

'Perhaps she's gone out.' Kim threw some sliced zucchini into the heavy pan and added more oil. With her dark hair and eyes and her plump figure – a testament to her fondness for her own cooking – Kim looked every inch the Italian mamma in the making for all she had been born in Romford and attended the same college as Jess and Steph. 'And she's forgotten to take her mobile.'

'That's probably it. I've reported the line at Ty Bran. They checked. It is broken.'

'Well, presumably someone will go and mend it.' Kim reached for her wine glass and took a sip before turning her attention back to the sauce. 'So, you can stop worrying, Steph. Jess is a big girl. She doesn't need you checking up on her all the time. In fact you never have before, so why now?'

Steph shook her head wearily. 'I don't know. I've got a strange feeling, that's all.'

'What sort of strange feeling?' Wooden spoon in hand, Kim paused in her stirring to gaze at her friend's face. 'You two aren't twins, are you?'

'You know we're not!'

'Then stop worrying. Go and see to our guests. Make sure everyone has got a drink. If you really want to know what is happening with Jess ask Carmella. She reads the cards. You'll find a deck in Stefano's old bureau.'

Steph wandered through the apartment towards the front door. From the grand reception room she could hear the sound of voices. Kim's penchant for cooking frequently led to these impromptu parties where her guests marvelled at the talent of their English hostess who could cook Italian food better than any of them.

Steph resisted the urge to mention the cards, but as they sat in the *salotto* later savouring their *dolci* and coffee Kim brought the subject up again.

'Steph needs some info about her sister, Carmella. Would you read the cards for her? Tell us what is happening over there in Wales?' She levered herself out of the deep sofa and went to the bureau, rummaging around in the drawers.

There was a general murmur of interest from the other guests at the suggestion as she drew out the small box she had been looking for.

Carmella, a tall, elegant woman in her forties, held out her hand languidly and took the box. 'I haven't seen these since Stefano died. Do you remember how often we would read them?' She smiled at Kim, raising one of her startlingly black, fly away eyebrows.

Kim nodded, suddenly wistful. 'He loved to watch you do it, but he would never let you do a reading for him. Perhaps if you had –'

'No!' Carmella started shuffling the deck. 'No, don't think of that. What was to be, was to be.' She flicked her dark hair out of her eyes and leaned forward to take a puff from the cigarette lying in the onyx ashtray near her coffee cup. 'Now, let me see what the cards have to say. This is about your sister, Steph?'

Steph nodded.

'Tell me her name.'

'Jess.'

'And do you have anything of hers with you? Perhaps a letter? A piece of jewellery to make the connection.'

Steph thought for a moment. 'I have a scarf of hers. I liked it so much she gave it to me.'

'That is good. Get it.'

Steph watched amused as Carmella cut the pack and then laid out the cards on the coffee table. It was years since she had seen anyone read the tarot. Probably not since she had been a student and done it herself. Carmella did it with superb style, she had to give her that. She lay back in her chair and sipped her coffee, watching as Carmella turned up the first card, Jess's scarf lying on her knee, a splash of emerald against the black of the woman's skirt.

'Ah, *il fante di denari*. The page of coins; pentacles you call them,

84

si? This is Jess. A page can represent a woman, you know that?'
She glanced round. Turning back to the table she ran her finger
thoughtfully over the card. The eyes of every person in the room
were fixed on her hands as she turned up the next and sat staring
down at the layout in front of her. She was frowning. *'Non capisco,'*
she murmured to herself. 'This is very strange. There are two
different people here. We have two women. You see? *Il fante di
bastoni*, the page of wands. But this one represents *una ragazza*. A
much younger woman. Very important in the reading. They are
linked in some way.' She turned a third card. 'And here with them
we have *il re di coppe al negativo.'* She paused, shaking her head.
'Here is violence, scandal, treachery. A bad man in the lives of
these two women.' She glanced up, concerned. 'And here. *Il matto*,
the fool. He heralds a journey for all these people. I think not
literally – maybe a step into the unknown. No, also a journey in
reality.' She turned up three more cards in quick succession. 'There
is so much here.' She spread her hands over the cards. 'They are
on a quest. Your sister, Steph, has set out on a journey she cannot
escape. She travels with another woman, maybe a child, and behind
them follows this man. The cards never tell a lie, but this and this
–' Her hand strayed over the cards, stroking them, reading them
almost like Braille. 'This is too strange. There is love here; new
love. Strong love, but also danger. And fear. And threats.'

'Oh God!' Steph whispered under her breath. She and Kim
exchanged glances.

'Perhaps,' Kim said suddenly, clearing her throat, 'this is not a
good idea. Why don't we have another drink and forget it.'

'No.' Carmella raised a commanding hand. *'Aspetta!* No, this is
important. It is telling me something very important about your
sister. She needs to be warned that she is in danger.'

'Oh God!' Steph repeated. She stood up as a murmur of concern
ran round the room. Everyone was looking at her. No one seemed
to doubt Carmella. No one was looking superior and cynical and
scoffing as they would at a dinner party in London. They were
all hanging on every word.

'Carmella, stop it!' Kim said. 'That's enough. You are frightening her!'

'So, you don't want to know? You don't want to save her?'

'Yes, of course I want to know.' Steph sat down again. She ran
her fingers through her hair. 'Go on.'

Carmella looked up at her for a moment, then she glanced back at the cards. 'There is another man here.' Her finger paused over the king of swords. She frowned. 'Your sister's father? He is wounded.'

'Our father is dead,' Steph put in sharply.

Carmella shook her head. 'I don't understand. This is definitely someone's father. The other girl, perhaps. Do you know who she is?' She looked up. 'And there are soldiers here.' She leaned closer to the cards for a minute. 'And here, I see danger again.' Her voice sharpened. 'Here it is clear. There are two lives here and this,' she tapped a card, 'is your sister and someone wants to kill her!' She sat back and stared at Steph, her eyes wide. *Dio mio*, we are told never to forecast a death. Never! This is awful!'

'And it's tosh, Carmella!' Kim looked really angry. 'This was supposed to comfort her, not make things worse.' She stood up. 'Enough! Let's have some Limoncello, then you should all go home!'

'I'm going to ring the police!' Steph hadn't moved. She was sitting staring at the cards.

'Don't be an idiot! You can't ring the police because of a tarot reading!' Kim bent forward and swept all the cards into a heap. 'That's it. Finished. I am going to put them away.'

'I'll ring the Prices. Meg and Ken won't mind going over to Ty Bran and seeing if she is all right.' Steph stood up. 'Don't be angry with Carmella. I knew there was something wrong.' She headed for the telephone, in the hallway, leaving the others all staring at each other.

The phone at Cwm-nant rang and rang. There was no reply. Steph slammed down the phone. Picking it up again she tried Ty Bran's number. The line was still dead. Then she tried Jess's mobile. It was still switched off.

'Leave it, Steph.' Kim appeared behind her. She had brought a bottle from the fridge in the kitchen and a tray of liqueur glasses. Pouring one out she put it down on the hall stand beside the telephone. 'Get that down you. I'm so sorry. It was a stupid, stupid idea doing the tarot. I should have remembered how melodramatic Carmella can be.'

Steph picked up the glass and sipped it. The strong cold shot of lemon revived her a bit. 'I don't know who to ring, Kim. Jess is all alone up there. There is no one there I know well enough to ask them to drive up into the hills in the middle of the night to see if my sister is OK.'

'I bet you she's fine.' Kim guided her back towards the kitchen and onto a stool by the table. 'I tell you what. Tomorrow, if you can't contact her by then, we'll ring the police and you can explain how worried you are, OK? Honestly. I don't think you can ring them tonight. Not on the strength of a card reading. They would think you were nuts. And they wouldn't go. You know that as well as I do. There is no point in even trying.'

'And what if someone is trying to kill her?' Steph took another swig from the Limoncello.

'Why on earth should someone try and kill Jess?' Kim grabbed Steph by the shoulders. 'Think about it, you idiot! What could Jess have possibly done that would warrant that!'

'Will was trying to find her. He rang –'

'Oh yes! And Will is trying to kill her? I thought you said he was still desperately in love with her.'

Steph shook her head. 'I'm being stupid, aren't I. I know I am. Sorry.'

'At last! Sense. There was love in those cards as well, remember? Right, I'm going to send the others home. Go to bed, Steph. Sleep well. It will all be all right in the morning, you'll see. The phone will be mended and you will find that Jess has been there all the time.'

For the second time Jess had locked the house and eased herself into the driver's seat. Terrified that she would meet Dan's car in the narrow lane she groped for the key and turned it in the ignition. The engine caught. With a little prayer of gratitude she eased up the clutch but as she began to turn the wheel to manoeuvre out of the yard the car engine coughed and died. 'No! Please God, no!' Leaning forward, her hands shaking, she turned the key again.

It was ten minutes before she gave up.

Nothing would persuade her to ring Rhodri again. She had her pride!

All she could do was take his advice after all, lock herself in and wait out the night. Perhaps Rhodri was right and Dan wasn't coming.

The doors were locked and bolted for good measure, the

windows closed, the curtains drawn, when Jess finally went to bed. Lying back on the pillows she stared at the window, not even bothering to open the book which rested on her knees. There was nothing to be afraid of. What could Dan do, even if he did come? She glanced at the clock. It was nearly midnight. Outside in the wood she could hear two tawny owls exchanging calls, the low hoots of the female echoing round the hillside, the sharp response of the male so loud he might have been sitting in the courtyard. She shivered and slid further down in the bed.

Publius Ostorius Scapula stood in his tent looking down at the woman who had been brought before him. She was dark-haired, slim, beautiful and very pale, the bruises on her face and throat still visible. One of his spies had given him some background on this woman. The eldest daughter of the last king of the Silures, the local and oh-so-troublesome tribe of these accursed southern Cambrian hills, she was Caratacus's second wife. The first had died in childbirth so he understood. This second he had chosen with great acumen from the tribe in whose lands he had settled to spearhead his opposition to Rome. And she had done him proud, giving him three children, two girls and a boy and, so he had heard, her unswerving loyalty and love. She had great dignity and courage, this Celtic queen, in spite of her position as his captive.

'I have news for you, lady,' he said at last. 'Your husband has been found.' He saw the flash of hope in those beautiful grey eyes. 'He was severely wounded but is, I understand, on the way to recovery.'

'Where is he?' The question came out as a whisper. She looked at him nervously, trying to be brave, meeting him eye to eye.

'He fled north,' he said slowly. 'To the land of the Brigantes, assuming he would find succour there.' His voice gave no clue to his feelings. 'He threw himself on the mercy of Queen Cartimandua, who is, I understand, a kinswoman of his.' She was smiling now. He moved across to the table, covered in maps and rolls of parchment and sat down, looking up at her thoughtfully. 'You do not, perhaps, realise that the queen is a client of Rome, sworn to the Emperor as our ally and friend.'

Cerys went white.

'She has done her duty to Rome and informed us that Caratacus is now her captive. When he is well enough he will be transferred to my custody. I shall have him taken to Camulodunum to await word of the Emperor's pleasure regarding his fate.'

To do her justice she did not flinch. Her shoulders remained straight, her face after that initial pallor without expression.

'I shall send you there as well, with your daughter. I understand she was attacked by one of my men?'

Cerys looked him in the eye. 'We were both raped by your men, General.'

'As soon as they are identified they will be punished. You have my word on that, lady. As to your other children,' his voice softened slightly. 'I understand every effort has been made to locate them.'

This time she could not hide the pain in her eyes.

'Has everything been done?' He raised his gaze to that of the praefectus, Justinus, who stood at her side.

He stood to attention and saluted. 'Sir. If they were there to be found, we would have found them. The search has been extended over a huge area. Either they have been found by local tribesmen and spirited away into the mountains, or –' He paused, with a glance at his commander. 'They are not there any more, sir.' Wolves. The word hovered between them. Out of pity for the woman's anguish neither man said it out loud.

Scapula was impressed by her dignity and courage. He sighed. He was as certain as maybe that the woman would never see her two younger children again. And he was prepared to waste no more of his soldiers' time on looking for them. Her capture and that of her daughter was enough to give him leverage over Caratacus, if any were needed. Now he was sure of the man's capture he had no real need of her at all, but no doubt parading them both before the people of Camulodunum, once the capital of this man's father, would add to the impact of the defeat.

Back in the tent where her daughter waited for her, Cerys sat down next to the child and put her arm around her shoulders. 'Your papa has been found alive, sweetheart. He is wounded but not too badly.' No point in saying he was a prisoner. No point in saying that the Queen of the Brigantes had betrayed them, betrayed her blood, her kin, her oath to her gods and to her people. She clenched her teeth desperately. They would never see Togo and Glads again. That had been made clear by the Romans. They were not unsympathetic; she had read that much in Scapula's eyes, but there was nothing more to be done. And never, never, she vowed as she cuddled her daughter to her, would she say anything that would cause Eigon to blame herself.

It was a game! Can we finish playing the game?
The voice echoed through Jess's head as she slept.
Please, can we stop playing now?
The words came not from Eigon but from a smaller child, her sister.

Restlessly Jess turned over and punched the pillow. 'She's alive! She's still alive! Glads is alive. Oh please, someone, go and look for her!' She called out the words in her head but no one heard them.

The lamps were burning low; no one had come to replenish the oil and the tent was full of shadows. Cerys could see the silhouettes of the two guards beyond the leather flap of the doorway, their profiles black against the firelight. She could see their spears as a cross, black against the flames.

And again the thin little voice echoed round Ty Bran:
Eigon, where are you? Can I tell Togo to come out now?
In her sleep Jess gave a little moan.

Outside the house a figure crept across the yard and stood for a moment at the front door. It was just growing light.

Dan reached out and pushed the door experimentally, soundlessly rattling the handle, then he turned and tiptoed along the front of the house, pausing as he reached the corner. In the holly bush the blackbird fluttered up to its look-out post, shrieking a warning into the cold morning and upstairs Jess jerked awake suddenly, startled by the noise. The dream fled as she sat up.

She listened nervously. Something was wrong. Throwing back her bedcovers she eased herself out of bed and moving silently towards the window she peered down. The courtyard was empty, lost in colourless pre-dawn mist. Soundlessly she pushed the window open and leaned out. There was a car parked in the lane. She could see the dull gleam of the bonnet beyond the stone wall. She couldn't distinguish the colour but she knew who it was. Closing the window silently she hurriedly threw on her clothes and tiptoed to her bedroom door, listening. She had locked all the downstairs doors and windows the night before; she remembered clearly touring the house one last time before she climbed the stairs to bed. He couldn't get in. Not without breaking a window. Almost as the thought occurred to her she heard the sound of breaking glass from somewhere downstairs. Bolting the door, she flew to the phone beside the bed and lifted the receiver. It wasn't until she had dialled 999 and waited, breathlessly, for an answer that she realised the line was still dead.

Oh please God, no. She shook the phone, tried again. Silence. 'Jess?'

Dan's voice was right outside her door. She saw the latch lift and heard the creak of the hinges as he tried to open it.

'Jess, come on. Open the door. I'm not going to hurt you. But we do have to talk, don't we.'

'What the hell are you doing here, Dan? You can't just break in! Go away. Now. I've called the police.' Her voice came over as remarkably strong. 'Don't be a fool. You are going to make things worse than they are already.'

There was a moment's silence. She thought she heard a chuckle. 'No, Jess. You haven't called the police. Your phone is dead, I tried it. I have your bag, and your mobile is here, in my hand.'

She spun round staring wildly about the room. She had left her phone downstairs, plugged in to charge. The thought that he had found it and that he had rifled through her bag as he was prowling through the house at five o'clock in the morning sickened her.

She tiptoed towards the window and peered out. Could she climb down? She doubted it. Anyway he would hear her.

'Go away, Dan. Please. I'm not coming out so unless you've got all day, in fact all week, you may as well give up now. Threatening me is not going to make things any better. Go and we can talk on the phone.' She clenched her teeth.

'Come on, Jess. You must realise I can't allow you to put everything I hold dear in jeopardy. I need you to make me some promises.'

'I'll promise nothing, Dan. Go away.'

There was a short pause. 'Open the door and we'll talk about it.'

'You know I'm not going to do that.'

'So you don't trust me, but I am expected to trust you?'

'There is a reason for that as you must realise.' She bit her lip. 'I've never lied to you, Dan.'

'Yes you have. You just told me that you had called the police. That was a lie, wasn't it.' His voice was silky.

She closed her eyes. 'I may not have called the police, but I've told someone what happened to me,' she said defiantly. 'And I have told him it was you. If anything happens to me he will go to the police for me and the truth will come out.'

'That was a mistake, Jess. We could have talked about this. I could have explained.' There was a long pause. 'Did he believe you, this person you talked to?'

'Of course he did!'

'You amaze me. No one else will, once the facts come out.' He laughed. There was a long silence. 'Really, Jess. There's no need for all this. We can talk it through.' There was another pause. 'We don't have to have a great confrontation. If I misunderstood what you wanted, I apologise. I thought you wanted it as much as I did. You did. How can you say you didn't? After all you can't remember anything about it, can you. So, you do need to take my word for this.' She heard his footsteps as he paced up and down the landing, then he was back outside her door again. 'No one needs to know anything about it. Come on. Open the door. We need to talk. You've been depressed, Jess. Things get out of all proportion when one is depressed. That is why you've been behaving so oddly; your friend Rhodri will confirm that.' There was another pause. 'Of course, it was Rhodri you talked to.' Another pause. 'It was, wasn't it? Large, extrovert, noisy Rhodri! Well, you didn't have to tell him how you were paranoid about ghosts in this house, how you hallucinated about people smashing up your paintings, how you broke bottles of wine and accused me of doing it. He knows. He saw it all.' She heard his footsteps again, heavy, angry, turning sharply at the end of the landing and returning to stop outside her door again. 'You realise I could break this door down,' he went on at last. 'You can't avoid me, Jess. Much better to talk about this. You don't want to make me angry.

After all, if something happened to you, who would ever suspect me? I would tell them how depressed you were when me met in Hay. Rhodri would confirm that, I expect! So, if you were found to have killed yourself, Jess, I doubt anyone would query your suicide. Look how strangely you've been behaving, even at school. Resigning. Not giving them notice. Refusing to go in even to collect your stuff. Oh Jess, no one would be surprised if it came to that. But we don't want it to happen, do we. Come on. I've got all the time in the world. I could just wait here!'

She had broken out into a sweat. He was threatening to kill her. She took a deep breath. 'You could never break this door down, Dan. It's solid oak.' She paused. 'OK. We'll wait then.' She kept her voice as light as possible. 'After all it won't be long. Rhodri will be here after breakfast. I'll just read till he comes, and you can wait there, on the landing.' She padded barefoot across the room and sat down on the bed. Turning on the lamp, she reached for her book.

In seconds she had put it down again. She listened hard. There was no sound from the door. Outside the blackbird had started whistling, its song beautiful as the sun rose in a blaze of stormy red.

Have the nasty men come back?

The voice was clearly audible in the room suddenly. Jess looked round, her heart thudding. 'Yes, they have.' She spoke out loud. 'Where are you, sweetheart?'

'What did you say?' Dan's voice was slightly muffled. He had obviously moved away from the door.

'I wasn't talking to you.'

'No?'

'No.' She gave a grim smile. She turned and addressed the empty space between the bed and the window. 'Can you fetch help, Glads?' Was it the younger child again? She thought so. The voice was lighter, more tentative. 'Can we find someone to make the nasty man go away?' She spoke softly, knowing he wouldn't be able to make out her words.

'Who are you talking to?' For a moment he sounded suspicious. Then he laughed. 'OK. You had me fooled for a second there, but only a second! I can wait all day, Jess.'

'Just till Rhodri comes!' She turned back towards the window. 'Are you still there, Glads?'

There was no reply. She sighed. It was insane to think there would be. For twenty minutes neither she nor Dan spoke, then at last she heard him walking across the landing. She didn't hear him come back. Had he moved away then? Exploring the house perhaps? She tiptoed towards the door. 'Dan? Tell me the truth. You might as well. Was it you who pretended to wreck my pictures? Was it some sort of practical joke?'

'And how exactly do you suppose I set up this joke?' His voice was very close to the door after all. Perhaps he was leaning against it. 'I brought glass and blood and a duplicate sketchbook with me, did I?'

'Doesn't sound very likely, does it!' she admitted ruefully. 'So,' she went on, 'where does Natalie think you are this morning?'

'London. So you don't have to worry about her expecting me back any time soon, Jess.' His voice had a mocking ring to it.

She retreated to the bed and sat down. What were the chances of someone coming to call? None at all. Unless Rhodri took it into his head to come over again before he went away. He might phone and find the line dead and worry about her. Was that likely? She bit her lip. It was as she could see her only hope.

Half an hour later Dan's voice woke her from a semi-doze. He sounded as though he was eating. 'I've helped myself to some breakfast, Jess. I hope you don't mind. Is there anything I can get you? Coffee? Toast? You must be feeling hungry by now.'

She grimaced. 'Thank you, Dan. I'm fine!'

'What time did you say Rhodri was coming?' He sounded amused.

'Soon.'

'I'll be waiting for him if he does.'

Shit! What was she going to do now?

There was water to drink in the bathroom, and she could go without food for the time being, surely. She wasn't hungry anyway, she was too scared. She could wait him out.

She tried to read but she couldn't concentrate. She did some sketching, thankful for the small sketchpad she had left on her bedside table and after a while she dozed. When she woke two hours had passed. Levering herself to her feet she went to the door. 'Dan? Are you still there?'

'Oh yes, sweetheart, I'm still here.'

'Just checking!' She forced herself to laugh.

It was almost dark when she finally heard his footsteps outside in the courtyard. She ran to the window, dizzy with hunger and exhaustion, dodging just in time behind the curtain as he turned and looked back at the house. He obviously hadn't seen her and in seconds he was once more heading towards the gate. Where was he going? Why had he given up? She didn't give herself time to think about it. Pulling a sweater on over her shirt and jeans and ramming her feet into her shoes she ran to the door and flung back the bolt. In seconds she was down the stairs and in the kitchen, unlocking the side door with shaking hands. Moments later she had ducked behind the studio out of sight of the front of the house and was running across the lawn towards the hedge.

Forcing herself through a gap laced with sheep wool, she was through, bleeding with scratches from the hawthorn and brambles and out into the field. Running as fast as she could she doubled back out of sight of the house and in moments she was in the shelter of the trees, gasping for breath. Desperately she tried to control her gulps for air as she listened for the sound of Dan's footsteps. Had he seen her? Why had he left unless it was to lure her out of her bedroom? All she could hear was the wind rustling in the treetops and the sudden sharp call of the owl. Below her in the valley it was already dark.

It seemed an age before she dared to move. Beyond the trees the sky was flooding with a colour wash of crimson and scarlet shot with green, silhouetting the distant hills. Cautiously she moved forward through the trees towards the house again, her eyes straining into the shadows until with a gasp of fear she saw his car below her, looming out of the darkness of the lane. She was far too close, coming out above the lane, much nearer to the house than she had expected and Dan was obviously still there. Somewhere. Her hope that he might have given up and driven away was a vain one. As silently as she could she melted back into the shelter of the trees and found her way back to the track. What now? There was only one option. To try and find her way across the fields to the Prices and pray that Rhodri was still there.

She glanced up at the sky between the branches of the trees. There was still a glimmer of light in the north west but down here amongst the trees it was growing pitch black as the sun slid behind the rim of the hill leaving nothing but a red glow on the highest branches of the summit trees. She glanced behind her. Was Dan following her or had he gone back into the house to wait for her?

She didn't have the courage to retrace her steps to try and find out.

All day she had kept the idea of Rhodri, with his broad shoulders and his deep strong voice in her mind, hoping against hope that just by conjuring him in her imagination she could bring him physically back to Ty Bran. It hadn't happened, but he would protect her if she asked. Just by being there he would protect her from the madman in her house.

With a shiver she knew she dared not wait any longer. Carefully she began her descent of the steep escarpment, sliding through the soft leaf mould, clinging to the branches, feeling her way between tree trunks rough with lichen, protecting her eyes with the crook of her arm against sharp twigs and whipping saplings.

At last she reached the fence that bordered the wood. She felt along the barbed wire cautiously looking for the wooden footrail of the stile and finding it at last, climbed over, pausing for a moment to catch her breath. The clouds had rolled back and the night was bright with stars. On the horizon there was still a bright green line of reflected light, the last trace of the dying sun. Far behind her a pheasant launched itself suddenly out of the tree-tops with a deafening squawk of alarm. She held her breath. Something up there in the wood had scared it. She listened, her fingers still clutching the top rail of the stile.

Togo? We've stopped playing now. Where are you?

The voice echoed softly through the trees, barely a breath in the wind.

The moss under Jess's fingers was damp. She could feel the moist warm velvet oozing under her nails. For a moment she clung tightly to the rail, paralysed with fear, then with a deep breath to strengthen her resolve she released it and set off across the field. It was rough under her feet, strewn with stones, uneven tussocks of grass and mudslips with here and there a patch of rushes catching at her ankles as she slid down into deeper puddles.

She felt horribly exposed as she crossed the field, but at least she could see in the starlight. As she reached the far side she found herself once again in the dark under the branches of a stand of ash trees as she made her way cautiously towards the gate.

She didn't know how long it was before she finally found her way to Cwm-nant. Almost weeping with exhaustion, she pushed open the heavy gate and let herself into the farmyard. The farm was in darkness. As she hammered on the back door she realised suddenly that the dogs were not there. Nor was Rhodri's car.

'Oh no!' She knocked again, beating on the door panels with her fists. 'Please, please be here!'

She already knew he wasn't. She was too late. He had gone. Too tired to do anything else she sank down into a huddle there in the porch, with tears of despair and exhaustion rolling down her cheeks.

Eventually she pulled herself together enough to climb to her feet and circle the house checking for open doors or windows. Rhodri had done a good job locking up and the dogs had gone. Feeling her way through the darkness into an outbuilding on the far side of the farmyard, she found some old sacks in which she could huddle as exhaustion finally overcame her. Her last thought before she fell asleep was that at least here Dan would not find her.

8

In Rome the morning was bright and already very hot. Steph stood for a moment at her open window, staring down at the street below, then with a sigh she reached out and closed the shutters against the heat. Still wearing her white cotton nightdress she padded barefoot down the corridor. 'I've tried to phone again. The line is still dead.' She found Kim in the kitchen. 'I'm going to phone the police.'

'I still think that is over-reacting. Call one of your neighbours. They won't mind now it's daytime, surely.' Kim poured a second cup of coffee for herself and then as an afterthought one for Steph as well. She pushed her tousled hair back off her face. 'You're fussing too much, Steph. She's a grown woman, for God's sake!'

Reaching wearily for the coffee, Steph sat down at the table opposite her. 'I know. And she'll be furious. It's just – I've got this feeling. And after last night –'

'Did you call the Prices?'

Steph nodded. 'No reply. Which is weird. How can a farm be empty? There has to be someone there for the animals.'

'Don't you know anyone else round there, Steph?'

Steph laughed. 'Of course.'

'Then ring them. Then you can relax.'

It was an hour and a half later that Sally Lomax rang Steph back from her car outside Ty Bran. 'Just to let you know that all is well. I have just talked to a nice chap who said he was called Will who is staying here with Jess. They know the phone is out of order and it has been reported. I didn't see Jess myself, but her car is here and he said he would get her to ring you this evening. Hope that puts your mind at rest.'

'There!' Kim grinned at Steph triumphantly when the message was relayed back to her. 'What did I tell you? And she's back with Will! That is fantastic news!'

* * *

Asleep in the outhouse Jess moved uncomfortably on her makeshift bed of sacks. Her eyes were flicking back and forth under her eyelids. They were leaving the lost and frightened children behind. This couldn't be. They had to look again.

But once the decision had been made there was no delay. A wagon was provided for Cerys and her daughter with an escort of fifty men. Many of the captives from the battle had already left on their way east; the remainder were being marshalled in chains to follow them, defeated, wounded, some half dead from illness and near starvation. Scapula watched as the woman and child were brought out of their tent and steered towards the vehicle. Cerys walked with stately dignity. Only her fists, clutched into the folds of the Roman tunic and mantle in which she was dressed betrayed her tension. Drawing opposite her captor she stood still. 'Promise me you will continue to search for my children.' Her voice trembled slightly as she held his gaze.

He nodded. 'We will continue to search.' They both knew he was staying to consolidate his victory and take the battle deeper into the mountains. There would be no time to search for children.

'Thank you.' The single austere phrase was all she said. She turned to the wagon, allowing one of the soldiers to take her arm and help her up the step. Eigon followed her, her face white and tear-stained. 'Mam, what about Togo and Glads?' She clung to her mother's skirt.

'The soldiers will look for them, child.' Cerys sat down on the bench which ran lengthways down the side of the wagon beneath the leather hood. She put her arm around her daughter's shoulders. 'We must pray to the goddess to take care of them.' Her voice faded to a whisper as she fought back her own tears. As the wagon lurched into motion they both looked through the double line of marching men as it fell in behind them, back towards the golden line of the hills, the broad river plain, the neat lines of Roman tents behind their fortifications slowly growing smaller as they lurched down the track. They were following the winding line of the great river towards the legionary fortress of Viroconium from where they were to start their journey east towards Camulodunum.

At Viroconium they were lodged in the house of the wife of one of the senior officers. She was kind and treated them with dignity. They were served with carefully prepared food at the family's table, but neither Cerys nor her daughter ate much, both locked in their own misery. It was the same wherever they stopped. At each day's end the procession halted at one of the forts, scattered a day's ride apart along the road, and at each one they were given hot food and beds. Several times the escort acceded to Cerys's demands that they be allowed to ride. Abandoning the imprisonment of the wagon with little regret they made better time, the legionaries watching the straight backs and easy riding style of the captive queen and her daughter with grudging approval. Even surrounded by the guards of her enemy with a lead rein from her horse's bit to the hand of a trooper Cerys felt better. At first she felt her spirits lift at the exercise but as the distance grew between them and the lands of the Silures and their northern neighbours the Ordovices she spoke to Eigon less and less, her heart torn with anguish for her two lost children. Eigon watched her miserably, huddling deeper and deeper into her cloak, her own guilt and loneliness growing greater with each step of her shaggy pony.

The countryside changed. Leaving the mountains of Wales faraway in the west they followed a route which became flatter with every day's journey. Eventually even the lower hills were gone and they plodded on across the flat midland plain through endless forests, areas of scrub, areas of burned cleared woodland, past small reclaimed areas of cultivated land, and larger fields, past small villages where the occupants cowered at the sight of the Roman soldiers and shook their fists at their backs as they rode by, always, endlessly heading towards the rising sun.

At Verulamium the party stopped for two days.

It was there, watching other children playing, that Eigon heard Glads's voice calling her.

Where are you? You told us to stay in the wood. Eigon? I can't find Togo. Can we stop playing now. I'm lonely!

The voice was hysterical, broken with sobs, echoing across the broad streets, threading over the sound of other children's laughter.

'Mam!' Eigon pulled at her mother's hand. 'I can hear Glads calling.'

Cerys looked down at her and her eyes were like flint. 'Don't mention your sister's name!'

'But Mam! Please! She's calling. She's lost and frightened!'

Cerys pulled her hand away sharply. 'You're lying!' She turned away to hide her tears. 'Don't think about them. They've gone.'

'But Mam, Glads is still there. She is waiting for us. She's lost Togo.'

Cerys let out a wail of anguish and violently pushed Eigon away. The child didn't try and tell her any more about what she had heard. Instead, quietly in her bed at night, she prayed, pouring out her heart to the goddess Bride, begging her to look after her brother and sister.

The goddess did not reply.

When Jess woke it was full daylight and she was so stiff she could hardly move. For a moment she couldn't remember where she was, then wearily she sat up and peered round, her dream receding, memories of the events of the day before flooding back. Hungry, thirsty and frightened she climbed to her feet and tiptoed to the door. The yard was deserted.

A second circuit of the farmhouse and its outbuildings confirmed the fact that the place was empty. Driven by hunger, she opened one of the old freezers which sat in a shed behind the barn and was confronted by a frozen mountain of various cuts of lamb. With a shudder she closed it. Megan's kitchen garden was much more help. Late raspberries and strawberries, blackcurrants, peas and a carrot or two brushed free of mud, restored her strength and confidence and by the time she had eaten her fill she had worked out a plan. She would go home, retracing her steps until she could look down at Ty Bran from the woods on the hillside above. If Dan was still there she would bypass the house, make her way down towards the road and the distant village.

Perched on the hillside above the house she had a good view of the courtyard and the lane outside the house. There was no sign of Dan's car. Cautiously she made her way down towards the gate and paused, scanning every corner of the yard, every tree and bush, every angle of the house. The place felt empty. The lean-to garage was empty. Her own car still stood uselessly in the middle of the courtyard. There was nowhere else his car could be. No space round the back; no hidden places up on the track. He had gone. She was sure of it. The blackbird was on his favourite perch on the roof of the studio. She smiled. If anyone had been here in the last few minutes the bird would have flown away, surely. As quietly as possible she pushed open the gate and tiptoed around the courtyard. The front door was closed. Silently, flattened against the wall, she edged towards the kitchen window and after a moment's hesitation, peered in. The room was empty. Ducking under the window she made her way round the side of the house. To her surprise the back door was ajar. She shrank back, frightened, and waited, holding her breath. Was he still there after all? It was a long time before she crept forward again and cautiously pushed the door open as far as it would go. There was no sound from inside. It took a lot of courage to go in; more to search the house. He had gone. There was no sign of him anywhere save the broken window in the dining room where he had forced his way in.

Her heart thudding with fear she stood in the kitchen again, trying to decide what to do. She couldn't stay here now. She was too much of a threat to him. She frowned. Where had he gone? Why had he left? Had Nat phoned him and demanded he go back? Perhaps his alibi had run out. She gave a grim smile at the thought, but she wasn't going to stay and wait for him to come back. He must realise she would tell someone about his threats. Or was he going to bluff it out; tell the world she was deluded. After all, he was right, there was no proof of what had happened, either yesterday or back in London. No proof at all. She had told no one. There was no evidence, she had seen to that. Miserably she paced up and down the floor, aware in some part of her that the blackbird was still singing outside from the studio roof, his reassurance her only comfort.

Where are you?

The words floated through the window suddenly, a child's voice from far away.

Jess shivered.

Where are you? Don't leave me!

'Oh God! I can't stand this any more!' Her mind made up, Jess turned towards the door.

Her handbag, the bag that Dan had presumably rifled through, was sitting on the kitchen table. She glanced through it. Her mobile was in there. He had put it back in the bag. And her passport, tucked into a side pocket. He had moved nothing. She found the name of a builder on Steph's list of emergency phone numbers and picked up the phone to get him to come and fix the window. The phone was still dead. Her mobile battery was still flat. Dan had unplugged it from the charger. Swearing, she tore off the piece of paper and put it in her pocket. She glanced round the house one last time to make sure she had forgotten nothing, as an afterthought scooped up Rhodri's CDs and tucked them into her bag, then she went outside, banging the door behind her. Unlocking the car she pulled one of her cases towards her. She needed a few things. She would put them in a carrier and lug them down to the village where she would find someone who would let her borrow their phone. It hardly seemed worthwhile to try to start the car again but she did it anyway.

It started first go. With a sob of hope she slammed the door and began to ease the car out of the yard. Pulling out onto the track she put her foot down and headed downhill. If Dan was still lurking in the lane and about to accost her as she drove past she intended to be travelling so fast he couldn't catch her. The car bucked and groaned as it lurched through the potholes but the engine seemed fine. She glanced in the mirror back towards the trees. The sun was glinting on the puddles, slanting through the branches throwing a network of shadows across the deep ruts.

'Goodbye, Eigon, Glads, Togo,' she whispered.

There was no reply.

She didn't stop until she reached the garage in the next town where an obliging mechanic found the loose connection within minutes. Within half an hour she had filled up with petrol, bought some sandwiches and called the builder to go up to the house and fix the window. She plugged her phone in to charge, then she leaned forward to select a CD.

The first that came to hand was Elgar's cantata *Caractacus* with Rhodri in the title role. She looked down at it thoughtfully, then pulled out the booklet tucked into the front of the case. Yes, Caractacus was the man she knew as Caratacus and his daughter was here too. Eigen, she was called. Jess frowned, looking down the cast list. Orbin. Who was Orbin? She read on swiftly. He was, apparently, Eigen's lover. Jess shook her head. No, that wasn't right. Eigon was a little girl. There was an Arch Druid in the cast, and of course the Emperor Claudius. She read on thoughtfully.

The scene had been set by Elgar in his beloved Malvern Hills. She slid the first disk from its case, slipped it into the player and as she pulled out of the garage forecourt she turned up the volume. Behind her, in the distance, the true site of Caratacus's defeat lay in the summer sunlight, gentle now beneath the distant escarpment of the hills, sleeping in the arm of the river, the site chosen with such care for his great confrontation with the forces of Rome and which had in the event served him so badly in the face of the greatest fighting force the country had yet seen.

The last leg of their journey took them from Verulamium to Camulodunum. Altogether, they had been some fourteen days on the road. This town had been the centre of the confederation of the two great tribes of the Catuvellauni and the Trinovantes. Cunobelinus, the father of Caratacus, Cerys's Caradoc, had been king here before the Romans came. Now it was the centre and the military base of the new province of Britannia. It was here, while she was lodged with her daughter in the legionary fortress, that Cerys learned their fate. As soon as her husband was brought south to join them all the captives were to be taken to Rome to be paraded as vanquished enemies before the people of Rome and before the Emperor in person and then consigned to their doom. Cerys did not need to read the expression in the eyes of the commander of the legion to know that he expected that they would be sentenced to a horrible death before the baying crowds, or that while waiting for her husband to be brought south from his incarceration by the queen of the Brigantes she and Eigon would be kept in close imprisonment. Their time as honoured captives was over, their new lives as prisoners and probably slaves about to begin.

She stared at the letter in his hand as though willing it to disappear; as though praying he would reread it, say he had made a mistake, but his eyes pitilessly confirmed what he had just read out loud. Already he had beckoned the guard forward. Already she was being led from the room, Eigon at her heels.

'Mam? Mam, where are we going? What is happening?' The child caught at the skirt of her tunic. Cerys ignored her. She clenched her fists in the folds of her cloak and straightened her shoulders. She would not show fear. She would not show grief.

She would not betray the honour of her tribe or the royal bravery of her husband before these men. And nor would her daughter.

'Be silent, Eigon,' she snapped. 'Remember you are a princess. Do not show them you are afraid!'

Eigon shrank back. Bewildered, she bit back her tears. One of the legionaries of their escort noticed the exchange. He glanced at his officer, noted he was looking the other way and smiling down at the little girl in an attempt at reassurance he winked. 'Courage!' he whispered.

The last chorus of the first CD came to an end with a flourish. With a start Jess realised she had driven miles without being aware of where she was, buoyed up by the passion of the music. She glanced round, looking for a signpost. She was still on track heading down towards the motorway and London. While Eigon's life had been unfolding inside her head some other part of her consciousness had been steering the car, turning corners, negotiating roundabouts and villages, heading away from Wales.

Pulling in at last at Warwick Services on the M40 she took stock of the situation as she queued up for coffee and a toasted sandwich, forcing herself to put Eigon and her family out of her mind and bring herself back to the present. She couldn't go back to her flat; her tenant wouldn't appreciate her sudden return and it would anyway be the first place Dan would look. She shivered, glancing in spite of herself at the crowds of people around her. No, she would stick to her plan. She had her passport, her credit cards, all she needed in the car with her. She would follow Steph – and Eigon – to Rome.

9

The gods were with her. She managed to get a flight that same evening. Leaving most of her belongings locked in the car in the long term car park at Heathrow, she settled into her seat with a huge sigh of relief as the plane took off and angled sharply over London.

She arrived at last at the palazzo in the early hours of the morning. When she climbed out of the taxi, paid the driver and dragged her case to the door the street was, she noticed wearily, as busy as it would be at midday at home. She had no time for any other observations. In seconds she was being enveloped in hugs and escorted up the great marble staircase which led to Kim's front door on the first floor. Minutes after that she was seated in front of a crisp glass of Frascati and a bowl of pasta in the echoing old-fashioned kitchen.

'So?' Steph sat down opposite her and leaned forward on her elbows. 'What happened?'

'What do you mean?' Jess took a mouthful of the *fettuccine alla marinara*, savouring the flavours with delight. She had not eaten since her motorway stop, so long ago it seemed like another era. A warm fuzzy sense of security was beginning to drift over her.

. Kim spooned the last of the sauce onto Jess's plate. She glanced at Steph. 'No questions now, Steph,' she said sternly. 'Jess is exhausted. We'll catch up on all her news in the morning.'

In less than an hour Jess had taken a long relaxing bath and fallen into bed. Almost before her head touched the pillow she was asleep. But her sleep was restless and it wasn't long before she woke suddenly and lay staring into the dark. Her head had been full of music. Elgar. The voice of Rhodri Price, filling the dark spaces of her brain. Except it wasn't Rhodri Price, it was Caratacus.

*   *   *

Tall, his strong weather-beaten features drawn with pain, his hair threaded now with silver amongst the thick auburn locks, he was standing in the doorway, his shoulder and upper arm still bandaged from his battle wound, his wrists shackled with heavy iron manacles, staring in towards his wife and daughter. 'Where is he?' he asked. 'Where is my son?'

Cerys clasped her hands in anguish as he stepped into the room. Behind him the guard slammed the door and they heard the bolt slide across.

'We searched. We searched everywhere. The Romans searched. They put the whole legion to the search –' Her voice rose in anguish. 'Eigon hid them in the wood above the battlefield. To keep them safe. But when we looked they had gone.'

Eigon had started to tremble. She stared at her father in terror, her eyes filling with tears. 'I told them to hide. I told them not to come out.'

For a brief second his face was consumed with anger; with an enormous effort he controlled it. 'They told me. Can we hope our own people found them? Can they be keeping them safe?'

'That is my prayer,' Cerys said softly. 'I pray every day to the goddess Bride to keep them safe. You must not blame Eigon. She did what she thought was right.' Her voice was softened by a smile as she turned towards her daughter but there was a hard edge of pain to it that Eigon heard with a small whimper of unhappiness.

Caradoc studied his wife's face. 'I had no intention of blaming her. Come here, child.' He held out his arms, awkward because of the chains and Eigon ran to him, leaning against his knees, worming her way into his embrace. 'You did what you thought was right, sweetheart, and you were very brave.' He dropped a kiss on the top of her head. 'And who knows,' he glanced up at his wife, his face strained. 'It may be that Togo and Glads are the ones who will survive to fight another day.'

The music faded and Jess slept again. Next time she woke she went and stood by the window looking out into the darkness, listening to the noises of the night. Her window faced away from the noisy street outside. From somewhere she could hear a tinkling of water, but behind it there was still a distant subdued hum of traffic. She smiled to herself. The Eternal City. She remembered how excited they had all been when Kim had announced her engagement to her Roman aristocrat. They had all vowed to keep in touch for ever, vowed with her, to learn Italian. Jess grimaced at the memory. Kim had become fluent over the years, of course she had. Her own and Steph's attempts at the language had flagged almost at once. Her promises to herself that she would one day read *La Commedia Divina* in the original had been ignominiously shunted aside, along with her recognition that her mastery of the language would probably be limited to a few useful phrases mostly involving food.

When she woke again it was late and she lay staring with delight round the large room to which she had been shown the night before. Too tired to take much notice of the room lit only by a shaded bedside light, she had taken in very little of its detail beyond the fact that it was comfortable and had its own en suite bathroom. Now she found she was lying in a baroque four-poster bed, its curtains open, tied back against the posts with brocade swags; at the windows the threadbare damask curtains were only half-drawn and sunlight poured through onto exotic old rugs filling the room with rich warm light. Climbing to her feet she went over to look out and found she was staring down into a courtyard garden somewhere in the quiet inner heart of the palazzo. The tantalising sound of water she had heard in the night, came, she discovered, from an ornate fountain at the centre of an intricate pattern of formal beds and gravelled paths.

'Are you awake?' Steph appeared in the doorway behind her. She was carrying two cups of coffee.

Jess turned away from the window and faced her, pushing her hair back from her face with both hands. 'This is heaven! I hope Kim really doesn't mind me turning up at such short notice.' She realised that for the first time in ages she felt completely safe.

'Kim is delighted. She rattles round in this apartment.' For a second Steph frowned. 'I think she is genuinely lonely, you know. It was fabulous when Stefano was alive but now I suspect she only has a few real friends here and most of them bugger off in the summer to go somewhere cooler. I met some of them the other night but most of them were about to leave Rome for the holidays.' Cradling her own cup she sat down on the bed, swinging her legs. Her feet were bare. 'I am so pleased you decided to come, Jessie. We're going to have such fun.'

Jess eyed her sister speculatively knowing it was only a matter of time before the cross questioning started. Ruefully she was remembering her recent enthusiasm for Wales, her pleas to go to Ty Bran, her longing to paint, knowing how illogical her sudden arrival in the middle of the night must seem. One thing was certain. She was not going to tell Steph and Kim the true reason.

'So, what changed your mind? Why did you decide to leave?' Steph had leaned back on her elbow amongst the pillows as she sipped her coffee, noting how pale and strained her sister looked.

Jess set her own cup down on a console table by the window. She rubbed her face with her hands. The music from her dream, from the long car journey was still there, at the back of her brain. She was not going to mention Dan, but she could tell them about Eigon. 'Did you ever hear a child's voice at Ty Bran, Steph? Eigon's voice.'

Steph sat up again. 'A voice?'

'Eigon. The daughter of Caratacus!'

Steph looked confused.

'The ghost! The little girl who haunts your studio.'

'Ah.' Steph stood up. She paced slowly over to the window and stood looking out. 'Is this why you changed your mind about staying up there alone? You got spooked.' Her voice was casual but Jess heard the tension there.

'I suppose I was,' she acknowledged cautiously. Better by far for Steph to think she had been chased out by ghosts than to know the real reason.

Steph retraced her steps to the bed and climbed onto it once more, sitting cross-legged against the pillows. 'Ty Bran is haunted. There's no doubt about it. I've often heard things, sensed things. Not really seen anything.' She picked idly at the silvery embroidery on the pillow case. 'But it's never frightened me. If it had, I would have warned you. I don't mind at all being up there alone. At least –'

'She didn't frighten me.' Jess sat down on the bed next to her. 'Not once I got used to her. But she made me sad. She is so lonely, so needy. Do you know the story? Eigon was captured by the Romans with her father and mother. And brought here. To Rome. They were prisoners in chains. But her baby brother and sister were lost in the woods at Ty Bran.'

'Lost?'

Jess nodded. 'They were hiding from the soldiers. They captured Eigon, but they never found the other two. At least, I don't think they did.'

'And you think she is still looking for them?' Steph shook her head. 'God that sounds awful. How do you know all this?'

'Rhodri Price.' Jess grimaced.

'Rhodri?' Steph stared at her incredulously.

Jess slipped off the bed again and went to rummage in her bag. She pulled out a CD.

'Elgar's *Caractacus*.' Steph read the label. 'That's mine!' She looked up.

'You might have warned me about him,' Jess said. 'I put my foot in it at once by not having a clue who he was!'

Steph chuckled. 'Oh dear. Sorry. That would really have upset him. He's a prickly so and so – much too big for his boots!'

'Isn't he just!' Jess grinned. 'I remembered you didn't like him much! I think I can see why.'

Steph dropped the CD on the bed. 'I'm surprised he was there. He doesn't stay at the farm much any more. He's based in London nowadays and he's always on tour somewhere or another. So, you've come to hear him sing? Megan told me he was due to appear at La Scala. But that's not in Rome . . .'

'No, I haven't come to hear him sing! Come off it. It's not my kind of music for a start.' The music which was nevertheless swirling and raging in her head; the music which wouldn't go away. 'And I wouldn't give him the satisfaction of letting him think I was even remotely interested in hearing him. My God, he might think I was a fan! No, I've come to do some research.' Suddenly she realised that was at least partly true. She wanted to get as faraway from Dan as possible, yes, but she needed to know what happened to Eigon as well. She wanted to find out about the children. 'I know what happened to Caratacus when he got to Rome, it's part of history, but I want to know what happened to her. It was Rhodri who told me who she was. He told me about the battle when Caratacus was defeated. After all, he has sung about it, their farm is part of the battlefield. He knows the story. And he got me to listen to a programme on the radio about it all.'

She repeated the whole story to Kim and Steph as the three women sat over a late lunch at a trattoria near the palazzo. Kim stared at her. 'Well, of all the reasons for anyone to come to Rome, that was the last thing that would have occurred to me.'

Steph grinned. 'I think it's wonderful. A quest!'

'But how does the dangerous man fit into all this, I wonder,' Kim went on thoughtfully. 'Did you tell her, Steph, about Carmella's warning?'

'What warning? What dangerous man?' Jess put down her fork.

'My friend Carmella read the cards for you and she said that you were in danger. Your sister here almost had the police out to you when she couldn't get you on the phone.'

'Really?' Jess met Steph's gaze thoughtfully.

'Really.'

'And now here you are with this strange mission,' Kim went on, her eyes sparkling suddenly. 'So, who is Caractacus? I know he was a king. I know that much from Rolf Harris! But I didn't know he was real. I didn't know he was dangerous. Caractacus I mean, Not Rolf.' She gave a gurgle of mirth.

'His real name was Caratacus, without the extra c. In Wales he's called Caradoc,' Jess said thoughtfully. 'The Romans defeated him in a battle in the valley below Ty Bran. He was the Welsh leader, a national hero. He was captured with his wife and daughter by the Romans and the Emperor Claudius ordered that they be brought to Rome in chains.'

'Bummer!' Kim reached out for the wine bottle. 'And what has this to do with your ghost?' She topped up Jess's glass.

'The ghosts at Ty Bran are his daughters.'

'Ghosts?' Steph put in. 'Are there more than one?'

Jess nodded. 'Eigon and her little sister, Glads. I've seen them both.'

'And they died at Ty Bran?'

Jess shook her head. 'No. I don't think so. That is what I want to find out. According to this –' she fished in her bag and produced the CD – 'Eigon came to Rome with her parents. In this opera, she is a grown woman. A powerful busty soprano! For me she is a little girl. Unhappy and lost.'

'Your first conundrum!' Kim pushed her plate aside and stood up. 'OK. I have to love you and leave you. I have a hair appointment. You two continue your sisterly reunion and I will see you later. *Ciao*, girls!'

'Right,' Steph said as they watched Kim duck out from under

the pavement umbrellas and thread her way down the street. 'And what happened to the other sister?'

Jess shook her head. 'I don't know.'

Steph raised an eyebrow. 'No, Jess, intriguing as all this seems I don't think I'm altogether buying this story. You're not a historian. Come on, I want the truth.'

Jess glanced at Steph, her eyes hidden behind her dark glasses from the blistering Roman sunshine then she looked down at the table and shrugged evasively. 'I've told you the truth. Now, what is this about reading my cards?' Firmly she changed the subject.

Steph shrugged. 'It was a silly game. One of Kim's friends does it as a party piece. Reading the *tarocchi*. She said you were in danger.' She looked surreptitiously at her sister. 'She talked about a man trying to kill you.'

Jess stared at her.

'I told them all that was nonsense, but I did worry a bit. Of course I did. That was why I tried to ring you.'

Jess tucked the CD back into her bag and reached for her purse. 'Can we go for a walk?' She found she was shivering in spite of the heat. 'Let me pay for this, then I would love to stroll for a bit.' Thoughtfully she pulled out a handful of euros. 'Why on earth should someone be trying kill me? Did she say?' She beckoned the waiter.

'No she didn't.' Steph hesitated. 'She also said something about love.'

Jess grinned distractedly. 'What tarot reader doesn't.'

'Good point. The thing is, you are still together, aren't you, you and Will?'

'No way!'

Steph glanced up as the young man appeared at their table. '*Il conto, grazie.*' Suddenly she was looking worried. 'He still loves you, you know.' She turned back to Jess.

'Not any more.'

'Why do you say that?'

'Because I was horrible to him. Because I thought he had done something.' She paused. 'It doesn't matter why, Steph. Just take my word for it.'

'Do you still like him at all, Jess?'

They stood up, leaving the tip on the table. The hovering waiter scooped it into the pocket of his long black apron with a wink.

Strolling slowly towards the Corso Vittorio Emanuele Steph glanced sideways at her sister. 'You didn't answer,' she persisted. 'Do you still like him?'

Jess shrugged. 'I don't know. I don't think we could ever be an item again, if that's what you mean. Too much water under the bridge.'

Steph swung her tote bag over her shoulder. The sun was reflecting off the pavement in a dazzling glare of pale stone. Car fumes hung in a haze over the crossroads ahead. The roar of traffic made it almost impossible to make themselves heard. Instinctively they crossed over to the shady side of the street and turned off the main road up a narrow alley, strolling more slowly still towards the Piazza Navona.

'But you wouldn't mind if you saw him again?' Steph went on doggedly.

'I suppose not.' Jess paused. 'Though I doubt if he would want to see me.' She pulled off her dark glasses, narrowing her eyes. 'Why are you asking me all this, Steph?'

'Because he's on his way. I'm sorry. I should have asked you first. I'm an idiot. But last time I spoke to him he told me how much he still loved you. Well, almost. And I thought . . . Well, he was up at Ty Bran, wasn't he and after you rang to say you were on your way, I rang him.' Steph heaved a great shrug. 'I should have told you last night. It was sort of Kim's idea too. She has so much room and we thought it would be fun, and Carmella said you had found love again –'

'Carmella!' Jess turned to face her angrily. 'Who is this woman who seems to have such an influence over you? She doesn't know anything about me! I don't want Will here! I came here for some peace!'

'I'm so sorry.'

Jess exhaled hard through her teeth. 'OK. I suppose it's not the end of the world. But I am not back with him. I am not wanting to be back with him, and that must be made clear. By you, Steph! I don't want to be put in the embarrassing position of him arriving and thinking I am going to fall at his feet. Or into his bed. Or have his bags delivered to my bedroom for God's sake!' She rammed her sunglasses back on. 'I have come here to do some research. I shall be out most of the time.'

'Sorry.' Steph shook her head again. 'So sorry.' There was a moment's silence. They had drifted to a standstill as they reached the piazza and around them people divided and passed them by on the busy pavement. They were surrounded by the smell of food from the restaurants all round them; the sound of water from the three great fountains filled the air.

'When is he coming?' Jess said, after a pause.

'Today.'

'Today?'

Steph nodded. 'Otherwise I could have rung him and told him not to come. He was very keen. He said you and he had had words and he was really sorry and he wanted to make up. Sorry.'

'Stop saying sorry!' Jess suddenly felt like crying. All the complications were coming back. Those wonderful moments of peace and happiness in her bedroom as she woke to a feeling of complete safety were gone. The wave of betrayal and devastation was swiftly replaced by anger. 'As I said, I shan't be there much.'

'How are you going to do all this research, Jess?' Steph said softly. 'When you don't speak Italian.'

Jess glared at her. 'I'll find a way. There are lots of websites. Besides, I shan't need Italian to walk around the ruins.'

Will arrived at about six p.m. He dropped his bags on the floor of the hallway and greeted Kim and Steph with a kiss on the cheek. Then he turned to Jess. He smiled.

'How are you?' He sounded wary.

'Better than last time we met. I'm sorry if I was rude.'

'Why don't you go into the *salotto*, you two.' Kim, forewarned by Steph that Jess wasn't quite as pleased by the arrival of the new guest as they had expected, ushered them into the large cool reception room off the entrance hall. 'Clear the air, then come and have a drink. We'll be in the kitchen.'

Will closed the door behind them and stood, his back to it, looking at Jess. He waited unsmiling for her to speak first.

'I'm sorry. I know I was awful to you.' Jess shrugged. 'I understand if you never want to speak to me again. Steph and Kim didn't realise. There was a reason I behaved the way I did.' She saw the sceptically raised eyebrow and plunged on. 'Can I explain?'

'I think you'd better.' He still hadn't smiled at her, she realised. He had made no move in her direction at all.

'When you came to see me in Wales I thought you had –' She floundered to a standstill.

'When I came to Wales you said all sorts of crazy things to me, Jess; you treated me as though I was a serial killer!' he filled in for her.

Shaking her head sadly she hesitated before going on. 'Almost. As you know, I thought,' she paused again. 'I thought you had done something. Broken into my flat.' She struggled to meet his eye. 'I know I was wrong. I want to apologise. I want to make it all right again.'

'Just like that?'

'Just like that.' She bit her lip.

'And did you find out who had broken into your flat?' He held her gaze.

She shook her head.

'Did they take anything?'

Only my self-respect. My peace of mind. Maybe a bit of my sanity. She didn't say it.

'Why did you think it was me?'

'Because –' She sighed. 'Because someone told me it was you and like a fool I believed them.'

'Dan?'

She was startled. 'How did you know that?'

'He's been saying some odd things lately. Tell me, if he thought I had broken into your flat, why did he suggest I come and see you in Wales?'

Jess shrugged miserably. 'He was setting you up. He knew you hadn't done it.'

His eyes narrowed angrily. 'He must have known you would throw me out.'

Dear God! She couldn't tell him the truth. If she did he would probably kill Dan. Everyone would find out what had happened. She would never be free of the horror and the scandal. 'He was protecting someone else. Look, Will, it doesn't matter why –'

'It most certainly does!' He strode away from the door towards the large circular table that stood in the middle of the floor. He ran a finger across the intricate marquetry. The room was dim, lit by the faint lines of sunlight which strayed in around the closed shutters. It smelled of beeswax polish and dust. 'Who was he protecting?'

She could feel the anger coming off him and it scared her. 'It was Ash,' she said hurriedly. 'He thought Ash had done it. He didn't,' she added quickly as Will's lips tightened. 'It was all a silly misunderstanding. That's why I wanted to explain to you why I had been so horrid.' She floundered to a halt miserably.

'A misunderstanding! And why did he think it was Ash who had done it? Because the boy's black, so he must be a thief?' Will's anger seemed to condense in the air around them.

'No! No, of course not. Dan saw Ash walking home with me after the school disco and assumed –' She faltered. 'Look, it wasn't Ash. And it wasn't you. And I'm so, so sorry for thinking that it was!'

'And you arranged to have me come all this way so you could apologise to me? May I ask why you didn't just telephone?' he asked acidly.

'I didn't know Kim and Steph had asked you. I didn't know you were coming till this afternoon.' She walked over and stood beside him. 'But I'm glad you have. It's given me the chance to explain. To apologise.'

'Well, I suppose I should be relieved all that venom wasn't for me after all,' he said with a sigh. There was a pause. 'What the hell are you doing in Rome anyway? I thought you were going to spend the summer painting in Wales.'

She forced a smile. 'I am researching a ghost, if you really want to know.' She gave him what she hoped was a disarming grin. How could she ever tell him the truth?

I'm here because I am scared Dan wants to kill me.

I am on the run.

I am not sure what I am going to do or how long I'm going to stay here or what is going to happen next.

At the moment I am not sure I shall ever dare go back to England!

No, she was hardly going to say all that.

He turned to face her. 'You know, I don't understand you any more at all! A ghost! What else? Why didn't I think of that!' He leaned forward and kissed her on the forehead before she could step back. 'Friends, but that's all, right? Do I read the message correctly now?'

She bit her lip and nodded.

'Fair enough.' He turned away. 'Where are the others? In the kitchen?' He strode away from her towards the door. Then as he reached for the ornate gilt handle he swung back. 'And you really don't know who broke into your flat?'

She shook her head.

'Did you call the police?'

'No.'

'Why not?'

'It was too late. No evidence.'

'And they didn't take anything?'

She shook her head. Nothing tangible.

He shrugged and pulling open the door, disappeared into the corridor.

Jess didn't move.

10

Someone had mended the broken window. Dan stood on the terrace looking at the clean pane of glass glittering in the afternoon sun. There was a small smear of putty in one corner. He scratched at it thoughtfully with a fingernail then turned to stare out across the garden. A slow tour of the entire property made it clear that she had gone. There was no sign of the car and his careful scrutiny of the rooms through the windows showed the house tidy; empty. He could sense the emptiness all around him.

He retraced his steps grimly to the front door and felt in his pocket for the keys; the spare set of keys he had found hanging on the hook in the kitchen before he left to face the wrath of his wife.

'For God's sake, you might have told me you were going to be away all night!' Natalie's voice replayed in his head yet again and he frowned in irritation. 'I was imagining all sorts of things. You might have been in an accident!' Then she had paused. Her eyes had narrowed. 'I suppose you're going to tell me you were book shopping again. But you weren't, were you! You spent the night with her, didn't you! You bastard! I might have known. You weren't book shopping, you were shagging the English teacher!'

He had denied it of course, again and again and eventually, he thought, she had believed him. But he had to make sure Jess didn't rock the boat. A bead of sweat appeared on his upper lip. He could not afford to wreck his marriage. Not now, not with his career poised to take off. Not ever.

Standing at the foot of the stairs he glanced up towards the landing. A stray beam of sunlight illuminated the ceiling, and spotlit the painting on the wall, an ink and wash scene of jumbled stones and yew trees not unlike the scene he could see from the window as he walked slowly upstairs.

The bedroom door was open. He walked across and stared in.

She had left no personal belongings there. The cupboards and drawers were empty, the chest of drawers had no clutter to show where her combs and cosmetics had lain. He went over to the bed, neatly made with an immaculately smooth patchwork quilt and with a sudden rush of anger bent to tear off the covers. He fell to his knees and pressed his face into the sheets, inhaling the faint scent of her body, almost masked by the odour of whatever laundry rinse had been used in Steph's washing machine. Digging his clawed fingers into the pillows he groaned. The silence of the room seemed to thicken as he knelt there and he shivered. And after a moment or two he looked up.

Where are you? Can we come out now?

The child's voice was very faint.

He clenched his fists into the sheets.

Where are you?

'No!' His face a rictus of fear and anger, he staggered to his feet. Hurling the pillow across the room, he threw himself at the door and out onto the landing.

In the kitchen he paused, trying to calm himself. Imagination. That's all. Stupid imagination. A reaction to Jess's insane behaviour. For a moment he had felt as though some alien force had gripped him. An anger like nothing he had ever experienced. He walked over to the sink and bent over it, splashing some cold water onto his face. He had to get out of there. Fast. And get back to Shrewsbury before Natalie became suspicious again.

As he headed for the door his fingers brushed against the bunch of keys in his pocket and he drew them out. Jess had gone for good. That much was obvious. He was not going to need them again. Better to hang them back where they were on the hook. Leave no sign that he had been here. He walked over to the noticeboard and stood staring at it. Someone had left a note there he hadn't noticed before. *KIM'S NUMBER*, it said. Followed by a string of figures. Kim. He smiled grimly. Was that where Jess had gone? It was obvious when he thought about it. She thought she could run away from him. Hide. Tell her sister a pack of lies about him. She had forgotten he had known Kim almost as long as she had; that Kim had even fancied him once, long ago, when they were all at college together. He scowled and reaching for the phone put it to his ear. The dialling tone confirmed that it had been reconnected. Only one way to tell where Jess was now and how much she had told them. Slowly he began to punch in the numbers. If she could get an invitation to Rome, so perhaps could he. He looked down at the keys, still in his hand. Perhaps he would keep them after all. Who knew when he might need them again.

'So, where do you suggest I start my research?' Jess directed her question at Kim as the four of them sat down to eat that evening. She helped herself to a chunk of focaccia from the bread basket.

Kim shrugged. 'How on earth would I know? Have you looked on the net? Libraries? Museums? Roman remains?' She reached into the oven with her padded gloves and produced a bubbling dish of cheesy pasta. 'We do all those in spades in Rome.' She slid the dish onto the table and chucked the gloves onto the worktop behind her. 'OK. Eat, *bambini*!'

'Have you heard your ghostly voice since you've been here?' Will asked thoughtfully.

Jess glanced at him suspiciously. 'No. Or, only in a dream.'

'So, she hasn't followed you.'

Jess shook her head. 'Ghosts don't do that, do they? Aren't they tied to specific places?'

They all shrugged.

'We need an expert on ghosts,' Steph said with a smile.

'Carmella!' Kim exclaimed. 'She knows all about this sort of thing. We could have a séance. Ask your little girl what she would like you to do.'

'Oh, I don't know.' Jess shook her head. 'Aren't séances supposed to be dangerous?'

'It might be fun,' Will put in. He grinned. 'You must have done table turning and stuff when you were students. "Is there anybody there?" sort of thing. We scared ourselves witless a few times if I remember.'

'We don't want to scare ourselves witless, Will,' Steph retorted. She was watching Jess's face. 'This is serious. And rather tragic. And I suspect it could be dangerous, yes. The little girl who haunts my studio is not above breaking a few things from time to time.'

Jess dropped her fork. She stared at her sister, stunned. 'So you do know more about her than you let on! It has happened to you! I thought I was going mad! She broke some figures in your studio and I blamed myself. I blamed a bird or a draught or something. Then she came into the house after me. She tore up my paintings and smashed a bottle of wine.'

'You're kidding!' Kim stared at her. 'No wonder you didn't want to stay there on your own.'

'I thought you said she didn't frighten you,' Steph put in quietly. 'That all sounds a bit frightening to me.'

Jess shrugged. 'It was frightening. I thought maybe someone else, I mean someone real, had come in and done it. It didn't occur to me that it was her to start with.'

'And someone real would be better than a ghost? Who on earth would do that?' Steph stared at her, shocked. 'Jess!'

Jess shrugged again. 'I wasn't thinking straight. But what was I supposed to believe? A burglar in the middle of nowhere? Or the resident ghost. Either way I was beginning to feel freaked out!'

She was aware of Will's eyes fixed on her face. She stared down at her plate, refusing to meet his gaze.

Kim stood up. 'Let's ring Carmella!'

'What? Now?' Steph shook her head dismayed.

'Why not? If she can summon your wayward child we can sort all this out and find out what is bugging her.'

'I don't know, Kim.' Jess looked from her sister to Will for support. 'This isn't a game. She is unhappy. Angry. Lost.'

'And we can help her. Find out what happened in Rome. Oh, come on! It will be fascinating.' Kim picked up the phone.

Steph leaned back in her chair and shrugged her shoulders at Jess. 'You are not going to stop her, I'm afraid.'

'And I doubt if anything will happen,' Will added. 'I don't see our Italian *signora* finding it easy to contact a two-thousand-year-old child from some weird British tribe!'

They fell silent as Kim's voice rose behind them in a torrent of excited Italian.

'Steph's right, you're not going to stop her now,' Will said quietly, with a rueful smile at Jess. 'I suspect we have to give in gracefully!'

The conversation on the phone had concluded with a fervent *'Ciao, a presto*!' and Kim turned to them flushed with triumph. 'She'll be here in half an hour. Just time to finish supper. Eat up, *bambini*. It's going to be a long night!'

*   *   *

121

'First, I read the cards.'

They were seated round a low coffee table in Kim's cosy sitting room, Steph and Will on the sofa, Jess and Kim on cushions, Carmella on a low chair at the head of the table. Behind her a cluster of candles flickered on the bookcase, otherwise there was no light in the room. The windows stood open onto the dark courtyard below with its gently trickling fountain. Theirs was the only one showing any light. Most of the occupants of the other apartments in the palazzo had left Rome for their summer residences in the hills or on the coast. Jess gave an involuntary shiver.

'OK. I start.' Carmella smiled at them. Her dark hair was tied back with a bright red scarf; the style emphasised her vivacious dark eyes.

This time she had her own deck of cards with her. She brought them out of her bag. They were wrapped in a length of black silk and reverently she unwound it and began a slow shuffling of the pack.

Carmella glanced up at Jess. 'Do you have something belonging to this child?' she asked.

Jess shook her head. 'She lived nearly two thousand years ago!'

'Ah.' Carmella was seemingly unfazed. 'No matter. Let me be silent for a few moments.'

She closed her eyes. The quiet of the room was broken by the faint sound of a police siren echoing from some distant street.

'*Va bene*. Let's start.' Carmella reached down and setting the cards on the table, cut the pack. Will looked up and caught Jess's eye. He gave a small grimace and she smiled. This wasn't going to work, but if it amused the others, then she was content to watch. She firmly pushed away the worm of unease which was beginning to rise deep in her stomach and reached over for her glass of wine, sipping it quietly as she studied the layout of cards which Carmella was setting out on the table. The warm polished surface of the old wood reflected the candlelight steadily. No breath of wind strayed in through the window. The night was hot and very still.

'OK. Now I start with the card of the child.' Carmella reached seemingly at random and turned over one of the cards. '*Il fante di bastoni*. So here she is again.'

Jess caught her breath. None of them said anything.

Slowly and methodically Carmella turned over the remaining cards in the spread. The silence in the room grew heavy. Will and Steph exchanged glances as Carmella sat staring at the cards. She leaned forward, tapping the table with a scarlet fingernail. Then at last she looked up. 'This young lady, she is in danger. Someone from her past is trying to find her. Hunting her down the centuries.' She frowned. 'I don't understand. This is complicated. *Molto pericoloso*. I have never read such a spread before. And you want me to try to speak to her?' She glanced doubtfully from Kim to Jess.

'Did she grow up to be a woman?' Jess whispered. 'Or did she die as a child? Can you tell from the cards?'

Carmella stared back down at the pattern on the table before her. 'She speaks from two worlds.' She trailed her fingers across the centre of the spread. 'She lived two thousand years ago, you said. So obviously she is in spirit now.'

'Yes, but did she live to grow up?' Jess leaned forward. 'Can you see her family? She lost a brother and sister. Are they there?'

'The cards speak of torment and fear. They speak of resolutions.' Carmella tapped her finger again. 'They speak of loss and of anger and sorrow. And they speak of love. At the end of her life, she found love, but for how long and with whom I cannot say.' She frowned. 'Perhaps it was at the moment of death.' Shaking her head she swept all the cards into a heap and leaned away from the table. 'I am not sure we should try and call her.'

'What!' Kim stared at her. 'Of course we should. How else will Jess know what happened to her? Jess has been talking to this girl. So has Steph. They know her already. She has been communicating with them in Wales. What we want is for her to speak to us here in Rome. Can you do that?'

Carmella shrugged. She half-turned on her seat and reached for her glass from the bookshelf behind them and turning back to the centre, sipped thoughtfully. 'To those in spirit all places and times are one. It does not matter where you are.'

'Unless she is anchored to the house in Wales. Doesn't that happen? A ghost hangs around in a spot where something special happened,' Will put in. He raised an eyebrow.

Carmella caught the quizzical smile. 'You do not believe. That does not matter. If she wants to speak, she will. Come.' She put down her glass of wine and sat forward on the edge of the chair. 'We hold hands like this.' She spread her arms and reached for Kim's hand. On the other side she beckoned Will to take her fingers. After a second's hesitation he did so, then he in turn reached out to Jess.

They sat in silence for a full minute, then Carmella spoke. Her voice was low and husky. 'Tell me her name again, this child from Wales.'

'Eigon,' Jess whispered.

Carmella nodded. 'OK. Now, sit quietly. Close your eyes. I will call her.'

Jess held her breath. Beside her Will was sitting, eyes closed as instructed, a slight smile on his lips. His hand was warm and firm in hers. On her other side Steph's palm was slightly damp. Jess opened one eye and peeped at her. Steph looked pale in the candlelight. Her face was composed; as still as marble.

'Eigon. We wish to speak to you. Show yourself here before us and perhaps we can help you in your unhappiness.' Carmella's throaty Italian accent rang out in the shadows. 'Eigon, I am asking you to appear before us here. Steph and Jess you know. You have asked their help before. Now we are here to try and answer your pleas.'

Carmella paused. The candles behind her guttered as a slight draught permeated the warm night air. There was someone else out there in the ether, listening, tuning in. She frowned. 'Please come to us, Eigon. We are here for you.' Her voice lifted as it grew stronger. She was no longer pleading. It was a command. 'Come and tell us your story, Eigon from Wales!'

'Wales didn't exist then,' Jess murmured. Her eyes were tightly closed.

Carmella shrugged. 'So. Eigon, of the tribes, can you hear me? The cards speak of love and sorrow and fear. Tell us your story. We are listening.'

The distant sound of a siren, faraway towards the centre of the city only accentuated the silence of the room as the candles flickered again. One of the flames faded and with a slight hiss it went out. Jess's mouth had gone dry. She was, she realised, clutching Will and Steph's hands as tightly as she could.

124

'*Bene*. She comes,' Carmella breathed. Her eyes were closed, her face still. 'Can you sense her in the room?'

The sudden jangle of the doorbell through the apartment jerked them out of the silence with frightening violence.

'*Dio!*' Carmella opened her eyes angrily. 'That is so dangerous! What fool rings the doorbell at *mezzanotte?*' She glanced at her wristwatch. 'It is so late!' They were all staring at each other, their link with one another broken.

Kim scrambled to her feet. She went to the door and flicked on the lights. 'Oh God, I am so sorry. I don't know who could be here so late. I'll send them away, then we can go on.'

'Too late! She is gone!' Carmella reached for her glass and angrily downed the last of her wine. 'The spell is broken. She will not come now.'

'She will.' Jess hadn't moved. She was still staring down at the table, her eyes fixed on the discarded heap of cards. 'I can feel her. She is still here.'

In the doorway Kim hesitated. 'I'll get rid of them, whoever they are. I am sure she will come back, Carmella. She wants to talk to Jess.'

The doorbell rang again. Kim disappeared into the hall. Will stood up and went over to the side table. He picked up the bottle of wine and brought it back to top up their glasses. 'You really think she was about to appear?' he asked softly.

Jess nodded. 'I could feel her in the room.'

Carmella glanced at her over her glass. 'Why do you need me? You can do this on your own. You ask. She comes.'

Jess bit her lip. 'It can't be that easy.'

'Why not? The dead are always with us. Did not one of your English poets say that? You are an English teacher, you should know.'

'The past. The past is always with us,' Jess said. She smiled. 'LP Hartley.'

'Is that not the same?'

'No. Not really.'

'All right. Then what about, *Il n'y a pas de morts*. That was Maeterlinck, I think.'

Jess smiled. '"There are no dead". That sounds a bit more like it. Did you see her, Carmella?'

Carmella shook her head. 'I could sense her. Hovering. In the shadows.'

'Does she really want to make contact –' Jess broke off as Kim appeared in the doorway.

'Guess who's here! It makes our old teachers' reunion complete!' Kim stepped aside.

Dan was standing in the doorway.

Jess felt a lurch of blind fear as he smiled round at them. 'I gather Kim forgot to tell you I rang. What a surprise to find you were all out here!' He was carrying a smart leather haversack. Dropping it in the doorway he walked into the room. 'Jess! How are you?' Before she could move he stooped and kissed her on the cheek. 'Steph. Will. A reunion indeed! And this must be – ?' He paused with a small bow in front of Carmella. She was staring at him, a small frown on her face.

'My friend, Carmella Bianchi,' Kim said. 'I am sorry. I didn't expect you quite so soon, Dan.' She glanced at Jess apologetically. 'We were having a séance. But I am sure we can stop for a bit to offer you some food after your journey.'

'No need,' Dan shook his head. 'I ate something on the plane. Please don't stop because of me. I'd hate to interrupt. And this sounds exciting.' He sat down on the sofa arm, between Jess and Steph. 'Go on, please.'

'No!' Carmella stood up. 'No, the time is not right now. We will do it another day. The energies have changed. The child has gone.'

'The child?' Dan raised an eyebrow. 'Let me guess. The child from Ty Bran?'

'You've seen her?' Carmella stared at him.

'Indeed. When I was staying with Jess.' Dan looked at Jess and smiled. His brown eyes were bright with malice; their colour seemed to have changed subtly. Now they seemed amber in the flickering candlelight. 'Didn't she tell you I was up there?' He reached across and rested his hand lightly on her arm.

'Yes,' Jess said coldly. 'I mentioned it.' She was aware of Steph and Will watching her. Standing up she moved away from the table. 'If Carmella is going, I think I might go to bed. I am very tired.' She paused and glanced back at Carmella. 'Can we try again some time?'

'You do not need me,' Carmella said softly. She went over to Jess and kissed her on the cheek. *'Dorma bene*, Jess. *Stammi bene*, OK.' She glanced over Jess's shoulder towards Dan. 'The cards I read for you,' she whispered. 'Before. I saw him. Do not be alone, eh?'

Jess stared at her.

Carmella shrugged her shoulders and bent to pick up her bag off the floor. Gathering her cards and wrapping them in their silk scarf, she pushed them into a pocket in the bag and zipped it up. '*Ciao*! See you soon!'

Kim frowned as the door closed behind her. 'I am sorry, Jess. That was so close! It was just getting exciting!'

'Did I mess things up?' Dan was contrite. 'I should have rung from the airport, I managed to get a flight sooner than I expected, but I wanted to surprise you all.' His glance brushed across Jess and went back to their hostess. 'I come bearing gifts, Kim. Does that make it better? Outside, in my case. Whisky. Shortbread. Pretty things.'

'So, where is Natalie?' Jess's question cut across the room.

He stopped in his tracks. 'In Shrewsbury with the children.' His voice was cold. 'We agreed that Rome in summer was not the ideal place for kids. Not when they have the chance to spend fun time with the grandparents.'

'And what was it that you had to do so urgently in Rome?' Jess asked harshly. Will and Steph were eyeing her speculatively.

He smiled. 'Don't you remember, Jess? I thought I told you exactly what I need to do. I told Nat I've come to attend an educational conference.'

'I didn't know there was one.' She managed to keep her voice steady as she walked towards the door. 'Goodnight.'

'Goodnight, Jess,' Will replied softly.

She flashed him a smile. For a moment she had forgotten he was there.

In the hall she stood for a second trying to gather her thoughts. Behind her she heard a burst of laughter from inside the room. What in God's name was she going to do now?

Pulling her bedroom door closed after her, she discovered a huge ornate key in the lock. It turned easily and she paused with it in her hand, trying to calm herself. She was safe for now. Never in a million years could he break down this huge heavy door. What was he going to do here anyway with three other people in the apartment?

Walking over to the window she pulled open the casements and stood looking out. The other three sides of the palazzo were all in darkness. The central courtyard below, with its formal pots and statues and its fountain were invisible. Only the sound of the water floated through the night on the hot city air. Leaving the windows open, she turned towards her bed.

A figure was standing about ten feet from her on the faded Aubusson carpet.

'Eigon?' she whispered. Her whole body went cold.

There was no mistaking her. The child was small, delicate, her wild dark hair tied into a bundle at the nape of her neck. She was wearing some sort of pale long tunic. There were silver bangles at her wrists. Jess stared at her. 'You came. You heard Carmella –' But the figure was fading before her eyes. She could see the carpet through the fine gauze of the dress, then the bed. Then she had gone.

'Eigon?' Jess called sharply. 'Wait! I want to help you!'

She sat down on the low velvet chair beside the window and suddenly she was shaking. She had seen the child; made eye contact. Eigon had come to find her.

Jess eyed the door. She wanted Steph. She needed to talk to Steph, but to do that she would have to unlock the door.

Getting up she tiptoed across to it and put her ear to the heavy panelling. What the fuck was Dan doing, following her here? A wave of anger shot through her fear. Did he intend to try and intimidate her into silence? Or did he still intend to kill her?

She paced away from the door, shaking her head. That was idiotic. Of course he didn't. He never had. That was sheer melo-dramatic nonsense. He had managed to scare her and she had overreacted. All she had to do was reassure him that she wasn't going to tell anyone what he had done. After all, she wasn't. Was she? She shivered suddenly. A cold breeze strayed in through the windows, stirring the heavy curtains.

There was a creak on the landing on the far side of the door. She froze. There was someone out there. Pressing her ear closer to the wood she listened intently. Silence. She sensed someone had paused outside the door. 'Dan?' She mouthed the word sound-lessly. Slowly the handle began to turn. The door creaked slightly as it was pushed from the outside. The lock held firm and she heard a quiet chuckle. A man's voice. Dan or Will? Did she even need to ask?

She hurried to the window and looked out. As she had thought, there was no way up to her room that way. The wall was high and there were no creepers or drainpipes on the outside. The lower part of the casement had an ornate wrought iron grille across it, more of a container for pots than a protection. There was no way anyone could get in from there. And no way of escape either.

11

Miserably Eigon hugged the pillow to her, muffling the sound of her tears. Outside she could hear the sounds of the big city all around her. The rattle of wagon wheels in the early morning light, the shouts of street vendors and in the distance the deeper throaty sound of a huge crowd gathering. It was a day of festival and triumph. The Emperor was to process through the streets of Rome to celebrate his successes. Behind him would follow symbols of his glorious victories, treasures of gold and jewellery, richly caparisoned horses, ornately collared hunting dogs, weapons and above all, his captives from Gaul and from Britannia, and most important of those was the captive king, her father, with his wife and daughter. The outer door of the prison clanged open and she heard the shouts of the men outside with a shudder. They were coming for them. Bringing chains to hammer onto their wrists and ankles. And after the procession, they would be dragged out into the sandy arena and killed. Her mother and father had tried to prevent her hearing their fate, but she had listened. She had crept closer and strained her ears to hear their whispered conversations. She had heard the guards talking, heard their cruel chuckles, seen their lascivious glances as they discussed how long it would take the beautiful wife of the British leader to die.

'We are proud and we are royal,' her father had told her again the night before. 'We will go to our deaths, if that is what the gods have ordained, with dignity and courage. Think of your next life, my child. This is just one of many. Our pain will be quickly over and there will be many lifetimes for you again. He had pulled her close to him and kissed her on the top of her head. 'I shall be proud of you tomorrow, Eigon. You will hold your head high and you will show the people of Rome that we are not ignorant peasants as they believe. We are noble and educated and as good as they are. Better. They have lost touch with the gods of the land in their quest for conquest. This city may be vast, there may be hundreds of thousands of people here, but if their spirits languish and their souls are lost then they are nothing compared to us. Remember that, my daughter.' He had glanced over her head at Cerys and smiled with sad resignation.

The sound of marching men rang through the stone walls and Eigon shrank further under her blanket. She heard the sharp bark of a command and the men came to a halt, the nails of their boots as they stamped to attention a crisp double report on the roadway somewhere nearby.

A shadow fell across the bed. 'Eigon. It is time to get up.' It was her mother. Cerys was pale, but resolute as she waited for Eigon to scramble miserably out of the bed. They had been brought fresh clothes. Cerys gave a wry smile. 'The more glorious we look, the better it reflects upon the Emperor that he has defeated us,' she said bitterly. 'See, they have given us beautiful tunics and mantles and even bangles of gold. They are calling your father king.'

'I don't know how brave I can be, Mam,' Eigon whispered as she pulled the tunic over her head. 'I am trying very hard.' She pulled the plaited girdle tight around her middle and held out her arms for her mantle. It was a smaller copy of her mother's.

'I know you are, sweetheart.' Cerys pulled her close. 'You will be a credit to us. Your father is certain of it.' There was a shout outside. Somewhere a door banged. Eigon shrank closer to her mother. 'Will it hurt? Being killed?'

Cerys shook her head firmly. 'No. The gods will bring you strength and comfort.'

They brought the chains at the last moment. Manacles and neck rings like those of slaves. Then they were ushered outside to their places in the procession which was forming on the barracks parade ground. Eigon caught her breath and gripped her mother's hand tightly. There was no sign of her father. There were hundreds of captives being ushered from the prison cells barefoot, emaciated, stinking from the filth of their imprisonment. Warriors. Farmers. Peasants who somehow had avoided being slaughtered, formed into ranks between the Roman guards who marshalled them into groups with swords and whips. There were noblemen from the tribes there too. Some smartly dressed like Eigon and Cerys. Others crippled with wounds or disease. All in chains. Somewhere at the front of the procession there were trumpeters, dignitaries in chariots, wagonloads of captured treasure, and interspersed with the prisoners were groups of horsemen and everywhere legionaries and auxiliaries of the Roman army. They heard the triumphant summons of the trumpet and knew the front of the long parade had started. It was a long time before it was their turn, walking hand in hand in their places as the procession wound its way through the baying crowds, towards the centre of Rome.

'Where is Papa?' Eigon looked up at her mother, clutching at her fingers.

Cerys shrugged. 'I can't see him.' Her face was white, but she walked proudly, her shoulders back, her head held high. Eigon bit her lips as bravely as she could and tried to copy her mother's stance. She would not let them down.

The procession wound its way through narrow streets lined with high buildings such as Eigon had never seen in her life before, some of wood, some of brick or stone, storey upon storey, some with balconies and windows and shutters, some just blank walls soaring up to tiled roofs, past temples and markets, through gardens and past villas and theatres and at last into the great forum where there were grander buildings than ever. The blinding light beat down on them and the heat was intense. The buildings here seemed to Eigon to reach to the sky; the temples were of glittering marble, their pillars like a shining forest of straight soaring trunks, the broad flights of steps banks of parallel formality, crowded now with the populace of Rome. She was awestruck. They came to a halt at last in front of the dais where the Emperor Claudius and his wife, Agrippina, were seated with their attendants beneath the arrayed standards of Rome. All around them the captives, surrounded by the crowded, baying audience of thousands, had fallen to their knees. Many of them were crying. Some were already begging for their lives, others, like her mother were standing proudly without bowing their heads as they were brought to the front of the crowd and halted before the Emperor. It was only then that Eigon saw her father. He had been escorted through the ranks of the prisoners by two men with drawn swords and brought immediately below the dais, where he was forced to look up at the Emperor. He was, as her mother had said, dressed as a king, and with his proud stance and calm, commanding face he surveyed the man before him with a quiet dignity which the neck ring and chains did nothing to diminish. If anything it was Claudius who looked uncertain.

'Do you have anything to say before we sentence you as traitors who have for so long opposed the might of Rome?' Claudius's voice did not carry far above the noise of the crowd and with its slight stutter it held little authority but the senators around him heard him. And so did the men closest to Caratacus.

He took a step forward and slowly the crowds around them began to fall silent. His guards stood back respectfully. He turned and beckoned Cerys and Eigon towards him. Their escort fell back and they came and stood one on either side of him.

'Great Emperor, I come before you as your prisoner,' he said slowly. 'But I come also as king of my people. A man of my bloodline and status would have come to Rome as an honoured guest instead of as a prisoner after only a fraction of the triumphs I have enjoyed and you would have been pleased to be the ally of such a powerful king. I was the ruler who defeated Rome and held her at bay!' He paused. Around him the great echoing space of the forum, framed by its two hills, enclosed by stately buildings, was totally silent as even the furthest ranks of the crowd craned forward to catch his words. 'As it is, you are the victor, I am the one who has been humiliated. I had horses and men, arms and wealth. Are you really so astonished that I regret their loss? You want to rule the world, but it does not follow that everybody else therefore wants to end up as a slave! Besides, if I had surrendered to you without a battle, neither my defeat nor your victory would have become famous.' He smiled gravely and there was a slight quizzical lift to his eyebrow as he held the Emperor's gaze. 'If you execute me and my family, we will all be forgotten. Spare our lives and my people and I shall for ever be a symbol of your mercy!'

His words were followed by a breathless hush. At last Claudius rose to his feet and stepped forward to the edge of the dais. He stared round, narrowing his eyes against the sunlight, his toga stirring in the light breeze, then finally he fixed his gaze on Caratacus's face.

'You are an eloquent opponent, King Caratacus. And a brave one.' His voice carried better now in the total silence which reigned over the crowded forum. 'I am minded to accede to your request and spare you.'

133

There was a short pause then slowly a sigh seemed to spread out across the kneeling sea of prisoners. It was taken up by the onlookers and at last someone cheered. Within seconds the cheer had spread around the seats and benches and then to the furthest ranks of the crowd high on the hills until the deafening ring seemed to resound through the whole city.

Claudius let it go on for a long time, a slight smile on his face, acknowledging the popularity of his words, then he raised his hand for silence. When, after what seemed like an eternity, he had it he took another step forward. 'I shall require your homage, great king. And that of your wife and daughter.' Suddenly he was looking straight into Eigon's eyes.

She felt herself gasp with fear. She sensed her father's hesitation, his struggle with his pride and she clutched at his hand, looking up at him pleadingly. Claudius had seen it too. He did not want this moment of triumph spoiled by the man's insane courage. 'Your homage, great king and your family and your people live. Without it they all die.' There was no mistaking the threat and the power in the man's voice now. For all his weaknesses Claudius could pull rank when he had to.

Caratacus took a deep breath. 'Remove our chains, and I shall kneel before you as a free man.'

Claudius bowed his head. He snapped his fingers and within seconds men had appeared to strike off their chains. Caratacus flexed his hands, then at last he stepped up onto the dais. The crowd fell silent again. Taking the Emperor's hand in his he went down on one knee and kissed the Emperor's ring. 'And now, you will pay homage to my wife.' Claudius gestured at Agrippina beside him. Caratacus raised an eyebrow but made no objection, taking her hand in his without noticing the frisson of disapproval which ran around the assembled senators and the Emperor's other attendants, as Cerys and Eigon stepped in their turn onto the dais and before thousands of witnesses paid homage to the Emperor of Rome. As she moved away from him Eigon felt the Emperor's hand on her head. She glanced up, scared, and for the second time caught his gaze. This time he smiled.

The day was not over. As the crowds in the forum began to drift away, the men on the dais made their way into the Senate building and it was there that Caratacus and his family were led next, once again to affirm their allegiance to Rome and once again

134

to allow Caratacus to address the Senate. And here they heard that the Emperor had granted them a house in which to live.

Cerys glanced at her husband. His face was impassive as he bowed his head in acquiescence. Was he accepting surrender, agreeing to a life of captivity in all but name? She couldn't decide. But for now it was all over. Their chains were gone, their attendants had been freed to serve them and as the Senate gave the Emperor a standing ovation their part in the proceedings was at an end. They were being escorted from the Senate building out into the blazing sunshine. The crowds were dispersing. The moment was over. They were free and on their way to their new abode.

Eigon's hand slipped into Cerys's and, hardly able to comprehend that their lives had been spared, her mother glanced down at her. 'Mam.' Eigon, tugging urgently at her fingers, was still pale, her eyes enormous in her small face. 'Mam, I need to tell you something.'

'Sweetheart, we are all safe. You needn't be afraid any more.'

Eigon stared up at her, scarcely comprehending. 'Not of anything?'

'No, my daughter, not of anything.' Smiling, Cerys glanced at her husband. His face was set. He did not appear to have heard the exchange. 'There is nothing more to worry about. We can forget all our worries and start a new life from this moment.'

Eigon nodded. She bit her lip. They had told her she had to say if ever she saw again any of the men who had hurt her so badly. She had thought they would have been left behind. But there, almost within touching distance in the Senate building she had seen one of the soldiers staring at her and her heart had stood still. She would recognise him anywhere. The hard golden wolf's eyes beneath the helmet, the sharp angular face, the loose red-lipped mouth which had lapped at her body like an animal, the grasping fingers which had torn at her and which now were holding a sword as he stood as an officer of the imperial guard. As soon as she saw him she had recognised him. And he had seen her gasp of recognition. Nothing registered on his face as he stood impassively at attention, but she realised at once that he knew who she was; he had seen her and he had seen Cerys. He now knew that he had raped the wife of the king of the British and their daughter and the child was probably the only person alive who could identify him.

Under Roman law the penalty for what he had done was death. As he held the child's gaze, just for one second the rigid figure moved and she saw him gesture sharply. He had drawn his finger across his throat. The implication was clear. If he saw her again he would kill her.

Jess woke with a start to the sound of knocking. Daylight flooded the room.

'Jess? Why have you locked the door?' The handle rattled up and down again. It was Steph.

Sliding from bed, Jess went to pull the door open. 'Sorry.'

'I've brought us coffee. Are you OK?'

Jess nodded. She grabbed her robe and pulled it round her, then taking one of the mugs from Steph she pushed the door shut. She had resolved not to say anything about Dan. 'Eigon came last night. She was here in this room. Carmella did summon her.' She was standing with her back to the door.

Steph sat down on the bed. 'Tell me.'

'She just appeared. She didn't say anything, but I could see her clearly. She sort of faded away, but I dreamed about her again. How she came to Rome and how Claudius pardoned her father. The family was given a house to live in.'

'Were you scared? I mean when she appeared.'

Jess nodded. 'I was a bit. It happened so suddenly and then she had gone. But she's not scary. Not really. She's a little girl.'

'A destructive little girl.' Steph drew up her knees. She balanced her mug between her hands. 'What is going on with you and the boys?'

'The boys?' Jess moved away from the door and went to stand in front of the window.

'Will and Dan.'

'I don't know what you mean.'

'Oh come off it, Jess. There was so much tension between you three it could have run a power station!'

'Not a good metaphor, Steph.' Jess was watching the fountain. At this hour of the morning the sun was blocked behind the building and the courtyard was shady.

'Maybe not. But expressive, I think you'd agree. So, what gives?'

Jess swung round to face her. 'How the hell did Dan know I was here?'

'Apparently he rang yesterday. Kim forgot to mention it. He has agreed to stand in at the last moment at this conference apparently and thought he would look in and see her. He had no idea we were all here.'

'Oh he knew all right! Is he still here?'

Steph nodded. 'As Nat and the kids are happily ensconced with her parents and that is not a scene he enjoys Kim suggested he stay for a few days until it starts. It will be like the old times. All of us together.' She hesitated. 'I know things are tricky between you and Will at the moment, I thought you were handling that. But is there something going on with Dan that I should know about?'

'Nothing. Only school stuff. I wanted to forget about school. I don't need anyone trying to get me to change my mind and stay there.'

'So that is what this is all about? Kim wasn't to know.'

'Don't worry about it.' Jess pursed her lips. 'Anyway, I'm planning to go out today. And I don't want to go out in a great gang, so can you tactfully tell Kim that she can include me out if she is planning any jolly excursions.'

'Of course. Where are you going?'

'Research. I want to follow Eigon's footsteps. See the Forum, the Senate. Find out where she lived. I'm going take my sketchbooks and wander round like a tourist.'

Steph smiled. 'I'll lend you a guidebook. Kim and I can take the chaps out and distract them. Dan mentioned the Spanish Steps and Keats' House.'

'Good idea. Anywhere but where I am going.'

She didn't see Will or Dan. Dressing in a loose cool linen shift and sun hat she put her sketchbook and pencils into her shoulder bag and slipped out of the apartment before either of them had appeared. In seconds she was lost among the throngs of people on the pavements as she headed, guidebook in hand, for the heart of the ancient city.

Nothing was as it had been in the dream. She smiled wryly as she sat down at a table under an awning outside a café just off the Piazza Consolazione and kicked off her sandals, exhausted. She had traipsed through the Forum for hours, staring at the ruins, briefly listening in here and there to other people's guided tours,

137

trying to visualise the place as it had been in the early first century AD. It was hard though she could easily imagine Eigon's awe. A child of the Celts, used to small domestic architecture, where the most awesome objects were forest trees, suddenly confronted with this. She climbed the Palatine Hill, grateful for the shade of the pines and cypress and evergreen oak, then moved on, ever watching for a small shadow behind a column, a child who was following her amongst the echoes of the past, but there was no sign of her.

When she did at last become aware of a figure standing over her and looked up it was not someone she wanted to see.

'Have you enjoyed your day?' Dan smiled. He pulled out the little wrought iron chair opposite her and sat down under the umbrella.

She stared at him, paralysed. 'What are you doing here? You followed me?'

'Of course. I can hardly claim to have arrived here by accident.' His face was hard. 'You and I have things to discuss, Jess.'

'Where are the others?'

'Mooning over Keats' grave in the English cemetery. They didn't even notice I had gone.' He smiled grimly.

She reached for her sunglasses and put them on. 'So discuss away. What do you want to say?' The guidebook was lying on the table in front of her. Beside it a glass of cold fresh orange juice. She grasped the glass and sipped it, hoping he wouldn't notice how her hand was shaking.

He was watching her intently. 'Have you told anyone?'

'No.'

He smiled. 'Sensible. It is not as though anyone would believe you.'

'I am not going to say anything, Dan, because I want to forget it. I don't want anyone to know what happened.'

'Nothing did happen. It was all in your imagination.' He glanced up as a waiter appeared and ordered a beer. 'You were drunk.'

She raised an eyebrow, feeling braver suddenly. After all, what could he do to her here, in front of so many people? 'You and I both know what happened, Dan. We both want to keep it to ourselves for whatever reasons. Let's leave it at that. I will try and forget what you did to me, and that when you realised that I had recognised you, you threatened to kill me.' She lowered her glasses onto the tip of her nose for a moment and peered at him over them. 'And you will forget the whole episode. I will not be blackmailed or threatened any more. You are a piece of shit. You have betrayed your wife and children and yourself. Having assimilated that point, I suggest you go back to England.' She stood up, her temper suddenly flaring. 'And I suggest that you give me a damn good reference, Dan, when I apply for a new job, otherwise I might start to remember what happened that night!' Groping in her pocket for some euros she threw them down on the table for the waiter and turned away, running down the steps to cross the piazza and climb towards the Tarpeian Rock, leaving Dan sitting staring after her.

The apartment was very silent when she arrived back. 'Hello?' she called. There was no reply. She went straight to her room and stepped out of her dusty sandals. Pulling off her dress she walked through to the bathroom and reached into the shower to turn it on.

The sound of the water spattering on the tiles was interrupted by a knock on the door behind her. She turned abruptly. 'Who is it?' she shouted. She fumbled behind her for the tap and turned it off. Grabbing at a towel she wrapped it around her. 'Who's there?'

There was no reply. She bit her lip nervously. The door was locked. 'Who's there?' she repeated. Padding across the tiles she pressed her ear against the door, listening. Slowly the door handle began to turn. 'Who is it?' she called a third time. 'Dan? Is that you? Leave me alone!' She was trembling all over. 'Go away.' There was no reply.

Then, faintly, she heard Steph's voice outside in her bedroom. 'Jess, are you back? Oh goodness, Dan! Sorry. Am I interrupting?'

Jess dragged the door open. 'No,' she breathed, clutching the towel around her, her fury erupting again. 'You aren't interrupting anything!'

Dan laughed. 'I'm sorry, Steph. I hadn't realised Jess was in the shower.' His lip lifted in a slight sneer as he glanced at her. 'I will leave you alone so she can make herself decent and then perhaps we can talk later.'

The two women stared after him as he walked out of the room. As soon as he had gone Steph turned back to her sister. 'What on earth is going on?'

Jess stormed towards the door and slammed it, turning the lock. She shook her head. 'It's a long story,' she said as she sat on the bed. She was shaking violently.

'So? I've got time.' Steph sat down next to her. 'The truth, Jess.'

Jess sighed. She couldn't keep this to herself any longer. She had to tell someone. 'He raped me, in London. After the end of term disco. That was why I left school.' Now she had begun, she couldn't stop the words pouring out. 'That was why I wanted to get away from him, Steph. He keeps threatening me. He's terrified I might tell someone. Like Natalie or the Head. He threatened to kill me in Wales. That was why I left Ty Bran. That was why I came here. I was trying to avoid him and now he's followed me here and today he followed me to the Forum and he threatened me again!' Her eyes filled with furious tears and she brushed them away angrily. 'I don't know what to do. I just don't know what on earth to do!'

Steph stared at her, white-lipped. 'Jess, do you know what you're saying?'

'Yes, of course I know what I'm saying! He raped me, Steph. He gave me some kind of date-rape drug and –' she took a deep shuddering breath – 'he raped me!' She was crying in earnest now.

Steph put her arms round her, hugging her tightly. 'Jess, my darling. My God, how could he!' She glanced over her shoulder at the door. 'Did you tell the police?' Releasing Jess she stood up and ran the few steps over to the door and tested the handle. The lock held. Coming back she sat down on the bed again. 'Well, did you?'

'No.'

'Why not?'

'Because I didn't want anyone to know. I couldn't face it. At first I didn't know who had done it. I couldn't remember anything. It only came back slowly; it was only then that I realised it was Dan. He didn't deny it. He claims I was drunk and that I egged him on.' She sighed heavily.

'Is it possible you did?' Steph frowned. She took Jess's hand and held it tightly.

Jess looked at her, appalled. *No one will believe you.* Dan's words echoed in her head for a moment. 'No,' she whispered. 'No, it isn't!' She snatched her hand away.

'But you just said you don't remember what happened. Some-times, when we've had a lot of drink –'

'My clothes were torn. My body was bruised – I was drugged. I went to the doctor.'

Steph's mouth dropped open.

'She tried to persuade me to go to the police but I wouldn't. I just wanted to get away.'

'So you resigned and went to Ty Bran.' Steph levered herself off the bed and went to stare out of the window.

Wordlessly Jess nodded.

'Why?' Steph turned to face her. 'I don't understand. If it's true, then why in God's name did you let him get away with it? You're a fighter, Jess. You should have crucified him. The bastard!'

Jess shrugged. 'I wasn't thinking straight. Besides, I've seen what happens to women who claim to have been raped. I went to the police with one of the girls from school. I was not going to put myself through that. After all, even you are wondering how much I had had to drink!'

'I believe you, Jess.' Steph shook her head. 'Of course I do. Oh my darling. I'm so sorry. He's a complete and utter shit, but I'm afraid I think he's right. Even if you went to the police, unless there was forensic evidence of what happened, even if there was ...' Steph paused with a shrug. 'It's going to be his word against yours.'

'Head of department. Married man. Respected teacher. Versus flighty vindictive frustrated colleague who was about to be sacked, you mean,' Jess whispered.

'Were you about to be sacked?' Steph asked gently.

Jess shook her head. 'Not as far as I know, but he could claim I was. He could say that was why I resigned. I jumped before I was pushed. He could say anything!'

'Would the Head believe your word against his?'

'Brian?' Jess shook her head again. 'Not against Dan, no. He's got him lined up to be his deputy. One day he'll get a school of his own.' She turned to face her sister. 'What am I going to do, Steph?'

Steph was silent. She was chewing her lips as she studied Jess's face. At last she spoke. 'To be honest, I don't know. How long have we known Dan? Years. Has he ever showed an interest in you before? I don't mean that unkindly, but I don't remember him fancying you. Not so we noticed, anyway.'

Jess gave a rueful smile. 'It was Kim who fancied him, remember, although I don't think he ever returned the compliment, did he? But I was with Will before.'

'Have you told Will about this?'

Jess shook her head. 'He and I have not been communicating lately, remember?' She paused. 'Did you hear what I said? Dan threatened to kill me, Steph!'

Steph turned to face the window again. 'So, he's thinks he's got away with it, but he is still after you.'

'He's afraid I will tell Nat.' Jess shivered and pulled the towel around her more tightly. 'I just wanted to put it all behind me. Start again. Paint. Maybe get a new job somewhere in the country. I never wanted to see Dan again. And now here he is.'

'He may be here, Jess, but he's not going to stay here. I'll see to that.' Steph turned purposefully towards the door. 'Leave this to me.'

In the kitchen Will was watching Kim frying onions in a heavy skillet when Dan walked in and sat down at the table, drawing the bottle of wine towards him. 'Listen, folks. I am going back to London tonight.' He watched Kim toss some garlic into the pan and swirl it round in the hot oil. 'But before I go there is something I need to tell you.' He glanced at Will. 'You both know that there is something odd going on between me and Jess.' He sighed and took a deep swig from his wine glass. 'I think you should know what's been happening. It is going to come out one way or another and I didn't want it to, but maybe it's better for Jess if you know about it.' He shrugged ruefully and took another sip. He looked at Will. 'You've probably guessed that things are not good for Jess at the moment.' He took a deep breath. 'Did she tell you about her breakdown?'

Will frowned. 'What breakdown?'

'I thought not.' Dan shook his head as Kim slid the skillet to one side and came to sit down beside Will. Frowning, she pushed up her sleeves and reached for her own glass. 'Jess hasn't had a breakdown. Steph would have mentioned it.'

'Steph doesn't know.' Dan pursed his lips. 'Look, I feel disloyal saying all this, but she is going to say some pretty vicious things about me, I suspect, and I need to put things right. She had it very tough after you two broke up, Will. It all got to her badly. I'm sure I don't have to tell you that. Well, she developed a bit of a thing for me. It wasn't on, of course. I mean, she's very attractive, but I'm happily married, as you know. I tried to put her off as gently as possible but she couldn't take rejection. She's made up some terrible fantasy that I've beaten her up. Raped her. She got very confrontational about it. Threatened to go to the police. I wasn't sure what to do. You wouldn't be, would you?' He glanced from Will to Kim and back, his fingers laced around his wine glass. 'I had to go to the Head. Ask his advice. I mean teachers are used to kids developing crushes or accusing them of stuff these days, but not a colleague. Not someone like Jess.' He studied his drink sorrowfully for a moment before taking another deep swig from the glass. There was a long silence. Kim and Will glanced at each other, stunned.

'I can't believe it,' Will said at last.

'No.' Dan reached for the bottle.

'And you say she has been sacked from the college,' Kim said doubtfully.

'Asked to leave,' Dan said softly. He topped up their glasses. 'More diplomatic. Working too hard. Needs to take a bit of a break. That sort of thing. Then it got even more weird. She somehow transferred all her accusations and frustrations into some kind of inner fantasy about a ghost. I was seriously worried after she disappeared from Ty Bran. She was rushing round the countryside fleeing Roman soldiers, yelling that one of them was trying to kill her.' He paused. 'Then I find she has headed for Rome itself. That was why I came after her. I mean, what would you have done? I was really scared for her.'

'So, there's no conference?' Kim said.

'No. There's no conference.'

'Shit,' Will whispered. 'I don't believe this.'

'No,' Kim said slowly. 'No, the bit about the ghosts she is not making up. Steph has seen the ghost. There is something there.'

'Roman soldiers?' Dan smiled cynically. 'Oh, please! OK, it's up to you if you believe her.' He threw back the last of his drink and stood up. 'I just wanted you to know the position about what happened at the college, OK? Don't say anything to her about this, it will only upset her more. And perhaps you'd better not tell Steph. She's never going to believe it anyway. Up to you. But

I'm going back to England. I didn't want to come, but I felt I should see if she was OK. And she will be safe here with you to keep an eye on her. I'm going to disappear now because my being here obviously upsets her and I need to get back to Nat and the kids. Can I leave it to you? Maybe she'll be OK once I've gone.' He shrugged. 'But I think you should be on your guard. Especially you, Will. She's not herself. She was quite violent when I was at Ty Bran.' He bit his lip and grimaced. 'Just don't hang around if she seems to think you're a Roman soldier or something.' He gave a wry smile and pushing his chair in turned towards the door.

'You're going now? This minute?' Kim called sharply.

'Better that way. Sorry to dump you in it, but you needed to know.' His bag was already in the hall. He heaved it up onto his shoulder. 'Take care, folks, and say goodbye to Steph for me. Sorry.'

'Dan –' Will scrambled to his feet but Dan had closed the door behind him. Seconds later they heard the front door bang, the sound resounding round the high-ceilinged, shady hallway.

'*Merda*!' Kim said. She stood up and went back to her pan, absent-mindedly pushing it back onto the heat and reaching for her wooden spoon.

'I knew something must be going on, but I never suspected anything like this.' Will resumed his seat and sat staring down at the tabletop in front of him. There was a long pause.

'Poor old Jess. That explains all that weird stuff about the Celts and the child. And the way she arrived so suddenly,' Kim said thoughtfully. 'Oh God, what are we going to say, Will?' She glanced up at him.

'Even if any of it is true, there's nothing we can do,' Will went on slowly. 'So we don't mention it. We'll just say Dan had to leave. Nat called him because one of the kids was ill. Something like that.'

Kim nodded. 'Do we tell Steph?'

Will sighed. 'I don't think so.'

'Shouldn't she know?'

'She wouldn't be able to keep quiet. She'd either be so furious with Dan for saying all this she would want to kill him, or she would want to rush poor old Jess off to a shrink or something in case any of it was true. Which I am sure it isn't! Let's give Jess a break. Dan has gone and he's right, his being here did upset her.

A lot. That much we could all see for ourselves. Perhaps knowing he's left will give her a chance to calm down.' He gave a deep sigh, then he frowned. 'I never got the impression she fancied Dan. Did you?'

Kim raised an eyebrow. 'If she did she is obviously well and truly over it now.' She began to pull fresh herbs off a bunch standing in a jug on the windowsill. 'Do you still love her, Will?' She glanced across at him.

He frowned. 'We split up, Kim.'

'That's not an answer.'

'Well, it's the only one you're getting.' He stood up and walked over to the window, staring down into the street. On the opposite side, Dan was climbing into a taxi. Will saw him glance up briefly towards the windows of the apartment. Then the door of the cab slammed and it pulled away into the traffic.

12

Eigon looked up at her mother and smiled uncertainly. The last few days had raced by in a whirl of confusing images. The family had been installed at once in a villa on the slopes of the Pincian Hill. Her father was treated as a king. Suddenly they had slaves and beautiful clothes and comfortable beds. She was to resume her lessons and she was to have companions her own age to play with. The only shadow of uncertainty was the nature of the guards on the gates of the villa, guards who were to escort them if they went out into the city.

'We are prisoners in all but name, Caradoc!' Cerys said to her husband as they stood looking towards the porticoed gateway.

'We are alive, Cerys. We have not been torn apart by lions.' He smiled down at her and put his arms around her shoulders. 'Let that suffice for now.' He was tired, her husband, somehow shrunken compared with the warrior he had once been, and he coughed incessantly. She glanced up at him, then leaned trustingly against his shoulder. He would not always surrender so easily to his captors, but he was right. For now they must be content and bide their time. Once he had regained his strength they would begin to plan their escape and their return to Britannia.

It was when she was alone with her daughter that Eigon had come to stand beside her and pulled urgently at her mother's gown. Cerys, still pale and drawn, was wearing a pale linen tunic and mantle. She looked down at her and smiled. It was the first time they had been alone together in many weeks.

'Mam! I keep having bad dreams about him. I saw him. He was guarding the Emperor.'

'Saw who, child?' Cerys sat down and pulled Eigon against her knees.

'The man who hurt me. He was there. I saw him.'

Cerys froze. Eigon felt her mother's hand tighten on her arm and she pulled away, frightened. 'You said I should tell you if ever I saw him again. He was there, near the Emperor. Part of his guard. He did this when he saw me.' She copied his gesture exactly, drawing her small fingers across the front of her throat. 'We can catch him, Mam. Then he can be punished.'

'No!' Cerys's face had frozen into a snarl. 'No. Not now. You must not mention him now. Your father doesn't know. He must never know what happened!'

'He does know.' Eigon remembered her father's gentle kiss, his assurance that the man would be punished, his promise that she would forget in time.

'He knows about you, but not about –' Cerys was silent suddenly. She had never dared tell her husband of her own violation and it had slowly dawned on her that for some reason of his own, neither Scapula nor anyone else had told him either. Perhaps Scapula had been too furious that men under his command had committed such an outrage. Perhaps he had been afraid it would devalue her as a hostage if her husband renounced her. She would never know. She pictured Caradoc's face, his gentle eyes, his strong arms around her, protecting her, cherishing her, comforting her for the loss of her son. She knew how the man who loved her before all others could change at the drop of a pin into a cold calculating killer. The leader of men, the warrior king who had defied Rome for seven long years would risk everything to find the man who had harmed his wife. He would not rest until the man was dead, but then – then how would he react? How could he ever love her again as he had loved her before knowing she had been raped by a common soldier from the enemy ranks. When she had realised that no one amongst the Romans had told him what had happened, she had seen it as a reprieve.

'Tell no one, Eigon,' she said urgently. 'We are safe here. We have a home. We have a new life. We must forget everything that happened to us before. That was a different world.' She paused. 'You imagined you saw him. Or if you did, I am sure he didn't really see you. That's it! He couldn't have recognised you. You have already grown out of all recognition, child. You are nearly a young woman.' She paused again. 'If he realised you had identified him, then his life would be worthless from that moment on. If that happened none of us would be safe ever again.'

'But he does know, Mam,' Eigon murmured, frightened, but

Cerys was already restlessly heading for the door into the courtyard. She never heard her daughter's words.

One of their first visitors was the lady Pomponia Graecina, the wife of Aulus Plautius, the man who had led the army that invaded the Britannic Isles and become the first governor of the province of Britannia. She was tall and slim with iron-grey hair pulled into a knot at her neck. She stood in the atrium of their villa and looked round, her expression austere rather than friendly as Cerys came forward to greet her.

'So, we are honoured by the presence of a queen,' Pomponia said. 'And the Emperor has made you welcome.' She waved away her attendants and sat down on a stone bench near the centre pool.

Cerys stood for a moment, dignified and regal in her turn, then she too sat down. From her position behind her mother Eigon noted their guest's fine clothes and her jewellery. She wore a lot of jet she noticed, and the gold rings and bracelets looked as though they were of intricate craftsmanship. They were probably part of the booty looted from the invasion of her own land.

'We met, did we not, in Camulodunum when the Emperor came to establish our rule?'

Cerys's eyebrow shot up. 'My husband was not one of those who went to bow the knee to Claudius, madam.'

Pomponia Graecina smiled. 'Of course not. Forgive me. He led the opposition, did he not.' She leaned forward. 'And a very brave man he is. I salute him.' She waved one of the attendants forward again from the doorway where they had been waiting. 'I have gifts for you and your daughter, madam. To help make you welcome to our city.'

The smaller box was for Eigon. She eyed it suspiciously and then looked up first at her mother and then at this very grand woman who was making herself so very much at home. Cerys smiled down at her. 'I am sure you may open it, child, so that you may thank the lady Pomponia Graecina for her gifts yourself.'

Eigon put the box down on the kerb around the edge of the pool and lifted the lid. Inside was a gaming board and a set of counters and dice. She picked out one of the intricately carved pieces and examined it, then she looked up at the donor. 'Thank you, lady,' she said shyly.

Pomponia smiled, delighted. 'She speaks Latin!'

'Of course.' Cerys nodded.

'And who is to teach the child her lessons?' Pomponia beckoned Eigon forward. She put her hands on either side of Eigon's face and tilted it up towards her. Eigon could feel the pressure of the heavy rings on the woman's fingers pressing into her cheeks.

'We don't know, yet.' Cerys arranged the folds of her mantle around her with a slight shiver. A draught had sent a drift of woodsmoke from the fires in the kitchens through the corridors of the building. Autumn was coming. 'It has been mentioned that she should have lessons. It is what her father wants, but he is not well. He suffers from a recurring fever. It is hard to make decisions; it is too soon to know who –'

'It is never too soon to have proper lessons.' Pomponia smiled down at Eigon. Eigon relaxed. The woman's eyes were warm and friendly. 'I have the very person for her in my household. He came with us from Britannia. He is one of your own people.'

Cerys frowned. 'Indeed, my lady?' she said cautiously.

'He worships your gods and follows your ways. He instructs me in the philosophy of your country,' Pomponia went on.

'A Druid?' Cerys whispered softly.

Pomponia nodded.

'But they are proscribed by your government.'

Her visitor shrugged. 'He does not advertise his beliefs.'

'Is he a slave?'

'Outwardly.'

'And if I agree, will that condemn me for condoning a forbidden practice?'

Pomponia sat deep in thought for a moment. 'You have not been forbidden the worship of your own gods. No one is forbidden the worship of their gods. Ours is a tolerant people. The Druids were condemned because they fought us. They fomented sedition. They plotted and organised the opposition against Rome. They still do. But this man, Melinus, is different. He is gentle and learned. He will teach her all that she needs to know.' She paused. 'I cannot force you to accept his services, Lady Cerys, but the offer is there. Wait until you feel more certain of your position. Consult the king your husband if you wish.' She gave a sudden almost mischievous smile. 'Ask about me. You will find that I am well known for my own opposition to the Emperor. He does not question me for it. He is wiser than to cross me as you will find out when you get to know us in Rome. You will be safe to take in this man. I do you a favour to offer him, for he is very dear to me. But this child needs someone to guide her.'

She gazed down at Eigon thoughtfully. Once again the beringed fingers strayed across Eigon's face. And then the visit was over. Pomponia called for her litter. The two women exchanged the stiff kisses of strangers who by circumstance must be sisters, and she had gone.

Eigon frowned. She had already found a private corner in the garden under a fig tree where she could hide. She had no desire at all for lessons, far less for them to be taught by a Druid. She remembered Druids as stern, austere, and rather frightening. They spoke to her father, his advisers and his companions. They had never concerned themselves with her and she did not want that state of affairs to change. When and if the Druid arrived, she fully intended to be missing.

He found her at once, of course. He was a man of middle height and late middle years, wearing the plain brown robe of a house servant. To Eigon's disgust Caradoc had agreed at once that he should be admitted to their household. He had already heard about Pomponia Graecina, and her reputation was formidable. He did not believe they would be in danger if they took the man from her. And so Melinus arrived the next day and within a very short time he had walked out into the garden in search of his charge.

'I see the small sparrow hiding in the bush,' he said softly. He had his back to her. 'She puffs her feathers against the cold, but they do not hide her. Come out, little bird. I need to see you.'

She didn't move. He turned and looked straight at her. He had a gentle face, deeply lined, with high cheekbones and sandy eyebrows topping intensely blue eyes. 'Come, child. Let us not waste time.' He put out his hand and beckoned and she felt the pull of his fingers as though they were touching her mantle. With a little squeak she burrowed further behind the gnarled old trunk of the tree, but she could feel him drawing her out as though his hand was on her neck, firmly gripping the edge of her tunic. Unable to resist, she found herself emerging into the sunshine, shamefacedly, brushing the leaves from her shoulders. He smiled and she found herself smiling back. His eyes were as blue as the skies of home, as blue as her father's, his hair the silvery colour of ripening oats. 'So, the reluctant pupil arrives on the scene.' He sat down on her mother's chair beside the pool. The pressure on her mantle had gone. There was nothing compelling her to stay but she found herself drawing closer to him, spellbound. She stared at him taking in the faded blue tattoos on his face, the laughter lines around his eyes, the way his hair fell across his forehead. She frowned. At home, Druids often shaved the front of their heads. They wore robes and carried a staff to denote their importance. Perhaps he wasn't a real Druid after all. The thought reassured her. Her father's Druids had been too preoccupied with the war to pay any attention to a small inquisitive child but their demeanour had frightened her. She moved closer, suddenly fascinated. He didn't stir, letting her approach of her own accord now. Trust must come in its own time. He hadn't realised yet that with this child no time was needed. Eigon made her mind up about people fast. In the last bewildering months after her father's defeat she had learned to fear men, but this man she knew instinctively she could trust with her life and she already felt in some inner part of herself as she moved towards him and reached out to put her hands into his that he would be not only her teacher but her friend.

Jess's eyes flew open. She stared round her bedroom. Outside it was just growing light. Her head was aching and the sheets on her bed felt hot and uncomfortable against her skin. Wearily she sat up. There was no point in trying to go back to sleep with the adrenaline pouring through her body, her mouth dry and her eyes gritty with exhaustion. Climbing out of bed she went to push open the half-closed shutters and stood staring out into the cool dawn. A pigeon was sitting on the fountain below in the shadowed courtyard garden, fluffing its feathers beneath the water spray. She watched it for several minutes, clearly enjoying itself until eventually it hopped away from the water jet, shook its feathers into place and positioned itself on the stone rim of the basin while it preened.

In the shadow of one of the neatly clipped little box hedges which surrounded the beds around the fountain something moved. Down there, away from the light it was still very dark. Jess felt herself tense as she focused her attention on the darker place within the darkness. It was a cat. She watched it crawl slowly forward, muscles taut, body compacted, almost on its stomach, each paw placed with such careful stealth she wondered if it was moving at all. Oblivious to its impending doom, the pigeon started to preen its other wing, the iridescent colours of its neck catching the first rays of light leaking from the sky into the centre of the garden. Jess's mouth went dry. It was too faraway to do anything. The cat was close enough to pounce.

'No!' She didn't realise she had shouted out loud until she had done it. She leaned forward out of the window. 'Hey!' She clapped her hands, the sound echoing off the sleeping walls of the palazzo like a pistol shot. The pigeon, startled, wheeled into the air, circled the courtyard and soared up over the rooftops out of sight.

When she looked back to see what had happened to the cat it had disappeared.

The others were already in the kitchen sitting at the table with their coffee and *panini* when she finally appeared for breakfast. She glanced round the room at once.

'Where's Dan?'

'He's gone, Jess.' Kim stood up and pulled out a chair for her to sit down. 'Back to England. Nat rang him. There was some crisis with one of the kids.' She glanced at Will. He was buttering his roll and did not look up.

Sitting down, Jess reached for the coffee jug. 'Well, I can't say I'm sorry.' She sighed. After the sleepless night and the early awakening her face was wan and her eyes circled in shadows. Her intense relief that Dan had gone was cut short as she sensed the atmosphere around the table. She looked up. 'What?'

Steph shrugged. 'Nothing. What are you planning to do today?'

'I am going to go on with my research.' Jess reached for the pot of home-made *marmellata* and spooned some onto her plate. 'I know it sounds daft but I dreamed about Eigon again last night and I can visualise the outline of the city where they lived. Their villa was high on one of the hills, looking down on the city. I'm going to take my sketchbook and camera and wander round a bit, to see if I can get a sense of the topography.'

'Stefano had lots of old books about Rome,' Kim said, reaching for the coffee pot. 'Why not have a root about in his library and see if there is in there? Old maps might be exactly what you want.' She glanced at Will. 'Why don't you go with Jess? Steph and I have plans this morning which involve shopping and shoes and doing girly things like that.'

Will grimaced. 'I have plans of my own, thanks. Unless you want an escort?' His glance towards Jess was less than eager.

She shook her head, colouring slightly. 'No need. I'd rather wander round on my own.'

'Well, that was less than subtle!' Kim turned on Will. After gulping down half a roll and a cup of coffee Jess had left the kitchen.

'I am not her minder!' Will retorted.

'And she doesn't want you to be,' Steph said slowly. 'What is wrong with you two? I'm picking up some funny vibes here. Do you know something I don't?'

Will shook his head. 'Dan made some rather derogatory remarks about Jess before he left. I don't know or care if they were true but I am not here to pick up the pieces.' Pushing his chair back he stood up and carried his own mug and plate to the sink. He ignored Kim's glare.

Steph rounded on her. 'Come on. Tell me. What is going on?'

'Dan says she set her cap at him after we split up,' Will answered for her. 'He says she became a bit unhinged.'

There was a snort from Kim as she tidied away the rest of the breakfast things.

'Dan said that?' Steph narrowed her eyes. 'And you think that sounds like Jess?'

'No.' Will's monosyllabic answer was almost lost as he headed for the doorway. 'No, I don't.' Ten minutes later they heard the front door bang behind him. Kim and Steph looked at each other.

'So, what's really going on here?' Kim asked as she reached for her purse and unhooked a bag from behind the door.

Steph shrugged. 'Dan and Jess have had a row. More than a row. A serious falling out. Will is upset. Jess is feeling better now Dan has gone.' She paused. 'Does that cover it?'

'Wounded male pride all round.' Kim shrugged as she led the way out of the apartment and down the broad marble stairs to the front door. Walking out into the blinding sunlight she and Steph headed up the street.

Behind them a figure stepped out from behind the passing crowds and stood watching them until they were out of sight. Dan glanced up at the windows of the apartment, his golden brown eyes narrowed in the strong sunlight. He gave a quick, hard smile. They had all gone out except for Jess. When she appeared she would be alone and he would be waiting for her.

Jess was poring over a book in Stefano's library, her fingers tracing the detail of an intricately worked etching. Stefan had collected books all his life, as had his father before him. There must have been thousands on the shelves of this high-ceilinged book-lined room with its beautiful leather-topped circular reading table and exquisite sets of library steps. If she could find Caratacus's villa anywhere it would be from information somewhere in this room. She glanced up. The shutters were closed against the sun to protect the leather bindings but narrow rays of light filtered through throwing dust-laden rays across the table. The whole room smelled of dust and age. She looked back at the brown, slightly foxed pages of the book lying on the table in front of her and shook her head in irritation. None of this was any use. The period when Eigon had lived was so long ago, nearly two thousand years. Why couldn't she get her head round the span of time? That was even before the building of the Colosseum. None of Stefano's histories was going to help. Nothing would help. Why had she thought it would? There was a reason no one mentioned the eventual fate of Caratacus and his family. It was because no one knew. And no one knew because no one cared. Their fate was irrelevant. He was no longer of any interest to the Roman historians once he had been defeated and brought here to Rome. From then on the only thing that had caught their attention was Claudius's extra-ordinary, but obviously self-interested gesture in sparing their lives. She pulled down another heavy volume of history and then another. They were all written in Italian but she could at least consult the index. Nothing. She wandered down the shelves helplessly gazing up into the shadows where the highest ranks of bindings blended into a monochrome wallpaper of tooled leather and gilt. One name caught her eye suddenly. Gibbon. *The History of the Decline and Fall of the Roman Empire.* That at least would be in English and might say something. Eagerly she dragged the library steps across and climbed up to pull out the first of the volumes.

She pored over the closely printed pages with their elegant but hugely difficult print face and long s's. This was a first edition, for

God's sake! She glanced at the chapter headings and turned to a page about Britain and began to read: 'Before Britain lo*f*t her freedom, the country was irregularly divided between thirty tribes of barbarians . . .' She glanced down the page. One of the tribes he mentioned was the Silures in South Wales. She read on: 'As far as we can either trace or credit the re*f*emblance of manners and language, Spain, Gaul and Britain were peopled by the *f*ame race of hardy *f*avages.' She shook her head with a wry smile and closed the book, pulling out instead the last volume to consult the index. But there was no mention of Caratacus there that she could see. This story was too early even for Gibbon. If Caratacus had escaped and made his way back to Britain, if he had made a great comeback in an attempt to free his people, Tacitus or the later Roman historian Dio Cassius would have mentioned the fact. They didn't. Gibbon didn't. No one did. No one cared what had happened to him. Why did she? That was easy. It was because of a bewildered child who was somehow lost wandering in the corridors of time.

She sat, staring at the table blankly, overwhelmed with disappointment. Where else could she look? Stefano had a copy of *The Annals of Imperial Rome* in the original Latin. She had found it earlier and laid it on the table. It was beautifully bound. She opened it carefully once again, hoping she might have missed something, then suddenly she stopped. Of course there was one possible reason that there was no mention of Caratacus. Perhaps he had died. That would explain everything. That first autumn they had spent in Italy he was ill. Eigon had implied as much and Eigon was her only source of information now. She frowned, deep in thought. He had been suffering from a recurring fever. Could that have been malaria? The warrior from the cold damp fastnesses of England and Wales had survived his hideous wounds after that last battle, but had succumbed to the curse of the Pontine Marshes. Had he died that first year? She closed the book and stood up. There was only one person who could tell her. Eigon herself.

Carefully replacing the books in their places on the shelves, she let herself out of the library. 'Steph? Kim?'

There was no reply. She glanced into the formal drawing room, the dining room, both with their closed shutters and air of summer sleep. Kim's more informal sitting room, pretty with flowers and with windows opening, like Jess's bedroom, onto the quiet courtyard garden at the centre of the palazzo, was deserted. So was the kitchen. Where were they all? She could see from the corridor the doors of the empty bedrooms beyond lying open. There was no sound save that of her own footsteps on the polished boards. 'Will?' They must have all gone out without her. For a moment she paused, hurt, then she gave a rueful grin. Her own fault for being so obsessive. They had probably called out to her, told her where they were going and deep in her study of the books she hadn't heard a thing. She looked at the front door. She had two choices. To go out and wander round, retracing her steps from the day before but this time looking out for landmarks such as the rise and fall of streets and the flights of steps that marked the ancient hills, or she could go back to Eigon. Hear more of the story. She hesitated. To go out was so tempting. She had spent hours in the semi-darkness of the library. Suddenly she longed for the sunlight and noise of the busy streets.

13

Exhausted, Jess found a small restaurant off the Via dei Serpenti and sat down beneath a red parasol in the shade. She ordered iced beer and a pizza and kicked off her sandals. The heat was appalling, the sunlight reflecting off the pavement. She had walked for miles up hill and down, trying to pinpoint the outline of the hills in a city of seven hills. She had threaded her way through crowds of tourists, climbed steps, crossed roads and followed winding alleys into shady courtyards and out again, exploring the whole area of the Esquiline, but nowhere had she had any impressions that this, though she had started at the site of Nero's Domus Aurea, was the city that Eigon had known.

Of course, she hadn't actually known it. The villa might have been outside the city. It probably was. After all, there were gardens. Not just courtyards, but gardens and trees. And a view of Rome. She sighed. Perhaps she was following completely the wrong lead. The Rome of Claudius was a small city compared to its successor. It had been so completely eradicated and buried, only a very few buildings, as far as she knew, still existed; even if they did they were irrelevant to the life which Eigon was now leading. Beyond her brief sojourn as a prisoner and that long parade from wherever they had been held to the Forum where Claudius and his wife Agrippina were waiting, she had seen nothing of the city of her jailors.

With a sigh Jess pulled her sketchbook to her and turned to a fresh page. Already it was full of little vignettes of Rome. People. Buildings. Piazzas. Fountains. Umbrellas. She gave a wry smile. Everywhere umbrellas and awnings to throw shade from the searing sunlight. Two men were sitting on a wall near her. They were talking to a third who balanced astride a motor scooter as he rolled a cigarette. They looked animated, relaxed, unfazed by the heat. Another man walked behind them and for a moment he paused. He turned and looked straight at her. Dan.

She froze.

A bus wheezed past and stopped with a hiss of brakes, blocking her view of the street as the three sets of doors flapped open then closed again. It moved on. Dan had gone. She looked left and right up the seething pavement. There was no sign of him. But there was no mistaking him. He had been only a few metres away on the far side of the road. She had seen him clearly; seen the smile on his face as he looked towards her.

'*Signora*?' A waiter had brought her food. He set it down in front of her and reached for the huge pepper grinder he carried under his arm. '*Pepe*?'

'*Si, grazie*!' She glanced round the man anxiously. She had imagined it. It was someone who looked like him, that was all. Dan had gone back to England.

'*Buon appetito*!' The waiter was already moving away, smiling at another customer. She pushed her sunglasses up onto the top of her head, scanning the street. Whoever it was, he had gone.

'Thank you.' Belatedly she smiled at the retreating back of the waiter. Her appetite had vanished.

It was after five when she returned to Kim's. The others were back. They were all seated in Kim's sitting room with Carmella.

'Ah, here you are at last!' Kim smiled at her. 'Come and join us, Jess.'

Jess stood looking at the low coffee table in front of the sofa. There, between the glasses and a bottle of chilled Frascati lay a spread of cards. She frowned. 'What are you doing?'

Kim and Carmella exchanged glances. 'Carmella felt there was something more we should know,' Kim said slowly. 'Sit down. Here. Let me pour you a glass of wine and she can explain.'

Jess looked at Steph and then at Will, who was seated on a chair a little back from the table, an expression of quizzical disapproval on his face. She sat down on the arm of Steph's chair as far from him as possible.

'I thought I saw Dan,' she said. 'Didn't you say he had gone back to England?'

There was a moment's silence. 'That's what he told us,' Will said at last. 'Is he coming back here?'

Jess shook her head. 'I didn't speak to him. He was on the other side of the road. He disappeared.' She hesitated. 'Maybe it wasn't him. It looked very like him.'

158

'A doppelgänger,' Kim said. She smiled. 'We all have them.'

There was another long silence. Will leaned forward. 'OK, Carmella. Let's hear what you have seen in the cards.' He glanced down at the table. 'One thing I don't understand. This is presumably a different – what do you call it, a spread? – from the one you did earlier. So how do you know that it is going to say the same thing?'

'The cards never lie.' Carmella looked up at him sharply. 'They will give the same warning, maybe in different ways, that is all.'

Jess took a sip from her glass, savouring the cold crisp wine on her tongue for a moment. 'So, do I gather that this is about me?' she said at last. Her voice was sharper than she intended.

Carmella shrugged. 'Forgive me, but yes. It is about you. We did not finish last time. We were interrupted. I was worried. About the child and about you.'

'And Dan. You warned me about Dan,' Jess went on softly.

Kim glanced at Will and frowned. His eyes were fixed on Jess's face. She tried to read his expression and failed. Clearing her throat she smiled at Carmella. 'So, shall we go on where we left off,' she said quietly.

Carmella shook her head sharply. 'We were going to have a séance. That is not what I intend to do. Jess does not need us for that. The child will speak to her direct, is that not so?' She looked up at Jess.

Jess's mouth went dry. She nodded. 'She spoke to me last night. Soon she will no longer be a child,' Jess said slowly. 'Soon she will be a young woman.'

'That is good.' Carmella smiled. She too was watching Jess's face. 'But this reading is not about Eigon. This is about you.' She tapped the cards with her fingernail. 'And now I shall shuffle the cards and we will start again with you here to cut the pack. Then if we get the same message, we know the cards speak the truth!' She transferred her gaze to Will for a moment. Sweeping the cards together she gathered them up and shuffled them slowly. When the deck was neatly together to her satisfaction she put it down in front of Jess. 'Do it.'

Jess put down her glass. She leaned forward and put her hand over the cards.

'Wait,' Carmella instructed. 'Before you touch them. Think for a moment, what it is you want to know. Do not tell me, just think about it and when you are ready then you take the cards.'

'This should be a question about Eigon?'

'Anything.' Carmella squinted up at her for a moment. 'Anything at all.' She sat back and reached for her glass. 'My grandmother always lit incense in the room before and after consulting the cards,' she commented quietly. Again she had had that strange feeling of unease, as though someone else, faraway was tuning in to the reading. 'She said the cards were sacred. This is not a game. This is a ritual.'

'So, you have incense?' Will looked more quizzical than ever.

Carmella shrugged. 'Stefano was horrified by such things, wasn't he, Kim?' She laughed. 'He loved the cards, but for him they were a joke. For other people. Part of me feels bad about doing this here. He would not have liked it. But I take seriously what it says. No, I have brought no incense in respect to Stefano's wishes, but here,' she thumped her breast, 'in my heart, I say a prayer as I did for your little girl.' She took a sip of wine, set down her glass, and sat forward again. 'You are ready, Jess?'

Jess nodded. Suddenly she was feeling nervous. She waited for several seconds then cautiously she cut the pack as instructed.

'OK. I need you to concentrate.' Picking up the cards, Carmella divided them into three piles.

'Wait a minute.' Will sat forward. 'Surely it is for Jess to pick out the cards.'

Carmella glanced up and frowned. 'That is not the way I usually work.'

'But in this case I think you should let her do it. The reading is supposed to be about her.'

'Will, I don't mind. I don't know how to do it,' Jess said quickly.

'You know about reading the cards, Will?' Kim put in. 'You sound like an expert suddenly.'

'I want to see it done right.' Will pursed his lips. 'No, I'm not an expert; no, I don't believe in this stuff, but I don't want to see you, Jess, being set up to panic about some ridiculous event that is not going to happen –'

'So, how exactly will who chooses the cards affect what Carmella says if you think the whole thing is a set up?' Kim retorted. 'I suggest you take a glass of wine and go and sit next door while we get on with this.'

'No.' Carmella held up her hand. 'No, he is right to be cautious. And he is right, sometimes people let the querent – that's the word they use in English, Will – choose the cards. I don't mind. Jess, please take out nine from the pack and lay them on the table face down for me in three groups of three.'

Jess glared at Will. She leaned forward and picking up the pack she dealt the cards and laid them down in front of her as she had been instructed. She reached to turn the first one over but Carmella stretched out her hand.

'No, I will turn them up, if Will does not object, and I will read them for you.' There were a few seconds of silence as she adjusted the cards to her satisfaction then finally she turned over the first. She caught her breath.

Jess frowned. 'What?'

Carmella said nothing. She proceeded to turn over the rest of the cards. They watched her as she studied the layout for a long time, then at last she looked up. 'I am not accustomed to being accused of cheating,' she glanced sternly at Will, 'but this reading proves that what I have read before and said before is right. The same card has come up.' She pointed. *Il re di coppe*. The king of cups and he is ill-dignified. Upside down. This is the man who pursues you, Jess. He came up before when Steph asked me about you, do you remember, Steph? He speaks of danger to you. This is a dangerous, vicious man. A man who is jealous and who feels threatened by you.'

Jess looked at Steph. Her face was white. 'I told you.'

'See here, and here.' Carmella pointed to first one card and then the next. *Il sei di spade e il otto di spade.* She shook her head. 'Both, *negativo*. This is so bad. You do know who it is I am talking about?'

Jess nodded. 'Dan,' she whispered.

'Oh per-lease!' Kim said impatiently. 'He said you would say this. He told us you were completely paranoid about him!'

'He said what?' Jess looked at her angrily.

'He said –' Kim looked at Will. 'Back me up here, Will! Look, Dan left because of you. He told us what happened in London.'

Jess froze. 'What did he tell you?'

'He's gone.' Kim scowled. 'There is no point in going over it!'

'There is every point!' Jess flashed back. 'What did he tell you?'

Kim shook her head. 'Leave it, Jess, please. I shouldn't have said anything.'

'I don't want to leave it.' Jess looked from one to the other round the low table. Carmella was staring down at the cards. Will was staring deep into the glass he was holding between his knees, twiddling the stem between restless fingers, refusing to meet her eye. Steph was staring from Jess to Kim uncomfortably.

'I think you should tell us exactly what he said, Kim,' Steph said at last. She glanced back at her sister. 'Jess has a right to know.'

'I'll tell you what he said,' Will said suddenly. He looked directly at Jess and held her gaze. 'He said that after you and I broke up you developed a serious crush on him. He said you threw yourself at him and when he didn't respond you accused him of raping you.'

'I knew it!' Jess stood up. 'The bastard! He's turned it all round! Tell them, Steph!'

'You knew about all this?' Kim swung to face Steph.

'Jess told me last night,' Steph said quietly. 'We had a long talk about it after Dan followed her to the Forum.'

'Like he followed her this afternoon?' Kim said. She raised an eyebrow.

The colour flared into Jess's cheeks. 'I'm not sure about this afternoon, I told you. It probably wasn't him –'

'It probably wasn't him yesterday either, Jess,' Will said gently.

'Excuse me,' Carmella put in at last. 'May I speak, please?' She looked at them all in turn. 'The cards do not lie. They see a dangerous man in Jess's life. They see a devious man. A man who can lie and cheat to get his way. They see accidents. They see the past catching up with Jess. They say she can no longer run away.'

'This is not about Dan!' Kim said firmly.

'Why not Dan?' Jess narrowed her eyes. 'What is it between you and Dan, Kim?

'Enough!' Will stood up abruptly. 'Let's stop all this right now. Take your cards, Carmella, and go home please. We don't need to listen for another moment to all this nonsense.' Stooping he swept the layout into a heap.

'No!' Carmella threw her hands across the cards to protect them.

'This is at best a party game, at worst, downright evil. You are exploiting someone's unhappiness and weakness. It is a complete nonsense!' Will said angrily.

'This is none of your business, Will!' Jess burst out, furious. 'How dare you interrupt.'

'Oh, I dare! Believe me, I dare. When I see you being exploited and damaged by all this superstitious clap trap!'

'I am not being exploited and damaged!' Jess stood up and faced him. 'It is you who should leave, Will. No one asked you to come here. None of this is anything to do with you any more. Go back to England and leave me alone!' To her fury she felt her eyes fill with angry tears. She turned away, determined he wouldn't see them and headed for the door. 'Forget it, all of you. None of you believes me. Just forget it!'

Carmella climbed to her feet. Stepping quickly round the table she caught Jess's arm. 'Wait. Here.' She pulled a wallet out of her bag and extracted a small card. 'If you need me, call me, OK?'

Jess stared down at the card. 'Thanks.' She pushed it into her pocket.

'Jess! Wait!' Will called after her but she had already opened the door and was heading down the hallway.

Will ran after her. Slamming the door on the other three he raced after her and caught up with her near the front door. He grabbed her arm and swung her to face him. 'Jess, I didn't mean to hurt you. I care about you, that's all. You can't believe a word Carmella says. She thinks she's helping you but she's not, believe me. You have to face up to the truth.'

'Face the truth?' Jess retorted. 'But you don't know what the truth is!' A tear trickled down her cheek and she dashed it away furiously. 'It is my word against his. Why does everyone believe him and not me? Except Steph. And Carmella. She believes me because the cards have shown her what kind of a person Dan is.'

'I can quite believe he has behaved like a bastard,' Will said quietly.

She wrenched her arm away from his hand.

'It's the whole thing. The drama. The accusations. The ghosts!'

'The ghosts?' Jess stared at him. 'You think I'm mad because of Eigon?'

'Not mad, Jess –'

'Not mad, but –?'

He shrugged. 'You've been under a lot of strain. Dan said they had asked you to resign.'

'And you believe him, of course.'

He hesitated.

'Did you actually ask Brian why I resigned?'

'I did actually.' He shrugged again. 'He said it was a private decision. Your decision.'

'Of course!' Turning away she almost stamped her foot in frustration. 'And so it was. I was hardly going to tell him that Dan raped me!'

Will stared at her, appalled. There was a long silence. She saw anger, disbelief, sympathy, flash in turn across his face. When at last he spoke his voice was gentle. 'If he raped you, Jess, why did you not go to the police? Why did you not tell someone. Anyone.' He put out his hand again. 'I still don't understand.'

She stared at him. 'Why not? What is so hard? I was violated physically and emotionally in my own home. For a long time I didn't know who had done it. I thought it was Ash. I thought it was you, for God's sake! I trusted Dan. I never suspected him. I confided in him.' She gave a sob of anger. 'I took his advice!'

Behind them the door opened. Steph appeared. 'Are you OK, Jess?'

'No! No, I'm not OK. Apparently I am a deluded paranoid liar!' She turned away and ran towards her bedroom. Reaching it she slammed the door in Will's face and turned the key.

There was a figure standing in the middle of the room.

'Eigon?'

Jess stood, her back against the door, adrenaline pouring through her stomach as the figure turned to face her. This was an older Eigon, tall, leggy, perhaps fourteen or fifteen, dressed in a creamy mantle and gown, her hair black as a raven's wing, bound with deep blue ribbon, gold jewellery at her wrists and throat.

It's not safe to go out. He's out there, watching. He's waiting. I didn't know it! I had made myself forget!

She was fading before Jess's eyes. Jess slumped where she stood, leaning against the door, too exhausted to move or react as the figure disappeared completely.

'I'm mad,' she said out loud. 'They are right. I am completely mad.'

Pushing herself away from the door she walked over to the window and looked out. It was growing dark. The courtyard seemed deserted as always although someone must go there occasionally, she thought wearily. Gardeners. The janitor. Perhaps even the tenants. The peace down there was tangible, broken only by the gentle patter of the water in the fountain and in the distance that all pervasive constant hum of traffic.

A movement in the shadows caught her eye. She frowned, aware suddenly that she was silhouetted in the open window against the dim light from her bedside lamp.

She leaned forward, trying to see what was out there. 'Eigon?' It was a whisper. Then she saw him. Dan was standing on a patch of neatly trimmed grass, surrounded by small immaculate box hedges, arms folded as he stared up at her window. She drew back sharply. Flying over to the bed she snapped off the light then she crept back to the window on tiptoe and peered out again, her heart hammering in her chest. There was no sign of him.

Behind her there was a soft knock at the door.

'Go away!' she called. Her voice was shaking.

'Jess, it's Steph. Please, let me in. We need to talk.'

'No.' She was scanning the garden, trying to see as the dusk thickened into darkness.

'Please, Jess.' Steph tapped again.

Jess could see nothing out there now. Only the sound of the water splashing into its wide stone basin disturbed the emptiness.

She went to the door and unlocked it.

Steph stepped into the room. 'Why are you in the dark?'

'Because –' Jess stopped herself in time. Because Dan is out there in the dark, watching my window. She had almost said it out loud. But he couldn't be. How would he get down there into the centre of the palazzo, into a courtyard surrounded by high walls with no door that she could see, save the French doors from the four downstairs apartments which led directly out onto the gravelled paths around the edge of the gardens. None of them had been open. All were locked and shuttered, their owners away to the cooler climate of the coast or the mountains. She sighed. Walking over to the bed she snapped the lamp on again, then she went to the window and pulled the shutters closed against the night. 'Has Carmella gone?'

'Yes.' Steph sat down on the bed. 'Apparently Dan had a long talk with Kim and Will before he left. He told them his version of what happened in London, and told them not to tell me.'

'And did he tell them what happened at Ty Bran?'

Steph shrugged. 'I don't know. They didn't mention it. He's

done a good job of trying to destroy your credibility, but they are your friends, Jess. They are not convinced. Not for a moment. Not even Kim, who used to be besotted with him.' She hesitated. 'Will is still in love with you, you know.'

'You said that before.' Jess sniffed. She came and sat down on the bed next to Steph. 'It doesn't seem to stop him thinking I'm mad. Perhaps I am mad.' She gave a watery smile.

'No. You are under a lot of strain.'

'Rhodri could tell you what happened at Ty Bran. He saw the way Dan was.'

'Rhodri Price?' Steph shook her head. She grimaced. 'He's in Milan.'

'And probably wouldn't back me up anyway.' Jess slumped back against the pillows. 'What am I going to do?' She glanced towards the window. Was Dan out there at this very moment, waiting for the chance to climb up to her window? She shivered.

Steph noticed. 'Can you try and put all this behind you, Jess? We'll pretend none of it happened. Dan has gone. Will says he will go home too, if you want him to. Then you can relax and have a really nice holiday. Go on sightseeing and concentrate on your painting. Get some colour back in your cheeks.' She reached out and put her hand over Jess's. 'For what it's worth, I never cared for Dan much. He's too plausible. Too charming. And he's got cruel eyes.' She shuddered. 'It's funny how I never noticed that before. I believe Carmella. God knows how she does it but she does seem to be very accurate with those cards of hers. Perhaps she's very intuitive or just a shrewd judge of character, but for whatever reason I think she's got Dan right.' Sighing, she shook her head. She drew her knees up to her chin and hugged them.

'And what about Eigon,' Jess said softly. 'Do you believe in her too?'

Steph glanced at her sideways. 'I believe that Ty Bran is haunted.'

'But not that she could follow me to Rome?'

Steph shrugged. 'I don't know anything about the way ghosts work, Jess. Isn't there a legend that they can't cross water or something?'

'Isn't that witches? Besides, I suppose technically she didn't follow me, I followed her.'

'Then I don't know. I don't know what to believe. I don't want you to get frightened. And I don't want to start wondering if you've become obsessed.' Steph hesitated. 'Dan talked about some Roman soldier who you believed was stalking you.'

'That's rubbish.' Jess slid off the bed impatiently and went back to the window. 'If anyone is stalking me it is Dan himself. I saw him in the garden down there just now before it got dark.' She spun round to face Steph. 'I didn't tell you because I knew you wouldn't believe me! Do you think I am hallucinating? Who knows, perhaps I am.' She pushed her hair back off her face.

'You are obviously very scared of him.'

'And that of course makes me paranoid. So, I go round and round in circles. I can't win.'

'Daylight and sunshine will help, Jess. And tomorrow why don't we all go out together. As long as you aren't alone, if Dan is following you then there is nothing he can do, is there.' Steph slid off the bed and stood up. 'Let's forget all this and go out on an excursion to the Villa Borghese or somewhere like that. Forget Dan.'

Forget Eigon.

Jess smiled wanly. 'OK. I'd like that.'

When Steph had gone she stood for a moment without moving, then she tiptoed towards the door and turned the lock. Seconds later she had closed the windows too and latched them securely. She drew the curtains across and went back towards the bed. It didn't matter how hot it was, she wasn't going to leave the windows open.

Hours later she was still awake. At two thirty exactly someone had tapped on the window. When she climbed out of bed and went to peer between the shutters there was nothing there but her own reflection.

167

14

They spent the day at the villa touring the Galleria Borghese and strolling in the gardens and parks around it, picnicking on the dusty grass under a huge old evergreen oak and then lying back in the shade as the heat of the day overwhelmed them. Later they wandered back, Jess trailing further and further behind the others. It was here. She was sure it was somewhere here, the villa that had been home to Eigon. There was nothing to recognise. No landmarks that she could make out, nothing but an increasingly strong feeling that this area was where she had lived. She paused and gazed round yet again, feeling the warm breeze stirring her hair. It was uncomfortably humid, almost hard to breathe.

'Eigon?'

Was she here, among the trees? She turned round, pushing wisps of hair out of her eyes, scanning the parkland for signs of life. There was no one there. There had been a party of children behind them, winding their way noisily through the trees. They had gone. All she could hear was the soughing of the wind in the great pines nearby. Then even that had died away and she was surrounded by a suffocating silence.

Julia!

The voice came from faraway.

Julia, where are you? Don't hide!

Jess stood still, trying to see where the voice had come from.

Please don't hide. I hate this game. Please, where are you!

'Eigon?' Jess called the name out loud.

'Jess! Jess, what is it! What's wrong?' Suddenly Steph was beside her. She caught hold of Jess's arm. 'Jess, for goodness' sake! Wake up!' The voice in her ear was sharp.

Jess stared at her sister for a moment, then she shook her head. 'I'm not asleep,' she said indignantly. 'I thought I heard someone calling. Sorry. The heat is getting to me.'

'Kim says there is somewhere nearby where we can get some *gelati.*' Steph scanned Jess's face. 'You were calling Eigon.'

Jess shook her head wearily. 'I thought she was here. I thought maybe this is where the villa was. There is something about this place. It has an atmosphere.'

Will and Kim had come to a standstill about fifty yards further on, in the shade of an old plane tree. They were looking back towards them, waiting.

'Don't tell them,' Jess said. She glanced at Steph pleadingly. 'They already think I'm mad.'

'No, they don't. We've all walked a bit too far, that's all. We'll get a taxi back once we've had a drink or an ice cream or something. Don't worry, Jess.' With a reassuring smile Steph turned and walked on towards the others. Jess glanced back over her shoulder. She could see the party of kids again now, hear them! They weren't faraway at all. How could she have missed them?

Pomponia Graecina's niece, the lively, pretty, Pomponia Julia, had been one of Eigon's first true companions and now she had come to live with them permanently. Her mother had died the previous winter and her other brothers and sisters being much older, Julia was bereft in her father's austere household. The chance to come and live with her friend Eigon had filled her with joy. Cerys was not so pleased. Julia was a bad influence. A bright, beautiful, intelligent girl, she was also a natural rebel, the perfect foil to the serious, intense atmosphere in which Eigon lived as the only child of her parents and the only pupil of Melinus.

He had established a strict routine, giving Eigon lessons every day, patiently repeating the information until she could say it back to him word perfect, never letting her write it down, training her memory ever more carefully and she absorbed every drop of wisdom he could impart. Her only other regular occupation was to play her lyre and to sing. She had a pure clear voice which soothed and delighted her father, and anyone else who happened to hear her, and she sang often, even when she walked alone in the gardens.

It was there sometimes she heard her sister calling. The voice came from so faraway it was hardly audible. Glads was still playing on the mountain, still looking for her lost family, still waiting for them to return. Eigon tried so hard to reach her with her thoughts, to reassure her that she was not forgotten, but Glads never seemed to hear and Eigon grew more and more lonely for her. It was a loneliness she couldn't share with her parents.

Eigon's father was increasingly ill. He had another violent recurrent fever that autumn which drained all his life force. Her mother stayed close to him and she and Melinus conferred with the Roman doctors to try and make him well so that he could go out and visit the Emperor who was asking for his attendance and growing impatient for a reward for the grand gesture of allowing them to live. From time to time Caradoc summoned the strength to come and sit in the gardens by the fountain. Sometimes he sat and listened to the water and the birds, and sometimes he called for music and Eigon would bring her lyre. Her mother had ensured that she had two or three friends and she would play and talk with Portia and Julia and Octavia, but most of all Eigon liked to give them the slip and wander alone around the formal square beds of the herb gardens with their carefully tended symmetry. They were like nothing she had ever seen at home; nature tamed and forced into straight lines. She would touch the little clipped plants and talk to them and commiserate at their imprisonment which she recognised perhaps at some level to be a reflection of her own. She grew to love those peaceful, healing beds of lavender and rosemary, but she was frustrated that she was never allowed out into the city. When the wind was in the right direction she could hear its howling and its rumbling from faraway, she could smell its stench and look down upon it from the cliffs beyond the walls at the end of the gardens, and she had to admit, it seemed a frightening place, but she was curious, oh so curious, about the outside world. She wanted to see what it was like.

The lady Pomponia Graecina had asked if the girls could visit her there. Eigon's mother refused. The others could go, but not her daughter. And Eigon knew why. The man who had raped them was out there in the city streets and the only way he could feel safe was to ensure that Eigon would never identify him. To do that he would have to kill her.

It was boring and Julia had a plan. 'We're going out! I've arranged it all. Flavius will meet us outside the gate with horses and he will come with us. Then we are going into the city!'

Eigon shook her head. 'I can't.'

'Why not?' Julia seized her arm. 'I don't understand why you won't go. I know your mother forbids it, but it is not the order of the Emperor. You are not a prisoner. You can go where you like! Come on, Eigon! There is so much to see down there. Your mother won't know. We'll be back before she misses you.' That was a cruel jibe. Eigon knew her mother wouldn't notice if she was out all day and probably all night too. Cerys had less and less time for her daughter, spending every minute with her ailing husband or with her dreams and memories of the distant past when she had three young children who scrambled and laughed and played among her skirts. Julia caught Eigon's hand. 'If you won't come, I shall go without you!'

'You can't. It wouldn't be safe.'

'Of course it would be safe. I go to the market all the time. As long as there are slaves with us we'll be all right. Don't tell Melinus. He makes you so dull. You work too much with him.' Julia's own studies had been sketchy. She had a good memory and loved stories and poems, often attending Eigon's lessons, but when the subjects became hard and serious she would creep away. She did not enjoy talking about astronomy and history and law and the proper rituals for the worship of the gods. She did not want to learn basic medicinal techniques and the properties of herbs. Flowers were for smelling; the stars were for gazing at and one day soon, she hoped, for kissing under. She was young and she was healthy. And she had found someone to flirt with, Flavius, the son of the house steward, Aelius. Besides, she was a little afraid of Melinus. He might dress no differently from the house servants, but he exuded a sense of power and authority which intimidated her; she sensed his disapproval of her frivolity and was in no doubt as to what he would think about their excursion. 'Come on! Just for a few hours. We'll be perfectly all right. I promise.'

Eigon shook her head. 'I've told you. I can't.'

'Can't, or won't.' Julia narrowed her cornflower-blue eyes sharply. 'Are you afraid?'

'No, of course not.' It was more than three years since they had arrived in Rome. It might as well have been thirty. The events which had led to her mother's warnings had happened long ago and they were buried so deep they never emerged now even in her nightmares. Eigon gave in.

171

The next day, swathed in cloaks they crept towards the villa gate as soon as Eigon's lessons for the day were finished. The guards had been bribed to keep silent. With a wink they stood back from the gates and turned to study the skies with interest while the two girls ran, smothering their giggles, to where the handsome young Flavius and two slaves were waiting with horses in the thick shelter of a clump of evergreen oaks.

It was a long time since Eigon had sat on a horse, but riding was not something one forgot. She settled into the Roman saddle with ease and almost at once her sense of guilt and terror at defying her mother was replaced by exhilaration and excitement. If she felt excluded almost at once by the attention that Flavius and Julia paid each other she didn't notice. There was too much to see. The track through the woods gave way almost at once to a paved road which ran downhill straight as a die through the gates of the city. The road was busy, with wagons and riders, carts full of produce from market gardens, travellers on foot and once or twice a litter carried by slaves, its windows curtained against the dust. They left their horses at an inn a short way inside the city gates and ventured towards the market on foot.

Julia clutched Eigon's hand with a giggle. 'See! Isn't it exciting. Did you bring money?'

Eigon shook her head. She had no money.

'Never mind. I shall lend you some. Come and see. There is a goldsmith near here where my aunt goes. He makes the most beautiful things.'

The streets were narrow and between the high buildings, deafening. They echoed with the shouts of vendors, the echoes of a thousand conversations all carried out at full volume accompanied by laughter, barking dogs, the rattle of wheeled barrows pushed over the cobbles. Eigon clutched Julia's hand more tightly. It was overwhelming. As were the smells. Some good. Some bad. Their arrival at the small doorway which led into a narrow inner courtyard in a street of jewellery makers and goldsmiths was a huge relief. The slaves, Dimitrius and Volpius, sat down on a bench there as Flavius led the two girls in through the door to the house at the back where the goldsmith plied his trade. He glanced up as they entered and obviously recognised Julia at once. 'So, is the lady Pomponia Graecina with you, child?'

Julia shook her head. The hood of her cloak fell back, exposing her black curls tied with a scarlet ribbon. 'I have brought my friend, Eigon. I want her to choose something pretty. Then we will put it on my aunt's account.'

The goldsmith studied her face. He was a short stout man of middle years with deeply wrinkled skin and merry brown eyes which read the girl's innocent expression with ease. 'So, does the lady Pomponia Graecina know she is going to present this young lady with a gift?'

Julia tried to look worldly and failed miserably. 'No. Not really. But she won't mind.'

'How can I be sure she won't mind?'

'Oh please,' Eigon interrupted, embarrassed. 'I don't want anything. I should just like to look.' Her eyes had already strayed to the tray of brooches and rings on a table nearby. Behind the counter which divided the room the goldsmith's assistant was working with a range of hammers, punches and chisels, concentrating on his work without looking up. Small crucibles, tweezers, snippets of silver wire lay around him on the bench.

The goldsmith smiled at his customers, raising an eyebrow at Flavius who was hanging back in the doorway. 'And this young man once again comes as your escort. So, young sir, have you saved enough to buy your young lady a gift?'

Flavius blushed scarlet. 'Not yet, sir,' he mumbled. He turned his back on them uncomfortably, staring out into the courtyard. Dimitrius and Volpius had settled at a table where a *duodecim scripta* board with its counters and dice had been left out for the amusement of people waiting; engrossed in the game, husbands and lovers would be less likely to try and hurry their ladies away from the choice of luxuries inside the workshop. Flavius sat down with them and in a few moments had forgotten the girls completely.

Eigon glanced at Julia who seemed unconcerned at Flavius's discomfort. 'It's not fair to tease him like that,' she whispered. 'You shouldn't bring him here.' She could feel the boy's embarrassment as a physical pain. She smiled ruefully at the goldsmith. 'I am sorry we have come without intending to buy anything,' she said gently. 'Julia was so keen to show me the beauty of your pieces she didn't realise that it's important for you to sell them. We're wasting your time.'

The goldsmith frowned. He studied her face closely. His customers were not normally the least bit interested in whether or not his time was being wasted or indeed whether or not they could afford his wares. He smiled at her encouragingly. 'I should enjoy showing you some of the things if you would like to see them, young lady,' he said gallantly. 'Sometimes it is enough to have one's handiwork admired by someone with a good eye and I sense you have an eye for beauty.' He called into the back of the house and a slave brought them a tray with a jug of pomegranate juice. 'I have here a selection of designs borrowed from the tradition of the Gauls.' He had spotted her Celtic cloak pin and noted the red glints in her dark hair, her fair colouring. Pomponia Graecina was noted for her love of the jewellery she had collected when her husband was governor of the distant province of Britannia; perhaps this child or her parents were also part of the lady Pomponia's collection of foreign memorabilia. 'See.' He turned into the body of the workshop and selected a few items from a row of caskets on one of the shelves. 'The craftsmen of the Celtic peoples are better than anything we can do here, but I have offered them homage with my attempts to reproduce their style.' There were rings and brooches on the small wooden tray. Swirling, glorious shapes incorporating here and there the animal heads and whirling wings and elegant limbs that characterised the style. Eigon gave a small smile. 'They are lovely.' She picked up a small silver ring and held it up.

'Put it on.' Julia watched her with a grin. Then she snatched something else out of the tray. 'No, try this, it's gold and much prettier.'

Eigon glanced at their host and saw he was still watching. He smiled understandingly as she shook her head. 'It is beautiful.' She couldn't keep the longing out of her voice. 'But too rich an ornament for me.'

Julia exclaimed crossly. 'Eigon! You are a king's daughter! What could be too rich for you?'

'Ah, I think I have guessed who you are, young lady. The daughter of the famous Caratacus!' The goldsmith nodded. 'I was there, in the crowd, the day the Emperor gave your father his freedom.'

Eigon put down the ring. 'We are still prisoners in all but name.' She gave the man a thin smile. He had reminded her of a day she would rather forget. 'My father is too sick to leave the house. My mother cannot leave his side. And I am being reared as a

174

daughter of Rome. That is not freedom.' She turned towards the door. 'Thank you for your hospitality, but we have to go back before I am missed.'

'Eigon!' Julia stared after her crossly as she went out into the courtyard. The three men scrambled to their feet as she stepped out into the sunlight. 'Eigon, wait! There is no hurry! Your mother won't know you have gone even if we stay out all afternoon.' But it was too late. Eigon was already heading through the gateway and out into the street.

Julia glanced back at the goldsmith. 'I am sorry. I don't know what's wrong with her.'

He laughed. 'She has pride, Pomponia Julia. That is what is wrong. And maybe it is not so wrong at all.' With a sigh he turned back into his workshop. An idea had just occurred to him.

As they retraced their steps through the market place Julia caught at Eigon's arm. 'Didn't you enjoy it?'

Eigon nodded. 'I enjoyed it very much.'

'Then what?'

'I couldn't pay him, Julia, that is what is wrong. I would love to have bought some of his things. Of course I would, but I will not owe money to you or to your aunt and I certainly will not leave him at a loss. I don't need jewellery. I have plenty.'

'You don't. You have a brooch, a few bangles and a small child's ring,' Julia exclaimed. 'Which you have to put on your little finger as it is!' She gave an exclamation of indignation as a man rushed past her, pushing her violently, almost knocking her into the gutter. Flavius was there at once, his arm for a few seconds protectively around her, the two other slaves drawing their cudgels from their belts.

'Idiot!' he yelled after the man. He turned to Julia, all concern. 'Are you all right?' Julia nodded, shaken.

Eigon was staring after the man who had dodged into the crowd out of sight. It had happened so suddenly and it had been so easy for the man to get near them. They were protected by three men and yet they had been helpless. Silently she slipped her hand into Julia's as they resumed their way back to the horses. 'Are you scared?' she whispered. She was still scanning the crowds.

Julia shook her head. 'No harm done. He wasn't a thief. Or if he was he was running from someone else.' She clutched her wrap around her tightly. 'These things happen!'

'Do they?' Eigon scanned the crowds nervously. In the distance a squad of soldiers was marching smartly away from the city centre towards one of the outlying barracks. They turned away across the market square and disappeared up one of the narrow streets out of sight, the rhythm of their nailed sandals ringing on the cobbles echoing round the square long after they had gone.

'He didn't see you. I'm sure he didn't see you.' Jess was talking in her sleep. She clutched at the thin sheet as in her dream she watched the small party of riders draw up at last. The two girls slid from their saddles and with Flavius ran into the outer court-yard of the villa as the slaves led the horses away. 'Don't go out again, it's too dangerous!'

Long shadows were lying across the paving slabs and the villa smelled of the great pine trees whose shade was thrown across the courtyard from the road outside. There was no one there to see them creep indoors and flee to their bedrooms to wash off the dust of the city. The house was very quiet. Eigon slipped on a fresh gown, brushed back her hair and tied it then she crept out of her room and went to find her parents. Her father was lying on a couch in the shade of the fig tree near the fountain. He seemed to be asleep. Her mother sat nearby busy with her spindle.

'Mam?' Eigon whispered.

Cerys looked up. 'Where have you been?'

Eigon shrugged. 'I fell asleep in the orchard. It is so hot down here.' She blushed, uncomfortable with the lie, but her mother didn't notice. She seemed to accept the answer. She glanced at her husband. 'Your father has been asleep for most of the day.' Her worry was engraved on her face.

'What does Melinus say?'

'He is trying a new medicine. One to bring the fever down. He is cross he can't find the right herbs here. He says he needs some-thing that grows only in the mountains at home.'

Eigon bit her lip. Her mother hardly ever mentioned their old life, before their exile. It was as if she had wiped it from her memory. 'Has he asked the doctor who comes to see Aelius's family? Flavius speaks highly of him. His father calls him in when any of them are ill.' She did not add that Flavius thought Melinus a terrifying magician.

Cerys scowled. 'All he does is tell me to sacrifice before the altar to Febris.'

'And you have no faith in a Roman goddess?' Eigon smiled. She went and sat down on the edge of her father's couch and took his hand. The powerful warrior had shrunk to a shadow of his former self, the scars on his shoulder and neck stark ropes of raised tissue against his skin. He was pale and weak as he opened his eyes and smiled at his daughter.

'She prays to every goddess of healing there is,' he said fondly. His voice was husky. 'But I fear our gods do not hear us from so faraway. I need a Druidess with the skills of Gruoch, who tended my wounds when I was a guest of Cartimandua.' His voice grew bitter. 'She brought the skills of the goddess. Melinus is good, but he lacks the gentle touch of a born healer and as your mother says he cannot find the right ingredients in this climate.' Stretching out on the couch he groaned with pain.

'Poor Papa.' Eigon bent to kiss his forehead.

He smiled. 'You have that touch, my daughter. Ask Melinus to teach you some of his skills.' His eyes closed and he sighed. 'If Melinus were to register as a doctor he would be given his freedom and the citizenship of Rome. It is our blessing that he chooses to remain with us. Learn from him, Eigon. As much as you can, my child. Now,' he stifled another groan as he tried to ease his aching limbs, 'sing to me, Eigon. That always soothes me.'

Eigon sat with him for a while, then as he drifted into an uneasy sleep she rose and went back into the house. Her mother did not notice her leave. Julia was in the atrium. With her was Pomponia Graecina.

'So, Eigon, I hear you paid a visit to my favourite shop this afternoon.'

Eigon glanced at Julia, furious that their secret was out, but Julia shrugged. 'The goldsmith told her,' she said crossly.

'I was not spying on you, children,' Pomponia said with a smile. 'I went there to select a gift for one of my friends. It is her birthday tomorrow. And he commented that you had just left. I am not cross. I think it is wonderful that you have been enticed outside at last.' She smiled at Eigon. 'So, did you enjoy your excursion?'

Eigon nodded. The fright they had suffered had already retreated into the shadows.

'And you admired his handiwork?'

She nodded again. 'Almost as good as the craftsmen at home.' She didn't remember the craftsmen at home. She didn't remember very much at all but it had become part of the good-natured banter between the girls to stick up for her barbarian origins.

'So, you wouldn't turn down a piece of his work if it was offered as a gift?'

Eigon laughed. 'Indeed not.'

'Good, because I have a gift for you.' Pomponia reached into the small basket she had put down on the edge of the fountain and produced a small packet wrapped in linen.

Eigon took it gingerly. 'You shouldn't have done this, Lady Pomponia!' She had already guessed what it was. The ring she had so admired and had put down so reluctantly, lay on her palm.

'Of course I should, child. You have few enough treats, shut away here with a sick father and a stern tutor monitoring your every move. Put it on. Let me see if it suits your hand.'

It fitted perfectly. They all admired it for a moment and Eigon smiled again, radiant.

'So, how is your father?' Pomponia Graecina asked.

'Not well. The fever returns and his scars hurt him so much. Melinus thinks there is infection deep inside the wounds.' Melinus was well aware that he was being compared unfavourably to the female Druid who had tended his lord's injuries in Brigantia and he had become convinced that the illness was the result of some magic the woman had performed, designed to reawaken far into the future and bring King Caradoc to his knees.

'My father thinks I should train to be a healer,' Eigon went on. The glitter of the gold on her finger caught her eye and for a moment she held her hand out, angling it in the last of the sunlight, streaming low through the doorway. It was an innocent feminine gesture which Pomponia Graecina noted with affection.

'And do you feel you would like to be a healer?' she asked.

Eigon nodded. 'I sometimes feel I want to rest my hand on Papa's head and draw away his pain. I can feel there is power in my hands, but I don't know how to use it.' She shrugged. 'Melinus has taught me some of his knowledge of herbs and how to gather

178

them when the stars and the moon are strongest. He knows I am interested.'

'And she's good,' Julia put in. 'She makes my headaches go away. Her hands are cool. They command the evil spirits that plague me to leave.'

Pomponia Graecina raised an eyebrow. 'I didn't know you were plagued by evil spirits, Julia. Are you sure they are not the spirits of laziness?'

Julia blushed. 'I'm not lazy!'

'Her headaches come monthly,' Eigon put in. 'I have noticed they are regular and they are very painful. It is part of being a woman.'

Pomponia Graecina looked startled. 'You noticed that by yourself?'

Eigon giggled. 'It is not something I would have discussed with Melinus! But I have found a soothing blend of plants here from our own herb beds which helps her.'

'As do your hands,' Julia insisted.

Pomponia Graecina looked thoughtful. 'If your father approves, then ask Melinus if you can study medicine with him in greater detail,' she said, 'but realise that he is an intellectual, a philosopher, he studies the properties of healing plants but is not necessarily the man to apply them. That takes a gentle kindness. He is an austere man, I have always found.' She nodded slowly. 'Do you pray to your own gods, Eigon?'

Eigon nodded. 'But Papa thinks they do not hear our prayers. They are too far away so I pray to the gods of the household here and to Febris for my father, but perhaps I am wrong to do that as I fear they do not listen to me.'

Pomponia Graecina shook her head. 'The gods hear one wherever they are, Eigon. If your gods are all powerful, pray to them, as I do.' She smiled. 'I found your gods in Britannia to be strong. Why do you think I brought Melinus back with me? He taught me their names and why I should pray to each one. They live in the mountains and rivers of Britannia and Gaul, but their power stretches across the world.'

'But don't they quarrel with the gods of Rome?' Eigon sat down on the rim of the fountain, her brow wrinkled in concentration.

Pomponia Graecina shook her head. 'This is something you must discuss with Melinus. Rome is a centre for all the gods. The

gods of Greece and Egypt, the god of the Jews, the gods from
North Africa and even the lands traversed by the silk road, they
all meet here and are worshipped in their way. Each one of us
must speak to our own gods. Rome accepts that men must be free
to worship in their own way as long as it does not conflict with
our loyalty to the Emperor.'

'Who is a god himself,' Eigon said softly. 'Do you believe that?'
She glanced up under her eyelashes.

Pomponia grinned. 'The Emperor and I do not agree about
many things,' she replied. 'He knows I do not fear him.'

'And you don't worship him either.' Eigon raised her eyebrows.

Pomponia shook her head. 'Such talk is dangerous, Eigon, even
for me. Concentrate on your healing and pray to the gods that
listen. Enough for now. I shall go and see your mother.'

Julia had been lost in her own thoughts, bored with talk of
gods and emperors, but the sight of her aunt rising to her feet
galvanised her into action. 'You won't tell Eigon's mother we went
into the city?' she put in anxiously.

'I will say nothing,' Pomponia Graecina said with a smile. 'And
next time you decide to go out you will come and see me, both
of you.'

Julia watched her depart. 'You are not serious about learning
to be a healer!'

'Why not? If I feel it is the right path for me.'

'Because it is boring. You want to go out and meet nice healthy
people, not sick ones!'

'You mean young men?' Eigon smiled.

'Of course young men.' Julia giggled. 'Don't tell me you aren't
interested!'

Eigon shook her head. 'I have met no one who interests me,
Julia. Perhaps I am not meant for marriage. My parents have
never mentioned it.'

Her parents had never so much as hinted that this was her
destiny. They had made no mention of her destiny at all.

Julia gave an exasperated sigh. 'Since when have girls waited
for their parents to suggest it!'

'Would your father approve of Flavius as your partner?' Eigon
asked.

'No, of course not. He's only the son of a freedman. Papa has
probably destined me for some old widower whose land borders

our estates.' Julia tossed her head. 'In which case I mean to have some fun while I still can. If my aunt has invited us to go out and see her I mean to go as soon as possible.'

Eigon shook her head. 'It is frightening out there.'

'Frightening!' Julia looked at her askance. 'What, that man who pushed us? Nothing happened. I don't suppose he even saw us, he was far too intent on running away. He had probably stolen something! Don't be foolish. Besides we would be perfectly safe going to the house of her husband, Aulus Plautius. They live on the Palatine Hill near the Emperor in a beautiful huge place with lots of visitors and relations and handsome young musicians. You can flash your lovely ring at them and twirl your gorgeous hair and bewitch whoever you please.'

Eigon knew it would be hard to refuse. The thought that the house was near the Imperial palace and therefore the Imperial bodyguard was something she did not even consider.

Instead she went to find Melinus. She would ask him to start her special training as a healer this very day. She glanced back at Julia. The poor girl seemed oblivious to the fact that she would be prostrate with her headaches and belly pain by this time tomorrow, as she always was at this quarter of the moon. So she would pick some *tenacetum* and some yellow iris from the pond in the formal gardens and make a decoction ready for her. She gave a wry chuckle. Just as well someone was paying attention to what was going on. Julia, her head in the clouds and her attention on her dreams, never would.

15

In her dream Jess stirred restlessly. As the moon rose, five days from the full, the light spilled across the gardens, throwing shadows before Eigon as she walked out to the pond, a basket on her arm, a small pair of shears in her hand ready to cut the iris. She smiled to herself in the moonlight. Melinus had been delighted with her request. Tomorrow they would set aside the studies they had been doing – for the time being at least – and begin to plan a course of ancient Druidic lore on the art of healing.

Wrapped up in her dreams she did not notice the movement along the top of the wall, or see the figure of the man heave himself up to sit astride it in the darkness, watching her every move.

They arrived home late from the Villa Borghese and with plates of spaghetti on their knees as they sat on cushions and watched a DVD, they had whiled away the heat of the evening until Jess, the first to admit to exhaustion, had made her way to bed. She fell asleep at once, oblivious to the fact that after she had left the room Kim had reached forward and turned off the TV. 'How do you think she is?' she asked.

'She's fine,' Steph said at once.

'No mention of Dan following us or anything?'

Steph shook her head.

'And no mention of Eigon and the Romans?'

Steph hesitated. Kim's gaze sharpened. 'I thought so. When you two lingered behind as we walked back she looked really weird. Sort of haunted.'

'She was talking about history,' Steph said defensively. 'She's interested in the story. We can't blame her for that. I'm interested too. After all it is my house where all this started. I want to know who Eigon is and what happened to her. Lots of rational people believe in ghosts.'

'I'm not denying it.' Will frowned. 'I'm just not sure I believe in them myself. I'm trying to understand. People like Carmella seem to have an intuitive ability to see things other people don't see. It's easy to mock her because she uses the trappings – the tarot cards, the mystical language, the faraway dozy expression.' He grinned and shook his head. 'Kim, you like Carmella, you brought her into the equation. Do you really believe her?'

'Yes, I do!'

'Are you sure?'

Kim shrugged. 'Perhaps it is better to say I want to believe her and I enjoy her card readings.'

'You shouldn't mock the tarot, Will,' Steph put in quietly. She wrapped the last of her spaghetti round her fork thoughtfully. 'Let me tell you something about them. They are an ancient system of archetypes, loaded with a symbolism which most so-called card readers don't understand properly themselves. Some packs are incredibly beautiful. The first tarot to appear in Europe were thought to be from Italy, you know. The secret of reading them is to allow the pictures to set the mind free to pick up on extra-sensory perceptions. Some people are better than others at doing that, of course. The standard meanings of the cards which come on the printed instructions are not worth the paper they are printed on.'

Will and Kim stared at her. 'Since when have you been an authority on the tarot?' Kim asked.

Steph smiled. 'I went on a course. Years ago. In London when I was a student. I bought myself a pack out of curiosity. Then another. Then another. I was fascinated by them. I stuck the cards round the walls of my bedsit. Then one of my boyfriends came over and he hated them. He was terrified of them. Screamed about evil and superstition and doom and death. He said I was a messenger of the devil and that I would go to hell. Needless to say we didn't meet again but it made me think. I realised I was looking at them purely as art forms, intriguing historical anachronisms, not as ways of telling the future and I had entirely missed the fact that some people are really scared of them. So I enrolled in this course. And I was very lucky because it could have been the kind of course which taught you to read them in the way that boyfriend imagined. I could have put a sequinned scarf over my hair and imitated one of the three witches moaning about doom and dark strangers and crossing my palm with silver. It didn't happen that way. Our lecturer talked about history and philosophy and the mystical origins of the cards in Ancient Egypt or somewhere in the Middle East after the Great Flood or in Ancient Rome in the time of Hermes Trismegistus – no one seems to know for sure. And he taught us to learn the symbolism, then to empty our minds and read the cards from our inner wisdom.'

'So, you know more about it than Carmella!' Kim looked at her askance. 'Why didn't you tell us before?'

Steph shook her head. 'I read them for myself. I never do it for other people. Sometimes I use them to meditate. You choose a card and think about it and explore it and then perhaps wonder why that particular card came up. It is amazingly helpful. A sort of potted session with a counsellor-stroke-psychotherapist. I don't do it better than Carmella, it's just that she does it differently. She is a natural. But a natural in a good way. She is not reading from a crib sheet. She is I would guess someone who has always done it. Who was taught by her mother or grandmother or someone like that.'

Kim shook her head, smiling. 'Her grandmother. Who was incidentally a good Catholic.'

Steph inclined her head. 'Because it is not evil.'

'No, but I doubt if the church approves.'

'Whatever. But the way she does it, she tunes in to whoever she has been asked to read for. She listens to some inner voice.'

'So the dangerous man was real, not her responding to the crowd?' Will pushed his plate away.

'As it happens I think it was.'

'Which brings us back to Dan.'

'Perhaps it wasn't Dan she was talking about. That is the problem: the interpretation of what she said, not the fact that she said it.'

'I think you are talking yourself round in circles, Steph.' Will stood up yawning. 'Will you forgive me if I follow Jess's example and go to bed? The heat is getting to me a bit.'

When he had gone Kim poured Steph another glass of wine. 'Did you bring your cards with you?'

Steph shook her head. 'I don't even know where they are. Packed away at Ty Bran somewhere.'

Climbing to her feet Kim went to the sideboard and brought out the pack Carmella had used on that first evening. She put them down in front of Steph. 'See what you can do.'

Steph shook her head. 'I told you. I don't do readings.'

'No. Pick a card. Meditate on it. About Jess.'

Steph reached out for the cards. She shuffled them and cut the pack then picked up the top card and turned it over. It was the king of cups.

Jess sat up with a jerk of fear and sat staring into the dark. She could hear the first rumbling of a storm in the distance. Was it the storm that had awakened her? She could hear the raindrops now, in the courtyard below the open window. The room was stiflingly hot. With a groan she threw back the sheet and sat up in bed. A flash of lightning lit the window and in that fraction of a second she saw a figure silhouetted against it. She screamed.

There was a slight click and a scraping sound, then silence save for the pattering of the raindrops. She scrabbled for the switch of the lamp and turned it on, trembling. The room was empty. Throwing her legs over the edge of the bed she padded over to the window and looked out into the dark. Another flicker of lightning illuminated the clouds overhead. It was enough to show her an empty garden. She leaned on the low sill to scan the paths and looked down at her hands suspiciously. They were wet. She stared down at the floorboards. Was that a footprint or just rain splashing in from the stone architrave? Her own feet were bare; the faint imprint there on the old oak was of a ridged sole larger by a couple of inches than her own feet.

'Jess?' There was a gentle tap at the door behind her. 'Jess, can I come in?'

Steph crept into the room. She too was barefoot; her hair dishevelled from sleep. She was wearing a pair of cotton pyjamas. She glanced round. 'I thought I heard you call out.'

Jess grimaced. 'I did. Sorry. I woke myself too.' She paused. She had been about to say she had heard someone in the room but already she had changed her mind. The print was almost dry. In seconds it would be gone. Perhaps it had never been a footprint at all. 'The thunder must have woken me up. The rain has made the floor all wet.' She leaned out to close the shutters. As she did so she saw a figure on the gravel path below. A flicker of lightning illuminated his face clearly. 'Dan!' she breathed.

'What?' Steph had heard. 'Jess, for goodness' sake! Dan has gone.' She came and leaned out beside her. 'Where? There's no one there!'

Jess shook her head. 'Of course not. It was a shadow.'

'Idiot!' Steph put an arm round her fondly. 'Come on. Do you want to get something to drink?'

Jess shook her head. 'I didn't wake everybody, did I?'

'No, of course you didn't. My room is next door and I was awake anyway.' Steph headed back towards the door. She paused. 'You've got to stop imagining things, Jess. Relax. Enjoy Rome. Dan's long gone.'

Jess overslept next morning. There was no sign of her when Steph wandered into the kitchen in search of coffee, and no sign of Will and Kim either. Presumably they too had been wakened by the storm which had long ago spent its fury in the distant hills. The sky was once more a clear intense blue as Steph reached for the jar of coffee beans. Pouring the coffee into a mug from the huge glass-fronted dresser she sat down at the kitchen table and pulled her mobile out of her pocket. 'Megan? How are you? Can I ask you a favour? My house plants have lost their babysitter.'

In the Welsh farmhouse Megan glanced at the ceiling in exasperation. Her voice however betrayed no hint of impatience as she answered, 'Of course. I'll go and water them. How is Jess? Rhodri rang yesterday. He told us he was worried about her.'

Steph took a sip of coffee. 'Really?' she said cautiously. 'Did he say why?'

Megan took her time before she answered. 'Is Jess there in Rome with you now?'

'Yes.'

'Did she say what happened?'

It was Steph's turn to be careful in her choice of words. 'She didn't say anything happened particularly. I think she found it a bit of a strain being there on her own. She said it was a bit spooky.'

'And yet you expect me to go up there on my own to water your plants!' Megan retorted.

'You'd be more than a match for any ghost, Meg!' Steph laughed.

'Yes, I probably would,' Megan agreed dryly. 'And anyone else who happened to be around.'

Steph put down her mug. 'Was there anyone else up there then?'

'I think she had one or two visitors. I wasn't here. She had gone by the time we came home.'

'But did Rhodri say something?'

'Not really.'

'Megan!'

'He said it wasn't his business.'

'What wasn't?'

'Well, he didn't say, did he!'

Behind her Steph heard the kitchen door open. Jess appeared, bleary-eyed. 'Hi!'

'Megan, I've got to go.' Steph grinned at Jess and pointed towards the coffee pot.

'Rhodri said he might look you up. He's got one more performance then he's finished in Milan. He's coming to Rome on the way back.'

Steph wrinkled her nose. 'Did you give him my number?'

'I did.' Steph could hear the laughter in Megan's voice. 'I knew you'd be pleased to see him!'

'What was that about?' Jess asked as Steph tossed the mobile onto the table.

'Rhodri. Megan said he might look us up on the way back from La Scala. I suppose I've got you to thank for that sudden interest in our activities?'

'I can't imagine why. I doubt if he would want to see me again!' Jess scowled. 'Where are the others?' She had seated herself at the end of the table and was sipping her black coffee.

'We're here!' Kim appeared in the doorway behind her, laden with brown paper bags. 'We went to get hot rolls for breakfast. How did you all sleep? Did you hear the storm?'

Will sat down next to Jess. 'Are you OK?'

She raised an eyebrow. 'Why?'

'You look very white.'

'Thanks for the concern.' She gave a wry smile as she returned her attention to the coffee. 'And yes, the storm did keep me awake.'

Kim pushed a plate towards her. 'Here. Have a roll. And some butter and jam. Did you know your sister was a tarot reader?' She plumped herself down in the wooden armchair opposite Jess and studied her face eagerly. 'It is really bizarre. She is better at it than Carmella!'

Jess shook her head. 'I remember you went on a course ages ago. You never told me you still did it, Steph! Somehow I can't believe it.'

'Good. Don't.' Steph frowned at Kim.

'It's true though,' Kim added, ignoring the sharp kick from Steph under the table. 'She showed me last night.'

'And what did the cards say last night?' Jess was tightlipped suddenly. 'That I am mad?'

'Jess!' Steph protested. 'Of course not.'

'But the card she turned over was the same old card. The king of cups!' Kim said. 'Weird or what.'

Jess blanched. 'I don't believe any of this.' She stood up. 'I'm not hungry. This coffee is enough for me. I'm going out. If we've nothing planned for today I thought I might do some more sketching. Indulge my fantasies a bit. Find myself a Roman ghost or two to talk to.' She headed for the door. 'I'll see you all this evening.'

Will caught her up outside the front door. The street was fresh and clean after the storm of the night before, the air much cooler. 'Look, Jess, don't rush off like this. It's idiotic. No one is trying to stitch you up. And no one is getting at you for being interested in Eigon. Can I come with you?'

Jess stopped in her tracks. 'Why?'

'Because I would like to spend the morning with you.'

She looked at him suspiciously. 'Are you sure?'

'Quite sure. I'm at your service. And I've brought a camera in case you need any photos of the topography.'

She raised an eyebrow. 'Learning the language of research, eh?'

'I'm doing my best. To be honest, I don't care where I go. I just like wandering around and I like your company. I've always liked your company, Jess. You know that.' He looked away uncomfortably. 'Sorry, I shouldn't have said that. Delete the last remark.'

'It's deleted.' Jess resumed walking slowly. 'OK. Let's go. I want to head over towards the Forum again. I have a goldsmith's house to find.'

And that was impossible. Wherever the jewellers' quarter was it probably wouldn't have been in the Forum, she realised that at once. They paused before the columns of the great temple of Saturn. 'I think this is one of the buildings left which dates from Eigon's time. It was old when she was here,' Jess said hesitantly. 'She must have stood near here before Claudius with her father.'

Will reached for his camera. 'So it is two thousand years old?'

'More. I think it dates from some time before Christ, according to my guidebook. Though it's been renovated. It must have been.' She swung her bag off her shoulder and fished out the book, pushing her sunglasses up onto her forehead as she riffled the pages. 'It's hard to get one's head round the age of all this stuff.' She glanced up at him. 'It's all so confusing, remains from so many different periods all jumbled up next to each other. I think most of it is too recent to interest me at the moment!' She smiled. The heat was intense by now, the air already dusty, the memory of the storm long gone.

'Like only nineteen hundred years old?' He snapped a few shots of the great columns in front of them as a hooded crow flew to perch on the battered marble architrave, staring down at them. He returned his camera to its case. 'Jess, all this Roman stuff. Eigon.' He shrugged. 'It's all a bit weird. When we – when you and I – were together you didn't talk about ghosts then.'

'I hadn't seen a ghost then,' she said defensively. 'I don't blame you for not believing it, Will. You've seen nothing, after all. But I do blame you for not taking my word about Dan. You still don't, do you, not really. I would have expected you to back me up on that one.' She turned away from him, suddenly afraid she was going to cry and headed down the crowded path.

He hurried after her. 'Jess! Wait!' The crowds parted to let them through, uninterested in a lovers' tiff, closing behind them again intent on their own sightseeing.

He caught her up. 'Jess, I want to know what made him do it.'

'You can't know.' She turned on him fiercely. 'No one can.'

He studied her face. 'If Dan raped you, Jess, I am going to have to kill him.'

She hesitated, half-believing him for a moment. Then she let out a small ugly yelp of laughter. 'No, thank you, Will. You don't have to go that far. I look after myself now.'

'Not very well, by all accounts.' He caught her arms and pulled her to face him. 'Jess, I still care, you know. You and I can't have what we had together without something remaining.'

She pushed him away sharply. 'I know that but I don't need you to gallop off on a white charger to defend my honour –' She broke off with a gasp.

'What?' Will swung round, following the direction of her gaze.

'Dan!' she whispered. 'There. Watching us.'

'Where?' Will was scanning the crowd.

'There!' She pointed at a flight of steps nearby.

Will ran up the steps and turned to stare down at the crowds around them. People milled in all directions. Tourists, hot and perspiring in summer dresses and colourful shirts, sunhats, dark glasses, water sellers, guides. The stream of people around the Forum was a never-ending tide swirling in and out amongst the pillars and stones. 'I can't see him. Where was he?'

'Right where you're standing.'

'Are you sure it was him?' Will scanned the crowd again.

She shrugged helplessly. 'It was only a glance. He was wearing dark glasses. I could be mistaken.' Her face was pale but she felt a quick surge of anger. She was making herself sound ridiculous. 'I am so sure he is following me, Will. I don't think he's gone at all. He threatened me. He wants to frighten me.'

Will nodded. 'I won't deny that's the way it looks.' He sighed, staring round again. 'Well, whoever it was is long gone now. I suggest we head somewhere we can get a cold drink. It is getting too hot out here. Are there any buildings left that Eigon knew which still have a roof on or do you want to go back to the palazzo and rest?'

Eigon was standing in the atrium. She had heard her sister's voice again in the night, the little plaintive cry coming to her over miles of land and sea and time.

Can we stop playing now? Eigon? Where are you? Please come back. I'm frightened.

She shivered miserably at the memory. It was a long time since she had dreamed of Gwladys and Togo. Those dreams were full of the rushing wind and the flare of torches in the darkness of the hillside. More often she dreamed of the gentle hills of her mother's home before they began following her father to the battlefield.

Those were dreams of sunlight and laughter, and the happiness of innocence. With a sigh she pushed her sister's voice gently away. She was near the open doorway into the gardens, listening to the gentle splattering of the water from the fountains. The trees, turning gold and russet with the autumn were drooping with the heat; she could smell the needles of the pine on the still air. Melinus had walked outside and was standing by the stone bench, talking to Pomponia Graecina. They hadn't seen her.

'How is he?' Melinus looked grim. For a moment Eigon thought they were discussing her father.

Pomponia shook her head. 'May the gods protect us all. It seems he will not last the day.' She lowered her voice and Eigon strained forward to hear. 'They say he ate poisonous mushrooms. It seems Agrippina has at last succeeded in doing away with him.'

'And who will succeed him?'

'Agrippina's son. Who else? I think we will find that Nero is already trying on the Emperor's golden wreath. The second his stepfather breathes his last Rome will have a new Emperor. A child on the throne, if you please, and not even the rightful heir, Britannicus.'

'A child with powerful connections. And a child on the verge of manhood.' There was a moment of intense silence. 'Will Nero honour Claudius's safe conduct for this family?' Melinus asked at last. The politics of Rome did not interest him apart from any threat immediately impinging upon this household.

Eigon took another small step closer, anxious to hear every word.

Pomponia Graecina shrugged. 'Their safety is, to my mind, guaranteed by Caradoc's illness.' She had taken to using the family's name for him. 'I doubt if anyone considers him a threat as he is at present. Nero's advisers will have other far more pressing worries in the Senate. Claudius's followers will no doubt find themselves suffering the same fate as his own if they are not very careful and a new set of masters will rise to rule the Empire.'

Melinus nodded. He was leaning on his staff, staring down into the square pool at his feet. The surface of the water was like glass. 'I see troubles a plenty ahead for Rome and for us here.'

He had spoken to Cerys earlier. When she had realised the implications of what he told her she had been distraught. He frowned. Emotion made him awkward. He had no idea how to comfort her.

'But surely the new Emperor won't go back on Claudius's word?' he said thoughtfully.

'Who knows what he will do.' Pomponia Graecina sniffed and raised an eyebrow. 'Will Caradoc ever recover, do you think?'

Melinus shook his head. 'I have used every piece of knowledge I possess. And I am teaching Eigon everything I know.' He gave a half-glance towards the doorway and Eigon shrank back out of sight. 'She learns fast. She is an intelligent girl and more importantly she has the blessing of Bride. She is a natural healer with hands which give her genuine power but even she, alas, does not seem able to rid him of this fever. It may be that it is his destiny to die here and be reborn in another life at home in Britannia. Only the gods know what lies in store.' He paused. 'If there are any gods out there I have not invoked you must tell me of them.'

Pomponia Graecina stepped closer. 'There is a teacher in Rome.' She lowered her voice. 'He's been here some ten years now and his reputation spreads all the time. I have recently been to hear him preach. His name is Peter. He heals in the name of Jesus, the Christ. I have seen Peter raise men who were far worse than King Caradoc. He produces miracles in the name of this god of his, who he says is the son of the only true god.'

Melinus raised an eyebrow. 'I have heard of him. Is he not a Jew?'

She nodded. 'But I gather his god is different to theirs. They call him the god of love. Many of the Jews from Greece follow him, as do a lot of people here. He has won many converts, especially amongst the poor.' She glanced at him thoughtfully, then she went on, 'Shall we go and listen together and you can see what he has to say?' She shrugged.

Melinus frowned. 'I suppose it could do no harm,' he said cautiously.

'He usually preaches in the house of one or other of his followers. I shall find out where he is likely to be and tell you.' She smiled. 'He speaks powerfully, Melinus. He is very persuasive.' She paused. 'Say nothing to Cerys. She clings obsessively to Bride, her goddess of healing and to Lenus and Ocelos, gods of her own people. She won't even sacrifice to our Roman Febris. But none of her prayers is answered.' She shook her head. 'You know how much I have admired your Druidic teachings, Melinus, since my husband and I were in Britannia and I heard their philosophers. Why else would

I have insisted you return with me?' She gave a small smile, suddenly embarrassed. This man was technically a slave though both had long ago forgotten it. 'But this man Peter attracts me too and I want to know what you think of him and his god.'

They began to walk slowly away from the house, inspecting the neat beds of herbs as they talked. Eigon stepped out of the shadows and went to stand in her turn near the pond, staring down into the reflections. What had Melinus seen there? She frowned. Whoever this teacher, Peter, was she prayed with all her heart that his god would be able to help her father.

Julia bounced out of the house behind her, making her jump. 'There you are! Come on. Have you forgotten? Flavius is going to escort us back to the market!'

Eigon frowned. 'Is it safe, Julia? Remember what happened last time.'

'Of course it is safe. And this time he and the others will be ready in case anyone comes near us. Please. Come with me. I don't want to go alone.' Julia blushed prettily. 'And I do want to buy another cloak pin to match the one I have.'

Eigon glanced into the shadowed interior of the house. In her parents' bedroom Cerys would be sitting with her father as he slept. There would be nothing to do until evening when they met over food her father was too weak to eat. Why not go and see some more of this city which looked like being her home for ever?

Less than two miles away the door to the mess in the barracks of the Praetorian guard creaked open and a figure peered in. 'Titus?'

The man sitting at the table looked up. He was writing notes on a tablet, a cup of wine at his elbow beside him. He was a tall officer, with dark rugged good looks, an aquiline nose and light amber eyes. He raised an eyebrow. 'Lucius?'

'My lookout has sent a message from the villa.' The other man came in and closed the door behind him. He glanced at the other occupants of the room and lowered his voice. 'The girls have gone out to the city centre again.'

Titus's eyes narrowed. 'Have they indeed! Are they escorted?'

'Only by a couple of slaves and Aelius's boy, Flavius.'

Titus shook his head in mock despair. 'What are they thinking of. Anything could happen to them! Especially with the unrest there is at the moment. Any news of the Emperor?'

Lucius shook his head. 'I believe he is still unconscious.'

'Then it is time to pay our respects to the heir presumptive, I think.' Wiping the tablet clear of notes with one sweep of the blunt end of his stylus Titus stood up, his cloak swinging back to reveal the sword tattooed on his arm. 'Are you with me, Lucius?'

Lucius grinned. 'As ever! What about your Celtic nemesis?'

Titus smiled grimly. 'She can wait. No hurry to deal with her. In fact the more they venture outside that villa the more vulnerable she will be. We want to catch her on her own for preference. The other girl has influential relations. I do not want to stir up Aulus Plautius and his followers. Something quick and quiet in the dark would be best, I think.' He hitched his cloak back onto his shoulder and tucked the tablet and writing implements into the pouch at his belt.

'So, we bow the knee to young Nero!' Lucius led the way out of the door.

Titus gave a grim smile. 'Unless you have a serious death wish, my friend, you will do nothing else.'

'And you think we will be chosen to be part of his personal guard even though we served Claudius before?'

'If we convince him of our loyalty and bribe the right men, of course!' The two men exchanged glances. After a moment Titus laughed. He slapped his companion on the back. 'I don't think we'll have any problems, my friend. None at all.'

For a moment Lucius frowned. 'If the little princess points the finger before you get to her? We could have taken her, you know.'

'She won't. She'll meet with an accident long before she gets the chance to set eyes on me again.' Titus grimaced. 'Pity though. I gather she is growing into an even more desirable little titbit now she's older.'

'And you don't fear the mother recognising you?' Lucius eyed his friend curiously. He had been half titillated and half appalled at his friend's story of rape and murder on a lonely hillside in a faraway province.

Titus shook his head. 'She was half-dead before I had her and there were others after me. And now I hear she's too taken up with weeping and moaning over the dying hero to care about me, or, I fear, her daughter.' He snorted derisively. 'Just make sure

194

your informant keeps me posted. They have no idea that I have been watching her all this time. And this way it is perfect. I prefer to tease her a little.' He grinned. 'She is no danger to me. Who, after all, would believe her after so long? No, I shall deal with our little princess when I'm ready. I'll have her when the moment is right.'

He led the way outside and snapped his fingers at the orderly holding Lucius's horse, ordering his own to be brought round at once. He restrained a smile. A delicious idea had occurred to him. It would be a waste to kill the girl straightaway. Not now that with every passing year she was growing more beautiful and more desirable. He felt himself hardening at the thought.

Glancing back as he grabbed the reins of his mount and hauled himself into the saddle Lucius caught sight of the expression on Titus's face and he shivered. Not for the first time he wondered to himself why he counted this man his friend.

16

Opening her eyes, Jess stretched and lay for a moment without moving, trying to recall the dream. She frowned, clinging to the wispy threads of the story as they dissipated into the air. A soldier. A horse. A cup of wine. The sun beating down on the raked earth of a parade ground and a sense of impending doom. That was all. With a groan she sat up, dragged herself off the bed and went to throw open the shutters. The sun had gone round now and her windows were in shadow. Leaning out she stared down into the garden. Then suddenly she turned. Slipping on her shoes she ran to the door.

Kim was in her sitting room. She put down the phone as Jess came in. 'Hi! Did you sleep OK?'

Jess nodded. 'How does one get down into the gardens here? Do you have any access?'

Kim nodded. 'We all have a key.'

'But there's no door.'

'There is. There is a passageway. It runs down the side of the building. The downstairs apartments have their own doors leading out, but we use the public access.'

'So, anyone can go down there?'

'If they've got a key, yes.'

'Have you?'

Kim nodded. 'It's on a hook in the kitchen. I don't go down there much. Too many windows looking down on you. It makes you feel you are being watched.'

'You probably are. Can I go and see?'

'Sure. It's the big old key hanging on the wall by the dresser. You can't miss it. Go out of the front door downstairs. Turn left. Then first left again down the alleyway between the two buildings.' She yawned. 'I won't join you, if you don't mind. I'll see you later.'

The key was heavy wrought iron. Slipping it off the hook Jess followed Kim's instructions. She ducked out of the busy street into a narrow passageway she hadn't even noticed before. It was dark and slightly damp after last night's rain. She shuddered in distaste. Not just rain. Judging by the smell for several hundred years it had been used as a handy latrine. She paused and glanced up at the sheer walls rising windowless several storeys towards the sky. The far end of the entry was blocked by a barred gate fastened by a heavy lock, itself a Renaissance historical artefact if the key was anything to go by. She glanced down at it, then carefully inserted it. It turned without a struggle and she pushed the gate open, hearing it grate slightly on the uneven paving stones. Closing it behind her she found herself in the secret oasis at the heart of the palazzo.

In deep shadow now, and cool after the blazing sun in the street she stepped out towards the paving and raked gravel paths and flowerbeds that surrounded the centre fountain. The small beds were weed free, obviously regularly and beautifully tended with neatly clipped low box hedges and patterns of intricately planted heliotrope and salvia and geraniums. She glanced up at the soaring walls of the building which surrounded her. Most of the windows, rising rank upon rank above the ground were shuttered now and blank. She stood staring up, trying to locate her own bedroom and found Kim's apartment easily. All the windows stood open, though her shutters too were closed against the heat in every window save one. Jess's. Behind her the fountain spewed its cascade of water down its ranks of sculpted bowls, draped here and there with iridescent green weed, gurgling at last into the stone basin at the bottom. She strolled slowly towards the wall where her own window looked out onto this scene of tranquillity, smelling the sweet scents of flowers and stood staring down at the bed below the window. There were no footprints in the carefully raked soil. No sign of anyone having been there at all. She took a step closer, then she saw it. Lying inside the box hedge deep in shadow where it was invisible except to someone standing as close as she was now, lay a hosepipe and a ladder.

'The bastard!' She stood staring at it for several seconds, then she turned and retraced her steps. Perhaps the others would believe her now. She was several paces from the gate when she realised there was someone standing behind the bars watching her. She stopped dead.

'Dan?'

In the dark passageway she couldn't make out his face, just the silhouette as he stared out at her.

Two hands came up and gripped the bars. *'Buonasera, signora. Vorrei entrare.'* To her relief the voice was husky. Old. It wasn't Dan. *'Vorrei entrare per visitare il bel giardino.'*

'Go away!' Jess called. 'This is a private garden! *Privato!'* Her heart thudded uncomfortably as the man rattled the gate. She had locked it, she realised, but the key was still there, sticking out of the lock only inches from his grimy fingers.

'Go away! *Basta!'* He must have followed her down the passage. She could see him more clearly now as her eyes grew used to the shadows. He had a haggard face with several days' growth of stubble. She could smell him from where she stood. She heard him give a hoarse chuckle, then he turned away. He shuffled a few paces back into the shadows and stopped. Creeping forward she grabbed the key out of the lock and as she did so she realised what he was doing. Relieving himself copiously against the wall he zipped himself up and with another chuckle turned towards the street. *'Arrivederci, signora!'* he called as he reached the corner. Then he had gone.

Kim was in the kitchen, wrestling with a corkscrew. 'Yes, we keep asking for a gate at the street end of the passage,' she laughed. 'Bad luck. But all cities have their sordid side as well as the beautiful!'

Jess collected the glasses Kim had put on the table. 'Did you know there was a ladder down there in the garden?'

Kim shrugged. 'I've never taken much interest to be honest. I'm not a gardener.'

Carrying the glasses through to Kim's sitting room, Jess put them down on the coffee table then went straight to the window and pushing back the shutters, leaned out. 'You can't see it from up here. It's completely hidden.'

'Why the interest?' As Will appeared behind them Kim waved the bottle in his direction. *'Aperitivo?* Where's Steph?'

'The interest is because that is how Dan got up to my window. I wasn't imagining it. He must have found another key or copied that one before he left.' Jess turned back to face them.

'You mean he was in your room after he left?' Kim looked at her askance.

Jess nodded. 'The noise of someone at the window woke me; it was the night of the storm. He'd gone, but it was raining hard and I found a wet footprint on the floor by the window.'

She intercepted the glance exchanged between Will and Kim with a rush of indignation. 'OK, forget it! My imagination. Obviously.' She sat down on the sofa with a groan. Kim poured the wine and passed her a glass. 'Maybe you should shut your windows at night.'

'Why not ask the janitor about the ladder, Kim?' Will suggested. He sat down next to Jess. 'Do you have such a person? Or the gardener. Someone must weed and water that glorious garden out there.'

'We have a *portiere*,' Kim said thoughtfully. 'I don't know who does the gardening, to be honest. But Jacopo would know. I'll call him.'

She was gone several minutes and returned shaking her head. 'No reply. He'll be down in the bar across the road I expect, that's where he hangs out most of the time. No point in ringing till tomorrow when he's sober. You know, something has occurred to me. Has anyone thought of ringing Natalie to check if Dan is with her?'

They both looked at Jess and she shrugged. 'I don't have her number.'

'What about Dan's?'

Jess nodded.

'I'll ring him.' Will put down his glass. 'His number is in my phone.' He stood up and reached into his pocket for his mobile.

Dan answered on the third ring. 'Dan? Just calling to see that you got back safely.' Will raised his eyebrow at the two women watching him. He chuckled. 'Something like that, yes.' He strolled towards the window and stood looking down into the garden. 'Shrewsbury? Well, it sounds much like anywhere else actually, but I believe you.' There was another silence. 'OK, yes. Great.' More silence. Will wandered back to the table and stooping, picked up his glass. Jess found she was clenching her fists. 'Has she? OK. No problem,' Will went on at last. 'Give her my love, OK? Ciao!'

He closed the mobile and tucked it back into his hip pocket, shaking his head. 'He says he's in Shrewsbury shopping with Nat. He guessed we were checking up on him at once and offered to let me say hello to Nat but then discovered she and the kids had wandered off into a shop and he couldn't see her.'

'So, she might not have been anywhere near,' Jess said quietly.
'Technically, no.'

'And he might have been anywhere at all.'

Will nodded. 'All I could hear was traffic in the background.'

'No way of checking where he took the call?'

'The police could, I expect, but not me. No.'

'So, he might have still been in Rome?'

There was a long pause. 'I suppose so.' Will nodded again.

Jess shrugged. 'So, nothing proved.'

Will shook his head. 'Not unless we can get hold of Nat's phone number and ask her. Look, Jess. You don't have to prove anything to me.' He glanced at Kim. 'Let's assume you're right. He or someone perhaps at his instigation is stalking you. So, we don't give them a chance to get near you. Don't go out on your own any more and keep your windows locked. Or better still why don't you swap bedrooms with me? Mine looks out onto the street which isn't so peaceful as yours but you would be safe there. No one is going to manage to climb up the front of the building and if he comes back to your present room he is going to have an awful shock when he tiptoes towards the bed ready to plonk a kiss on your brow and finds me there.'

Jess grinned. 'That would be worth seeing.'

'You're welcome to stay in the room with me, of course.' He raised an eyebrow. 'That would be even better.'

She shook her head. 'A step too retrograde, I fear. Sorry.'

He shrugged. 'The offer's there.'

Kim cleared her throat. 'Would you two rather be alone for this discussion?'

'No!' Both spoke at once; both laughed.

Kim eyed them. 'Just so I know,' she said.

When Steph appeared a few minutes later they were sitting in silence. Kim was playing with her pack of tarot cards. 'At last!' She pushed the cards across the table towards her. 'Sit down and have a drink. We need to consult the oracle.'

'Kim!' Steph shook her head. 'I told you, I don't do this.'

'Not even for your sister?'

'Come on, Steph,' Will cajoled. 'I've never seen you in action.'

'And you won't.' Steph took the proffered glass of wine. She pushed the cards away.

'Jess needs advice,' he said softly. 'About Dan.'

'Forget Dan!' Steph slid off the chair to the floor and sat leaning against the seat, her ankles crossed in front of her. She was wearing cropped trousers and new sandals she had bought in a boutique just off the Campo de' Fiori. 'The more we think about him the more he's managing to ruin Jess's stay, whether he's here or not.' She leaned forward idly and picked up the pack. 'One cut, OK?' Almost absent-mindedly she shuffled them and cut the cards into two piles, pausing to sip her wine as she stared down at her hand hovering over them. Will leaned forward and picked up the top card. He tossed it on to the table, face up.

The king of cups.

Dan pushed another measure of grappa across the table. Two empties already stood in line in front of the *portiere* from the palazzo and the man's eyes were glazing over. 'So, you have the keys? *Le chiave*?'

'*Si. Si*.' Jacopo nodded. He reached for the glass.

'Keys first.' Dan drew it back a little, just out of reach.

With a phlegmy sigh Jacopo groped in his pocket. He produced a set of keys. They were shiny; newly cut.

Dan smiled. He pushed the drink over.

'*Soldi*!' The rheumy eyes were suddenly focused. Jacopo clicked his fingers under Dan's nose.

Dan reached into his pocket and produced an envelope. He pushed it across the table, leaving a smeared trail amongst the wine stains. 'Nice doing business with you, Jacopo.' Dan stood up. 'Now, remember. *Silenzio. Capisce*?'

Jacopo nodded. He glanced into the envelope, ruffled through the wad of euros then raised the glass in a silent toast but Dan had already turned away. In the doorway he paused and gazed across the street. He could see the corner of the palazzo from there, its graceful lines rising austerely between its more raffish neighbours. He chinked the keys in his pocket with a small nod of satisfaction.

'So, no unwelcome visitors in the night?' Kim greeted Will next morning as he appeared in the kitchen, drawn by the smell of perking coffee.

'No sign, no.' Will grinned. 'Poor Jess. Nice though all your guest rooms are, I got the better end of this deal. That view over the garden is fantastic and far more peaceful than the street.'

'I'm going to make English toast,' Kim announced. She reached for a loaf of crusty bread. 'Do you want to give Jess and Steph a shout.'

There was no need. Seconds later Jess appeared in the doorway. She was wearing a bathrobe, her hair awry. 'He's been in the night!' she said huskily. 'Look.' She threw her sketchbook down on the table. With a glance up at her face Will reached for it. Slowly he opened it and turned the pages. Every one had been defaced.

'Good morning, guys.' Steph walked in and stopped behind him, looking over his shoulder. 'What's happened?' Her voice sharpened.

Will put the pad down on the table and went on turning the pages so they could all see Jess's delicate pen and ink drawings, the pencil sketches, the water colours. Every one had been scribbled over.

'Jess.' Steph put her arm round her sister's shoulders. 'I don't understand. How could anyone have done this?'

Will and Steph were standing staring down at the final pictures. It showed a young woman wearing a long gown and mantle, her hair tied on the top of her head by pale pink ribbons. She had slanting, sad eyes and high cheekbones and her hair was the colour of polished jet. The line which sliced across the page had cut through the paper.

'It can't have been Dan,' Kim said slowly. 'I double-locked the front door last night.'

'Then he must have come through the window.' Jess looked at Will. 'He saw I wasn't there and searched the apartment until he found where I was.'

He shook his head. 'I tied thread across the window. It was unbroken this morning. And the door was still keyed on the inside.'

'But – you don't think I did it?' Jess stared at each one in turn.

'Is it possible that you did it in your sleep, Jess?' Kim asked gently. 'You've been under a lot of strain.'

'You can't think that! Of course I wouldn't!' She looked from one to the other wildly. Her gaze sharpened. 'I couldn't lock my door. There was no key.'

'That's true,' Will said.

'Anyone could have done it.'

'Are you accusing one of us, then?' Kim's mouth tightened.

'No. Of course not. But it wasn't me.'

'Sit down, love, you're shaking.' Steph put her hands on Jess's shoulders and guided her to a chair. 'Jess needs coffee, guys, not accusations. Her lovely pictures are ruined.'

'It wasn't Dan, it was Eigon.' Jess's voice was shaking. 'She did this. It happened before. At Ty Bran.'

They were all staring at her.

'Dan was there, but so was Rhodri when it happened. She ruined all my paintings and broke some glasses and bottles of wine. Then later,' she paused, shaking her head wearily, 'I went in again, to clear it up and it was all as it had been. No damage done.'

Steph pulled up a chair next to her. 'You say Dan saw this?'

She nodded. 'And Rhodri. It wasn't my imagination.'

Will whistled. He pulled the sketchbook towards him and gently turned the leaves over. 'Well, this is not going to magically mend itself.'

'I'll go and get dressed.' Jess pushed back her chair and stood up. She took the sketchbook out of Will's hand and picked up her mug with the other. Without another word she walked out of the kitchen.

They watched her go in silence. 'Ghost or Dan?' Kim said at last.

'She might have done it herself,' Will said quietly. 'I don't think she's lying. If she did do it, I think she's unaware of it. You are right, Kim, she might have done it in her sleep.' He shook his head thoughtfully. 'She's so stressed about Dan. She could wreck his career by accusing him of raping her,' he went on slowly, 'so he is going to want to destroy her credibility. It's her word against his. But if there was any doubt at all or it went to a court case, or if the school held an enquiry, then whatever the outcome, his career is compromised. You know the way these things work. If he has any ambition to become a head one day it would be well and truly scuppered. If she is totally discredited and no one believes a word she says then it would save his bacon.'

'So, you think he could have come in last night,' Steph said.

'If he did, he came in somewhere other than my room.' Will glanced at her. 'I don't suppose he could have put the ladder up to your window? It's next door. Could he have crept across your room without waking you and gone to look for Jess? Or yours, Kim?'

'How would he know she wasn't in the same bedroom any more?' Steph said.

'He would have found the door locked. So he might just have looked around the apartment to see if there was some other mischief he could do, and found her by accident.'

They looked at each other. Kim shivered. 'I don't relish that idea one bit.'

Steph leaned back in her chair. She fixed Will with a thoughtful stare. 'You want to believe her, don't you?'

He nodded. 'Dan has always been a shifty bastard. And I know – knew – Jess very well. She is not neurotic and she is not a liar.'

A door banged in the depths of the flat. Kim frowned. 'That's the front door.'

'She hasn't gone out by herself!' Will leaped to his feet. They heard his footsteps in the corridor outside. It was several seconds before he returned. 'She has. She's gone.'

'Supposing he's waiting for her?' Steph looked at him anxiously. 'Run after her, Will!'

This time it was ten minutes before he came back 'There's no sign of her. She could have gone anywhere. There is no point in me trying to follow her.' He slumped back into his chair, defeated. 'I told her not to go out on her own. She knew I would go with her.'

Jess crossed the Corso Vittorio Emanuele and with a quick glance over her shoulder to check she wasn't being followed, headed towards the Pantheon. From there she made her way towards the Corso. Turning up the Via Condotti she walked towards the Piazza di Spagna. She didn't think Dan was behind her. She had crossed each road several times, ducking in and out of the crowds. Climbing the Spanish Steps she resisted the urge to turn round and scan the piazza behind her. If Dan was there he would be looking up, trying to spot her. In front of the twin towers of the Trinità dei Monti she turned left. She was going back to the Villa Borghese. This road was quieter and shaded by trees. Bougainvillea trailed over the walls and oleanders filled the shade with colour. The air was full of the scent of flowers and the spiced smell of the great stone pines. She cut down past the Villa Medici and crossed the bridge into the Borghese Gardens.

It was hard to find the spot where she thought she had seen Eigon before. She wandered into the shade of the trees, staring round, resisting the urge to look over her shoulder. Dan could not know where she was. There was no chance he had followed her this time, she had been too careful. For once she was alone and could concentrate on the matter in hand.

She was an idiot to have shown her sketchbook to the others. If she had given it any thought at all she would have known it was Eigon who had done it, as it had been at Ty Bran. Dan could not have got into the apartment and now she had made a fool of herself in front of them all.

She paused under the shade of an old pine, staring round. It was early. The park was relatively empty. No parties of foreign school children visiting Rome in their summer vacations this early in the day; no guided tours yet. Only one or two riders quietly walking their horses down tree-shaded paths.

She stared into the distance between the trees, trying to locate the place where she had had the strange feeling that she was near Eigon's home. A heat haze hung over the park, making it impossible to see very far. There was dust in the air; a strange feeling of expectation. She turned round slowly in a full circle, trying to find the slight shift in the perception of reality where she could slip through that invisible curtain which divides past from present. She put out a tentative hand. 'Eigon?' She whispered the name uncertainly. 'Are you here?'

The room was crowded with people. Pomponia Graecina and Melinus slipped into the back and took their places amongst the others. All around them people were greeting each other with hugs and kisses. Everyone seemed to know each other. They had found their way to the house with little difficulty, following the small crowd of people clearly intent on the same destination.

'Welcome, strangers.' Someone stepped forward and greeted them. He eyed them closely but without animosity. 'You haven't joined us before, I seem to think?' His face broke into a smile.

Pomponia shook her head. 'Is it all right to be here?'

'Of course. Everyone is welcome. Peter is here. He will speak to us soon.' The man was about forty years of age, dressed in the toga of a wealthy citizen though the crowds around them were mixed, some clearly slaves, some tradesmen, perhaps half of them women. Pomponia found herself next to another woman, wrapped in a warm cloak. Moving up to make room the woman smiled wanly at her neighbour.

'I have come to receive healing.' She took a deep, laboured breath, glancing beyond Pomponia to Melinus who had seated himself beside them, his face a carefully guarded blank. 'Are you Christians?'

Pomponia Graecina hesitated. Then she shook her head. She felt that this was somewhere one should remain honest. 'I've never heard him preach. But we are here in the hope of finding healing for a close friend.'

'Is he here with you?' The woman glanced at Melinus.

Pomponia shook her head. 'He is too ill to walk at present.'

Her new friend nodded. 'As I was. My friends carried me here the last time I came. I want to be baptised.'

'What is that?' Pomponia frowned. Near them a rustle of expectation heralded the arrival of an elderly man who was threading his way to the front of the crowd. 'Is that him?'

The woman nodded. She smiled radiantly. 'Just wait till you hear the message. He is amazing and the Lord he serves more amazing still.'

It had grown dark many hours since when at last the crowds began to disperse and Pomponia Graecina and Melinus made their way back to her house on the Palatine where Melinus kept a room, though to all intents and purposes he now lived out at the villa. The slaves brought them wine and food and left them to talk softly by the fountain in the central courtyard.

'So, what did you think?' Pomponia glanced at the old Druid, eyebrow raised.

'Astonishing man. Full of charisma. A powerful story. Convincingly told.' He nodded.

'So, are you convinced?'

'That the son of God was born as a man and died as a man and then rose as a God himself? This is a story I have heard before. Our gods frequently came to earth as humans. As did the gods of Rome and Greece.' He was being cautious.

She frowned. 'The difference is that Peter says there is only the one god. The others were not real.'

Melinus shook his head. 'I'm not so easily convinced of that.'

'And the healing?'

'Oh, Peter is a powerful healer, I would not deny that. And this Jesus Christ is a god of power. I would not deny that either.' He reached thoughtfully for his goblet of wine. 'The Gauls have a god, named Esus.'

'Is he the same god?'

He shook his head. 'I think not. This Jesus hails from Judea. His lands are the hot desert places; his people the Jews. I doubt if he would bless our mountains and rivers and forests at home.'

'But he is the universal god. From what Peter says he is as much the god of your country as of mine.'

'And as such I will greet him with our own gods. And I shall go again to listen to Peter. He is an astonishing man. Irascible,' he chuckled, 'but compelling. I can see he doesn't suffer fools gladly and yet he radiates a strange warmth and compassion. My neighbour told me he originated as a simple fisherman working for his father with his brothers in his own country. Yet he is clearly an educated man. He speaks with learning and authority, and I have to say with more conviction than I have heard for many years.' Melinus nodded thoughtfully. 'It is that conviction which has brought him to faraway countries spreading the word about Jesus.'

That night both prayed to the Lord Jesus, one fervently, one with a certain amount of caution. Both in their prayers mentioned Caradoc.

The next morning when they arrived back at the villa the invalid was out of bed and with unaccustomed vigour strolling slowly in the gardens. They exchanged glances but said nothing. Both of them pragmatic by nature, they were waiting to see what the new god could achieve.

'Eigon?' Jess's eyes refocused abruptly. 'What happened. Where were you?'

But the vision had gone. She was alone in a patch of deep shadow just beyond the Viale del Muro. Crossing out of the park, back over the bridge across the chasm made by the fast road circling outside the ancient wall she walked through the Pincian Gardens, past the famous water clock towards the belvedere which looked out from the height of the hill across Rome towards St Peter's and she gasped. Surely this was the view from the villa wall. Eigon's home had been somewhere like this, on a height above the city, looking west. The Pincian Hill. She remembered the name now. Eigon herself had mentioned it. In Eigon's day it would have been so different it was hard to visualise it, but the skyline would have been the same and where now there were churches, cupolas and domes there would have been marble temples. She stood for a long time staring out over the Piazza del Popolo below towards the distances, trying not to see the forest of aerials which sprouted from every rooftop, trying to fade out the two thousand intervening years. Giving up at last, she turned away and went to find a seat where she could rest in the shade of the plane trees and holm oaks, cedars and palm trees which filled the gardens. It was peaceful there in spite of the roar of traffic in the distance and she pulled out her sketchbook and opened it. If she had hoped the drawings and paintings would be miraculously restored she was disappointed. Sadly she looked at the portrait of Eigon with its angry slash. What message was she trying to convey?

The afternoon was very hot.

Where are you, Jess?

The voice seemed to be coming from somewhere very faraway. A man's voice. Dan. She shrank back, scouring the area round the trees. He couldn't be here.

You know I'll find you, don't you.

The mocking tone was carried on the warm breeze. Slowly she stood up, her eyes frantically probing the shadows, black in contrast to the dazzling sunlight.

'Dan?' Her own voice sounded flat by comparison. It hit the humid atmosphere as though it had been absorbed by damp rags and it disappeared without resonance.

Jess! He was further away.

'He's not here,' she murmured to herself. 'All I have to do is ignore him. He's thinking about me from far away. Playing with me. Messing with my head! It proves he doesn't know where I am.'

She sank down onto the parched grass under a tree and leaned back against the trunk, her arms wrapped around her legs. 'Leave me alone, you bastard!' She muttered the words under her breath. She closed her eyes tightly. 'Eigon? What happened? Where are you?'

There was no reply.

Opening her eyes again, she sighed. She shifted her weight against the tree and heard the slight rasp of stiff paper from her pocket. Groping for it she drew it out. She had forgotten all about Carmella's card.

Carmella lived in a small rooftop apartment in a narrow street off the Piazza di Spagna. Consulting her guidebook Jess retraced her route; running down the long sun-baked flight of the Spanish Steps she headed past the Fontana della Barcaccia towards the Via delle Carrozze. Ducking into the shade of the narrow street past bars and cafés, threading her way between scooters and parked cars she found Carmella's street of faded ochre and terracotta buildings and managed at last to locate the house. The entry phone admitted her at an ancient door, probably in itself a museum piece but covered in torn faded posters and there at the top of four exhausting flights of stairs she found Carmella waiting for her. She was ushered into a low-ceilinged, bright flat with stripped floors and shuttered windows looking on to the street far below.

Carmella's furnishings were an eclectic collection of bright artistic fringed and beaded comfort, the walls crammed with paintings, most donated by her artistic friends from the quarter, some good, some frankly crap, as she confided, ushering Jess past one riot of colour towards another. One of the windows opened out onto a small roof garden, a blaze of flowers and greenery in even more colourful ceramic and terracotta pots, with views across the rooftops towards the towers of Trinità dei Monti and round towards the Pincian Hill.

'I can't believe how pretty this is,' Jess exclaimed in delight as she was gently pushed towards a cushioned wrought iron chair shaded by potted ferns. Nearby a wind chime played a gentle ethereal sequence of notes in the almost non existent breeze.

Carmella smiled. 'It's better you've come here on your own. There are things we need to discuss alone, no?' She brought two glasses of white wine and a dish of olives, setting them down on the glass-topped table. Then she went back into the living room. She reappeared with a woven bag which she set on the floor between their chairs. 'My kit for *chiaroveggente*. Kim calls this clairvoyance. You have no word for it in English which is strange!'

'Fortune telling; seeing the future. Prediction. Second sight?' Jess said softly. 'I think we have many words as we do for everything.'

Carmella shrugged. 'OK. Well, my kit has my cards. My *sfera di cristallo*, the I ching, everything I need for *predizione del futuro*.'

Jess smiled. She felt safe for the first time in ages, relaxing back into her chair, strangely content to put herself and her future in Carmella's hands.

'I couldn't do this in front of the others. They mock these things. They do them for a side show.' Carmella leaned forward in her own chair and held out her hands for Jess's. 'Show me your *palmi*. We call this *la chiromanzia*.'

'Chiromancy. Palmistry.' Jess grinned.

Carmella took her hands in her own and stared at them for a long time, tracing lightly the lines with the little finger of her right hand. Jess waited in silence. She felt nervous suddenly.

At length Carmella let go of her hands. She sat back and smiled. 'Your hands tell me about you. For your friend Eigon I need *la sfera*. She produced a black velvet bundle from her bag and reverently unwrapped a crystal ball. It was some five inches in diameter, filled with strange occlusions and rainbows as she balanced it on a small padded ring on the table in front of her.

Jess gazed at it in awe. 'It moves as though it is alive.'

'It is. This was made hundreds of years ago. It was in my family for generations and my grandmother left it to me.' Carmella looked up and smiled. 'Don't tell Kim. She would tease me for this as well. This bag,' she gestured to where it lay at her feet, 'stays behind the sofa when Kim comes to see me. She knows only about the cards.'

She moved her hands gently across the surface of the crystal, cupping them against the sunlight. 'Normally I read the ball in the dark by candlelight, but today we need the sun.'

Jess was sitting on the edge of her seat watching closely. 'Why?'

'I want to throw light on the past, not dig in the shadows. Your Eigon wants to tell you her story. We do not have to spy on her.'

'And Dan?' It was a whisper.

'Dan is in your cards and again in your palm. And he is in your head.' Carmella looked up suddenly. 'He is, isn't he?'

Jess's eyes widened. She had said nothing about the voice in the park. 'You know I heard him?'

'You are a sensitive. It would be hard not to. His voice fills the space around you.' Carmella shivered. 'So. First, I will teach you to blank him out. Pouf! Like that!' She snapped her fingers. 'He is very afraid and a frightened animal is a dangerous animal, Jess. You have the power to ruin everything in his life and he is not acting with logic. He is in a panic.'

The two glasses of wine sat untouched on the table between them, condensation running down the stems in the heat of the afternoon to pool on the glass of the table. A wasp flew towards the dish of olives, hovered for a moment and then veered away.

Jess shivered.

'Eigon is here. You are both afraid. Both running away from a man,' Carmella said quietly. 'Listen to her first. Hear her story. Then we will go on.'

17

They had visited the goldsmith and again stayed longer than they should. It was growing late and darkness was nearly upon them as they made their way back to where they had left the horses. The gates were open and already the wagons and carts, banned during the daytime, were beginning to make their way into the city, increasing the noise and congestion tenfold. Flavius kept looking round, nervously scanning the crowds. He had a bad feeling about this. The whole area seemed too busy. The atmosphere everywhere was volatile and angry. He wasn't sure what was happening. The mob was gathering and this was not the time to be out in a public place, never mind with two vulnerable young women and a couple of unarmed slaves. He had grown careless, bringing them out on these excursions, each time wondering if it was safe to let Eigon wander the streets against her mother's wishes. But nothing had happened. Time had passed. Four years of study for her which had been hard. She deserved her excursions. And they gave him plenty of time to spend with Julia. No one had ever approached them though several times he had had the feeling they were watched. Wordlessly he moved closer to them. He strained his ears to try and hear what people were talking about. The Emperor. The young Emperor and his friends were out in the streets again, fighting and carousing and causing chaos as they taunted the mob. Cursing silently, Flavius hurried his charges on, dodging through gaps in the crowds. Then almost in front of them they saw a fight break out. A dozen young men surged towards them, shouting. The leader seemed to be looking straight at them. Flavius's blood ran cold. They were heading for the girls. Grabbing Eigon's arm he dragged her off the road, looking round frantically for an escape route. Behind him the slave Demitrius had seized Julia's hand. They huddled together as they ran and behind them the young men changed course after them with a shout of anger.

'Fend them off!' Flavius screamed at the second slave, Vulpius. 'Give us a moment's start!' The mouth of a dark alleyway opened up near them. Flavius headed for it desperately, shoving the girls into the shadows as the gang of youths reached Vulpius and pushed him out of the way. Behind them more men were surging in their direction. Shouts turned to screams. Someone grabbed a flaming torch and pushed it into the faces of the combatants; someone else set about them with his fists and Flavius found himself forcing his way back to Vulpius's side. 'Run!' he shouted over his shoulder. 'Run, now!'

Terrified, Julia and Eigon shrank away into the darkness. They stopped, transfixed with terror. 'We can't go without Flavius!' Julia cried. 'Go on. Run. I'll wait for him.' Vulpius had gone down. For an instant Flavius saw the man's anguished face beneath a scrum of heaving bodies, then it was gone. He couldn't even see where he was. Desperately he tried to fight his way back out of the crowd, away from the angry flying fists, his nose running with blood. Then Julia was there. Behind them the crowd bayed as someone else fell to the ground. Julia clutched at Flavius's arm and dragged him into the shadows. 'This way! Quick!'

'But Vulpius! We can't leave him!'

'We have to. There's nothing we can do!' It was Demitrius who took the lead. 'This way. They won't follow us in the dark, they're too interested in the fight.'

Somehow they had ducked away from the crowds into a narrow cut between two buildings then on down another alleyway, doubling back away from the Forum. Eigon reached for Julia's hand. Behind her Flavius pounded at their heels, glancing over his shoulder. In seconds they had left the noise behind. When at last they stopped they were gasping for breath.

Flavius wiped his nose on the edge of his sleeve. 'Are you all right? Did you see what happened? Someone had a knife. What on earth was that all about?' He put his arm protectively around Julia's shoulders. 'Come on. If we go this way we can work our way round the back to the horses. I've got to get you out of here!' He glanced behind him again.

'What do we do about Vulpius?' Eigon cried. 'We can't abandon him.'

'We can't help him, either. I'll get you home, then Demitrius and I'll come back and look for him.' Flavius wiped the blood from his face again. 'This way. We'll try and work our way through the backstreets.' He thought they were in the Subura area now, rough even in daylight. He cursed under his breath, looking round. If they could head eastwards up the Esqualine Hill it would be safer there.

It was not long before they realised that they were completely lost.

'We've been down this alley before, Flavius.' Demitrius gestured at a house sign. 'At the sign of three goblets.'

Eigon nodded. They were all panting. 'He's right. I can't hear the crowds any more either in the distance. It's almost too quiet.'

Huddling together they looked round at the crowded buildings. The lane was barely more than the width of a man's outstretched arms. The sky was a narrow strip of stars between the uneven roofs.

'So, what do you suggest?' Flavius tried to steady his breath. He wiped his nose again, trying to hide his growing unease. He was responsible for these two girls, they were already late, he had brought them to hideous danger and they were all hopelessly lost in an area of slums and brothels to which he would never have exposed them even in daylight with an armed escort of the Praetorian guard.

There was a burst of shouting suddenly from the end of the street. A crowd of figures appeared in the distance wielding torches, baying like hunting dogs.

'I don't believe it. They can't have followed us! Come on. Round the corner so they can't see us.' Flavius set off at a run. The others pounded after him ducking down another even narrower alley into total darkness. Demitrius crept forward ahead of them, his eyes like a cat's in the dark. 'This is a dead end.' He paused and turned to face them. 'We're trapped.'

'Keep quiet then,' Flavius murmured through gritted teeth. 'Maybe they won't see us.'

'Did they go down here?' a voice called behind them, echoing between the buildings and for an instant they saw a figure silhouetted against the flame as someone held a torch up high above his head. The light ran up the walls. It almost reached them as they cowered into the shadows, but not quite. 'Where are they, did you see? We can't go back without her. We have to find her or our lives won't be worth living! I saw people running away.

They must have gone down here.' He was heading down the alley after them, the torch held high above his head when a shout from the main street stopped him in his tracks. 'This way! We've spotted them. Come on!'

The figure hesitated. Eigon and Julia were holding their breath. Eigon could feel herself trembling. 'I don't think so,' the man went on. His voice was quieter now, projected in their direction. He held his torch even higher. 'I think there is a band of frightened little mice hiding up this passageway, and I think I'm going to catch them!'

Julia gave a moan of fright. There was nowhere to go. They pressed themselves further into the shadows. Eigon could feel the unyielding stone against her shoulder-blades, then level with her hip a smooth colder protuberance from the wall. It was a ring. Turning with a little gasp of hope she fumbled at it and found a door handle. Desperately she grabbed at it and turned it and behind them a small wooden door creaked open. In seconds they were through it, pushing it closed behind them over rough paving stones which caught on the wood.

'Is there a bolt?' Eigon scrabbled desperately at the back of the door in the darkness. 'Help me! I can't find one. It won't close properly.' She felt a hand cover hers, then rough fingers gripped the handle as Demitrius put his shoulder to the wood. A bolt rasped into place and the door was secure.

'Thank the gods,' she sobbed as Julia clutched her arm and the two girls clung together, turning to survey the darkness around them. It was hard to see anything, but from the cool air and the sound of running water and the scent of flowers they seemed to be in a small garden. On the far side of the wall they heard shouting. It was followed by a volley of thuds and crashes as someone tried to force the door open. A stream of obscenities echoed over the high wall.

'Greetings, friends.' Another door had opened suddenly behind them. Light flooded into the garden and they stood blinking as a figure appeared in the doorway at the top of a steep flight of steps leading up towards a house, a torch in his hand, the flame streaming sideways in the draught. 'I gather you are in need of sanctuary. Please come up.'

The four of them climbed the steps and found themselves in another world. It seemed they had climbed out of the slums and into an area on the higher slopes of the hill which housed a world of calm wealth and elegance. They trooped into the house and stood huddled together as their rescuer closed the doors behind them and locked them. He was tall and dark-haired, with a thin aesthetic face, perhaps a year or two older than Flavius and far better looking. 'Grandfather, it seems we have guests.'

As their eyes grew used to the lamplight they realised that an elderly man was sitting at the end of a long table in the room to which they had been led. Various maps and scrolls were spread out before him, a goblet of wine at his elbow.

Felicius Marinus Publius nodded at them graciously as though dishevelled, frightened visitors frequently arrived in the middle of the night via his besieged garden. 'How delightful. Please, come and sit down.' In one movement he had gathered all the documents together and swept them into an untidy pile and taken in the condition of the newcomers. 'Julius, my boy, one of these men is hurt. Will you call Antonia to bathe his face? And these young ladies seem distressed. What's happened?' Suddenly he became alarmed.

'It was kind of your grandson to let us in. He saved our lives.' Eigon stepped forward as Julia and Flavius both looked at her and she realised suddenly that even though Julia had instigated their excursion and Flavius had organised it, now at least she was the designated leader of this bedraggled party. 'Please don't be alarmed. We were going home from the city when some sort of riot developed. A group of men were fighting and they started chasing us.' She paused. They were chasing *her*. The realisation made her blanch. She bit her lip and ploughed on with the story. 'We tried to dodge them and we lost our way. I don't know what we would have done if your door hadn't opened. I think they would have killed us.' She tried to steady her voice, overcome with weariness and fear. 'One of our number, our slave, Vulpius, was caught by them . . .' Her explanation trailed away miserably into silence.

Julius frowned. 'The door should not have been unlocked. It seems that God was on your side. We'll send out a search party for your slave tomorrow – I fear it is unlikely anyone will find him now in the dark and with the streets so full of people.'

Eigon glanced at him gratefully. 'We were foolish to be out so late. All because Julia couldn't decide which bangle she wanted to buy!'

216

There was a trace of sharpness in her voice. She had already noticed that the younger man's gaze was turning almost involuntarily towards her friend and she watched as at her words he glanced towards Julia again. What was it that Julia did to so effortlessly attract men's gaze? And why did she care? Cross with herself at so unworthy a thought at such an inappropriate time, she was completely unaware of the coquettish little toss to her head which she gave or that the movement had caught the eye of the handsome Julius as he turned his attention thoughtfully back to her.

It was only a short time before food and wine had appeared and Flavius's face had been attended to by Julius's sister, Antonia, who had brought towels and a basin of warm water. At his protest she smiled. 'Who else would attend you but me?'

'Ask a slave, please, don't dirty your hands, lady –'

She grinned impishly. 'I would trust no one to do this but one of us and you would fare better at my hands than those of my clumsy brother or a servant, I assure you!'

Julius grinned broadly. They were clearly fond of each other and it was he who took away the bowl and towels. As they all approached the table a few minutes later Demitrius hung back. 'Perhaps I should join your slaves, sir,' he mumbled. 'It is not appropriate that I sit here.'

The old man frowned. 'If that is your wish. But I feel that as you have shared your experience with the others and risked your life with them, it is right that you should share food with them now. Do you not agree?' He fixed his gaze on Eigon's face.

She nodded. 'Demitrius has been very brave.'

'They are worried, Grandfather, about another member of their party. Vulpius was separated from them in the riot,' Julius reminded him. He smiled at Eigon. 'I suggested that there is nothing we can do while it is still dark.'

The old man looked concerned. 'Then we will pray for him. Please, come to the table.'

As they took their places the old man raised his hand for silence. 'We should give thanks to God for the food and drink set here before us and for your safe delivery, my friends, in the name of Our Lord Jesus Christ, and we pray that your companion Vulpius is delivered safely back to you.'

There was a brief moment of silence. Julia and Eigon exchanged

217

glances. Flavius frowned. He leaned forward. 'You are Christians, sir? My father has spoken about people like you.' He broke off abruptly and looked down at his plate, embarrassed by his own tone.

'And not very complimentarily, obviously, if your expression is anything to go by, young man,' Julius's grandfather chuckled. 'Have no fear, we are not going to proselytise. Nor will we make you a human sacrifice as I believe you may suspect. Eat. Enjoy. Then our servants will escort you safely home.'

As the evening progressed however the sound of rioting in the streets surged closer. Several times they heard banging on the door as the mob poured down the street outside and once Eigon was sure she heard her own name called. She shuddered and glanced round. The others appeared to have heard nothing beyond the general noise but slowly one by one they set down their knives and spoons and nervously pushed the food away.

'You can't let them go out tonight, Grandfather,' Antonia said at last. 'They must stay. The crowds will grow tired of all this in the end. They'll disperse as daylight comes. It will be safer then and perhaps we'll find out what all this is about.'

'I agree.' The old man nodded. 'Please, be our guests. We have plenty of room. Antonia, my dear, take the young ladies and see that they are made comfortable.'

The two rooms they were given led off the peristyle. Exclaiming in delight they settled in, the lamplight flickering on painted walls and mosaic floors, examining ivory combs and soft towels.

Eigon was standing staring down into the basin of warm water that a young woman servant had brought her to wash in when there was a quick knock at her door. It was Antonia. 'I came to see if you have all you need.' She smiled. Tall and slender, very like her brother in looks, she had sent Eigon several friendly glances as the evening progressed and had seemed fascinated by all Eigon had to say. 'May I come in and talk or are you too tired?'

Eigon beckoned her inside and closed the door softly. 'I don't know what we would have done without your help. We are so grateful.'

Antonia sat down on the edge of the bed. 'One of our servants has been out on the streets to try and find out what is going on. The Emperor gave one of his concerts and then got drunk with his friends. Somehow a riot started, but it is quieter now.' She

studied Eigon's face for a moment. 'The mob is always mindless.'
She shivered. 'But you were afraid of something other than the
mob. You thought someone was after you personally, didn't you?'

Eigon looked up in astonishment. 'How did you know that?'

Antonia shook her head. 'I was watching you. You didn't seem
surprised at what happened.'

'They were calling my name. They knew I was in here. No one
else noticed.'

'Do you know why anyone should do such a thing?' Antonia
asked gently.

Eigon shrugged. 'I do, yes. But it's a long story –' She looked
away. 'Maybe not for tonight.'

'I understand. It's none of my business.' Antonia didn't seem
upset. 'I just hope your family aren't going to be too worried.
Would you like a messenger to be sent –'

Eigon shook her head. 'We are not supposed to be out at all.
It may be that they haven't noticed that we've gone. My father
isn't well. Sometimes my mother goes for days without speaking
to me or even registering that I'm there.'

'How sad.'

Eigon nodded. 'My tutor will notice, but he will check and
realise that Julia and Flavius aren't there and guess we've got
caught up in this trouble.'

Antonia's eyebrow shot up. 'How old are you? You seem too
old to have a tutor. I gave up studies as soon as I could.'

Eigon laughed. 'I think I'm about fourteen or fifteen. I'm not
sure.' She shrugged. 'Am I too old? Melinus says one can remain
a student all one's life. I enjoy my studies.'

'That sounds very serious.' Antonia made a face.

'Not all the time. That's why Julia and I came into town. We
were shopping.'

'Even so. Where do you live?'

Eigon told her and Antonia seemed impressed. 'I thought that
was an Imperial villa.'

'It did belong to the old emperor. He saved our lives. He gave
us the house.'

'Why?'

'My father was – is – a king in our own land. He was captured
and we were brought to Rome to be paraded and killed but the
Emperor spared us. It's a long time ago now.'

Antonia shivered. 'It is a cruel world we live in.' She sighed. 'You must have been so scared.'

Eigon nodded. 'But Claudius was good to us. And so far the Emperor Nero has left us alone.'

Antonia shook her head. 'He seems a very wild young man. Hence his enthusiastic part in the riots tonight!' She sighed. 'But while Seneca and Burrus rule for him, while he amuses himself, Rome is relatively safe. They are sensible men and in a few days everyone will have forgotten all about the riot and Rome will have calmed down again.'

'He seems foolish in the extreme!' Eigon was still in shock. 'Aelius, that's our steward, tells us that the mob are always coming up with rumours and horror stories about him.' She bit her lip. The events of the night had shocked and frightened her.

Antonia put her head on one side. 'What land was it where your father was king?'

'We lived in the Pretannic Isles. Claudius calls it – called,' she corrected herself, 'Britannia. My father was – is – king of the Catuvellauni and the Silures, which was my mother's tribe. Our tribes had the bravest warriors and the land was beautiful beyond dreams. I sit sometimes and conjure up the memories. Gentle green hills and forests and cattle and sheep and beautiful ponies and dogs. And soft wooden houses with rounded walls and thatched roofs. We never went to cities like Rome. Perhaps there were none. Camulodunum was the largest I saw there, but that was a village compared with Rome.' She edged round to study Antonia. 'And you. Where do you come from?'

'My grandfather's family have lived in Rome for many years Our mother and father died several years ago when a fever swept through the hills around the summer villa where we were staying.' Antonia gazed down sadly at her folded hands. 'Julius and I came to live here with Grandfather who is a senator.'

'And what are Christians?' Eigon asked. 'Flavius seemed to know, but I haven't heard of them, I'm sorry.'

'We are followers of Christ. God's own son, Jesus Christ, became a man. He lived amongst the Jews in Judea and taught and healed and the Roman governor, Pontius Pilate, sentenced him to be crucified. He wasn't as lucky as your father. He was killed. But then God woke him up and he is alive again, in heaven.'

Eigon frowned. 'He is one of your Roman gods then?'

220

Antonia shook her head. 'There is only one God. That's the point. The Roman gods are not true gods. And neither is the Emperor.'

'Something one should not dare to say out loud!' Eigon raised an eyebrow. 'And our gods from Britannia?'

Antonia shrugged. 'The same, I suppose. We are taught that perhaps,' she tried to soften the remark with an apologetic smile, 'the old gods were angels. Servants, messengers of God.'

Eigon sighed. 'Melinus would not agree.' Or would he? She wasn't sure. He had never mentioned Christians to her.

'Who is Melinus?'

'My tutor. He is a Druid.' Eigon laughed at the look of incomprehension on Antonia's face. 'What you would call a priest and a philosopher. A learned man.'

'And he came with your father as a prisoner?'

Eigon shook her head. 'Another long story, I'm afraid.' How could she tell her new friend that Melinus was a slave? They had already gathered that their host had given all his slaves their freedom. As freedmen and women they still worked for him but that was their choice and they were paid for their work.

Behind them the door opened and Julia stood there wrapped in a shawl. 'I thought I heard talking. Aren't you two tired?' She yawned as though to underline the point.

'You are right.' Antonia stood up. 'I'm sorry. It was thoughtless of me to keep you awake. We will talk some more in the morning. Goodnight.'

They watched as she hurried down the peristyle and out of sight. 'Did I interrupt something?' Julia plumped down on the bed beside Eigon.

Eigon shook her head. 'We were talking about the gods.'

Julia looked incredulous. 'Why weren't you talking about her dishy brother? Is he spoken for?'

Eigon laughed. 'Julia!'

'We must find out. First thing in the morning. Then I shall ask my aunt to introduce us to the family formally. I think he would make a very good husband, don't you?'

'For me?' Eigon could feel herself blushing.

'No, you idiot. For me!'

* * *

221

The rooftop garden had grown dark. Jess stretched out on the chair with a groan.

'Ah, at last you are awake!' Carmella appeared in the doorway. 'I rang Kim in case she was worried about where you were and I told her you were going to stay for supper with me.' She put a glass down in front of Jess with a chink of ice cubes. 'Campari. Now, the story goes on for Eigon,' she smiled. 'but we need to sort you out. To keep Dan out of your head.'

Jess could see a spread of cards lying on the table. It had not been there before. 'Have you been doing another reading?'

Carmella nodded. 'And I saw him in the *sfera di cristallo* He is nearby.' As was that other listener who she sensed stirring whenever she looked into the cards for Jess. It was another woman; another reader of the inner pathways. But who was she and how did she fit in to this story? Carmella didn't know.

'So, Dan is in Rome.'

Carmella nodded. 'Of course. Where did you think he was?'

'He told us he had gone back to England, but I didn't believe him.'

'You're right, he is here. And very near.' Carmella glanced up at her. 'I am sorry, Jess, but he does not mean you well. And there is something strange about him now I have had the chance to watch him closely. There is another man – a vicious man – inside his head. If I were to guess, I would say he was possessed.' Her face was full of concern. 'This other man feeds off Dan's hatred and fear.'

Jess stared at her. 'Another man?' She couldn't take this in.

Carmella nodded. 'A dead man, Jess. You do understand. A ghost.'

'Oh my God!' Jess felt herself grow cold. 'Do you know who?' Her mouth had gone dry.

Carmella shrugged. 'I do not see him as a face. Just a shadow. But I feel the cold of his grip. He is an evil man. And I fear they are plotting terrible, irrational things. Something dreadful is going to happen, Jess!'

'What do I do?' Jess whispered.

'You must avoid Dan.' Carmella held her gaze for a moment. 'Do not let him find you. Why he lets this other man into his soul I do not know. Perhaps he doesn't know it has happened. I will teach you to fight him off psychically, but better you do not let him come near you. I am afraid of what he may try and do.'

Jess shivered. She nodded bleakly. 'You don't have to tell me to be afraid of him. I am terrified. And you are sure he is here in Rome still?'

Carmella nodded.

'Then you must help me convince the others. They will not believe me. They think I'm mad.'

It was well after midnight when Carmella led the way downstairs and guided Jess to her car. 'I will not let you walk at this time of night alone. Not with someone like him around.' She unlocked the neat maroon and silver Smart car, which had been parked nose to the wall in the next street, behind a rank of overflowing rubbish bins. 'It will only take us a few minutes to reach Kim's.'

They roared through warm streets, ducking and weaving with terrifying speed past floodlit piazzas and fountains, busy bistros and trattorias, drawing to a halt at last outside the palazzo. 'Take care, *cara mia*, and remember what I have taught you.' Carmella leaned across to plant a kiss on each of Jess's cheeks. She unlatched Jess's door and pushed it open. 'See you soon, OK? *Ciao!*'

She waited, her foot toying with the accelerator as Jess climbed out and made her way across the street. As soon as the front door was open, Carmella let in the clutch and with a wave roared away.

Jess closed the door behind her and stood for a moment in the vestibule listening to the silence of the old building settling around her. She was exhausted. It seemed to have been a very long time since she had left the building that morning. Heading across the marble-floored hall towards the staircase she was about to start up towards Kim's front door when a figure stepped out of the darkness. 'Good evening, Jess. I thought you were never going to come home.'

She spun round. 'Dan!'

'The very same. You've become an elusive woman lately. Strange when you think how pleased you used to be to see me.' He smiled.

She stared at him. He was unshaven and unwashed. She could smell his sweat from several paces away. 'Dan, I thought you had gone back to Nat.'

'I have.' He grinned. 'I think you will find that everyone knows I am in England with her and the kids.' He took a step towards her.

'Where did you get the key?'

'Same place you did, I expect.' He paused and folded his arms. 'Kim seems to keep dozens of spares in the kitchen. She is too generous by half when it comes to giving her guests free access to her apartment. I bet she doesn't even know how many she's got. Not that I took them for long. I copied them and then put them back so there won't be any missing.'

'And what are you planning to do now?' Her heart was hammering with terror, the palms of her hands clammy. She reached out to the bottom of the heavy swirl of banisters which led up to the first floor, steadying herself.

He smiled coldly. 'To tell you the truth I am not sure.'

'I could scream.'

'You could. But I doubt if anyone would hear. Not even Sir Galahad. I saw you and Will together, you know. You still love him, don't you? You hate me and you love that stupid, ineffectual prat! Well, he can't save you; no one is going to hear if you scream. The apartments on this floor are all empty for the summer and Jacopo is probably drunk and fast asleep. Even if they heard you upstairs, by the time they came it would be too late.'

'What do you mean, too late?' Her mouth was dry.

He laughed. 'What indeed? Maybe you would already be lying dead on the floor, robbed, mugged and murdered in this oh-so-dangerous city. Or maybe you would tell them that Dan was here and attacked and threatened you even though nothing actually happened and even though they know he is in England and can prove it. They would shake their heads and look at each other and sigh. Poor Jess. Imagining things again.'

'You are enjoying this insane game of yours.' She was clutching the newel post as though her life depended on it.

'Indeed.' He smiled. 'If you threaten to ruin my life, Jess, you can expect no less.'

'I have told you I don't intend to ruin your life.'

'But it is going to happen. You've told Will, haven't you? Did he believe you? He's besotted enough to. Some time, somewhere, it will get out. You will always hold it over me and for the rest of my life you will have power over my destiny.'

'I won't –'

'Oh, I think you will, Jess. And I can't allow that, can I?' He stepped towards her, his hand outstretched.

With a cry of fear she turned to flee up the stairs just as with a rattle of keys in the lock someone began to push open the heavy front door behind them.

Dan swung round. Not waiting to see who was coming in, he dived towards the door, elbowed the newcomer aside and fled into the street.

A flood of Italian invective echoed round the hall as Jacopo staggered in. '*Che cosa*?' He stared round blearily. '*Signora*?' The front door hung open. Dan had disappeared into the night. The old man pushed the door closed. He could barely stand.

Jess took a deep breath. Trying to steady the thunderous beat of her pulse in her ears she turned back to the staircase. '*Buonanotte*, Jacopo!' she called back slowly. He was shuffling across the floor towards the doorway in the corner that led into his own quarters and didn't hear her.

Somehow she managed to haul herself up the stairs and let herself into the apartment, locking the door behind her. The flat was in darkness. They hadn't waited up. She stood for several seconds staring at the back of the door and finally found the bolt. Drawing it across she made for her bedroom.

She was halfway across the room when the bedside light came on and Will sat up in the bed. 'Jesus, Jess!'

'Oh God!' Jess stood still, her heart thudding with fright. 'Oh Will, I'm so sorry. I forgot we'd changed rooms.'

He grinned, running his hands through his hair. 'Don't worry about it. Are you OK?' Concern registered on his face as saw how white she was.

'Dan was downstairs. Inside. He's copied Kim's keys.' She sank down on the chair by the table.

'Shit.' Will climbed out of bed. He was naked. She smiled wanly as he turned and with his back to her hauled on a pair of jeans.

'Where is he now?' he asked as he dragged a T-shirt over his head, turning back to her.

'I don't know. Thank God the concierge came home. Dan pushed past him and ran for it. He's long gone now. He's been living rough as far as I can see. He stinks and he hasn't shaved and he's convinced you all think he's back in England with Nat and that you all think I'm mad.' She rubbed her face with her hands wearily. 'Perhaps I am mad. What am I going to do, Will?'

Will sat down on the end of the bed. 'Perhaps you are the one who should go back to England. Leave him playing his little games here.'

She stared at him. 'But what about Eigon?'

He sighed. 'What about Eigon, Jess? You saw her in Wales. No doubt you can go on with your research or whatever you call it there.' He shook his head. 'Is she really that important? Compared with your safety?'

She nodded. 'Yes, she is. I can't explain it, but that's the way it is. I don't want to go home, Will. Not yet.'

He sighed again. 'Well, the important thing is, you're safe now. Go to bed, Jess. We'll discuss this in the morning, OK?'

'He said you wouldn't believe me if I told you I'd seen him.'

'I believe you.'

She nodded miserably. Turning towards the door she glanced over her shoulder. 'Thanks for being here, Will.'

'My pleasure!'

'See you in the morning.'

He nodded.

As the door closed behind her he wandered over to the window and stood staring thoughtfully out into the darkness.

In the garden a figure stood staring back, though Will couldn't see him in the deep shadows. Dan's eyes narrowed in anger at the sight of him silhouetted against the light. So, the bastard was even sharing her bedroom again. He swore under his breath and then on tiptoe, turned for the gate. Carefully locking it behind him, he ducked through the alleyway and crept back towards the street. He paused. Then a small grim smile strayed across his lips. He turned and retraced his steps into the garden. Tiptoeing across the lawns and gravel paths he made his way to the flower-bed below Jess's window and bent to look for the ladder.

No one in the villa expected the agitated arrival of Aelius that morning as they settled on the chairs with Cerys to sit by the fountain in the warm October sunshine. The man had hovered for a second respectfully by the door, still wondering what he should tell them, then, too upset to wait to be called forward he came to stand behind Caratacus.

'The two young ladies went out yesterday, my lord.' He wrung his hands in consternation. 'They did not return last night.'

Caratacus stared up at his steward, his face blanching. 'What do you mean they went out?'

'They wanted to go to the silk stalls at the market and then on to the goldsmith who lives behind the Via Sacra.' He glanced at Pomponia. 'My son Flavius escorted them with two slaves. They should have been perfectly safe.' They had all heard about the rioting overnight.

Cerys let out a wail of fear. She jumped to her feet. 'Eigon should not have left the villa. She knows she must never go outside!'

'There is no need for despair, lady.' Melinus stepped forward. 'I am sure they are safe.'

Pomponia who had arrived early with a new scroll for Caratacus to read, scowled. 'Julia is a scatterbrain! She knows Eigon is not to go outside without a proper escort! But she is also resourceful.' Clearly. To have circumvented Cerys's clear instructions. 'Perhaps they decided to stay somewhere overnight. Flavius is a sensible young man. When he saw there was trouble in the streets I am sure he would have seen to it that they were safe.'

'They might have stayed at your house,' Caratacus said thoughtfully. He looked up at her with a ray of hope. 'It is far closer to the centre of the city.'

Their guest shook her head. 'Alas, no. We have just come from home. They were not there.'

'Then we have no option but to send out a search party,' Caratacus said. His face was growing more pinched by the minute, his voice weakening as he used up the last of his strength. 'See to it, Aelius.'

'Sir!' Aelius retreated.

'Stop crying, Cerys!' Caratacus ordered. He glared balefully at his wife. 'I've never understood your reluctance to let Eigon go outside in the first place, and this is the direct result of your prohibition. It's all your fault. She felt she had to go secretly and she's gone without a proper escort. Aelius will pay for this dearly! He had no business to let this happen!'

Cerys gazed at her husband tearfully. She could neither tell him the reason, nor ever explain the full extent of the danger. No one knew the secret she shared with Eigon and no one ever would.

But that meant that no one else knew that out there somewhere in the city was a man whose vowed aim was to kill their daughter. She shuddered. She and Eigon had never discussed the threat since that very first day in the villa all those years ago and yet she knew it was still there. She could feel it. Eyes watching them, waiting, a cat beside a mousehole, biding its time with infinite patience. Why the man had waited for so long she couldn't guess, but somehow she knew that he was still out there somewhere, watching.

The small bedraggled party was escorted back to the villa later that morning by Julius Marinus Publius and a group of his grandfather's servants and after due thanks and gratitude were expressed and their rescuers had departed, they faced the combined wrath of Cerys and Caratacus. Julia retreated to her bedroom and closed the door firmly to wait until things had blown over.

Eigon was still with her mother trying desperately to still the storm of tears and anger when one of the household slaves came and sought out Aelius. They had found Vulpius's body in the orchard. His throat has been cut and his body thrown over the wall.

Aelius stood looking down at it in horror then he called his son, tight-lipped with rage. 'How many times have you taken Princess Eigon and Lady Julia out into the city?' he asked.

'Often, Father. There has never been any danger. No one has ever threatened us. We were perfectly safe.' Flavius was white as a sheet.

'This is a warning,' Aelius breathed quietly. His fists were clenched. 'They knew where he came from. Whoever did this is watching this house.'

'But why, Father?' Flavius was trying hard not to show his fear. 'The riot had nothing to do with us. The mob is always rioting about something or other! The Emperor and his friends were winding them up again!'

'Quiet, stupid boy!' His father glanced over his shoulder even though they were alone in the orchard now. The body had been taken away. 'Don't let me hear you say anything like that out loud again. Walls have ears.'

Flavius bit his lip. The sight of the dead man had horrified him more than he dared admit to anyone, even himself. 'Surely the likely reason they targeted us is that someone saw us coming away from the goldsmith's and thought we might have something worth stealing. That's why they attacked us. Poor Vulpius had nothing on him to steal.'

Aelius scowled. It was possible that his son was right. But it was also possible that there was something more to this. For a start, how did they know where Vulpius came from? The man was a slave. He had nothing on him to identify him at all. This household did not require its slaves to wear tags with their address and owner's name. Had he been tortured, he wondered, to give information to his killers, and if so, what information did they want? He sighed. To all intents and purposes this villa belonged to Caratacus who was the head of the household and treated with all the deference offered to a great man. But the fact remained that he was also, though no one seemed to remember it, more or less a prisoner. Nobody, not even Aelius's wife or his son knew that Aelius had been ordered, when they had first come to the villa, to spy on the king. He turned away thoughtfully and began to walk slowly back towards the house, his son trailing miserably behind him. A sick and acquiescent man was no danger to the Emperor. But if anything in Caratacus's demeanour changed, then Claudius had wanted to be the first to know about it and no doubt Nero's advisers would also.

'What did you say to your mother?' Julia appeared the moment Eigon was alone.

'Just that we wanted to visit the goldsmith.'

'Was she angry?'

'Yes, she was angry.' Eigon looked utterly deflated. Angry didn't even begin to cover her mother's reaction to everything that had happened. Or the news that her daughter had been defying her orders for so long. The news of the death of one of the slaves had been kept from Caratacus who was feverish again and had taken to his bed, but Cerys, after reining in her emotions with such strength in front of her husband had let fly at her daughter the moment they were alone again. 'I am going to send Julia away!' she shouted. 'She has been nothing but a bad influence on you. How could you be so thoughtless and stupid? Does your own safety mean nothing to you?'

'But Mam, nothing has ever happened to me!'

'I forbid you to set foot outside this house again, do you hear? Not even the orchard. There are people outside the walls spying on us. Criminals. Who knows in whose pay they are.' Suddenly she was sobbing, and Eigon had put her arms around her. 'Hush, Mam, don't cry. I'm sorry to worry you so. And I won't go again, I promise.'

A quiet knock sounded on the half-open door and Cerys pushed Eigon away. Their moment together was over.

'My lady?' It was Melinus. 'I have been looking for Eigon. It is time for her lessons.' It was a rescue of sorts.

'Of course.' Cerys sniffed, straightening her shoulders. 'Go with him, Eigon. But remember what I've said.'

Eigon followed her tutor outside, biting her lip. He glanced at her, raising an eyebrow as they seated themselves at the table they had commandeered so long ago for their studies. As the evenings drew in and grew colder they did not work late in the garden any more. 'So, what really happened?' His voice was gentle but his eyes were stern.

She told him everything. When she had finished he sat back thoughtfully and for several heartbeats said nothing. When at last he did it was the last thing she expected.

'How strange that you should have been given shelter by Christians. The Lady Pomponia Graecina and I have been to several Christian meetings. We listened to their teacher, Peter.'

Eigon stared at him, astonished. 'But surely you don't believe in their god? Just one god, when we know that there are gods of every river and mountain and forest.'

He shook his head slowly. 'Their god, who I think is the god of the Jews in a gentler form, is a powerful god and Peter himself impressed me with his learning and his eloquence. There is much there to think about. He knew this Jesus and travelled with him and was his friend. I would like to speak to these people you met myself one day, but for the time being be content that they are kind and hospitable. You could have chosen no one better to look after you.'

She frowned. 'We were saved, but we caused the death of a man.'

'No, princess; the man who killed Vulpius is responsible for his death. But he died in your service and so should be remembered with honour.' He sighed. His intuition told him there was more to this killing than an attempted robbery or even mob violence. The whole villa knew by now that the body had been thrown over the wall and all guessed that it was a message. But to whom, and why? Pulling a pile of scrolls before him he resolved to concentrate on the matter in hand. Eigon needed the distraction. He hated to see how haunted she looked. Whatever he said she was going to blame herself for this death, whilst the flibbertigibbet, Julia, would probably give it not another thought.

Will tensed as something moved in the gardens below, catching his eye. He moved sideways behind the half-open shutters and peered down. Was there still someone out there? Crossing the room in two strides he snapped off the light and tiptoed back to the window. At first he could see nothing in the darkness, then he saw the figure almost immediately below on the gravel path. He could see the pale moon of a face as it looked up, too indistinct to make out the features but he was certain it was Dan. Who else would it be? The face disappeared and the figure foreshortened suddenly. He was bending over, looking for something – the ladder Jess said was hidden there? Will smiled grimly. If he was coming up to the window he was in for an unpleasant shock. He waited silently. Nothing happened. Cautiously he looked out again. The figure had moved. He heard the rustle of dead leaves and a muttered curse and suddenly he guessed what had happened. Someone had moved the ladder. In which case, perhaps it was time he went downstairs and had a word with Dan himself.

Slipping on his shoes he let himself out of the room, closing the door silently after him. He glanced towards Jess's room. All was quiet. Good. What he needed to say to Dan was best said without her there. Clenching his fists he headed towards the apartment front door, let himself out and padded down the main staircase on silent rubber soles. This much at least perhaps he could do for Jess.

The street had grown quiet. Glancing both ways Will set off along the wall, guessing the entrance to the garden must be along there somewhere. When he reached the corner he paused and edged cautiously forward to glance round into the pitch dark chasm which was the alleyway between the two tall buildings. He could see nothing. He listened. Was that the faintest squeak of a rusty hinge? He edged closer. There would be a gate at the far end of the alley. Had Dan come through it? Was he too waiting and listening? He held his breath.

Nothing. All he could hear was the beat of his own heart. There! Was that someone moving? A cautious footstep heading up the alleyway towards him?

He tensed, ready. It had stopped again. He moved closer to the corner. One inch further and he could see round.

And suddenly there was an explosion of movement. It seemed to come from behind him, then from all around. An arm clamped round his neck and he heard a breathless gasp. 'So, Sir Galahad, you thought I couldn't see you, eh?' The grip tightened and Will felt himself swept with blind rage. He was the fit one, the sportsman and yet he was impotent. He couldn't breathe. He felt his neck wrench backwards and for an instant he saw Dan's face an inch from his own. 'What were you going to do, Will? Save her reputation? Her life?' Dan laughed. 'Make the noble sacrifice?' He angled his arm higher. Will was beginning to see stars. He clawed desperately at Dan's arm when suddenly everything went black.

18

Jess woke abruptly and lay staring at the ceiling. It was already daylight and the roar of traffic outside was building. The smell of coffee was drifting through the apartment. Reluctantly she climbed out of bed and headed for the shower.

Kim and Steph were in the kitchen. Someone had already poured her a coffee when she appeared at last. 'Dan was here last night,' she said. 'He was downstairs waiting for me when I got home.'

'What happened?' Steph whispered. She and Kim were staring at her.

'He threatened me. Luckily Jacopo came back and he ran off. Then I saw him in the garden. Will saw him too, I forgot we changed rooms and woke him up.'

Steph grinned. 'Poor old Will. Well, it proves Dan is still around. I wonder where he is staying.'

'What did Carmella say? Did she mention him?' Steph asked.

'She was helpful.'

'And?' Steph raised an eyebrow.

'She thinks I should stay and fight him. Stop being afraid.'

'Sounds good.' Kim nodded approval.

'But Will thinks I should go back to England. Leave Dan here, thinking I'm still around.'

Steph and Kim glanced at each other. 'If he's watching you, Jess, he'd soon realise you had disappeared.'

'That's true.' Kim reached for the coffee pot. The phone rang and she pushed back her chair. '*Pronto*?'

She listened for a moment, then she glanced at Steph and held out the phone. 'Rhodri Price for you.'

Steph waved at Jess. 'You take it!'

'Why me?'

'Because he must want to talk to you, he never talks to me if he can help it!' Her voice barely rose above a whisper.

Jess frowned at her. She climbed to her feet and went to take the phone from Kim. 'Hi Rhodri, it's Jess.'

'I'm staying at the Hassler and I wondered if you and Steph and your hostess would like to come and have a drink with me on the terrace at the Palazzetto before I head off home. What about breakfast thrown in?'

Jess grinned. She had noticed the hotel at the top of the Spanish Steps. It was one of Rome's best. 'That's kind, Rhodri. We'd love to.' She was surprised at how pleased she was to hear his voice again.

Steph was shaking her head, waving her finger – no!

Jess turned her back. 'There's the three of us and also our friend, Will.'

'Bring him. Bring everyone.' Rhodri sounded euphoric. Jess glanced at her watch. It was still technically breakfast time by her reckoning. She smiled at Steph as she hung up. 'You needn't come. Champagne breakfast at the Hassler is probably not your thing.'

Steph made a face. 'I'll force myself. Just to keep an eye on you two. Shall I go and wake Will?'

Minutes later she had reappeared. 'He's not there. He must have gone out early.'

'Leave him a note.' Kim stood up. 'He can follow us if he wants to.'

On the terrace, Rhodri, relaxed in an open-necked white shirt and cream designer chinos, greeted them with effusive kisses all round and led them to a table which gave them a panoramic view of the Spanish Steps and the Piazza di Spagna below. 'It's great to have someone to celebrate with.'

'Celebrate?' Jess couldn't resist the naïve question. She took the proffered chair. They were surrounded by urns of white petunias.

'A successful gig! I fly home tomorrow.'

'This was opera in Milan?'

'Of course.' He grinned broadly as he sat down next to her. 'You don't like my kind of singing, Jess, do you?'

Steph and Kim glanced up from their menus.

Jess shrugged innocently. 'Actually I'm beginning to appreciate it more than I used to. I pinched a couple of Steph's CDs.' She found she enjoyed teasing him.

'Oh.' He beckoned the hovering waiter. 'May I ask which?'

'*Caractacus.*'

234

He laughed. 'So, it was research, not a quest for musical enlightenment?'

Steph raised an eyebrow. 'You know about Jess's fascination with Eigon then?' she said stiffly. Her antagonism towards this man was still there.

'Oh yes!' Rhodri nodded as they gave their orders. The waiters, they noticed, seemed to treat him as an old friend. 'I was there. I saw what she could do.'

'Eigon?' Kim stared at him. 'You saw her? So, you believe in ghosts?'

Rhodri considered her question for a moment as the waiter brought their coffee. Another produced a bottle of champagne for his inspection. He nodded and glanced at Kim. 'I'm a Welshman. We invented ghosts!'

Jess's mobile rang as she lifted her glass. With an apologetic shrug, she put the glass down untouched. 'Will? Where are you?'

'Jess, help me!' The voice was faint, the line full of static. 'I'm somewhere near the villa –' The name was muffled by crackling. 'Please, come . . .'

'Will?' Jess shook the phone. 'Will, can you hear me?' The others were watching her closely. 'Will, are you all right?' The noise worsened till his voice was inaudible. Then the line went dead. She looked up, her face tense. 'He's in trouble.'

'What sort of trouble?' Kim demanded.

'I don't know. The line was bad. His battery cut out. He said "Help me".' She looked desperately round the table. 'Dan! Dan has done something to him!'

'Did he say so?' Kim asked sharply.

'No, but what else could it be? Dan was in the palazzo last night. Will must have gone down and confronted him after I went to bed. Oh God, this is all my fault!'

'What on earth is going on?' Rhodri put in. 'Will someone explain?'

'It's a long story!' Steph snapped. 'We'll explain later. Let's just say Will and Dan have issues.'

'OK.' Rhodri leaned forward, focusing on the practicalities. 'Did Will say where he was?' He put his hand over Jess's, calming her.

Jess shook her head. 'It sounded like two words. Villa Maya – something like that?' She didn't move her hand away. She looked at Kim pleadingly. 'Does that mean anything to you?'

Kim shrugged. Rhodri called the hovering waiter back and addressed him in a stream of fluent Italian. The waiter thought for a moment and replied in equally fluent English with one or two suggestions. They all looked at Jess and she glanced around despairingly. 'I don't know, it doesn't sound right,' she replied at last.

The waiter shrugged. 'No? *Mi dispiace.*'

'What do we do?' Jess looked at the others pleadingly. 'We have to find him. Should we call the police?'

'There's not much to go on,' Kim said doubtfully. 'Are you sure you didn't hear anything else? We don't actually know he's in trouble, do we. He might just be stranded somewhere.'

'Carmella!' Steph said suddenly. 'She'll know if anyone does. Let's ask her.'

Jess stood up. 'I'll go. She's only down there and round the corner.' She gestured down at the piazza below.

Rhodri pushed back his chair. 'I'll go with you, Jess. You two, enjoy your breakfast. Drink the champagne. We'll have ours later.'

'There's no need, Rhodri.' Jess hesitated. 'Stay with the others –'

He shook his head. He was already threading his way between the tables. 'I'm coming with you, Jess. It sounds as though you might need someone with a bit of muscle.' He grinned at her. 'And I want to hear what you've been up to. No arguments.'

Carmella drew the two of them through her door, listened to Jess's introductions, and took them straight out onto the roof terrace. Waving them into chairs she leaned forward anxiously. 'Tell me again, slowly.'

'Will is missing,' Jess repeated. 'He's in trouble of some sort. Please,' she went on in a whisper, 'will you look in your crystal ball? You must be able to tell where he is.'

Rhodri raised an eyebrow but he sat down in silence.

Carmella nodded slowly. 'Wait. I will fetch my cards!' She reappeared moments later with her bag. Drawing out the pack she began to shuffle them slowly.

'I don't suppose you have something of Will's with you?'

Jess shook her head miserably.

Carmella glanced up. 'Don't worry. We will try anyway. Here. Give me your hand.' She took Jess's hand in her own and held it for a few moments, her eyes closed, concentrating. Rhodri sat back, his arms folded, a bemused expression on his face. Releasing

Jess's hand, Carmella picked up the cards again and cut the pack, dealing several onto the low table in front of them. The noise of traffic from the streets below, the endless rattle of tyres on the cobbles, seemed to fade as Jess and Rhodri watched her hands hovering. She reached for another card and then another, staring at them with a frown deepening between her eyes. It was a long time before she looked up, shaking her head. 'I can see nothing about where he is. I'm sorry.'

'What do you mean, nothing?' Jess cried out.

Carmella shook her head. 'I do not sense that he is injured. I would see that, I think.' She put her hand out to Jess with a gentle almost motherly gesture. 'But something is wrong. There is a blackness round him. Confusion. I guess, maybe he is concussed. Or unconscious. Could he have had an accident?'

'I don't know! He spoke to me on the phone half an hour ago begging me to help him. We need to know where he is!' Jess said urgently. She sat forward on the edge of the chair. 'Please, try. You knew what had happened to me in Wales, you must be able to do it.'

Carmella settled back into deep silence. She didn't sense that other woman listening today. Was she not interested in Will then, only in Jess or Eigon? She moved one of the cards to the top of her spread and took another to set beside it, studying them intently. 'I think he is in the dark. He is either asleep or in a darkened room. I don't think he is injured. If I could see through his eyes I might get a clue where he is but there is nothing.'

Rhodri sat forward suddenly. 'Can he hear anything?'

She glanced up as though seeing him for the first time, then looked down at the cards again. 'Bells. He heard bells.'

'Close by?' Rhodri was concentrating on her face.

She nodded.

'Church or clock?'

'A church. The angelus.'

'Good. Several bells or one?'

'Two. Perhaps more.'

'Can he hear traffic?'

She shook her head.

'Water? Fountains?'

She nodded. 'Very faint.'

'Birds singing?'

There was a long silence. Carmella smiled. 'A dove cooing some-where in the distance.'

She opened her eyes and surveyed him. 'How did you know what to ask?'

He grinned. 'My aunty Blodwen used to go to a clairvoyant in Radnor. You're not reading those cards. You've tuned in to Will psychically.'

Carmella shook her head. 'No, I read the cards.'

'Whatever!' He shrugged. 'The important thing is we have a clue. Now, try again. We know a certain amount but not nearly enough to find him. We need a name.'

'But supposing he doesn't know where he is, Rhodri?' Jess put in.

'He does. He told you. You couldn't hear it because of the phone, but it was there in his brain. Come on, Carmella. Try!'

Carmella frowned. She shook her head. 'This is too hard.'

'No it isn't. Forget those damn cards, woman. Just tune into him!'

Jess saw a flash of anger in Carmella's eyes. She shrugged. Letting her hands fall into her lap she sat back and after a moment did as she was told.

There was a long silence. She shook her head at last. 'Nothing.'

'Not good enough.' Rhodri leaned forward and took Jess's hand in his. He passed it to Carmella. 'Use Jess as the link again. Will is thinking about her.'

Carmella raised an eyebrow sharply but again she did as she was asked. Holding Jess's hand loosely in her own she closed her eyes.

'"They are never going to find me!"' she said at last. '"Dear God, what has he done to me?"'

Jess and Rhodri were watching her face. Jess held her breath.

'"My phone. Where is my phone? I can't find my phone."' There was a long silence, then Carmella went on, '"Jess. Jess will come."'

'Speak to him,' Rhodri murmured. 'In your mind tell him we are coming. Ask him where he is.'

There was another long silence. 'I can see it. I can see the house. A beautiful villa across the road. He is in a small bedroom. Upstairs. His head is aching. The door is locked. He can see the villa through the window.'

238

'Where is the villa? Is there a sign? A street sign? How does Will know where he is?' Rhodri's voice was very calm. Jess closed her eyes trying to breathe steadily so her hand in Carmella's wouldn't shake.

'I can see through his eyes. A long driveway. Gates. They are chained and there is a notice beside the gates. It has hours on it. Hours when the villa is open.' There was another long silence. Carmella was frowning. 'I can't read it. It is too far away.' She paused again. Then her eyes flew open. 'I recognise it! I have been there. I remember the wrought iron over the gates. The, what you call it, a coat of arms? It is the Villa Maria Paollo.'

Rhodri stared at her. 'I know it too. I've been to a recital there. Well done!' He stood up.

Jess stared up at him. 'How will we get there?'

'I've got a hire car. It's up near the hotel.' He turned to Carmella and taking her hand he kissed it with a grin. 'Forgive me for bullying you, but it worked, didn't it! Can you tell the others where we've gone? I know the way, don't worry,' he said over his shoulder as Jess hurried after him. He led her back up the Spanish Steps at a run, past the hotel, towards a red Mercedes drawn up into a parking space under the trees in the Piazza Trinità dei Monti.

'It is Dan, isn't it,' Jess said as she climbed into the car. 'But how could he make Will go with him? How could he get him to go to this place?'

'We'll know soon.' Rhodri headed into a network of streets, driving with all the speed and enthusiasm of a citizen born and bred.

Jess clenched her fists nervously. 'Is it far?'

'Not very. Maybe ten miles.' Rhodri braked sharply and turned up a side street, the sound of the engine reverberating between high walls, blank windows shuttered against the heat.

He swung the car down another street and then onto a main road heading south and put his foot down. Very soon they were driving through suburbs in an area of blistered tatty hoardings, sunburned houses and empty roads, washed by mirages.

The car speeded up on a dead straight stretch of country road then slowed again as they approached a village. Rhodri pulled into the side of the road. 'We're just about there. A bit further, round the corner on the left as we get into the village. There are gates

239

and a long straight drive going up to the villa. I came to a recital here a couple of years ago.' He didn't say if he was part of the audience or the star of the evening and she didn't ask him. He glanced at his watch. 'It's probably closed for lunch at this time of day.'

He was right. They drew up outside the tall elegant wrought iron gates which were, as he had anticipated, shut fast and climbed out. There beside the gates was a notice which listed the opening hours of the villa just as Carmella had said. The gates, topped by an elegant wrought iron coat of arms, gilded in the bright sunlight, were not due to reopen that day.

Jess bit her lip. She looked from left to right at the high walls. The street was deserted. The village seemed locked in sleep. There was no house across the road.

'Supposing we've got it wrong,' she whispered. She had filled him in on some of the story as they drove south.

Rhodri wandered a few paces away from her, staring thoughtfully around. 'We've nothing else to go on.' He paused and glanced at her. 'It was Will's voice?'

She stared at him. 'You mean someone else had his phone?' Her optimism was trickling away. 'It was a dreadful line. I suppose it could have been someone else.' She broke off with a small shiver. 'Dan?'

'Maybe. I'm trying to work out what is happening here. Could Dan have actually made the call? To lure you out here by yourself?'

'If Will fought with Dan,' she whispered. 'I suppose he might have dropped the phone.'

'Is that likely? Can Will handle himself?' Rhodri sounded calmly practical.

'He's fit. A sportsman.'

'And he was expecting Dan to be there. It's not as though Dan could have jumped him.'

They looked at each other for a moment. Rhodri scanned the empty road again. 'I can't help wondering what would have happened if you had arrived here on your own.'

Jess paled. 'But Carmella was talking about Will. She could see Will here.'

Rhodri shrugged. 'Good point. But where is this house across the road?'

They both turned to look at the high stone wall behind them.

'Shall we walk further into the village?' Jess whispered at last. 'There are houses further on.'

'Is it possible Carmella made a mistake?' Rhodri asked after a moment. He was feeling increasingly uncomfortable. 'Supposing Dan picked up Will's phone after they scuffled. Dan thinks you're in love with this man.' He paused as though waiting for her to deny it and when she didn't he went on. 'He obviously fancies you himself, he's insanely jealous and he has the perfect way of bringing you to him.' He glanced round again. 'Jess!' He put his arm round her shoulders suddenly. 'Get back in the car. Now.' He was guiding her away from the gates.

'Why?' Instinctively Jess resisted, trying to pull away from him.

'Because we're being watched. Don't turn round. Just head back to the car slowly. Now.' He manoeuvred her round to the passenger seat and opened the door. Closing it behind her he walked casually round to the driver's side, car keys in hand. Climbing in, he rammed the key in the ignition and pulled away from the kerb.

'Someone was standing in the street further down, watching us.'

'Dan?'

'I couldn't see.' He pulled up a side street and checking the mirror again he drew in and parked. 'Just how dangerous is this guy, Jess?'

She lay back in the seat and closed her eyes for a second. She was going to have to tell him everything. 'He's threatened to kill me,' she concluded when it was done. 'Perhaps I'm exaggerating, but I'm so scared of him.' She hunched her shoulders. 'He's convinced me he wants to kill me. I've told him I'm no threat. I've told him I won't say anything to anyone but he doesn't believe me.'

'The bastard! He's not going to get away with this!' Rhodri was silent for a moment as he digested everything she had said. 'So what have you done about it?'

'Nothing.' She shook her head. She felt strangely comforted now that he knew the whole story.

'You don't strike me as the kind of person to be intimidated.' It sounded like a reproach.

She gave a wry smile. 'Well, I am.'

'You could stop all this by going to the police.'

'They wouldn't believe me. There is no proof. It would be my word against his. That is why he has been trying to convince everybody that I'm mad. So no one will believe me about anything. You believe me, don't you?' She turned and looked at him intently.

He nodded. 'Oh yes, I believe you. Maybe I'm becoming as paranoid as you, but maybe not.' He threw a quick smile in her direction. It was warm, reassuring. Not for the first time she was aware of just how safe she felt in this man's company. 'I think I should go and have a look at the house where that man was standing.'

'You're not going without me.'

'It's you he's after, Jess.'

'Yes, and I'm not going to wait here alone!'

Rhodri frowned. 'OK. We'll go together. I tell you what. I'll drive straight to the house and knock on the door, OK? You wait in the car with the doors locked.' He grinned at her. 'I can't believe we're doing this.'

Reversing back the way they had come they turned back into the main street and drew up outside the end house of a terrace of shabby two-storey dwellings, their pitted and crumbling plaster relieved by pretty balconies woven with jasmine. Locking the car behind him, Rhodri strode to the front door. He knocked. The door wasn't properly closed and it creaked slightly as it swung open.

'Hello?' Rhodri called. 'Anyone there? Will?'

There was no reply.

'*C'è qualcuno*?' Still no reply. He glanced round. 'I'm going in,' he whispered.

Jess climbed out of the car and ran after him as he stepped into the hallway. Rhodri glanced at the table inside the door. 'It's some kind of B and B,' he murmured. 'Look. Visitor's book.' It was lying open on the table. The last entry was dated several days earlier. 'Will?' he called again more loudly this time. 'Are you there?'

And this time there was a reply. A faint sound came from upstairs. Rhodri ran up two at a time, Jess immediately behind him. Only one door on the landing was closed. There was a key in the lock. Rhodri gestured at her to stand back. He tiptoed across and turned the key. Pushing open the door he paused for a moment, listening. They both heard a man groan.

'Will?' Jess stepped forward.

Rhodri caught her arm. 'Let me go first.' He pushed the door back hard against the wall, then walked in and looked round. Will was lying on the bed, fully dressed. His face was white, one eye swollen. There was no one else in the room.

'Will? Will, my God, what has he done to you?' Jess ran to him.

Will tried to sit up and fell back against the pillow with a groan. 'Hit my head,' he murmured. 'Can't seem to see straight.'

'Is Dan here?' Rhodri had gone straight to the window. He could just see the villa gates in the distance.

'Gone.' Will's voice was very weak. 'He gave me something. Drug. Used my phone.' He gestured feebly towards the bedside table where his phone lay.

'Right. Can you stand, mate?' Rhodri walked over to him. 'We've got a car outside. Let's get you out of here before he comes back. Whose house is this?'

Will shook his head. 'Haven't seen anyone at all.' He stared at Rhodri, puzzled. 'Who are you?' he mumbled.

Rhodri grinned. 'A friend of Jess's from Wales. Knight errant and not a bad right hook, at your service. You might say I am Dan's worst nightmare. So, come on, my friend. Let's see if you can walk.'

Between them Jess and Rhodri managed to get Will to his feet and down the stairs, pushing him into the back of the car.

Drawing away from the kerb Rhodri glanced into the rear-view mirror. A man had appeared and was standing in the road watching them go.

'Jess can't stay here a moment longer.' Steph shook her head emphatically. They were in Kim's sitting room. 'Dan's got keys to this house and to the garden and to the apartment and he's getting more and more brazen. Either you go to the police, Jess, or you go back to England. It's the only answer.'

Jess and Rhodri had taken Will to the nearest hospital on the way back. He was badly bruised and disorientated and the hospital had insisted on keeping him in for observation. Before they left he had forbidden them to go to the police.

'This is a private matter between me and Dan,' he said, through gritted teeth. 'I'm not involving the police. Think of the complications.'

'It's all my fault. Just by being here I am putting you all in danger,' Jess said miserably. 'Dan must have gone completely mad. If he's going to threaten Will and kidnap him, what else is he capable of?'

'He needs to be stopped,' Steph said with conviction.

'And soon,' Kim agreed.

'And that is best done in England,' Rhodri put in. 'If he follows you home then we will go to the police and say he is stalking you. There are laws about that. And the best weapon of all is that if you tell his wife what has been happening, then there is no point in his trying to silence you. Even if she doesn't believe it at least it will all be out in the open.'

'And you have another secret weapon as well. Carmella.' Steph grinned. 'With her on your side, you're always going to be one step in front of him, and your spies are always going to be on his shoulder. After all she sensed there was something wrong when you were in Ty Bran before she'd even met you.' There was a pause. 'So, where is Dan now?' she went on. 'He is still out there.'

Jess stirred uncomfortably and opened her eyes, staring towards the window. It was still dark. She listened intently. The apartment was sunk in silence and she was safe. The windows were locked, the shutters barred. The ladder, when Rhodri went to look for it, had gone. The front door had been triple-locked and bolted behind him when he had at last left for his hotel in the early hours of the morning. No one was coming into the flat tonight.

19

Pomponia Graecina had sent her litter for the girls. 'You'll be perfectly safe, Eigon.' She smiled when she issued the invitation. 'No one will know it's you. But we won't tell your mama. She has enough to worry her.'

Caratacus was in bed, too weak to rise, his body racked by rigors which left him barely conscious. His gaunt frame was emaciated now almost beyond recognition.

'Don't tell Aelius either,' she added. 'Get one of the girls to cover for you.' She giggled suddenly, her normally austere face lighting up at the thought of her plan.

Julia and Eigon climbed into the litter, their heads swathed in their stoles and pulled the curtains across. The Aulus litter, carried by six slaves in front and six slaves behind moved fast and smoothly down the dusty track towards the road which led towards the Via Flaminia which would take them down into the city.

'So, what do you think is behind the invitation?' Doffing her stole, Julia was tweaking the ornately pinned curls of her hair-style into place.

Eigon shrugged. Melinus had given her a clue. And sworn her to secrecy. If events transpired as he suspected then Julia was to be whisked away on a shopping spree exciting enough to distract her for weeks to come.

Beyond the curtains the day was hot and airless, the great pine trees that lined the road the only green things in a dusty parched landscape. Pedestrians and riders were tired and slow as they plodded in and out of the city.

The attack when it came was sudden. At the approaching thunder of hooves, the slaves had moved smartly to the side of the road to allow the party of soldiers to pass. They didn't. The riders had surrounded them in seconds, swerving towards the litter, forcing them to stop. They wore the scarlet uniform of the Praetorian guard.

'Stop in the Emperor's name!' The side curtains were swept back on the point of a sword as the slaves dropped the litter and stood back. Eigon and Julia huddled together, terrified as one of the men dismounted. 'Out!' He wasted no time on pleasantries. The two girls climbed out and stood staring at him.

'What is the meaning of this?' Eigon found her voice first. 'How dare you!'

The officer looked her up and down, and then looked at Julia as if not sure which one of the young women he was to address. 'I dare, sweetheart, believe me! Which of you is Julia Pomponia Graecina?'

Julia shrank back. 'Why do you want to know?'

'Answer, lady!' The man's voice was harsh.

'It's obvious, Marius!' one of the men commented. 'Look at the colouring. This is the one we want.' He nodded towards Eigon.

Eigon straightened her back. 'What is this outrage?' She was trying desperately to keep her voice steady.

'You.' The first man pointed at Julia. 'Back in the litter.'

Julia stared at him. 'I will do no such thing.' She gathered all her courage. 'How dare you! Do you know who my uncle is? You will suffer for this!'

'You are not to be harmed, lady,' the second man commented. 'Please get back in the litter.'

'Eigon! You first!' Julia's voice was shaking.

Eigon did not need to be asked twice. She dived back into the litter, trembling. Julia followed her. Neither man had moved to stop them. Marius sighed. 'Very well, if you both want to come. No doubt that can be arranged. You,' he addressed the slaves. 'Pick it up and follow us.' The armed guard had posted themselves at the four corners of the litter.

'No!' Julia's whispered voice was barely audible.

'There are people coming, lady,' Marcello, the senior slave muttered. 'Hang on. Help is on the way.' He glanced at one of the leading litter bearers and gave a slight nod. A cloud of dust in the distance heralded another party of horses coming from the city.

'Move on!' Marius's voice sharpened.

The slaves bent to their burden. Then the man in front stumbled. The litter lurched; the two girls clutched at each other in terror. In the short time it took for the litter bearers to sort themselves out, the second troop of soldiers had arrived, drawing to a halt in a cloud of dust. They bore the same insignia as the guard. The senior rider drew up alongside Marius. 'What is this? Is someone hurt?'

Marius shook his head.

The newcomer nodded. 'Come on then, my friends. We'll race you back to the Castra Praetoria!' His horse was snorting, bucking against the tight rein.

Marius reined in his own cavorting mount. He drew his sword. 'Out of the way. Our orders are to escort this litter to the villa of Titus Marcus Olivinus.'

'No! Take us to my aunt's house. Please, Marcello, tell him.' Julia leaned forward. 'This man was trying to kidnap us!' Her face was white.

Abruptly Marius shrugged. He pulled his horse away from the litter. 'Rubbish! What nonsense the girl talks. Very well, lady. If you refuse my master's invitation, that is your loss.' It had all gone wrong. Now there were witnesses and besides, he had not been instructed to use force. 'Don't kill anyone,' Titus had said with a grin when they had set up the plan after one of Titus's spies had told them of the impending excursion. 'For the gods' sake don't bring down the whole weight of the Senate on my head. Just grab the girl and run.' He had snorted with mirth.

'Away!' Marius raised his arm to his troop. He gave a brief salute towards the litter and his men wheeled and galloped up the road followed at once by the second party of riders. In seconds they were out of sight.

Eigon was shaking. 'That was not a robbery.'

'No, indeed it was not.' Marcello wiped the sweat off his forehead. 'Are you all right, princess?' He gestured at the litter bearers. 'Let's move quickly. It's not far to the gates of Rome.' He glanced back over his shoulder. In seconds they had resumed their journey.

'What happened?' Pomponia Graecina received the girls in her boudoir, her face set.

Julia shrugged. 'They were Praetorians. They seemed to be looking for Eigon.'

Pomponia looked at Eigon, concerned. 'Do you know why?'

Eigon was pale and drawn. She shook her head. 'Was it something to do with Papa?' She shivered.

Pomponia shrugged. 'I somehow doubt it. But one never knows with Nero what he may have decided on next. If it was anything to do with Nero.' She sighed. For a moment the three women stood in silence, then Pomponia forced herself to a cheerful smile. 'Well, whatever it was I am not about to allow a group of silly guards to spoil my plans. Julia, I am sending you on a special mission for me, first to the Vicus Unguentarius to pick up a flask of my special scent. You may buy something for yourself there. Then I want you to call in on my dressmaker. I have torn my favourite gown and you can leave it with her to be mended and look at some of her new materials. And as I know such an excursion would bore Eigon, she and I are going to talk about healing with a new healer I have met. We will gather together again this evening and you will both stay here tonight. I will send word to the villa that you are both safe here. No,' she raised a hand as Eigon opened her mouth to protest. 'I will see to it that your parents are not concerned. As long as Aelius knows you are both safe no one will worry.'

An excited Julia was equipped with a heavy purse, two young ladies to escort her, plus four slaves armed with heavy cudgels. Eigon watched the preparations half amused. Another part of her was knotted with fear. She knew exactly who had been behind the attempt to abduct her. And now she knew his name. Titus Marcus Olivinus.

When Julia and her chattering friends had gone, Pomponia turned to Eigon. 'Are you all right, sweetheart?'

Eigon nodded. Fond though she was of this woman who was as much an aunt to her as she was to her genuine niece, Julia, she could never tell her the terrible secret that she shared with no one but her mother.

Pomponia scanned her face. She nodded sadly. She suspected Eigon knew more than she was saying about the strange attack, but if the girl was not prepared to share the knowledge then she would respect her silence. She tucked Eigon's arm through her own. 'Today is a very special day for me. I want you to share it. I have some friends of yours here. Come.'

She led the way towards the main reception hall. The first person she saw was Melinus. He smiled gravely. Standing next to him was Julius. Pomponia led her over to them. 'Here is my special guest. Tell her, Julius, what is to happen, while I prepare.' With a smile she took Eigon's hand and put it into Julius's.

For a moment Eigon caught her breath. The touch of this young man's fingers in her own had the power to send a bolt of excitement through her veins. The emotion frightened her. For a second they stared at one another, unable to look away. Embarrassed, it was Eigon who dropped her gaze first. Gently she removed her hand from his. She glanced towards Melinus who had been watching them with quizzical amusement. 'What is happening?'

'Peter is coming.'

'Pomponia wants you to ask him to pray for your father,' Julius said softly.

'Peter the Christian?' Eigon frowned. She glanced round at Melinus.

Julius nodded. 'You know that my grandfather and Melinus have become firm friends.' He looked down at her, his brown eyes warm with amusement.

It had happened almost as soon as they had met a few days after the terrible night Julius had rescued her and Julia from the mob. Julius had brought his grandfather out to the villa so Caratacus and his wife could give their thanks in person for saving their daughter. Later in the afternoon Melinus and the older man had found themselves alone. The two men had started to talk and had quickly recognised in each other the many qualities they shared in spite of the vast differences in their backgrounds. Their interests, their approach to life, their philosophies, though Melinus remained a Druid and Felicius had been baptised as a Christian, gave them occasion for many happy hours of debate. Melinus had admitted his respect for the teacher Peter, the head of the Christians in Rome, and had gone with Felicius to hear Peter's colleague and fellow apostle, Paul of Tarsus, when he had arrived to preach in the city and he had told Eigon much of what he had heard.

Christians were more numerous in Rome now, amongst the dozens of religions and superstitions which flourished there in the hugely mixed population, but although most beliefs were by and large tolerated by the Roman authorities men did not openly declare their allegiance to the Christian faith. Nero and his advisers were suspicious of them as were the ordinary people who, hearing rumours that they ate the flesh and blood of the son of their god, accused them of cannibalism, one of the few perversions no one in Rome would tolerate. From time to time they were arrested almost arbitrarily on charges of treason and worse and their fate was terrible. It was better to keep quiet about their faith.

'It must be very frightening sometimes to think that people are spying on you. Don't they notice that you don't go to the temple for public sacrifices?' Eigon asked quietly.

Julius smiled. 'People are more tolerant than you think. And our family is sufficiently respected for people to turn a blind eye to our eccentricities.' He smiled again. 'You are not afraid of being here, I hope, with so many Christians?'

She shook her head. Unable as always to resist his smile she glanced round again. 'Does Pomponia know you are Christians?'

'Of course. She has asked Peter here today. Partly to meet you. Partly so that he can baptise her.'

Eigon's eyes rounded. 'She is to become a Christian? Does Aulus Plautius know?' Pomponia's husband was known for his conservative support of Roman ways.

Julius shrugged. 'I guess not. He is away from Rome at present, as are most of his servants.' He winked at her. 'The lady Pomponia has always had her own way of doing things.'

'Including getting rid of Julia.' Eigon glanced up at him expecting his expression to soften at the mention of Julia's name. His eyes were however still fixed on her own and she thought she saw a twitch of amusement at the corners of his mouth.

'Julia is not one to show much interest in either religion or philosophy,' he said softly. She had the impression that he was not paying Julia a compliment.

A buzz of excited talk near the door interrupted them. Peter had arrived. The old man leaned heavily on his staff as he climbed the steps into the room and came towards them. On every side people were greeting him as an old friend. Julius's grandfather was at his side, Eigon realised, and they were coming towards her.

Peter's eyes were a deep warm brown. They held hers for several seconds, then he put out his hands to hers. He was smiling gravely. 'So, this is Eigon. I have heard much about you, my child.' She could feel the warmth and love radiating from him. 'I hear you are a healer.'

She lowered her eyes with a little shrug. 'I do my best, sir.'

He laughed. 'Don't call me sir, child! My friends call me brother. Your father is ill?'

Eigon nodded. 'He has been ill for so long. It's more than an illness. It's unhappiness. He misses our home so much.'

Peter nodded. 'And your home is faraway in Britannia?'

Eigon nodded. She glanced up. Melinus was standing behind Peter. He met her gaze and she saw him smile. He nodded encouragingly. 'Will you pray for my father?' Eigon asked.

'Of course I will. And I will pray for you, Eigon. Jesus will bless you both.'

'And my mother and my little brother and sister who were lost,' she burst out. Her eyes filled with tears. It was a long time since she had mentioned Togo and Gwladys to anyone. It was strangely easy to speak to this man. It was as though by unburdening her fears on his stooped shoulders a great weight was lifted from hers.

'Jesus will hold your whole family in his arms, Eigon. Pray to him, child. He will hear you.' He rested his hand for a moment on her head, then he turned away distracted as someone else came forward clamouring for his attention.

Eigon stood still. Julius smiled at her. 'You understand now why we love him?' he said quietly.

She nodded. 'Will my father get better now?'

Julius shrugged. 'Sometimes people are healed instantly. Other times, if it is the time for them to die then they will die, but they are enfolded in Jesus's arms. He takes them to heaven to live with him. They aren't frightened any more, Eigon. They are comforted and reassured.'

Eigon frowned. 'My father isn't frightened. He is a warrior. His gods expect him to die bravely. Then he will go to the land of the ever young.'

Julius shrugged. 'That sounds to me like heaven,' he said. 'Not Hades. There is no River Styx to cross. In heaven there is sunshine and flowers and angels.'

Eigon nodded with a smile. 'The Isles of the Blest,' she whispered.

'Look,' Julius said suddenly. 'Peter is going to baptise some of the people here. Sometimes they take people down to the river and do it there, but that is too public in Rome. Watch.'

Pomponia Graecina was the first in line. Peter blessed a bowl of water and used it to mark the sign of the cross on each person's forehead. He baptised Pomponia with the name Lucina. As they walked away from him dripping and laughing, the room seemed filled with happiness.

Infected by the feeling of joy all around her Eigon reached for Julius's hand. She wasn't even aware that she had done it. The terrifying moments in the litter earlier were forgotten. 'This is a wonderful house to be in,' she said. 'I feel so safe here!'

Jess stirred and smiled in her sleep. The silence of the apartment was very deep. Outside on the landing at the top of the flight of stone stairs Dan stood listening, his ear pressed against the door. Silently he raised his hand and pushed. The door stood firm. Reaching into his pocket he produced a set of keys and inserted them into the lock. They turned easily but the door didn't move. He gave a wry smile. It was bolted.

In Jess's dream Eigon seemed suddenly older now, taller, more elegant, her hair the deeper, richer black of a raven's wing. She was sitting in the sunshine with her friend Antonia at her side.

'Julius is hoping you will come to his birthday party.' Antonia glanced up with a smile. She was making notes on a tablet with a stylus, crossing off items on a long list.

'Me? Or Julia?' Eigon smiled wistfully.

'You!' Antonia laughed. 'You know it's you he wants there. Are you never going to have pity on the poor man?'

Eigon blushed. 'You know it's pointless.' She would rather have died than admit that she had dreamed about Julius; that almost every day when she should have been studying recipes for herbal cures she found herself daydreaming about his handsome face, his warm laughing eyes. 'Mam has forbidden me to go out. She has set Aelius to watch over me to see I can't slip outside.'

'And you still obey her like a small child!' Antonia frowned. 'Are you going to stay locked in this place like a prisoner for ever, Eigon? Your life is passing. You study with Melinus every second of the day and when you're not studying you are working with the sick or tending your father. You never go out to the shops any more or to the theatre or to the games with Julia. You're always working with Melinus on your healing and I know most mornings people queue up to consult you and that is wonderful. It is what God would want of you, but, for goodness' sake, have you no *unicia* of healthy rebellion in you? Is it Melinus who is stopping you coming to us? Has he some sort of hold over you? Are you under a spell? Or is it because of our faith?' She scowled.

'You know it's not that!' Eigon was indignant. 'Melinus has great respect for your faith. He went to the city to visit your grandfather yesterday.'

'So?' Antonia was not to be deflected. 'Do you not think my brother deserves a visit too? Do you not find him attractive?'

Eigon smiled. She glanced up under her lashes. 'You know I do.' She heaved a great sigh. 'It's just not going to happen, Antonia. You know it can't. I shall never marry. My parents are in no position to give me a dowry. They have no money. Anyway, we are prisoners here. Slaves, in a way. The Emperor would have to be asked and he would never allow me to marry.'

She closed her eyes, feeling the sun on her lids. This was a subject she did not want to pursue. She was human. She had longings and dreams and Julius appeared in all of them. From time to time she abandoned herself to tears in the dark loneliness of her bedroom, after allowing herself to wonder what would happen if she gave way to her longing to follow him into the darkness of the gardens in the evening and raise her face to his for a kiss.

'Grandfather could persuade the Senate to agree; and he would not insist on a dowry!' This time Antonia was not going to be deterred from her theme. 'It is nonsense to say you are slaves. Your father is a king! No one will stop you if you both want it. But maybe your parents would not want you to marry a Christian? Have you told them that's what we are?'

Eigon shook her head.

Antonia shrugged. 'Our next door neighbour on one side became a Christian himself last year. He comes to the meetings in our house. The senator on the other side is an old friend of grandfather's. I am sure he would ignore any rumours about us. He must have guessed.' She smiled and the sadness vanished from her eyes. 'You do like Julius though, don't you?' she persisted.

Eigon nodded.

'And his religion wouldn't be a problem for you?'

Eigon shook her head. 'I love hearing stories of your Jesus and his miracles. And he was one of the greatest healers of all time from what I hear.' She grinned. 'If I'm honest I think Melinus is halfway to believing that your Jesus was actually a Druid.'

253

Antonia looked shocked for a moment, then she laughed. 'Maybe he was.'

'Julia likes Julius, you know.' Eigon changed the subject abruptly.

'I thought she loved young Flavius. You said they had been a couple more or less for years.' Antonia smiled. 'She's always out with him.'

Eigon nodded. 'They've been friends since we were all children. The trouble is that Flavius is nowhere near her league socially. His father is our steward here. He's a freedman. Julia's uncle was governor of Britannia. She could never marry Flavius. He knows that and so does she. She's set her cap at your brother since that first day we met you.' She sat back for a moment with a sigh. 'How does it feel to have two women in love with your brother?'

'Ah! So you do love him!' Antonia pounced.

Eigon smiled. 'Only one of us is in a position to do anything about it and that is Julia. He could do a lot worse. Her family is rich and well connected. And her aunt is a Christian.'

Antonia shook her head. 'I don't think Aulus Plautius knows that even now! I doubt if he would allow Julia anywhere near Julius if it was suspected that we are Christians.' She broke off abruptly, turning towards the house. 'Who's there?'

The doorway was empty.

Eigon frowned. 'What's wrong?'

'Someone was there, listening, I'm sure they were! They must have heard me.' Antonia had gone pale. She jumped to her feet and running to the doorway she stared into the atrium. There was no one there. The place drowsed in the silence of the hot afternoon.

'I don't think anyone heard,' she whispered as she came back to the chairs. 'But we must be careful. Even here there are spies.'

Especially here. Melinus had warned Eigon to be on her guard with Aelius a long time ago. If he had been listening how much of their conversation had he overheard? Her heart sank.

But already Antonia was laughing again. 'I'm talking nonsense. This must be the safest place in the world!'

'. . . Safe! The safest place in the world!'

The words echoed in Jess's head. She woke again, her eyes wide, staring round the room. It was still dark, but thin rays of sunlight were beginning to find their way through the closed shutters onto the carpet.

Eigon had met St Peter. Jess sat up, amazed and energised. Had that been a dream, or was it real? She stared round her again, half-expecting to see the room filled with shadowy figures, the men in togas, the women in gowns of beautiful colours with stoles around their shoulders, the old man with white hair bestowing his blessings amongst them with so much love and warmth she could feel it now herself. And the two girls. Friends. Chatting about love in the afternoon sun.

She glanced at her watch, memories of the previous day suddenly flooding back. It was just after six and the shadows had gone. Rising wearily from the bed she went over to the window and threw the shutters open. The street was dazzling in the early sunshine, the traffic already heavy.

There was a quiet knock at the door. 'Are you up, Jess?' Steph pushed it open. 'Kim has told Jacopo to call a taxi. We'll all help you down with your stuff.'

Jess turned round. 'Let me jump in the shower and I'll be with you.'

'Any sign of Dan out there?'

Jess shook her head. 'The street is already crowded. He could be anywhere. Are you sure this idea is going to work?'

Steph shrugged. 'I can't think of a better one, can you?'

Kim had told Jacopo to call a taxi for the airport. The instruction was to be given loudly to the taxi driver as well. If anyone was listening, or if the old man was bribed to tell, the story would be the same. Jess was going back to England.

Rhodri was waiting for her at his hotel. Within seconds her bags had been whisked away, the disappointed taxi driver paid off and she was with Rhodri in a corner of the restaurant garden. They settled at a small table, surrounded by vivid clusters of plants. The early morning was wonderfully cool and fresh. He smiled at her. 'Are you OK?'

She nodded wanly. 'Will?'

'I've been in to see him first thing. He's fine. They will release him later this afternoon. I have suggested he goes straight home.'

'Home?'

Rhodri nodded. 'Back to London.'

'So Dan will think we are both going back there.'

'Will will be OK, Jess.' Rhodri put his hand over hers for a fraction of a second. 'He can go straight to his parents. He said they live somewhere deep in the country.'

Jess smiled. 'They do. Cornwall.'

'He'll be safe there. Stop worrying.'

'And what about me? Where am I going to go? I can't stay here.'

'You can. As long as you like. I've checked you in with me.' He chuckled. 'Sorry. Will it ruin your reputation? The thing is, I have a suite here. Stupid extravagance, but you have to allow the star a few perks!' He signed the chit as the waiter brought them some coffee. 'As soon as we are sure that Dan has gone racing back to England after you, you can, if you'd rather not stay with me, go back to Kim's flat and get on with your holiday.'

'And if he doesn't go?'

'I'll smuggle you back to Wales.'

Their eyes met for a moment and he grinned. 'Best I can do for now!'

She shrugged. 'You've been fantastic, Rhodri. I'm so grateful.' She gave a small embarrassed smile. 'Sorry. That seems a bit inadequate considering you probably risked your life to rescue Will.'

He considered for a moment. 'I probably did, didn't I. But then, so did you. I hope he's duly grateful. He has at least asked me to convey his apologies to Carmella for ever doubting her abilities. He's not such a bad guy, Will.' With another quick glance at her, he leaned forward and picked up his cup.

She sat for a moment in silence, frowning. He sat back in his chair, watching her, content to wait for whatever thought was distracting her to surface. When she spoke it was the perfect non sequitur. 'Are you a Christian, Rhodri?'

He looked startled. 'Now, that is a question I was not expecting! Why do you want to know?'

She hesitated for a moment. 'I had a strange dream last night. About Eigon. I dreamed she met St Peter here in Rome.'

'Ah.' He nodded. 'I see. Well, the answer to your question is yes and no. Officially yes. I was baptised. I sing a lot of religious music and it moves me. But I'm not a churchgoer as such.'

'Nor am I. I never have been,' she said thoughtfully. 'My parents weren't into that sort of stuff, so I missed out on the family tradition thing and I've never really understood what it was all about.

I absorbed my philosophy of life from literature and it's pretty eclectic. But I felt the most extraordinary love coming off him. Magnetism. It was so real I can still feel it.'

Rhodri raised an eyebrow. 'You've been blessed then.' He gave a bark of laughter. 'Literally perhaps.'

She smiled. 'I suppose I have. It was a shock to wake up and think about Dan.'

'That would be a shock for anyone.'

A shadow fell across the table and they both looked up.

'Did I hear someone mention my name?' Dan was standing looking down at them, his hands in his pockets.

Jess gasped. For a moment she was too shocked to speak. She had allowed herself to relax. To feel safe. How could she have been so stupid?

'How did you know I was here?'

'I followed you. All that loud talk of airports. Did you really think I would be fooled by that?' He helped himself to a chair from a neighbouring table and beckoned the waiter. 'Oh you sad people! How pathetic. So, Rhodri. Has she been filling you up with more lies? More madness?' His face was set with dislike.

Rhodri hadn't moved. He contemplated Dan almost idly from behind his dark glasses. 'It was not Jess's madness which left Will drugged and imprisoned in the countryside yesterday.'

'Oh but it was. Yes, I heard from Jacopo that he had returned a gibbering wreck. Jess filled his mind with drivel and he chose to believe it. Was he drugged? No, I don't think you'll find he was. Was he imprisoned? No. He was, so I hear,' he smiled, 'holed up in a cosy B and B in a popular tourist area outside Rome where he had gone in order to recover and probably hide from our Jess's terrifying revelations. I expect she's driven you the same way with her talk of ghosts and hauntings. Has the beautiful Eigon scribbled on any more of your drawings, sweetheart?' His voice was heavy with sarcasm.

Jess bit her lip. 'I don't think that was Eigon. I think that was you. You had keys to the flat.' She managed to keep her voice steady.

'Ah yes, I told you that, didn't I.' He laughed out loud. He seemed perfectly relaxed, enjoying himself. 'So, Rhodri. What has she been telling you? The latest instalment in the great Roman saga?'

257

Jess went cold. Only minutes before she had been confiding in Rhodri that she had been blessed by St Peter. She glanced at him helplessly but his face was impassive, his eyes hidden behind the dark glasses.

Dan picked up on her moment of hesitation at once. 'Ah, I see she has. So, what was it this time? Packs of Roman ladies rushing down the street pursued by satyrs and gladiators?' Once again he gave a chilling laugh.

'Jacopo did not see Will last night,' Rhodri put in at last, his voice lazy and unconcerned. He still had not removed his glasses. 'We took him straight to the hospital where they gave him blood tests while I stood and watched to make sure all was done correctly.'

For a moment Dan seemed disconcerted. Then he shrugged. 'So, Jacopo got it wrong. He's such a drunken sot I doubt if he is on the same planet as the rest of us most of the time.'

Rhodri said nothing, his face falling into a sardonic half-smile as he inclined his head, waiting for Dan to go on. Which he did.

'So, did they find any drugs? I've always had Will marked down as a user on the quiet.'

Jess opened her mouth to protest. Then thought better of it. She followed Rhodri's example and smiled.

Dan glanced from one to the other. 'Oh, I see. A conspiracy of silence. Pathetic!' He leaned back in his chair and folded his arms. 'Well, you might like to know that I have been busy. I thought it wise to tell a few people about Jess's mental condition. It seemed kinder to warn them before she starts blurting her fantasies to all and sundry and putting them in the embarrassing position of having to work out what the hell she is talking about.' He paused. 'Starting with Nat. Nat has always thought you were a bit of a fruitcake, Jess. She wasn't even surprised when I told her about your nervous breakdown. And of course she wasn't the least bit surprised to hear that you thought you'd fallen in love with me!'

Jess was about to retort when Rhodri put his hand on her arm. He gripped it firmly. 'Take no notice, Jess. Don't give him the pleasure! I think it's time you went on your way, Dan. They have very strict stalking laws in Rome, you know.' He hauled himself up out of his chair and stood looking down at Dan. Jess suppressed a smile. Rhodri was a big man. It was only seconds before Dan was intimidated into standing up himself.

'Don't say I haven't warned you,' Dan retorted smugly. He

turned away. Then he stopped. 'You're right about the stalking laws,' he threw over his shoulder. 'As it happens I have already reported Jess to the police myself. If you had gone to the airport I think you might have found a big fat policeman there ready to escort you onto the plane after stamping your passport to make sure you don't come back to Italy. Ever!'

He turned and walked away.

'No, Jess, leave it!' Rhodri commanded sternly. Flinging himself down into his chair he leaned over and took her arm again, preventing her from standing up. 'We both know that's rubbish. He's just making himself sound even more crazy by the second. Let him go.'

'The bastard!' She was spluttering with fury.

'He's trying to wind you up and he's succeeded. What a poisonous worm. At least I've seen him in action myself now.' He released her. 'Drink your coffee, girl. We've got to think about this.'

'So you don't think he's really reported me?'

'No. Not for one second. Besides, it doesn't work like that. They're not going to take his word for something like that, any more, unfortunately, than they would yours. They would want proof.'

'I can't believe he just followed me here. I was so confident. You'd made me feel safe.'

He grimaced. 'I'm sorry. I underestimated him.'

She took a long gulp of her coffee. It was cold. 'It was clever of him to tell Nat. Now whatever I say she won't listen. No one is going to listen to anything I say ever again. I'll never get another job.'

'I think you will. But we do need a master plan at this stage. We'll let him go now. See what he does. You're safe as long as you're with me. I think Will is safe too.'

'Won't he be afraid of what Will is going tell people?'

Rhodri thought about it for a minute. 'I doubt it. Will is in love with you.' He raised a hand. 'Yes, he is! So his evidence would be regarded as biased. Do you both know Dan's wife?'

'Nat? Yes, we do. We've all been friends and colleagues for years. Of course we know her.'

'Hmm.' Rhodri leaned back in his chair again. Then he frowned. 'Jess, what is it?' Her eyes had opened wide and she was staring across the terrace. 'Has he come back?' He followed her gaze.

'It's Eigon.' She whispered. 'Look.'

'I can't see her, Jess.' Rhodri scanned the terrace. Several people were wandering about. He could see a waitress with a tray heading for a neighbouring table. He frowned uneasily. 'Tell me what you can see.'

She turned to look at him suddenly. 'Oh shit! You think I'm imagining it. Perhaps I was.' She sighed. 'She's gone. Of course she's gone. What would she be doing here in a hotel, for God's sake!'

'This hotel like every building in Rome will be on an ancient site, Jess,' he said gently. 'Eigon could have been anywhere in her lifetime. And who's to say she had to have been here anyway. Perhaps she is looking for you.'

Jess stared at him miserably. 'You think?'

He smiled. 'If you actually saw her, there must be a reason.'

'If.' She shrugged. 'That crucial if. Don't think I haven't wondered if Dan isn't right. Who's to say I'm not completely mad.'

'Then so is your sister. She's seen Eigon too.'

'We don't actually know that. Steph thinks Ty Bran is haunted. That's all. It's an old house, full of funny noises and shadows.' Her voice trailed away.

Rhodri followed her gaze. She was looking into the middle distance. Two women were sitting at a small table, facing away from them, examining the contents of a carrier bag with a Via Condotti address on it. As they giggled softly together a waiter brought them a bottle of mineral water and two glasses. He chuckled. Both on a diet then, but what woman wasn't, in Rome. Beyond them he could see faint moving shadows as the sunlight began to ease its way through the leaves of some carefully sited lemon trees. Was that a ghostly figure in the corner? Frowning, he leaned closer.

'Is it true?' Cerys stared at her daughter coldly. 'Are you seeing this young Roman?'

'Not really. We talk sometimes, that's all. I like him. Mam, please –'

'I forbid you to see him again, Eigon, do you hear? Ever!'

'But why?'

'Because we must do nothing to bring ourselves to the attention of the Emperor. Don't you understand how precarious our position is, you stupid child! We are a threat to him.'

'But Papa is ill –'

'Especially with your papa ill. Don't you see, if you should have a child, Eigon, the grandchild of Caratacus, the people at home might hope he would come back to save them. Nero would never allow that. You know what happens to people he even suspects of being a threat to him.' Cerys shuddered.

'But Mam, the people of Britannia have forgotten us.'

'Never! No, they are still waiting for your father to return.'

Eigon held her mother's implacable gaze for a moment then she looked away. What was the point of arguing. 'Anyway, you don't have to worry,' she said miserably. 'I'm not "seeing him" as you call it. He is far more interested in Julia.'

'I'm glad to hear it!' Cerys stood up and pulled her wrap around her shoulders. 'We want no Romans in our family. They are the enemy and never forget it!'

20

Titus Marcus Olivinus was sitting on the steps of the steam bath next to his uncle, Senator Caius Marcus Pomponius. The two men were deep in conversation.

'It was part of my duties to follow these men; there is suspicion of treason in the making,' Titus confided quietly. He raised a hand to acknowledge a colleague as he walked across the wet floor towards the benches on the other side of the room. 'As you know the Emperor has begun to have grave reservations about Christians. They spread like a mould through the underbelly of the city.'

His uncle smiled at the simile. 'Not just the underbelly, Titus. There are men in the Senate, the army – all over the place – who subscribe to these beliefs. We used to think it was limited to slaves and women, but now!' He shrugged.

'Peter the Fisherman was at the house of Pomponia Graecina with a huge gathering of them,' Titus whispered, 'and he baptised her.' He stared down at his toes seemingly uninterested in his uncle's reaction. 'There were several people there from the household of Caratacus the Briton, whom Pomponia Graecina has befriended. It is my information that he is recovered from his illness. Peter healed him with prayers to this Jesus. And now the first thing he does is to plot against the Empire.'

Caius formed his lips into a soundless whistle.

'Caratacus's daughter is a dark horse,' Titus went on. 'A quiet mousey little thing, so my informants tell me.' He paused with a small private smile. Quiet and mousey were not the words that had been used to describe her to him. Far from it. She was clever, feisty and beautiful, and, he scowled, it seemed, she was carefully guarded. So far in spite of several attempts to snatch her she had remained tantalisingly safe from his attentions. His combined frustration and fear kept him constantly on edge about her. The idea to implicate her friends and family in treasonous activity had occurred to him only recently after a particularly long drinking session with his friend, Marius. 'She has wormed her way into several households, spreading sedition and unrest with her large beautiful eyes and her sweet innocent smiles.' He paused abruptly, aware that his uncle had looked sharply at him, his eyes narrowed keenly, a touch of amusement playing around his mouth.

'I thought you said she was quiet and mousey,' Caius said innocently.

Titus laughed. 'Always the most dangerous type!' The words of one worldly man to another.

Caius nodded. 'So, you think we should investigate this treasonous little lady and her father?'

Titus shrugged his shoulders. 'Maybe not investigate as such. I would start with Pomponia's household. Her husband should be warned of her activities.'

'He knows.' Caius dabbed at his face with the corner of his towel.

'Then perhaps he should do something about it and take an interest in his wife's friends. It would do his own reputation no good for it to be known that she is not only a Christian but also cosying up to traitors. Surveillance on the people around her would do no harm at all.'

Eigon sat unmoving, staring at Melinus in horror. 'What do you mean, Pomponia Graecina has been arrested? Who has arrested her?'

'The Senate has accused her of practising a foreign superstition to the detriment of the safety of the state and the Emperor!'

Eigon's mouth dropped open. 'A foreign superstition,' she echoed. 'She is a Christian! We saw her baptised!'

Melinus nodded grimly. 'Exactly.'

'But why? Why suddenly? I know many people are suspicious of Christians, but they are not persecuted for their beliefs as long as they do not question the Emperor's divinity. And most just keep quiet about that like the rest of us!'

'I do not recall the lady Pomponia being discreet about this emperor any more than she was about Claudius. She's accused him of being implicated in the death of her son, you know.'

Eigon was silent. 'That was stupid. Even if she had proof it was foolish to let it be known what she suspected. No one dares say things like that about the Emperor.' She sighed. 'But whatever the truth of the situation who would betray her?'

Melinus shrugged. 'And who else has been betrayed ...' he said thoughtfully.

She guessed at once that Melinus was thinking about his friend Felicius and about Julius. She felt herself grow pale.

'What will happen to her?'

'She will be made to appear before her husband and his family to answer the charge.'

'And what will they do?'

Melinus shrugged. 'I don't know.' Why suddenly? Why now? And why were the members of Caradoc's household suddenly being watched openly? Everyone, even the slaves. He studied Eigon's face, concerned. 'Be careful, when you go out. I know you seldom do. And I know you are always escorted. But there is something amiss here.'

For a moment Eigon held his gaze. She shivered. 'You know something?'

He shook his head. 'My senses grow dull with age!' His voice was suddenly full of frustration. 'I gaze into the sacred pool and I see nothing but ripples in the water; I listen to the wind in the trees and it speaks a foreign language I no longer understand. I feel surrounded by messages I cannot read and dangers I cannot foresee. There is no future there.'

Eigon shivered. 'What should I do?'

'I don't know!' His anguish frightened her. 'Consult the gods, Eigon. Listen. See if they speak more clearly to you. Speak to your father. He is stronger now. He is a wise man.' Gathering his cloak around him with a shiver he walked away from her, disappearing into the house, heading, shoulders slumped in despair, towards his own room.

Eigon watched him go, overwhelmed with loneliness. Melinus was her mentor, her teacher and her friend. More and more recently he had withdrawn from her. She watched his uncertainties and his unhappiness with increasing helplessness. He was the one she turned to. Now he was drawing away from her and she didn't feel ready to take up the burden he was passing on.

She made her way thoughtfully to her private office, the room where she saw the sick and injured who came to consult her skills. She felt the room wrap its peacefulness around her as it always did. She loved this place. Her own sanctum, which smelled of dried herbs. Before the small shrine to the goddess Bride a lamp burned, the sweet oil adding to the scent of the room. She stared at the shrine thoughtfully. The gods they worshipped in this house were many. The gods of the household, the gods of healing, the goddess of fever, gods of Britannia and gods of Rome and now, since Peter had come to speak to her father, and pray for him, his hand on Caratacus's forehead, the Christian god, Jesus. She stared at the small carving of a fish she had set on the shrine. The secret sign the Christians used amongst themselves. She smiled. Like so many educated people in Rome she spoke Greek, painstakingly taught to her by Melinus over the years and it was Greek which was the key to this symbol. *Icthus*, a fish. The letters stood for *Iesous Christos Theou Huios Soter*, Jesus Christ, son of God, Saviour.

The Christian god was full of love and kindness. Peter promised that He would take care of people and indeed as soon as Peter had spoken to her father he had begun to recover, though he had not consented to be baptised. Not then. She pondered. What was the prayer they used? 'Our Father,' they said. And their father was a kind and caring father. A shepherd who looked after his sheep. A host who fed his guests. And ensured their wine did not run out. She smiled to herself. She remembered her father's face when he heard that story. The twitch of his lips, the appreciative glint in his eyes. That as much as the touch of Peter's hand had started him on the road to recovery. She bit her lip. She did not yet dare hope that he was cured. This had happened again and again over the years. A few weeks or months' respite, then as the summer heat grew and the air festered, he would be struck down again, in days as weak as he had ever been. But he was stronger than she remembered him. His old wounds were troubling him far less. Maybe Jesus had healed him.

She stared round the small room, eyeing the lines of jars with their waxed seals, the bunches of dried herbs hanging from a ceiling beam, from a line of forged hooks worked into the shape of birds' claws, a gift from Julia, made by some friend of Flavius's. She went to stand in front of her work table. It was neatly swept of the crumbs of dried herbs which so often littered it; on one side a stack of small empty pots, on the other wax notepads and a stylus. A couple of scrolls lay there with carefully copied recipes for herbal mixtures for various ailments, the most common suffered by the members of the household who routinely came to her now for help when they were ill.

The door opened behind her and she swung round. Aelius stood there. His face was white. 'Lady Eigon. There are soldiers in the courtyard. They are demanding to see you.'

'Soldiers?' Fear knifed through her.

'Praetorians.'

'Did they say what they wanted?' Her fists were clenched into the folds of her gown.

He shook his head. 'I assumed they would want to speak to the king, but they insist on seeing you.'

She took a deep breath. 'I will speak to their commanding officer in the atrium, Aelius. His men are to remain outside. And I want you to stay with me when I speak to him.' She drew herself up and took a deep breath, trying to steady her voice.

It wasn't him. For a moment she had been terrified that he had grown tired of waiting for her guard to drop and had come looking for her. This man she didn't recognise as he saluted before her.

'Lucius Flavius Corbidum, madam.'

Eigon greeted him calmly and waited in silence to hear what he had to say.

For a moment he hesitated. Then he proceeded. 'I have a warrant for the arrest of your slave, the man known as Melinus. It was suggested that I speak to you directly rather than the king as he is ill. You would not want him to be drawn into any accusations of treason.'

Eigon stared at him. 'You are accusing Melinus of treason?'

The young man nodded. 'It would be better for you to call him than for me to send my men into the villa to search for him by force, princess.'

'Melinus could not be guilty of treason,' Eigon stammered. She glanced at Aelius who was standing by the door, his face a careful blank. 'It is not in his nature. He is a kind, gentle man, not interested in politics –'

'That is for the judges to say, princess.' Lucius eyed her brazenly. Titus was right. She had turned into a looker, this child he had himself found all those years ago in a soggy wood in a far corner of the Empire. And her reaction proved Titus right. Melinus was one of her friends. And one by one her friends were about to disappear. If she believed that a slave was going to get a trial she was more naïve than she looked. But all he wanted was to get the man out of the house as quickly as possible with the minimum of fuss.

A figure had appeared in the doorway behind them. Melinus was standing there watching them. With a thoughtful glance at Aelius he stepped forward. 'You have come for me?' His face was grave.

'If you are Melinus.'

Melinus bowed assent. Lucius shivered. This man, he had been told, was a Druid. A feared and proscribed priest of the vicious Celtic religion of this young woman and her father, and he looked every inch the part with his long silver hair and his carved staff. He found he had to nerve himself to look the man in the eye.

'I have a warrant for your arrest. You are to accompany me to the Mamertine prison where you will be held pending your trial.' He suspected that Melinus would know there would be no trial. The man could probably already hear the roar of the hungry lions waiting to tear him apart. He stood to attention, ready to shout for his men but Melinus merely shrugged. It was as if he had been expecting this to happen. Lucius shivered. Druids were fearsome in so many ways, not least because they could foretell the future.

Melinus turned to Eigon and smiled. 'Do not fear, princess. I will be all right.'

'But Melinus –'

'Do not come after me.' He frowned sternly. 'Do nothing. What happens to me is written in the stars. Stay with your father.' Ignoring Aelius, he turned to Lucius, his voice even, almost friendly. 'We should go, my friend, before the storm breaks.'

'What storm?' Lucius gazed towards the open roof of the atrium, above the central pool. The sky was an unbroken blue.

Melinus gave an enigmatic smile. 'The storm which will be sent by my gods to show their displeasure at my arrest.' He strode towards the doorway.

Lucius hurried after him. He paused almost as an afterthought to bow towards Eigon, then he had gone. Eigon stared after them, her mouth dry, her stomach tight with fear as, almost too faint to hear, a first low threatening rumble echoed around the distant hills.

*   *   *

267

'Did you hear the thunder?' Jess whispered. 'The gods of the hills are angry. It will be the worst storm Rome has ever seen.'

She refocused her attention slowly from the glitter of sunbeams filtered through the narrow leaves of the plants shading their table to find herself sitting opposite Rhodri in the corner of the terrace. He was watching her intently. 'Welcome back.'

She frowned. 'What do you mean?'

'You've been two thousand years away, somewhere.' He gave a quizzical smile. 'Tell me what happened?'

She hesitated, still dazed, then a wave of embarrassment swept over her as she glanced at her watch. 'How long have I been dreaming?'

He shrugged. 'Not long. But you weren't asleep. You were in some sort of trance, gazing into the distance. You called out someone's name. Melinus.'

'Melinus was arrested. He was a Druid.' Her embarrassment had disappeared as quickly as it had come. She was, she realised, comfortable talking to him about it.

Rhodri raised an eyebrow. 'A Welshman?'

She nodded. 'I suppose so. He was Eigon's friend.' Her eyes flooded with tears suddenly. 'He was going to be killed. They were going to throw him to the lions.'

'Why?'

'Because he was a Druid. They were banned. The Romans were terrified of them. And he was gentle. Kind. A scholar.' She brushed her hand across her face. 'I'm sorry. Now you know I'm mad!'

'"You are but mad north north west!"' he quoted. 'Remember your *Hamlet*?' He gave her a sideways glance. 'And Eigon. What happened to her?' He had a generous smile, she realised. Not mocking after all.

'I don't know. They took him away –' She broke off suddenly. 'Rhodri! Dan's still here!'

Rhodri straightened. 'Where?'

'Don't move. Don't look round,' she murmured. 'He's down there, leaning on a wall in the piazza, waiting.'

Rhodri sat back in his chair. He crossed his legs casually as though getting more comfortable. It gave him a view of the whole area. 'I think we need that master plan,' he said quietly. 'He can presumably sit there all day if he chooses to. I must confess, I don't like the thought of him following us wherever we go.' He smiled suddenly. 'But then we don't have to go out that way, do we!' He raised his hand and summoned the waiter. 'This gentleman will show you out by the back door, so to speak. I will sit here until you have time to be well clear, then I will stroll out past Dan and have a few words on my way by.' He put on his dark glasses and folded his arms, a picture of bored inattention, aware of Dan watching him through narrowed eyes, alert to their every move. 'I've had second thoughts about all this, Jess. I think you should go straight to the airport. Get out of the country.'

'But what about Eigon?' She was amazed at the wave of anguish that hit her. 'I can't go without knowing what happens to her and to Melinus.'

'You can find that out when you get back to Wales.'

'No, you don't understand! I can't, that's the whole point. She is a child in Wales. She must be, otherwise why didn't she come to me as an adult? I will go back to Ty Bran and she will be a small child again, playing hide and seek in the wood. I have to be here!'

'Jess!' Rhodri sat forward, his fists on the table. 'Be sensible! Now I've had the chance to look into the man's eyes, I don't like what I see! He is a psychopath! Wherever you go he seems to be able to find you. He wants you dead! You can't stay here in Rome.'

There was a moment's intense silence. 'I know he said that, but he didn't mean it, he just wants to make sure –' She paused.

'He wants to make sure you can't hurt him, Jess.' Rhodri leaned forward, his face inches from hers. 'He is terrified of what you could do to him.'

'But he's cancelled anything I could say by telling everyone I'm mad. So I'm not a threat!'

Rhodri sighed. 'Let's hope so.' He paused. 'You remember what we were talking about before he so rudely interrupted us? Religion. I think now might be the time to try the odd prayer. You never know. It might help. Now, just go, Jess, before he twigs what we are doing. I'll be in touch, OK?'

'So, you are a prisoner in Rome, like Eigon!' Carmella looked at Jess with a quizzical smile as she let her in.

Jess nodded. She watched Carmella put the chain across the

door then they made their way through into Carmella's small sitting room.

'Please. I desperately need you to read the cards for me.' Jess sat down. 'They spell things out clearly. I need to know what happened to her. And I need to know what will happen to me.' Her face was drawn and pale. 'I can't get away from Dan. He follows me everywhere. He seems to know everything I do. He wants to kill me but I can't leave Rome till I know what's happened to Eigon.'

Carmella sat down opposite her. Wearing a black silk bathrobe, her hair piled on top of her head straight from the shower, she looked strangely serene, almost ethereal. It was several seconds before it dawned on Jess suddenly that maybe she had been about to go out. 'I'm sorry. I won't stay long. But I have to know.'

Carmella nodded. She reached for her cards and began to unwrap them. Jess's eyes were fixed on her hands as she carefully shuffled the big cards, with a rhythmic, hypnotic motion. Finally she laid them on the table. 'Cut for me, please!'

Obediently Jess reached forward and lifted a small section of the pack, putting them neatly down beside the others. She waited, holding her breath. Carmella gathered them up and held them for a moment against her breast, her eyes closed, then slowly she began to deal them out face down onto the table.

'*Ancora il re di coppe al negativo.*' Her finger rested for a second on the card. 'We expect to see him, do we not? He is still here. Still angry. And he is coupled with another. *Spade*. Swords. *Molto combattivo*. You have many swords in this reading.' She paused, studying the cards. The other listener was there, silent. Concentrated. For a moment Carmella had a vision of a face, intelligent, amused, watchful, then it had gone. She brought her attention back to the cards with an effort. 'Swords can mean danger and stress and even death.' She hesitated. Her hand was hovering over the king.

'Upside down,' Jess murmured. 'That's bad, isn't it.'

Carmella frowned. '*Il re di spade*. Powerful. Arrogant. Obsessed with his needs to control a situation which he sees slipping from his grasp.' Her finger had reached the Tower. '*La casa di dio*,' she murmured. There was a long pause. She said nothing. Her finger moved on. 'Dan is pushed, driven, by another man,' she said softly. 'An overshadow. A man with darker hair, amber eyes, a taller man –'

270

'Titus,' Jess whispered. 'Titus Marcus Olivinus. The man who raped Eigon. The man who is pursuing Eigon.' There was a long silence. Outside, from four storeys below they could hear the sounds of Rome drifting in through the open windows.

Carmella leaned forward suddenly, chewing her lip. Briskly she dealt three more cards from the pack and turned them face up. 'The ten of swords,' she whispered. She shook her head and moved on. 'OK. Here we see what they will do, these two men in one body. This is danger for you.' She paused. 'Here is the joker, the fool. He heralds a journey for you all. There is so much here. You cannot escape what is to happen, Jess. You are linked to Eigon in some way now, which is why you feel you cannot leave her.' Her attention was still fixed on the cards. 'Here is *la luna*. She warns that you are becoming too fixated on this inner life. You are not possessed by her?' Carmella looked up suddenly.

Jess shivered. 'No, I don't think so. No. Definitely not.'

'But you are obsessed by her. Why?'

'I suppose I was touched by seeing her as a little girl, so frightened and unhappy. So guilty about losing her brother and sister. She haunts Ty Bran as a child. Here in Rome she is a grown woman. I want to know what happened to her.' She reached forward and ran her finger across one of the cards. The page of wands.

Carmella smiled. 'You have found her.'

'Eigon?'

'Of course.'

'But it is a boy.'

'Also known as *la principessa*!' Carmella put her head on one side. 'You think she cannot come to you as a grown woman when you return to Wales? Why?'

Jess shrugged. 'Just a feeling. I want to make it better for her, but I can't, can I. It is all in the past. I can't change the past!'

'Can't you?' Carmella said the words almost casually, gently challenging.

'How?'

'You have already changed things. By thinking about them. By drawing attention to them. By dipping your finger into the waters of time and causing ripples. You have awoken Titus and brought him into the present.'

Jess was shaken by a wave of nausea. 'To possess Dan. Does

that mean he will leave Eigon alone in the past and come after me instead?'

It was a while before Carmella answered thoughtfully. 'It would not have happened were Dan not open to him. Dan needed the anger and the fear. They need each other.' She looked up suddenly. 'But this makes it twice as dangerous for you.'

'So how can I escape them?' Jess met Carmella's eyes. She took a deep breath, trying to match Carmella's serenity.

'You, Jess, share one characteristic with Eigon which is very marked.' Carmella dealt another three cards. She scanned them and looked up. 'Neither of you is prepared to rely on someone else. You are not prepared to rely on a man. There are men prepared to help you, as there are men prepared to help her. You do not trust them. You do not think they are strong enough.'

'Which men? Will? Rhodri?'

Carmella glanced up at her. 'At least you know who they are.'

'But it's not fair to drag them into this. It is not their problem.'

'I think they are both in your story already, Jess. Will, from the beginning. He is, as we *tarocchi* readers say, at the heart of the matter. Then Rhodri comes in, at the same moment as Titus enters the drama. Is he going to be the *deus ex machina*, who will bring resolution to the story, or will he be the catalyst who stirs the pot? Or,' she glanced up, 'will he turn out to be the villain?'

In spite of herself Jess laughed. 'What a hotchpotch of mixed metaphors! But surely, this is what the tarot can tell me?'

Carmella shook her head. 'I merely lay out the scenario at this stage. I tell you to beware. I tell you to trust Will.' She pointed to the king of Pentacles. 'Trustworthy. Loyal. Patient.' She glanced up again. 'Perhaps not exciting, but do you need any more excitement at the moment?'

'And Rhodri is exciting?'

Carmella grinned mischievously. 'Ah. Our *cantante lirico*, our *divo*. He is a big character on the stage. The lead role!'

'Does he feature in Eigon's life?'

She frowned. 'I don't see him there. But I don't see you there either, Jess. You are silent watchers. You are not characters in her play. But in your own, it is you who are the greatest danger to yourself, Jess. To escape Dan you should leave Rome. You won't go. To be safe you should stay inside; you go out. You court danger. Why?' For a moment she held Jess's gaze.

Jess shook her head helplessly. 'I can't help it,' she whispered.

The conversation was interrupted by the doorbell, jangling intrusively through the intimacy of the moment. Jess stood up, frightened. 'Is that Dan?'

Carmella shook her head. 'It is my date. I am sorry, Jess. But I have to go out.'

'I'll leave.'

No!' Carmella sailed past her towards the front door of the apartment. 'No, you can stay here as long as you like.' She pulled the door open and let in a tall, grey-haired man. Pulling him into the room she introduced them. 'Henrico, this is my friend, Jess. Jess this is my dinner date. I will get dressed quickly. *Cinque minuti, carissimo.*' She winked at Henrico as she headed for the bedroom door. 'Jess, I want you to stay in the flat. Please don't go out. Think about what I have said. There is food in the fridge. You know where things are. Stay here and stay silent. Don't ring anyone. I've called Kim. She knows you are safe. Stay the night. If I don't come home this evening,' she glanced coquettishly at Henrico, 'do not worry. I shall return *domani* and we will talk some more, but before I go, there is something I must say to you. Come in here.' She led Jess into the bedroom and closed the door. 'I must teach you more to protect yourself psychically. Eigon is leading you into dangerous places and there are things you can do to keep yourself safe. Do not follow Eigon into the past. Watch, but don't take part. Imagine a circle of flames around you. Light the dark places. Be aware of the dangers. Protection, Jess. Never forget it. And remember, never say Titus's name! Make sure you are on your own ground. Surround yourself with guides and angels; there is no point in Christian prayers and platitudes. Hit him with his own gods. Call on your power animal. Whoever you see as your inner friend, call on them to protect you. And clear the space physically. Wait, I will show you what to do.'

The apartment was very silent after they had left. Jess walked slowly out of the opened windows onto the roof terrace and stood looking round. It felt safe here; otherworldly. She sat down at the small wrought iron table thinking about Carmella's revelations. She was a silent watcher in Eigon's play. That much was true. She wasn't a character; she wasn't there. There was nothing she could do to influence the past one way or the other. But, protected by Carmella's rituals, she could watch it. And perhaps if she watched it enough she could reach into the open window of their lives and lightly touch them in warning.

Julius defied Cerys's ban to bring Eigon the news himself. 'It was very quick. He would not have suffered.'

She was shredding the edge of her stole between nervous fingers, fighting back the tears.

He swallowed hard. He had gone to visit Melinus in the dungeon of the Mamertine before the day of the executions. Nero had seen to it that there was a good selection of men and women, some Christians, feeling the weight of the city's suspicion, some murderers, traitors who Nero felt had threatened him personally, all condemned to die the worst of deaths. And Julius had forced himself to go to the arena to watch. 'I will be there for you, my friend,' he had said before he left. 'Grandfather should not come. He is not strong, but I will be there and I will hold you in my prayers. Your gods and my God will stand firm beside you. You will have one friend in the stands who will see to it, I promise.'

Melinus had smiled a little wanly. 'It is my belief, Julius, that I shall go to the land of the ever young, in the country of my forebears. It will be a happy day for me. I bless the creature that chooses to end my suffering and I forgive it.'

'That is a Christian sentiment, old friend.' Julius teased gently. 'I see now why Eigon always calls you her Christian Druid.'

Melinus gave a wistful laugh. 'Eigon is probably right, as with so many things. I give her into your care, Julius.' He took a deep breath. 'Last night the powers of foresight which have forsaken me for so long returned. I saw her enemy. And mine, it seems. There is a man out there in the city. A member of the Praetorian guard who seeks her death. He is afraid of her and angry at her. The gods did not tell me why. They veiled the past where the reason lies, but I have my suspicions. This man was behind my arrest, and the arrest of Pomponia Graecina. Because he is Eigon's enemy he is also your enemy. He is the enemy of all who love her. Take warning, Julius. Be strong, my boy. Take her away from Rome if you can. As long as she remains here she is in terrible danger.'

Julius frowned. 'Who is he? Did you see his face?'

Melinus shook his head. 'The gods enjoy their games. They

warn but they do not reveal. That is for us to work out. Ask your Jesus to protect her, Julius. She has had little love in her life. A god of love would be a kindness now.' He paused and a small smile lit his eyes. 'I think your attentions might be welcome too, my boy!'

Julius blushed. 'I don't think she has even noticed me in that way.'

'Oh, I think she has. You know her mother has forbidden her to see you? Why would the lady Cerys do that unless she sensed an interest there. Eigon has an iron will, Julius. She has been well trained. By me.' He grinned again. 'She is clever and witty and educated. She is a talented and blessed healer. She could be a priestess in our own land.' He raised an eyebrow. 'I am sad not to see what she will become, but perhaps I will be granted a new life to do just that, who knows. She thinks she will not marry. She thinks the powers that be in Rome have decided that there should be no bloodline of Caratacus to focus dissent in Britannia. The rest of her family died. She is the last.' He put out a thin hand to rest on Julius's arm. The iron manacle around his wrist clanked uncomfortably and Julius felt the weight of it dragging the old man down. 'Someone must see to it that she returns to her own country.'

Julius looked round nervously. The other prisoners, all wrapped up in their own terror and misery were paying them no attention. 'Do you know what you are saying?'

Melinus nodded. 'Go now, my boy. Take my blessings. Pray for my soul.'

The lion killed him with a single clean bite to the neck. It must have been instantaneous. As Julius stood in the baying crowd watching the blood of a dozen victims soak into the sawdust of the arena he felt a soft touch against his cheek, the smallest breath of wind. 'Courage, my boy. It was easy.' Were those words whispered in his ear? He stared round. The crowd was focused on the gore and the roaring of the beasts as their prey was dragged away from them on hooks, taunting them, luring them to look round for other victims. Blindly Julius turned away and fought his way towards the exit. He wasn't the only man to vomit into the bushes outside.

* * *

He reached out and gently he took Eigon's hand. 'I had a long talk to Melinus last night, before –' He didn't finish the sentence. There was a moment of silence, then he went on. 'He saw into the future and he saw a man who he said was your enemy.' He was watching her face and he saw the colour drain from her cheeks. Reaching out he stroked the tears away. 'You know who he is, don't you?'

She nodded wordlessly.

'Are you going to tell me?'

She shook her head slowly. 'He's a shadow from my past. Best forgotten.'

'You can't forget him if he is hunting down your friends.'

She stared at him. 'What do you mean?'

'Melinus said this man was the one who had accused Pomponia Graecina and the one who had named him. He said he was going to take your friends away one by one.'

Eigon turned away sharply. 'Then you must go. You mustn't come here again.'

'It is too late, Eigon. Everyone knows you are my friend.' He smiled gently. 'Just as my family are your friends. Antonia and Grandfather are just as much in danger as I am, if indeed there is any danger – we will be the judge of that. But if I am in danger, I need to know where it is coming from. Melinus said he is a member of the Praetorians.'

Eigon nodded slowly.

'And he obviously has influence.'

She nodded again.

'Then why has he not been able to reach you?'

She shrugged. 'I have often wondered. I suppose my father's household look out for me.' She paused. 'But I suspect sometimes that, maybe, he is playing with me.'

He raised an eyebrow. That could be a shrewd deduction. He glanced towards the doorway as a figure appeared in the shadows. 'Julia!'

'Julius!' She giggled as she ran towards them. 'Why did no one tell me you were here!' She threw her arms around his neck. 'Eigon, you selfish woman! You have been keeping him to yourself.' She planted a kiss on Julius's cheek. 'Have you come to collect me and take me to the games?'

Eigon turned away sharply. She went to stand by the fountain staring down at the water, pitted by the gentle waterdrops cascading from the central figure.

'I have been to the games, Julia,' Julius said sternly. 'I do not intend to go again. I went to watch Melinus die.'

Julia stared at him in horror. Then she turned to Eigon. 'Did you know –' She broke off, shrugging. 'Of course you did. I'm sorry. That's awful.' She sat down on one of the chairs under the fig tree, smoothing down her skirt. 'I can see that would spoil the games for you.'

'A trifle,' Julius said dryly. He walked back to Eigon. 'I should leave. Will you be all right?'

She nodded.

He put a hand on her shoulder gently. 'Take care, won't you.'

'And you. Be careful, all of you.' She looked up through her tears.

He turned away. 'Look after her,' he said to Julia as he passed her, then he had gone.

Julia looked up. Her face was white. 'Poor Melinus.'

Eigon came over and sat down beside her. 'At least he is free now. Free to go home, to the land of the ever young. Perhaps from there he will see the mountains of my home too.'

'You sound as though you still miss it,' Julia said, puzzled. 'Can you still remember it?'

'Of course. It wasn't that long ago.' Eigon sighed. 'I may have been a child but I can remember it well. The mists and the rain, the soft sunlight, sucking up the clouds and leaving the land bathed in gold, the apple trees, the gentle breezes, the hills full of mysterious shadows and wild rushing rivers. Eagles soaring above the mountains.'

And ravens. The thought came to her suddenly. Ravens, harbingers of death, gathering over the battlefield, warning them, crying at her father not to engage the enemy. He had ignored the portents. And his people had paid with their freedom and their lives. And his younger children, had they also been sacrificed to the goddess of war? She shuddered.

'They won't send Aunt Pomponia to be torn apart by lions, will they?' Julia had finally realised the significance of what had happened that morning. She bit her lip. 'Eigon, we have to save her!'

Eigon smiled. 'Your aunt will be fine,' she said gravely. Julius had already told her the news. Pomponia Graecina had, as the law demanded, been called to face a court headed by her husband but he had immediately decreed the accusations against her arrant nonsense. She was already free.

So one of Titus's targets had slipped through the net. Standing up she wandered back to stare down into the waters of the fountain again. She was beginning to understand her persecutor now. Who would be next, she wondered sadly.

It would not be long before she found out.

Jess lay back in the comfortable cushioned chair, staring up at the sky. It was evening now. She could smell the kitchens of Rome firing up, readying to prepare the evening meals of three million people. She gave a wry smile. She had never felt less like eating. She wanted to ring someone. Steph. Kim. And Will. How was Will and where was he? But Carmella was right. She mustn't do it. She mustn't even think about it. Dan and Titus were marauding the streets out there somewhere, somehow plugged into her every thought.

Titus had taught Dan to listen. Not with his ears, but with his inner senses. It was something he had never done before and it astounded him: the sheer amount of 'stuff' there was out there, waiting to be heard. Of course he wasn't a fool. He knew what had happened. And when. Parked up on the edge of the field near Ty Bran. He had climbed into the car, empty. Afraid. Not knowing what to do, knowing only that he had blown everything – his career, his marriage, his future. Then, unexpectedly, suddenly, he had sensed that other person there, next to him. He had been afraid, terrified, but he hadn't fought it. What had he to lose?

He was sitting now on the rim of the fountain below the Spanish Steps, watching the world go by as it grew dark. She was nearby, he could feel her. Something was changing. It was almost as if he didn't have to follow her any more. He just knew. He smiled. He wasn't sure what Titus intended but it didn't matter. He would know when the time came what he had to do. He closed his eyes. In the meantime he had, he was sure, covered all the eventualities. Will was a spent force. Weak. Maybe he should have despatched him

278

while he had the chance, putting him out of his misery like a broken animal, but maybe better this way to add to the confusion. Nat, her friends, the headmaster, even that weirdo opera singer were all in the picture now. They all knew about her 'breakdown'. No one would listen to her; she had nowhere to go. If in the end she decided to cut her losses and end it all, who would be surprised? He smiled to himself. No sweat. If he wasn't so comfortable watching the crowds he might get up and go and check into some small hotel; enjoy his last few days in Rome. After all, it couldn't be long now. He felt Titus stir, somewhere there inside his own head. An uncomfortable presence, living off him, draining his energy, but it was something he was prepared to put up with for now. For now they could help each other.

21

Will directed the taxi along the street towards the palazzo and then got the man to drop him off on the corner. It was late, but he could see there were lights on in the apartment windows. He glanced both ways down the street and loped across to push the intercom. 'Kim? It's me. Can I come in?'

'So, how are you?' Kim drew him inside.

'OK. He must have hit me on the head and then slipped me some sort of Mickey Finn. It left me with a foul headache.'

'The bastard! I thought you were going back to London?' Kim and Steph had been sitting in the half dark, the windows open onto the courtyard.

'I was, but I thought better of it.' Will's lips tightened. 'Dan is going to need dealing with. Is Jess safely away?'

Kim and Steph glanced at each other. 'We had a plan, but she blew it. Rhodri was supposed to get her away from his hotel, but Dan found them. He must have followed her from here. It is all right. She is safe with Carmella. We don't know where Dan went.'

'Shit!'

Kim produced a bottle of wine. She fetched three glasses. 'Jess is her own worst enemy. She keeps going off on her own. She doesn't trust us. I don't think she trusts anyone.'

Will banged his glass down on the table. A little wine slopped onto the surface of the wood and stood, a small pool in the darkness.

'What about Rhodri?'

Kim grinned. 'Rhodri is scouring Rome for Dan as we speak. The trouble is no one has any idea where to look.' She had found a paper napkin and was dabbing at the spilled wine.

'So where do we go from here?'

'We can't just wait. We have to do something.' Will stood up restlessly. He went to stare down out of the window. 'That's where I saw Dan. Down there in the garden.'

'Well, he's not there now. I've had the locks changed!' Kim said crisply. 'Jacopo has had the telling off from hell. He's lucky to have kept his job.'

'Not his fault,' Will commented. 'He was out of his league. As we all were.' He took a thoughtful sip from his glass, still looking out into the dark 'It's this damn obsession of hers. It's not rational. Supposing she goes off into one of her daydreams and never wakes up?'

Steph moved away restlessly. 'We must do something. We have to persuade Jess to leave.'

Kim walked over and put her hand on Steph's shoulder. 'But how?'

Titus and Lucius were off duty, wearing togas, strolling towards the Senate to hear the debate. They were also engaged in deep conversation.

'I've put word about,' Lucius murmured. 'As you suggested. I don't think there is any doubt that the whole family are Christians.' He sighed. 'Pity. I rather liked the look of Antonia. And she would come with a first-rate dowry. But if she has befriended our princess she will have to go.' He gave an uncomfortable laugh. 'It's not easy always to find a way to incriminate people, though. Christianity is not in itself illegal.'

'All the more reason to make sure our Emperor becomes more and more suspicious of it. I grant you he's not interested in politics. He prefers his music and plays and orgies in the palace, but we need only sow seeds.' Titus grinned. 'The mush he calls his brain is fertile ground for seeds!'

The two men roared with laughter. Titus glanced across at his friend. He had a good instinct for weakening resolve. 'It seems unfair for me to plan my own delicious dalliance with the princess and leave you out. Why don't we give you the gentle Antonia? It would be unkind to send her to the wild beasts as a virgin. What a waste!'

Lucius frowned. 'I'm not sure I like this, Titus.'

'Oh, you will like it, believe me.' Titus slapped him on the shoulder. 'And I have far richer plans for you, my friend, when

281

it comes to the matrimonial stakes. You needn't worry about that. Do this for me, and I shall see you rewarded beyond your wildest dreams.'

It was so easy when men were short of cash. Lucius had already spent his allowance. Titus had made it his business to find out which moneylender he went to and how often he had written to his mother to beg for extra funds. His father had long ago stopped responding to his son's desperate pleas for loans, refusing even to read the letters carried back to the estate by a succession of winsome slaves chosen by Lucius in the hope they would tempt his father to look favourably on him.

'I think we should start to plan more urgently,' Titus went on. 'I'd hate to hear that either lady had been snatched from under our noses by prospective suitors. They are already suspicious. Maybe it was a mistake to take Melinus. But I want Eigon isolated. I want her to feel the fear.' His face hardened. 'Right. Antonia must wait her turn. Our next target is Julia Pomponia. No one can call her a Christian, so that won't work. I think she just needs to disappear. Any ideas?'

Lucius shook his head.

'An accident, I think. Plain and simple. The girl is out of control anyway. She's pretty,' he paused reflectively, 'but she's greedy and stupid. She can be lured by gold bangles and earrings. I'll see to that. You don't need to get involved with this part of the plan.' He glanced ahead at the Senate building. 'Are you still coming? It is always worth hearing Seneca. Then we can go on to the baths.'

'Flavius!' Jess heard herself scream. 'Flavius, Aelius, you have to guard her! Eigon, tell Julia to be careful . . .'

She stared round frantically into the luminous darkness. Only the pelargoniums and bougainvillea on Carmella's roof terrace heard her warning. Climbing up out of the chair she went to lean over the railing, looking down at the lights far below. She found she was trembling. The streets were still crowded, cars threading their way slowly between pedestrians, the sound of music reaching her from the bistro further up the narrow street, tables and noise and the flavours of the menu overflowing onto the street and drifting up towards her. She was shivering and there were tears on her cheeks. She brushed them away impatiently. The dream had gone and there was nothing she could do. In the depths of the flat the door buzzer rang. She spun round and stared at the entry phone, her heart thudding. There was a long pause then it rang again. She held her breath. She was safe. No one could get in. But the sharp noise of the buzzer had spoiled her sense of calm safety. She was agitated again. Her head was aching. She needed Eigon. She wanted Eigon's cooling hands on her brow, a poultice of green herbs, the gentle patter of water from the fountain in the atrium, the peace of a gentle healing darkness.

'Eigon? Where are you? I'm leaving now. Are you sure you don't want to come?' Julia was standing near the door, her best stole around her shoulders. 'I've ordered the litter. They could carry us both.'

Eigon shook her head and smiled. 'Not this time. I have someone in the side room. A woman with a hangover.' She turned and glanced at the retching woman. There was a black bruise on the side of her head.

Julia grimaced. 'Rather you than me!' She turned away and headed out into the sunlight, scowling. Flavius was supposed to be coming with her but at the last moment he had been called back by his father. She'd furiously told him not to obey, and he had hesitated, torn between his duty to his father and his desire to protect her. But duty had won. 'Wait for me, Julia! I won't be long,' he had shouted before he disappeared into the house.

'He will,' one of the slaves had commented with a laugh. 'Aelius is fed up with Flavius jaunting off to the shops with you. You can kiss goodbye to the trip if you wait for him.'

Julia raised an eyebrow. 'Is that so? Then we'll go without him. I shall be perfectly safe with you. You know where we're going.' To the silk vendor, then on to her favourite sandal shop and then on to her aunt's to exchange gossip over a carafe of grape juice with some of her friends. Climbing into the litter she pulled the curtains against the dust and sat back on the cushions with a little sigh of pleasure. It was quite exciting to be on her own for once. An adventure. If she was honest she was beginning to tire of Flavius's doe-eyed devotion. And Pomponia Graecina had pointed out more than once that at her age Julia should be thinking more in terms of a good marriage than dalliance with the son of a freedman. She closed her eyes thoughtfully. She had always known that Flavius was not for her. Not on any longterm basis, but he was useful. A compliant escort who denied her nothing. All right, so the money for her gifts was always hers, but that meant she always got what she wanted. She smiled to herself. If she had been a cat she would have purred.

When the litter lurched to a halt she didn't react. Her daydreams were too pleasant. She felt the chair descend with a jolt and at last she sat up and pulled back the curtain. A pair of bright eyes were staring in at her. They belonged to an exceedingly handsome man. 'Greetings, lady Julia!' He saluted. 'I have been sent by a friend of yours to bring you to his house. He has a goldsmith there he is sure you would like to meet.'

She saw the worried face of the senior slave. She saw the two front littermen look at each other in concern. Then she glanced back at the green-eyed god who had waved the litter down. 'Just give the order and your litter can follow me.' He was rich, she noted, accustomed to spotting the detail of people's clothing. The neat stitching, the finely wrought pins and buckles, the expensive barbering, the heavy signet ring, the accoutrements of his horse. Even the horse itself.

'All right. Why not.' She gave him a flirtatious smile. 'It would be rude to refuse.'

'NO!' Jess was screaming inside her head, but no sound emerged. She was powerless to intervene.

The slaves carrying the litter had followed the man up a long avenue of pines and round the back of an old house. It appeared to be closed up. The windows were shuttered and there was no sign of anyone there.

Julia leaned forward and peered out in excitement. She frowned. It was a nice enough house, but not quite the huge place she had expected. And where were the slaves, the grooms, the chariot and litters which she would expect in a rich man's villa? The slaves put the litter on the ground near the door.

The young man swung down from his horse. 'Take the litter back to your master's house. The lady Julia won't be requiring it again.

I shall bring her back on my horse later.' Money changed hands then he pulled back the curtain and handed her out. 'This way.' He smiled at her warmly enough, but there was something in his eyes which gave her pause. She glanced round. 'There's no one here.'

'There is.' He waved towards the stables. 'The horses are inside out of the sun. This way. You'll see.'

She followed him up the steps. The door opened easily and she stepped in behind him with only the smallest of misgivings.

Jess groaned. 'Don't go. Don't trust him. Please!'

Julia screamed. She stared at the two men and turned to run, but they came after her so easily, catching her, stripping her naked and tying her to the bedframe in the shadowed empty house. 'There you are, Lucius. A delicious gift.' Titus laughed. 'More beautiful than I had imagined.'

The two men had not bothered even to wear masks. She gazed up at them in terror. 'Please don't hurt me. Do whatever you want. Please –'

'We intend to do whatever we want, sweetheart, have no fear on that score.' Titus smiled down at her coldly. 'Shall I leave you, Lucius? Or do you prefer an audience?'

'Leave me.' Lucius was pulling at his clothes, excited beyond endurance in spite of his qualms.

When he had finished, Julia was sobbing quietly, her struggles over. It had not been so bad. He had been quite considerate and it was not as though it was the first time. Flavius had been the first. She opened her eyes and smiled up at the tall young man with his lean, athletic body, who was lying exhausted on top of her.

'That was nice after all.' She paused. 'Please, let me go now. I won't tell anyone.'

She turned her head slightly at the sound of footsteps nearby and paled. The other man, Titus, had appeared.

'My turn now, I think.'

Lucius climbed off the bed and bent to gather up his clothes. 'Don't hurt her, Titus.'

Titus laughed. 'Of course not.'

Lucius heard her screams from the courtyard where he had gone to sit near the horses. He put his hands over his ears. He had not liked this plan from the start. It was vicious and cruel and deeply sadistic. Climbing to his feet he went over to his horse which was moving uneasily at the end of its halter and he patted its nose, murmuring reassuringly in its ear.

The screams behind him reached a new, terrifying intensity, then abruptly they stopped. The silence, reverberating in the hot shadows beneath the pines and ilex which shaded the stable block was almost worse than the agonised noise. He bit his lip and turned towards the house, frowning. Perhaps Titus had relented.

It was several minutes before Titus appeared. He was fully dressed and his face was pale. There was blood on his hands. 'It is done,' he said. He walked over to the well and began to pull up a bucket of water. 'Go, Lucius, if you haven't the stomach for the next bit. I'll see you back at the barracks.'

Lucius closed his eyes. For a moment his stomach lurched, then he was in control again. Untying his horse's rein he led it out into the sunshine and vaulted into the saddle.

'No! No, Julia!'

Jess moved her head from side to side uneasily. She stared round, dazed. She was lying on the sofa in Carmella's sitting room, wearing Carmella's black and scarlet dressing gown. In the corner the TV was on quietly. A half-empty glass of wine was sitting on the table near her. The curtains were still closed. She groaned and sat up. Her head was spinning. She didn't remember drinking anything, or turning on the TV. She frowned. When had she got undressed? What time was it? She staggered into Carmella's kitchen and with shaking hands reached into the fridge for a jar of coffee beans. She had to concentrate. Drawing back the curtains she took the mug of black coffee out into the blazing sunshine on the roof terrace. Her hands were still shaking.

'Jess?' Carmella's voice woke her from her reverie about twenty minutes later. She appeared at the terrace window. 'I thought I smelled coffee. Wait, I will get myself some.'

Only when they were sitting down did Carmella look at her closely. 'Jess, what happened?'

There was a long silence after Jess finished talking. Carmella leaned forward, elbows on knees, staring at her intently. At last she shook her head reproachfully. 'You have forgotten already what I told you, Jess, about protecting yourself,' she said gently. She stood up and went inside, reappearing almost at once with her cards. She dealt six onto the low table and paused. 'I am asking here about Dan.' She sighed as one by one she turned up the cards. She hesitated. Was she there, the unknown watcher? She couldn't sense her presence. Not yet. 'We have here two men. Dan and this Titus. They are linked so closely like this,' she crossed her fingers, 'that they can read each other's minds. Both of them are losing their grip on reality.' She glanced up. 'If Titus can find you, Jess, I am afraid that perhaps so can Dan. They are both such dangerous men.' Carmella stared down at the cards and shook her head. She was conscious of her now, the enigmatic smile. The overview from faraway. Watching. She stood up. 'I am going to ring Steph. You should have your friends around you and we need to think what to do.'

'Wait!' Jess leaned forward and caught her sleeve. 'You've seen something else. Tell me what.'

'No more than you already know, Jess. You are in danger. I think Dan on his own might be content to try and ruin your reputation and then threaten you. With Titus in his head he is not responsible for his actions. Something happened to him and Titus on your Welsh hillside. It has forged a link which is growing stronger and stronger. And now Titus has blood on his hands.' She shook her head. 'My grandmama told me, when I was learning the cards, that there was something no one should ever, ever do and that is warn of a coming death. It is not for us to foretell the death of someone. The cards cannot do that. At least –' She paused. 'Even now, they cannot say for sure, but they warn me. They are afraid and they are telling me that you are in mortal danger.' She leaned forward and stroked her finger over them gently. 'We cannot ignore them, Jess. But I do not know how to advise you. I don't know how to keep you safe.' She straightened. 'So, I go and ring Kim, yes?'

Jess nodded. 'Yes, please.' Her mouth had gone dry.

Kim, Steph and Will were there in twenty minutes.

There weren't enough chairs and Will seated himself cross-legged on a cushion at Kim's feet as they sat down around the low table on the roof terrace. Carmella's spread was still lying there, the colourful cards bright in the sunlight.

'I think we can all agree that Dan has seriously lost it. But what can we do about it? There is no proof of anything apart from our word against his. He's been bloody clever.' Will shifted his weight, trying to get more comfortable as Carmella appeared with more coffee. 'I owe you an apology, Carmella, for not believing you can do whatever you do.' He grinned. 'You've saved my life in your own mysterious way.'

'I am glad to have helped you, Will.' She smiled back at him.

He held her gaze for a moment, then he turned back to the others. 'So, what if Jess did go back to London? Would she be safe there?'

Carmella shook her head. She took her place again in front of the cards. 'I don't think that is enough.' She looked down at them in silence for a long moment, then she glanced up at Steph who had been studying them in silence. 'You have seen what they say?'

Steph nodded.

Will frowned. 'Hang on a minute. What do they say exactly?'

Carmella shrugged. 'That Jess should disappear, as you suggest. But I don't think she would be any safer in London than here.'

'I suppose I could change my name. Dye my hair.' Jess gave a wan smile. She looked up. 'Where's Rhodri?' she asked suddenly.

'Don't worry, he's still in Rome.' Kim grinned suggestively. 'He rang to say he's not going anywhere until he knows you're safe.'

'That's nice of him.' The knowledge was reassuring. Jess rubbed her face with her hands. She was near to tears. 'Changing my identity isn't going to help, though, is it; Dan is going to find me through Titus.'

'I think one thing can save you,' Carmella put in thoughtfully. 'You must forget about Eigon. No more questions. No more research. No more Rome. Don't let Titus – or Eigon – into your head. I told you this before. And I told you how to do it. Surround yourself with light. Call for angels to protect you. These are time-honoured ways to keep yourself safe, Jess. You must use them. If they cannot reach you inside your head, they cannot find you.'

Jess scrambled to her feet. She went and stood by the parapet, staring down. 'But I can't put them out of my head,' she whispered. Her voice was full of anguish. 'I have to know what happened.'

*   *   *

Dan was sitting in a bar three streets away. He lifted a grappa to his lips with a shaking hand. He had seen what happened to Julia. Through Titus's eyes he had seen him cut her throat. They raped her, then she was killed. It was so easy. And so quick. Too quick. He swallowed some more grappa and wiped his lips on his sleeve. He had looked through Titus's strange amber-coloured eyes. He had felt what Titus had felt. It had been exciting. He enjoyed it. It was not the same as fighting in battle. It was not man to man, even combat. It was a sacrifice. An offering to the god of love.

And then through Titus's eyes he had seen what it would be like when it was his turn and the woman lying helpless before him was Jess. What if he raped her again? Titus would be there watching, he would taunt Dan for holding back and this time, Dan would kill her. And it would be real; powerful. Exciting.

He still didn't know why he had done it, that first time. He hadn't planned it. Or had he? He had been carrying that drug around with him for a long time after he had confiscated it in a locker search at the college, almost as if he knew, one day, he would want to use it. He had drunk too much at the disco. He had been turned on by so many young nubile girls displaying their wares to him on every side, the smell of sex exuded in that hall that night had been overpowering. He could have had any of those girls but he had watched Jess. Seen her dancing with Ash, seen the boy grinding his hips against hers provocatively, seen her laughing; then she had danced with Will and he had seen them holding each other more and more closely. And who did he have to dance with? His wife was at home with the children. He was a senior master and he had danced with the headmaster's wife. And the French student teacher. That was better. And Jess; she could hardly refuse. But she had held him at arm's length. She had looked at him with a disengaged smile and listened politely. And then she had gone off to dance again with Ash. It was then he had decided. He would show her what love-making was like. What it was really like. And he had.

He beckoned the waiter and ordered another drink.

It was only the next morning that he realised what he had done.

At first he had thought he'd got away with it. She obviously couldn't remember anything about it. But then slowly she had begun to piece it all together. He should have known the silly bitch wouldn't let it go. As soon as she remembered he knew he had blown his career, his future and his marriage.

The threats to kill her hadn't been real. Of course they hadn't. Not at first. He just wanted to terrify her into silence. But it hadn't worked. It had probably made matters worse. After that the plan had been to make people think she had suffered a breakdown. Not difficult. She had completely lost it as far as he could see, with her ghosts and her voices and her visions, and the blood-stained sketchbooks. He shuddered at the memory. But then the voice had started murmuring in his head. The voice of another man. The voice which had been following him ever since that day at Ty Bran when she had fled into the fields leaving him to face his demons alone.

He hadn't really intended to take it any further. Of course not. He was a civilised man. But in his dream, when he saw the flare of terror in Jess's eyes, it had excited him and when he woke up, sweating in his bed, he had found himself engulfed not just by lust but by a visceral excitement which had everything to do with wondering what it would be like to kill her for real. The man in his head knew. The man in his head was egging him on.

22

Eigon had called Flavius into the atrium. 'When did Julia say she would return?' It was dark outside. Heavy thundershowers were drifting in from the north. Normally she gave no thought at all to Julia, far too preoccupied to worry about her friend's flighty comings and goings, but this time she was uneasy.

'She didn't say.' Flavius shuffled his feet. 'She was angry because I wouldn't go with her. We quarrelled.'

'Send a messenger then, to the house of her aunt. She may have decided to stay as the weather has turned so horrible. She should have thought to tell us though.' Eigon sighed. All afternoon there had been a succession of men and women at the gate asking for her services. She had dressed wound after wound. Handed out herbal pills and potions. Given advice. Since Melinus had died she was working alone in the herb room and finding out just how many people he had been helping in his strange gruff way. Exhausted she walked across the atrium and stood staring down into the pool of water. The rain was draining into it from the gutters on the roof with a steady drip. The sound was comforting.

Flavius reappeared almost at once. His face had cleared with relief. He knew he was wrong to have allowed her to leave the house without a proper escort and he felt guilty and afraid. 'Her litter has returned with a message to say that she is staying away tonight.'

'Good! So at least she had the decency to tell us in the end.' Eigon shook her head in exasperation. 'Very well, tell the cooks they can serve the evening meal. I will go and see if Papa is well enough to get up for it or if he would like it in his room.'

Antonia was sitting with Caradoc. He was sitting up looking more cheerful than she had seen him for a long while. 'This charming young lady has been entertaining me, Eigon, while your mother has some well-earned time to herself,' he said as his daughter appeared. 'She came to see you, of course, but you were busy so I captured her.' He reached over and patted Antonia's hand.

Cerys joined them however when they sat down together in the dining room, reclining on their couches as the slaves brought in their evening meal. She seemed unaware that this girl whose company gave so much pleasure to her husband was the sister of the man she had forbidden Eigon to see.

Caradoc's colour was good; he ate with enthusiasm and he engaged the three women with him in lively conversation. 'I can see your talks with Peter have done you good, my lord.' Antonia smiled at him gently. 'I have heard you will not ask for baptism, but you must admit that Jesus is a powerful healer.'

Caradoc raised an eyebrow, nodding. 'I grant you that, child. He is indeed and Peter had won our Melinus over to his cause.' There was a moment's uncomfortable pause.

'Did you see Peter, Mam?' Eigon quickly jumped into the silence.

Cerys shook her head. 'I worship no gods but my own.' She leaned across and clasped her husband's fingers. 'And neither does my lord and husband. The very idea! And neither I hope do you.' Her eyes narrowed as she glanced at Eigon.

'Mam!' Eigon coloured. 'You are being discourteous to our guest.'

'No.' Cerys turned a weary face towards Antonia and smiled. 'Antonia knows I love her. But I do not have to love her god. He has caused nothing but trouble for his own followers and for my dear Melinus.' She sighed.

'Melinus was not a Christian, Lady Cerys,' Antonia corrected quietly. 'It was not for that reason that he was arrested.' Her shoulders slumped.

Eigon glanced at the slave waiting to clear their dishes and nodded. He was a young man, barely more than a boy, thin, with bright darting eyes and a ready crooked smile. He came over at once and noisily gathered up the plates. She glanced up at him, amused. He had clearly been listening and had decided to ensure a change of subject in his own manner. 'Bring the fruit, Silas, thank you.' She looked up and caught his eye. 'And

292

more wine for my father.' She had noticed this boy before and liked him. She would make sure that Aelius gave him more responsibility. Her train of thought was interrupted by an unearthly cry from the courtyard. They looked at each other in consternation. Caradoc sat up and threw his napkin down on the table. 'What is that?'

'Wait, Father. I will see.' White-faced, Eigon ran towards the door. Aelius was standing in the atrium with three of the house slaves. Two of the men were dripping wet from the rain. Aelius turned towards her, his face the colour of a linen shroud.

He opened his mouth to speak but no words came.

'What is it?' Caradoc appeared in the doorway behind her, leaning heavily on the door frame for support. 'What has happened?'

Aelius shook his head. He had put his hands over his face and his shoulders were heaving with sobs.

Eigon ran towards him and seized his arm. 'What is it? Tell us!'

'It is the lady Julia,' one of the slaves said, his voice barely audible. Rain was pooling round his feet and his hair and tunic were soaked. 'I went out to fetch more firewood and I found her by the wall. She looked as though she was asleep.'

Eigon felt the blood in her veins turn to ice. She stared from the man to Aelius and back. 'Where is she? Show me.'

'No, lady!' The slave shook his head. 'No, you mustn't.'

'But you will show me.' Caradoc's voice was strong. He stepped forward shakily. 'Now, Aelius.'

The courtyard was noisy with rain, great drops splattering onto the cobbles, turning the dust to rivulets of mud, hissing on the torches as the slaves led the way. A dark shape lay by the gates to the road, wrapped in a blanket. The corner had been folded back to reveal Julia's face. She looked serene, her face unmarked, her hair streaked back by the rain. Eigon stooped and pulled the coloured blanket away with shaking hands. The wound across Julia's neck had been washed clean of blood by the rain. Her throat had been severed almost to the bone. She was naked but for the blanket and for a dozen gold bracelets on the arms which were crossed on her breasts. With a little moan of grief Eigon turned away. It was her father who ordered Julia to be brought indoors and laid decently in a side room. Then he walked into the atrium and summoned the household.

'I want to know who did this and why.' His face was grim. The warrior and king, so long effaced by illness had reappeared. 'Thieves do not leave their victims with more gold than they have taken. They do not select Celtic gold, and wrap the body in a Celtic plaid for the Roman friend of a Celtic household, without a good reason.'

Eigon hadn't even noticed the intricate carving and design of the bangles or the tartan design of the rug. Impressed that her father had taken in the scene so quickly and in such detail, she glanced at her mother. This was another message that no one in the household was safe. The people closest to her. The people she loved. Desperately she tried to restrain her tears, trying to copy her father's strength. Her mother was stony-faced. In shock. Not registering, not acknowledging what had happened. But she must know. She must have realised as Eigon had realised that this was a message from Titus Marcus Olivinus.

'Mam –'

'No!' Cerys turned on her ferociously. 'No! Don't you dare say anything, Eigon, do you hear me? The girl was out of control. Foolish. She behaved like a slut! She asked for this!' She turned and fled towards her private rooms.

The others stared after her, shocked. 'I am sorry, Eigon,' Caradoc said slowly. 'Your mother is overcome with the horror of this. And she is wrong. No one deserves this. No one, least of all little Julia. I don't know how we are going to tell Pomponia Graecina.'

'Jess!' Someone was shaking her arm. 'Jess, wake up. Now!'

Jess shivered. Somehow she refocused her eyes to find Will standing beside her. They were alone together on the roof terrace.

'Jess, you have to stop this. Disappearing into your own little world is not going to help you,' he said gently. 'I want you to come back with me. We'll go to my parents' down in Cornwall. As far as I recall Dan doesn't know about them, and even if he does, it would be very hard for him to get near you there. They live in a small village where everyone knows everyone. If a stranger arrived word would get round in seconds.'

'I can't hide for the rest of my life, Will.'

'No, I'm not suggesting you do. But it will do in the interim. While we work out a plan.' He put his hands on her shoulders, staring into her eyes. 'I can't let Dan hurt you any more, Jess.'

For a long moment they stared at each other. He leaned forward and gently kissed her on the lips. She pulled away sharply. 'No! No, Will! I'm sorry. I just can't bear anyone to touch me. Not yet.' She shuddered. 'Oh God!' She buried her face in her hands.

'I understand.' He moved a couple of paces away from her. 'It was insensitive of me. But don't turn your back on my offer, Jess. Please. You need help.'

'Will, Dan has already tried to kill you!'

'I don't think he did. He had every opportunity to kill me when he drugged me.'

'Well, he might not be so restrained next time.' She pushed past him and stepped through the windows into the apartment. The three others were standing in there looking anxiously towards them.

'Jess –?' Kim said.

Jess shook her head. 'No! Please leave me alone.' She started to run towards Carmella's bathroom. There she locked the door and subsided onto the floor, tears pouring down her face.

'Mam, you have to listen!' Eigon had cornered her mother in the dining room where Cerys was watching the slaves put away the cups and bowls in the cupboard.

Cerys jumped. She turned a tear-streaked face to her daughter. 'Your father is ill, Eigon. He collapsed after Pomponia Graecina and Aulus Plautius left with Julia's body.'

Eigon headed for the door. 'I'll go to him.'

'Leave him for now. He is asleep.' Cerys sighed. 'Without Melinus there is no hope for him.' She was hugging her arms around herself. Another tear coursed down her cheek. The slaves glanced at each other and quietly disappeared towards the kitchens.

'Mam, I can treat him,' Eigon said. 'You know I can. I have the medicines that Melinus taught me how to make, and I can help with those. And we can ask Peter to come again and pray with him. I know,' she rushed on as she saw her mother's face close, 'I know you don't approve of him, but his Jesus is so powerful.

295

Papa likes Peter. He trusts him.' She shook her head in exasperation. Her mother was impossible to pin down. Every time she tried to speak to her about Peter and the Christians she changed the subject, just as she managed to sidestep the issue of Titus. There was no arguing with her. Eigon shivered. What could they do anyway? His viciousness knew no bounds. They were never going to escape him. He was there, lurking, an unseen enemy in the shadows, waiting. And one day he would catch her alone.

'Tell her,' Jess murmured. 'Insist. Don't let her fob you off. You are too vulnerable. You have to be protected.'

Eigon turned. She scanned the shadows of the room and frowned. 'Can you hear me?' Jess sat up. 'Eigon?'

'Jess!' Will's voice reached her through the door. 'Jess, open up. I need to speak to you.'

'No!' Jess shook her head. She turned back towards Eigon. 'Tell your mother he is ruthless. Pretending he is not there will not save you!'

Eigon had gone pale. She put her hands to her head. 'Leave me alone!' She was staring round in confusion.

'Tell her!' Jess called out. 'Tell her. He will kill you if you don't.'

'Jess!' Will was knocking on the door. 'Who are you talking to? Open up.'

'No! Go away, Will!'

She could see Eigon but her figure had grown less substantial. She was fading. Scrambling to her feet furiously, she dragged the door open. 'You idiot! Why can't you leave me alone! Now she's gone.' She turned tearfully and stared round the room. 'I can't see her any more.'

'You can't see her because she's not there, Jess.' Will caught her arm. 'Calm down and come through here. Carmella is making us some more coffee. Come and sit down.'

'Will?' Steph appeared behind him. 'Leave her to me. Jess, come on. Will's right. She's gone. There is nothing you can do.'

'You don't understand.' Jess shrugged stubbornly. 'None of you understand. I'm the only one who can save her.'

'You can't save her, Jess. That's the point.' Steph put her arm round Jess's shoulders and guided her through to the sofa. She pushed her down firmly. 'Sit down and calm down. When you can think rationally you will see this is all nonsense. You can't save anyone. You can't speak to Eigon.'

'Why not?' Carmella appeared in the kitchen doorway. She had a large cafetière in her hand. She set it down on the table. 'Of course she can speak to her.'

'But she can't change what happened!' Steph insisted. 'She can't make whatever happened in the past better, can she?' She straightened up and stared at Carmella accusingly.

'I can warn her,' Jess repeated. 'I am sure I can warn her. She heard me. She knew I was there.'

Will came and sat down beside her. 'Jess, darling. Please listen.'

'Don't you call me darling!' Jess turned on him. 'Just leave me alone! All of you, leave me alone!' She stood up and fled into Carmella's bedroom.

Carmella followed her and closed the door. 'They don't understand, Jess. That is natural. But you must be careful. Please don't do anything without me there. I can at least watch your back.' She gave an apologetic smile. 'We are in such controversial country here. Steph has seen your Eigon herself but she still can't bring herself to believe it all completely. Will doesn't believe anything much at all. Kim thinks it is all a party trick, no more than that. We know it is real. But we also know it is dangerous. If you can't do as I suggest and stop thinking about her, we must at least go with a book of rules and back up, yes?'

Jess stood in front of the mirror for a moment, then grabbed Carmella's comb and ran it through her hair. Her face was very pale. 'We are having a bad time, you and I, Eigon,' she murmured. She leaned forward, peering harder. The second face in the mirror was indistinct. She turned round. It was as though she was staring into another room through some kind of a glass wall. She could see Eigon standing in front of her work bench. She was making up a herbal brew. Carefully adding hot water to her bowl. She could see the small brazier and the pan where she had heated it, the shelves of bottles and jars and boxes on the wall behind her, the neat line of probes and tweezers, a small scalpel, a bowl of what looked like moss and a pile of linen bandages, neatly folded. By her shoulder a bunch of some kind of herb was hanging from the ceiling.

'Eigon? Can you hear me?' she whispered.

Eigon looked up. She frowned. Then she went back to her task.

'I'm in trouble too.' Jess glanced at the door. She was speaking in a whisper. 'Titus has invaded Dan's head. I don't know what to do.'

She paused. Eigon had turned away from her table. She was looking not towards Jess but at the door. It opened and an old man came in. Jess caught her breath. It was the leader of the Christians in Rome. Peter.

St Peter.

'How is he?' Eigon asked. There were tears in her eyes.

'His heart is weak, Eigon.' Peter shook his head.

'Can Jesus not heal him? I thought he could do anything.'

Peter smiled. 'Indeed he can, my child. But sometimes he knows that another course is best. We cannot live for ever. That is not part of God's plan for us. Your father is tired, Eigon. You know that.'

'And he won't be baptised.'

'He is like my friend Melinus. He wants to cover his options.' Peter laughed quietly. 'As does another young woman who stands not a large distance from me at this moment. Jesus wants our whole commitment,' he added sternly, but then he went on more gently, 'but he knows how hard it is to change. He knows that we are only human and frail. He will bless your father.'

'My father wants to go to the heaven of our own people. He wants to go back to the country of his birth. He told me that Jesus's heaven sounded like Nero's gardens. He doesn't want to go there.'

Peter gave a short sharp bark of laughter. 'The Lord Jesus does not base his gardens on those of the Emperor of Rome.' He looked at her and put a gentle hand on her arm. 'Jesus told us that his house has many mansions; I am sure there are as many gardens. There is one there for your father. And there is one there for you.' He pulled up a stool. 'I have prayed for you, Eigon, many times. Melinus saw much strength and good in you, my daughter. He begged me to look after you.'

Eigon frowned. 'Melinus was a good man.'

'He was. And I will tell you a secret. I baptised him in the prison, Eigon, the night before he died. He died in the knowledge that he would go to my father and your father in heaven. And he knew that the Isles of the Blest would be there waiting for him.'

Eigon stared at him, awestruck. 'You know about Tir n'an Og?'

'It is but another name in another language. God has told me to preach to all men, of whatever race and language. I have to spread his word amongst people everywhere.'

'But –'

Peter held up his hand. 'Listen to me. Jesus has chosen you for a special task.'

'Me?' She went white. 'No!'

'When your father dies, and he will die soon, Eigon, you must resign yourself to that.' He paused and gave her a gentle smile. 'You are to return to your homeland. And you will tell them about Jesus.'

'But I'm not baptised.'

'No.'

'You want me to be?'

'Of course. But that is your decision to make. You must pray. Jesus will speak to you himself.'

'Do Pomponia and Felicius know about this?'

He shook his head. 'This is between you and me and the Lord.'

She realised suddenly that she had been shredding a bunch of thyme. The dusty leaves were scattered over her work bench. She threw the stems down. 'I'm forbidden to return to Britannia.'

He nodded. 'It will take courage.'

'I don't know anyone there.'

'You are the daughter of their king.'

'And their king still needs me here.' She turned away from him. 'I can't go.'

He smiled. 'When Our Lord asks you, you will go.' She could feel his will beginning to bend her own. She swung round ready to argue, but his stern smile stopped her in her tracks. He shook his head. 'Do not fret, Eigon. He will not ask you to go as long as your father needs you. He told us to honour our fathers and our mothers.' He rested his hand for a moment on her arm. She could feel the strength and warmth of his grip. It reassured her.

'Jess? Come back.'

Eigon turned and stared at Jess, as though hearing something in the distance. Jess bent closer, listening hard.

'Rhodri is here.' The voice was indistinct. Irritating. She shook her head, trying to push it away.

'Come on, Jess.' A deeper stronger tone now. Rhodri. The hand on her wrist was his. Not Peter's. Peter had his hand on Eigon's wrist. Not hers. She closed her eyes.

'Wake up, Jess. Come on.' There was a murmur in the background. Carmella was saying something. Jess felt the words drift past her.

Peter had gone.

Eigon had turned to follow him but in the atrium she stopped. Antonia was standing there, waiting for her. The two young women embraced.

Jess went on watching, aware that she felt suddenly on the outside, no longer part of the scene, rejected as Eigon and her friend sat down together, their heads close, their tears for Julia and for the dying king mingling as they clutched one another's hands.

They looked up suddenly and both young women smiled, and Jess saw Julius making his way through the door towards them. He held out his arms and Eigon ran into them. It was a simple, brotherly gesture of comfort and support, the three of them locked together in their misery and confusion.

'Jess!' Rhodri put his hands on her shoulders. He shook her gently. 'Come back now, girl. No more of this!'

'She hasn't told them. They don't know about Titus!' Jess tried to pull away. 'She must tell them!'

'Later. She can tell them later.' Rhodri was still holding onto her. 'Jess! Pull yourself together.' This time his voice was loud; commanding. She blinked and shook her head. 'That's right. Come on. Pay attention!'

'Get off me!' Suddenly she was there in the room with him. She gave him a push, wrenching herself free. 'How dare you!'

'Jess, Rhodri is here to help you.' Carmella sounded reproachful.

'I've got the car outside. Your stuff is in it. We're heading out now.' Rhodri calmly ignored her fury. 'It's up to you. Either you come with me now back to Wales or I dump your stuff here and I go without you. Your choice.'

She stared at him, confused. She hesitated. 'I don't know, Rhodri. It's kind of you, of course it is.'

'Too right!' he snorted. 'So? Your decision.'

'I can't go. I have to warn her –'

'No, you don't have to warn anyone about anything!' He glanced heavenwards in exasperation. 'For God's sake, woman!'

'Jess, go with him.' Will came and crouched on his heels next to her. 'You have to get out of Rome.'

'Just go, Jess.' Carmella shivered. 'While you can.'

Jess was shaking her head, glancing one way then the other, confused and anxious, her brain in turmoil.

'Jess, if you won't go with Rhodri, come with me. We'll go straight to the airport.' Will caught her hand.

'Eigon –'

'If Eigon wants to communicate with you she will do it wherever you are, Jess,' Carmella put in. 'She showed herself to you in Wales before, didn't she?'

Jess stood up. Will was too close. He was crowding her. So was Rhodri. She looked from one to the other feeling the pressure. Beginning to panic. 'I can't go. I have to know what happens. I've seen St Peter. Think of that!' She pushed between them. 'I have been given the chance to see into their world. Can't you understand what that means? How amazing it is? I am privileged! I can't just go.'

Will sat back on his heels with a sigh. 'Are you ready to risk being murdered?'

'Dan's not going to murder me. He thinks you think I'm insane.' She gave a wry laugh. 'That's enough for him. He's done what he wanted.'

She saw Will and Rhodri glance at each other in exasperation. 'It's my decision, after all,' she said after a moment. Her voice was calmer now. 'You can't force me to go with you anywhere. You're not like Dan. You are rational, very, very nice men.' She smiled from one to the other. 'Thank you for everything you have done for me. But I can't go on putting you two at risk. Or you.' She turned to Carmella. 'I will go and stay in a hotel somewhere where no one knows me. I will lock myself in and be perfectly safe, then I can contact Eigon as much as I like and find out what happens to her. I can warn her about that bastard, Titus. She can see me and hear me. I've realised that at last. She is looking through a

301

window into the future just as I am looking through a window into the past. I can reach her.'

There was a long silence. Jess grimaced. 'Oh God! You are all looking so shocked. I'm not mad. I promise.'

'No?' Steph raised an eyebrow.

'No.' Jess shrugged.

'Dan has followed you everywhere else. You think he won't follow you out of this flat, today?' Kim said slowly.

'I've given him the slip before.'

'Not very effectively, if I may say so,' Rhodri said caustically. He was eyeing her with a certain sneaking admiration. She was standing in front of them with a defiance which he was beginning to think was not only insane but rather wonderful. He saw her gaze shift thoughtfully to his face and he winked at her. 'OK. What do you want to do with your stuff?'

'Could you take it back to Wales? If I collect a few things just to tide me over.' If she did what Carmella told her this time and avoided thinking about Titus, wouldn't that keep her safe? She gave Rhodri a watery grin.

'Whatever you like.' He nodded.

'You're driving back?' Will asked sharply.

Rhodri shrugged. 'I've arranged to keep the car on a bit longer now. I may as well.'

Will leaned forward suddenly. 'I've had an idea. What about a decoy? When were you thinking of going home, Steph?'

Steph shrugged. 'Soon, I suppose. Kim is going up to the lakes in a week or so when Rome gets too hot even for her!' She glanced at Kim who nodded.

'Then why don't you go with Rhodri. Borrow Jess's top. Her glasses. Her scarf. Anything. Set off at dead of night. Look furtive.'

Rhodri laughed at the look of horror on Steph's face. 'It just might work this time. It might get him off your back for a while, Jess.'

'Would you do that?' Jess looked at her sister in weary amusement. The thought of Steph and Rhodri driving across Europe in the confines of a single car, however powerful, filled her with wistful glee.

Steph frowned. 'I think I could bring myself to do that if you think it would do any good. Why not? It could be fun.' She couldn't hide the lack of enthusiasm in her tone.

'What if he doesn't rise to the bait?' Will asked. 'He does seem to be able to find you every time!'

'You stay and keep an eye on Jess,' Rhodri said. 'That way every eventuality is covered.' He was watching Jess's face. Her eyes had narrowed at the last suggestion.

It was the only idea they could come up with in the face of Jess's intransigence and in the event the whole strategy, once decided, proved extraordinarily easy to perform. Kim and Will went back to the palazzo almost at once and Will left a while later by a hitherto unsuspected service door at the opposite side of the building to the entrance to the gardens. He was going to check in at a cheap hotel for a few days while he did some sightseeing of his own and stay within reach of Jess's mobile should she need him. It was the only concession she would make towards him.

Rhodri and Steph left at midnight, looking suitably shifty, climbed into the hired Mercedes and drove slowly and carefully out of Rome, resisting the temptation to look back.

Next morning Jess strolled out of Carmella's flat wearing a pair of Carmella's Versace jeans and a Prada shirt, Carmella's huge dark glasses, a scarlet Hermes headscarf covering her hair. The leather haversack over her shoulder was Carmella's, as was the bright lipstick. The disguise would fool no one who was close enough to see her in detail, but a figure lounging on a street corner in the distance might be misled for a while. The two women were of similar build and Jess briefly studied Carmella's swaying walk and elegant posture, even borrowing a pair of Gucci sandals for her exit sashay down the street. It was hard to keep a straight face, easy to forget, just for a few minutes, her fear and anger as she walked away towards the Via Condotti and freedom.

In the ladies' room of a terrifyingly smart store she admitted defeat and slipped out of the high-heeled shoes and put on a pair of her own from the haversack. She left by a different door from the one she had entered and at last able to move faster headed towards her new refuge, a *pensione* belonging to an acquaintance of Carmella's. Ironically it was quite close to Kim's apartment, on the far side of the Campo de' Fiori in a narrow winding street of medieval houses.

The whole house was ancient, built into the surviving wall of a long-gone church, with rooms crammed with antiques and curios, curtains swagged with heavy tassels, pictures and ornaments vying for space on the walls, the dark oak staircase creaking like a ship in a storm as she followed her hostess, whose name was Margaretta, up to the top floor. She stared round her room in delight. It was small, one wall the rough stone of the old church against which the house huddled, the furniture charmingly eclectic in style. Left alone to settle in, she dropped the haversack on the floor and sat down on the bed with a sigh of pleasure.

Remember to protect yourself all the time. Do not allow Titus into your head or you are lost. Carmella's parting words echoed for a moment in her ears. *Make this place a refuge and a base from which to conduct your research. Do not become a slave to him, or indeed to Eigon or you will lose your own soul!*

Jess bit her lip. Now she was here, safe from Dan, on her own, if their plans had worked, she felt a strange reluctance to do anything except lie down on the bed and close her eyes. She glanced down at the haversack. Her mobile was in there. She could call anyone if she wanted to. She could ring Steph and see how far they had got; see if Dan was following them. She frowned. She should ring Will, tell him she had arrived safely and as far as she could see un-followed. He would be worrying. She gave a wistful smile. He was doing so much for her sake. She stood up and wandered over to the window. The street was narrow and she could see nothing below; opposite a woman appeared briefly at a window in the house across the street, shook out a duster then stood back out of the sunlight, pulling the slatted shutters half closed as she disappeared. The action was almost symbolic, the final cutting of the connection between Jess and the rest of the world. She turned back into the room.

Eigon was standing watching her, a strangely quizzical expression on her face.

'Hello.' Jess was surprised into the greeting. She gave a small sharp laugh generated by embarrassment more than anything else. 'Can you hear me?'

The figure did not react. She was shadowy now. Jess could see the outline of the bed through her. 'Don't go! Please!' Her voice was sharper. 'I need to talk to you. To warn you.' But the figure had gone. Jess stepped forward, her hand outstretched trailing her fingers through the air, trying to feel the substance of the apparition. There was nothing there. Her shoulders slumped. She gave a small sigh and sat down on the bed again. She had already forgotten Carmella's warning.

23

'He's taken the bait. We are being followed.' Rhodri glanced in the mirror again. 'Where the hell did he get a car so quickly?'

Steph looked over her shoulder nervously. 'I can't see anyone.' Behind them the road stretched emptily back towards the curve in the hills which hid whatever it was that Rhodri had thought he'd seen.

'He's keeping well back. I'm pretty sure it must be him.' He grinned. 'The trick is to keep him on our tail without him getting too close.' He couldn't get over how alike the two sisters were when they put their minds to it, like now, with Steph wearing Jess's distinctive turquoise top and her sun glasses. Only a physical likeness mind you. They couldn't be more dissimilar when it came to personality. He gave a rueful smile. Still, this seemed to have had the desired effect on Dan. 'Take a look at the map. Is there a turning up ahead we can take which will bring us back onto the main road after a few miles? If he follows us we'll know it's him. Then I can put my foot down when we get on the autostrada.'

Steph opened the book. She squinted at the maze of roads tracing their route with a finger. 'Here. There's a by road about three miles ahead.'

'OK. We'll take that.'

'What happens when we stop for lunch?'

He laughed. 'Hungry already? We'll have to make sure he doesn't get close enough to you to get a good look. Should be OK. I doubt if he wants to get that close. Just close enough to frighten Jess. If you were Jess.'

'He can't be allowed to get away with this, Rhodri.'

Rhodri raised an eyebrow. He was concentrating on the road. Ahead a signpost signalled the road they were going to take. 'He won't,' he said succinctly. 'Will and I have discussed it.' He gave her a quick almost feral grin as he swung the heavy car onto the side road. 'Once we are home on our own turf, so to speak, I think we can put the fear of God into Dan Nicolson, don't you worry about it.'

She tucked the atlas down into the footwell. 'You fancy my sister, don't you?' She gave him a quick sideways glance from behind her glasses.

He gave a shout of laughter. 'I wouldn't say that. She seems to me to be a perfect pain! Like you!'

'But an attractive pain?' She ignored the insult.

'Both of your mother's daughters are attractive.'

She shook her head. 'Welsh blarney.'

'No such thing!' He glanced into the mirror. 'The car behind us is drawing a bit closer now we're not on the fast road.'

'So, he did see us turn.'

'Looks like it. It's dark red. Large. Powerful. Can't see what it is yet.'

'So, if it is him, he could catch us if he wanted to?' She felt a knot of anxiety deep in her stomach.

'Not if I put my foot down. This baby is faster than his.' He was enjoying himself. 'And I don't want him to catch us. Not for a long way yet, certainly not while we are still in Italy. Preferably not till we reach the Channel. I'll head for the autostrada north. He won't get close once we're on it but we'll make sure we don't leave him behind.'

In her pretty room at the *pensione* Jess saw that once again it was summer in the past. Eigon was sitting outside on the terrace near the fig tree. Antonia was with her. Jess smiled. The young women were enjoying the peace of the garden, a basket of dried herbs lying between them on the paving at their feet. Eigon had been singing softly as they stripped the leaves and packed them into labelled jars. The courtyard was very still in the shelter of the walls of the house but out in the orchards on the slope behind the house the trees were bending before a stiff summer wind. Brushing herb dust off her skirt Eigon reached for another handful of dried plants, filled her jar and pushed in the stopper firmly. She had picked up some more dried thyme, her slim fingers running down the stems to dislodge the tiny leaves as Antonia began stacking the jars onto a tray. She straightened her shoulders with a grimace as Eigon reached the end of her song and a companionable silence fell upon them.

'It's so hot, in spite of the wind. Look at the sky. I think we're in for a storm.'

Eigon followed her pointing finger and frowned. The sky over the city had turned to a strange brazen colour. 'It's not a storm. It's smoke!' she cried suddenly.

The two young women stood up. They ran across the gardens towards the far wall where the hillside dropped away cliff-like to the south and they stood staring down towards the city. Below them the marshy ground which bounded the Tiber gave way very quickly to the built up area of slums which clustered around the great walls of the city. Beyond the wall the sky was dark with smoke.

There was a sound behind them. Both young women spun round. It was Aelius.

'There's a fire in the city centre! It's a bad one.' He shifted his feet anxiously. 'One of the slaves has just returned. He says the city is in chaos. The roads are blocked with people fleeing.' He paused. 'My son is there.'

It had taken Eigon a long time to forgive Flavius for letting Julia go out alone to her death. Even now Aelius was reluctant to mention his name in her presence. 'I didn't like to speak to the queen your mother about it. She has enough to worry her with your father so ill.' His face was pinched with exhaustion and worry.

'No, you did right to tell me.' Eigon sighed. 'Where are Julius and your grandfather?' She turned suddenly to Antonia. She felt a shiver run down her back. They stood for a moment in silence.

Antonia shrugged. 'I'm sure they will be all right,' she said at last. They were both staring out across the wall. 'The alarms must have been sounded and the cohorts and the vigiles will have been on the scene at once.' She was reassuring herself as much as anyone. Fires in the ancient city with its crowded wooden tenements and shops packed tight between the safer stone buildings were a common occurrence. 'There is nothing we can do except pray that they are safe.'

Aelius raised an eyebrow. 'May Vulcan be merciful.' He bowed formally.

'Let me know if you hear anything,' Eigon called after him as he turned towards the house. 'I'm sure Flavius will be all right,' she added. He did not appear to hear her.

She sat down on a stone bench and she shivered. 'I pray to your god and to mine that they will all be safe.' Both young women stared at the sky. The billowing clouds in the distance had turned the colour of molten iron.

'Blessed Lord, keep the people of this city in your hands,' Antonia murmured quietly. 'Send rain to help the fire brigades.' She bit her lip. 'I heard my grandfather talking only yesterday about the prophesies the Apostle Peter has spoken of. He said the prophets described Rome as a harlot and that the sages of Egypt predicted that a great city would fall on the day that the Dog Star rises. They said it was Rome.'

Eigon stared at her, her face aghast. 'That is today,' she whispered. 'The fourth day after the Ides of July. The rising of the Dog Star. It's in my almanac.' They both turned again to the sky.

'I must go!' Antonia was suddenly galvanised into action. 'If the fire is in the centre of the city I have to make sure that Grandfather and Julius are all right.'

'No!' Eigon caught her arm. 'You can't do anything! You'll make matters worse. At least they know you are safe if you are here.'

Time passed and the sky to the south grew darker. Occasionally they saw the bronze of the flames reflected on the clouds. The smell of burning carried towards them on the wind, then blew away again as its direction changed and on the road outside their barred gates the stream of refugees from the burning city grew more crowded. Men, women and children, exhausted, scared, sooty, their possessions loaded onto carts and wagons, plodding onwards, many of them not knowing where, so long as it was away from the fire. News carried as fast as the ash on the wind. The fire had been contained. It had spread out of control. It had been extinguished in one quarter only to leap the wooden roof shingles to another. A woman near the cattle market had been lynched after her neighbours thought it was her lamp, tangled in the sheets suspended to dry across her room which had started it. Others blamed a forge on the Viminal, yet others a bakery on the Aventine. The Praetorian guard had been called out at once, as had the vigiles. As night fell the full horror of the blaze was emphasised by the darkness. There was no word from Julius.

Flavius still had not returned. Caradoc and Cerys had come for a while to stand in the orchard watching the sky, then Caradoc, exhausted, had finally been persuaded to return to his bed. Cerys had stayed a while longer, clutching her daughter's hand, then she too had disappeared indoors.

'It's out of control.' Aelius joined the two young women at last. 'I have forbidden the slaves to go. What's the point? A handful more men won't help now. They must stay here and watch our walls. There is looting everywhere.'

'Are we in danger here?' Antonia looked at his pale face. The man had aged ten years since morning.

He shook his head. 'The wind is blowing away from us. Besides, there are fields and the cliffs and gardens between us and the suburbs.'

'Where did Flavius go, Aelius?' Eigon asked gently. She knew he would not tell her anything without her prompting.

'He had taken a parcel from your mother to Pomponia Graecina, princess. Once he had done that I told him,' he paused and gave a great shuddering sob, 'I told him to stay and amuse himself for the rest of the day. He works hard here. He deserved a treat.' He looked at her pleadingly.

'I know he does, Aelius.' She forced herself to smile at him. She knew he was right. Flavius had worked without ceasing since Julia had died, as if he was afraid to stop in case he had to confront his own guilt. She knew her father had called him in the end and told him that whoever had planned Julia's murder would not have been deterred by his presence. All that would have happened had he been there, was that he would have died as well. He meant it kindly to take some of the load from the young man's shoulders. Whether or not it had helped no one could tell. 'I am sure he will be all right,' Eigon said softly. 'The last report was that the fire has been contained.' She looked up at the sky to the south and they all fell silent. Contained was not the word that any one of them would have chosen as the glow spread ever higher into the clouds.

Flavius returned just before dawn. His hands were blistered, his hair singed and his face was black with soot when he called to be admitted at the northern gate. Eigon and Antonia had fallen into an uneasy sleep in the atrium when Aelius appeared with his son in tow.

'Ladies,' Flavius's voice was so hoarse he could barely speak. 'Felicius Marinus Publius and his grandson Julius are safe. I saw them as it grew dark. They have evacuated the whole area round the Forum and the Palatine. They went with Aulus Plautius and his family to their villa in the hills. They are all safe.' His voice cracked for a moment. He took a deep breath to steady himself.

Eigon understood at once. The young man had gone to help Julia's family. He had put them before his own safety. Deeply touched, she stood up and went to the table to pour him a beaker of wine. She put it in his hands and when she found they were shaking too much to hold it she closed his fingers around it herself. 'The fire had reached the Forum?' she prompted quietly.

He nodded. 'The whole area has gone. The senators' houses. The entire quarter. The Palatine. The Esqualine. The Domus Transitoria.'

'What? The Emperor's palace?' His father stood staring at him, slack-jawed.

Flavius nodded. His voice was stronger after the sip of wine. 'They say the Emperor has returned from Antium. He is leading the fire-fighters himself. People are saying the fire was set deliberately.'

'No.' Antonia was pleating her stole between nervous fingers. 'Who would do such a thing? It must have been an accident. There are hundreds of fires every day from accidents.'

Flavius glanced at her. He hesitated for a moment then he went on. 'I heard the Emperor is blaming the Christians.' The words came out in a rush.

There was a moment of silence broken only by the splashing of the water in the fountain. The two young women were staring at the mist of droplets drifting in the sudden breeze from the west. There was a splatter of cold water on the paving stones then the wind dropped and the water jet shot skywards again. 'Why?' It was Eigon who asked the question in the end.

'He says they have been predicting a fire. There are tracts all over the poorer areas where they are ripe for trouble, saying that only a fire can clean up the city. He says they started it them-selves to make sure the oracle is fulfilled.'

Antonia and Eigon glanced at each other. Outside in the vast swathe of the dawn sky the Dog Star's rising had been masked by the glow of the fire.

'He says,' Flavius went on, stammering, 'that he will make the Christians pay with their lives.'

Jess opened her eyes and stared down at the carpet. She could smell the burning, see the reflection of the flames in the sky. All around them a fine rain of ash had begun to fall. She brushed impatiently at her arms, and then realised there was no ash on her. No burning. Nothing but a quiet empty room. Almost without realising she had done it she climbed to her feet and walked over to the wall and put her hand on the rough stones. As she climbed up the staircase behind her hostess she had clutched in her hand a small leaflet, handed she supposed to every guest, describing the delights of the *pensione*, including the fact that the back wall of the house was an original wall from 200 BC which had been incorporated into the later church. This wall had survived the great fire of Rome. Leaning forward she rested her forehead against it and closed her eyes, willing herself to see the story it could tell. Was that why Carmella had chosen this house as her friend's refuge? She must have known the story. Jess could feel the cold stone against her skin, but no pictures came. No smoke. No crackle of flames. Nothing. After a few minutes she moved away and went back to sit on the bed.

'I'm going to have to stop for petrol soon.' Rhodri had been glancing more and more frequently at the dashboard. 'Can you see him?'

Steph stared at the wing mirror hard. 'He's about four cars behind, I think.'

'Damn!' He smacked the steering wheel with the flat of his hand. 'Look at the map. See if there are any turnings off. Perhaps we can duck down one and let him sail past. Sooner rather than later.'

Steph studied the page intently. She knew it by heart already. There were no turnings for several miles. 'Perhaps I can run into the ladies and stay there out of sight so he won't know I'm not Jess. And you never know, he might not notice we've pulled in until it's too late.' She was feeling twitchy again. He was staying too close. Somehow she had thought they would be able to lose him before now, but there he was, always just in sight, accelerating when they did, slowing down when they did, a malevolent maroon shadow on their rear horizon.

'Can't help it. We'll be out of fuel if I don't stop at this next service place. Hold tight.' As the service station came into view Rhodri waited until the last moment to brake hard and swerve in. The car immediately behind him sat on the horn for several long seconds as it swerved past them and disappeared up the road. Rhodri pulled past the pumps and swept behind the buildings to draw up out of sight of the road. There was perspiration standing on his brow. 'Sorry about that shocking piece of driving. Did it work?'

Steph turned round. 'I can't see.' She was shaking.

He closed his eyes and put his head back against the head rest. 'I'm knackered!'

'If we've lost him we can get a coffee here perhaps.' She gave an exhausted grin. 'And use the loo!'

Rhodri pushed open the car door and climbed out. He glanced round. 'Wait here. I'll go and peer round the corner. See if the coast's clear.'

Opening her own door she swung her legs out and sat there for a few minutes, elbows on knees, head in hands, waiting for him. When he didn't appear she levered herself to her feet and headed after him. There was a dusty maroon BMW standing at the pumps. She stared at it, goosepimples crawling up the backs of her arms. There was no sign of the driver. She turned away quickly and headed for the ladies' loo as fast as she could. Ducking inside she headed for a cubicle and bolted herself in. Now what? Had he seen her? Where was Rhodri? She waited for several minutes, listening as other people came in and used the facilities and walked out again, their footsteps ringing on the tiled floor. No one spoke. She strained her ears for the sound of voices outside but could hear nothing above the rushing of water. Cautiously she pulled back the lock and peered out. The cloakroom was completely empty. Washing her hands and face she ran a comb through her hair and at last turned towards the doorway. She hesitated, glancing at her watch. She had been ten minutes. If the maroon car was nothing to do with Dan it would have gone by now. She reached for the handle on the heavy swing door and pulled it open. The parking lot and the approach to the pumps were dazzling in the bright sunlight. Far above swifts wheeled against the intense blue of the sky, thin cries barely audible in the still air.

The heat hit her as soon as she stepped outside. She scanned the pumps in the shade of the roof. The car had gone and Rhodri had pulled up in its place. With a sigh of relief she stepped outside and heading towards their car she climbed in and sat back in the seat, the window down, waiting for Rhodri to pay. When she next glanced up Dan was standing beside the car looking down at her. He gave her a cold smile as she let out an exclamation of fright at the sight of him.

'Steph! Well, well. I might have known.' He folded his arms. 'How foolish of me.'

'Dan!' She pretended surprise. 'How extraordinary to see you here. Are you heading home as well?' The palms of her hands had broken into a sweat as she looked up at him and she rubbed them surreptitiously on her knees. He was wearing dark glasses and she couldn't read his expression. Glancing beyond him she saw Rhodri appear, carrying cartons of coffee and a bag of pastries. At the sight of Dan he speeded up and came to a standstill beside him.

'I thought it was you! You utter shit! I am going to beat the living daylights out of you for what you've done to Jess!' Rhodri dropped the bags from the coffee shop through the window into Steph's lap. 'By the time I've finished with you, you will be sorry you were ever born!'

Dan took a sharp step backwards as Rhodri reached out to grab him, then he turned and ran.

Rhodri didn't bother to follow. 'Coward!' he bellowed after him. 'Give up, man! She's already gone. You won't find her!'

Dan paused and looked back. 'She hasn't gone,' he shouted back. 'Don't you understand anything? She won't leave until Titus has killed her nemesis.' He gave a humourless laugh. 'I should have known better than to follow you. What a farce. Now he's angry!' A few seconds later they saw his car heading back onto the carriageway from where he had parked it amongst some lorries behind the coffee bar. With a screech of tyres he did a U-turn on the quiet road and accelerated back the way they had come.

'Bastard! Get your mobile, quick.' Rhodri lowered himself into the driving seat and pulled away from the pumps. He parked again almost at once. 'There's no point in chasing him. Ring Will. Warn him he's on his way back. Bugger! Bugger! Bugger!'

314

'What are we going to do?' Steph had her mobile to her ear.

'See what Will thinks.' Rhodri took back one of the coffees and took off the lid, blowing froth and steam from the cappuccino inside.

'I'll get her to the airport,' Will said as Steph reported what had happened. 'He doesn't know where she's staying. That is a bonus. We'll go out to Ciampino. My plan is to get her down to Cornwall. There is no way Dan could find her there.'

'What shall we do?' Steph asked. 'Shall we come back?'

'No point if we're leaving. I suggest you carry on driving back. Enjoy the trip. But be careful if you go to Ty Bran. You might find he automatically heads there if the trail goes cold.'

Titus Marcus Olivinus threw back his head and laughed. 'I couldn't have done better if I had set the fire myself!'

Lucius glanced at him doubtfully. 'Are you sure you didn't?'

Titus touched the side of his nose. 'Who knows? A word here. A word there. They say it started in several places at once. If I played a modest part, it would only have been to make suggestions as to who did what, where.' He gave a satisfied grin.

'So, you would destroy an entire city to isolate your little princess?'

'You must admit, such a plan has style.' Titus sat back in his chair. Outside the barrack block men ran to and fro, changing shifts, coming back exhausted from fighting the fire, throwing themselves into their bunks as the men who would replace them formed up on the parade ground ready to march towards the seat of the flames. 'There will be nothing left by the time this finally goes out. It is right out of control. Our Emperor at least will be ecstatic. He can put into effect all his plans to build a new city once he's routed out the elements he decides to blame.'

'And he will decide to blame Eigon's friends?'

'They will certainly be amongst those he picks on, yes. Christians and anyone he considers his enemy. I would be very wary if I was a member of the Senate at the moment.' Titus gave a cynical laugh.

'Has it occurred to you that Eigon might get swept up in the clean-out herself? My informer thinks she's been baptised,' Lucius commented gravely.

Titus grimaced. 'Then I will have to see that she is reserved for my own personal attention before they start rounding them up.'

'It's already started. The mob is out in force. They want someone to blame, and they want that someone now.'

'Then Nero has found the perfect scapegoat. Christians are everywhere. You know, it's my guess he started at least one of the fires himself!' Titus went on with a guffaw of laughter. 'I wouldn't put it past him. He's been trying to get his plans for a huge new palace approved by the Senate for ages. He wants that and he wants the power of the Senate curtailed. What better way than to smoke them out.'

'And put the blame squarely somewhere else.' Lucius shook his head. 'And be elsewhere giving one of his appalling concerts when it starts. What an alibi!' Somehow he preferred the idea of the Emperor being behind the conflagration to the suspicion that it might have been started by this cold calculating man beside him.

Titus levered himself to his feet. 'Time to make one or two plans, I think.'

'You're not going in to do a bit of fire-fighting?'

Titus raised an eyebrow. 'I'm not rostered on. And I'm not going to volunteer. What is the point? One more man throwing a bucket of water at the flames is hardly going to make a difference. I have more exciting things to do. Are you with me?' He held Lucius's gaze.

For a moment Lucius hesitated. Then he shook his head. He was not prepared to witness the culmination of Titus's sadistic plans for Eigon. He had long ago decided that. Julia's fate had shocked him more than he cared to admit. It had shaken his friendship with this man to the core and he was not sure that friendship would survive much longer. He gave a grim smile, gathering up his cloak and heading towards the door. 'I'm going to put in a spot of fire-fighting. There are men and women and children dying out there. Whoever is to blame, it sure as Hades wasn't them!'

Titus shrugged. 'Up to you. I think maybe it is time Eigon and I were alone together anyway. And what I have planned doesn't need an audience!'

*   *   *

316

The sound of her mobile ringing made Jess jump. She was dry-mouthed and terrified. She had to warn Eigon. Somehow she had to contact her. To make her listen. The mobile rang on and on. With an irritated exclamation she bent to the bag, lying on the floor by the dressing table and rooted around until she found it. She turned it off without looking to see who it was. Carmella and Will had both emphasised again and again that she must keep it on at all times, but not now. Not while she was trying to contact Eigon. Throwing it down she went back to the bed and sat down again, closing her eyes. *Remember to protect yourself.* Once again Carmella's voice echoed for a moment in her head. There was no time for that now. No time for anything but direct action. 'Eigon,' she whispered. 'Eigon, are you there? Listen. Please, listen to me. You have to be careful.' There was a long silence. Nothing happened. Jess opened her eyes as a sudden thought struck her. Lucius had said that Eigon had been baptised. She was a Christian. Why had she not seen that happening? How could she have missed something so important? Was it so secret that even Jess had been excluded? She frowned impatiently. 'Come on!' she murmured. 'Where are you?'

Even now she didn't know how this process worked. Sometimes she dreamed. Sometimes she appeared to go into a trance. Sometimes she was just awake and watching the scene running before her eyes like a film. Did Eigon consciously facilitate what was happening? Did she want Jess to know her story? Did she want help, as she seemed to do as a little girl, crying in the woods in Wales? Or was this whole process something inside her own brain? Somehow, without her knowledge or her intention it had tuned to a faraway frequency. She clenched her fists. 'Eigon. Please, listen to me! Be careful. He is coming to find you.'

The fire finally burned out after six days. It would take far longer for any semblance of order to be restored to the wreckage of the city. Everything was in disarray even in the areas which had been preserved. Even out here in the suburbs routines were still haywire. But the gates to the villa were open. Titus smiled. He watched a wagon turn in and rumble across the dusty forecourt drawing to a halt in front of the main doors. Slack. That is what he would call their entire household.

Aelius was going to pieces. Too old. No strong direction from the top, he had been allowed to go his own way too long and the shock of the fire and not knowing where Flavius was had turned the man into a lump of dough. And he still had no idea what Flavius was up to. Titus smiled. It had been easy to subvert Flavius. A few denarii here and there and the lad would do anything he asked. He frowned, moving back into the shade of a roadside tree as another wagon approached. This one lumbered on past, heading out of town. He hadn't realised quite how fond the lad was of Julia of course. It had been a tactical error telling the young man to delay his trip into Rome that day so she had to go out alone. He obviously was a better judge of female character than Flavius was himself. He knew she would go on her own rather than be disappointed. But it might have made Flavius suspicious. It had certainly rendered him useless for months afterwards as he grieved for the stupid woman. His frown melted into a smile as he remembered and he felt himself growing hard. Dealing with Julia had been far more exciting than he had ever dreamed possible. And now the long planned moment had come and he was about to do the same thing again.

Eigon, however, was going to be much harder to winkle out of her lair. More of a challenge, but then he liked challenges. He peered out of the shadow at the gateway. There were guards there, he had established that much but they were lounging in the shade, not paying attention. If he rode in smartly dressed, well horsed, he would be waved towards the house where the house slaves would be expected to look after him. If there were any around. He turned, untied his horse and swung himself into the saddle. Eigon wouldn't see him. Her routine was unfailing. All morning she would be in her rooms seeing to a long queue of ailing peasants and slaves. Taking no payment. Giving them her undivided attention, her gentle smiles, her creams and pills and potions until her father woke and demanded his turn. Ye gods, the girl would probably thank him at the end for the excitement he was going to provide for her last hours on earth! He headed the horse towards the gate at a leisurely walk and drew up inside to wait for someone to come and accost him.

'Hey there!' he called imperiously. 'Is there no one here?'

The shelter where the gate porter normally sat, out of the weather, was empty. Titus snorted derision. If it was going to be this easy he was going to feel cheated. All the long hours of planning, the dreaming, the lusting over his goal looked to have been a waste of time. He could have walked in and taken her just like that!

'Can I help, my lord?' The voice behind him made him jump. There was someone in attendance after all. His horse sidestepped nervously and he jabbed viciously at its bit. The man reached out for Titus's bridle and quieted his horse with a hand on its nose. 'I'm sorry there was no one to receive you. The guards have escorted a wagon round the back. Did you wish to see King Caratacus?' He was a slave, but immaculately dressed and well spoken. Titus reined back away from his hand forcing the man to release the horse. 'I came to see his steward, Aelius,' he said sharply. 'There is no need to bother the king himself.'

The slave nodded. He reached for the horse's bridle again. 'If you would care to dismount, sir, and go to the door I will send for someone to tell him you are here.'

Titus sat still. 'Call him out here,' he said curtly.

The slave frowned. He said nothing however. Stepping away from the horse a second time he turned and walked towards the main entrance to the villa, disappearing under the portico into the black shadow of the interior. Titus narrowed his eyes, watching. There was no other sign of life. No dogs, no scurrying servants. The place seemed to be asleep but that didn't mean there weren't other guards he couldn't see.

When the servant returned he was alone as Titus had known he would be. 'I am sorry, lord, Aelius went into the city early this morning. He will not be here until nightfall. Would you like to speak to anyone else?'

Titus shook his head. 'I will return another day.' He wheeled round and cantered towards the gate without another word. The man would recognise him if he saw him again, but that meant nothing. He smiled to himself as he spurred the animal into a gallop on the hard roadway heading back towards the city.

'*Signorina*!' The knock at the door was loud in the room. 'Someone is on the telephone for you. Are you there?' There was a pause. '*Signorina*?' Another few seconds of silence then came the sound of footsteps as the woman ran back down the stairs, her sandals

319

clopping down the wooden treads, the sound fading into the distance.

Jess moved uneasily on her bed but she had heard nothing. Her attention had moved inside the house now, through the dark entranceway into the atrium which was flooded by sunlight through the open centre to the roof above the still pool of water in the middle of the room beneath it. She moved towards Eigon's rooms, drifting like a shadow herself through the deserted reception area to the passage where a bench had been placed so that patients could wait more comfortably for their turn inside her small still room.

Eigon looked tired. Somehow Jess had passed through the door to stand inside watching. She was bandaging the infected arm of a small boy. He was crying, trying to hide in his mother's skirt. The woman was ragged and distraught. 'I don't know why he does it! I tell him not to climb the wall. I tell him to be careful!'

Eigon smiled without looking up as she concentrated on the wound. 'Boys will be boys. There. That is better.' She patted the child on his head. 'I'll give you some ointment for the wound, Cilla. Try and keep the dirt out of it or it won't heal.'

When the woman had gone she stood for a moment, her hands to her back in the classic pose of a woman overburdened. Jess heard her sigh. She was still beautiful, still young, but there was a heaviness about her that spoke of total exhaustion.

'Eigon!' Jess's voice was urgent. 'Eigon, can you hear me? You have to hear me. Titus is nearby. He is coming to try and kidnap you. He will kill you. Please, please, listen to me!'

Eigon straightened. She looked round with an expression of faint puzzlement on her face. 'Is there someone there?'

'Yes!' Jess was exultant. 'Eigon! You can hear me! Listen!'

Eigon shook her head and put her hand to her forehead. 'Glads?'

So, she still thought about her sister. Still perhaps heard that lonely voice from her childhood. She looked round again, then she walked to the door and opened it, beckoning the next patient inside.

Jess groaned. 'No, please! Please, listen –'

'*Shsss!*'

The sudden hiss in her ear almost knocked Jess over. 'Stop it!

Leave her alone! I know what you're trying to do!' The whisper was harsh, husky, almost lost in a dusty echo.

Jess lurched to her feet and stared round, terrified. It had been so close she could feel it reverberating in her head, but the room, her room, in the *pensione*, was empty. One of the shutters had swung open and a broad band of sunlight lay across the carpet near her feet. The atmosphere felt tense, utterly silent, without air. She put her hand to her chest, swallowing hard, feeling her heart thudding uncomfortably. Her mouth had gone dry. Her doorway into the past had closed. She couldn't see Eigon any more, but she could feel someone in the room near her. Trying to regain her breath she backed towards the door. 'Who's there?' Her own voice cracked with fear. 'What do you want?'

She was staring at the line of sunbeams, whirling with dust, which lay across the shadows. Was there a figure there, just for a moment, a hazy outline, no more, then gone?

'Titus?' She breathed the word and immediately felt the atmosphere change. It was like an electrical charge in the room. She felt her head tighten uncomfortably as though someone had drawn a ligature around her forehead.

Protection, Jess. Never forget it. And remember, never say his name. Do not even think his name! Carmella's words rose in her head from somewhere. *No point in Christian prayers and platitudes.* Carmella was no churchgoer either. *Hit him with his own gods!*

'Go back to Hades where you belong, you vile murderer!' Jess's voice was still husky.

Surround yourself with light. Make sure you are on your own ground. Surround yourself with guides and angels. Call on your power animal. Whoever you see as your inner friend, call on them to protect you!

Jess clenched her fists. She had no inner friends or guides; she had never heard of a power animal. She should have listened better. She had been an idiot, so obsessed with finding Eigon, afraid that any steps she took to protect herself would shut out Eigon as well. And now here she was alone and vulnerable with this vicious bastard in the room with her. Then suddenly she knew; of course she knew. There had been one animal in her life who would fulfil every criteria Carmella had described.

'*Hugo*!' The cry she gave echoed round the room. It was a scream for help, for protection, calling for the dog she had so adored as a child, her mother's great shaggy French sheepdog, who had taken it upon himself to be guardian and tutor and protector of her and Steph. And incredibly, suddenly, he was there, a whirl of black shadows in the room with her, a scrabble of claws on the rug by the window and Titus had gone.

Jess sat down on the bed, crying. The room was suddenly still again. She felt a slight, quick, pressure against her leg, the weight of a dog, leaning against her, pleased with itself, and it was gone.

The footsteps on the stair were running this time. '*Signorina*? Are you all right? *Signorina* Jess, please open the door!' Jess staggered to her feet. She unlocked the door with shaking hands and pulled it open.

Margaretta, her hostess, was standing on the landing. 'Is something wrong?' Her eyes were wide. 'You called out? I could hear you downstairs.'

Jess nodded. She gave an embarrassed laugh as she groped for a tissue. 'I'm sorry. I was asleep. I was dreaming about the dog my mother had when I was a child. I thought he was here in the room with me.'

'*Dio*!' Her hostess shook her head. 'You were asleep. That is why you didn't hear me before!'

'Hear you?'

Margaretta nodded. 'It was your sister. She said you weren't answering your mobile. She said it was important.'

'I must have been very tired if I didn't hear. I didn't mean to worry you. I'm sorry.' Jess shrugged.

The woman stared round again suspiciously, then she stepped back. 'If you are OK. You will call her now, yes?'

'I will. I promise.' Somehow Jess managed a smile as she closed the door gently in Margaretta's face; she had no intention of returning the call. Behind her the room was empty.

Dan pulled into the side of the road. He felt slightly sick. He had been driving for hours and he couldn't remember when he had last had anything to eat. The urgency inside him to drive on was immense, pushing him forward, the picture in his head relentless. He had to find Eigon. He clasped the wheel in front of him tightly and shook his head. Not Eigon. Jess. He had to find Jess. If he didn't sort her out, she would destroy him. He could feel the sweat standing out on his forehead. Once she was in the litter no one would see her. The slaves would never dare question him. He would use drugs as he had before. He slipped his hand into his pocket. The small bottle of pills was there. She would know nothing about it. She wouldn't be frightened or hurt. He would deal with her quietly and leave her somewhere to be found when he was long gone from the scene. But the voice was there again pushing, always pushing. *You are not going to leave her, you are going to enjoy her first. You enjoyed it before, didn't you? Seeing her helpless. Watching the fear in her eyes. Isn't that what you want?*

Dan dashed the back of his hand across his face, wiping away the sweat. Why couldn't the voice leave him alone! The crazed sadistic bastard was there inside his head all the time. He couldn't think straight. He couldn't function rationally any more without him interfering. His knuckles were white on the steering wheel. He rested his head on his hands for a moment and took several long deep breaths. It was all irrelevant anyway. He didn't know where Eigon – Jess – was. They had hidden her somewhere. Or taken her back to England. Or to Ty Bran again.

He frowned. Had she gone back to the cold misty distance which was Britannia? The posting they all dreaded because it was about as far as you could get from Rome without falling off the edge of the world. He shuddered. Those wild Celtic women with their flying hair and their bright mocking eyes, luring men on, even the children desirable; the children of the enemy, to be subdued and punished and destroyed. But she hadn't been destroyed. She had lived to watch him with those reproachful eyes, lived to recognise him, to identify him, to threaten his position, his future, his life.

So, where is she, Titus? You'll have to find her, because I can't. Dan sat up and put his head back against the headrest, his eyes closed. I can't do it. She's gone. Escaped. If you want me to kill her then you have to help me. He opened his eyes again suddenly and stared ahead out of the windscreen. So what did you do, Titus? What did you do when you finally got your hands on her? Did you live out your fantasies? Did you rape her and torture her and kill her? Was it her spirit that escaped you? Is that what this is all about? Even with your hands around her throat did she look into your eyes and smile, knowing you couldn't follow her where she was going!

* * *

323

Julius closed the door behind him and came to stand near her in the still room. He was out of breath, his face pale. Turning to him she reached out her arms to him and smiled. 'Julius?' The smile faded on her lips. 'What is it? What's wrong?'

'Eigon, are you all right? Has there been any trouble out here? The streets of the city are crawling with soldiers. Nero has decreed a vendetta against Christians. He blames us for setting fire to Rome. He is rounding us all up. People we know, our friends, have been taken to the dungeons on the Esquiline. They are going to be thrown to the wild beasts.' There were tears in his eyes. 'He is crazy, completely crazy!'

He put his arms around her and rested his face for a moment in her hair. 'Oh, Eigon, what are we going to do?'

For a moment she snuggled against him, clinging to his tunic, then with a sigh she pushed him away. 'Your father? And Antonia? Where are they?'

'My father has left. The house was burned to the ground. He and the servants have gone to the country. I think he's safe – but who knows? I don't know why this is happening.' He shook his head in genuine bewilderment.

'And Antonia? Where is she? I tried to persuade her to stay here, but she wouldn't. She was so worried about you and your grandfather.' Eigon held his gaze fiercely. 'Where is she, Julius?'

He shrugged. 'I don't know.' His voice was so husky the words were barely audible. 'That's why I came. I know your mother has forbidden me to come to the house but she loves Antonia. Surely she would understand my worry.'

'Of course she would.' Eigon dismissed her mother's views without hesitation. 'Where have you looked?'

'Everywhere. I've asked everyone.'

'Won't Antonia have gone to your country estate? Surely that is the safest place?' The worm of unease in her stomach was growing. She paused. 'What about Peter?'

'He's safe for now. I don't think Nero would dare touch him.'

'Could she be with him?' Eigon caught his hands. 'Isn't that what she would do? When she found the house gone, and no sign of you or your grandfather, she would have gone to him. Or to Paul. Is he still in Rome?'

He shrugged 'It's a thought. Everything is so confused. I'll ride

324

back and check. But you, Eigon.' He gazed down at her. 'I don't think you are safe here. That is why I came. You must hide. People are whispering that you are a Christian. You have been seen too often in our houses; you have been seen sitting at Peter's feet.'

'And still I prevaricate.' She smiled sadly. 'Peter sees me as a challenge but I have told him I cannot give up the gods of my mother and father's country.' Standing on tiptoe she kissed him on the cheek. 'Go, Julius. You must find her. Take her to your grandfather.'

'I can't go without you. You are not safe.' He put his hands on her shoulders and looked down at her sternly. 'You know I love you, don't you.'

She smiled. 'I know, Julius.'

'And do you love me?'

She nodded. 'I believe I do.'

'Will you marry me?'

'Even if I'm not a Christian?'

'You are in your heart. Jesus sees that.'

She smiled. 'Whatever Jesus thinks, my mother and father must come first, Julius. I cannot go against their wishes.'

The door opened so suddenly behind them that they had no time to jump apart as Aelius appeared. He surveyed them for a moment, his lips pursed. 'There are two officers of the Praetorians in the courtyard asking for you, princess.'

'No!' Julius caught her arm. 'Don't go.'

Eigon hesitated. 'What do they want, Aelius, do you know?' Her stomach knotted with fear.

The steward shrugged. He eyed Julius with open dislike. 'Why not go and see what they want, lady. They asked for you to go out to them particularly.'

'No!' Julius was still holding on to her. 'You must not go out there.'

'Shall I refer them to the king your father, then?' Aelius asked. 'I am sure he would be able to deal with their request, whatever it is.'

'No.' Eigon pulled away from Julius. 'You know we can't do that, Aelius. My father is resting. I shall deal with it.' She turned to Julius. 'I want you to go. Now. Go and search for Antonia. I shall be quite safe out here.'

'I don't think you will.' He looked down at her sternly. 'At least

325

let me come out to see these men with you. Find out what they want.'

'And let them see me consorting with a known Christian?' She smiled. 'Then it might be you who is in danger, Julius, and it would make things worse for me. Go, please. Go out through the kitchens, take your horse, and leave by the north gate. It will do none of us any good if you are arrested; and even if you aren't, what use are you to Antonia and your grandfather here? Please.' She stood on her toes again and kissed him.

Aelius raised an eyebrow. 'Shall I come with you to see these men, lady?'

'Yes, please.' She took a deep breath. 'Come now,' she instructed as she hurried past him.

To her relief she did not recognise the two officers in the court-yard. They saluted as she appeared and one of them stepped forward. 'I have a letter for you, lady.' He held out a scroll. 'We have been instructed to escort you to a house in the next village.'

She frowned, glancing from one man to the other as she unrolled the letter. The taller of the men had green eyes. His face was tired and dusty.

'You've been fighting the fire in the city?' she asked. He nodded. The other man was smarter, his back straighter, his eyes hard, the colour of flint. She found herself disliking him instinctively. The letter was short and to the point: *Eigon, I need you. Please come. Tell no one. Antonia.*

The writing was shaky but it was Antonia's. Eigon glanced up at the taller man. 'Who gave you this?'

'One of my colleagues, lady. He was to have delivered it himself, but he was injured in the fire.'

'Do you know what it says?'

He nodded. 'We're to take you to a house a couple of miles or so away from here up the Via Flaminia. There is a young lady there. She has been injured, I believe. She needs your care.'

'Aelius, quick! See if Julius is still here!' Eigon called over her shoulder. 'Tell him this is from Antonia. Then ask a slave to fetch my bay mare.' She turned to the officers. 'Wait. I shall go and collect up some medicines and bandages.' She paused. What if this was a trap? 'What is wrong with her?' she asked suspiciously.

They both shrugged. The shorter man smiled. 'It is serious, lady, from what I hear.' She studied his face thoughtfully. His expression

326

did not reassure her, but what could she do? She could not abandon Antonia. Turning on her heels she ran back into the atrium and through towards her rooms. It took only a minute to throw some phials of tincture, some small clay jars of medicine and some linen bandages into a bag. She pulled a light cloak off the hook behind the door and was out in the courtyard again in seconds.

Aelius had reappeared. 'I was too late, lady. He had gone.' He hesitated. 'I should come with you, myself.' He too seemed worried.

'There is no need.' The taller officer spoke as he stood forward. 'We shall escort the princess Eigon. She will come to no harm with us.'

Aelius hesitated. 'Someone should go with you. It isn't fitting –'

'Hurry, lady.' The shorter man dragged the reins of his own horse over its head and swung himself into the saddle as the slave, Silas, appeared with Eigon's pony. 'Come or don't come but don't keep us waiting.'

'You go!' Aelius directed the slave as the young man knelt and put out his hand for Eigon's foot, tossing her onto the horse's back. 'Run with her. Stay with her. You are her escort, understand?'

'Sir!' Silas nodded. He grinned at the officers as the second man mounted in his turn. 'Just don't ride too fast, sirs!'

They set off at a fast trot, veering onto the Via Flaminia at the end of the track and following it for some two miles before turning off up another dusty road towards a ruined villa which had belonged to one of their neighbours who years ago had moved away to Actium.

Eigon scanned the surrounding countryside warily. It was so seldom that she rode outside the gates she was for a moment disorientated. She reined in her horse. 'There's no one living here. This can't be right.'

'Your friend is in hiding, lady, as I understand it.' The younger officer with the flinty eyes reined back alongside her and reached for her rein. 'That's why she is here. Where no one will find her. I think we should hurry. She doesn't want to be found by the authorities, now, does she. As a Christian.'

Eigon stared at him, their eyes meeting across the horse's neck. 'You are the authorities, are you not?' she challenged tartly.

He shrugged. 'I just do what I'm told. I've nothing against anyone in particular. I carried a message; I am bringing you as instructed. Then we go back to the barracks.' He urged the horses on.

They dismounted in a weedy, abandoned yard behind the villa. Eigon stared round, full of misgivings. 'This doesn't feel right.' She glanced at Silas. He was carrying her bag, still trying to regain his breath after trotting on foot after them. 'Where is she?' She turned to the taller man.

He shrugged uncomfortably. 'I'll go and knock.'

The door opened almost at once. The doorway, deep in shadow, hid the man who stood there. Eigon took a step towards him. 'Where is Antonia?' Suddenly she was frightened. She shouldn't have come with just one slave. She should have brought an escort.

'She's inside. She can't stand. Her ankle is sprained.' The deep voice was reassuring. 'Antonia, can you hear?' he called over his shoulder. 'Your friend is here with her bandages. You'll soon be fixed up.' He was answered by a whimper of pain. He glanced at Silas. 'I suggest you ride back, young man, with the lady's horse. Come and collect her tomorrow with a litter for her and her friend who by then will be well enough to be moved.' He stood back waiting for Eigon to enter. She glanced at Silas doubtfully, anxious to get to Antonia, reassured by the voice of the man looking after her, yet worried at the thought of remaining on her own.

Silas was hesitating. 'I should stay, lady.'

Another moan from Antonia made up her mind. 'Do as he says but tell Aelius where we are.' She took the bag from the young man and walked past him into the house.

Antonia was lying on a pile of straw covered by a filthy rug. There was a rag tied across her mouth. Her eyes were frantic. Eigon spun round but the man who had ushered her in had gone. There was no sign of Silas. Someone else stood in the doorway. She recognised him at once. Titus Marcus Olivinus.

Dan smiled. So, you caught her at last. You caught both of them. What a bonus! Was she really so naïve she walked in like that without even hesitating? He sighed, glancing out of the windscreen. Black storm clouds had massed on the horizon. The heat was intense inside the car with the air conditioning off. He didn't want to be caught in a storm by the side of the road; time to head into Rome. He gave a grim smile as he reached down for the ignition key and turned on the engine. If Titus wanted him to find Jess, Titus would find a way to tell him where she was.

24

Jess took a deep breath. She was being a fool. She had to follow Carmella's instructions and protect herself psychically against Titus. There was no way she was going to allow that evil bastard into this room again. Thoughtfully she picked up the bag. Inside, with her things, was a do-it-yourself psychic protection kit Carmella had put together for her: a candle, a clove of garlic – not that Titus was a vampire, she thought wryly. A bowl for water. A clean duster. 'Make sure there is no dust or dirt anywhere. Open the window, turn on all the lights, bring in the sunshine,' Carmella had called after her as they parted. Jess glanced at the window. The sky was dark. 'If you sense him, picture a sword in your hand, Jess. A strong sword made of flame.' And what was it Rhodri had said? Now might be the time to try the odd prayer.

Jess sighed. She had needed none of that. Not in the end. Just her beloved old Hugo.

She sat down on the bed again.

'Eigon? What happened next?'

Titus walked slowly towards the straw bed where Antonia lay and pulled out a dagger. She gave a moan of fear as he casually reached out with it and flicked it lightly across her cheek. A line of red appeared; it hardly bled at all. Her hands and feet, Eigon could see now, had been tightly bound. He turned towards Eigon. 'So, princess, at last we meet face to face, properly. I have waited so long for this moment. You do, of course, know who I am? And that we met before, a long time ago.'

'Titus Marcus Olivinus.' She said the words softly, her voice steady.

He looked startled for a moment. 'So, you knew who I was all along?'

'I've known for many years.'

'And you told no one?'

She shook her head. 'You were in no danger from me.'

'Why?' He folded his arms.

'My mother did not want my father upset by something so trivial.'

He coloured slightly. 'Trivial!'

'To us, yes.' She tried to keep her voice calm. It was important she didn't upset him. It would be harder to kill in cold blood, she suspected, even for a man like him.

He smiled, as if reading her mind. 'It was so easy to kill Julia. She was a whore, ready to do anything to try and save her own skin, but in the end she didn't think what I did was trivial.'

'I'm sure she didn't. Was she tied and helpless too, like a sacrificial lamb?' Eigon glanced at Antonia who moaned again. 'That can't have taken much courage on your part.' She took a step towards him and was pleased to see him take a step back. 'If you are a courageous man, you will let Antonia go. Then you will have me on my own to do with what you will. That is your plan?' She raised an imperious eyebrow. 'To kill women who are bound hand and foot is the mark of a coward.'

He gave a bark of laughter. 'You call me a coward?'

She smiled. 'I do. Only a coward would rape a child.'

'You and your mother and those other slaves were scum. The enemy. Defeated. Bound for the arena. You were ours to do with what we wanted.'

'The punishment for the rape of a queen and a daughter of the royal house was death!' she flashed back at him. 'Why else have you lived in craven fear all your life since? We were not destined for the arena! We were destined to live in state as the guests of the Emperor of Rome.' She smiled at him coldly. 'Whatever you do now, you are doomed to die. I have left instructions as to what to do and where to look should anything happen to me. I wrote them down years ago when I first realised you were watching me.' Her fear seemed a million miles away, walled off behind a sheet of adamantine crystal. She took another step forward, her eyes fixed on his.

This time he stood his ground. 'Your death will destroy your father, princess,' he said quietly. 'Doesn't that worry you?'

'My cowardice would worry him more,' she retorted.

He looked at her mockingly. 'And does he know you are a Christian?' The change of tack was so sudden it took her by surprise.

She glanced at Antonia in spite of herself. 'I'm not a Christian.'

'No?' He laughed. 'Well, almost. The thing is that it seems I don't have to kill you, Eigon of the Silures, as my Emperor will do it for me.' He grinned. 'He feels that an example must be made of the Christians who have fired his city. People can't go around doing things like that, can they; they have to be made an example of, enough of an example to terrify the rest of the population into submission. That has always been the way with our leaders. You know that as well as I do. You are an intelligent woman. Do you know what he is doing with Christians, men, women and,' he smiled, 'even children?'

'I'm sure you are going to tell me,' she said dryly.

'Last night the first batch were dealt with. I understand it was an amazing sight.' He moved back a little to lounge against the wall. 'They are going to repeat the show tonight. They are setting up posts along the paths in the royal gardens. Posts soaked in tar. To light the way in the dark.' He paused. 'Each one had a Christian lashed to it last night. They lit up the skies of Rome like candles, and it was only right, after all. Think of all the innocent Roman citizens who died in the fire they themselves had lit.'

Antonia groaned. Eigon felt her stomach tighten with fear.

He smiled. Pushing himself away from the wall he moved towards her. He reached out his hand and touched her face. She stood her ground. 'Such a shame. You are beautiful. It is hard to imagine your skin wrinkled and blackened, hanging off your skull in shreds as the flames lick round you.'

Somehow she managed to stand upright and hold his gaze without shrinking from his touch. 'Christians believe in everlasting life, Titus Marcus Olivinus. They go to the land of the ever young, to sit at the feet of their God and the Lord Jesus and they know that God will punish those who hurt them.'

'Somehow that thought doesn't scare me at all.' He grinned again. 'Besides, you just said you weren't a Christian.' His hand was still there, near her face. He stroked his fingers gently, almost affectionately, down her cheek and across her throat. She was tempted to spit in his face. Somehow she managed to keep herself still. To enrage him would make matters far worse. At least if she kept him talking it was giving them time. Time for what she wasn't sure, but time was the only weapon she had at the moment.

His hand moved lower to the neckline of her tunic. He plucked gently at the material, teasing. Then he brought up his other hand. In it was the dagger. Eigon held her breath. She was sure he must be able to hear the panic-stricken beating of her heart as he placed the point of the dagger against her flesh and pressed. It wasn't a strong movement. Not enough to draw blood this time. Then suddenly he pushed it down between her breasts, ripping through the linen of her tunic to the waist, where it met the plaited leather of her girdle and stopped. He seized the flapping wings of material and pushed them back, leaving her half-naked before him. This time she did spit. She got him directly in the eye. Without hesitation he raised his right hand and hit her hard across the face. She staggered back against the wall with a cry of pain but he had already seized her arm. He threw her to the ground, grabbed his dagger from where it had fallen at his feet and proceeded to cut the rest of her clothes from her body. She was almost insensible with terror when the sound of hoof beats on the stones of the yard outside caused him to pause and look up, panting. It sounded as though a large party of horses had arrived. A shouted command echoed through the room and then another. Titus swore. Stepping over her body he went over to the window, sheathing his dagger in his belt. A troop of legionaries had ridden into the courtyard and were dismounting, leading their horses to the trough to drink, shouting to each other.

Titus whipped round. He bent and seizing a piece of Eigon's torn tunic he rammed it into her mouth, tying it there with a section of the girdle. He rolled her into his cloak and tied it round her with the rest of the girdle, then heaving her off the floor into his arms, he threw her on the straw beside Antonia. He glanced down at them with a grin. 'It seems I have reinforcements. Earlier than I might have hoped, but then there are so many more of you to round up!' Stepping to the door he flung it open and walked out into the sunshine.

Jess opened her eyes. She was sitting on the floor, her back against the wall. Outside the window it had grown dark. She felt sick and frightened. The palms of her hands were sweating. For a long time she sat still, gazing in front of her into space, her mind a whorl of shadows and voices.

The senior officer strode straight into the farmhouse and stood looking down at the two women. 'Who are these?' he asked curtly.

Titus had followed him back inside. He shrugged. 'Two more Christians, sir. This area is a hotbed of them. We were about to take them to Rome.'

'No need. Throw them in the wagon with the others.' The man barked a command over his shoulder and two more legionaries appeared.

He overruled Titus's protests with a few short commands to his men and that was that. Titus saluted, his eyes smouldering with fury as he watched the two women being dragged from the straw and tossed through the rough leather flaps at the back of the covered wagon to crash onto the floor in the semi-darkness. There were other people in there already. Two small children, beyond screaming now, too frightened even to whimper. A woman, perhaps their mother, lay on her back, her eyes open. She was dead. Two men had been tied together, their wrists fastened to the hoops of the wagon roof. They sat quietly, reciting prayers. They made no attempt to speak to the two young women who had been thrown in with them. It was a little boy, one of the children, who crawled across to them as the wagon lurched into motion, heading south towards the city and with bleeding hands tried to undo Eigon's gag. He managed it at last. Then he set to work on the knots of the leather rope which bound her. Forcing her bruised lips into a smile, she tried to speak. It was several minutes before the whispered words of encouragement began to form. When at last he managed to free her she forced her agonised arms to move and caught him against her, comforting him, dropping a kiss on the top of his head. Then she crawled across to Antonia. She managed to tear the gag away but it was a long time before she could undo her bonds. By now the men were watching. She put her finger to her lips, hushing them, then moved to them. 'In my pack. Over there.' The husky whisper of one of them was in her ear. 'There is a knife.'

334

She found it at last, bracing herself against the lurching of the wagon, her ears straining for a sign that one of the soldiers sitting on the front of the wagon would take it into his head to look back and check what was happening to his human cargo. She could hear their voices, exchanging banter with the escort, shouting to make themselves heard above the sound of horses' hooves, moving at speed.

One of the men moved forward to the dead woman. He bent and kissed her forehead. 'May our Lord Jesus Christ bless you, my darling.' Then, his lips firmly pressed together, he pulled her stole away from her shoulders and gave it to Eigon. 'You need it more than she does,' he said quietly. She blushed. She had tried to pull Titus's cloak around her for modesty's sake but she knew her nakedness must be obvious to all of them. The other man moved carefully to the back of the wagon and lifting the edge of the leather cover peered out. There was no sign of anyone behind them. The escort must be in front or at least alongside. They were travelling through a wooded area, shaded from the sunlight. He looked at Eigon and raised an eyebrow. 'Shall we jump for it?' He had to put his lips to her ear to make himself heard. 'It might be the only chance we'll get.' She nodded. The light wagon was high above the road and moving at speed. Anyone jumping from the back was risking being badly hurt but anything was better than meekly awaiting their fate. 'We'll have to go quietly. When you hit the ground roll off the road into the trees. Get out of sight.' He glanced at the other man and then at Antonia. 'You two women go first. We'll each take a child and follow. Go!'

There was no time to argue. No time for thought. Eigon caught Antonia's hand. Together they perched for a second on the back of the wagon then they leaped out into space. The ground hit with enormous force, winding her, but Eigon was on her feet and running for the trees before she had given herself time to think. As she ran she saw the two men jumping out too. Each had a small child in his arms. One of the men landed on his feet, he staggered forward, saved himself and dived into the woodland out of sight. The horses were travelling at a canter, the wagon bucketing along behind them. The sound of the hooves on the road surface drowned any noise they might have made and almost before they had time to catch their breath the wagon had disappeared around a bend in the road and they were left with nothing but dust.

'Are you all right? Where are the others?' The man with the little boy in his arms beckoned to her from the shadows. The child seemed stunned.

Eigon shook her head. 'I can't see them. They must have rolled into the trees. I'll look.' Her ankle was agony. She had turned it over as she landed and she had grazed her arm. It burned fiercely as she crept to the edge of the trees and peered out.

'Eigon?' Antonia staggered towards her. She was covered in leaves, and her face was bruised, but she seemed to be all right. 'Where are the others?'

They found the second man and the little girl sitting in a ditch, too stunned to move. It took several minutes of coaxing and re-assurance before the child would release her grip on his neck, then at last he managed to climb to his feet.

'Come on. They will notice we've gone and come back to look for us. We have to get away from here.' The older of the two men took command. 'We'll go deeper into the wood. We must get right away from the road. Does anyone know where we are?'

Eigon had torn a piece of material from the stole she had wrapped around her and was binding her ankle tightly with it, gritting her teeth against the pain. 'We can't be far from the farm-house where Antonia and I were captured. I know where that was. I rode there willingly.' She grimaced half from the agony of her foot as she put her weight down, half at her own stupidity. 'It was not far from my home.'

'You don't want to lead them there, Eigon,' Antonia put in quietly. Her teeth were chattering. 'That is the first place he will look.'

Eigon sighed. 'You're right. So, what do we do?'

'We should pray.' The younger man, the father of the two chil-dren, had his arms around them now. He glanced at the two women. 'My name is Stephen. These are Maria and David.'

'And I am Marcellus,' the older man said. He glanced up as a low rumble of thunder echoed through the trees. 'Can you walk, Eigon? Then let's go. My instinct tells me to walk towards the thunder. That has been coming all afternoon from the hills. It will lead us away from the city and the road. Mountains are always a good place to lose oneself. We will pray as we go, Stephen. God will guide us.'

Eigon smiled to herself. The instinct to run and hide in the hills had never left her. In her dreams of home the soft hillsides were a background to happy memories. That last terrible night when she and her mother had been raped and her brother and sister had disappeared into the hills was something she had put so firmly to the back of her mind that it was almost beyond recall. She glanced at Antonia. 'Can I borrow your shoulder to lean on?'

Antonia nodded. 'This is all my fault. You came to rescue me.'

'That is not your fault.' Eigon winced as she put the foot to the ground. 'It was mine for being so trusting. I was a fool. We won't talk about it any more. Except –' she glanced at Antonia suddenly. 'Your grandfather? Where is he? Julius came looking for you both.'

'He is safe. Or he was when I left the villa. I was tricked too.' She shrugged. 'I was an idiot!'

'Did he –?' Eigon hesitated. 'Did he rape you?'

Antonia shook her head. 'He didn't hurt me at all. Only my dignity.'

'Thank God!'

Antonia smiled. 'That sounded heartfelt.'

'It was.'

'You said thank God, not thank the gods.'

Eigon gazed at her for a moment in astonishment. 'So I did!'

They walked on for a long time, heading as Marcellus had suggested towards the thunder clouds which hung above the hills. It was late, and they were exhausted and hungry when at last they came to the first rising ground and spotted a house lying amongst its market gardens against the woods.

'I will go and see if I can buy bread and goat's milk for the children and find out exactly where we are,' Marcellus said softly. 'You all shelter here.' They had come to a halt at last on the edge of a rocky ravine, a tumbling river at the bottom, steep banks forming a natural hiding place amongst the interwoven tree roots.

They watched him stride off towards the house. 'He's a good man,' Stephen said slowly. 'Dear God, please keep him safe.'

Maria and David had huddled together in the muddy shelter at once, too tired and frightened to complain, falling into uneasy sleep as Eigon sat with them and sang gently one of the lullabies she remembered from her childhood.

Later, Stephen, Antonia and Eigon sat close together on the edge of the river listening to the roar of the water. 'Do you think we are safe?' Antonia asked at last. She was shivering.

Stephen shrugged. 'From our own captors perhaps. Who knows? This outbreak of hatred against us is so strange. As if we would set fire to the city.'

'Someone has to carry the blame.' Eigon was hugging her knees.

'And Julius had heard that the Jews are also suspected of badmouthing us,' Antonia whispered, her voice still hoarse. 'The Romans respect them. They weren't interested in Christians before; they thought we were just another Jewish sect. Then the Jews began to be afraid at how many people are being baptised as Christians, especially amongst the poor of Rome.'

Eigon was shivering. 'Rome is a big city. One fire or a dozen fires, who knows. Perhaps it was just an accident.' She sighed. 'Marcellus said he was going to try and buy food. Does he have money, then?'

There was a long pause. 'I don't know him,' Stephen said at last. 'When we were arrested he was already in the wagon. I don't know where they picked him up.'

'That was your wife, in the wagon, Stephen?' Antonia asked at last. 'I am so sorry for her death.'

He nodded. For a moment he put his head in his arms on his knees. Then he looked up. 'At least she is with Jesus.'

'And she is watching over you and her children,' Eigon said. She leaned forward and put her hand on his for a moment. 'I sense her very close to us.'

He stared at her. 'How do you know?'

She shrugged. 'I just do.'

A rattle of footsteps behind them made them all look up, frightened. Marcellus appeared. He had a bag on his shoulder, and a heavy cloak over his arm. 'I have food and warmth, my brother and sisters, look.' Sitting down beside them he opened the bag and produced two loaves of bread, still warm from the oven, a jug of milk, a wedge of goat's cheese and two pasties. He blessed the food, they woke the children and shared everything he had brought with him as the storm grew ever louder, then huddling

338

into the back of the cave they wrapped themselves in the cloak and prepared to wait out the night.

The children fell asleep again at once and almost as fast Antonia, snuggling against them, began to doze. The other three leaned against the mud walls of their shelter and watched as the rain began in earnest.

'You think the river will rise? We're in the wrong place if so,' Stephen said at last. The torrent was churning near the top of the bank.

Marcellus shook his head. 'It's steep here and it's moving too fast. We'll be all right. It's safe to sleep.'

Several minutes later Stephen was snoring. Marcellus glanced across at Eigon. 'You still awake?'

She nodded. 'I'm content to rest like this.' She settled more comfortably on the ground. 'You're not from Rome?'

'No.' He gave a throaty chuckle. 'Nor are you, though your language is fluent.'

'I'm from Britannia.' She grinned.

'And I am from Ephasis. I heard Paul teaching there, ten or so years ago; he baptised me and I became one of his helpers. I came to Rome with him three years ago. After his trial and acquittal he asked me to stay to carry on his work here while he travelled again.'

'So you are in more danger than us,' she said thoughtfully.

He chuckled. 'I don't think there are relative degrees of danger in these circumstances.'

She bit her lip. 'Would you do something for me, Marcellus?'

He raised an eyebrow. 'That depends.'

'Will you baptise me?'

There was a long silence. 'I should be honoured.'

'You don't ask if I know what I am doing?'

'I don't think there is any need.' He hauled himself to his feet. 'Come down to the water.'

Leaving the others asleep they stepped out into the rain. In seconds they were both soaked to the skin. Marcellus laughed. 'God is baptising you himself with his own holy water!'

She laughed. 'I should call Antonia. She would want to be here!'

'She is here.' He glanced behind her. 'We must have woken her. She shall be your sponsor. Leave Stephen with his children.

They need sleep to give them strength for whatever comes tomorrow.' He half scrambled, half slid down the bank towards the rushing torrent, holding his hand out to steady her. Behind her Antonia stood, her hair streaming down her back.

'What is it? What is happening?'

'Marcellus is going to baptise me,' Eigon called. 'Come. Be my witness!'

Antonia gave a cry of delight. 'Oh, Eigon, at last! Oh, my dear, you will be my sister in Christ!' She slid down the bank after them, her skirt tangling round her legs as a clap of thunder reverberated down the ravine.

It took only seconds, then the three of them hugged one another and prayed. At last, shivering and exhausted they crept back into the meagre shelter of the bank, and, huddling together for warmth in their soaking wet clothes, tried to compose themselves for sleep.

Eigon stayed awake a long time, staring out into the rain as the thunder died away. She felt deeply at peace. What she had done was not after all a betrayal of her family's gods, but an acceptance that she had been drawn into a greater circle of love and tenderness and strength which would sustain her for the rest of her life. She murmured a prayer that somehow her mother and father would know that she was safe and that they would soon be reunited.

As the rain died away, no longer rattling on the leaves, silence descended on the woods, broken only by the decreasing rush of the river. Slowly it grew light. Faraway from the higher hills in the distance she heard the long lonely howl of a wolf. She smiled. Behind her the little boy stirred. He crawled out of his father's arms and came and sat beside her without a word. She reached out and put her arm round him, drawing him close. He must be about the same age as her little brother was when she last saw him. 'Are you all right?' she whispered, terribly aware suddenly that this little boy had seen his mother die only the day before.

He nodded. 'I'm hungry.'

She smiled. 'So am I. Marcellus is going back to the house when it's properly light. He'll try and get us some more of that lovely bread and cheese.'

'Then where are we going?'

340

'I don't know,' she said. She was trying to hold back the tears. She had no idea at all.

Jess shivered. She had grown so stiff, sitting on the floor leaning against the wall, she could hardly move. She glanced at the window. Here too it was nearly light. Aching, she dragged herself to her feet and went into the small bathroom. A shower made her feel a lot better. She climbed into bed and fell asleep at once under the sheet. When she awoke it was nearly ten o'clock. Her obliging hostess provided her with hot panini and coffee and, much restored, she retraced her steps to her bedroom.

'What in Hades are you going to do now?' Lucius was standing beside Titus, watching the farrier running an expert hand up his horse's leg, gently pressing at a swelling on its hock. 'She'll tell her father and then you will be in trouble.'

'She won't tell her father, that's the beauty of it.' Titus gave a rueful smile. 'I've finally realised that her mother didn't want him to know that I had the queen of the Silures in a sheep's byre on some sodden hillside in a land of barbarian peasants, otherwise why didn't the story come out at the time? Anyway she never saw my face. I'll wager I never was in any danger! What an irony. It's worthy of an entire satire by Horace!'

'So, you're going to forget her?' Lucius felt a huge wave of relief sweep over him. The thought that he might be any more enmeshed in his friend's plans sickened him.

'No chance! I want her. And I'm going to have her.'

'How? They escaped.'

Titus scowled. The discovery that their prisoners had escaped by the simple method of jumping out of the back to the wagon was not something he was going to live down in a hurry. An entire cohort of the Praetorian guard had been duped. They had not noticed until they were back inside the camp ready to move the prisoners on to the dungeons on the Esquiline, constructed hastily from the cellars of houses which had been pulled down in an attempt to create a fire break. From there the Christians were to be taken either to the Circus on the Vatican plain, or to the Emperor's pleasure gardens to act as Roman candles.

'Her escape was providential as it happened,' he said with a harsh laugh. 'It would have been such a waste if she had been lined up for the Emperor's entertainment. I would have been cheated of my pleasure.' He stepped forward as the farrier straightened. 'Is it worth saving the horse?'

The man nodded. 'A couple of days' rest and it'll be as good as new. I'll take it round the back and dress the swelling.' He glanced at the officer suspiciously. He'd known men like him before. He would as soon knock the animal on the head as waste time trying to save it. Gentling the sweating creature he gave Titus no time to change his mind. He led the animal away.

'So, how will you find her?' Lucius asked as they strode towards the officers' mess.

Titus shrugged. 'I have a feeling she will turn up. There's a voice in my head.' He gave a roar of laughter. 'It tells me where she is.' He tapped his nose. 'Perhaps I can smell her out.' He paused so suddenly that Lucius almost bumped into him. 'I'll cross young Flavius's palm with some more silver. That will bring me news if there is any. You are right. Eigon is sure to send a message to her parents; perhaps she will even be stupid enough to go back to them and wait for me to try again. I'll tell you something, Lucius. She's a brave woman. She stood up to me.' He grinned. 'I liked that. The other one, Antonia, snivelled like a whipped pup.'

Dan grinned. He had stopped for a meal at a service station the night before and then, exhausted, decided to book himself into a nearby *pensione* for the night, leaving the car in the lorry park. It had been a good decision. He felt more alert than he had for a long time, and he had dreamed about Titus. It was extraordinary. Just like a film. The detail had been incredible. It would have enthralled the kids at school. And not even an 18 certificate! He gave a wry grin. He had been looking forward to seeing Eigon get her deserts but it hadn't happened. Somehow she had escaped. As had Jess.

He paid his bill and walked out into the clear sunlight. The heat hit him with breathtaking ferocity as he pulled out his car key. It wouldn't take long to get back to Rome and return the car; then perhaps he would stroll round to the palazzo and pay a visit to his friend Jacopo. The combination of money and threats had worked very well before. If there was anything to find out then Jacopo was his man – unless Titus had any luck in the meantime. He was sitting for a moment, the car door open, touching the accelerator with his toe, reluctant to close the door in the furnace heat when his mobile rang. He reached into his pocket and took it out. 'Hello, Nat?'

'Where the hell have you been, Dan?' Natalie's voice seemed to echo round the hot car. 'I've been trying to reach you.'

'I'm sorry. I've been out of town and my mobile was off. Is there anything wrong?'

'The headmaster has been trying to get in touch with you. Something to do with the police.'

'What?' He turned off the engine and climbed out of the car, standing beside it staring across the parking lot towards the distant hills. His hands had started to shake. 'Why?'

'I don't know, he wouldn't tell me, would he.'

'No. I suppose not.'

'He wants you to ring him urgently.'

'Does he know I'm here?'

'Yes, of course he does. I told him.'

'Shit!' Dan was sweating hard. 'Look, there's no point in me contacting them from here. I'll leave it until I get back which will only be a day or so. Can you ring Brian and tell him you couldn't contact me, but I had left a message on your phone saying I'm heading back home overland. That will give me a bit of space.'

There was a moment's silence. 'What is wrong, Dan? What's happened?' Her voice was sharp with suspicion.

'Nothing's wrong. It is probably something to do with the school. But whatever it is, I can't do anything from here, can I! And I'm damned if I'm going to spoil my holiday worrying about what-ever it is. I'll be back soon.'

'Since when have you been on holiday, Dan?' Natalie's voice hardened imperceptibly. 'You're supposed to take your family on holidays, remember? You told me you'd been invited to take someone else's place at the last moment at an educational conference.'

'And so it was.' Dan swore silently. 'It's just, I don't want to cut it short unnecessarily, do I.' He dashed the sweat from his eyes with the back of his hand. 'Look, Nat, I've got to go. The next speaker is arriving. I'll ring you tomorrow, OK? Just stall everyone if you can and I'll sort it when I get home.' He switched off the phone and tossed it into the back. 'Shit! Shit! Shit!' He exhaled loudly and stood for a moment unmoving as a huge lorry started its engine nearby with a throaty roar. After a few moments it began to pull slowly out of the crowded park, leaving him enveloped in a cloud of exhaust fumes. She had been on to the police. Well, he knew she might. That was the whole point of making people think she was mad. Not that he needed to do any more about that. She was mad. Mad as a hatter. She had only to talk to them about Eigon and Titus and the ghosts of Christmas past and they would close their little black notebooks and prosecute her for wasting their time. He lowered himself stiffly back into the car and restarted the engine. So, what to do? If he could find her, well and good, though it was bad that he had admitted to being in Italy still. That was a tactical error. He should have claimed to be back in England. Or in France on the way home. He tensed suddenly. He was on the way home. Rhodri and Steph could verify that. They were miles from Rome when he had caught up with them. It was their word against his about where he was headed.

But he had told Nat he was still at the conference. Shit again. He would deny it. She would think she had misheard. She was paranoid anyway that he was having an affair with someone at school. He would say it was her jealousy talking. He glanced in the rear view mirror and headed out onto the road. He had a day or two at most to find Jess and deal with her. He would ring Nat again and confess he was in Switzerland. Make up some story to pacify her. Exhaustion would be good. And true. Confess there was no conference – the police would check that easily, so there was no point in sticking to that alibi, perhaps beg Nat to come out to him. Cry on her shoulder. Get her to bring the kids. No, not the kids. On her own she was more vulnerable. Less of a mother tiger. On her own, he could win her round easily, and she would back him up. She always did.

Now all he had to do was contact Titus. Titus would help him. Titus was sharp and he was hard. He would know what to do. He would know where to find Jess. He smiled as he put his foot down, closed the windows and cranked up the air conditioning.

Someone in Rome was going to know where she was. If it was Kim then Jacopo would find out. If it was Carmella then it was up to him. And he had just realised how to do it. God, it was so obvious. How could he have been such a fool!

25

'I can see no one watching the entrance,' Marcellus said quietly. They were hidden by darkness, beneath the stone pine near the high walls of Eigon's home. The gates were open and a torch burned in the holder by the door.

'They could be in the porter's lodge, or inside,' Eigon whispered. 'Normally the gates would be locked at night.'

'Normally you would be at home at night,' Antonia said tartly. 'This is madness. Anyone could be watching from the orchards, and anyone could be inside. You said the man who brought the message walked straight in. He was an officer.'

Eigon bit her lip. 'If I could get a message to Aelius or Flavius it would be all right.' She glanced at Marcellus. 'They don't know you.'

'Our enemies do.' He stood up straight. 'But as you say, we'll be out here all night if we don't do something. I'll walk in and knock.'

He strode out into the moonlight before they could say a word, approaching the gates in full view of anyone who was on watch. The others held their breath. He walked right up to the gates and stepped through them, calling out. There was no reply.

Eigon bit her lip. 'Something is very wrong.'

Stephen put his hand on her arm. 'Stay here with the children. I will go and see. No one knows me either.' Marcellus had walked across the courtyard and was approaching the front door. They all watched as he raised his hand to the bronze eagle which served as a knocker. The sound echoed out to them on the road.

'No, wait.' Eigon put her hand on Stephen's arm. 'Someone is coming.'

The door was opening. They saw Marcellus speak to someone inside. He turned and beckoned.

'It's all right.' Eigon stepped forward.

'No, let me go first.' Stephen moved out of the shadows and approached the gate as Antonia caught the children by the hand to hold them back.

Marcellus met him and exchanged a word. They beckoned the others.

'Eigon, I'm afraid your father is very ill,' Marcellus said gently. 'The whole household is at sixes and sevens according to the servant girl I spoke to.'

Eigon gave a small cry of distress. 'Let me go to him.' Pushing past him she ran ahead of them and into the house.

Caradoc's bedroom was filled with the light of dozens of torches and lamps. Cerys sat beside him, her hands clasped around his. He appeared to be unconscious.

She glanced up as Eigon appeared. 'Where have you been?' Her face was swollen with crying. 'He's been asking for you incessantly.'

'I'm sorry, Mam. I couldn't help it. I will explain later.' Eigon tiptoed towards the bed, aware that a dozen or so people were standing round the room. 'Papa?' She turned a stricken look to her mother. 'What happened? He was fine last time I saw him.'

'Someone came. They said you had become a Christian and that you had been arrested and would die in the arena!' Cerys cried. 'I told them it wasn't true, but they said they had proof. They brought your gold bangle.'

Eigon clapped her hand to her wrist. The bangle was missing and she hadn't even noticed. 'Oh, Mam. I'm so sorry. Antonia and I were arrested but we escaped. We came back as soon as we could.' She glanced round the room. 'Someone close the gates and bar them!' she cried. 'Why were they open?'

'They were open for your spirit to come home, child,' Cerys said, more gently now. 'We have heard what they are doing to Christians in the city. To lose Melinus was enough. My own child –' She shook her head. 'I could not bear that. I told him that it wasn't true. That you weren't a Christian. That you never had been, but he didn't believe me and it has finished your father.'

'Papa?' Eigon sat down on the bed and took her father's hands in her own. 'Papa, it's Eigon. Can you hear me?'

Caradoc didn't stir. His face was grey, his eyes closed.

'Papa, I am safe. I came back as soon as I could.' She leaned forward and kissed him on the forehead. She looked up again. 'Who was it who came and told you I had been taken?'

Cerys shrugged. 'An officer of the guard. He said he felt it was his duty to inform us.'

'Did he speak to you personally?'

'To both of us.'

'And you didn't recognise him?' She held her mother's gaze.

Cerys blanched. 'Not – him?' She shrugged. 'I never saw his face, how would I recognise him?' she protested at last. Her voice trailed away.

Eigon nodded. 'All these years he's been waiting.'

'What did he do to you?' Cerys took a deep breath. Her voice was shaking.

'Nothing. Oh, he intended to, but his escort arrived and he thought better of it in front of so many witnesses. He contented himself with throwing Antonia and me into a wagon with Marcellus and Stephen and the children.' She indicated the others who had hung back near the doorway, awed by the situation. 'He was right. We were destined for the palace gardens.'

Cerys gave a moan of misery.

'And then he realised of course that he could hurt me far more by coming here.' Her face was white. 'He decided to destroy me, by hurting you.'

Cerys held her gaze. 'He would have told your father everything had Caradoc not collapsed and lost consciousness. That was what he wanted. It was so easy. To kill a king.' She paused. 'But it's not that easy, is it. Now you are here. Aelius?' she called. 'Where are you?'

There was a shuffling of feet at the back of the room and the steward stepped forward.

'Have you bolted the gates?'

'It has been done, my lady.'

'See that these people are looked after. They are our guests.' She recovered some of her composure. With it came new resolution. 'And clear the room.' She looked round as though seeing the crowd of servants and slaves for the first time. 'Give my lord some air. Now Eigon is back she will help him. Everything is going to be all right.' In a very short time the room was empty but for Eigon and her mother. 'Do you need anything from your healing room?' she asked quietly as Eigon sat holding her father's hand.

348

Eigon shook her head. She was praying.

'Shall I order them to make soup for him?'

'No, Mam.' She looked up at last. 'There is nothing I can do. Papa is dying. We must just be here for him. He is going home.' She gave her mother a sad smile. 'His heart has not been strong for a long time. You know that. I can feel it under my hand. It is very weak. Scarcely beating. Already he can see the hills of home.'

Cerys stared at her, blind with tears. 'No,' she whispered.

'It will be time, soon.' Eigon moved slightly, making room for her mother beside her. 'Here. Come and hold him. Let him know we are both with him.'

'He was better!' Cerys wailed.

'I know. Perhaps that was the last of his strength.' She leaned forward and kissed her father on the forehead.

They sat in silence for a long time after he stopped breathing. When Eigon broke the silence at last it was with a quiet prayer. 'Dear Jesus. My father never had the chance to know you. But bless him and keep him safe, I beg you, in the land of the ever young.'

Cerys looked up. 'So it's true.' She stood up furiously. 'How dare you pray to a foreign god over your father's body! When that man said you were a Christian I didn't believe him. Oh, I've long known that Antonia and her family were. Your father thought they were, but he said it didn't matter. He said Christians were good people. But they are not. They have destroyed the city. They have destroyed my family and now they have destroyed my beloved! You have destroyed him!'

'Mam! Please, no one destroyed him.'

She thought of Titus's eyes as she spoke the words. He had been here. In this room. He had destroyed her father's love for her; his faith in her; his last vestiges of peace. He had destroyed everything that she held dear and in so doing he had destroyed her.

'Get out of this room!' Cerys threw herself across her husband's body, weeping. 'Go away! You lost me Togo and Gwladys! Now you have lost me Caradoc! Just go with your Christian friends. Get out of this house. You no longer have a home here. I never want to see you again.'

Behind them a door opened quietly. 'Eigon?' It was Marcellus.

Eigon wasn't sure how much he had heard. She turned blindly towards him. 'He's dead.'

'My dear, I'm so sorry.' He moved across the room, glancing down at the dead man, and the distraught woman who was clinging to him. 'Eigon, I'm sorry, but one of your slaves has told me something disquieting,' he whispered. 'About the son of your steward. Flavius, is it? The slave thinks he took money from the Praetorian officer. When we arrived Flavius slipped out before the gates were barred. The slave thinks maybe he has gone to tell them that we are here.'

Eigon turned miserably to her mother. 'Mam, did you hear that?'

'Go!' Cerys didn't look up. 'Just go. And never come back!'

Marcellus put a gentle hand on her shoulder. 'I am sorry to have brought so much distress to this house.'

Eigon bit her lip. She reached out to her father's body, changed her mind and moved away from the bed. 'We must go now, while we have the chance so we don't bring any more misfortune here,' she said as resolutely as she could. 'Where are the others?'

'The slave, Silas, has taken them to the stables.'

She followed him to the door then she paused and glanced sadly over her shoulder towards the bed. 'Goodbye, Mam. I love you.'

Cerys made no sign that she had heard.

They rode all night, each man with a child before them on the saddle. Marcellus knew of a place, he said, where they would be safe and as dawn broke they were again in rough wild country, but this time there was no sign of pursuit. Before they left Eigon had ransacked her room for fresh clothing for her and Antonia and cloaks for the children and Silas had made them up baskets of food hastily grabbed from the kitchens to sling from the saddles. He had gone with them to the Via Flaminia. There they paused.

'Do you want to go back?' Eigon asked him. 'You will be safer there.'

He shook his head. 'I'll come with you, lady, if you let me.' He glanced at Marcellus whom he seemed to regard with something like awe. 'Please.'

She smiled. 'We will be in danger.'

He nodded. 'I can help. I'm strong and I know this country-side. I shouldn't have left you before. I want to make up for it.'

'Then you can come, lad.' Marcellus put a hand on his shoulder. 'We will be pleased to have you with us.'

The place they were seeking turned out to be a half-ruined village. There were some dozen Christian families there already, fleeing the horrors of the city. Marcellus knew some of them and they were instantly made welcome. Antonia and Eigon found themselves allocated a small room with two straw mattresses in one of the half-collapsed cottages.

'Your mother didn't mean it, you know.' Antonia put her arm round Eigon's shoulder. It was the first time they had had a chance to talk alone. 'She was shocked and unhappy. She will always love you.'

Eigon shrugged. 'I don't think she ever did. She blamed me for the deaths of my brother and sister.'

Antonia shook her head. 'We all say things in the heat of the moment. She was terribly distressed. Let's pray for her.'

Eigon shook her head. 'She wouldn't want that. She has always been loyal to our own gods.'

'We can still pray. And we can pray for Grandfather and Julius.' Antonia bit her lip. 'I so hoped they might be here.'

Eigon nodded. 'So did I,' she admitted.

'Do you think they are all right?'

'They got away from Rome. Julius would have seen to it that your grandfather was somewhere safe.' Eigon sighed. What if she never saw Julius again? He couldn't have been caught. He couldn't have been killed. His image kept appearing in her dreams. She kept thinking about him. His kind eyes, his strong arms, his merry laugh. He would have kept them safe. He wouldn't have let anything happen to her.

Those who had brought food with them donated it towards a communal meal that night. The women prepared it while the men finished repairing the shelters then they all sat together to eat. Marcellus stood up and blessed the food. He was, Eigon was beginning to realise, very senior in the hierarchy of the newly developing church. At the end of the meal he stood up again and surveyed the bewildered, frightened group of people.

'Friends, we have all lost someone we love. We have all been fleeing for our lives. We don't know why God has seen fit to allow the Emperor to turn against us like this, but I am sure there is a reason. Perhaps to test our resolve. And we will have resolve. We will rest tonight, then tomorrow we will decide what to do and where to go. We will be strong.' He smiled at them all. 'God bless you, my children. Sleep well.'

Antonia pulled off her sandals with a groan of pain as she and Eigon settled into their makeshift beds. 'My feet are agony. The ropes that brute tied me with have taken all the skin off.'

Eigon leaned forward to see. Her own ankle was still aching almost unbearably. She ignored it stoically. 'Peter always used to say we should wash one another's feet as an act of humility, do you remember? But there is no water, tonight, and I have no medicines. I left my bag in that room where Titus tied us up. One day I will fry that man's eyeballs for what he has done to us and to my mother and father.'

Antonia gave a wan smile. 'We are not supposed to say things like that. Jesus told us to love our enemies.'

'He obviously hadn't met Titus Marcus Olivinus,' Eigon retorted. She pulled gently at Antonia's skirt where it clung to the bloody wound on her ankle.

'Ouch!' Antonia flinched away from her. 'Can't you make some more remedies? There are all sorts of wild herbs growing round the village. There are a lot of people here who look as though they need your care.'

'I'll look tomorrow. I am sure I can find something to help.'

Antonia lay back with a sigh. 'Why do you think this village was deserted?'

Eigon looked up. She stared round the room in silence, then she shivered. 'There was sickness here. Can't you feel it? Sickness and fear.'

Antonia stared at her. 'You're doing it again. Seeing ghosts.'

'I'm sorry. I've always done it. It is something my people seem to be good at. The dead are not dead to us.'

'Or to us.' Antonia looked doubtful. 'But Christians believe they go to heaven. They don't hang around in dark corners.'

'These people weren't Christians,' Eigon said slowly. She sank down onto her mattress and pulled a rug over herself. 'They had no gods at all. They thought their gods had abandoned them.'

'Perhaps we should pray for their souls,' Antonia said after a long silence. 'Would that make them go away?'

Eigon smiled. 'It would give them peace,' she said. Somehow she knew it was true.

'Why don't you sing,' Antonia murmured after a while. 'Something soft and gentle. I'd like that.'

Eigon smiled. The song soothed them both. Antonia was soon asleep and it wasn't long before she too closed her eyes.

Sometime later she opened them again and found herself staring into the darkness, her heart thudding with fear.

Jess stirred uncomfortably. She was lying on her bed. Outside her own window it had grown dark again too. She should get up, get undressed and get into bed properly. But she was too tired. She tried to relax, her head on the pillow staring up at the ceiling. Then she felt it. The same strange sensation that had awoken Eigon. The eerie feeling that she was being watched; that there was someone in the shadows, waiting.

Jess sat up.

Lights. Camera. Action. Carmella's words. Fill the room with light. Surround yourself with it. Look round. Focus. And fight. 'Hugo?' Jess whispered. 'Are you here? Keep watch, good dog.' There was no sound of claws on the wooden floor. Nothing. Cautiously she swung her legs off the bed and stood up. She reached for the bedside light, then went over to the door and turned the switch. It worked the lamp on the dressing table and another on the table by the window. She surveyed the room. She could see nothing unusual. Nothing had been moved. It felt all right. Warm in the night air from the window, and safe. As she watched a white moth sailed in and began bashing around inside the lampshade on the table. A moth. An ordinary moth. Nothing sinister in that. And no danger from the window. It was far too high for anyone to climb in. She walked slowly over to the table and reached to switch the lamp off at the stem. The moth settled at once, its wings trembling slightly as it clung to the inside of the shade.

There it was again. Someone was trying to access her brain. She gave a wry grin. Computer speak. Stupid, but that was what it felt like. Creepy fingers insinuating their search inside her head, parting through the fibres and synapses. She shuddered. Somehow she had to keep him out. It had to be Titus. But how could she fight him? Think! That is what she had to do. Set the whole apparatus whirring so she could distract him. Not allow him to access her thoughts. He wanted to know where she was. That was it, of course. He needed her address. She mustn't think it. Mustn't picture it. Mustn't let him know anything about this place at all.

Recite. That would distract him. Fill her head with something else.

> 'I know a bank where the wild thyme blows,
> Where oxlips and the nodding violet grows,
> Quite over-canopied with luscious woodbine,
> With sweet musk-roses, and with eglantine;
> There sleeps Titania sometime of the night,
> Lull'd in these flowers with dances and delight;
> And there the snake throws her enamell'd skin,
> Weed wide enough to wrap a fairy in.'

She paused, listening to the echoing silence. 'That got you, you bastard. You didn't expect that, did you!' She spoke out loud. 'Try and get inside my head, and you can expect more of the same:

> '"The lunatic, the lover, and the poet,
> Are of imagination all compact:
> One sees more devils than vast hell can hold,
> That is the madman; the love, all as frantic,
> Sees Helen's beauty in a brow of Egypt –"'

She paused. 'Want some more? Recognise yourself there, do you? You lunatic! I can go on for hours. Mess with an English teacher, and you find a head full of quotations!' She turned slowly round and round, listening. He had gone. She was sure of it.

What about Eigon? Had he left her alone too?

She walked slowly back to the bed and climbed onto it, still fully dressed. Leaving the light on she huddled back against the pillows and with a last wary glance round the room she closed her eyes.

Eigon was sitting up, her back pressed against the cold stones of the ruined wall, her eyes open as she peered through the darkness. Something had woken her. Titus was searching for her, wondering where she had gone, resenting her escape with such fury she could sense his anger against her skin. Desperately she tried to blank him out. What would Melinus have told her to do? She tried to think. He would have invoked the gods as a protection. But the old gods would not come to her as a Christian; and Jesus would not be invoked against a Roman who believed in his own gods, if he believed in any gods at all. Or would he? She tried to remember the words of the prayer Peter had taught them. There was a bit of it which always comforted her: *Deliver us from evil*. Titus Marcus Olivinus was the most evil man she had ever encountered. She shivered, pressing her hands against her ears.

She dozed, then she woke again. The voices she could hear were louder and to her relief she realised that this time they were real. There were people talking quietly and urgently outside. Pulling the rug around her shoulders she crept out, leaving Antonia asleep.

Several figures huddled round the fire. As she crept closer someone bent and threw on a log. A blaze flared up and she saw the faces of the men. They looked weary and distraught.

'What's wrong? Has something happened?' She joined them, shivering in the pre-dawn chill of the hills.

Marcellus sat down on the log they had dragged over to the fire as a bench. He rubbed his hands over his face, his palms rasping against his unshaven cheeks. 'There is bad news. Felicius Marinus Publius and his grandson, Julius, have been taken.'

'No!' Eigon stared at him in anguish. 'Oh, please, no.'

One of the other men nodded. 'I'm afraid so.' He was a newcomer who must have arrived after the others had gone to bed. Dust-covered and exhausted the man sat down next to Marcellus. 'The Praetorian guard came to the villa where we were all hiding. They knew exactly who they were looking for. No one stood a chance. They put most of the household to the sword and took away Felicius and Julius in chains.'

'So, by now they are probably already dead.' Marcellus stared between his knees at the ground. His shoulders had slumped.

'Not yet. They are destined for Nero's circus. I was told they are running out of Christians after burning so many in the palace gardens. They tied them to posts soaked in pitch and lit them at dusk, even children –'

'We know!' Marcellus cut him off. 'What has happened to Peter?' He changed the subject quickly. 'Is there any news?'

'He's safe. In hiding with several others.'

'And when are – the games at which our friends are to provide the entertainment?' Marcellus's voice was husky.

The newcomer shrugged. 'They have been taken to the Mamertine prison. Nero is said to want a good show to cheer up his citizens.' His voice was heavy. 'Maybe they will wait a few days till they have enough victims to make it worthwhile. I hear the lions are sated,' he added bitterly. 'They will have to wait until they grow hungry again.'

Eigon was fighting back her tears, her fists clenched until her palms bled, looking from one man to the other. 'But we can rescue them. Surely we can rescue them?' Her voice rose in a panic.

They turned to her. Marcellus stood up. He went over and put his arm around her shoulders. 'Julius and his grandfather are Roman citizens. It is forbidden to torture them. They can't be thrown to the wild beasts.'

The man gave him a pitying look. 'Mistakes are made. Men who are dragged to the arena in chains can scream all they like that they are citizens. Most do. No one can hear them in the roar of the crowd. If a mistake is found to have happened it is too late. The state merely promises to pay compensation to the family. It never happens.'

There was a moment's silence. Marcellus cleared his throat. 'If there is any way to get them out of those dungeons we will try, I promise you. But they are in deep beneath the ground, barred and guarded day and night.' He guided Eigon to the log and she sat down near the fire. Beyond the circle of warmth and light the ruined village was very dark. No one else had woken. Somewhere in the woods an owl hooted. 'We will pray for guidance. There must be a way.'

Eigon took a deep breath. 'There is.'

The others looked at her. Marcellus raised an eyebrow. 'You've thought of something?'

'I know the man who captured them. Almost certainly it was a Praetorian officer called Titus Marcus Olivinus. The man who captured me and Antonia.' She tried very hard to keep her voice steady. 'He and I –' She paused, fighting her rising terror. 'He and I have an ongoing argument. He would give a great deal to get his hands on me again.' She gave them a humourless smile. 'When your wagon arrived and we were thrown into it, he had been about to settle a personal score with me which might have deflected him from his ardour in hunting down Christians. He knew Felicius and Julius are my friends. He knew Antonia was my friend. We have a quarrel going back many years to something that happened in Britannia when my mother and I were captured after my father's defeat.' Her voice had grown so soft the men had to lean forward to hear. 'He is afraid I will tell the authorities something he did which incurs the death penalty. He raped my mother the queen. And he raped me. I was only a child.'

Her fists were clenched so tightly now that her hands had turned to white marble in the firelight. 'I could say nothing as my mother did not want my father to find out. He could not have borne the humiliation, but now he is dead.' She pressed her lips together to hide her grief, then took a deep breath as the men stared at her in silence. 'I think I am sufficiently important to Titus for a deal to be made. Felicius and Julius in exchange for me.'

There was another long silence broken only by the crackling of the flames. At last Marcellus moved towards her. He knelt stiffly down in front of her and taking her hands in his own he kissed them. 'You love them so much you would give up your life for them? Bless you, my child. Your bravery is without comparison. But we cannot allow you to do this.' He glanced at the others, who all nodded agreement. 'Every life is precious before God and it is my belief that He has not called you to die in someone else's place.'

For a moment she stared at him, panic-stricken. 'But I have to do something.' She blinked away her tears. Her head was whirling. 'Then I have another idea. Perhaps we could pretend you are going to give me in exchange. At least it might lure Titus out into the open and he might be persuaded to bring Felicius and Julius to an exchange point?'

'That's good thinking, Marcellus,' Stephen said quietly. She had not noticed him amongst the others in the darkness. 'This young lady is a good strategist, a worthy daughter to such a great warrior king.' He smiled at her. 'If this man is so desperate to get his hands on her he might not be thinking too clearly. We can demand he has no escort otherwise we would all be in danger. He might agree.'

'He would cheat and hide a whole army if he could,' Eigon put in. She straightened her shoulders. 'He is not a man of honour.'

'Nor are we when it comes to saving our own,' Marcellus said grimly. 'It's worth a try. So, how do we reach him?'

'We send a messenger. And that person must be the bravest of us all,' Stephen said gloomily. 'I suggest we draw lots. Let God decide.'

Dan rang Carmella's doorbell and waited by the speakerphone. To his surprise there was a buzz and a click and the door swung open without anyone asking him who it was. He smiled.

He had had no luck at the palazzo. Jacopo, when he had finally managed to rouse him had been so drunk he could barely utter a coherent word, but he had at last managed to come up with the information that *la signora* Kim had closed the apartment and gone to spend the rest of the summer with a friend in the Lakes.

Dan took the stairs two at a time and found Carmella's door on the latch. Pushing it open, he sniffed appreciatively. Garlic; onions, some sort of meat sauce. She was obviously expecting guests for lunch.

'Henrico?' Her voice came to him from the kitchen above the hiss of frying. '*Ciao, carissimo*. Help yourself to a drink and bring me one too! This is almost ready.'

Dan smiled. The gods were with him so far. He walked into the sitting room and glanced round. There were fresh flowers on the side table and a bottle of Barolo on the desk with two glasses. Carmella's mobile was lying on the coffee table. It was that easy. He wasn't even going to have to use threats. He picked it up, blew a kiss towards the kitchen and slipping it into his pocket, he crept back out of the room, carefully pulling the door behind him, leaving it exactly as he had found it. Taking the stairs two at a time he had reached the street and was several yards away before a car drew up, tucked itself into a gap, and a silver-haired man climbed out. Dan strolled across the road, watching out of the corner of his eye. He grinned. She was going to think it really strange when Henrico made a second appearance. He wondered how long it would take her to miss her mobile.

He struck gold with the call register. The fifth number he tried was a *pensione*. The girl who answered said yes, there was an

English lady staying there, on the top floor and she believed her name was Jess but she didn't appear to be registered in the book. She sounded very vague; almost simple. Dan smiled. The house was half an hour's walk, if that, from the bar where he was sitting over a very pleasant glass of chianti classico, making his calls. He tossed a couple of olives into his mouth and continued to scroll through Carmella's phone. He hadn't decided what to do yet. He could not afford to fail again. He had a very narrow window in which to find Jess before he got back on the motorway and drove north.

He ordered another glass of wine, leaning forward to see the screen better as he began to go through Carmella's undeleted text messages. Old Henrico seemed to be a devoted follower; he also, so it appeared, had a wife about whom Carmella knew. They seemed sanguine about her. He chuckled. How civilised. How very Roman. How unlike the tempestuous events he seemed to find himself embroiled in. He downed the wine and prepared to leave. It was time to find the *pensione* and case the place, see how he could get in, see where he could hide if necessary. Making his way towards the door he glanced over his shoulder to make sure no one was looking, then slid the phone into the brass cachepot of a large aspidistra near the doorway. It was only as he turned up the street that he wondered if he ought to have wiped his fingerprints off it.

He stood at the corner for a few minutes, watching the quiet street with its old houses drowsing in the heat, their soft earthy colours punctuated here and there by ancient stone walls. The front door of the house was open. Did everyone in Rome leave their doors open at lunchtime? Walking swiftly up to it he raised his hand to knock and peered inside. 'Hello? *Buongiorno? C'è qualcuno a casa?*'

The hall was elegantly furnished with Afghan rugs and exquisite antiques. The place smelled of beeswax. *'Signora?* Hello?' He walked further in.

The staircase, a wonder of carved oak finials and twisted banisters led up into the cool centre of the house which was shady and appeared deserted. Helping himself to a couple of letters off the table in the entrance hall to use as an alibi if he met someone, he set off upstairs.

At the top there were two doors leading off the landing. Neither was locked. He shook his head in disbelief. The first room he peered into was neat and tidy and as far as he could see unoccupied. He paused outside the other door, listening. Then he knocked softly. There was no reply. Carefully he clasped the handle and turned it. There was no one inside. A bag lay on the floor near the door. A brush and comb sat on the dressing table and he recognised the pale sweater thrown across the chair. He went in and closed the door behind him very quietly. One set of doors in the room concealed a wardrobe area with several empty hangers. The other led into a small shower room. Someone had left a pile of fresh towels on the side of the basin. He turned back and surveyed her sanctuary, wondering where she was. The shutters were closed against the heat. He went over and pushed them open. The window looked out across a narrow declivity between the buildings and then over a vista of red clay tiles broken here and there by the tops of trees. The only living things he could see were pigeons. Smiling he pulled the shutters closed again and turned back into the room. It was going to be too simple. All he had to do was wait for her to come back.

26

Eigon had drained every ounce of energy that Jess possessed. Her head ached and her whole body had cried out for a rest so when the girl at the *pensione* had knocked on the door, wanting to clean her room, she had seized the excuse to go out. After all, there were still places she wanted, no, desperately needed, to see, places that resonated through history. Places where Eigon had been. Dan was almost certainly long gone, following Rhodri across Europe, and she had foiled Titus's attempt to access her brain so it would be quite safe; no one could find her now and she would only go out for a couple of hours so no one would know. She was very careful leaving the house, scanning the street in both directions, sunhat and glasses hiding her face and hair. There had been no one to see her, she was sure of it, and before leaving the house she had taken all the precautions she could think of to block Titus out of her mind. This time she was reciting TS Eliot.

Slowly Jess walked towards the river, threading her way between the crowds, heading towards the Vatican. Nero's circus, the scene of Melinus's death, had been somewhere here, at the foot of the Mons Vaticanus. 'On the left facing church', as her guidebook said tersely. She smiled as she gazed in front of her at the great basilica of St Peter's. This traditionally was the site of St Peter's tomb, nestling deep beneath the great dome. And the obelisk in front of her now in the centre of Piazza San Pietro, which had been brought to Rome by the Emperor Caligula in AD 36, had stood for years at the centre of the circus and marked the spot where Peter had died almost where she was standing now. Her recital of poetry forgotten she riffled the pages of her guidebook, staring up at the obelisk. What sights it had seen. For two thousand years it had stood here or nearby. It had seen the lions tearing apart the so-called enemies of the state, heard their screams, watched the sawdust raked clean and every trace of their passing removed. It had seen an old man crucified and witnessed the growth of the faith he had so loved, marked now by Michelangelo's great dome rising to dwarf everything around it. Slowly she turned away. She had no wish to go into the building. Now was not the time for architecture and art; nor to be reminded of the church militant as it evolved. That was the bit she couldn't get her head around. The inquisition. The fundamentalism. The politics. The vast riches. The church of the Peter she felt she knew, the Peter who had known Jesus, been his rock, the church of Eigon and Marcellus, was one of small gatherings in people's homes; private heartfelt prayer and the celebration of meals of bread and wine. They had built no special buildings, not then, not yet. Their church was one of love. People. Faith.

The enormity of what she was witnessing was slowly coming home to her. She gave a wry smile. How many of the people wandering round here with their guidebooks, just like hers, their cameras, their passion for this place, would believe that she had seen St Peter? Heard him speak. She frowned as she headed back towards the Tiber. She had witnessed amazing things in her dreams, a stunning awesome privilege. And now she had breathed the same air as them, walked the same contours, seen the river they had seen. Dan was forgotten as the story she was following once more enveloped her.

There was one more place she wanted to go. The Mamertine prison where Julius and his grandfather had been held, and where, later, as she knew from the guidebook, Peter himself had been imprisoned. It was still there, according to the book in her hand. It was possible to visit it, tucked beneath an old church at the foot of the Capitoline hill. It was something she wanted, needed, to see. To reach it she would walk almost past the door of the *pensione*, heading back towards the Forum. She hesitated at the end of the street. She was tired and longing to go back to her peaceful safe retreat; it would be nice to rest out of the heat. On the other hand she wanted to see for herself the place where Julius had been held and she knew she would not be able to pluck up the courage to go out on her own again if she went back now. Seconds later she had crossed the road and headed on up towards the Campidoglio.

The entrance to the church below which lay the prison was at the foot of a long flight of steps. After a moment's hesitation she joined a small queue outside. They seemed to be admitting people in small groups and when at last she groped her way down the steep stone staircase that led into the dungeon she realised why. It was small, low-ceilinged, dark and claustrophobic. For a moment she felt like running away. Her arms were covered in goosepimples. She could feel whispers of fear tiptoeing up and down her spine. Taking a deep breath she forced herself to stay calm and made her way inside, keeping close to the wall as the other people in the group clustered round the guide. He was speaking fast in Italian and she gave up trying to understand almost at once, contenting herself with looking round. Faint light came through a hole in the ceiling, the hole down which, so her guidebook had told her, the prisoners were dropped. There had been no staircase then. Against the far wall was a small stone altar and at its foot another hole in the floor at the bottom of which she could see water. This was the spring which had sprung into existence, so her book said, so St Peter could baptise his guards the night before his execution. Behind her the group of visitors suddenly revealed themselves as pilgrims. They were praying out loud in unison. For a moment she was swept up in their devotions; she could feel the hairs on the back of her neck standing on end. She could feel the specialness and holiness of this place. Seconds later it was over, and the crowd was surging once more up the staircase and out towards the fresh air. For a brief second she stood where she was, alone in the dungeon, feeling the atmosphere alive with memories, then as the next group of visitors began to make their way down the stairs she hurried to meet them, suddenly desperate to get outside, overwhelmed with the sadness and awe of knowing what Eigon and Julius could not have known, the momentousness of the events of which they were a part.

The *pensione* was deserted as she walked in. She had bought herself some pastries, a bag of figs and some bottled water. Climbing exhausted up to her room she pushed open the door and went inside. She put her paper bags on the table, threw her bag down on the bed and went straight into the small bathroom to splash her face with cold water.

When she came out Dan was leaning against the door to the landing. He was swinging the key in his hand. *'Buongiorno*, Jess. Have you had a pleasant day?'

She closed her eyes for a moment, too shocked to speak.

He smiled. 'This is a nice room, very restful. When I heard you coming up the stairs I thought I would just step into the cupboard there, to give you time to make yourself comfortable.'

'How did you find me?' She found her voice at last. She sat down on the edge of the chair near the desk. Her legs had begun to shake. 'Titus?'

'Not Titus. Not this time. Something much more mundane! I stole Carmella's phone. I rang everyone she had spoken to lately and the girl who picked up here joyfully confirmed that you were indeed a resident.'

'And now you're here what are you going to do?'

He was still standing leaning against the door. He changed position slightly, making himself more comfortable. 'Now, that is the thing. I'm not sure. Not sure at all. I'm waiting for instructions.'

'Instructions?' She crossed her arms across her breasts, aware that she had taken off her linen shirt as she came upstairs and that now she was wearing only a skimpy camisole with her trousers.

He nodded. 'That is the problem. Titus is always wanting more.'

'You are not Titus, Dan!' Her voice sharpened. 'You are a good man; a teacher with a great future in front of you. If that future is wrecked it will be your fault not mine. No one knows anything at the moment. Why not leave it at that? Forget me. Go back to Nat.'

He shook his head. 'Ah, but that is the trouble. I've spoken to Nat. It appears the police want to talk to me. Now why do you suppose that is?'

She shrugged. 'It's not because of anything I have said. I told you, I haven't reported you. If anyone has said anything it's Will, and I think you know why that is.'

'Ah yes, Will. But then there is also Steph. And Kim. And Carmella.' He was counting on his fingers. 'And the inestimable Welshman, of course. You have so many friends.'

She bit her lip. Seeing it he gave an angelic smile. 'And none of them are here, are they.' He shook his head. 'Carmella is shacked up with her Henrico for the afternoon. Rhodri and Steph must be clean across France by now. Kim has closed up her palace and gone to stay with her friends in the Lakes. Only Will is an unknown quantity and he is clearly not here.'

'But he is on his way.' She said it at once without thinking.

His face closed. 'That of course makes things a little more urgent.'

'No, it doesn't, Dan. It just means you should leave now. Before he comes. Just go. We'll forget you were here.' She gave him a pleading smile. 'Please. You don't want to hurt me any more. You are not Titus. Titus was a complete shit!'

'He was, wasn't he.' He smiled. 'What a rôle model! But the trouble is that he is in my head. I know I accused you of madness and as far as other people are concerned that is probably true, you are as mad as a hatter, but I am a bit afraid I might be mad too.' He sighed thoughtfully. 'You are just being haunted by a ghost, Jess. With me it is something much more profound. It's very strange having someone else inside one's head. An odd sensation. It somehow exonerates one from whatever actions one decides to take. One can stand back and watch. And yet one is taking part.' He paused. 'Twice the fun, I suppose.' He put his head on one side. 'When I made love to you after the school party it was just a bit of a joke. Slip you something to make you sleepy. Stuck up, snooty Miss Kendal, who wouldn't look twice at me, performing in the sack like a true whore at my command. It was wonderful. But not worth losing my job over. When you said you knew it was me, when you put everything in jeopardy I knew I had to do something. The rage I felt was amazing. That is what attracted Titus. He loved the energy. He recognised at once that we were soul mates.'

She found she was shivering uncontrollably.

'Dan. Please. Fight him.'

Dan smiled. 'Why? It's a fantastic feeling. Such a buzz!'

'Can you see him?' Somehow she had to keep him talking – not rise to his taunts, talk him down. As you did with a child who lost it in school. Calmly leading the conversation back to sanity. 'Describe him. I want to know if he is the same Titus I see.'

He paused. She could actually watch him scanning some inner screen up in the air in front of him. 'He's tall. Dark. Roman nose. Good-looking. Tattoo on his arm. Just the man one would cast in the part if one was a film director. Shifty eyes, strange golden eyes.' He paused thoughtfully. 'I must admit, I wouldn't want him as my commanding officer.' He chortled. He switched his attention abruptly back to her. 'So, does he look the same?'

Jess nodded. 'And Eigon?'

'Dark hair. Pale complexion. Tendency to freckles. Fabulous clear grey eyes. Good bones. Beautiful. Nothing like you!'

'Thanks!'

'I meant she doesn't look like you.' He adjusted his stance against the door again. He must be getting tired, she thought. That was good. Wasn't it?

'She is getting a bit pious though,' he went on thoughtfully. 'Signs of spirit now and then, but this Christian stuff is a bit of a trial. What she needs is a good seeing to!' He grinned.

'Do you know what happens in the end?' Jess ignored the last comment.

'No. Do you?'

She shook her head. 'But I know where she is now. Where Titus can't find her.'

'Where?'

'They are holed up in the hills in a ruined village quite a way from Rome.' She made herself smile too. 'An awful lot of Christians survived to spread the word, you know. Obviously.'

'I could tell him where she was. Is.' He narrowed his eyes. 'He listens to me.'

'Does he? Really?' If she could get him out of this room, out into the street she would have the chance to escape. In here she was at his mercy. 'I suppose I could guide you there,' she said, casually, almost reluctantly. 'I'm not entirely sure where it is, but I know how they got there. I wonder if it is still there or if it's just a pile of stones now?'

'What are they planning?' He stood up straight suddenly. 'Tell me.'

'They are discussing what to do.'

'They can't hope to rescue the captives,' he sneered. 'It's impossible. Have you seen the dungeons?'

Jess shuddered. He knew what was happening in her story. He was part of it. He could see what she could see but through someone else's eyes. 'I went out to Mamertine today,' she said as calmly as she could. 'That is where St Peter spent his last days as well. There is a church built on top now. There is an inscription outside. I couldn't quite understand it, but it seemed to say that by making a pilgrimage there one could earn oneself time off from purgatory.' This was surreal. They were like two historians, discussing the what happened and the what ifs of history. 'There were other dungeons as well, on the Esqualine, did you know? There wasn't enough room for all the prisoners in the Mamertine. The houses of people like Felicius Marinus Publius and Julius, which had been burned in the fire or pulled down to make a fire break, were being cleared. With them gone there was nothing to stop Nero constructing his amazing pleasure palace and before he got round to that, the cellars of those houses were converted into dungeons to hold all the prisoners he was planning to throw to the lions.' She clasped her hands together to stop them shaking. 'Titus is a clever man. If he can hear you, see you, he must wonder how this is all working, just as you and I are wondering. If he knows that you know something about where they were and are withholding the information, won't he be angry?' The illogicality of what she was saying did not strike either of them.

Dan shrugged. 'We'll just force it out of you.'

She shuddered. 'There is nothing to force. I can't describe how they got to wherever they were. I would have to follow the route. Work it out.'

'And I would have to let you leave this room.' Dan grinned amiably. 'I am not that stupid, sweetheart. I can see what you're doing.'

She shook her head ruefully. 'You're so clever. OK. What do we do now?' Before he could answer she reached for her paper bags. 'I don't know about you but I'm starving. I've pastries and fruit. Do you want some?'

He shook his head. 'You go ahead. I'll watch.'

She found it impossible to eat. The food turned to concrete in her mouth. She managed to swallow one or two pieces, then put the pastry down. She could feel him watching her and could picture the amusement on his face but she refused to look up. She broke open a fig with her nails and sucked out some of the sweet pith.

'Nice?' His mocking tone goaded her into glancing up. She knew she had fig juice trickling down her chin. A figure was standing beside him. Shadowy. Tall. Watching her with as much amusement as he was. She gave a small cry of horror, dropping the fruit on the table.

'What? What is it?' Dan stared round tensely, his eyes wide.

She pointed, speechless with fear. 'Can't you see him?'

'Who?'

'Titus!' The word came out as a soundless whisper.

'Where?' His face had gone white. 'Where? I can't see him. You're lying.'

'I'm not lying!' She stood up and backed away, putting the table between herself and Dan. The apparition was standing close beside him, almost touching. It was touching.

'Oh shit, Dan. Can't you feel it? He's on top of you. He's all around you.' Then she remembered. 'Hugo! Oh God, Hugo, boy, come to me. Help me. Please!'

'What are you talking about?' Dan was rigid with fear. 'I can't see him.'

'Can't you feel him? Dan, he's all over you. HUGO!' This time it was a scream and the dog was suddenly there, standing in the middle of the room facing Dan. It was motionless. Huge. Black. Solid.

'Dear God in heaven, what is that?' Dan was ashen, his lips white, his arms held out before him. 'Keep it off me!'

Jess smiled. 'Leave. Now. Calmly. Just go. I can't hold him back.'

Dan scrabbled behind him for the door handle. He turned it but it wouldn't open. He tugged at it furiously.

'You locked it, Dan,' she said quietly. She could see the dog beginning to quiver. 'Get the key and put it in the lock quickly. You haven't much time. I can't control him.'

'I can't find it!'

'You had it in your hand. You were taunting me with it!'

'What the hell is it, Jess?' He was searching his pockets frantically. He found it at last, inserted it into the lock, turned it and the door opened. In seconds he was running down the stairs.

Hugo turned and looked at her. She could swear he was smiling. 'Thank you,' she whispered. 'You've saved my life.' She held out her arms but already he was fading. She could have sworn his tail was wagging as he disappeared.

She was by the door in two steps. Slamming it shut she squatted by her bag and scrabbled frantically for her phone. With shaking hands she switched it on, praying there was still some life in the battery. 'Will. He was here. Dan. He was threatening me. Please come.'

'I've been trying to reach you, Jess. Rhodri warned me.' Will's voice was breaking up. 'Stay there. Lock yourself in. I'll come as soon as I can.' The phone cut out. She stared at it in disgust. Had his battery gone, or hers? She redialled but there was no reply. Wherever Will was, the signal had failed.

'Show yourself quickly then duck back behind the wall.' Marcellus was close beside her. 'That's enough for them to know you're here.' They could see the group of men in the distance but it was too faraway to identify any of them.

Their messenger had been specific. Eigon would give herself up if Felicius and Julius were released unharmed. There had to be neutral negotiators there to ensure that the deal was done fairly and cleanly. Except the negotiators were not neutral. They were going to stand forward at the last minute between Eigon and her would-be captors, just long enough for the party to be whisked out of sight under cover of darkness. Marcellus had arranged it all, with many misgivings, as being the only way to get Julius and his grandfather out of the dungeons. The games were nearly upon them. The stadium was being prepared and the wild beasts were hungry again.

Eigon was determined. She was ready to do anything to save Julius, and now at last, she would meet Titus again face to face. It was as though she had been preparing for this encounter all her life. This time they would meet as equals. She was not at a disadvantage. She knew where and when the meeting would take place and she was ready. She was no longer afraid. The anger inside her had reached boiling point. He was threatening the people she loved. He had been terrorising her ever since she could remember. He had killed her friend, almost killed her. He had caused the death of her father. Now it was her turn to bring the encounter to him on her terms.

Marcellus glanced at her. He found he was almost feeling sorry for Marcus Olivinus. 'Ready?' he whispered. He still had the feeling this was madness, but what other alternative was there?

She nodded. 'I can't see. Is it them?'

'We don't move until we are sure.' He gave her a quick smile. 'Stephen is going to go first. He has met Julius and his grandfather. He knows them well enough to be sure it is them.' He glanced over his shoulder at Stephen who grinned. He raised his thumb. 'Shall I go now?'

'Give them time to come a few paces closer. They are nowhere near halfway.' Marcellus could feel his nerves tightening. He glanced round into the darkness. It had seemed so easy, so foolproof, this plan, but now it was dark he was full of doubts. He and Eigon were planning to play tricks. Then so too could Marcus Olivinus.

'Why are we waiting?' Eigon was beside him now. He could see her nerves were stretched almost to breaking.

'We can't be sure it is them yet. It's too dark,' Marcellus murmured.

'Call out.'

Marcellus glanced at Stephen. 'Shall I?'

Stephen nodded. 'It's not as though we are trying to get closer in secret. This is a meeting. It should be completely open.'

Marcellus stepped forward. 'Marcus Olivinus? Are you there? Show us our two men.'

There was no response. The group of figures moved closer to them.

'Julius?' Stephen called out. 'Are you there?'

There was no reply. The group moved closer.

Eigon bit her lip. She could feel the palms of her hands growing clammy. And suddenly she knew. 'They're not there. They've tricked us!'

Marcellus cursed. Grabbing her arm, he turned to flee. And suddenly there were men all round them. Torches flared in the night. They were surrounded. Eigon flinched back, dazzled by the flames. She couldn't see anything. Her arm was wrenched from Marcellus's hand and she found herself being dragged away from him. Screaming, she pushed her fingers into the eyes of whoever had grabbed her. Someone swore. He lost grip of her and she managed to wrench away from him. Turning she ran blindly through the crowd of men, not knowing where to go, panicked by the noise and the turmoil. Somewhere a horse screamed. She could hear the thud and scrape of hoofbeats on the paving of the road. Then someone else had grabbed her. 'This way! Quick!' She recognised Stephen's voice. 'Down here!'

'Julius?' she cried. 'Where is Julius?'

'He's not there. He never was.' Stephen sidestepped a group of men and dragged her with him through a gate and into the darkness of a vineyard. 'This way. Leave the others. They will cope. They weren't expecting us to have extra men as well.' They pounded down between the vines, seeing dimly in the hazy moonlight, and then turned at right angles towards an area of scrub. In the distance the silhouette of an aqueduct snaked massively across the landscape, throwing arched moonshadows over the plain. Stephen made towards it. They found a gap in a wall and ran through it. Now they were in an area of market gardens, dotted at intervals with orchards and small farmhouses. He paused, glancing round. 'I can't hear anyone, can you?' His breath came in tight gasps.

She was too tired to speak. She shook her head, swallowing frantically, clutching at the stitch in her side. 'What about Marcellus?'

'He'll be all right but we have to get somewhere safe. It's you they want, don't forget.' He did not tell her that Marcellus had persuaded one of the young men in their group to put on a robe and cloak and a wig in the event that something like this happened. By now he would have ditched his disguise, but for a few important moments it would have distracted them and with luck they would have followed him. He held his breath, listening. Nothing. A light wind whispered through the leaves of a grove of olive trees nearby.

'What do we do?' Eigon's earlier courage seemed to have trickled away. She could feel her voice shaking. 'Where is Julius?'

'I doubt if they brought him,' Stephen whispered. 'It was always a risk.'

He saw her look of misery swiftly followed by a visible straightening of her shoulders as she took a deep breath. 'We have to go and find him. We can't leave him there.'

Stephen shook his head. 'Leave it to the others, Eigon. We can't risk you. You know that. You are our only bargaining counter.'

She knew that was true; it was the only way to make her listen.

'But they cheated. They won't agree again.'

'Marcellus will think of something. He's a good strategist. Leave it to him. We have to find somewhere safe to hide till it's light. Then we have to meet up with the others. The plan was to make our way to a house belonging to some sympathisers about five miles from here.'

'Five miles?'

'I know. It's a long way. We'll go slowly and stop to rest once we're further away. It's too open here for my liking. Once we get there we'll be safe.'

'And Julius and his grandfather?'

Stephen bit his lip. 'We'll pray for them. You must keep faith, Eigon. God is on our side. He will protect us.'

'God wants martyrs,' she said bitterly. 'I've heard Marcellus say so. He wants people to prove their faith by dying in agony for him. I thought he was supposed to be a god of love.' She pulled her cloak around her with a shiver.

Stephen said nothing. With a sigh he set off, walking fast down the track. She had to run to catch him up. His silence had reminded her that his wife had already died for her faith. Biting her lip at her lack of thought she pulled at his arm. 'Stephen, where are your children?'

'They are being looked after.'

'You left them to come to help me?' She forced him to stop, looking up into his face.

'It was my duty.'

'No, it wasn't your duty. It was an act of love.' She shrugged. 'I'm sorry. I'm not a very good Christian yet.'

He gave a wry smile. 'Are any of us? We are struggling to do what Jesus would have wanted us to do, but he would understand. He knew we are not as strong as him. Look at Peter. Even he denied the Christ when he was afraid.'

Eigon dropped his arm. Resolutely she began walking again. 'You are right.' They walked on for a bit. 'Melinus was brave,' she said after a while. 'He was a Druid. They were persecuted by Rome as well. I don't think I could be so strong.'

'You would. You are one of the bravest people I've met.' Stephen grinned at her. 'Julius is a lucky man.'

She blushed. 'I never hoped for him. My parents wouldn't have allowed it.'

'And you wouldn't have defied them?' He raised an eyebrow.

She smiled. 'Not my father, no.'

'But now he's gone.'

She nodded sadly. 'Now he's gone.'

'So, what is standing in your way?'

She laughed out loud. 'Apart from a dungeon wall nothing at all.' She thought sadly about her mother, alone now in the villa with her memories. Had she given even one thought to the daughter she had thrown out? She would probably never know.

They reached their destination as it grew light. Weary and covered in dust they made their way into the gardens of the villa and Stephen tapped at a side door. It opened at once and they were ushered inside. Their hostess was a tall white-haired woman, elegantly dressed even at that hour, her face pale and soft-skinned, every inch a patrician, though her eyes were a bright cornflower blue which with her pale skin betrayed an ancestry far north-west of Rome. At once Eigon was whisked away by a pretty well-dressed slave who cheerily helped her to bathe, brushed out her dusty hair, dressed her in new clothes and in no time at all brought her back to join Stephen and their hostess for breakfast.

'I am Junilla Gallica, my dear. Welcome. You are safe here.' Her hostess smiled as she held out her hands and drew Eigon close enough to kiss her cheek. 'Sit down. There is bread and cheese and honey on the table and *calda* to drink.' She pushed a carafe of the warm, weak spiced wine towards them. 'Please, Stephen, will you bless it for us?'

As warm sunlight crept into the room Eigon found her eyes closing. She forced them open in embarrassment. But again they began to close. Her hostess smiled. 'Don't fight it, my dear. Go to the guest room and sleep. We will call you when the others arrive.'

It was several hours before there was any news. Marcellus and a party of six other dusty weary men, including Silas, walked in at last as Eigon and Junilla were sitting together in a shady court-yard talking.

'We gave them the slip soon after you and Stephen got away,' he said, throwing himself onto a stool beside them. 'No one was seriously hurt, no one lost. And we have news,'

The two women looked up expectantly.

'Felicius has been freed from the dungeons.'

'What?' Eigon jumped to her feet. 'And Julius?'

'As I understand it they are both being held under house arrest by order of the Emperor. We don't know why. You know Nero and his whims, but I suspect it is because Felicius is a senator and has friends in high places. My source told me that Marcus Olivinus is furious but there is nothing he can do. But we have to be wary. This was against everything he wanted, but he can still turn it to his advantage by using Julius as a lure, so,' he held up his hand as Eigon tried to speak, 'we will not rush in and do something stupid without thinking very hard about how to handle this.'

By next morning they had a plan. They talked it through again and again until it seemed foolproof. It depended on Junilla Gallica.

She and Eigon both wore heavy veils. They were dressed soberly and unostentatiously so as to attract as little attention as possible. Both were wearing two loose-fitting gowns beneath their cloaks, any added bulkiness well hidden. Attending them were two slaves, carrying clubs for protection, as was usual for ladies from less well off but patrician households who could not afford better armed bodyguards. One of them carried a bag slung over his shoulder. In it were extra veils and two spare cloaks. The intention was to give the impression to anyone watching the house that they were in mourning.

It was the first time either had been into Rome since the fire. They were horrified by the devastation they saw around them. Whole areas had been levelled; all around were deserted houses, half-ruined; roads and streets piled high with stone and rubble and heaps of ash and burned wood. In other places the fire seemed to have had no effect at all. The city went on as before, but with a quiet, more thoughtful air. The house where Felicius and Julius were lodged was in a quiet area of smart homes on the Caelian Hill, an area which seemed to have missed the fire. There was no outward sign of guards save the two at the front of the house, one on either side of the front door. Junilla walked slowly but seemingly with confidence towards the entrance. She turned towards one of the slaves and graciously nodded her head. Neither woman gave any hint of the fear they were feeling. The slave bowed and stepped forward to rap on the door with his club. They waited in silence. Under her veil Eigon held her breath, scanning the houses on either side of them as, nervously, she clenched her fists. The two guards ignored them. The street was quiet, sunlight playing on the deserted paving slabs. There was no sign that anyone was watching them. At last they heard footsteps inside and the door opened. Junilla stepped forward. 'I have come to visit my brother.' Her voice was convincingly weak and shaky. 'Is that you, Septimus?' She peered short-sightedly through her veil. 'Please, tell him I'm here.'

She stepped inside, followed by Eigon and the slaves. The door shut behind them and Eigon closed her eyes in relief. Up until that moment they hadn't been sure that their message with an outline of their plan had arrived. She had chosen Silas to carry it ahead of them. If anyone could get through, he could and she would trust him with her life. Septimus, a spare figure with balding hair, wearing the smart but plain tunic of a senior house servant, put his finger to his lips. He led them quickly through the passage and into the inner rooms. 'In here, ladies,' he said out loud. He went on in a whisper, 'Please say nothing rash. We don't know who might be a spy.'

Junilla sent a warning glance at Eigon who nodded without speaking, her heart thudding with fear and excitement.

It was several minutes before anyone appeared. Tempus Decimus, the owner of the house arrived at last and with him, both looking tired and thin, were his two guests. Decimus was a tall man in his early forties, his face etched with deep lines of worry. For the moment though he was smiling. Eigon clenched her fists under her cloak as she felt Julius's gaze run over her. Other than that no sign of recognition passed between them. 'Refreshments, please,' their host ordered. The two slaves who were waiting by the door bowed and disappeared. Junilla's slaves followed them. For a moment the room was empty but for themselves.

'Quick. You first.' Junilla's persona as a bent old lady vanished. 'Take off your gown and veil. And your cloak. Give them to Julius.'

With a grin, Julius turned his back as Eigon did as she was bid. She reached over and handed him her gown and he pulled it over his head. Then came the cloak and the veil. They subsided into soundless giggles as his broad shoulders strained beneath the sleeve brooches of the gown. 'Will it do?' Eigon asked Junilla.

She smiled. 'If the guards are blind! You will have to walk like her, Julius. And she will have to walk like me, all bent and old!' She pulled off her own cloak and stole, handing them to Eigon.

'They're coming back!' Decimus was standing near the door. 'Quick, Junilla, out here in the courtyard.'

When the slaves returned there were, as before in the room two ladies, now seated side by side on a couch, both still veiled. Decimus was standing near them. Two other ladies, half concealed by the pots of plants in the courtyard were standing staring down into the pool, their backs to the room. The slaves put the refreshments down on the low table without comment and after a moment retired.

'How are we going to do this?' Decimus asked when the door closed behind them. He went to the window and beckoned Junilla and Eigon back inside.

'After we have taken refreshment Eigon and I will leave with our escort as before,' Junilla said firmly, taking off her cloak and throwing it over the back of the couch. 'Except of course it won't be me.' She smiled at Julius. 'Luckily Eigon is fairly tall. I doubt the guards will notice the difference. They scarcely looked at us when we arrived.'

'And how will you leave later?'

'With you, my dear, after they have changed the guard.' Junilla smiled at Felicius. 'We will wear cloaks and veils and we will walk out arm in arm openly, as we arrived. Even if someone mentions that we have already left, no one is going to question two old ladies leaving the house.' She frowned. 'But what will happen to you when they find out your birds have flown?' She turned to Decimus.

He gave a wry grin. 'I don't plan to be here when they find out. I know who I can trust amongst my servants. It's the others I'm not sure of. But we have a plan. I shall leave almost as soon as you do, to go to the baths. There, I plan to disappear. I shall join you, my dear, in the country as soon as I can.'

'You will lose much for us, Decimus,' Junilla put her hand on his arm, 'when they find out your guests have gone. Your house will be at risk. Your property. Your place in the Senate.'

He smiled again. 'It won't be the first time I will have been in self-imposed exile for the good of my health! I'll be back.' He poured a cup of wine for her, then another which he passed to Eigon. 'Drink this to give you courage. Then you two,' he nodded to Eigon and Julius who was standing so uncomfortably in women's clothes, 'should go before they change the guard. Shall I call your slaves back?'

Junilla nodded. 'Remember, Eigon, you are me. You are bent and aching with old age, my dear. And grief-stricken. But you must talk if they address you,' she laughed. 'Don't let Julius say a word or you will be lost with his deep tones.'

Eigon went first, slowly, wrapped in Junilla's cloak and stole. Behind her Julius walked lightly, trying to remember the way Eigon normally held herself, so carefree, so upright, so graceful. Behind them the two slaves were holding their clubs loosely, shambling a little as the front door opened and they all stepped out into the sunlight. It was so hard to walk slowly, to turn left and walk up the street, keeping to the shady side, leaning together a little. At the corner they paused for a moment to cross over, still in sight of the guards. 'Keep going,' Julius murmured. 'Don't do or say anything yet. When we get to the square get one of the slaves to hail a litter. Then we'll have a bit of privacy.'

They were clinging together now but it didn't look strange. Women often walked like that. If there was any tension in the group people would have put it down to the urgent conversation they appeared to be having.

In the square one of the slaves stepped forward and hailed a litter from the rank near the baths. They climbed in and drew the curtains as the litter lurched upward. The slaves would run behind.

Eigon sat back. She was shaking all over. Julius pulled back his veil. The sight of his undeniably male face with a shadow on his chin, his hard handsome features and his strong eyebrows peering out from the pale silk made her subside into giggles again. He leaned forward and kissed her on the cheek. Again he put his finger to his lips to keep her quiet. Even litter bearers could be spies. They stared at each other for a long moment, then he leaned forward again. This time he kissed her on the lips. In the shadowed privacy of the curtained seats they were in a world of their own. She slipped forward until she was half-kneeling as his arms went round her and he kissed her again and again until she was fainting with desire and excitement. The enforced silence was strangely erotic. They could say nothing, could hardly move in the cramped space. One of the litter bearers tripped and stumbled and the litter lurched. They bumped sideways and both of them laughed. 'Hush!' Julius put his finger to her mouth. He sat back on the seat and pulled his veil across his face, fluttering his eyelashes coquettishly. 'People will think we are ladies from Lesbos!'

She smothered another giggle, quickly sliding back onto her seat as the litter was set down. They had arrived already. Climbing out, their veils clutched over their faces they waited whilst one of the slaves paid the men and the litter was borne away, then made their way towards the *mansio* where their wagon waited. This would take them out into the *campagna*. Only then would Julius be able to throw off his disguise. Two more staging posts, then they would at last be able to turn towards Junilla's villa.

Walking quickly into the inn they looked at each other and smiled again. They were safe. Julius picked up his unaccustomedly long skirt and leaped up the steps into the house two at a time.

Standing lounging against the wall nearby, a man noticed the sturdy somewhat hairy legs beneath the skirt, the muscular arm holding the veil, the masculine stride, light feminine footsteps forgotten, and sniggered. He didn't think much of it now, but if he was asked he would remember; and he would remember in great detail the wagon they climbed into a few minutes later in the inn yard.

27

Rhodri dropped Steph's last case on the floor in the kitchen. He was exhausted. He glanced round briefly. The house seemed in order. Nothing terrible seemed to have happened in her absence. 'I'll go straight on back home, if you don't mind. I'm knackered.' He grinned. 'Talk tomorrow, yes?'

She nodded wryly. Rhodri and she had not forged an undying bond on their drive back across Europe. Far from it. They had quarrelled almost incessantly, worrying about Jess, disagreeing on what to do about her, disagreeing about what to do about Dan, disagreeing about the route, in the end driving almost non stop, taking turns at the wheel as they headed across France.

'We should have dumped the car and flown,' she said flatly.

'Too much luggage.' They had Jess's bag as well as their own. 'At least we had the foresight to pick up some bottles at the Tunnel.'

She smiled wanly. 'See you later, Rhodri. Say hello to your mum. I'll come over and see her in a day or two.'

She watched as he climbed back into the car, reversed in the yard and drove out of the gate then she walked slowly into the kitchen. The fridge of course would be empty. There was probably no food in the house at all.

She stood staring out of the window with a sigh. 'So, Eigon, my love. Are you still here with your little girl voice and your habit of throwing my pots around the studio?' she said out loud. There was no reply. She turned back towards the hall and walked through to the dining room. The window Jess said had been broken was mended. The builder had left the bill on the table. Outside the grass on the small back lawn had grown to about a foot high. She sighed again. The house felt very empty.

Walking back into the kitchen she reached for the phone and

dialled Jess's mobile. It was switched off. She tried Will. That was off too. Great!

Unlocking the door into the passage through to the studio she walked into the room and looked round. It was as always dusty, smelling of paint and clay and varnish. She wandered over to the work table and ran her fingers across the surface, blowing off the dust before going over to the range of shelves, looking at the work she had left there ready to go to the gallery in Hereford, to the shop in London. Apart from the one box of broken pieces, nothing appeared to have been touched. Everything was as she had left it. Suddenly she longed to get started again, to bring life to the studio, to fire up the kiln.

Where are you?

The voice was so faint she almost missed it. She felt her nerves tighten.

Where are you? Can we come out now?

'Shit!' Steph swore out loud. 'No, you bloody can't! Go away! Leave me alone. Isn't it enough to be making Jess's life a misery in Rome? Just leave us alone!'

She walked out of the studio, slamming the door behind her and went back into the kitchen. 'You are not going to drive me out of my beloved house and you are not going to scare me, is that clear! I am not listening. Not! Not! Not!'

One by one she lugged the bags up the stairs. Jess's she put in the bedroom which her sister seemed to have been using. Hers she took into her own bedroom. She dropped them on the floor and looked round. There, on the bed lay a crude broken doll. She went cold all over. For a moment she was too frightened to move, then she shook her head and laughed. Of course, Jess must have put it there. As a joke? A gift? Who knew with Jess.

She walked over to the doll and picked it up. The moment she touched it she froze with fear, then she dropped it on the floor, shaking her hands in horror. The doll was wet with fresh moss and leaves. She stood looking down at it, unable to move, smelling the damp of leaf mould. 'Shit!' It seemed to be the only word she was capable of saying. Spinning on her heel she ran downstairs and out of the front door. The air out there was fresh and clean, the sky a bright clear blue, patched with white lambswool clouds, moving at speed across the broad river valley towards the English border. Above she heard a deep throaty croak. A raven was flying towards the wood with ponderous wingstrokes. As she watched she heard the yelp of a buzzard high above. The buzzard suddenly descended like a stone towards the raven which side-slipped out of reach and the two birds circled each other in anger for a minute or two before the buzzard soared up and angled away and the raven resumed its journey, disappearing into the leaf canopy where it was safe.

Turning, Steph looked at the front of the house. It was slumbering in the sunshine, roses climbing round the door, the curtains in one of the front windows half-drawn across, a splash of blue against the stone. It was a happy house.

But there was unhappiness in this valley.

And now there was the doll.

She walked cautiously back inside. Picking up the phone she was about to ring Megan when she paused. If she did that, Rhodri would come. He would assume she needed help. His large overpowering complacent help. Dear God, she didn't want him back so soon. Instead she rang France.

'Mummy? Are you there? Pick up, please.'

There was a scrabbling sound on the end of the phone and a breathless voice echoed out into the room. 'Steph? Hold on, dear. Let me get this thing the right way up.' Another crash then at last her mother came on the line. By now Steph was smiling. She pictured her mother, her hippy clothes, her wild grey hair, her hands ruined by too much gardening when she was at home in her cottage in the Basses-Pyrénées, her skin leathered by the suns of a thousand countries where she had wandered and written and gossiped with the locals, her eyes a piercing blue, not the pretty china blue of Victorian portraits, or the gentle blue-grey of her daughters', but the steel blue of someone who stares long and hard into the distance to see the skies and mountains which are the frame of a country's soul.

'Sorry about that, dear. I was just bringing in a basket of veg.' Aurelia was still out of breath. 'How are you? I haven't heard from either of you for ages.'

Steph bit her lip. 'Mummy, awful things are happening.' She hadn't meant it to come out like that, but the sound of her mother's voice triggered all kinds of childish dependency. Suddenly she wanted more than anything to see her mother, to hear her infectious laugh, to smell her wonderful smell of the shampoos she made herself out of rosemary and lavender and the strange floral scents she picked up on her travels.

In her untidy, warm, chaotic kitchen in France Aurelia sat down with a worried frown. 'Tell me, darling,' she said.

It took Steph a long time. As she talked she realised she was clutching the telephone receiver so tightly her hand had gone numb. She changed hands as at last her story drifted to a halt.

'Where is Jess now?' Aurelia asked at last.

'Still in Rome. Will is going to take her to Cornwall to stay with his parents. We thought she would be safe there.'

'And you are alone at Ty Bran?'

Steph nodded, suddenly near tears.

'And what have you done with this doll?'

'It's still there. Upstairs.'

'I think you should put it outside, darling. Don't touch it again. Use some tongs or something. Just put it gently outside. Don't chuck it about. Put it somewhere safe. This might be very precious to the child who left it there.'

'The child who left it there has been dead for two thousand years!'

'I know. That doesn't change anything.' Aurelia sighed. 'Shall I come?'

Steph nodded soundlessly. Then she took a grip on herself. 'No, you don't need to do that. Just tell me to pull myself together.' She attempted a laugh.

'I was planning to come and see you next month as it happens,' Aurelia went on calmly. 'I need to talk to my publisher about my next book. Why don't I bring my visit forward? I can be with you tomorrow. Now, what are you going to do tonight? I take it from your comments that you don't want to go to the Prices, though Megan would welcome you, if I remember right. I know, why not go and stay at the pub? Sandra would put you up. She's still there, isn't she? She'd love to have you.'

Steph smiled. 'Don't worry. I'll find somewhere. It would be nice if you could come, though. It really would. I need my head banging together!'

Aurelia laughed. 'I'll bet you do.' She was already making plans. 'I'll get on the first flight I can, darling. I'll ring you from London and perhaps you can collect me off the train. Love you.'

As Steph hung up she felt much better. She glanced towards

the stairs. Do it now. At once. Tongs. Did she have tongs? She walked over to the wall and stared at the line of hooks where her cooking equipment hung. They were still there, where she had left them. Picking them up she took a deep breath and headed for the stairs.

The doll lay where she had left it, on the floor. She stared down at it. It was real, no doubt about that, she had felt it, smelled it, seen the damp patch it had left on her bedspread. But it had been left there by a ghost. It had to have been. If Jess had put it there it would have dried out long ago, and before drying out it would probably have made a huge patch of mould on the bed. And it would have smelled foul, whereas now it just smelled of the woods.

She reached for it with the tongs. Then she changed her mind. A little girl had left this here, a little girl who might or might not have regarded it as her most treasured possession. She was not going to pick it up with tongs. She bent and lifted it up between finger and thumb. It was still wet and cold but it felt real. Carrying it at arm's length she ran down the stairs and out of the front door. She walked over to the wall which separated her courtyard from the wood and laid the doll on top. 'Put it somewhere safe,' her mother had said. That was right. She should look after it. She glanced towards the wood. Jess said the voices came from there. Turning, she went to the shed where she kept her spade and her wheelbarrow. There were one or two old boxes in there. She found a wooden box which had once contained a bottle of especially nice champagne. It was exactly the right size. She put the doll in it, replaced the lid and tucked the box into a sheltered niche in the wall. For a moment she paused, looking over towards the wood. She heard nothing. Turning she went back into the house and closed the door behind her. Running upstairs she went into her bedroom and tearing the bedspread off the bed she took it back downstairs and rammed it into her washing machine.

Julius was waiting for her when she woke up. As she appeared at the doorway of her hut he slid off the wall where he had been sitting, and walked towards her. 'How are you?' He smiled at her and she found herself melting at the sight of his warm brown eyes as he put his arms round her and kissed her forehead.

'I'm well. Is there any news of your grandfather?'

He nodded. 'They are safe. Junilla took him to a house nearer Rome. It is where Peter is staying.'

'Thank God!' She stood for a moment unable to believe that they were all safe now. He pushed her away gently and took her by the hand, leading her to the log they were using as a bench. There was no one else there. A low fire smoked fitfully in the centre of its ring of stones; a cauldron of water was hanging over it, newly filled and not yet warm. They sat down together.

'Eigon, I have to tell you something,' he said gently. 'It is not all good news, my dear.'

'What?' She looked at him anxiously. 'Antonia?'

'Antonia is fine. She is here somewhere. We are all well and safe for now, but the messenger who came from Grandfather brought other news, for you, Eigon.' He reached for her hand. 'It is about your mother, my dear.'

She felt her stomach clench in sudden fear. 'What about her?'

'It appears she could not face a life without your father.'

'What do you mean?' Eigon stared at him.

'She has killed herself, Eigon. I am so sorry.'

Eigon's eyes widened. 'But, she wouldn't! Why? No –!' But already she knew why. With her beloved husband gone, and Togo and Gwladys dead, and Eigon gone from her life, Cerys had no one left at all. She had followed her beloved Caradoc into the land of the ever young, certain that one day they would both be reborn together into a new life. Her eyes flooded with tears and for a moment she stood unable to move, overwhelmed with grief.

It was a long time before she stood up and walked away from the fire, staring out over the hedge towards the hills. An orange butterfly danced round her for a second, then flew away. Now she in her turn was alone.

Julius did not attempt to follow her. He waited, sitting on the log, staring down into the fire until at last she came back and sat down beside him. 'What did she do?'

'I believe she took poison.'

She bit her lip. 'She must have been so unhappy.' She looked at him, her cheeks still wet with tears.

He nodded. He lifted a hand and gently brushed them away with a fingertip.

'And it is a sin, is it not? To take one's own life?' Eigon whispered after a long pause. Her voice was trembling.

Julius shrugged. 'Your mother was not a Christian. Nor was your father.'

'So they are damned in our eyes?' She stood up again and began to pace up and down restlessly. 'That cannot be right.' She turned to him passionately. 'It means everyone who ever lived is going to go to hell except for us few souls.'

Julius shook his head helplessly. 'I don't know if that is true. You will have to ask Peter. He wants to see you, Eigon. I told the messenger you and I would find a way to ride down there this evening.'

'What if someone sees us?' She had walked away from him again, abstracted, her thoughts still with her mother.

'We'll make sure they don't.'

She didn't point out the futility of that remark. As far as Titus Marcus Olivinus was concerned every tree and every wall in Rome seemed to be in his pay.

Their only hope was disguise and the protection of their fervent prayers. It had worked before; why shouldn't it work again? Somehow they had to reach Peter and it seemed sensible to go, at once in broad daylight, as people with nothing to fear. They set off in the late afternoon with baskets of produce as gifts which served the double purpose of helping them look convincing in the roles of a farmer and his wife taking their wares to a customer in time for his dinner party that evening. They were dressed in simple home-spun clothes and alone, without any slaves or escort. Eigon was riding on a mule; Julius walked at her side. He grinned up at her. 'So, how do you like life as a simple farmer's wife?'

The remark jolted her out of her reverie and she smiled, blushing. 'I like it very much.' Her eyes were still red with tears.

He reached up and took her hand as she guided the mule with the other. The amphora of wine which was slung from the saddle jolted between them, the panniers of fruit and vegetables and country bread on either side behind her. 'Would you consider, ever, becoming the wife of someone who wasn't a farmer?' He glanced up at her, his eyes twinkling.

'I might.' A wave of happiness swept over her, and for a moment or two her sadness receded.

'I thought I might speak to my grandfather when we get there,'

he said softly. 'I would so much like his blessing when I get married.'
He was still holding her hand.

'And had you thought who you might marry?' She studied the
mule's ears.

'Indeed I have. I thought I might marry someone a bit different.
Nice Roman girls are so predictable. So,' he waved his free hand
airily, 'Roman.'

She smiled. 'And would Felicius countenance your marriage to
someone unpredictable and not Roman?'

'You know he would. He has been hinting for months that I
should hurry and ask someone otherwise someone else might ask
her first.' He paused. 'But I suspected your father would not give
his consent.' He put his hand to the rein and brought the mule
to a halt. 'I did not want to jump in and ask you today, when
you are so unhappy, Eigon. I know it is insensitive.' His voice was
very gentle. 'But times are dangerous and uncertain. This is my
chance to ask Grandfather, and if you agree, I should like to ask
Peter to marry us.'

She stared down at him. 'Today?'

'Well, maybe tomorrow!' He shrugged, feigning deep thought.

For a moment she stared at him incredulously then she let out
a small cry of joy. Hurling herself sideways out of the saddle she
flung her arms around his neck as the mule let out a bray of
protest. They stood there in the middle of the road together for
a long time, lost in a passionate kiss. Only the arrival of a cart full
of cabbages brought them to their senses as the driver whistled
and yelled obscenities at them to get them out of his way. They
dissolved into laughter and Julius helped her back into the saddle.

'We will have our whole lives together to kiss, my darling. Let's
get there before it begins to grow dark and Grandfather gets
worried.' He smacked the flank of the mule which indignantly
broke into a trot, still holding her hand as the dust of the passing
wagon rolled over them.

It was late when they eventually arrived at the suburban house
where Peter had been living for the last few weeks. It was a plain
dull building from the outside, but the inner courtyards and the
rooms they were shown into were beautifully furnished and
comfortable.

Peter greeted them each with a kiss. He looked older and more
careworn than when Eigon had seen him last as he led them into

the inner sanctum he used for his letter writing. He turned to them, puzzled.

'Whilst I am very pleased to see you, I don't understand why you are here. We had a message that you were waiting for Felicius at the farmhouse. He rode off this morning to meet you there.'

Julius frowned. 'That can't be right. We were told Grandfather was here. We have brought you produce from the market garden.' He glanced at Eigon. 'Our messenger brought news for Eigon, too.' He paused. 'There must have been a misunderstanding.' His voice had sharpened. 'Surely we couldn't have got the message wrong?'

Peter looked worried. 'I'll call Drusilla and find out who brought the message to Felicius this morning.'

He hurried out of the room, leaning heavily on his staff. Julius looked at Eigon. 'I have a bad feeling about this.'

She nodded, shivering. Her excitement and happiness had trickled away leaving a cold sensation in the pit of her stomach. 'Is it possible that Titus found out where Felicius was?' she whispered. 'And us. That he knew all the time?'

Julius grimaced. 'Who knows, my darling. Please God you are not right.'

Peter reappeared almost at once. With him was a pretty woman, somewhere in her mid-thirties, with black hair and dark eyes. She looked troubled. Drusilla it emerged was Pomponia Graecina's cousin. 'It was a young man,' she said. 'He knocked on the door and he said you had reached safety in the hills and that you would like your grandfather to go there to join you as soon as possible.'

'What did he look like?' Julius asked sharply.

She shrugged. 'I didn't see him. He spoke to one of the slaves. He said he couldn't wait as he had other households to visit with the news.' She licked her lips nervously, looking from Julius to Peter and back. 'Do I gather you didn't send the messenger?'

Julius shook his head. 'I did not. I'm going back.'

'I'll come with you.' Eigon reached out for his hand. He shook it off. 'No. Better if I go alone. It will be quicker and I want to know you at least are safe.' He looked down at her sternly, then his face softened again and he took her hands in his. 'I'll borrow a horse and be there in no time at all. The chances are that this is a misunderstanding and that Grandfather will have already turned round and set off back here when Marcellus told him where we are and I'll meet him on the road.'

She clung to him for a second. 'Please, be careful. I couldn't bear to lose you again.'

He leaned across and kissed her on the lips. 'I shall be back as soon as I can. Then we will ask Peter to marry us!' He grinned at the old man. 'I was going to ask Grandfather's blessing first, but now I shall ask yours, sir, for my journey. I'll find Grandfather and I shall bring Antonia back as well. She would be furious if we got married without her there.'

And he was gone.

Eigon stared at the ground. Suddenly she was near to tears again. Drusilla put an arm around her shoulders. 'He'll be all right. You'll see. Come with me and we'll talk. We'll leave Peter to his correspondence and his prayers.' She smiled at the old man.

He nodded. 'I will take great pleasure in marrying you two,' he said with a reassuring smile. 'That will be something we can all look forward to.'

Eigon was woken just before dawn. For a moment she stared round the unfamiliar room, forgetting where she was, then she sat up anxiously. There was someone standing in the doorway. 'What is it?'

The boy who had knocked at her door carried a lamp. Shadows slid up the wall and across the ceiling. 'Please come, lady, quickly.'

She pulled a wrap around her shoulders and followed him. A group of people were gathered in the main room. One of the slaves was going around lighting the lamps. Drusilla was there. She was crying.

'What is it? What's happened?' Eigon was suddenly more afraid than she had ever been.

Peter was standing there leaning on his staff. He was still dressed in the old blue tunic he had been wearing the night before. His face was haggard. 'My dear, I am afraid I have the worst news.' He held out his arms to her. 'You must prepare yourself for a shock.' He pushed forward a young man who was standing nearby. He was covered in dust and his clothes were torn. It was a moment before she recognised him as Silas who had followed her from her father's villa.

'What's happened?' Her mouth was dry. She saw their faces and shook her head desperately. 'No. Please, no.' Almost without realising it she had moved forward to Peter. He put his arm around her shoulders. 'Be strong, child.'

'We were betrayed.' Silas shook his head. His shoulders began shaking with sobs. 'I had gone down to the stream to fetch more water when a troop of soldiers came up the hill. They didn't even bother to arrest anyone. They put everyone to the sword. Everyone. The women. Stephen's children, Marcellus.' His voice cracked. 'Felicius Marinus. Antonia.'

Eigon froze. She knew he was speaking but she could no longer hear him. Julius's face swam before her eyes. His smile, his mouth. His eyes. His arms outstretched towards her.

'We were sharing a meal.' The words went on. 'Felicius had arrived. He was looking for you and Julius.' He was shaking his head again. 'It was a trick. They must have followed him.'

She wasn't listening. She pulled away from Peter's arms and moved over to the door. Dreamlike she walked out into the atrium and stood staring down into the pool at its centre. If she expected to see scenes of slaughter there she was spared that at least. The water lay quiet and clear, rippling across a mosaic design of acanthus leaves.

When Peter came to her at last she met his gaze with calm clear eyes. 'It is my fault. Titus Marcus Olivinus is behind this. If it had been Nero's men they would have arrested them all and taken them to the dungeons so that they could make a spectacle of their deaths. This was personal. He has killed every single person I love. For all I know he was behind my mother's death as well.'

Her voice shook slightly.

Peter took her hand. 'Let us pray together, my dear. Pour out your heart to Jesus. Let him comfort you.'

She stayed with Peter and Drusilla for five days. Then she set out to return to Britannia.

28

Jess was sitting, gazing out of the window. The sky was growing darker, the colours less vibrant. She glanced at her watch and realised with a shock that it was already after eight o'clock. Where was Will? Stiffly she stood up. If only she could feel the certainties that Eigon felt; take comfort from a faith which would sustain her through so much. Eigon had spent the best part of a week in prayer, supported and comforted by Peter and by a houseful of kind, gentle Christians. It was Peter who sheltered her from the horrors recounted by the men who had gone up to the farm to bury the dead. It was Peter who talked to her each day about the people she had lost; Peter who prayed with her and reassured her, Peter who explained that Julius and Antonia and Felicius would be now amongst the angels; that she would see them again one day; that maybe her father and even her mother had had sufficient contact with the wonder of Christ to beg for his intercession in their hearts as they died.

Eigon was the one who had remembered Peter's earlier suggestion that one day she might go back to the land of her birth. There was nothing in Rome for her now but danger and sadness. To plan the trip was to take her mind off the aching emptiness inside her. She was to go to Ostia and take a ship to Massilia; from there she would travel overland, heading west over regular and well maintained trade routes, taking with her the message of Christ's love. She wasn't going to go alone. Peter chose two companions to go with her. One was Drusilla herself, who had proved a firm gentle friend over the last days. She was a widow with no children and had it seemed a surprising appetite for adventure. The second person he selected was Commios, a freedman, who had been brought to Rome with his parents from Gaul and was now one of Peter's most trusted disciples, anxious to return to the lands where he had originated. Pursing his lips, Peter told them all his decision.

There was no time to finesse their departure. Word on the street was that Titus Marcus Olivinus had openly let it be known that he was searching for Eigon and that he was offering a substantial reward for her capture. Praetorian spies were everywhere. They had very little time. Peter kept that news to himself. To add to Eigon's burden would be unforgivable. As long as he got her out of Rome as soon as possible she would be safe. He had no way of knowing that barely two streets away at the baths Titus was sitting on a towel in the steam room listening to the very interesting information being passed on to him by one of the tradesmen who that very morning had brought a consignment of olive oil to the house.

The knock on her door brought Jess out of her reverie with a start. '*Signorina*?' It was Margaretta. 'Carmella has arrived. She is waiting for you downstairs.'

'Jess! Thank God!' Carmella was sitting in the front room. She jumped to her feet. 'Are you all right? Will rang me in such a panic! Has he arrived yet? He said he was on his way. He was so worried. His phone couldn't get a signal and then when he rang you back there was no reply so I said I would come and make sure you were OK.'

'I'm sorry. I lost track of the time as usual.' Jess joined her and threw herself down in a chair. 'I suppose my phone was switched off.'

Carmella shook her head. 'You make life very difficult for that poor man, Jess.' She sighed. 'Stupidly I've lost my mobile. So I had to wait to call him again from here.'

'Dan had your phone.' Jess scowled. 'Would you believe he walked into your flat and took it? He said you never even saw him.'

Carmella blanched. 'When?'

'You were expecting someone to lunch and you left your door open. He was so pleased with himself. He got the number from your phone and just rang up and asked them the address then he came here and found me. It wasn't supernatural. It was that simple. Even this place wasn't safe in the end.'

Carmella shook her head. 'Oh, Jess. I am so sorry. That man. He is the devil. But you are all right? What did he do?'

Jess gave a wry grin. 'You might say he was chased away.'

Carmella sighed. 'You need a drink. Wait.'

Jess closed her eyes as Carmella left the room. When she opened them Carmella was offering her a small glass. 'Iced Limoncello. It will help you feel better. I will go and phone Will from the kitchen, OK?'

Exhausted, Jess closed her eyes and lay back in the chair. So much had happened; she had had so little proper sleep over the last few nights, she wondered if she would ever be able to stand up again.

Was it the right thing to do, to go back to England with Will? Was Eigon herself going there now? Her eyes flew open. She couldn't be sure that Eigon escaped. Titus knew where she was staying. Peter was preparing to ship her out but she hadn't gone yet. How long did it take to prepare a journey like that? Supposing Titus came before Eigon had the chance to leave? Jess could feel the adrenaline pouring through her veins suddenly.

'OK. I found him.' Carmella came through from the kitchen. 'He is on his way.'

'How long will he be?' Jess stared up at her in a panic.

'Not long.' Carmella sat down beside her. 'Don't worry, Jess. You will be all right. Dan can't get to you now. We are all here.'

'No! You don't understand. It's not Dan. It's just –' She clutched at Carmella's arm. 'Please, you have to look for me. Now, before he comes. What happened? What happened to Eigon? Did she escape? Where are your cards? Did you bring them?'

Carmella shook her head. 'No, Jess, I didn't bring them.' She scanned Jess's white face. 'Leave it now, eh? You've done as much as you can. You know enough. Protect yourself, Jess. Leave Eigon to the past.'

'I can't! Don't you understand? I need to know. It would only take you five minutes. Please.' Jess snapped her fingers suddenly. 'I know!' Before Carmella could stop her she ran through into the kitchen. Margaretta was standing at the table chopping zucchini. She looked up in astonishment as Jess erupted through the door.

'Please, I'm sorry. Can I have a bowl of water? Here, this will do.' She seized the empty salad bowl off the table and ran to the sink. Half filling it with water she carried it back next door, leaving her hostess open-mouthed, staring after her. 'Here. Look in here.

You said water would work as well as your *sfera di cristallo*.' She put the bowl down on the table, slopping water over the polished walnut surface.

'Jess –!'

'Go on, quickly before Will gets here. Just look. Please.'

Behind them Margaretta appeared in the doorway, drying her hands on a cloth. She looked mildly put out at having her bowl snatched from under her nose.

'Carmella?'

Carmella glanced up. She muttered something quick and incomprehensible. Jess ignored it. 'Go on. Look. Please.' She glanced up. A taxi had pulled up outside the house. 'Two minutes. Before he comes in. Please, Carmella!'

Carmella sighed. She leaned forward over the bowl, pushing her hair back from her face with one hand as she leaned closer looking deep into the water. She was there. The enigmatic face from the past, staring back. She could see the woman's features, the veil over her hair, the bright intelligent eyes, watching Carmella as Carmella was watching her.

Jess had scrambled to her feet and ran to the door as Will appeared. 'Wait. One second.' She put her finger to her lips. 'Just one second.'

Will stared over her shoulder at Carmella. 'What's going on?'

'She's just checking something for me.'

Carmella sat back abruptly. Whoever this was, it was not Eigon. She shook her head. 'It's no good, Jess. I'm sorry. I can't do it like this. I can't concentrate. Nothing is coming.'

'But I have to know.' Jess could hear herself. She sounded more and more pathetic.

'I will look when I go home, Jess. I promise you.' Carmella climbed to her feet. She walked over and put her hands on Jess's forearms, holding her firmly. 'Now you go with Will. I will ring you, I promise. As soon as you get home we will be in touch. I will do this tonight when it is peaceful and safe and I can concentrate. Now go and get your things.'

'Have you told him where to go?' Jess said wearily as they settled into the taxi.

'I've told him.' Will sat back with a sigh. He closed his eyes with a groan. 'I thought I'd lost you again.'

She bit her lip. Part of her was still in the front room at the *pensione* peering over Carmella's shoulder into the bowl of water. There was nothing there. Carmella was right. Just a swirl of restless patterns.

'I rang the airline this afternoon,' Will said as the taxi hurtled through the streets. 'We have seats on the last plane out to Stansted tonight.'

Jess gave him a wan smile. 'I've been a pain, haven't I. I'm so grateful, Will. You've been my knight in shining armour.'

'Have I?' He shrugged.

'You know you have. You put your life in danger for me.' She reached across and kissed him on the cheek.

He put his arm round her. 'Glad to have been of service.'

He left his arm there as the taxi wound its way through the suburbs. 'Have you thought what you are going to do when this is all over?'

She shook her head. 'I can't see beyond it somehow.'

'We can't just leave it. We must go to the police The man is a serious menace. He's dangerous, Jess.'

She bit her lip. 'There is no proof, Will. None at all for any of it. Even if you tell them what he did to you, I bet there isn't any evidence. Your bruises – you could have got them by falling, just as I could. No one saw it happen, did they. And the drugs he gave you. Have they left any traces? Even if they are still there in your hair or somewhere, you can't prove he did it, can you? And the worst I could claim is that he has been stalking me. I suppose you could all be witnesses to that. But even then there are no CCTV pictures, or phone calls. Nothing. He only has to deny it.'

'Are you going to let him go back to school next year as though nothing has happened? You expect me to work alongside him?'

She shook her head wordlessly.

'So, what can we do?'

'I don't know, Will.' Their faces were very close. He leaned forward and kissed her on the lips. 'Jess.' She didn't move so he kissed her again more firmly this time. 'I was such a fool, Jess. We should never have broken up.' He reached to cup her face in his hands, staring deep into her eyes. 'Jess?'

She shook her head, drawing away from him. 'I'm sorry, Will. I can't. Not at the moment. Not after everything that's happened.' She turned away from him, staring hard out of the window at the blur of passing lights. The sun had set and it was growing dark.

He sat back with a sigh. 'Of course. I'm sorry. Stupid of me.'

'No!' She turned back. 'No, Will. It's not stupid. It's wonderful of you. It's me. I just can't respond at the moment. I've switched off somewhere deep inside me. I'm sorry!' She was fighting tears.

The taxi driver glanced in the rear view mirror and pouted sympathetically. He had seen it all before so many times. Didn't matter what nationality, what age. Not even what sexes these days. *L'amore* was hell! 'La Via Appia Antica,' he called over his shoulder. 'See? Ancient Roman road.' He said it to every tourist leaving Rome on this route for Ciampino.

'I don't know if I'll be able to love anyone ever again.' Jess had turned back to the window, her voice tight and painful. 'Not after what he did.' The straight narrow road between high walls was floodlit by the taxi headlights. She shivered.

Will's face set in a grim line. 'He's going to pay for this, Jess. One way or another, I swear it.' He reached for her hand. 'I'll still be your knight in shining armour. Don't ever think you're alone, will you.'

She gave a wistful smile. 'I know. Thank you.'

They checked in and made their way straight through into the departure lounge. Only once they were there did Jess stop glancing over her shoulder at the teeming crowds, expecting to see Dan at every moment.

Will managed to find them somewhere to sit. 'Are you OK?'

She nodded. Exhaustion was beginning to take over. Her eyes were closing and the sounds from the TV monitors mounted below the ceilings had faded away. She was still in Italy. Why in God's name wasn't she trying to contact Eigon? She glanced at Will. His eyes were closed. She could do it now. Summon Eigon from the past. Ask her what had happened. Closing her lids she took a slow deep breath, trying to relax. Nearby two people were laughing loudly. She half-turned away from them, hunching into the chair. 'Eigon?' she murmured. 'Where are you?' She screwed up her eyes, looking inwards, searching the darkness inside her head for pictures, but nothing came.

'Eigon?'

She sat up suddenly and stared round. Had she called out loud? She glanced at Will. He seemed to be soundly asleep. Settling back again she closed her eyes once more. She tried again to picture the house, the bright sun-filled rooms around the various atria, the sound of tinkling water from the fountains; Drusilla's bright laughter, never intrusive, never insensitive after the terrible events that had passed but so much a part of her personality that it seemed to follow her wherever she went; Eigon discussing with her and Peter the route they were to follow; Commios busying himself with arranging the passes and collecting the money they would need for the journey, the items to go in the panniers of the mules they would buy once they landed in Massilia.

They would have spent a long time praying with Peter. They would have sat at his feet and listened to his instructions and his wisdom and his stories about Jesus. Jess scrunched up her eyes even tighter, trying to conjure them from the darkness. Nothing happened.

She dozed.

It seemed like only seconds later when she was woken by Will. He was shaking her shoulder. 'Come on, Jess. They've called our flight.'

'No!' She stared round. 'I can't go yet.'

'What do you mean you can't go?' He had stooped to pick up his rucksack. He turned on her. 'Please don't do this, Jess.' He sounded very weary.

'I don't know what happened to Eigon –'

He groaned. 'If I never hear that name again it will be too soon. Forget it, Jess. You're coming with me now.' He picked up her bag and held it out to her. His face was thunderous. She took the bag meekly. 'I should go to the ladies.'

'Wait till you're on the plane.'

'But –'

'No buts, Jess. This is it. We're going back to England.'

Dan stretched out on the bed and opened his eyes, slowly taking in the room with its torn ugly wallpaper, its cheap battered furniture and the threadbare towel hanging on the rail. He'd had to pay extra for that and soap. He had checked in late last night in the cheapest hotel he could find near Termini. All he wanted was a good night's sleep on a horizontal bed. He scratched reflectively. He had been bitten by something in the night. Serve him right for not being more choosy. He glanced at his watch. It was early still but the noise from the street outside was growing louder by the moment. He could smell the traffic fumes through the crack in the window which he had left open last night as he tried to clear the fug of cigarette smoke from the room. He washed, redressed and left.

He found a café open. A black coffee and he was beginning to feel more human. He sat back in his chair and stuck his legs out in front of him. What to do next? Go and find Jess. He pictured her in that cushy little *pensione* with its beautiful antiques and its rooftop bedrooms and he scowled. Whatever it was she had summoned to chase him out he would be ready for it this time. It wasn't real. Titus could deal with it. He sighed and ordered another coffee. He was a fool to have left her and now he had to move fast before the police got the chance to interview her. Mind you, she had no credibility left anyway. They wouldn't believe her. But they might just wonder. If there was some bloody female feminist person interviewing her they might decide to follow it up just because they hated men. And whatever they did, it was going to damage him. He gave a tight determined smile as he stood up and headed for the door. Time for Jess to give way to her paranoia and top herself. Walking out into the sunshine he gave a snort of amusement. Where was Titus when he needed him? It was time to work out just how she was going to do it. He and Titus could discuss it on the way back to the *pensione*.

Titus was waiting for Lucius. The man was late. He stamped his feet a couple of times, walking up and down the room slowly, growing more and more impatient. Surely he'd got the message? He needed him this morning, not next month. He swung round and did another length of the room, aware that some of the other officers were eyeing him warily. They were distancing themselves more and more from him, he knew that. And he knew why. Word of the massacre at the farm had spread. Not that anyone cared one way or another about a bunch of renegade Christians, but the way it had been done seemed to have shocked them. It had been a private matter, a vicious, very personal vendetta but it had involved the killing not just of slaves, who loved this new religion, but also of women and children and several Roman citizens and that made it different. He wondered if he was going to be interviewed by a tribune praetor. If so he would bluff his way through it. In the meantime there was one more person to catch. The only person he really wanted. And he knew where she was. All he needed was for Lucius to call at the house, speak to Drusilla, who, wonder of wonders turned out to be a distant cousin, and he would be in. But Lucius still hadn't come.

'Sir.' A timid voice at his elbow stopped him in his pacing. He swung round. 'Sir, a message.' It was a boy, one of the stable lads. He proffered a tablet on which was scribbled a note. *Sorry. Can't make it. On leave until calends next month. L*

Titus swore viciously. He aimed a kick at the boy and hurled the tablet into the corner of the room. 'Bastard!' Lucius had double-crossed him. He didn't want any more to do with him. Leave, indeed. He had no leave planned. He must have gone to the legate to swing this one. Well, he would pay. He would see to it that every person in that house was arrested. Including Drusilla! He looked round for the boy. He had fled. The other men in the room strode purposefully one by one towards the door and left. Yet again he found himself alone.

The raid was carried out by a cohort of the Praetorians. Titus did not go with them. They returned to their camp disgruntled. They had found the house empty. There was no one there, not even a slave. They reported to headquarters that they had been given duff information and moved on to scour another quarter of the city. The trail had gone cold. Titus walked down the street looking thoughtfully up at the shuttered windows. He had to find her soon. He did not have long. If she told her story to anyone it might get out. Whoever and whatever she was now, she had been the daughter of a king. Interest would be directed towards him. He sent a spy out to the villa to see if she was there. The place had been left empty. Aelius and Flavius had taken anything they could carry and disappeared into the night. The Emperor's men had taken everything else. The horses and anything else saleable had been put up for auction. The rest had been taken away on carts. The house was awaiting a new tenant. The gardens were growing over with weeds, the orchards were bare, in the autumn winds the fig trees had shed huge flabby leaves all over the courtyard.

Titus sat for a long time after he received the report, deep in thought. Then grimly he rummaged in his money chest and drew out a bag of coins. He took out a handful, thought swiftly and added some more, before throwing a cloak over his uniform and striding out towards the city centre. He was going to find Marcia Maximilla. She was clever; she was beautiful; she was greedy; she was famous. She was a seer. She could, if she chose, find Eigon for him without moving from her couch.

29

With a jolt Jess awoke. She clutched the armrests in a panic, wondering for a second where she was, then reassured by the drone of engines remembered. She glanced sideways at Will. His seat was reclined, his eyes closed. Looking down out of the window she could see nothing.

Closing her own eyes again she sighed. In barely another hour they would once again be back in England and her chance to follow Eigon's story would be over.

Unless.

She willed herself back into Eigon's past, picturing the house in Rome, its peaceful atmosphere, its warmth, its elegant shabbiness, the people around her, the gentle kindnesses of Drusilla, who made sure she was alone when she needed peace to pray, and that she had company when she needed to talk, the fierce determination of Peter as he rallied them from their misery and led them in their communal prayers, the decision to leave Rome, the hasty procurement of passports, the raising of money to pay their way. But the detail wouldn't come. The pictures had stalled. The characters waited for her to put words into their mouths. Turning her head to stare once more out into the darkness she felt herself near to tears. 'Where are you?' she whispered. 'Please. Show me.'

As waves slammed against the decking, soaking the hard-reefed sails, the passengers huddled below decks in terror. Some dozen people had taken passage with the trader, laden with supplies for the occupying legions, heading for Massilia in Narbonensis on the southern coast of Gaul, little realising that they were heading out into the first of the autumnal storms which had suddenly out of nowhere raked across this narrow stretch of sea. Drusilla was prostrate, groaning with the others over evil-smelling buckets. Commios looked round searching for a sign of Eigon.

He found her on deck, clinging to the shrouds, staring out across the white-topped rollers. Her eyes were shining, her hair, torn free of its combs, whipping round her head like so many ebony snakes. He came to stand beside her. 'The captain has commanded everyone below deck.'

She turned to him. His words had been snatched away and she couldn't hear them above the roar of the waves. 'Isn't it wonderful? I didn't know anything could be so exciting!' Water streamed down her face; her clothes were soaked, clinging to her like a second skin. He grinned. He couldn't hear what she had said, but he got the gist of it. It was wonderful and wild out here, away from the stench and the wails of the other passengers, and if the boat foundered it was better surely to be up here under the sky, part of the storm, rather than below, trapped in the wooden box which could so easily turn into a water-logged coffin.

'How far now?' she cried.

He shrugged. Either he hadn't heard her or he didn't know. They had been out of sight of land for so long it was impossible to gauge their progress. For all he knew they were drifting backwards towards Ostia, or heading out across the Mare Tyrrhenum towards Carthago or Hippo Regius. The journey was supposed to take two days, two and a half at most. He tried to count the number of times the sky had gone dark and gave up. Just so long as they did not end up back where they had started. He had seen the weight fall from Eigon's shoulders as they left the Roman mainland behind. With it went her fear of being pursued. He and only he had been told by Peter of Titus's single-minded vendetta. He had sworn to keep it to himself but it meant he would keep an eye out until they were truly safe. Her excitement was infectious and he found himself laughing with her as a fresh smack of water hit the deck near them and they were soaked yet again.

It was nearly dusk when the storm began to ease and the ship picked up speed. The sky cleared and they found they could see the coast on their right-hand side, far closer than they had expected. As the other passengers crawled up on deck word began to go round that they were indeed nearly at their destination and that the captain's astonishingly accurate navigation was due solely to the offerings he had made to Neptune before they left land.

The port was noisy, dirty and crowded. Commios took charge as they staggered ashore, trying to find their land legs, conscious of how wretched and ragged they looked in their wet clothing. They assembled their belongings, in the end no more than they could carry between them, and headed away from the quays to find the house of Tullius Gaius, a freedman whose father had worked for Drusilla's grandfather and who was now a successful merchant and entrepreneur in the city, importing and exporting in a huge ever-increasing market. They were directed to a substantial house in the centre of the trading quarter and shown into a luxurious and comfortable home.

Gaius wasn't there, but his wife, Aemilia, greeted them warmly and at once set about finding them rooms. At her suggestion they made their way almost at once to the nearby baths. When they returned, clean, rested, wearing fresh clothes they found a meal waiting for them, their host had been summoned from his office and he and several of his friends were already arrayed on couches around the table, agog for news from Rome. It was soon clear that none of them knew of Drusilla's conversion to Christianity or that their guests were members of the sect. At a warning glance from Commios Eigon kept silent on the subject, and they emphasised instead their need to travel on as soon as possible towards the north.

In Eigon's room later she and Drusilla sat on the bed, talking softly. 'I want to stay here for ever!' Eigon said, laughing. 'This place is wonderful!' Her sorrow had been walled temporarily away in some inner recess of her mind. It was too great, too all consuming to bear. She would face it one day again and deal with it, but not now, not while it was so fresh and so raw.

Drusilla nodded. 'And it doesn't rock up and down being sloshed with sea water,' she added fervently. 'Commios was asking if we could buy a passage on a barge up the river Rhodanus. I'm not so sure that is a good idea.'

Eigon smiled. 'Have no fear. Barges don't rock up and down. You've seen them on the Tiber. Flat and steady is what they do best.'

Drusilla nodded. She glanced at the door. 'We shouldn't really tell anyone where we are headed,' she whispered. 'I'm sure we can trust these people, but I'd feel better if there were no clues left behind us.'

Eigon's face sobered rapidly. She shivered. 'You're right,' she said reluctantly. 'We should move on soon, shouldn't we. Just as soon as our clothes are dry.' She stared round the room suddenly, and shivered again. 'Drusilla,' she whispered. 'Can you feel it? As though someone is watching us?'

Drusilla shook her head. 'Don't be silly. I'm sorry, now I've frightened you. I didn't mean to do that.'

'No.' Eigon took her hand. 'No, you haven't. You are absolutely right.' She leaned forward and kissed Drusilla goodnight.

She watched the door close behind her and stood for a moment, numb with exhaustion. Her guard down, her eyes filled with tears as loneliness overwhelmed her. It was when she was alone like this that it was at its worst. Her longing for Julius flooded back as she remembered that last journey with him into Rome, his last kiss. With a deep sigh of misery she knelt down beside the bed and prayed. For Julius. For his grandfather. For Antonia. For Peter and his ongoing cause. And she prayed for her own safety. Then once again she pushed her unhappiness away.

As she rose to her feet at last she stared round once more. It was still there, the feeling that someone, somewhere was watching her. Not Julius. It wasn't any of the people she loved, of that she was certain. She sat down on the edge of the bed for a moment, her eyes fixed on the guttering flame of the oil lamp on the exquisitely carved oak table beside the bed. The patterns in the wood reminded her of her childhood. They were the curling interlaced designs of home. She had heard Celtic being spoken in the port almost as soon as they had docked, one of a dozen languages being shouted on every side, and seen in several faces the unmistakable colouring of men and women from the northern edges of the Empire. It was a long, long time since she had allowed herself to feel homesick, but now suddenly she couldn't wait to see again the green hills and misty distances, cooled by gently falling rain which had so haunted her dreams.

She tensed suddenly. There it was again. The atmosphere in the room had grown heavy; the temperature had dropped. She stared round wildly. Then she closed her eyes. 'Pray, surround yourself with prayer and with the golden light of safety.' Melinus had taught her that. Peter had said much the same. 'Send away demons in the name of Christ, my child. Surround yourself with His love. He will keep you safe. Pray.' She shook her head. She wasn't sure if her prayers were fervent enough, if they were working at all, because someone was out there trying to find her. Titus. And he was using an adept, someone who was having no trouble at all in locating her.

'Oh my God!' Jess woke with a start. 'He's on to her. He's following her.'

Will sighed. He didn't have to ask who she meant. 'So, she's even haunting you at thirty thousand feet?'

She shook her head. 'I was dreaming –'

'Never mind. We're practically at Stansted. Look.' He indicated the window. The plane was losing altitude. Already they could make out the patterns of lights below them. 'You're safe, Jess, that's what matters now.'

'But don't you see, Titus is following her. And if he is, then Dan is following me.'

'I doubt it.' Will sounded grim. 'But if he is, Jess, it doesn't matter. We're on home territory now. If necessary we will call the police. And anyway he is not going to find you. I'm taking you straight down to Cornwall. You'll be safe there. He will never think of looking for you there in a million years. You'll have time to decide what you want to do, and you'll be able to relax and stop worrying.'

The captain had started speaking. They would soon be landing. When he finished his announcement Jess turned back to Will. 'I'm sorry, you have been so good to me, Will. You probably saved my life,' she said gently, 'but I'm not coming to Cornwall.'

'Why not?' He frowned.

'You know why not. I have to go back to Ty Bran. That is where Eigon is going.'

'No, Jess. It's the first place Dan will look.'

'I'll have to take that risk.' She reached over and put her hand over his. 'Will, you've done more than I expected or deserve. I can't ask you to do any more for me.' There was a slight bump as the plane wheels were lowered. 'I want you to go and see your parents. Enjoy what's left of the summer. I'm going to stay with Steph.'

He frowned. 'Are you sending me away?'

She grinned. 'That sounds a bit bossy. It's not what I meant. I just don't want you to feel responsible for me.'

He had coloured slightly and she couldn't sense whether he was hurt or just angry. 'Are you going back to see him?' he burst out suddenly.

'Who?' She was genuinely puzzled for a moment.

'Rhodri.' His lips tightened.

'No! I doubt he wants to see me ever again.' She laughed out loud. She glanced at him sideways then turned to look out of the window. The plane was only a few hundred feet above the ground now. She could see the layout of roads below, the headlights of cars threading their way through the night. Rhodri. She pictured him for a moment, his broad shoulders, his weathered complexion, the neat but somehow rakish beard, the laughter in his eyes and the protective anger. He was an attractive man, there was no question about that. But that was his job. He was charismatic and she had been sucked in by his image. That was it. 'You're not jealous, Will?'

'Hardly. As you reminded me, we are over.'

'And that was your choice,' she said quietly. 'You left me, remember? At the time our break up nearly destroyed me, but you had sensed that all was not well between us long before I did. And now I realise you were right.'

'I was a fool.' He was staring straight ahead at the back of the seat in front of him. 'Does it have to be for ever? No scope to change my mind?'

'No one can know about for ever, Will, but for now.' She glanced across at him sadly. Will had done so much for her. He had laid his life on the line, that was true and she was still fond of him; the anger and the hurt had gone. But gratitude and fondness wasn't enough to base a relationship on.

He was still looking away from her. 'So, you'll go straight to Wales?'

She shrugged. 'I've got to make my way to Heathrow first. I left my car there.'

Will looked at her. 'Shit! I'm sorry. It never occurred to me.'

'It's OK. I'm sure there are buses or trains that go there. Then I'll go on to Wales.'

'And wherever Eigon goes you go, I suppose.' He sounded bitter. 'You'll ring me if you need help? You know I'll come.' He and Rhodri had made a pact to deal with Dan; could he work with Rhodri? He sighed. Probably, if it meant freeing Jess from this torment.

'I'll ring you, Will.' She was smiling at him. 'Are you still going to Cornwall?'

'Later perhaps. I'll go back home first. Remember you can come any time you like. No strings.'

She grinned. 'Then we might have each other's company for a while yet. On the train into London.'

She said goodbye to him at Liverpool Street Station. She was heading towards a connection to the Piccadilly Line and Heathrow, he was going back to South London. On tiptoe she reached up and kissed him once lightly on the lips. 'Take care, Will.'

'And you.' He gave her a quick hug. 'Don't let Titus get you.' For a moment she thought he was going to say something else, but he had already turned away.

Dan sipped thoughtfully at a cappuccino, staring across the street. The sun was blinding, the heat reflecting off the cobbles. The air smelled of traffic fumes and hot stone. He was tired, depressed and so angry he couldn't cope with the waves of fury which rolled through him with frightening regularity. There had been several messages from Nat, each growing more worried, more cross, more impatient. She had demanded to know where he was. He had promised to be home by now. The police, she said, had rung her three times now; so had the headmaster. What on earth was going on? He took another sip from the cup, wiping froth off his upper lip and called for a prosecco. Jess had disappeared. There was no trace of her. He had no idea where the others were. He had staked out Carmella's flat. They weren't staying there and they weren't at the *pensione*. He drained the glass and put it down with a bang.

And there was no sign of Titus.

Shit! He slammed his fist down on the table suddenly, making the cup jump in its saucer. The woman at the neighbouring table turned to stare at him, then she turned away, shifting her chair slightly on its spindly legs so she had her back to him.

'Up yours too, lady,' he muttered. He stood up, threw some coins on the table and strode away.

Titus sat quietly watching the woman as she consulted her oracles. Prophetesses were expensive and this was his third visit. Each time she gave him just enough to tantalise him, just enough to convince him that she could indeed see deep into time and space beyond the dark room where they sat. 'I see others; patrician families, caught up in these plots. I see a lady, two ladies talking. They befriended your princess. They have friends in high places. They are beyond your reach.' She gave him a look which was nothing short of withering. 'I see a woman from faraway watching you, as you are watching her.' She smiled enigmatically. She had felt this woman's quest before; she was searching for the truth across time just as they were. But she came from another era. Marcia Maximilla was intrigued. She came back to the business in hand. 'Do you wish to find out more about the princess?'

Titus fought the urge to reach out and strangle her. 'That is why I am here, lady.'

She glanced at him obviously wondering if this was the moment to up her charge. Thinking better of it she looked away. She was getting an uncomfortable feeling about this particular client. Better to give him what he wanted and send him on his way as fast as possible. 'She's gone. Over the sea. I see the waves rough and turbulent. She stood at the prow of the ship, staring ahead into her dreams, and she has put Rome behind her for ever.'

Titus clenched his fists. 'Tell me where she is going.'

For the first time the seer frowned. 'I see her swathed in veils. Her destiny is unclear. No!' She screamed as he lunged across the table at her and caught her by the shoulders. 'I would tell you, lord, if I could see. She too is an adept. She senses me searching for her. She has surrounded herself with mist.'

He subsided into his seat. What was the point of killing her? She was the best Rome could offer. 'There must be something. Some clue. Has she gone to Gaul? Is she going back to Britannia?'

The woman resettled herself, trying to be calm. She wanted nothing so much as to be rid of him. She glanced up and her face cleared. 'I have it. Her thoughts betrayed her for a moment. She is going to Britannia.'

It was the furthest place she could think of.

Britannia! Dan picked up the thought as a blinding flash. She has gone back to Britannia. And if Eigon had gone back to Britannia, then so would Jess. He went cold. He had to get there fast before she did. He had to get to her before she had the chance to reach anyone with her stupid accusations and her petty obsessions. Particularly he had to make sure she didn't get to Nat.

Jess's car was still there next morning when she reclaimed it at last. So much had happened it felt as though it was months since she had left it there in the long-term car park. Clutching her ticket, she opened the door and climbed in. Slamming it shut she lay back and closed her eyes. She felt safe for the first time in ages.

Reaching for her mobile she dialled Steph. No reply. She dialled Kim. No reply. She resisted the urge to ring Carmella. She was on her own, by her own choice. Will, reluctantly, had gone. It was up to her now. She had to make her own decisions and she had to find somewhere where she could contact Eigon and that was not going to be the car park at Heathrow airport. Leaning forward with a sigh she inserted the key in the ignition and began to back out of the parking space.

'We have to go. Now.' Eigon was shaking Drusilla's shoulder. It was first light and already the streets outside were noisy with the shouts of traders. 'I'm so sorry, but we can't stay here. He's coming. He knows where we are. I've been warned in my prayers.'

Drusilla did not question her. At once she climbed out of bed and began to pack her things.

The travellers caught a river trader, boarding it soon before it sailed. Drusilla and Eigon were given a small curtained-off area to themselves on the flat-bottomed, wide-hulled barge laden with goods which was making its way laboriously northwards. Commios was content to find himself a corner to sleep amongst the crew. It made the cost of the trip much cheaper and he was able to talk to the men who worked the boat, one of whom he established at once was a fellow tribesman.

'He is happy,' Drusilla whispered to Eigon. They were leaning against the rail, watching the banks of the river slide by.

'And we'll lose him, if we are not careful. He has come home.' Drusilla sighed. 'He's an attractive man, isn't he?' She gave a wistful smile.

Eigon glanced at her. 'I've noticed you watching him.'

Drusilla was gazing out across the river watching a flock of ducks paddling against the tide. 'And he has eyes for no one but you. If he stays with us that will be why. He won't leave you.'

'That's not true. He watches over both of us. Peter gave him that charge, Drusilla!' It had never occurred to Eigon that anyone would ever fall in love with her again. She couldn't even contemplate the thought.

'And I am sure he will carry it out as long as he feels he can.' Drusilla shook her head. 'Take no notice of me, Eigon. I am a jealous rusty old woman; no man will look at me now. You can have him if you want!'

Eigon stared at her aghast. 'You talk such nonsense. You are not rusty!' She gazed at her for a moment. 'I can see a mature, beautiful woman without a blemish on her skin, overflowing with charm and accomplishments. But,' she paused. 'We mustn't forget why we are making this journey.'

'Peter didn't swear us to celibacy!' Drusilla said it rather sharply.

'No.' Eigon sighed. 'Have no fear, Drusilla. I don't want Commios. He is a fine man and I am fond of him and I treasure his friendship but there was only ever one man for me.'

There was a pause. Drusilla bit her lip and reached across to touch the back of Eigon's hand where it gripped the wooden planking on the ship's side. 'Sorry.'

After a minute Eigon turned back to her. 'You don't think Commios would really leave us?'

They both turned to watch him as he laughed and joked with his fellow tribesman. He noticed them watching him and raised a hand.

'No,' Drusilla said at last. 'I think he will see us safe to our destination.'

'And if he doesn't? If he decides to stay in Gaul, would you stay with him?' Eigon was watching the ducks with fierce concentration.

Drusilla smiled. 'It's not going to happen. Don't worry. I shall stay with you. If you want me,' she added.

Eigon caught her hand and gave it a squeeze. 'I want you. I am so afraid. I was ten years old when I left Britannia. I barely remember it. And the more I think about it the more frightened I get. There will be no one there who remembers me. I don't even know where to go. My father moved so often. He was a general.

409

A soldier. He came from one tribe and ruled another. Perhaps neither will welcome me.'

'Where did your mother come from?'

'She was a Silurian. Her father's tribal lands were in the western mountains.' She hesitated. 'My father's first wife came from the Trinovantes, the tribe he ruled with the Catuvellauni. She died in childbirth, so I was told. Then when he led his armies westward to consolidate the opposition to Rome he met and married my mother. I suppose it is her hills I remember as home; the places I see in my dreams. But mostly I remember travelling with my father endlessly across the length and breadth of the land as he fought the Roman invasion.' She smiled. 'Your people were our worst nightmare!'

Drusilla nodded. 'I can imagine that, my dear. It must have been terrible for you. We assume the world awaits our arrival with longing for our civilisation and our rule. The gods of Ancient Rome promised their followers the whole world.' She waved at a small child who was paddling in the shallows at the edge of the river. He stared then made a rude gesture which made the women smile. 'There's another unsatisfied new Roman!' Drusilla said quietly.

Eigon laughed. 'People value their freedom more than their lives.'

'Yet your father never tried to return to Britannia?' Drusilla asked. 'I'm sorry. That is an insensitive question.'

'He dreamed of it,' Eigon said slowly. 'He talked about it a great deal when we first arrived in Rome, but his health was so bad he knew he could do nothing to help his people until he recovered. We had messages from time to time, that they still looked to him as their redeemer, but they fought on without him and slowly the messages stopped coming. I suspect the people at home thought my father was dead.' She bit her lip.

'You think they no longer fight?'

Eigon shrugged. 'I hear most of Britannia is quiet under the yoke. There was a rebellion four years ago under the queen of the Iceni, but it was quashed in the end. There are still parts of the land where they will not accept defeat, but news has been hard to come by.'

'You don't think you will be hailed as queen as your father's heir?'

Eigon looked shocked. 'I don't think so.'

'My dear, I think you must be wary. It is possible the governor might suspect your motives for return. We have assumed we can slip into the province and move around freely, and so take them Christ's message as He commanded, but I was talking to Gaius before we left without giving him any clues of course about our real plans. He was less sanguine. We must assume that we know nothing of what to expect. The governor is a man called Marcus Trebellius Maximus. He is, I gather, managing to convince the provincials that life under the Roman Empire can be good. He may not welcome us.' She smiled suddenly, her eyes shining. 'We will have to wait and see. It's very exciting! Commios likes excitement. We will have to remind him that this is an adventure! That will keep him with us.'

Eigon glanced at her with a worried frown. It cleared and she found herself smiling back. 'You are good for me, Drusilla. You are such a strong woman. And so optimistic. I feel myself wobbling. My fears, my doubts.' She paused. 'My loneliness sometimes overwhelms me in spite of my prayers.' She looked down into the water. 'I never had the chance to be with Julius, not properly.' She bit back a sob. 'Yet I miss him so much.'

Drusilla put her arm round her shoulders. 'I know.'

'I thought I would sense him near me.' Eigon shrugged. 'Our people feel things, you know? We sometimes can see those who have died. But he's not there.'

'He is with Jesus, Eigon. He is safe and at peace now.'

Eigon fought back her tears. 'I sense no peace. If I sensed anything it was anger. But now with every mile we move further away from his shade.'

Drusilla frowned. She wished Commios would join them. He would distract Eigon and cheer them both with his humour and strength but now he was engaged in an argument with one of the boat's crew, waving his arms about, pointing out across the countryside as the boat slid ever northwards. She turned back to Eigon.

'Do you still sense this man Titus trying to find you?' she asked quietly. Commios had felt it best that she know that this man might be following them and she had been impressed by the force with which Eigon had been able to convince them all that he was already on their heels. These Celts believed in a world of shadows

411

and hints and echoes which were an enigma to those who were Roman born. But there was no doubt that they knew things beyond the normal range of people's perceptions.

Eigon gave a deep sigh. 'I am afraid to open myself to the window in the darkness he has penetrated. It is a two-way road. If I can see him he can see me.'

Drusilla shuddered. 'Let us hope he is still in Rome and that he can get no leave, and no passport!'

Eigon turned as Commios joined them at last. 'So, did you win your argument?'

He raised an eyebrow. 'What argument? The man knew he was on a hiding to nothing, taking me on!'

'Should we ask what you were discussing so animatedly?' Drusilla queried.

'Not a subject for a lady!' Commios chuckled. He smiled at them both, Eigon noted, carefully even-handed. 'Now you will be glad to hear, the boat is going to tie up at the next village where there is a *mansio*, and a *taberna* which will provide food and parts for some crucial bit of the rudder which they think has been damaged. We will get some time ashore to eat and maybe even to stretch our legs a bit.'

And they would leave a lasting impression on one of the barmen. Two Roman women with one man for escort were unusual travellers on the river. Especially when the two women were good-looking and trying so hard not to be noticed.

Will threw open the double doors which led from the small sitting room of his ground floor flat and stepped out into his pocket-handkerchief garden with a feeling of enormous relief. He always loved coming home. This was his haven, his space; the place he had licked his wounds after he and Jess had split up. No, after he had split from Jess. She was right. That gentle remonstrance on the plane served him right. He thought what he had done for her in the last few days had changed things, made up for the misery he had caused her. It hadn't. Of course it hadn't. If anything her whole problem was his fault. If they had still been together he would have walked her home from the dance or they would have come back here. Dan would never have had the chance to stalk her and force his way into her flat and do what he did to her. He shivered with distaste. The bastard. The absolute fucking bastard!

The policeman listened to his story with calm attention. He wrote down names and addresses then he sighed and shook his head. 'Unless Miss Kendal chooses to pursue this I don't think there is anything we can do. And if there is no proof, she is right, we can't follow it up.'

'But you can write down his name. You can keep an eye out for him. You can watch and wait and then if he does something –' Will shook his head. 'He's dangerous. He tried to kill me in Rome. And he has threatened Jess's life. The man is deranged. There must be something you can do!'

There wasn't. With advice to get in touch if he had any further reason to worry the policeman politely drew the interview to a close. Will walked out into the street and headed towards the school.

Catherine Barker answered the door of the house which was directly opposite the school campus. She burst into smiles. The headmaster's wife was a stunningly attractive woman with flaming red hair and eyes the colour of emeralds, ten years younger than her husband. She had the slightest lisp of Ireland in her voice. 'Will! How lovely to see you. Come in. Brian is upstairs. I'll call him.'

Brian, tall, thin and wiry with a shock of white hair and a ruddy, battered complexion led the way into his first floor study and closed the door leaving Catherine standing at the bottom of the stairs frowning up at them.

'I'm sorry, Brian. I hope she doesn't mind. I felt we should keep this private for now.' As Brian didn't invite him to sit down Will moved a pile of books off a chair himself before launching into the story.

'Jess didn't want anyone to know all this. She was adamant that no one was told. There is no evidence. No proof. Her word against Dan's and Dan has spent the weeks since it happened trying to destroy her credibility and destroy her emotionally.'

'And he followed her to Rome, you say,' Brian said thoughtfully. 'Does Nat know about any of this? I've been trying to contact him and she didn't seem to know where he was.'

'I'll bet,' Will said caustically. 'I can't see him telling her anything, can you!' He paused. 'Why were you trying to contact him?'

'One of his pupils. Ash. He's in trouble with the police. Such a

413

stupid thing. A misunderstanding as far as I can see, but the boy is black and –' he shrugged – 'you know how it is. It could ruin his prospects and he has so much promise.'

'He was Jess's protégée. You should have called her.'

'I didn't know where she was. I rang her flat and the woman I spoke to told me she was the tenant and that Jess had gone away for six months. Don't forget, she has left the school.'

Will grimaced. 'She went to her sister in Wales. Dan followed her.' He paused. 'Perhaps I can do something for Ash. I taught him too.'

Brian nodded. 'I'll give you the number to ring.' He wandered over to the window and looked down into the street, his hands rammed down into his pockets. 'What a mess. What a goddam mess! I had recommended Dan for promotion to headship of his own school, you know. He has – had – a lot of potential.' He paused. 'The police aren't interested, you say?'

Will shook his head.

'I can't say I'm surprised. They'll follow up on someone like poor Ash instantly, or someone who might be a kiddy fiddler, but a man who might be a potential murderer – no chance.' He turned round, leaning on the windowsill and sighed. 'Can we tell Catherine? She'll keep it under her hat and she's pretty shrewd. She might think of something we can do.'

Will nodded. 'Of course.'

'Are you still in love with Jess, Will?'

Will laughed wryly. 'If I am, it's too late. I've lost her.'

Dan stood for a while on the pavement looking thoughtfully at Will's front door. He gave a malicious grin. It was serendipity that he had hung on to the spare key Will had given him two years before when they had been working together on a school project. Not deliberately. Will had forgotten to ask for it back and Dan thought he may as well keep it. It had lain all that time in the glove pocket of his car and when he had rummaged around for it amongst all the children's sweets and rubbish and old pens and parking tickets after he returned to the house this afternoon, it emerged sticky but, it appeared, still functional. He inserted it into the lock and pushed open the door. 'Will? You there?'

The flat was empty, Will's bag lying just inside the door. He hadn't even unpacked before rushing off somewhere. Dan looked down at it thoughtfully. Now where would Will have gone in such a hurry? He walked over to the phone and pushed redial.

The police station.

Swearing viciously he threw himself down on a chair and sat, his head in his hands, trying to think.

The Elgar discs were still in the car and Jess sat quietly by the side of the road, only a few hundred yards from her flat, listening to *Caractacus*. The music surged and flowed round her carrying her back and forth with it, depicting his beloved Malvern hills, the surge of battle, the anguish of defeat. Eigon sounded so wrong; they all sounded wrong. None of it was right, but the music was powerful. Nationalistic. Bracing. Lyrical. It finished at last and Jess closed her eyes. She was exhausted and she had nowhere to go. It was such an irony. She was only a few yards from her home; she had headed back here out of habit, too tired to face the long drive to Wales yet, forgetting all about her tenant. She should have accepted Will's invitation to go and stay with him. She picked up her phone and dialled Steph again. There was still no answer and no answer machine.

With a groan she sat back and closed her eyes. At least she had a permit to park her car round here. She could leave it parked up and go and get herself some food. She bought a takeaway from her favourite Indian: rice, a chicken Madras and a poppadum to cheer herself up. The boy behind the counter recognised her and greeted her as an old friend. That cheered her too. She bought a can of lager as well and returned to the car. It was growing dark when the light in her flat went on. Scrunching up the wrappers and foil containers she knotted them into the carrier bag, climbed out and went to stuff it into an overflowing bin on the corner of the street. Returning to the car she sat sipping her lager, staring up at the light in her sitting room window. After half an hour it went out and as the streetlights around her came on, the flat sank into darkness.

Rummaging for another CD she found a Classic FM compilation of peaceful music that Will had given her years before after a particularly stressful Ofsted which had reduced them both to a quivering mass of nerves. She smiled sadly. Dear old Will. Why did her thoughts keep going back to him? Had she made a terrible mistake turning her back on him so abruptly? She couldn't get the picture of the wistful look in his eyes as they said goodbye out of her head. Suddenly she made up her mind. She would drive over to his flat and throw herself on his mercy yet again. That would give her the chance to make sure she thanked him properly this time for all he had done, make sure he realised that she knew just how much he had risked for her. See to it that they parted as friends. Slotting the disc into place she started the car and pulled out into the traffic to the gentle sound of Debussy.

Inserting his key into the lock, Will pushed his door open and walked into the flat. He had spent the evening with the Barkers, eating a pot luck supper with them in their attractive, chaotic kitchen with two of their teenage daughters ducking in and out around them, distracting them from the dark mood which hung over them. When at last the girls went out Catherine turned to Will as she waited for the coffee to perk.

'You have to go and find her, Will. I bet she's changed her mind by now. She's probably already bitterly regretting sending you away.'

Will grinned. 'You think so?'

'I would be, in her shoes.' She smiled. He must know how attractive he was to women. 'Ring her up and grovel, Will. Tell her you will be her slave, her escort, her armed guard, whatever. Just don't leave her to face this alone.'

'I wanted to take her to Cornwall. I thought she'd be safe there with my parents.'

'Did you ask her or tell her?'

Will stared at her. Then suddenly he laughed. 'Oh God, you're right. I probably didn't ask her. It just seemed such a good idea.'

'Ring her. Now.' Catherine pointed at the door. 'Go on. In there where we can't hear you pleading.'

Will was back after only a couple of minutes. 'There's no reply.' He put his phone down on the table. Catherine glanced at her wristwatch. 'She's probably checked in somewhere for the night. Try again in the morning.'

Will frowned. If she had turned the phone off it would have gone straight to the message service. If it wasn't turned off, it would have been in her pocket or her bag and she would hear it. A worm of worry began to gnaw away inside him.

He left only half an hour later.

Pushing open his door he paused. Something felt different. The flat was in darkness. It was silent, but he could feel a presence there.

'Jess? Are you here?'

He couldn't remember if she still had a key. At least he had another reason to talk to her now, to discuss work. 'Jess, I've been talking to Brian about Ash.' He reached for the lightswitch and flicked it. Nothing happened. He clicked it up and down a couple of times in irritation and stepped forward, groping for the table lamp just inside the sitting room door. 'Jess? Is that you?'

He never saw the figure behind him. There was a slight noise from the darkness. As he spun round a hand was raised, holding something hard and heavy. It came down on his head with a thud. Will fell without making a sound.

30

Catherine waited until Brian had disappeared into the bathroom and turned on the shower then she crept downstairs into the sitting room and closed the door quietly behind her. Turning on a single table lamp she picked up the phone. The room was shadowy, cosy, almost as cluttered as her husband's study upstairs with books and newspapers everywhere, and piles of well-thumbed music stacked untidily on the ancient piano against the wall.

'Nat, how are you?' She had found the number in the over-stuffed organiser in her shoulder bag. 'How are the holidays going?' They talked for a few minutes, then Catherine went on. 'There is something I need to speak to you about, Nat. Is this a good moment? Are the kids in bed?' She slid into the deep armchair, cradling the receiver under her chin, talking softly. 'You remember you told me that you were frightened of Dan,' she said a little awkwardly. 'That he'd beaten you up a couple of times. Has that ever happened again?'

The voice the other end was suspicious and angry. Catherine paused until Nat had finished her tirade of denial then she went on patiently. 'No, listen, I haven't told anyone. I promised, didn't I? It's just I heard something this evening which has terrified me. He has attacked someone else, Nat.'

Nat was silent for several seconds. 'Who?' she whispered at last.

'I can't tell you. I've given my word. Just believe me, it was bad. Have you heard from him?'

'Not today. He's still at a conference in Italy.'

'Well, he's certainly been to Italy,' Catherine said repressively. 'I think you should be careful, love. He might be on his way back. And it sounds as if he's acting very strangely. Stay there with your parents? Keep out of his way.'

'Shit!' Nat sounded as though she was already in tears. 'If I tell Dad, he will kill him, Cath. He's never trusted Dan. Never.'

'Sounds as though he's a good judge of character,' Catherine replied ruefully. 'Look, I've got to go. Just take care, OK?' She could hear footsteps on the stairs. Guiltily she dropped the receiver back on its base. When Brian opened the door she was glancing innocently through a magazine. 'Have you finished in the bathroom?' She looked up. 'I was just trying to find an article I saw earlier. I wanted to tear it out to keep.' She threw the magazine down on the table. 'Never mind, I'll look for it tomorrow. Now my clean and shiny husband has relinquished the shower it's my turn.' She smiled at him. Climbing to her feet she went over and put her arms round his neck. 'We are so lucky, Brian, to have each other.' She kissed him tenderly on the lips. 'Some people have such an awful time.'

Brian drew her close and kissed her lovingly then he turned and led her towards the door. 'Bath and bed,' he whispered. 'Not necessarily in that order!' He knew she had been on the phone. He had heard the rattle as she dropped the receiver.

At any other time of the year it would have been impossible to find a parking space near Will's flat. By this time of the night cars would have been jammed bumper to bumper down both sides of every single residential road, leaving one lane, barely passable, down the centre for people who actually wanted to go somewhere. In the summer, thank God, lots of people went away, desperate to get away from the crush and the heat and the stress of London and it meant there were one or two rare spaces to be had. Even so it took Jess several minutes to find one a couple of streets away from the flat. Climbing out and locking the door she walked slowly through the luminous darkness along pavements lined with cherry trees, stepping round building skips, recycling bins, groups of late-night diners returning home. The air was warm and fragrant with the scents of summer, lime tree flowers somewhere nearby and strangely in this so urban environment the smell of mown grass, the fresh cool smell from one or other of London's lungs – a park or a heath or perhaps just a small garden square like her own. Turning the corner she followed the once familiar route to Will's flat and with a strange poignant surge of affection looked at the windows. They were dark. She glanced at her watch. It was barely midnight. Would he mind if she woke him? He must be as tired as she was. Taking her courage in both hands she ran up the flight of steps to the front door and rang the bell. There was no reply. For the first time she bitterly regretted throwing his keys at him when she finally accepted that their affair was over. She tried once more then with a sigh of disappointment she turned and retraced her steps to the car. Perhaps he had gone down to Cornwall after all.

Having found the parking space she stayed where she was in the darkness, huddled down into the passenger seat softly playing her CDs as the hum of traffic from the main road two streets away grew slowly less. Some time in the early hours it had almost stopped save for the occasional car or motorbike determined to waken the world. Twice she played *Caractacus*, smiling softly as Rhodri's baritone drifted round the car, the volume turned well down, only half-aware of how much the sound of his voice comforted her, then she switched to something more peaceful. As dawn broke a blackbird started its serenade to the morning from the top of a laburnum bush in the garden next to her and she stopped playing the CDs altogether. Lulled by the sound of the bird she drifted at last into an uneasy sleep.

Having reached Lugdunum Eigon, Drusilla and Commios had disembarked from the boat and were now following a straight well-made road cutting due north and east across the centre of Gaul. They had bought a mule and it cheerfully carried their possessions and whichever of the two women whose turn it was to ride. Commios laughed at them, saying he would rather walk now he had found his stride and seemed content to march at the mule's head. Each night they found a *taberna* or at the very least a *mansio* where they could stop and find food and beds of varying squalidness. Once or twice they asked for shelter at a farmhouse or villa near the road, as by law they were entitled to. Their reception varied from generous and friendly to downright rude.

Twice they were overtaken on the road by a squadron of soldiers riding fast, leaving them choking in the dust. The second time it happened Commios stopped, rubbing the mule's nose to comfort it and turned to Eigon who had been walking doggedly behind him, one hand on the mule's rump. Above them Drusilla seemed asleep in the saddle. 'You know, perhaps we should pull off when we hear them coming. Just in case. We don't know how much influence your friend Titus has, do we? Would he be able to send messengers ahead to look for us?'

Eigon stood still, her shoulders slumped. She was exhausted. 'I wouldn't put anything past him.'

'But you haven't sensed him nearby?' He looked intently into her face. He had enormous admiration, almost awe, for Eigon's mysterious insights, but for the last four days she had seemed more and more depressed and withdrawn. He reached out gently and touched her hand.

She drew away a little and shook her head. 'I haven't had the chance. Last night was awful.' She and Drusilla had paid for beds in a *mansio* but had been driven out by the filth and the fleas. The insolent barman, the only person there who seemed to be in charge, had pocketed their denarii, refused a refund and sworn at them obscenely when they complained. Commios had slept better sharing a stall with the mule. The previous nights had not been much better. The roads were more overgrown here; whoever was in charge of cutting back the undergrowth and keeping them maintained had given up the effort. Once or twice they sensed that they were being watched from the trees. The eyes spying on them did not seem friendly. The mule, normally a placid animal, had grown jumpy and spooked at the slightest sound from the woods which crowded near them from the surrounding hills. At night they could hear the howling of wolves.

'I vote we stop soon. When we find somewhere nice,' Commios said cheerfully. 'Take a few days to rest the animal. And our feet.' He glanced down ruefully at his sandals. His feet were covered in blisters and sores. 'Did anyone notice what the last milestone said? A chap in the stables last night said that Lutetia is not a bad place. Maybe we can stretch the finances a bit and find ourselves somewhere decent to stay.'

He glanced up at Drusilla. She had opened her eyes and was staring round. Even her endless cheerfulness had waned. She smiled down at them wearily. 'That sounds good to me. Have we enough money left?' Commios was in charge of the purse.

He nodded. 'If we resist the urge to buy luxuries beyond our dreams!' he said brightly. 'I calculate we still have fourteen days until we reach the coast. More if we stop. Maybe I can earn some money while we're here.'

'Earn some?' Eigon looked at him with a raised eyebrow. 'What can you do?'

He laughed. 'Ah. So, you don't rate my earning power! I'll show you when we get there.'

He was as good as his word. That evening to their delight they found a reasonable-sized township on the banks of a broad slow flowing river. They were directed to a pleasant boarding house with clean sheets and even better, clean water. While Drusilla and Eigon sat down to talk to their hostess and accepted her offer of a meal, Commios slipped away. When he returned he poured out a bag of coins onto the table with a look of triumph.

Eigon stared at him. 'How on earth did you get that?' They looked at the money, a mixture of Roman asses and sestertii, a couple of denarii and a handful of Gallic bronze and silver coins, most clipped almost out of recognition.

Their hostess smiled. 'Your fame has preceded you home, sir. Don't you know what he was doing?' She laughed at Eigon's startled face.

'Nothing bad!' he put in hastily. 'I sang for my supper.'

'Sang?' Drusilla looked at him. 'I didn't know you could sing!'

He shrugged modestly. 'I've never done it for money before. It's too much like begging.'

'But you haven't sung for us. You didn't sing for our brothers and sisters at home.' She was reproachful.

Again he shrugged. He looked abashed. 'I didn't want to push myself forward. I only knew songs of my homeland my mother taught me. No one would have liked them in Rome but I thought they might go down well once we came back to Gaul. It was worth a try.'

'It was certainly worth a try.' Eigon reached forward and put her hand over his. 'You are what my father used to call a dark horse.' She did not admit that she sang herself or that she had wondered if in the end she would resort to singing for money to tide them over.

That night when everyone was asleep Eigon crept from her bed out into the garden. Autumn had wreaked havoc with the neatly tended flowerbeds, but she could still smell the herbs above the cloying blanket of damp leaves and the scent of the sodden fields of stubble behind the town wall. Woodsmoke drifted across the garden. Staring up she could see Cassiopeia, which Melinus had called Llys Don. She tried to remember some of the other stars from her childhood. The morning star, which Peter called Christos Helios, the star of Christ, and the Romans called Venus was called by her mother Berlewen, the blessed light of the God Lugh. The sky was hazy now, slowly being veiled by a drift of smoke.

There was an old wooden seat at the end of the garden. She made her way there and sat down, pulling her cloak around her with a shiver. The winds were growing colder as they made their way north and soon the first storms of winter would make themselves felt. She sighed. She had almost lost track of the days but at supper her hostess had mentioned that the festival of Samhain was upon them. It appeared that she had been baking and making preserves for weeks. Eigon had glanced at Drusilla who was looking blank. 'It is the same time as the games of Sulla in Rome,' she explained. 'But it is a major festival to bid goodbye to the old year and welcome in the new, it is a time when the gods and the ancestors speak to us.'

'Are we allowed to celebrate it?' Drusilla had asked. She glanced at Commios. There was so much to remember about Christ's teaching. What Peter had taught them, his sermons, had been heard and reheard and absorbed and his letters read and reread, as had the letters of Paul which had been circulated amongst the Christian community and read avidly by them all, but sometimes they were left wondering. And now there was no one to ask. They were left with nothing but their prayers.

Carrying their message was a responsibility they could not forget, but they had all agreed that it would be foolish to draw attention to themselves too soon. Better to travel quietly and to travel fast. Once they reached their destination then was the time to start to tell people their exciting news.

Their hostess had watched them curiously. 'Why would you not celebrate?' she asked, astonished.

Eigon shook her head. 'Of course we are going to celebrate,' she said with a smile. 'And Commios is going to sing to us all.'

Drusilla and Commios had nodded in agreement, both relieved she had taken a lead and made the decision for them.

As she gazed up a shooting star streaked out of Taurus across the sky. She smiled at the sign. Then she bit her lip. She could no longer assume such things were messages from the gods. Her God, Jesus Christ, hadn't said anything about shooting stars, had he? Sadly she shook her head. Yet another certainty she had had to give up. She wondered yet again if she was truly the right person for this mission. She felt so under-prepared, so ignorant. 'Pray, child, if you have doubts. Pray. Ask Jesus to help you. He will tell you what to do.' Peter's voice rang in her ears.

'Our Father which art in heaven.' She paused. She was still looking up in wonder but the mist and smoke had crept back across the heavens and she could no longer see the stars. 'Am I doing the right thing? And please, tell me if Titus is still a risk to us. Dear Lord, I'm not sure if I am doing this right. Help me. Speak to me. Amen.'

She closed her eyes and waited. She shivered. The night was suddenly colder. Her happiness had gone.

And there he was behind her eyes, inside her head waiting, hunting, searching. She felt herself tense with fright. He was with the soothsayer, Marcia Maximilla, the best fortune teller in Rome. He had piled gold into her greedy hands and she was hunting the byways for her prey. Eigon could see her face, her eyes like cold flint, peering into her scrying dish. As Eigon watched she grew more tense. She looked up straight into Eigon's startled gaze and she smiled. 'So, there you are, little princess. I have been looking for you. There is someone here who needs to know where you are. You have unfinished business together, I hear.' Her eyes were bright with malice.

Eigon couldn't move. She was pinned to the spot with horror and fear. 'Do you want me to tell him?' The icy gaze hardened. 'You are so afraid, little princess. Why? Doesn't your Jesus protect you any more? Do his arms not stretch as far as Gaul?'

'How do you know where I am?' Eigon whispered soundlessly.

The thin mouth stretched into something like a smile. 'I know everything. My sight is infinite. I see the limitless distances.'

'And you sell your talent for gold?' As so often happened Eigon's fear was evaporating as her anger built. 'To men like Titus Marcus Olivinus! Do you have no pride, Marcia Maximilla?'

Surprise flared in the eyes. 'You know who I am?'

'Of course.'

'You see the back ways of time yourself.'

Eigon smiled. 'When I choose.'

'And your God allows this? Have you been initiated as a priestess of his cult?'

Eigon paused. Perspiration was standing out on her brow as

she struggled to hold the link. The cool breeze stroked her face and she felt a gentle sense of peace envelop her. 'If you mean, have I been baptised, yes, I have,' she said quietly. 'And you are right, I have no reason to be afraid. Titus cannot touch me now.'

Marcia smiled. 'He can if I tell him where you are.'

'You haven't told him?' Eigon was surprised. She didn't allow herself to feel any relief. She guessed the woman would sell her if she chose, and enjoy doing it. 'You should be careful. If he finds out you have withheld information he will be angry.'

'I too can be angry.'

Eigon raised an eyebrow. 'So, lady, is he there with you now?'

Marcia's eyes narrowed. 'He is here.'

'And he can see nothing?'

'Nothing! The fool sits and pants in the corner like a dog, slavering over a promised bone.'

Eigon grimaced. She was the bone. 'Sweet Jesus, blessed Lord, protect me. Veil my presence from them. Keep me safe to do Thy work. And keep Drusilla and Commios safe too. Do not let them suffer for being my friends, I beg you.' As she murmured the prayer she saw Marcia's face grow hazy. Smoke from the bonfire was drifting over her, swirling round the bench.

'Wait –' She saw Marcia's hand, clawed, grabbing at the air, dissolving, trying to hold the image, then she was gone. Eigon was left with a sense of peace and safety and warmth which had nothing to do with the increasing cold of the night.

'Thank you,' she murmured into the darkness.

A loud knocking on the window woke Jess abruptly. She stared round, her heart thudding with fright. She was in the car and a traffic warden was bending down to stare at her. 'Oh shit!' She pushed herself up in the seat and wound down the window.

The woman studied her suspiciously. 'How long you been here? You been drinking?'

'No!' Jess tried desperately to gather her woolly thoughts together. One moment she had been in a dark garden two thousand years ago with Eigon and suddenly she was confronting a furious black face swathed in spite of the heat in an authoritative grey jacket and cap. 'I'm sorry. I was waiting for someone. I must have dozed off. What time is it?'

'It's nearly nine and this is a residential parking area.' The woman started pressing buttons on her electronic pad.

'Oh please, no.' Jess felt an overwhelming urge to cry. 'Look, I'll go. I wasn't parked. I was still with the car. I haven't left it.'

'I been watching you. You been here a long time.' The woman stood back from the window, presumably content she couldn't smell drink on Jess's breath. She walked round to the front of the car, punching in the registration number.

'Shit, shit, shit!' Jess muttered under her breath. This was all she needed.

'You said something?' The woman was back. Her face was smooth and shiny and full of aggression under her peaked hat as she put the ticket in a polythene bag and tucked it under Jess's windscreen wiper.

Jess shook her head. 'Not a word,' she sighed. Meekly she waited until the woman had gone, opened the door, reached for the parking ticket, then climbed back in and started the engine. She had been planning to walk back and try Will's house again but she changed her mind abruptly. If she left the car now the warden would be bound to return. No, it was time to get out of London and go back to Wales.

She stopped twice, once for a breakfast of black coffee and a toasted teacake at the Reading Services on the M4 and then again in Abergavenny where she found a coffee shop for lunch. Before she went in she had rummaged in her bag for her mobile and her credit cards and paid the fine. It was her way of washing her hands of London and the traffic warden, and of Dan too. Even if he ended up back at Ty Bran, here at this moment she was safe from him. He had no idea where she was.

It was late afternoon when she pulled at last in through the gate and parked next to Steph's old four-wheel-drive. She sat still for several seconds listening to the sounds of the car engine cooling down, staring at the house as it dozed in the sunlight. The front door was open, a robin was singing sadly and sweetly from the lilac bush near the studio and a clump of meadowsweet was blossoming in a patch of long damp grass near the door. Behind her on the wall she could see valerian and hedge parsley hanging from cracks amongst the moss.

Pushing open the door at last she climbed out stiffly. 'Steph? Are you around?'

There was no reply. She went over to the door and peered inside. There were the remains of a meal on the table which had been set for two. She stood looking down at the half-eaten salad, the crumbled bread rolls, the half-drunk glasses of wine and frowned. It looked as though Steph and whoever she was with had got up suddenly in the middle of eating and abandoned the meal. 'Steph? Where are you?'

She wandered through to the dining room. The French doors were open, the pane of glass mended, she noted. She stepped out onto the lawn. The grass was far too long, the garden unkempt. There was still no sign of anyone. 'Steph?' Suddenly she was feeling nervous. She walked back inside and through to the kitchen, staring round. She felt the kettle. Cold. Turning she went back into the hall and ran upstairs two at a time. Steph's room was a mess, but her usual mess and the bed was made, more or less. She looked into the room that had been her own. It was as she had left it and her own case had been put there just inside the door. The third bedroom was now occupied. She recognised the clothes, the cases, the tote bag. Her mother was here. She went over to the dressing table and looked at the array of combs and brushes, the aromatherapy oils, the organic face cream and she smiled. If Aurelia was here everything was going to be all right.

Running downstairs again she went out to her car and began to unload her stuff, carting it all back to her former bedroom. When she had finished she glanced at her watch. They had been out for a long time and it still seemed strange that they had left the house in the middle of a meal. Refusing to allow herself to think about Dan she walked over to the phone and dialled Cwm-nant. Megan answered.

'Hi Megan, are Steph and my mother there, by any chance?' She turned to look out of the window as she spoke.

'Jess? Is that you?' Megan sounded delighted to hear her voice. 'No. They're not here. Is Aurelia staying? That's great. I do enjoy it when she comes. But no, I haven't heard from them since Steph and Rhodri got back. Hold on, dear, Rhodri just came in.' Jess heard a muttered exchange of conversation then Rhodri came on the line. 'Jess? How are you? When did you get back?' His voice was full of warmth. 'Is everything OK? Is Will with you?'

'Hi, Rhodri. No, he stayed in London!' She found she was smiling as she explained the reason for her call. It was so good to hear his voice again.

'No sign of them here, Jess. There hasn't been a word from Steph since we got back.' He chuckled. 'Not best mates, Steph and me.'

Jess bit back a gurgle of laughter. 'Oh Rhodri, I'm so sorry. Was she a pain?'

'She was.' He didn't sound too worried about it. 'Our leisurely drift through rural France turned into a breakneck race for the coast before I was minded to strangle her.'

'Oh dear.' She grimaced. 'Look, Rhodri, I'm a bit worried. They seem to have got up and gone out in the middle of lunch leaving everything open. Wine half drunk, that sort of thing. It's like the Marie Celeste.'

He refrained from making a remark about Steph's wine-drinking habits. 'You don't think Dan has turned up?' His voice had sharpened suddenly.

Her heart sank. 'Oh God, Rhodri, I hope not.' She turned to stare out of the window. 'There's no other car here. I was so sure he would still be in Italy. Wishful thinking, I suppose.'

'Could he have hidden it up the track?'

She sighed. 'I don't know. I suppose I'd better go and look.'

'No. Jess, don't go up there on your own. Look, hang on. I'll come straight over.'

He didn't give her a chance to reply. The phone was hung up.

Opening the door into the studio she stood looking round. It was neat and tidy; it didn't look as though Steph had done any work since she had come home. The kiln was cold. A butterfly was fluttering against the window near her work bench. Jess walked in and pulled the window open. Gently she shepherded the butterfly out and stood watching it soar up towards the sun.

Are we still playing the game?

A child's voice sounded close to her in the room. Her blood froze. She turned round slowly. 'Eigon? Glads?'

I don't want to play any more. I'm cold.

The voice was tetchy. She could hear the fear behind the indignation.

'Where are you, sweetheart?' she called after a moment.

Eigon's gone. I can't find her! Suddenly there were tears in the child's voice.

Jess caught her breath. 'Glads? Is that you?'

I don't want to play any more! I don't like this game!

Jess swallowed her fear. These were young children. Abandoned. Alone. There was nothing to fear from them. She was astonished at the wave of maternal love that swept over her. 'Listen, little ones. Eigon has gone away. But she's coming back.'

That was a stupid thing to say. She didn't know that. She didn't know anything. She didn't even know what millennium she was in. With a groan she headed out of the door. 'Steph? Mummy?' Suddenly she was calling too, overwhelmed with loneliness and fear.

Rhodri arrived some half an hour later, pulling up in a flurry of dust. 'Any sign of them?'

She was sitting on the wall, waiting for him in the sunshine. She shook her head. 'I didn't go up the track to the wood. I thought I'd wait for you.' She was very conscious of the relief and happiness that flooded through her as she saw him. His solid frame, dressed in an old check shirt and distinctly moth-eaten cords was immensely reassuring as was his smile as he looked down at her. He bent and kissed her on the cheek. 'Glad you made it back safely.'

'Me too.' She moved away from the wall. 'You don't really think Dan turned up here do you?'

He shook his head. 'Steph would have shrivelled him with a glance. And your mum is a formidable woman. If she can quell a tribe of nomads in Uzbekistan with a toss of the head she is not going to be scared of our Mr Nasty.'

Jess smiled. 'I'm so glad you're here.'

'So am I, girl.' He looked down at her for just a second longer than necessary and she felt a quick throb of excitement deep in the pit of her stomach.

The moment was gone in a flash. 'Come on.' He was heading for the gate. 'Let's go and have a quick look up in the wood before we do anything else.'

There were no signs of fresh car tracks leading up the lane. They reached the gate into the wood, puffing slightly after the climb and walked in under the trees. It was very still in the shade. The birds were silent and there wasn't a breath of wind. The only sound was the humming of a bee in a clump of honeysuckle near the holly brake.

Rhodri bent, examining the path. 'Can you see any footprints?'

Jess smiled. 'Were you a boy scout when you were young?'

He shook his head. 'But I was always on the side of the Indians in cowboy and Indian films on the telly. I loved the way they could track anyone anywhere. Look.' He was pointing at a mark in the soft earth at the side of the path. 'Someone has been here recently. Someone with quite small feet, not wearing proper boots.'

Jess laughed out loud. 'That could be my mum. Which way was she going?'

'Up the track, I think. Come on.' He walked ahead of her and stopped again a few paces on. 'Yes, look. Two different sets of prints walking side by side and here –' he paused, frowning. 'Suddenly they are deeper, less well defined. They are running together side by side. Here, where it is still muddy, someone slipped.'

Jess followed him, her mouth dry. 'Why are they running?'

'Well, they are not being followed by anyone. Otherwise there would be prints on top of theirs, wouldn't there.' He stopped, looking round, his hand raised for silence, listening intently. 'I should have brought the dogs. Shall we risk shouting?'

Biting her lip, she nodded and jumped, her hands over her ears, as he let fly. The voice of a top notch Welsh baritone is designed to carry. The echoes rang for several seconds. All around birds flew up squawking with fright. Pheasants from the undergrowth, pigeons from the treetops, a lone raven croaking its dismay as it launched itself from an oak tree deep in the centre of the wood. Two jays crashed screaming out of the old mother ash which overhung the stream far below. As the noise of the birds died away they listened again, turning round slowly.

'Nothing?' Jess shrugged.

Rhodri shook his head. He looked down at the path again. 'There is still the odd footprint. We'll see where it leads.' He set off ahead of her uphill now, steeply climbing towards the summit where someone a hundred years or so ago had planted a clump of redwoods. They were clustered round an ancient earthwork, standing up above the surrounding wild woodland like a group of sentinels.

Rhodri slowed down as they approached. 'There is someone there, look.'

Jess stared through the undergrowth. He was right. A figure

was standing up there in the distance with its back to them peering down at the foot of the old stones which crowned the hill. 'It's my mother!' Jess said suddenly.

'Thank God!' Rhodri raised a thumb. 'Come on, girl. What are you waiting for?' They set off up the last bit of track, and as they approached he shouted again.

Aurelia swung round. Her hair had grown longer and if anything more wild than when Jess had last seen her; her skin more tanned. She was dressed in a gypsy skirt and a silver-blue shirt, the sleeves rolled up to her elbows, the buttons at the neck unfastened to reveal a necklace of crystal and lapis beads. She raised her hand and waved. As they drew close her face broke into a smile. 'Jess, darling! Rhodri! What on earth are you doing up here?' She didn't give them a chance to respond. She hugged Jess briefly then she grabbed her hand. 'Look. In there. Steph has crawled inside. We could hear someone calling. We thought a child had got trapped in there.'

Rhodri and Jess exchanged glances. Rhodri squatted down. 'Are you all right, Steph?' he shouted. 'Have you got a torch?'

There was a scrabbling sound and Steph's face emerged from deep inside the stones. She crawled out, covered in mud and climbed to her feet. It was only then they realised that her face was white and she was shaking. She didn't even acknowledge Jess's arrival. 'There's a skeleton in there. A child.' She bit her lip. 'It's curled up against the stones. It must have been buried and a fox or something has dug it up. The bones have been scattered.' Her voice wavered. It was as though she hadn't seen Rhodri or Jess. 'Oh God, it's awful. They are so small!'

'Are you sure they're human?' Rhodri said gently.

'Of course I'm sure!' she flashed back at him. 'What kind of stupid question is that. It's a child!' Tears had streaked the mud on her face.

'How on earth did you find them?' Jess asked at last. 'What were you doing up here?'

Aurelia had stepped forward to wipe Steph's face with the handkerchief she had dug out of her pocket. 'We heard the child calling,' she said. 'On and on. It was heart-rending. It was obviously lost. Steph thought it was your ghost, but we couldn't be sure. Of course we couldn't be sure! We both heard it and . . .' She paused, shaking her head. 'We abandoned our lunch and came out to find her. We followed the sound up the track. We kept calling back, saying we were coming. Then up here at the top it stopped. Suddenly. Completely. Steph thought she was hiding in there.' She pointed at the stones. 'We kept saying we were here and that we would look after her. But she had stopped crying.' For the first time her voice wavered. 'There was this terrible silence.'

'Did she ask if she could stop playing?' Jess asked huskily after a moment.

Steph nodded. Aurelia looked from one of her daughters to the other. 'Is this your ghost? Eigon?'

'It's not Eigon,' Jess said. 'I think it is her little sister – or her baby brother. They were lost when she was captured.'

'Oh God!' Aurelia looked distraught. She glanced back at the rocks. 'You mean she – or he – crawled in there and died? Oh, that's too awful to think about.'

'They searched the hills for days but they never found them,' Jess whispered. 'In the end they gave up and they took Eigon and her mother away. Their mother and father died in Rome.'

'And Eigon?' Aurelia looked at her younger daughter. Both women were white-faced.

'I don't know. I don't know what happened to Eigon in the end.'

'What are we going to do about this?' Rhodri asked after another silence. 'We can't leave the little one here.'

'We can't tell anyone either,' Jess put in hastily. 'You know what would happen. The police would come. They would want to make sure it wasn't a modern child. They would take the bones away. The papers would get hold of the story. People would be everywhere in our woods. If the bones are ancient they would give them to a museum or something and they would stick them in a glass case and label them "Iron Age child" or "Romano-British child" and I will not allow that to happen!' Her eyes were full of tears. 'It would be a travesty! We can't tell anyone. We have to let her rest in peace.'

'But she's not at peace, Jess,' her mother put in gently.

'No, but she knows we know where she is now.' Jess dashed the tears out of her eyes. 'I'm going in to see her.'

'Are you sure?' Steph shook her head. 'It's awful.'

'I'm sure.' Jess nodded. She walked away from the rocks for a moment and bent to pick some foxgloves that were growing in

432

the dappled shade beneath one of the tall redwoods. Turning, she glanced at Rhodri. He nodded encouragingly and crouching down after a moment's hesitation, she inched her way into the darkness.

'Can she see in there?' Rhodri asked quietly. 'You haven't got a torch.'

Steph nodded. 'It's hard, but the sunlight seeps through between the stones.' She sniffed, rubbing her face with her hands. 'The bones have been disturbed. They've been scattered around. Something's dug them up.' Her voice broke into a sob.

Aurelia put her arm round Steph's shoulders. 'I hope to God this is an archaeological find,' she said dryly. 'If it is a modern burial then we are in trouble.'

'We have to be sure before we make any decisions about what to do,' Rhodri said after another long pause. They were all watching the darkness of the crack between the stones where Jess had disappeared. 'I wonder if Jim Macrae would be up for confirming if they are old or not.'

'Dr Macrae?' Steph looked at him in horror. 'You can't tell him. He would have to tell the police. I am sure he has to report dead people, however old they are. I seem to remember someone telling me you have to get a doctor to certify that someone is dead even if they are a skeleton! Then don't you have to get a coroner involved and everything? Jess would skitz! No.' She shook her head. 'Let's think about this very carefully. We were led here. That child called us.'

Rhodri had wandered over to the rocks. He crouched down and peered in. 'Are you all right?' he called softly.

Inside, Jess was sitting on the ground beside the pathetic little heap of bones. She had laid the flowers next to them and put her hand for a moment gently over the scattered joints of the tiny fingers. 'I am so sorry no one came,' she whispered. 'Eigon tried. She tried so hard to find you. They all did. Did you crawl in here to keep safe? Oh my darling, I am so sorry.' Tears were running down her face. 'Your mother never recovered from losing you. She missed you so much. Did she find you in Tir n'an Og? That's what she wanted.' She closed her eyes. 'However faraway she was, she never stopped loving you.'

Which child was it? She wished she knew. The bones were so small. Gently she picked one up. It was light as a feather, brittle as a twig. She put it back reverently. She kissed her finger and laid it for a second on the forehead of the small skull then she turned and crawled out into the sunshine.

The others looked at her in silence and for a moment no one moved, then Rhodri stepped forward and put his arms round her. 'Are you OK?'

Burying her face in his chest she nodded. For a moment she clung to him, aware of his strength and the nice male smell of his shirt. She realised with a small jolt of surprise that she wanted to stay like that, savouring the feel of him, the safety of his arms, but she forced herself to move away with an apologetic grin.

'Sorry. Don't know what came over me.' She took a deep breath, trying to steady her voice. 'I don't think there is any doubt but that they are old bones. They are so light and friable. They are certainly not modern.'

'What do you think we should do?' Steph asked shakily.

Jess stood for a moment in silence. She was a picture of dejection, her arms hanging helplessly at her sides, her face miserable and exhausted. 'Can we leave her there for now?' she said at last. 'If we tell someone they will move her.'

'That's what we thought.' Rhodri glanced at Steph. 'You are right. She shouldn't be in a museum. I think that would be so wrong.'

'Maybe you could ask your friend, Eigon?' Steph added quietly. 'Does she talk to you like that? Will she know what's happened?'

Jess shrugged. 'I can try.'

'Let's go back to the house,' Aurelia said at last. 'This little one has lain here so long another night is not going to make a difference. If her soul is wandering the woods here she knows now that we have found her and that you took her in some flowers, Jess. Tomorrow we will decide what to do.'

Jess woke suddenly from a strange dream. She stared round the room in the dark. The four of them had spent the rest of the day together; they had had supper in the kitchen and then at nearly midnight Rhodri had at last driven back to Cwm-nant. The only thing they agreed about was that the bones should not languish in a museum. When Jess went to bed she had lain still, talking gently to Eigon in the darkness. There was no reply.

When at last she slept she dreamed about Will. He was calling her again and again, standing behind the door of his house. 'Jess, the traffic warden's gone. You can come in now.' When she woke it was to a feeling of utter panic. Creeping downstairs so as not to wake the others she went into the kitchen and poured herself a glass of water. Standing at the window she stared out into the moonlit garden. A wind had arisen and the branches of the trees were dancing, casting moonshadows across the courtyard and up the walls of the studio. 'Togo? Glads?' she whispered. 'Are you there?'

There was no reply.

When at last she went back to bed she fell asleep at once.

31

So Eigon's Isle of the Blest was a real place after all.

Julius lay staring up at the ceiling above him in sleepy wonder. He could see trees and children and wild animals and mythical beasts frolicking and entwining around each other up there. Now and then a flaxen-haired child came and bathed his head with muslin cloths soaked in something that was cold and soothing and smelled of exotic herbs. He dozed and woke again. The scene was the same but instead of sunlight above his head there were shadows and he could hear the wind blowing through the cracks in the door. Time had passed, he knew that, but how long? The effort of thinking was too much. He tried to move and winced with pain. His shoulder was on fire and something stabbed at his gut as though it had been pierced with a bodkin.

He frowned. He had been wounded. He vaguely remembered the fight. Figures pouring out of the darkness. Screams. The clash of iron. The awful gurgling of someone dying at his feet from a throat sliced through. He shuddered and again the wave of pain cut through him. 'In the name of Jesus Christ –' It had been Marcellus. He had risen from the fire to greet him with a smile and a hug and his blessing had been drowned in a froth of blood. Julius groaned. Immediately a light appeared. The shadows raced up across the ceiling making the animals writhe more terribly and a figure appeared at his side. 'Are you awake, my son?' An old man peered down at him. Not his grandfather. A stranger. The stranger laid a gentle hand on his forehead and nodded. 'I think I see improvement at last.'

Julius tried to smile. His lips were cracked and sore. His voice husky. The effort was too much for him. His eyes closed and everything went black.

When he next woke it was daylight again. He frowned, staring round the room. Compared to the ceiling the walls were relatively plain, painted with columns and arcades with the occasional tree for relief. Somewhere he could hear something scratching. A pen racing across parchment. Licking his lips experimentally he tried to call out. The result was no more than a croak but it had the desired effect. The scratching stopped and he heard a stool being pushed back. The old man appeared in his field of vision. 'Awake? Good.' He smiled. 'Now, don't try and talk this time until I have managed to get some medicine down you!' Whatever else was in the medicine there was poppy juice to make him sleep away the pain. He felt himself sliding once more into blackness. It was a warm, safe place to be. In wakefulness there was too much anguish to bear.

Jess woke to the sound of rain beating down on the roof of the studio outside her window. She lay still trying to gather her scattered dreams. Had she seen Eigon? No, it was Julius. Julius who had somehow escaped the slaughter at the farm and who didn't know that his sister and his grandfather were dead, or that the woman he loved had in despair left Rome to go back to the country of her birth. And Will. Why had she dreamed about Will? She would ring him in the morning. She glanced at her watch. It was just after five. Too early to get up. Too early to think about the day to come and the decision that had to be made about the bones of the child.

She turned over restlessly, pulling the sheet over her head. Rhodri thought they ought to bury them somewhere nearby. Not in the churchyard, the child was a pagan, but somewhere special. Somewhere sacred. 'There are loads of special places on the farm,' he had said as he left. 'They are two a penny in Wales. The whole country is sacred!'

They had said goodbye outside the front door and he had stooped and kissed her quickly on the cheek. With a wink he had turned away. 'Don't worry, lovely, we'll find somewhere for her.'

Snuggling down on her pillow she smiled, wrapping her arms around herself, thinking about his handsome face, his strong muscular body. Steph couldn't stand him, but Jess was finding him more and more attractive. And he was a comfort. With him there she felt so much less afraid. With him in the next valley, if Dan turned up again, she could cope.

Sleep had deserted her. Climbing to her feet with a groan Jess wrapped herself in her bathrobe and went downstairs. Her glass from the night before still stood on the draining board where she had left it. She ignored it, going instead to the kettle. She was sitting sipping the tea at the kitchen table, listening to a thrush tuning up outside the door when she heard the little voice in the distance.

Can we stop playing now? I want to go home.

Dan had been driving all night, hurtling up the M40, stopping at a service station to grab a couple of hours' sleep in the car park and yet more coffee. It was just after eight when, almost too tired to function properly, he turned into the gate of Natalie's parents' house in the outskirts of Shrewsbury.

'Daddy!' Georgie must have seen him from the window. The front door opened and a small figure hurled herself out to greet him. He caught her in his arms and swung her off her feet.

'Hello, my darling! How are you? Where is Jack? And Mum? And Granny?' Carrying her, he made his way into the house. His mother-in-law was standing in the hall. 'Hello, Belle. Good to see you!'

She was a tall graceful woman in her sixties with overly-darkened hair, too strong a colour for her complexion which made her look hard, an expression which he knew hardened even more in his presence. Belle Foxley did not like her son-in-law and went to very few lengths to hide the fact. He bent and grazed her cheek with his own. 'There are some Italian goodies in the car for everyone. Where is Nat?'

Belle looked at him quizzically. 'She is upstairs with Jack. He had a bad night. Get down, Georgie. Go and tell Mummy that your father is here.'

As the child scampered up the stairs she walked ahead of Dan into the kitchen where her husband, Stephen, was sitting behind the *Daily Telegraph*. He glanced round the side of the paper. 'Dan.' That was the sole greeting he warranted as the older man went back to the cricket reports. His father-in-law intimidated him even more than Belle. The tall patrician figure, the upper-class, cut-glass vowels which made him feel like an upstart from the gutter immediately antagonised him as always.

He walked over to the teapot and shook it experimentally, helped himself to a cup and saucer from the cupboard above the worktop and poured himself a cup without asking. After all, no one had offered and to him that seemed the greater insult. 'I've been driving most of the night.'

'Why didn't you wait till morning?' Belle said, eyebrow raised.

'I wanted to see you all. I've missed you.' Dan tried a smile. He didn't like the way she surveyed his face, the long cool stare as always cutting him down to size. Had Nat ever told her what went on, he wondered, in the privacy of their bedroom? He felt himself break out into a cold sweat at the thought of just how much he had to hide. And how much he had to lose. And how much worse he had made things in the last twenty-four hours.

The landslide arrival of young Jack relieved the silence. 'Daddy! We went to see a cow yesterday. It leaked lots and lots of milk into a bucket!' The little boy with his long wild golden curls clambered onto his knee and threw his arms around Dan's neck. 'I drank some and it was warm and disgusting!'

Dan smiled. 'So where was this?' He glanced over his son's head towards Belle.

She shrugged. 'Natalie took them out to some farm open day. They came back with lots of things, didn't you, Jack. Cheese and eggs.' She wasn't actually looking at the child. She was still studying her son-in-law. He grew more uncomfortable as Jack tried to wriggle down off his knee.

'Why not stay with Daddy for a minute.' He clung to the little boy. 'I've missed you both.'

'Hello, Dan.' Nat appeared in the doorway behind him. Her ethereal beauty was worn now, her face beginning to show the strain of marriage and children and exhaustion. Her face was white. She didn't come forward to kiss him.

'Hi, darling.' He smiled at her. 'How are you? It's so good to see you all.'

'Really?' Her expression was cold, her eyes shuttered.

He licked his lips nervously, holding on tightly to Jack who was beginning to wriggle in protest.

'Give him to me!' Nat moved towards him suddenly. She held out her arms to Jack who reached up to cling to her. 'Why didn't you go back to London, Dan, to wait for us there? I am sure you have a lot to do with preparing for the new term. You need to get in touch with the headmaster, too. And the police.' There was an infinitesimal pause. 'Why are the police looking for you, Dan?' She pushed her long shiny hair back from her face impatiently.

Stephen lowered the paper slowly and began to fold it with quiet precision. All eyes were fixed on Dan as even the children seemed to be waiting for him to speak. For a moment he panicked. 'I've no idea. None at all.' His palms were sweating. 'It must be about something at school. One or other of the kids is always getting into trouble.' He glanced from one to the other with a look of astonished innocence. 'Don't tell me you thought it was me that had done something?' He managed a laugh.

Stephen stood up, his lips pursed. 'That would never occur to us, Daniel. I'm afraid I have to go out. I am sure that Natalie will be very sad that you have to go straight back to London to deal with this problem, whatever it is, but I assure you, we can take care of her and our grandchildren for the rest of the summer.'

Dan watched his father-in-law walk out, his face set in a mask of dislike. Glancing at Belle, he realised with a start that his expression had probably betrayed him. He forced himself to smile. 'Perhaps you could look after the children, Belle, for a little while, and give Nat and me a chance to catch up before I go back.' He had no intention of going back, but it would be Natalie who was going to change their minds and beg him to stay. 'Darling, why don't we go upstairs so we can talk on our own for a bit?'

Her face was still white. 'I'd prefer us to talk in the garden, Dan,' she said quietly. 'Come and look at Mummy's plants. They are so beautiful.' She walked ahead of him out of the kitchen door.

The second they were out of sight of the window he grabbed her wrist. She gasped with pain as he pulled her towards him, his fingers like a vice round her slender bones. 'What the hell has been going on?'

'Nothing.' She looked guilty. 'I just think it would be boring for you here and I am sure they need you in London.'

'They don't need me. My family needs me. I arrive back, having slogged through the night to get here as soon as possible imagining in my naïveté that they will be pleased to see me and I am more or less instructed by your father to go back to London!'

She flushed uncomfortably, hopelessly trying to wriggle her wrist free of his grasp. 'Dan, Daddy just thought you would have to go back and call the school –'

'No, he didn't. He can't stand the sight of me and he wanted

440

to tell me to get the hell out from under his roof. Well, I am going to disappoint him. I am staying. And I am staying in the same room as my wife, and if the children are still in the room with you, you will ask your mother to put them somewhere else so we can have some privacy. Do you understand?' He pushed his face close to hers.

Two specks of colour appeared on her cheekbones. 'Stop bullying me, Dan.' She finally managed to wrench her wrist free. 'I am not a slave or a chattel for you to order about –'

Dan stared at her. A slave. Titus had used slaves for whatever he wanted. Whenever he wanted. Where was Titus? He stared at his wife blankly, suddenly distracted by the thought, then he smiled. The vision of his oh so posh, well bred wife in chains was thoroughly appealing.

She saw the expression and for a moment panic showed in her face, replaced at once by steely reserve. 'Get out, Dan,' she hissed at him. 'Go back to London. I am not going to do as I'm told like some scared child. I am the mother of your children and an independent woman and I have no desire at the moment to see you ever again. I may change my mind, I don't know, but for now I would like some peace this summer.'

He grabbed at her again. 'What are you talking about? Have you been speaking to Jess?' His eyes were blazing.

She looked genuinely astonished for a moment, then she sighed. 'So, it is Jess. I did wonder who. I can't say I'm surprised. You've always fancied her, haven't you?' She shook her head. 'Poor Jess. Did you hurt her badly?'

'What?' He was suddenly incandescent with rage. 'I haven't hurt her at all! I don't know what you're talking about!'

The look she gave him was one of utter pity as she turned away and walked back into the house. He stood where he was for a moment without moving, then he threw himself towards the side gate. In seconds he was back in his car and reversing out of the drive. With a scream of tyres he had turned the car and was heading back the way he had come. It wouldn't take him long to reach Ty Bran and if that was where she had gone he would find her and make her sorry she had spoken to Nat. He would make her sorry she had ever been born.

* * *

Togo? Togo? Where are you? Don't leave me alone!

Jess was standing at the open window of her bedroom looking out across the yard.

She bit her lip. 'Was it Togo in the tomb, sweetheart?' she whispered. 'Did you go and look for your sister, then when you went back you couldn't find him either?' Her eyes filled with tears.

Togo! Togo!

The voice was drawing away now, up the track.

'So, what happened to you, my darling?' Jess called in a husky whisper. Turning away from the window she opened her door silently. The others were up now. She could hear their voices from the kitchen. Steph giggling, then her mother's deep throaty chuckle. She couldn't face them. She needed to be by herself. It was all too much. Those tiny bones, the thought of the child, creeping away, lost, frightened, exhausted, all alone in the woods where he could have heard the lonely howl of a wolf and the croak of a raven or the wild cry of an eagle scanning the ground below for prey, hiding, even perhaps hearing the calls of the people looking for him, but too frightened to come out because his big sisters had told him to hide.

Walking softly down the stairs she went out of the front door and across the yard. She could see them in the kitchen through the window. Steph was doing something at the cooker while Aurelia was laying the table.

Staring ahead at the cool sweet-smelling shadows under the woodland canopy she let herself out of the gate and slowly she began to walk back up the track and into the trees.

Something was pressing her neck, just below the ear. For a moment Eigon lay staring up into the darkness, wondering what had awakened her, then she heard a whisper. 'Ssh! Listen.' It was Commios. He was kneeling beside her bed, his hand on the pillow next to her head. He had used the old soldiers' trick to wake her gently and completely without a sound. 'Titus is in the village. He has been asking about us at the *mansio*. Three Roman travellers. We were easy to spot. We have to make a run for it.'

'Drusilla?' Eigon sat up, her heart thudding with fear.

'She's awake. She's packing our stuff. There must be no trace that we were ever here. We can't go near the river. They have the boat stations covered and there are men on the road at both ends of the village. We have to go now, over the back wall into the woods and pray they don't think of using dogs till we can cross water and break the trail.' He had pulled off her bed covers. 'Dress quickly. Wrap yourself in your cloak. We'll be waiting by the kitchen door. And don't light the lamp!'

'What about Felix?' she whispered as they crept across the garden only minutes later. They had all grown very fond of their patient plodding mule.

'Our hostess can keep him. She will make good use of him. We carry our own bundles from here on.' He had explained to the woman that it would be best for her as much as for them if she forgot that her guests had ever been there, and she had accepted the mule in payment for their stay. He was pretty sure she would not betray them.

He had spied out an easy place to climb the wall and one by one he helped hoist Eigon and Drusilla into the pear tree which had been trained across the stones and helped them scramble and slither over into the nettles on the far side. He tossed their bags after them, quickly and carefully tidied away any traces of their passing from the leaves and moss, scattered fresh leaves over the scene and vaulted over himself. Faraway at the western end of the village they heard a burst of sudden shouting. Flames flared up into the night.

'They are searching every house,' Commios muttered. 'I'm sorry for the families that resist. Come on. We can't spare time for prayer. That can come later! Luckily when I sang for my supper I left in the other direction and doubled back in the dark. No one knows we were staying here.'

He plunged ahead of them, sure footed, somehow sensing where the tracks led between the trees. There had been no time for consultation; no thought of which way they were going as long as it was as faraway from the village as possible.

On they went into the depths of the forest. There was no sound of pursuit, no flare of fire in the sky, nothing save the sudden alarm note of a bird as they put it up and the scattered panic of a herd of deer sleeping by a deep hidden pool. It was a long time before Commios allowed them to stop. The two women could hear nothing above their own laboured breathing, but Commios seemed to be alert to the sounds of the forest in a way that escaped them. He held up his hand and they both held their breath, straining their ears.

'Can you hear it?' he asked at last. He spoke in a normal voice which was somehow shocking in the silence of the trees. 'Water. There is a stream near here, running in spate.' Eigon realised suddenly she could see his face; the gleam of his teeth as he smiled. Without her noticing it was gradually growing light. 'We'll cross the water, perhaps wade in it a bit, so our trail is broken, though I've heard no dogs behind us.' Already he was on his way again. The two women glanced at each other in mutual sympathy, picked up their bundles and struggled on in his wake.

It was full daylight when at last he allowed them to stop. They had crossed the stream, and then another, changing the course of their flight, doubling back and forth into ever deeper forest until at last they came to a line of low cliffs, perforated with shallow caves. Into one of these they crept, so exhausted they could barely move. Within seconds the two women were asleep. Commios sat for a while in the mouth of the cave, staring down the gorge below them, alert for the slightest sign which would betray anyone amongst the trees. He was fairly sure they had given their pursuers the slip, but one could never be sure. 'Dear Lord Jesus,' he murmured. 'Be with us here. Keep us safe so we can do your work. Guide us to our destination and hide us with the veils of your mist.' He glanced at Eigon, leaning back against the wall, her eyes closed, her face lost in the darkness, her hair loose beneath the hood of her cloak slipping in gentle coils across her breast. He gave a fond sigh. His gaze did not stray to Drusilla who had moved further in, and was lying, her head cushioned on her arm. She dozed and then woke again, trying to get more comfortable. With a small pang of jealousy she saw his expression soften as he watched Eigon and determinedly she closed her eyes.

Commios watched for a while longer then at last he allowed himself to lean back against the wall of the cave to sleep.

They awoke some two hours later shivering as a cold wet fog lapped into the cave. Commios went outside to listen. He came back nodding. 'I can't hear anything. I think it's safe to stop here for a bit but I don't think we should light a fire.' He reached for his knapsack and opened the flap. 'Bread, ladies?'

Drusilla's eyes widened. 'Where did you get that?'

He grinned. 'I'm afraid I stole it as we ran through the kitchen.

I'm sure our hostess won't miss one loaf. It's yesterday's bread. She was probably going to throw it to the dogs anyway.' He tore it into pieces and passed them to each of the women. 'Eigon, would you like to bless our food?' She nodded, repeating the prayer, before sinking her teeth into the coarse bread. For a while there was silence as they ate, then at last she glanced up at him again. 'I heard you pray for mist last night.' They all glanced at the cave mouth, veiled in a damp white blanket. 'Our Lord was listening to us.'

He shrugged. 'It was an old Druid prayer to conjure the weather.'

She smiled. 'I thought so. Melinus taught me prayers like that. But we are forbidden to pray to the old gods. It is a sin.'

'I don't believe that.' Commios drew up his knees, leaning on his elbows thoughtfully as he chewed. 'Our ancestors knew nothing of Christ. They called God by different names, that's all. The spirits of the countryside are still there. You can feel them. See them. How could they have gone? Christ is our God. Our Lord. He knows the spirits exist. He calls them angels, that's all. We are no longer in Rome, Eigon. We are in Gaul. We are heading for your country, and in our own lands we have to deal with our own gods.'

She glanced at him doubtfully but said nothing. It was Drusilla who shook her head. 'I am the Lord thy God: thou shalt have no other gods but me.'

Eigon smiled. 'And that is right. He is the father God. But Commios is right too. Peter spoke of angels all the time. God's messengers. And they are all around us.' She shivered. 'Can't you feel them, in the mist?'

Drusilla frowned. 'You're wrong,' she said sharply.

Commios and Eigon stared at her. It wasn't often that the gentle Drusilla raised her voice.

Commios shook his head. 'Well, whoever is out there, let us pray that they and the Lord will lead us out of this wilderness,' he said ruefully. 'Because once we have eaten this bread, we have nothing but what we find in the forest. There are nuts and fruits a plenty but not for long. The birds and animals are gorging themselves as we watch.'

'We should go, while the mist is here to hide us, Commios,' Eigon said. She threw the last crumbs from her piece of bread to the floor, an offering to the spirits of the cave.

He noticed her act and grinned. 'Crumbs for the angels?'

'Or for the little animals that live here,' she countered. 'It is their home and I thank them for allowing us to stay here safely.'

'But it is cold and damp and the mist you summoned from God is very uncomfortable!' Drusilla said sharply.

An eerie sound echoed suddenly out of the forest below them and they froze. 'A hunting horn,' Commios said grimly.

'Do you think they are on our trail?' Eigon felt the blood drain from her face.

He shrugged. 'They may be hunting boar; they may know nothing about us, but you are right, we should move on.' He broke off as the sound of the horn echoed again from the trees far away. 'They are far to the east of us, and moving away,' he said quietly. 'We'll follow the stream down the gorge in the opposite direction.'

In seconds they had gathered up their belongings and were once more climbing down the rocks away from the cave mouth.

By the evening they had put many miles between them and the cave they had rested in, guiding themselves by the westering sun as it rose late from the blanket of fog, sucking mist in spirals out of the trees. They skirted several villages, crossed a dozen more streams and rivers heading ever west until at last they found a deserted shepherd's hut on the shoulder of a hill where they could spend the night in relative warmth and safety. Commios, looking now as wild and unRoman as it was possible to look headed alone into the village with some coins. Speaking their language he aroused less suspicion and was able to secure food and ale and a couple of stout cloaks woven in the local design.

They slept well that night, and next morning set off into bright sunlight feeling much more cheerful. Their mood made them careless. Even Commios had not seen the group of men hiding in the trees waiting for them. One moment they were walking in single file along a sunlit track at the bottom of the valley and the next they were surrounded by tribesmen and Commios was being held with a knife at his throat.

Drusilla screamed. Someone slapped a dirty hand across her mouth and the three of them were dragged off the path and into the undergrowth. A growling voice spoke in Commios's ear. 'Who are you? Where are you going?'

The language was that of his own tribe and he swore at their captors so roundly and comprehensively in the vernacular that they stood back in astonishment. Eigon glanced round. There were some dozen men standing in a semi-circle around them, swords drawn, their hair wild, their eyes angry, their clothes primitive and ill-made. She risked a glance at Commios who had moved on from swearing at them to demanding who they thought they were manhandling and were they intending to rob them as well? Two young men who had already seized the bundles from the women dropped them shamefacedly on the ground. One man stood forward. He was, it appeared, their leader. He and Commios exchanged some lively conversation during which their attacker looked more and more shamefaced. At the end of it they were all gazing at Eigon in awe.

'What have you said, Commios?' she asked suspiciously. She addressed him in Latin.

He grinned. 'I have told him you are Queen of the Silures, daughter of the great Caratacus and that you will demand their heads as payment for the insult they have offered you.'

She raised an eyebrow. 'Good Christian sentiments, Commios.'

He snorted. 'They are not Christian. And I have never understood this rush to be martyred unnecessarily.'

'And lies. I am no queen.'

'You don't know that. And you are the daughter of Caratacus are you not?'

She nodded meekly.

'Then act like it. Be regal!'

She surveyed their captors nervously. Every pair of eyes was fixed on her face. Squaring her shoulders she assumed as haughty a look as possible and was gratified to see one or two of them quail. 'Who is your leader?' Her own Celtic was rusty, but she remembered enough to make herself understood, and she did after all come from a distant tribe from across the ocean. Her voice after a moment's huskiness rang out true and strong. 'Did you attack us on his orders?'

She noticed Commios standing back respectfully as she spoke. He was muttering to Drusilla out of the corner of his mouth. 'Even if you spit in her soup later, please act deferentially. Just for now you are her servant.'

Drusilla's eyebrow shot skywards, but she was quick to realise that at this moment, their lives depended on Eigon's ability to act like a queen.

It wasn't hard. Eigon had only to think of her father's combination of gentleness and natural authority and the power he used to wield before his illness. She added a touch of her mother's arrogance to the mixture and straightening her back even further stepped forward into the ring of men. 'Take us to your village. I will speak to your leader myself.' She turned to the two would-be thieves. 'You two, carry our belongings. You will tell him that you planned to rob the Queen of the Silures. You,' she fixed their spokesman with a steady thoughtful gaze which told him she would never forget his face, 'will explain to him why you rob travellers on the roads of your kingdom and have so completely forgotten the sacred code of hospitality.'

The village lay in an arm of a small river. Two or three large wooden houses were surrounded by several smaller rectangular buildings, all thatched with reed, the whole settlement surrounded by a double ring of strong palings, with a guard house at the entrance. She stared at the place, memories flooding back.

'Commios! It's so primitive!' she whispered. 'I had forgotten.'

He raised a haughty eyebrow. 'To those brought up in the court of an emperor, perhaps. You had better get used to it. This is the life we will be leading from now on.'

He strode ahead of her and at the gateway turned, bowing, gesturing extravagantly that she should enter the outer courtyard at the head of the file of men. Drusilla scurried behind her, tugging at her cloak to straighten it. 'You wait, great queen, till we are alone. I will want my share of this special treatment,' she murmured with a smile.

Eigon grinned. 'All are equal in the sight of the Lord, Drusilla. When we are alone, we will go back to being sisters.' She paused and looked around her with a suitably regal air. The courtyard was deserted. There was no sign of anyone at all, though smoke rose from two fires outside one of the buildings. 'Where is your leader?'

There was a scuffle from one of the larger houses and an elderly man appeared. He was wearing a robe significantly richer than those of the men around them. He strode forward and came to a halt a few feet from Eigon, leaning on his staff. 'Greetings, lady. To what do we owe the honour of your presence?' He glanced at the man behind her who shuffled his feet uncomfortably.

'This lady is an honoured guest. She is Queen of the Silures tribe.'

The man's face remained impassive. 'I find that unlikely.' His eyes bored into Eigon's. 'I have visited the land of the Silures and heard no word there of a queen.'

Stunned by this revelation Eigon nevertheless continued to hold his gaze. 'Caratacus was my father, sir.' If this man really knew the Silures surely he would know her father's name?

The man raised an eyebrow. 'Caratacus was a great king but he was captured many years ago and taken to Rome. As far as I know he is there still.'

Eigon shook her head. 'You are right. We were taken to Rome and I am sorry to tell you that my father has died. I am his only heir.'

'And you were elected by the elders of his tribe?' His face was like granite.

She sighed. 'No. I have not been back to the lands of the Silures since our capture. I am on my way there now with my father's commendation and his blessing as his successor.' She paused. 'May I ask, sir, who you are?'

He gave a humourless smile. 'You may ask. I do not choose to tell you. Madunos?' He addressed their escort. 'Make our guests welcome. Give them food and beds for the night as they expect in the name of hospitality. Tomorrow give them food for their journey and show them the road west.' He bowed towards her with grudging respect and turned away, walking back into the shadows of his house.

Commios blew loudly through his lips. 'He's your Druid, yes?' he guessed, addressing Madunos. 'Friendly fellow. Well, all we require is food and shelter as you have taken us off our road. It is not our concern if you do not recognise Queen Eigon. She is travelling in disguise to avoid the Romans anyway. Where do we go?'

Madunos was hesitating. He wasn't sure whether or not to treat them with respect or scorn, if they were impostors.

Eigon read his thoughts and took a step towards him. He flinched back as though she had struck him. 'Obey your Druid, fellow,' she ordered sharply. 'I will deal with him later. He dishonours our God with his disbelief, but he has commanded you to give us food and shelter so bring our belongings and show us where we are to sleep.'

'Don't face up to the old one, Eigon. He seems a hard man and suspicious,' Commios said as they stared round the small building which had been put at their disposal. 'Let's just eat, sleep and get out of here.'

'The Druids have no love of Romans,' she said firmly. 'He is clever and he has travelled to western Britannia and he could be an ally. He suspects us for our Roman clothing under our cloaks. We will talk to him, you and I, later and convince him we are genuine. And I think we should change our clothes. We will ask them to sell us Gaulish clothing so we can pass for villagers as we journey on. We have to avoid the town centres if Titus is following us, so we should follow the forest tracks and keep out of their way. We need to blend in.' She glanced at Drusilla's face and laughed out loud. 'Do not look so horrified, Drusilla! Their clothes are comfortable and warm.'

'And stinking!' Drusilla said with a shudder.

'Then we will ask for clean ones. These people are poor,' Commios retorted sharply. 'Shame on you! Poor people in Rome stink as much, if not more. You know that from when we worked amongst them spreading the word of the Lord.'

Drusilla bit her lip. She nodded reluctantly. 'I'm sorry.'

To their surprise they were invited to join the people in the settlement around the communal fire for food and singing that evening. Having been told to accept their visitors by their Druid they had obviously decided to make the most of the unexpected company and they made them welcome. It was late when Eigon stood up and beckoning Commios and Drusilla bid their hosts goodnight.

Drusilla ducked into their bedchamber alone as Eigon and Commios headed towards the Druid's house. They were stooping to enter the low doorway when someone stood up out of the shadows and put out his hand to stop them. 'Where are you going?'

'We want to speak to your Druid,' Eigon said softly.

'Taxilos? He's not here. He has gone to his private house in the woods.'

Eigon glanced at Commios. 'Then we'll go and see him there,' Commios said firmly. 'Take us there and ask him if we can speak to him urgently.'

Somewhat to their surprise their request was acceded to at once. They found the old man seated at a table in a small hut some way into the forest outside the stockade. He looked up as they entered and smiled coldly. 'I was expecting you.'

Eigon glanced round the room. It was lit by three lamps which cast a warm golden glow around his desk. On it lay a pile of scrolls, some wooden leaf notebooks and a wax tablet and stylus. There were stoppered jars, an intricate metal instrument which she guessed was a miniature astrolabe and a complicated calendar, the dates engraved into a fine sheet of bronze. His staff rested against the wall. He looked extraordinarily weary as he waved them towards the two spare stools and turned away from the desk to face them, his hands folded in his lap.

'So, what can I do for you?'

'We've come to ask your help,' Eigon said slowly. She did not look at Commios who sat beside her in silence. 'By now you will have consulted your gods and they will have told you that we speak the truth about who we are.'

He inclined his head.

'We would like to buy clothing and food for our journey and ask advice about the best way to travel on towards the coast. We are being pursued by a Roman officer who means me harm. I need to avoid him by travelling the back ways.'

He raised an eyebrow. 'Titus Marcus Olivinus.'

Her mouth dropped open as she stared at him, shocked. 'You know?'

'He has sent messengers all over the country. He is a very determined man. He has offered a vast sum of money as reward for information about your whereabouts.'

She was speechless for a moment and Commios took the opportunity to speak. 'We couldn't blame you or your clan for wanting to earn that reward.'

'To do so would dishonour us and betray you,' Taxilos said sternly. 'You have nothing to fear from us, but I should warn you that he has a powerful ally in Rome. She walks the inner pathways and can see into the distances as well as the past and the future.'

'Marcia,' Eigon murmured. 'I have seen her.'

He gave her his full attention again. 'Then you have been trained by a Druid, lady, for all your Roman ways.'

She nodded. 'Melinus. He was my tutor for many years.'

'And now he is dead?'

She bit her lip. 'He died in the Roman circus.'

He frowned. 'They call us barbarians! You know that he still watches over you? Consult him when you need to.'

She glanced at Commios. He shrugged. His face was pale and he glanced round the room uncomfortably. She tensed. Was there danger here?

Taxilos noticed and smiled thinly. 'You need have no fear of me, lady. I do not run messages for Roman soldiers. I will see to it that you have what you need tomorrow. Now I suggest you go and sleep. You still have a long journey to the coast and the winds grow stronger and the waves that protect your isle grow larger as each day passes.'

He turned back to his desk and they rose without a word. It was only after they had gone that he looked up from his scroll and thoughtfully stared at the window. Marcia Maximilla was a powerful enemy. Her greedy fingers clawed their way throughout the Roman world from her power base behind the temple of the Vestals. Even here in furthest Gaul they had heard of her and quailed at her name. He smiled and wondered idly for a few delightful moments if he was up to the challenge of thwarting her. It was tempting. It was hard to decide which way to jump.

'Where are you, Titus, you bastard?' Dan thumped the steering wheel with his fists. He was sweating hard and he could feel his shirt sticking to his back. He lowered the window, swerving round a cyclist with a vicious curse as he steered one-handed down the narrow road and pulled up at last in a lay-by. In the distance he could see the line of hills behind Ty Bran.

'What do I do if she's here?' he asked out loud. 'You want her dead, don't you, you sicko bastard, but you won't do your own dirty work! You want to watch me do it!'

Pushing open the door he climbed out. His legs were shaking and he could feel a wave of nausea building somewhere at the base of his stomach. He stood by the hedge staring out across the valley, waiting to see if he was going to vomit. There in the distance he could make out the cottage nestling just under the ridge below the woods. From here he could see just how far those woods stretched, hundreds of acres spread like a soft green rug over the tops of the hills and down into the next valley with the higher, treeless mountain peaks rising far behind them. Someone could get lost in there and never be seen again even in this day and age! He gave a cold smile, wiping his forehead with the back of his hand. The nausea was passing.

He could still hear the scorn in Nat's voice echoing in his head. It had followed him up the road and round the corner and he had felt a hundred middle-class suburban eyes looking at him from behind their hedges as his car accelerated through the peaceful streets. He pushed the sound away. That part of his life was over. He could never go back now. And why would he want to? Even the children were lost to him already, little clones of their mother who probably secretly despised him. He shook his head, pushing away the memory of his little son's arms clinging round his neck, and his mouth downturned into a vicious sneer. Forget them. They had always stood in his way. Now he was free to go wherever he wanted and to do all the things he had dreamed of. He glanced at his watch. Tonight, for a start, he would find himself a comfortable bed. He was damned if he was going to spend another night in some cheap motorway lodge or worse still in the car. Tonight he would have all the luxuries, but before that, Titus and he were going to pay Jess a visit, a visit which he was planning to enjoy enormously.

32

'Jess, wait!' Rhodri was hurrying up the track behind her. He had arrived at Ty Bran shortly after nine that morning to find Aurelia and Steph had put breakfast on hold until Jess got back from her walk. He had volunteered to go and meet her.

She paused, smiling. 'You sound out of breath. Surely the maestro should have better control of his lungs than that!'

'Even the stage at La Scala hasn't got a rake on it like this hill!' he retorted. 'That's where it matters that I keep my breath controlled. Not here. Where are you going? Not back up to those rocks, I hope.'

She shrugged. 'I just needed to get outside. Mummy and Steph were acting so normal, getting breakfast, going on with life as though nothing had happened. I can't get it out of my head. That little boy all by himself.'

'I understand, Jess.' His voice was gentle. 'So you think it's the boy?'

'I don't know.' She shook her head. 'Yes. It is. I'm sure. A little lost boy, knowing there has been a massacre of his father's army just down there.' She waved her arm. 'Knowing there are enemy soldiers looking for him and his sisters. Knowing they will be skewered on Roman swords if they are found.'

'I don't think he did know that, Jess,' he said quietly. 'His sister told him it was a game, remember? You told me that. She was trying to protect him from that knowledge.' He studied her face. 'You have to put this out of your head, Jess. It is too painful to think about otherwise. Imagine him cuddling up in the dry under those rocks and going to sleep. Perhaps it was a cold night and he got hypothermia. He would have known nothing about it. He would have sunk deeper and deeper into sleep. It would have been a kind death.'

She sniffed. 'My thoughts sometimes race out of control.'

He laughed fondly. 'You're telling me!'

She looked up. 'Have I been a pain?'

'I'd say that was an understatement, but it has certainly been a different kind of summer for me, that's for sure.' He pulled her against him and kissed her forehead. 'I was sent to bring you back for brunch.'

For a moment they stood without moving. She held her breath. If she looked up he would kiss her again, properly. She knew it and she wasn't sure if that was what she wanted. Part of her ached to stay in his arms for ever, it felt so safe, but part of her was tugging impatiently away from him, wanting to go back to the world in another time and place.

'Jess –?'

She broke away. 'Rhodri, no. I'm sorry! I can't.'

He didn't move. 'Why?'

'Because – I'm a disaster at the moment. I'm confused and muddled and frightened.'

He paused. 'I want to stop you being frightened,' he said softly. 'I want to protect you.'

'I know.'

'While we're getting things clear I need to know. Is it Will?'

She shook her head. 'Will and I are finished.'

'Does he know that?'

She nodded. 'I think so.'

'So, it's Eigon.'

She nodded. 'I can't inflict her on you, Rhodri. I'm a total mess because of her. I don't understand why I'm so involved, but I can't get her out of my head day or night. There is something I have to do for her.'

'Bury her little brother?'

She looked at him, startled. 'You understand?'

'Of course I understand. We all understand. Your mother and Steph know exactly what you are thinking. I am probably thinking the same thing. Don't bottle it up, Jess. And give us some credit for knowing how you feel. In fact give us some credit for having feelings too. You seem to think you have the exclusive right to them!' Suddenly he was angry. 'For goodness' sake, let us in!' He turned and stamped away. A few paces further on he stopped. 'Well, are you coming?'

She gave a penitent smile. 'OK.'

'Good! Because I'm getting a bit fed up chasing after you all the time.'

There was a pause. She knew she should say something. Anything to delay him. She should tell him she wanted him to go on chasing her. She should run to him and kiss him. She did nothing. Paralysed by indecision, she stood still and watched as after half a second's hesitation he turned and walked away down the track. In a few moments he had turned the corner and was out of sight.

The postman in London had just pushed a handful of letters through the letter box when he paused. From somewhere behind the door he thought he heard a groan. Normally he would have ignored it, but he had got to know Will Matthews over the months he had been on this round, often running into him on the doorstep as he left for school and he liked the guy. 'Hello?' He stood at the door and called up at the windows, then he crouched down and pushing open the flap put his eye to the letter box.

The ambulance arrived at the same time as the police. They forced the door and went in. Nothing seemed to have been touched. There had been no robbery that they could see, just the man lying on the floor only feet from the front door, in a pool of blood, his head smashed in by some kind of a blunt instrument. He had obviously regained consciousness for long enough to cry out when he heard the post hit the doormat. He had also regained consciousness for long enough to scrawl one word on the wall in his own blood:

DAN ~

But by the time the police rang Brian Barker, headmaster of the local sixth form college whose name and number they had found on Will's desk, he was dead.

Steph took the call from Catherine in the kitchen at Ty Bran. They had given up waiting for Jess and settled down to a late leisurely breakfast and were lingering over their coffee. Jess had still not reappeared and Rhodri was about to leave as the phone had rung. One look at Steph's face halted him in his tracks. He sat down again as they all waited in silence for her to finish, staring at her in horror as they listened to her end of the fragmented conversation.

'What's happened?' Aurelia asked as Steph tipped the phone back onto its cradle. Steph's face was white with shock.

'It's Will.' Steph's eyes filled with tears. 'He's dead.' She swallowed, groping her way back to her chair and throwing herself down. 'Apparently the postman found him this morning. He had been bashed over the head. He . . .' She paused, unable to speak for a moment. 'He had written a name in his own blood. They asked Catherine and Brian if they knew anyone called Dan.' Her voice faded to a whisper.

Rhodri stood up, pushing the chair back so violently it fell with a crash onto the floor. 'The bastard! The absolute bastard!' He clenched his fists. 'Where is he, do they know? Have they caught him?'

Steph shook her head. She glanced at her mother who was sitting staring at her in shocked silence. 'Catherine didn't know. She wanted Jess to hear about Will from us. She said the police might come and question her.' She hesitated. 'I gather they saw Will. He went straight there when he got back from Rome and he told them he had been to see the police. He warned them about Dan.'

Rhodri bent to pick up the chair. 'I'll go and meet Jess. She must be on her way back by now. I thought she was following me.' He paused on his way to the door. 'Shall I break the news to her? Or would it be better coming from you two?'

'You tell her,' Steph whispered. 'I don't think I can do it.'

Rhodri retraced his steps to the spot where he had last seen Jess and stopped, looking round. There was no sign of her, but he had hardly expected her still to be there.

'Jess?' he called. 'Where are you?'

The woods were completely silent. Not even a bird answered him. He sighed. He knew where she would be. He started to climb the track towards the summit, but when he reached the rocks there was still no trace of her. He crouched to peer into the hollow space under them. 'You there, love?' he called softly. After a few seconds as his eyes became used to the darkness he could see the faint outlines of the bones lying exactly where they had left them on the ground and beside them the pale limp shape of the foxgloves Jess had put there. Otherwise the space was empty. He sat back on his heels with a puzzled frown. In the far distance he could just hear the drumming of a woodpecker. The sound echoed through the trees, emphasising his sudden loneliness. Jess hadn't been back here. He could sense it; the little boy wasn't here in any sense either; his spirit had long ago gone elsewhere. He sat down with a sigh on an old moss-covered tree stump. Poor Will. They should have seen this coming.

Where was Dan now, that was the question. He felt himself tensing uncomfortably. Where would Dan go after killing Will? He would want to get out of London, that was for sure. There would be two things uppermost in his mind. Avoiding the police and silencing Jess. And he would guess that if Jess was not with Will, then she would have come back to Ty Bran. He exhaled sharply. Could he be here already? A wave of panic hit him. Jess had been up here alone. He might already have found her.

He gazed round wildly. 'Jess!' His shout echoed across the rolling hills unanswered and as far as he knew, unheard.

Julius was sitting in a chair staring at the fire. There was a rug around his knees; his hands shook. He tried to steady them around a cup of warm wine, lifting it cautiously to his mouth, aware that he was dribbling it down his front as the woman came in. He looked up and tried to smile, horribly aware that half his face felt as if it were paralysed. He had asked for a mirror. It had not been forthcoming, but even with hands as shaky as his he could feel the raw jagged scar which ran from just below his eye to his chin.

'The wine is good,' he said, articulating the words with difficulty. 'Strengthening.'

'Good. That is what it is intended to be,' she said as she came over and began tidying the table, casually relieving him of the half-empty cup before he had time to drop it as had happened only the day before when its predecessor had smashed to pieces on the elegant floor tiles. 'Are you comfortable?'

He managed a nod. She was a striking woman, tall, in her mid-forties perhaps, with dark hair already greying at the temples, swept back into a serviceable knot which seemed to hold itself in place without the need for any ornate comb or pins. She had the gentle capable hands of a born nurse. He forced his mouth into a smile. 'When are you going to let me see the doctor who cared for me?'

She returned his gaze calmly. 'You are looking at her.'

He stared. 'No. I saw a man. An old man with white hair.'

'My pharmacist.' She smiled briskly. 'He makes my remedies and copies the recipes to circulate amongst other doctors in the city. But don't worry. I am properly trained. The stitches in your cheek are the neatest you will find anywhere for the money.'

He was frowning with concentration, trying to get his head around her comments. 'You charge? I don't know if I have any gold –'

She shook her head. 'That was a joke, fine lord.'

He rubbed his forehead, trying to assimilate what she was saying but her voice was receding on a tide of noise inside his head, washing slowly back and forth, the words jumbled and incomprehensible. 'Where is this?' he managed a sensible question at last.

'We are near Tibur,' she said. She saw his struggle and hiding the worried expression in her eyes, came to put a practised hand on his brow. He was slightly feverish. 'But half a day's ride to the east of Rome. You were brought to me many weeks ago, lying in the back of a cart. You were in so many pieces, I thought they had brought me a test case for my students to practise their stitchery on.'

'You teach as well?' He was faintly incredulous.

'There is no end to my skills, lord.' She smiled again. Her smiles were, he decided, of incredible warmth. Just to look at her was healing.

'What I can't tell you,' she went on, 'is your name or what happened to you.' She shook her head. 'That is a mystery. The man who brought you found you unconscious in his wagon. As you could not possibly have walked there someone must have put you there. There was a coin and a note asking for you to be brought here.' She paused, her head a little to one side. 'Don't think about it if it's too painful.'

He was breathing deeply through his nose, trying to recollect his scattered nightmares, the flashes of noise and pain, the fear and the stench of death. 'They came out of the darkness. They must have followed me.' He paused in anguish. 'There are screams in my head. My friends –' He could feel tears trickling down his face. 'My sister. They killed my sister.'

'That's enough for now.' She came over and laid a cool hand over his burning wrist. Calmly she snapped her fingers in front of his face. 'Remember the elephants!'

He stared at her, trying to understand. 'Elephants? What elephants?'

She smiled. It always worked, breaking the train of thought. Every patient she had seen knew about the elephants in the Emperor's collection. Giant gentle creatures and a total distraction if only for a moment from whatever memories were pouring through out of the darkness.

Nothing would stop his memories returning in the end, though. She had sat at his bedside hour after hour as he raved and screamed and sobbed. In his dreams he remembered it all: the massacre, the blood, the death. She knew only too well what had happened to him for she had listened to his horror and his fear and his helplessness. He had lost his sister and his grandfather and his friends. He had seen them spitted and butchered in front of his eyes and then he had watched the descent of the vicious two-handed blow which had been intended to cleave his own skull and divide his body in half. It very nearly had. She had guessed they were a Christian family. It had happened to too many of them. His beliefs did not bother her. She saw him as an interesting case with not only a body but a mind to heal. She was more confident of managing the former and in the interests of the latter she had no intention of informing him that one of the leaders of his faith, if that indeed was his faith, Peter, had been arrested, in Rome, and sentenced to death.

'My children are here,' she said quietly. 'They will bring you some more wine. I'll put a sleeping draught in it for you so you can rest now.'

He shook his head. 'I don't want to sleep.' He looked at her pleadingly.

So, he did remember his dreams. 'Then I will ask Portia to come and play for you a little. You like her music.'

He nodded. He had always loved music.

She used to sing to him.

She.

Who?

Her face hovered just beyond the reach of his memory. All he knew was that it belonged to the person he loved most of all. And that he had lost her.

Whoever she was she was dead with the others. Everyone he loved was dead. He should rightly be dead himself.

Rhodri and Aurelia were once more seated at the kitchen table listening to Steph. She was on the phone to Nat. When she hung up and turned to face them at last her face was grim.

'Dan left them first thing this morning. He had driven there overnight, straight from London. Presumably straight from killing Will.' Her voice shook. 'She told me he's been violent before. He's beaten her up several times in the past. They had a row and he left. She doesn't know where he went. The police have been there though, asking for him. She said they told her it was urgent and asked her to contact them the moment she heard from him. They told her to be careful.'

'And she didn't know where he had gone?'

'No.'

They looked at each other. 'You think he came here?' Aurelia said softly.

Rhodri nodded. 'Everything has been about Jess, hasn't it. He would have guessed she had come here.' He had liked Jess and Steph's mother immediately they had met. She was calm and sensible in spite of her anguish.

'We should call the police,' Steph said resolutely. 'I can't think why they aren't here yet!'

'I'll ring the local boys. I know one of the inspectors.' Rhodri stood up and went over to the phone. 'We can't just wait and see if Dan turns up. He might already be here. I searched everywhere for Jess. There was no trace of her. Where could she have gone? I left her there on the track. I'm such an ass. I should have made her come back with me. She said she was coming –'

'No one blames you, Rhodri.' Aurelia laid her hand on his arm. She gave him a wan smile.

'I blame me!' He was punching the numbers into the phone. Then he rang his mother. Jess had not made her way over to the farm or, when he rang the post office, to the village either.

The police arrived in less than an hour. Rhodri's mate, DI James Lloyd and the sergeant who had accompanied him sat with them at the kitchen table making notes as Steph and Rhodri told them the whole story. They had, it appeared, already been alerted to the fact that Dan might well be heading towards Ty Bran by the Homicide Assessment Team in London. That Jess had disappeared was a worrying development. They all tramped up the path to the rocks, fanning out once more into the woods, calling till they were hoarse. Eventually they gathered at the highest point of the woods and stood within yards of the place the little child had crawled to die but no one drew their attention to it. That was Jess's secret. The two policemen looked round everywhere, even stooping and glancing into the heart of the rock pile, but they didn't notice the pathetic scattering of little bones. There were no signs of Jess, or anyone else, no tracks other than their own and the ones that had been left earlier. No clues; nothing to say that Dan had been anywhere near. There was no strange car parked in any of the lanes nearby.

'Dogs?' Rhodri suggested.

The inspector shrugged. 'Jess has been all over the place up here so the scent would be confused. We'll speak to London and Shrewsbury. They are sending more men and they may feel we should call out a helicopter; maybe it's too soon. I can promise you, as soon as there is any news we will be in touch, and if Jess appears or there is any sign at all of Mr Nicolson please let us know at once. I'm sure we don't have to tell you not to approach him.'

'So, it's up to us,' Aurelia said tersely as the two policemen climbed back into their Range Rover and disappeared back down the lane.

Steph glanced at Rhodri. 'Carmella?' she said.

'Who is Carmella?' Aurelia was sifting through Steph's wine rack with a look of faint disgust. 'I need a drink!' Her hands were shaking with exhaustion.

'She's a friend of Kim's. A clairvoyant and tarot reader.' Steph ventured uncomfortably.

Aurelia straightened from the wine rack and stared at her.

'She knew Jess was in trouble before,' Steph said defensively. 'That's how all this started!'

462

'Then ring her.' Aurelia turned back to the rack and selected a bottle. 'Where is your corkscrew?'

'It's screw top, Mummy!' Steph went to the phone after rummaging through her diary for the number. 'Sorry it's not French but I rather like Australian. Carmella? *Ciao*! It's me, Stephanie!'

Megan arrived while they waited for Carmella to ring back after she had consulted her cards. A plump, energetic woman with wind-reddened cheeks and curly sand-coloured hair, she surveyed them in turn in utter horror as they told her what was happening.

'This sounds like a gangster movie!' she said at last. 'Rhodri? Why didn't you tell me all this?'

He sighed. 'To stop you having a fit, Mum! Why do you think?'

They had to wait a long time for the call from Italy. Carmella was apologetic. 'I can't get anything about her, Steph. I'm so sorry. I don't know what has happened. I have never had this experience before. The cards read like wooden bricks. They are playing dumb. The messages spin in circles. They say she is in danger, then they say she is safe. They say she has found the one she was looking for then they say she has lost the one she sought. They say she is on the threshold of her life's desire, then they say she has lost everything.' Her voice rose in frustration. 'I am sorry. I don't know what to tell you. Except that I don't know where she is. I went to my *sfera di cristallo* and asked it to show me what she could see. I saw trees and leaves and branches dancing in the wind. I saw birds circling overhead. I saw the sky. It could have been anywhere.'

'But she is alive?' Steph's mouth was dry.

There was a fractional hesitation the other end of the line. 'I think so. I pray so. I don't know, Steph. The vision was hazy. Not clear.'

Somewhere in the background Steph heard a deep voice talking in Italian. 'Carmella, I'm sorry. You have visitors and I've interrupted.' Steph tried to disguise her own misery.

'No. No. That was my friend and he has brought me a cup of coffee to wake my head up.' Steph thought she could hear the wry smile. 'He understands that I must do these things.' There was a pause, then, 'Steph, I have an idea. I will ring you back in half an hour, OK?' The phone went dead.

Steph turned back into the room. She shook her head. 'No news,' she said. There was a sob in her voice.

'Why didn't you ask her about Dan?' Rhodri asked sharply.

'I was going to, but she thought of something else to try. She is going to ring back in half an hour.' Steph flung herself down in her chair.

Megan got up and went to put an arm round her shoulders. 'She'll be all right. You'll see. I have a feeling in my bones!'

Aurelia looked up sharply. 'Wait a moment, if we are into consulting occult specialists, I know who we can ask. Do you remember Meryn Jones, Megan? Does he still live round here? He'd know what to do.'

Megan frowned. 'You're right. He was an amazing man. Didn't you take a bit of a shine to him, Aurelia?' She gave a small teasing smile. 'I haven't heard from him for years. He went to the States, didn't he? Then I think I heard he went to live in Scotland?'

'Mummy?' Steph stared at her.

'It's a long story,' Aurelia said with a rueful shrug. 'I'll tell you some time. Not now.'

It was when she too had lived in these hills. Jess and Steph had left home. She was alone. Her daughters were both independent, committed to their own careers, and recognising this she had decided to move on. She never told them about him and she and Meryn had drifted apart before any firm commitments had been made. But she had often wondered where he was and what might have happened if they had stayed in touch.

Rhodri sat up. 'Meryn Jones was the consultant on the programme on the radio about Cartimandua. I knew I remembered his name from somewhere. Jess heard the programme too. That was what started all this obsession with Eigon and Caratacus.'

'But who is he?' Steph asked sharply.

'He does stuff like Carmella,' Rhodri said. 'He can see into the future and the past and talk to the spirits. I don't think he does tarot and crystal balls; he's more of an academic, but he's also some sort of pagan priest and shaman, I think, as well as being an expert on the Celts. A Druid!' He shrugged. 'I don't know where he is though, but you might be right. I think that programme came from Scotland.'

'Can you find out?' Steph asked. 'You must know people at the BBC. Couldn't you get someone to tell you?' She turned back to her mother. 'Mummy, why have you never mentioned him before?'

'I know who'll know where he is,' Megan interrupted. It was her turn to go to the phone. She dialled a Hereford number and within seconds was beckoning someone to pass her a piece of paper and pencil. She scribbled down the number and then began to dial again.

'I don't know what he could do, though,' she said over her shoulder as she waited for the phone to pick up. When it did it was a message service. Her face fell, but she spoke anyway. 'Meryn? It's Megan Price. From Cwm-nant. Remember me? Listen, could you ring me? I need a favour. I need help. Urgently. I'm at my neighbour's, at Ty Bran in the next valley. Their number is –' She recited it slowly and carefully and then hung up with a shrug. 'Just pray he is around.' She hadn't mentioned Aurelia, Steph noticed and with a look at her mother's face, she let the matter drop. Whoever this chap was, if her mother hadn't seen him for so long whatever there had been between them, must have died the death.

When the phone next rang it was Carmella again. 'OK. I have consulted the cards about Dan and Will.' There was a pause. 'Will is in trouble.'

'Will is dead, Carmella!' Steph replied sharply. 'Dan killed him.'

'*Dio mio*!' There was a moment's silence. 'I am so sorry. Well, that explains Dan's reading. Do you want to hear it?' Her voice quavered, then she went on. 'I think you must. This is not good.'

Steph swallowed hard. 'Go on.'

'Titus is heading your way. Perhaps he has already arrived in England. He is on the trail of Eigon and of Jess. Someone else is watching them. A soothsayer, a woman from Ancient Rome. I have been seeing her; she comes when I tune in. She told Titus where Eigon was, but then she was sorry she had done it. She knows that he is someone evil. I don't know how this works, whether he has possessed Dan or is following him or is using him, but he is heading back to the place where it all started.'

'Ty Bran.'

'Yes. And he is very close. I sense him as out of control.' Carmella took a deep breath. 'Tell me what happened to Will.'

'Dan seems to have broken into Will's flat in London and beaten him to death.' Steph's eyes filled with tears.

'How do they know it was Dan?'

'Will wrote Dan's name in blood. Before he died.'

'The police told you that?'

'No. Or at least they told the headmaster of the college where Dan and Jess and Will teach. Taught.'

'*Dio Mio*!' she breathed again. 'This is awful.'

'Do you think he had been possessed by Titus?'

Carmella gave a short bitter laugh. 'I don't suppose that is an excuse that will stand up before a judge! I saw him, Steph, in the *cristallo*. I saw him dressed in Roman uniform, like a legionary and he had a sword, dripping with blood. You know, the short swords the soldiers carried.'

'Titus?'

'Dan.'

'But Jess? You didn't see Jess?'

'He was with a woman, Steph. I saw her. She had her arms bound behind her and her eyes were blindfolded.'

Steph was breathing heavily, trying to hold back her panic. 'It can't have been Jess. You said before, Jess could see leaves and trees.'

'I don't know what she can see, Steph. But I have a bad feeling about this. Very bad. I will go on trying. But you have to find Dan.'

'The entire police force is searching for Dan, Carmella.'

She turned back to the others. 'Did you get the gist of that? She only told us what we already know. Jess is in danger and Dan seems to have been possessed by the vicious Roman. In her vision he is brandishing a bloody sword.'

There was silence round the table. 'What can we do?' Aurelia whispered at last. 'We must do something!'

'I'm going out to look again!' Rhodri pushed back his chair. 'I can't just sit here waiting for something to happen!'

'Wait! Has anyone rung her mobile?' Megan said suddenly. They looked at each other. Steph went back to the phone. Seconds later they heard the reedy ring tone from upstairs.

'Damn!' was all she said.

They were standing on the beach staring out at the waves crashing onto the shore, sucking at the sand, breathing in and out at their feet like a living creature. Eigon shuddered. 'Is it a long way to the other side?'

Commios looked at their guide enquiringly. The man shrugged. 'Long enough.'

'Where do we get a boat?'

'You walk along to Gesoriacum and you pay someone.' The guide grinned. 'My job is done. You are here. You are safe.'

Commios raised an eyebrow. 'You were supposed to take us to the port, friend.'

Their guide shook his head. 'The coast was what we agreed. It's only a short way over the dunes there. You can't miss it.' He gave a leering grin which showed the gap where his two centre teeth were missing.

Commios shrugged. 'I don't suppose you fancy coming across the Oceanus with us?'

'No.' The man was adamant. He turned to Drusilla and bowed. 'May the gods go with you, lady. And you, oh queen.' He bowed to Eigon with reserve tinged by awe. 'And with you, friend.' He clasped Commios by the wrist. Then he was gone.

They stood staring after him. 'That was sudden.' Drusilla's face was touched with colour. She had enjoyed his company, the Gaul who had led them for the last few days through the forests and farmlands and river valleys towards the coast. His departure had been so quick it had taken them all by surprise.

Suddenly Commios stiffened. 'Quickly. Here. Hide!' He dragged them with him back towards the trees as two horsemen appeared in the distance, galloping up the beach from the south-east.

They drew back into the shadows, peering from behind the trees. The two figures approached and galloped past without drawing rein. They were wearing the uniform of Rome, leaning forward on the necks of their horses, their faces set against the cold wind as they rode.

Eigon held her breath as they disappeared into the murk. 'Titus,' she breathed.

'I can't believe he is still following us.' Commios swore under his breath. 'How did he know where we were?'

'Our guide?' Drusilla said bitterly. 'Could that be why he was in such a hurry to leave us? Perhaps he was paid. Last night at the *caupona* where we stopped, I had a bad feeling about some of the men there. We should not have gone in.'

467

Eigon and Commios stared at her then reluctantly they both nodded. 'It makes sense,' said Commios bitterly. 'He owed us nothing. And who will ever know. He brought us to the coast as we asked and he earned his pay.' He sighed. 'On the bright side, Titus didn't see us so we are still one step ahead of him. We know he's here, whereas he hasn't seen us. And as our so kind escort has gone, he won't find out that we have arrived until we choose to tell him.'

'If we choose to tell him,' Drusilla said.

'Which we won't,' Eigon added. She shuddered. 'Will we ever be rid of the man?' She stared out across the waves in despair. A line of cold silver light had appeared on the horizon where the sun was sinking beneath the sea, throwing its beam up for an instant onto the low line of cloud. She sank down on her knees. 'Sweet Lord, send us safe across the sea. Protect us and bless us and keep us from our enemies.' For a long time she knelt where she was, lost in the rhythm of the ocean, then slowly she climbed to her feet. 'God is going to send us a boat. All we have to do is wait.' She smiled at them, her exhausted face lighting with humour. 'Don't look like that. I just have a feeling my prayer is to be answered. We have no need to go to the port. Titus is not going to find us there.'

They made a fire and sat round it, making a supper of the bread and apples they had begged from a house they had passed a few miles back, then they huddled down in their cloaks at the edge of the beach as darkness fell. It was cold and the wind was growing in strength. Drusilla and Commios exchanged glances. Both were thinking that they could find warmer safer accommodation in the town without Titus ever knowing where they were staying. Eigon sat up, swathed in her cloak, her eyes on the sea.

It was full dark when they heard the creak of oars and the sound of men's voices carrying in across the waves. 'There's a fire on the beach.' The boat turned in towards them.

Commios swore quietly. He had been about to kick sand over the embers and extinguish them when Eigon had put her hand on his arm and shaken her head. 'This is the boat God has sent us,' she whispered.

'Maybe it is, maybe it isn't,' he replied. 'Don't go rushing out till we see who they are!'

At least she had the grace to see the sense in that. They waited quietly as the boat grounded on the sand and two men climbed out. 'Wind's veering,' one of them said. 'We'll get a good night's fishing at this rate. So, what have we here?' They walked up towards the trees and came to a stop beside the fire.

'Hello?' The taller of the two shadowy figures stared towards them, searching the darkness of the trees. 'Anyone there?'

Commios stepped forward alone. 'Greetings, friends.' He raised his hands away from his sides to show he was unarmed. 'You are welcome to our fireside.'

'Our?' the second man queried. He stared round. There was no sign of the two women who were waiting, holding their breath out of sight.

Commios nodded. 'We have been expecting a boat. Are you the sailors who have been sent to take us across to Britannia?'

The two men exploded into laughter. 'I think not!' one of them said. 'We are just inshore fishermen, earning our living and minding our own business. If you want to cross, you should go up to Gesoriacum. You'll find plenty there who will take you over with their cargo.' He stepped back and his eyes widened as Eigon appeared from the shadows, followed by Drusilla.

Eigon went straight up to the taller of the two men who seemed to be in charge. 'Please, is your boat big enough to do the crossing?'

'No!' That was the man's companion.

'Yes!' The boat owner was bragging.

'We would make it worth your while. How much would you make from a night's fishing?'

The man hesitated. He was obviously doing some quick sums in his head; too much and he would lose them. Commios quietly put his hand into the purse at his belt and clinked some coins gently with his fingers. The sound galvanised the two men. 'Payment in advance.'

Commios nodded.

'And landfall wherever we end up. I don't know the coast across there.' He glanced over his shoulder towards the gently heaving swell behind him. The wind had fallen still further with the darkness but it was backing, blowing off the land behind them.

'One condition.' Commios raised his hand. 'You tell no one you have seen us when you come back. If you do the wrath of God will fall on you.'

The man grimaced. 'The wrath of my wife will fall on me if she hears where we've been. Don't worry about that, my friend. We tell no one. No one at all.'

33

Jess stirred. Something was touching her face. Her eyes flickered open. Above her she could see the canopy of leaves; they stirred a little in the light, casting dappled shadows over her. She tried to move and let out a gasp of pain. Every bone in her body was screaming with agony. She bit her lip and lay still for a moment before trying again. Sweat poured off her, then moments later she started to shiver. Sunlight played over her face and she tried to open her eyes again. Someone was there above her, standing over her. She screwed up her eyes trying to see more clearly. 'Help me.' Her whisper was inaudible.

There it was again. The light touch on her face. She could feel whatever it was moving down her cheek towards her neck. Cold. Sharp. The tip of a sword. He was holding it to her throat. She was shaking now, gazing piteously up at his face. She could see him smiling coldly down at her, his eyes as hard as flint, his head silhouetted against the shimmering leaves.

Something dripped on her face. She flinched. It was blood. She could see it trickling down the broad flat blade. 'Please help me.' She could feel the words sticking to her tongue, cloying. No sound came out.

'Jess!'

Someone was calling her in the distance. 'Jess, where are you?' 'I'm here!' she tried to answer, but it was no use. The only sound was the gentle cooing of a pigeon high up in the trees.

The stiffened leather straps on his tunic creaked slightly as he moved. She could see his fingers tightening around the hilt of his sword, his knuckles white.

'Titus,' she whispered. 'Please don't hurt me.' She was sobbing now, soundlessly, tears running sideways down her cheeks into the moss on which she was lying. 'Where's Dan? Please, don't let him find me.'

He said nothing.

Then from somewhere close by she heard the low threatening growl of a dog. She tried to move her head, to see. A black shadow hovered near her. 'Hugo?' her whisper was almost soundless. 'Help me.'

The growl grew louder. Titus half-turned to face the animal. She closed her eyes, holding her breath. When she reopened them he had gone.

'Hugo? Help me.' She tried to reach out. She felt a moment of warmth and comfort on her hand, a dog's lick. Then it had gone.

From somewhere in the distance she heard the voice calling again. It was further away this time. She tried to change her position to ease the pain in her bones and hesitantly, as though speaking a language of which she had little grasp, she began to pray. The effort was too much. Slowly her eyelids closed and she slid gently into the warm darkness where there was no fear and no pain.

As the sun rose out of the sea behind them the boat ran aground on the soft sand and the two men jumped out. Commios stepped over the side after them, ankle-deep in water and began to haul their bundles out of the boat, throwing them up the beach.

'You've done well, my friends. Thank you.' He gave his hand to Eigon, helping her up onto the edge of the boat. Then he swung her onto the beach. She was smiling for all her exhaustion, energised by the sea crossing. Unable to resist he leaned forward and kissed her cheek. Before she had a chance to react he had turned back to the boat. 'Drusilla?' He grinned. She was huddled on the bottom boards, groaning, half-hidden by the sail the men had dropped as they coasted in on the tide. 'We're there. Come on, up you get! No more sailing!'

Somehow she sat up and trembling with exhaustion, hauled herself to her feet. Commios lifted her onto the beach and she collapsed clutching her stomach.

'Hope you don't plan to go back any time soon!' One of the sailors eyed her in amusement. 'Not a born sailor, that lady!'

Commios chuckled. 'She'll be fine! Bless you, my friends.' The fare was already paid but he felt in his pouch for an extra coin or two and tossed them over. Already they were pushing the boat away into the deeper water. 'Safe journey back!' The light from the rising sun was shimmering in a scarlet stream across the water, glittering through the mist. They watched as the men hauled up the sail, catching the changing wind to carry them down the coast. In no time at all they had vanished into the haze.

'Right!' Commios looked round. 'So, where do we go next?' He raised an eyebrow at Eigon.

She shrugged. 'I know no more than you! Presumably we make our way to a town where we can find lodgings. Then we will start.'

'Start what?' Drusilla pushed her bedraggled hair back from her face with a shiver. The promise of the sunrise had already gone; the day was turning grey, the wind cold. They were all shivering by the time they turned their backs on the sea and headed up the beach towards the scrubby woodland which topped the low cliffs before them.

'Our mission.' Eigon tried to smile. They had been heading westward so long, with their goal to reach Britannia. But now they were here it was hard to know what to do next. They didn't even know which part of Britannia they had landed in.

'At least if we had taken a regular trading vessel we would have put in at a port and been on a proper route,' Drusilla said sharply.

'And Titus could have been on the next boat,' Commios reprimanded gently. 'We can't be far from somewhere.' He grinned. 'Let's pray for guidance.'

There was a track at the top of the cliff. They followed it for some time, feeling more and more miserable as the weather grew colder and more windy. They were about to call a halt and find a sheltered spot to make a fire when Commios paused.

'Someone has second guessed us. Can you smell burning?'

'I can smell food!' Eigon smiled encouragement. 'Let us hope the natives are friendly!' She was about to move on when he caught her arm.

'Until we know how friendly, I think from now on we should keep to ourselves who you are and what we are doing here, agreed?'

She nodded. They both glanced at Drusilla. She shrugged. 'Don't look at me like that. I am hardly likely to be the one to blurt anything out, am I!' She pulled her cloak around her shoulders more tightly.

Almost around the next corner in the woodland scrub they stumbled upon a small encampment of charcoal burners. To their surprise they were made instantly welcome and for the first time in fourteen years Eigon heard the Celtic of Britannia spoken in her native land. The cauldron hanging over the fire contained savoury hare stew, thickened with dried peas and flavoured with wild garlic, in the clay oven there were loaves of bread, and bean cakes. To drink there were jugs of ale. With the head of the family was his wife, their three children and two of his brothers. The men were shy but the woman and the children were curious about their visitors and eager to talk. When they heard that they had come across the sea in a small fishing boat they were awestruck. They were not totally isolated though. They were, they said, part of the Cantiaci tribe and they had been to the Roman settlement Durovernum Cantiacorum. There they said there were people and houses, tradesmen and shops and temples and an open air theatre. It was a huge place, full of riches. Their visitors should go there first, they advised, and then maybe follow the road to Londinium.

They slept in one of the charcoal burners' huts that night and next day set off, restored by the rest, towards Durovernum.

They had expected a great trading town like Massilia. This place was far smaller; although there were good houses and as they had been told shops and temples they found they could walk the breadth of the town in a short time. They found themselves lodgings in a private house near the outer walls of the fort. It was clean and neat, owned by the widow of an officer in the XIV legion. A tall, striking woman, Octavia Candida had strong bones, faded fair hair and light blue eyes which betrayed her British origins. As her slaves brought in an evening meal she quizzed them about their travels, eager to hear where they had been. Discovering that they came from Rome itself her eyes widened. 'Is it as wonderful as they say? I have never been further than Verulamium. I came from the Catuvellauni originally. I expect you guessed that I am British. My husband and I came here when he retired from the legion.'

Eigon suppressed a little gasp at the name, but Commios gave her a warning frown. 'So, what is life like in Britannia, lady?'

She shrugged. 'After the rebellion it was very tough. So much damage was done. Verulamium was burned you know, by Boudica. All my family there were killed by her followers. She could not forgive those who supported Roman rule.' She sighed. 'Even here there was rebellion and fighting as British tribesmen went to her support. But at least this town was not burned. You will see, there is a lot of building going on. We are becoming ever more wealthy. They are constructing new baths and another temple.' She smiled up at the young slave who was placing the bowls of food before them. 'Where are you going?'

'Siluria.' Eigon had said it without thinking.

Octavia's eyes widened. 'That is a long way.'

Eigon nodded. She raised an eyebrow at Commios to silence him. 'My family came from there many years ago. I wanted to go back, to see what was there.' She gave a disarming smile.

Octavia shrugged. 'There is a fort, I know, at Isca Silurum. My husband was stationed there before the battle with Caratacus when they were trying to subjugate the Silures and again after they defeated him. They are a fearsome warlike people, I gather. They still give the authorities much trouble.' She paused, realising she might have been tactless. 'I'm sorry. If that is your tribe, forgive me, my dear. It is hard sometimes not to say the wrong thing!'

Eigon smiled. 'I can see it is difficult. We have crossed Gaul and things are much the same there. We found hospitality with Roman families and with people of the land. Both were kind, but they were suspicious of one another.'

Octavia nodded. 'It is better here. Being on the main road from Rutupiae to Londinium we constantly have travellers going in both directions from every corner of the Empire. That is why I decided to welcome people to stay here. It's interesting and,' she shrugged without embarrassment, 'it augments my husband's pension. I had a party from Rome only three days ago.' She paused for the first time, seeming to choose her words with care. 'Things seem to have been very difficult in Rome since this terrible fire. You knew about that?'

They nodded. Commios reached for more bread. 'We were there. It was dreadful.'

'I hear they blame a sect who follow a man called Jesus Christ.' Octavia picked up the wine jug and topped up their beakers. 'Nero has exacted a terrible revenge on any he can capture. It seems strange that a man who proclaims himself a god of love should be blamed with so much.' She shook her head. Putting down the jug, she was not looking at their faces and didn't notice the sudden tension of the guests at her table. 'I hear their leader has been crucified, like their god, Jesus.'

'Their leader?' It was Drusilla who managed to blurt out the question. Octavia looked up and at last saw their anguished faces. 'Oh, my dears. Don't tell me you follow the Christ. I am so sorry. I spoke so carelessly.'

'Do you know the name of their leader? Who was it?'

'A man called Peter. The Rock, they said. He was an old man apparently.' She sighed. 'Nero has done so many terrible things, but this –' She paused. 'They told me he had been crucified upside down, in the Neronian circus. I expect you know where that is?'

Commios nodded. His mouth had gone dry. 'It is where Nero goes to amuse himself.' His voice was heavy with bitterness. There was a moment's silence. Drusilla and Eigon were holding one another's hands, trying to hold back their tears.

Octavia looked from one to the other in deep sympathy. 'You knew him? But of course you did. Forgive me for having to break such awful news.' She stood up. 'Let me leave you alone for a little while,' she said in a whisper. 'I am sure you will want to pray for him.'

Commios looked up sharply. 'You have had Christians staying here before, lady?'

She smiled. 'Of course. As I told you, we have all sorts here. All are welcome to my house.'

'I can't believe it!' Commios hit the table with his fist as the door closed behind her. 'How can he have been caught! Did someone betray him?' There were tears in his eyes too now. 'Is no one safe?'

'Perhaps he knew,' Eigon said sadly. 'Perhaps that is why he sent us away. And others. If there are other Christians in this country perhaps they were sent by him, or by Paul.' She gave them a watery smile. 'At least now he is with Our Lord and I expect he is watching over us at this very moment.'

Drusilla gazed up at the ceiling nervously. 'Do you think so?' She glanced at Commios and blushed. 'Do you think he can read our thoughts?'

'If he can,' he retorted sternly, 'he will know that we are about to pray together for his soul, and that we are thinking only of our duty to spread the word.' He bit his lip. 'We have been very remiss in not doing that so far.'

'We had to get here,' Eigon said sharply. 'There would have been no point in telling everyone who we were and being caught at the first place we stayed. We had to avoid Titus.' She shivered. 'Do you think he will follow us over the Ocean?'

Commios nodded wearily. 'Yes, I think he will. So I think we should get away from here tomorrow. This town is obviously the first stop for people who are coming off the boats from Gaul. We need to plan a route across country, away from the main roads, so we can give him the slip for good. I am so tired of always running from this man!' He thumped the table with his fist again. He glanced from one woman to the other. 'So, let us pray together now for Peter and our friends in Rome.'

They bowed their heads.

As they did so a weary horseman was riding through the town gates, his horse covered in dust, his uniform muddy and salt-stained. He dismounted at the first *mansio* and beckoned a lounging boy to take his horse. 'Do you have friends, boy?'

The young man gazed at him vacantly without deigning to reply. 'If you have and they want to earn themselves some money present yourselves here as soon as my horse has been fed and watered. I have a job for you.'

It had worked at every town he had visited across Gaul. Enquiries at every *hospes, taberna, mansio* or *caupona*, every temple, every Jewish settlement, every house that had ever been known to take guests, every by way, every crossroads, every ferry. People remembered strangers, even in a town that was used to them. And a man with two women was not that usual on the road. He gave a grim smile. All the time he had been getting closer and now he was so near he could feel them by the tingling in his fingers. He smiled to himself. Perhaps it was time to act. And he would start, of necessity, with Commios. He reached without even knowing he did it for his sword and loosened it slightly in its scabbard.

Rhodri stood staring down across the folded hills towards his own home, nestling just below his line of sight across the valley. Behind the hills the sky had grown dark. Thunder grumbled in the distance and as he watched he saw a fork of lightning cut across the sky.

Where was she? If Dan had her, he could not have taken her far unless he had managed to get her to his car. But there had been no sign of a car parked up on the track. It wasn't a place that passers-by came to; the only tyre marks were those of his own vehicle and the local tractor and trailer. The more recent tracks were from the police car and from his mother's. Before that the rain of the last few days had smoothed the mud clean. If Dan had driven up within the last twenty-four hours there would have been signs. Rhodri sighed.

Supposing it wasn't Dan. Supposing they were guessing completely wrongly? Supposing she had fallen in the steep woods? Or been taken ill. Supposing Titus was there, patrolling the trees.

He took a deep breath. The only way to search such a huge area was with dogs. The police had felt it was too early to bring in tracker dogs; but he could fetch up the dogs from the farm. He groped in his pocket for his mobile. If there was anything to be found they would know. And while he waited for Megan to bring them over he would go on looking. He ached with misery. His loss was so acute he could feel its presence in his soul. If he had ever doubted it he knew it now. He had fallen in love with her.

'Jess?' His voice echoed uselessly down the hillside. 'Jess, are you there, my lovely? Jess –'

'That's Rhodri calling.' Steph and Aurelia were standing in the yard as Megan climbed into her car and pulled away to go and collect the dogs.

'He's devastated,' Aurelia said thoughtfully. 'He should have gone back to London by now. He's singing at the Proms in a few weeks and he said he had a lot of work to do on the piece but he won't consider leaving while all this is going on. Did you know he was so fond of Jess?'

Steph shook her head in bewilderment. 'He does seem to have fallen for her, God knows why!'

'Does Jess feel the same way?'

Steph paused to think, then she nodded. 'I think she might. I think she was still fond of Will, but that was all it was. He had hurt her so badly she could never have trusted him again. Poor Will.' She sighed.

Come and find me! Where are you?

A child's voice came to them from the distance, far away up the track. Aurelia paled. 'Did you hear that?'

Steph nodded.

'Is that your ghost?'

'I think so. There aren't any real children wandering around in the woods.'

They both looked up at the distant rumble of thunder.

'That poor little soul lying up there,' Aurelia murmured. 'I can't take it in.' She hugged her arms around herself with a shudder. 'But they are talking English?'

Steph shrugged. 'Perhaps it is because it's us listening. Doesn't it filter through our brains or something? Otherwise we wouldn't understand.'

'I hope Meryn gets in touch soon. He will know what to do. About the child. About Titus. He will probably know what to do about Dan.' Aurelia shook her head. 'I wish Rhodri would come back. I feel so vulnerable here, just you and me.' She glanced round, shivering. 'This is such an isolated spot, Steph. I can't think how you can live here on your own.'

Steph gave a wan smile. 'And that comment is from our intrepid lady explorer who traverses unknown wastes alone and lives in the Pyrenees miles from anywhere and lived near here herself once upon a time!'

'My mountains aren't haunted,' Aurelia said pointedly.

'I bet they are!'

'Well, if they are they aren't bothering to haunt me.' She shivered again.

Behind them the phone rang in the kitchen. Steph ran indoors with Aurelia following more sedately behind.

Steph handed her the phone. 'Your friend Meryn.'

At the end of their conversation she was smiling. Meryn had listened to her story, asked some questions and suggested he drive down at once from Scotland.

'He'll be here some time this evening. I think he was glad of the excuse to come back.'

Steph raised an eyebrow. 'I suppose it's no good me asking about him?'

Aurelia shook her head. 'If you mean about him and me, I've told you, there is nothing to tell. The important thing is that he has devoted his life to studying weird stuff and he will help.'

Steph sat down at the kitchen table and rested her chin on her hands. 'I suppose nothing comes much weirder than this! I hope to God he can sort us out.' She blinked rapidly, trying to hold back her tears. 'I am so glad you are here.' She reached out across the table and clutched her mother's hands.

Returning with the dogs Megan parked her ancient Land Rover in the yard and climbed out as the two dogs leaped down from the back. 'Where's Rhodri?'

'He hasn't come back yet.' Steph was wearing her walking boots and carrying a stick. 'Mummy is going to stay here by the phone. I thought I would walk up with you. The dogs will at least find Rhodri, won't they? Then the three of us can spread out.'

Rhodri was sitting on a tree stump in a clearing some mile and a half from the summit. He had followed a barely perceptible track through the undergrowth, wandering without much thought wherever the path led. His throat was sore from shouting. He was exhausted. As the dogs raced up to him, their tails wagging he looked up. His eyes were red and puffy.

'I've brought Jess's scarf.' Steph rummaged in her pocket. 'So the dogs can smell it.'

Rhodri smiled. 'They're not trained for tracking, Steph. Just for sheep. Better just to tell them to find Jess. They probably won't know what they're looking for, but they'll rush around a lot and we'll know if they find something. Anything.' He glanced at his mother. 'Dad didn't want to come?' It was beginning to rain. He brushed raindrops off his face with the back of his wrist.

She shook her head. 'He wasn't there. I think he went into market this morning. Doesn't matter. I'll send them. Might as well start here as anywhere?' She turned and called the dogs. At her command they both sniffed at Jess's scarf with interest, wagging their tails, then she sent them away. They shot off into the trees and within seconds they had disappeared from sight as a louder rumble of thunder echoed round them.

They worked across the hill in circles, to no avail. By midafternoon it was raining hard and they were too exhausted to go on. Disconsolately trailing back to Ty Bran through the rain and wind, they flung themselves down at the kitchen table, watching as the dogs drank frantically from the large bowl of water Aurelia put down for them.

'The police rang.' Aurelia looked at Rhodri. 'They are going to put up a helicopter as soon as the storm has passed.' She tried to keep her voice steady. 'Have something to eat at least. No one can go on without food and rest. You all look completely done in.'

'Is there any word about Dan?' Rhodri pushed his hair back from his face with both hands. There was a long bramble scratch across his forehead.

Aurelia shook her head. 'They are looking.'

'There must be something else we can do. I'll ring them again.' Rhodri climbed wearily to his feet and went to the phone.

When he turned back to them he was frowning. 'They have found Dan's car. They were going to tell us, apparently. Maybe next year! It was locked and parked in Newtown. In the town centre car park. No trace of him.'

'So he was on his way here.'

Rhodri shrugged. 'They said they are doing forensic tests on it.' He paused. 'Maybe he hasn't got here yet after all.' He sounded hopeful.

'So Jess's disappearance could have nothing to do with him.' Aurelia stared out of the window, her face drawn with anxiety. Rain was streaming down the glass. Lightning flashed across the yard and another clap of thunder shook the house.

'Or he had been and gone before we even realised Jess was missing.' Rhodri threw himself back into his chair. 'It's all my fault. If I had just waited for her!'

Megan leaned across and touched his hand. 'Don't waste energy beating yourself up, son. We'll find her.'

Meryn was exhausted when at last his car pulled into the courtyard. Megan and the dogs had long gone back to the farm. Rhodri was still there though, refusing to leave.

A tall distinguished figure with thick grey hair brushed back from a lean, weather-beaten face, Meryn pulled two bags out of the car into the rain and headed into the house. The smaller contained his toothbrush and razor and a change of clothes, the larger the items he might need in his professional capacity as a walker between the worlds. Dressed in faded jeans and an open-necked shirt he looked more like a retired school teacher than the be-robed Druid that Steph and Rhodri had been expecting. He bent to kiss Aurelia on the cheek, shook hands with the others and followed them into the farmhouse. Already he could feel the turbulent energies whirling around the building. Some were from the present, but some, far more interestingly, were from the distant past.

Aurelia had tried to distract herself from her anguish while they were waiting by cooking a meal and the house was full of the savoury smell of a slow-cooking stew.

'You must be hungry after that long drive!' she insisted. She passed Meryn a glass of wine. 'We can tell you everything while we eat.'

It was Steph who did most of the talking. From time to time she glanced at Rhodri for support but he was picking at his food, lost in misery. She saw Meryn watching him too, but most of the time he gave Steph his full attention, his thoughtful eyes fixed on her face.

When at last she had finished there was a long silence broken at last by Rhodri as he pushed aside his plate. 'Can you help, do you think?'

Meryn nodded. 'I will do my best but until I have had a chance to wander round and get a feel of things, I can't tell you much.' He looked at Aurelia. 'That meal was a feast for the senses, my dear.' He pushed back his chair and stood up. 'Now, if I may I would like to feel my way around the house on my own, then I will go into the outbuildings. After that I might want to walk up the hill along the track you have mentioned. While I do that I suggest you all try and get some rest. Distract yourselves. Have a cup of tea.'

'Can't I come?' Steph looked up at him anxiously.

He shook his head. 'I would rather you didn't at this stage. I find I can hear and see things better on my own. If I need your help I will ask for it. If I'm reading the situation aright, the two people at the centre of this whole conundrum of yours are Eigon and Titus. Jess and Dan have been dragged in and to a greater or lesser extent used by them in their on-going battle. I hope we will find them soon but it will probably be through Eigon. I need to contact her and I will do that better alone.' He glanced at Rhodri. 'I use shamanic techniques to do this. Later I may need your help.'

Rhodri raised an eyebrow. He shrugged. 'I'll do whatever I can.'

'I believe so.' Meryn inclined his head with a trace of a smile.

'Let me at least show you my studio.' Steph stood up hastily. 'According to Jess that's where it all started.'

Meryn stood for a while, his thumbs tucked into the belt of his jeans, listening to the silence. The storm had moved on. He could still hear it rumbling away in the east, but the full force of it had passed. The rain had lessened. From somewhere in the yard he could hear water gurgling down a drainpipe; occasional drops reverberated on the roof, but otherwise it was very quiet. The atmosphere in the large room was strangely muffled by the clay; he was intrigued. He hadn't worked in a studio before. The overlay of earthy materials plus the agitation of the creative technique clogged the messages he was getting from the surroundings. He walked slowly round, gazing down at the pots and sculptures on the shelves, the huge cold kiln squatting in the corner, the dusty table, the sacks of materials, the tins and bottles of pigment and glaze. Slowly he was feeling his way down through the layers. Before this was a studio it had been a byre. For storage and for animals. Men had sheltered here; and sheep. Long passages of time had passed where the place had slept untroubled by any usage at all. There had been trees here, growing up through the jumbled stones of the walls. They had grown old and rotted and fallen. Others had been cut down. Elders had been ripped up without apology, their roots torn screaming from the soil. Piles of slate had stood against a wall, moss growing through and over them, pulling them back into the native rock from whence they had been wrenched. They had been removed and the builders had come in to neaten and tidy the site. He gave a half-smile. Their thoughts and fears and jibes were recorded in the echoes of the building as much as the hesitancies of the current owner in her creative torment. Perhaps he could help her see where she should be going. Her talent was flailing without enough confidence to drive it on.

He shook his head slightly. He had to get past all this. Further back. Down the years into the darkness.

Now he could see it. The place was a byre again, the stones had tumbled and it was half-roofed against the winter snows. But here was a group of men. Their lust was like a slash of vicious scarlet across the darkness of the night. They had lost control of themselves in the bloody battle in which they had been involved. They no longer thought. They no longer reasoned. Titus Marcus Olivinus was their leader. Where he led, they followed.

Meryn watched, a shadow from the future, as the men thrust again and again into the screaming helpless women. He saw the child dragged out; he saw the others hesitate but Titus, his eyes filmed with bloodlust, threw her down and fell on her.

When he had finished they went back to their horses, leaving the women and the child for dead. Titus was exalted, triumphant, his followers subdued as the hoofbeats echoed into the darkness of time.

Meryn waited. He had learned to empty his mind, to wait without judgement, without involvement. If he was to act he had to be in control.

He saw the second band of soldiers come. He saw their leader's compassion, the men's revulsion. These were disciplined legionaries acting under a code of war.

The women were removed. The byre sank back into the darkness, but the stench of fear and blood remained. Then after a while a small child appeared, nervous as a young deer with huge dark-blue eyes. The little girl peered round. 'Eigon?' Her voice was tremulous. 'Eigon, where are you? Are we still playing the game? Can we come out now?'

He could feel the watching trees, bending closer. There was nothing they could do. She wandered into the enclosure sniffing at the atmosphere like a small animal, knowing that what she sensed was bad, yet not knowing how to interpret it. He saw her stand still suddenly. In front of her a patch of blood showed black on the grass. She glanced up. It was growing light. Merciful darkness was drawing back. Soon she would see blood everywhere.

'Eigon? Where are you?' The little voice was tremulous. 'I don't know where Togo has gone.' Suddenly she was crying. 'I'm all alone.'

Meryn watched helplessly. For a while she hung around then, disconsolate, her little shoulders slumped with misery, she turned back and trailed away into the trees.

He shook his head. So much pain and fear and unhappiness etched on the surrounding countryside. The battlefield below in the valley, death and destruction everywhere, up here this small but anguished scene, one man's vicious crime crying out for retribution.

He waited. The scene darkened. Day followed night; the weather changed. Ravens circled the battlefield, servants of the goddess of death. Kites picked clean the bones that had remained unburied. It grew cold; the snows came. The little girl never returned. He sent feelers out after her into the woodland. There was nothing there. He searched for the little boy. It was a small spark, so easily extinguished; a life force gone almost before it had lived. He caught a glimpse of the small body curled in the darkness. He was sucking his thumb, his eyes closed tightly against his fear and loneliness. A fox trotted past his hiding place and paused, paw raised, its nose quivering to test the air. It smelled human; it smelled fever. It turned away and fled. A wolf mother might have sensed a lonely cub and suckled him; the fox turned about its business and disappeared without a backward thought into the night. By morning the little boy was dead.

'So,' Meryn breathed. 'We have two little girls. Eigon and Glads. We know what happened to Eigon but where is her sister?' He waited. A stray beam of light crawled across the floor of the studio towards him as for a moment the storm clouds parted. He watched it thoughtfully. The sun had almost set. She was older; maybe she had gone elsewhere to find help.

The byre's story was told. Tomorrow he would cleanse it of its memories. For now it was time to go outside. He let himself out into the courtyard and walked slowly towards the gate into the lane. An owl was calling in the distance. He smiled. She was hunting away from the hills this evening, flying out across the fields looking for voles in the wet grass. If he could see through her eyes he might be able to find Jess. When Steph told him about the dogs looking for her this afternoon she had indicated with a nod the crumpled silk scarf they had used to try and show the dogs who they were looking for. Before supper he had quietly picked it up and put it in his pocket. He drew it out now, winding it round his hand, tuning into the woman who had been wearing it.

And there he was. Titus Marcus Olivinus. Older now, with greying hair, and deep-set watchful eyes, heart and soul heavy with hatred and fear. Obsessive, his whole being centred on one person.

Eigon.

Jess.

485

Eigon.

They were not the same person. There was no sign there of a soul reborn; no kindred; no descent, but Titus connected them in his twisted mind. No, not his. Meryn ranged wider, following secret pathways through the air around him. This was where it had happened. Where the lines had become crossed. Jess had been interested. Sympathetic. Vulnerable. She had been caught up in Eigon's memories and somehow a pathway had opened between them.

But it had worked both ways. Dan. Dan and Titus. Meryn rubbed his chin, pondering. Dan had followed Jess here and Titus had followed Eigon. He could see Dan. Tall, intense, jealous. Dan had brought hatred and anger back to the mountain; his emotions had acted as conductor. The life stories had flared and run like wildfire between the four characters who had met here at this house and the destruction had begun.

'But are you still alive, Jess?' Meryn walked across the courtyard and opened the gate, standing for a minute in the lane. The thunder and lightning had cleared the air. Now he could sense more clearly. She had turned right and walked up the path to the summit; then she had come halfway back. She had moved off the path, following some subconscious urge. It had led her into the trees and eventually round behind the cottage.

She had heard someone singing; that was it. A voice had led her deeper and deeper into the woods. It was like a fairy story. He tensed, listening. This voice had been ghostly. The voice of a woman keening for her dead love.

Jess had followed it as Glads had followed it all those years before. The woman had been kneeling beside the body of her man, a Celtic warrior, dead on the field of battle, naked but for his shield, his sword stolen by the ghouls who follow battles everywhere, his eyes taken by the ravens.

Glads stopped beside her and stood staring down at the dead man's body. The woman looked up, tears still running down her cheeks and saw the little girl with the wan face, the muddy dress, the bramble-scratched legs and arms.

Meryn watched as they clung to each other in their loneliness and misery. Glads stared down as the woman buried her man, scrabbling mud over his body until it was hidden from the birds; she watched as the woman prayed for his soul, then hand in hand, much later, the woman and the child walked away from the battlefield into the mist.

He sighed. For some reason he couldn't follow them. Someone had set up a barrier. He looked round for Jess. She had heard the woman singing too; she had followed the sound. So where was she? He turned left down the lane walking slowly in the darkness between the hedges and then turned left again through a gate into the field. He could see better here. In the coming darkness the moon had risen. Moonlight lay scattered across the rough ground. The track was leading back behind Ty Bran towards the darkness of the gorge cut by the brook into the edge of the hillside. There the ground was thick with oak and birch and fell away steeply towards the roar of the water far below. If she had fallen down there she could be badly hurt. He needed help and he needed a torch. 'Wait for me, Jess,' he breathed. 'Hang on. I'm going for Rhodri. We're coming. Soon.'

34

'I sent to ask as you wished.' The doctor smiled sadly at Julius. 'The house is empty, I'm afraid. There is no one there.'

He was sitting by the fountain in the old courtyard behind her house, his walking stick leaning against the bench beside him. 'Did your messenger ask where they had gone?' He struggled to his feet, leaning on the stick with a grimace of pain.

'He asked. No one knew. It is dangerous in Rome, Julius. No one will admit to knowing a Christian at the moment. The lady Drusilla was a known friend to Peter the Apostle. The messenger went on to ask at the house of Aulus Plautius for Pomponia Graecina as you suggested. The lady has gone away to one of their villas in the mountains. The house steward he spoke to said she had been ill and wasn't expected to return to Rome.'

'Did anyone go with her?' Julius asked. His face, still dreadfully scarred down one side, was ravaged with anxiety. The doctor shook her head. 'The man didn't know. He thought it unlikely. He said she had gone, as far as he knew with a couple of house slaves.'

'One of them might have been her. She might have been in disguise?' There was so much hope in his voice.

A whirl of wind whipped dust devils round the courtyard, spinning dead fig leaves at his feet. It had taken him a long time to remember; to separate what had happened when his friends and family had been killed from his visit to Drusilla's house in Rome. Eigon had been there, in Rome. She had been safe. She wasn't killed with Antonia and his grandfather. So what had happened to her?

The doctor noticed he had begun to shiver. She guided him slowly back inside the house. The day he had remembered the woman he loved she had known he would go. It was just a matter of time now. All she could give him was enough care and rest to make him strong and complete his cure. She sighed. She had come to love him more than she would like to admit, this most wayward and tricky of patients, but he was not for her. All she could do for him was to help him try and locate his Eigon and send him on his way.

Word came sooner than she expected. Her messenger had, it seemed, had the wit to leave a scratched note for anyone in the household who returned, a note beneath the secret sign of the fish; only three days later someone picked it up and within a week a messenger arrived at the doctor's house. It was someone Julius knew, Silas, who had once been a slave in the villa of Caratacus.

The young man stared at Julius in horror. He was the first person outside the household to see him since he had been wounded. His expression, swiftly veiled, told Julius that he was no longer a handsome man.

His heart plummeted. Leading the newcomer outside where they couldn't be overheard he asked him what had happened. It was only now he discovered the awful train of events which had followed the massacre at the farm. As far as he knew Silas had been the only one to escape the massacre. He had fled to Drusilla's house, so they had heard almost at once what had happened and that everyone had been killed. 'Including you, lord, so we thought.' He shrugged miserably. 'Princess Eigon was devastated. No amount of prayers would comfort her. In the end Peter sent her away.'

'Where?' Julius held his gaze. He already knew that he would not follow. How could she love a man as disfigured as he was?

'To Britannia.'

'What!' Julius stared at him.

'I think Peter knew the end was coming, lord. We persuaded him to flee, and he left Rome when we did, going to friends where he would be safe from the Emperor, but, the story goes,' he moved a little closer and lowered his voice, 'that he met our Lord Jesus on the road and Jesus asked him where he was going, when He himself was going to Rome to be with his followers in their hour of need. Peter knew then he could not leave his poor persecuted flock and he turned round and went back. He was captured almost at once.' The young man's face tightened into a mask of misery. 'You know he's dead?'

Julius nodded.

'The lady Pomponia Graecina has asked me to take you to her.

You can stay at the villa with her. It is a long way from Rome. You will be safe there.'

'Thank you.' Julius gave a faint smile. 'I should like that.'

The doctor had other ideas. 'I'm sorry, he's not well enough yet. Soon. I will let you come and take him soon, but while he still needs a stick and medication I can't let him go.'

Julius smiled when he heard Silas had gone without him. 'So, you can't bear to part with me?'

She nodded. 'You are too good a specimen for my students to practise on.' She gazed at him with her steady clear eyes fixed on his. 'Did he tell you where your Eigon has gone?'

He nodded. 'Far beyond my reach.'

'She's not dead?'

'No.' He shook his head. 'Not quite that bad. She has gone to Britannia with Drusilla and a handsome escort called Commios. She has no need of me.' He groped for his stick.

She could see his pain in every movement; not just physical pain now but the pain of loss all over again.

'Did she love you, Julius?'

He nodded. He was biting down hard on his lip.

'And you think she will have given her heart away already?'

'Why not? She thinks I'm dead. I might as well be. Look at me!' His barber had never let him look into a mirror, but he had in the end got hold of one belonging to the doctor's pretty daughter. It was made of polished bronze and he stared for a long time into its depths. It told him what he already knew from leaning over the basin in which he washed his face, and from running his hand endlessly over the great rough ridges down his cheek. He was ugly.

The doctor rested her hand lightly on his chest. She moved it to his face and stroked it. 'She will see the man behind the scar, Julius. Besides, I take pride in my stitchery. It will get better. It is hardly healed as yet. Go after her.' She gazed up at him.

'You said I wasn't well enough.'

'I lied.' She smiled. 'I want you out of my house before I lose my own heart to you!' She already had, but she was never going to tell him that. 'Take my son, Drusus. He is but fifteen, but he is strong and as the eldest he craves adventure. I charge you to take care of him as if he were your own. He will look after you and help dress your wounds and he has a good sense of direction! I

490

will lend you the money you need for your journey. I am a wealthy woman; you didn't know that, did you!' She managed to laugh. 'I have to spend it on something so why not on him. It will cover you both. You can travel for a while, as his tutor!' Again she laughed. 'If you travel fast you will manage to get there before the weather changes and the roads close for the winter. May your God go with you, Julius.' She stood on tiptoe and kissed him, just that once, on the lips, then she swept out of the room to tend her other patients.

They found where Jess had been lying. She seemed to have missed her footing, slipped down the steep bank, and rolled down between the trees at the bottom to come to rest near the brook at the foot of a young oak tree with half its roots overhanging the red-brown water that raced down off the high mountains. She had torn her blouse; a fine strip of green cotton was caught on a bramble, its pattern easily identifiable and Rhodri found some of her hairs tangled among the thorns. How long she had remained there no one could tell but there was no sign of her now. No footprints; nothing to say she had slipped into the stream. If she had she would have been caught on the rocks and mossy stones; it was not deep enough here, for all its speed after the storm, to carry someone away.

'So, where is she?' Rhodri sat down, his head in his hands. Steph and Aurelia sat down near him; they had brought torches and a length of rope, and a first aid box in a backpack.

'Could someone have carried her away?' Steph asked at last. For 'someone' they all understood Dan.

'If he had, we would have seen his footprints,' Aurelia said wearily. She gazed up at Meryn, her eyes brimming with tears. 'Tell us what to do.'

Meryn was thoughtful. He wandered away from them upstream, scrambling over the slippery rocks, illuminating the water with the torch they had given him. In the lightbeam the water was clear. He crouched down near a small backwater where it was still, fringed with green fern and tried to focus his eyes into the depths. For a short while, before he had descended the slope, he had made contact; he had sensed her near him. So where had she gone? There were strange forces here; he wasn't alone for

491

one thing. There were others poking around in the atmosphere, muddying the water. He glanced back towards Rhodri and the two women, studying their anxious faces in the torchlight as they huddled together. It was very dark down here, apart from the occasional flashes of light from the water as small crests and waves broke against the rocks. The noise of the water hurtling down from the faraway tops of the hills was deafening, funnelled between the rocks and banks. If she was calling they wouldn't hear her; but she wasn't calling. He sensed a total quiet which worried him more than he would like to admit. He scrambled back towards them.

'Does the name Marcia mean anything to any of you?'

Steph exchanged glances with Rhodri and shrugged. They both looked blank. He looked at Aurelia, who didn't know either.

Meryn shook his head wryly. 'Someone else is out there looking for Jess. Not your friend Dan.' He paused, then shook his head again. 'I think we are looking into the past here. At Titus.'

The name reverberated strangely in his head; he flinched.

'Meryn?' Aurelia whispered. 'What is it?'

'Marcia Maximilla,' he murmured. 'Ah, lady, there you are. I can see you. Very clever.' His eyes were shut. 'Very powerful. Impressive.'

The other three glanced at each other; no one spoke.

'So, have you found her yet? Is it Jess you are looking for?' He seemed to be talking to himself. 'No, I see it's Eigon you are after, but Jess is your route to her. What a tangled web you've woven down the years. Eigon has sealed herself away from you hasn't she. She's been taught well.' His torch went out suddenly. He didn't seem to notice. 'Jess has been taken into her protection.' He breathed out slowly then he opened his eyes. 'We are wasting our time here. I'm sorry to have brought you on a wild goose chase.'

'But she was here!' Aurelia pointed at the fibres hanging from the brambles.

'Yes, she was, but she's gone.' Meryn reached out a hand to help her stand up. 'Come back to the house. She may be back there already.'

They followed him in silence back up the steep muddy gorge, hauling themselves up from tree to tree panting until they were once more in the field and then back in the lane. Exhausted, Steph fumbled in her pocket for the key and pushed the front door open. She paused. The sitting room door was open, the light on. 'Jess?' She hurried across the hall, the others following.

Dan was sitting on the sofa near the window, his back propped up with cushions, a cup of coffee on the low table in front of him. A shotgun lay on the table.

Steph stopped. 'Dan!' She scanned the room, aware of the others behind her clustered in the doorway. 'How in God's name did you get in? Where's Jess?'

Dan stared at them. The spare keys he had taken so long ago from the board in the kitchen were lying on the table in front of him. He ignored her question. 'About time. Where have you been?' His voice was husky with exhaustion. His jeans were muddy, his shirt rumpled. 'You've been so long I had to make myself something to eat and drink!'

'We were out looking for Jess,' Steph said slowly. 'Where is she?'

He gave a grim smile. 'Not here,' he gestured round the room, 'as you can see.' His glance flicked behind her to where Aurelia and Rhodri were standing in the doorway. 'Come in, please. Do I know this lady? I wondered whose car that was outside.' He focused on Aurelia.

'I'm Jess's mother,' Aurelia answered. 'You, I take it, are the man who has been pursuing her.' Her voice was acid. Behind her Meryn had melted out of sight, tiptoeing unseen towards the kitchen. Well and good if Dan thought his car belonged to Aurelia.

'Your daughter is a silly little flirt!' Dan said conversationally. 'But I do need to speak to her. Why else would I come to this godforsaken hole! SIT DOWN!' His voice hardened as Rhodri put his hands on Aurelia's shoulders and moved her aside so he could enter the room. Dan leaned forward and pushed aside his coffee cup almost casually as he pulled the gun towards him and hefted it onto his knee.

'Where did you get that?' Steph whispered.

'I stole it!' Dan smiled. 'Astounding really. I parked next to this ancient Land Rover in Newtown. The old farmer just got out and walked off. Never even locked it. There was the gun lying half-covered with a blanket in the back. What is more the old fool had left his keys in the ignition. I took the car as well!' He chuckled. 'Full box of ammunition in the glove pocket. I'll bet he hasn't even reported it missing. He could go to prison for being so careless with a firearm!'

He moved the gun fractionally, easing his position, loosely hooking his finger round the trigger.

'Is that loaded?' Aurelia asked softly.

'I'd be more of a fool than even you could dream of if it wasn't!' Dan retorted. 'Yes, Mrs Kendal, it's loaded. And cocked.' He smiled. 'So, I ask you again. Where is Jess?'

'We don't know. That's the point!' Rhodri put in. 'We have been looking for her all day. We thought you had taken her.' His eyes were fixed on the gun.

Dan shook his head. 'Obviously not.'

'If you're serious, then she's in trouble. She's out there somewhere, lost!' Rhodri said tautly. He was holding his temper in with difficulty.

'Lost and waiting for me to find her!' Dan raised an eyebrow.

Steph was staring at him, mesmerised. 'We know you killed Will,' she said, her voice shaking. 'How could you!'

'Ah, you probably shouldn't have told me that,' he said, shifting his gaze imperceptibly so he could see her face. 'Now I know I have nothing to lose by killing you as well.' He paused thoughtfully. 'At least two of you, anyway. A left and a right. That would be easy at this range. After that of course I would have to reload. That would be harder with one person left, afraid for their life. The question is, which two will I shoot first? Rhodri of course because I dislike him intensely. But you two.' He shook his head as he looked with mock concern from Steph to Aurelia and back. 'That I don't know.'

There was a sharp bang on the window behind him. Dan leaped to his feet, the gun held low in front of him and backed towards the wall. 'What was that?'

'Perhaps it was Jess?'

Rhodri stared at the window. Meryn must be out there. He had caught a glimpse of movement in the dark as a figure dodged across the window out of sight. Another bang on the pane caused Dan to lift the gun to his shoulder. 'Who is it?' he shouted. 'Come out or I'll shoot!'

Another bang. Someone was throwing stones at the glass. Dan swore. He was finding it hard to hold the gun steady. 'Who is it?' He swung it at Rhodri. 'Who's out there?'

494

'Jess!' Rhodri shouted. 'Jess, for God's sake keep away. Call the police.'

Dan swore again. He edged round towards the French window. 'You said she was missing!'

'Obviously she is found!' Rhodri retorted. He stepped closer to Dan as Dan's attention veered between them and the window and stopped as the gun swung towards him again. Behind him something flew at the window out of the darkness. The glass smashed and Dan swung the gun back. He fired off one barrel, the sound deafening inside the room as a flowerpot landed on the floor, scattering earth and geranium petals at Dan's feet.

'One shot gone,' Rhodri said, taunting. 'So this one's mine?' He lunged forward into a rugger tackle which managed to put him under the gun's barrel, pushing it violently upwards. The second blast hit the ceiling between the beams and chunks of plaster fell round them as with a roar of fury Dan hurled the gun away and leaped forward eluding Rhodri's clutching fingers, pushed between Steph and Aurelia and hurtled out into the front hall.

'Out of my way!' Rhodri threw himself after him. 'I'm going to get that bastard!' In seconds the two men had vanished into the courtyard and out into the night.

'She's betrayed us!' Drusilla burst in through the door, her face white. 'There are soldiers outside.'

Commios leaped to his feet and ran to the doorway. 'Where?'

'Outside! I had gone to the latrine! I turned the wrong way in the passage outside and there they were at the outer door. Our oh-so-kind hostess was talking to two men in uniform. She was pointing over her shoulder towards this room.'

Commios turned round, frantically searching the room for another exit. 'This way!'

He led the others through the door which led directly to the kitchen quarters. A single slave was in there languidly finishing rinsing through the bowls and plates they had used at dinner. He turned in surprise as they burst in.

'Which way to the street?' Commios shouted in Celtic.

The man pointed at an open door. It led into a deserted alley, strewn with windblown rubbish. A dog, nosing through the piles of refuse, took one look at them and fled. They followed it away from the main street to where the alley debouched into a quiet back road lined with high walls. 'There's nowhere to hide!' Commios swore. 'This way!' They followed him a few paces, then doubled back with him into another doorway. It led into the kitchen of another house two doors down from the one where they had been staying. He paused, holding up his hand to stop them in their tracks. They waited, trying desperately to quieten their breathing as they crept forward. There was no sign of anyone there. Then they realised what had happened. The sound of raised voices from the street outside had attracted the people in this house to the main door where they were clustered staring out at a party of soldiers, swords drawn, who were pushing their way into the house from which they had escaped.

'Which way?' Commios stared round. 'Where do we go?'

'Upstairs?' Drusilla pointed behind them at a steep ladder which led from the kitchen up into some kind of store room. 'We can hide there until it's dark.'

They climbed as fast as they could, pulling themselves up to a loft area filled with boxes and barrels, and quietly made their way into the far corner where they settled down behind some sacks of flour.

Commios leaned back against the wall and closed his eyes. 'That woman deserves to be fried in pig's lard.' He was still out of breath.

'And we've lost all our things,' Drusilla wailed, 'everything!'

'Have you still got our money?' Eigon said to Commios sharply.

He nodded. 'The purse is on my belt. We'll have to get out of here once it's dark as you say, then somehow get out of the town at dawn when they open the gates.'

'They'll be watching those like hawks,' Eigon put in. 'Once they know we have escaped from the house.'

'Will they look here?' Drusilla's voice shook.

'I doubt it.' Eigon reached across and pressed her hand. 'Don't worry. God is with us. He has kept us one step ahead so far.' She sighed, closing her eyes against the dusty darkness around them. 'We'll travel faster without our bundles. Jesus travelled with only a staff and a purse, did he not?'

'Then we will need a stout staff each!' Commios commented dryly. 'We haven't even got that much!'

'We'll cut them tomorrow when we get out into the forest!' Eigon said. There was a trace of amusement in her voice.

A sound below them made them all tense. Someone had walked into the kitchen. There was a rattle of pots and pans and the sound of water being poured from a jug into a basin. Someone was pottering round, tidying up. For a while the noises continued then they heard the squeak of the outside door being closed. Two bolts were shot into place, someone – a man – cleared his throat, then his footsteps pattered away into the distance. Silence ensued. Commios put his finger to his lips. No one made a sound. Outside it was growing dark.

Eigon leaned across towards Commios. 'Why not stay here till dawn?' she whispered. Her lips touched his hair. 'It's safer than going outside where we don't know our way round.'

He turned towards her. Her face was so close to his. He nodded imperceptibly. 'Good idea.' He mouthed the words, nodding.

On his other side Drusilla leaned towards him. 'What?'

He explained, quietly repeating the plan to her. She leaned closer and he felt her hand on his arm. She edged closer still, snuggling against him. He resisted the urge to move away but silently in the darkness he reached out with his other hand towards Eigon. His questing fingers found the edge of her skirt and he touched it lightly, taking comfort from the feel of something which was a part of her.

They were awoken by the sound of someone drawing back the bolts in the door downstairs. A glimmer of light strayed up the steep stairs and with it a breath of fresh air from the open door. Commios swore under his breath. He had intended that they be out of here long before this. To their horror they heard someone climbing the steps and a figure appeared silhouetted against the square hatchway. The figure moved confidently across the floor and opened one of the flour sacks. He scooped several measures of flour into a wooden bucket, knotted the neck of the sack and turned away without seeing them to feel his way back downstairs again.

Commios breathed a sigh of relief. He crawled forward to the edge of the steps and peered down. The man was kneading barley flour and oatmeal into a soft dough with some milk. He watched as the man added more milk from his jug, forming it into small cakes, setting them onto one side, concentrating as he worked. Nearby he had set a griddle to heat over the stove. Whistling softly he began to place the cakes onto the hot griddle. They sniffed hungrily as the appetising smell filled the air. From somewhere in the distance they heard the sound of a bell being rung. The man swore. He glanced at his scones, obviously decided they wouldn't burn if he was quick and left the kitchen.

In seconds the three of them had descended the stairs. Commios scooped three steaming hot scones from the griddle with a knife as they passed. He winked at the two women as, when he found they were too hot to carry, he wrapped them in a dishcloth and followed them out of the door. In seconds they were out in the street and had turned down a second alley, on their way towards the town gates.

It was harder to get out of the town. As they approached the town walls they could see an armed guard searching the wagons which were queuing to leave on the road which led northwards towards Londinium. Commios drew back into the shadows. They had eaten their scones with great enjoyment. 'Now what do we do?'

'We don't look like wealthy Roman travellers any more,' Drusilla put in piteously. She had even lost her precious ivory comb, left behind in the bedroom at the guesthouse.

Commios grinned. 'The perfect disguise. I vote we wait for a likely looking wagon and join the driver. I am sure for a silver stater he would give us a lift onwards. As long as you don't speak, Drusilla. We are going to have to teach you some Celtic otherwise your impeccable cut-glass Roman accent will betray us.'

Drusilla flushed scarlet. She shrugged. 'I will be as quiet as a mouse.' She gasped suddenly. 'Is that Titus?'

Commios swore. 'I don't believe it! Is it?' He glanced at Eigon who had blanched visibly as she shrank back into the shadows. 'It is. He's checking everyone who goes through the gate. Look!'

Titus was sitting on his horse beside the archway through the wall watching every single person that passed. When there were people travelling inside wagons they were being made to climb out and walk beside the mules or the oxen pulling the load. Women who had shawls or veils round their heads were being made to unveil so he could scrutinise their faces.

Commios drew them quietly back away from the queue which was beginning to form. 'What about the gate the other end of the town?'

'He obviously expects us to head for Londinium,' Eigon said

softly. 'But I expect he has the other entrances covered as well.'

'We should separate,' Drusilla said, brushing the crumbs from her tunic. 'The three of us separately would excite no notice at all. And Eigon is the only one he would actually recognise, surely.'

'That's true.' Commios nodded. He glanced at Eigon. 'We should all leave on the road south; we can meet once we are safely outside.'

They went back to the south gate via the market place. There they bought a basket and some fruit for Eigon to carry and a blue and red veil embroidered with red swirls and coils to cover her hair; they bought a new blue and green cloak for Drusilla to replace the one she had left lying on the bed in her bedroom, and a cheap bone comb.

For Commios there was a serviceable hunting knife and a leather pouch to hang from his shoulder on a strap. In it he put two more loaves of bread and some fruit. 'For lunch,' he said with a reassuring smile, 'when we meet outside the gates.' For safety they divided up the money from Commios's purse, then they split up.

Drusilla went first. She walked slowly behind a group of giggling women who were heading out towards the fields. The guards on the gate did not even glance at them twice. Drusilla slipped out behind them, her eyes downcast and before she knew it she was walking down the road, coughing as a covered cart rattled past, raising the dust.

She paused at the first milestone as arranged, sitting down to wait in the shadow of an old oak tree, russet in the low autumn sunlight.

Eigon came next. She had struck up a conversation with a husband and wife who were heading towards the coast, their belongings carried on the back of a sturdy mule. The woman was garrulous and did not stop talking as they approached the guard, barely giving him a glance as she talked on. The soldier waved them past with a lewd comment and they were through. When they reached the milestone Eigon bade them farewell and went to join Drusilla in the shade on the rustling carpet of fallen leaves.

They waited and waited. There was no sign of Commios.

Drusilla shaded her eyes, trying to see who was coming down the road. 'Where is he? He can't have got lost!' Eigon could hear the fear in her companion's voice.

Eigon leaned back against the tree trunk. 'I don't see why anyone would have stopped him. He had nothing to incriminate him. Even if Titus saw him he wouldn't know him.'

They waited a while longer. 'Should we go back?' Drusilla was biting her nails. 'Perhaps this isn't the right place?'

'Of course it's the right place. The first milestone on the road. How wrong can one go? I managed to find it!' Eigon was growing more and more anxious. 'He's been caught.'

'He can't have been.' Drusilla shook her head. 'Who would recognise him? Without us he is just another man.'

Eigon stared at her. 'Just another man,' she echoed. She gave a faint smile. 'A tall, striking, handsome man who would stand out in any crowd. I'm going back.'

They retraced their steps, pausing when they were in sight of the gates. A constant stream of traffic was still going in and out of the town; there was no sign of Commios. 'What are we going to do?' Drusilla asked nervously.

Eigon shrugged. 'He might have been delayed for some reason. We don't want to go rushing back to find that he is on his way. On the other hand if he has been arrested we have to try and do something.'

'Everywhere we've been, we've been betrayed,' Drusilla said miserably. 'Everyone who has befriended us or sheltered us has sold out once Titus comes along with his money.'

'They owed us nothing, Drusilla. They gave us food and shelter – that was all we asked of them. If he's been caught it is up to us to try and rescue him.' Eigon shook her head. 'But how?'

'What would he do?'

'Go back. Find out what has happened.' Eigon took a deep breath. 'All right. On our own we are in a way safer. We are less recognisable. We are just two women. We could be anyone. We are wearing local clothes; we are weather-worn.' She gave a wry smile. 'We have baskets.'

'Which we should fill.'

'Thank goodness we have some money. Perhaps we can buy some stuff from a pedlar.' They had noticed the itinerant sellers wandering amongst the travellers heading in towards the town. Some had sold all their wares before they ever reached the gates. Drusilla bought a bundle of beautifully woven scarves which she could claim to be taking in to sell if she were stopped. Eigon filled

500

her basket with apples from the panniers of a mule being taken in by a farmer's wife. They headed in together and were both waved in without comment. Inside the town was seething with people brought out into the streets by the sunlight. They wandered around for a bit then separated with the intention of making enquiries. Drusilla heard news first. She chatted up one of the ostlers at the inn next to the guardhouse. He was lounging outside after dumping a bucket of water in front of a thirsty horse, waiting for it to drink, cursing amiably as it dripped water over his feet. He had watched as the big man with red hair had been questioned; he had taken a swing at the guard and been overpowered and dragged away to the fort. He glanced at Drusilla and raised an eyebrow. 'You a friend of his?'

She managed a cheeky grin. 'I wouldn't have said no if he asked!' She shrugged eloquently, managing to mangle her Latin with such a broad country drawl he found it hard to understand. 'I thought he might be a friend of my brother who is on his way over to Gaul. I was going to ask him to take a message. No use to me in the fort though, is he!' She managed a convincing flounce and strolled back into the crowds.

Eigon was waiting for her round the corner. She too had news. 'I went back to the house where we had hoped to stay,' she whispered. There was a large woollen bag at her feet. 'Look. Our stuff. I bribed the boy. He said the soldiers came and did a quick search but they didn't touch our things because she had already stolen them and hidden them in her bedroom. He said she was a tight-fisted cheat. I gave him some money to get our belongings out of her room where she had stacked it up to sell, then he said he was off. He wasn't going back. She'll think he stole it but he didn't care. He said the soldiers were searching the whole town. We were lucky to escape.'

'They caught Commios,' Drusilla said. 'He's in the fort.'

Eigon stared at her, aghast. 'So what do we do?' They looked towards the end of the street where the high walls of the fortress rose above the local houses. 'We can't do anything on our own,' Eigon went on miserably. 'Somehow we have to have help. And that's not easy. As you say everyone seems ready to cheat and lie!'

'Perhaps that is to our advantage,' Drusilla said thoughtfully. 'Thank the Good Lord that we have some money. We can bribe someone to rescue him. Can't we?' She gazed at Eigon hopefully.

Eigon shrugged. 'But who? And how?'

Drusilla straightened her shoulders. She was screwing up her courage visibly. 'It is going to have to be me. Titus knows you. He has no idea what I look like. If I can get in there and wander round a bit perhaps I will get an idea.'

'But you might be taken, too.' Eigon caught her arm, shaking her head. 'You can't take the risk.'

'I have to. What else is there? We can't go on without him.' She gazed at Eigon intently. 'He'll be in the guardhouse, won't he? Perhaps I can bribe a guard. Give me your share of the money. How much have we got between us?'

They picked over the coins; Roman aurei, sestertii and denarii, silver staters, coins from Gaul. 'They'll only want the gold,' Eigon said thoughtfully. 'Put that on top of the bag so it looks more.' There was a coin amongst them with the head of Caratacus. Eigon stared at it in shock. It was a stark reminder of the time when her father had been a king in this country.

'What is it?' Drusilla gazed at her. Eigon shook her head. 'Nothing.' She dropped the coin back into the bag and gave Drusilla a hug. 'Good luck. May God go with you.'

'What will you do while I'm in there?'

Eigon shrugged. 'Wait for you.'

Meryn came back indoors, breathless. 'I saw them both rush up the track towards the wood but I lost them in the dark. At least he had dropped the gun.'

'He's completely mad!' Aurelia said. 'Oh God, Rhodri! I hope he's careful.' She was shaking violently. Sitting down she looked at Steph. 'Where's Jess?' Her voice cracked in a breathless sob.

Steph glanced at Meryn. 'I don't know, but at least he hasn't got her.'

'I called the police,' Meryn said. 'They will be here fairly quickly. The mention of a suspected murderer and a firearm usually makes them get their skates on. You wait for them; I'm going to go outside and have a bit of a think.'

He let himself out into the garden behind the studio and wandered across the dew-wet grass. The violence of the last minutes had shaken him more than he cared to admit. He could feel it reverberating in the air around him, screeching in jagged and red scars on the ether like fingernails on glass. He glanced round into the night. He could hear sheep calling to each other in the distance. They seemed calm; there was nothing out there to worry them at the moment. He turned slowly, listening to the sounds of the night, trying to still himself, to feel who and what was out there. In the far distance an owl called, then a fox. Slowly his breathing returned to normal. He stilled it further, reaching out. Titus. Where was he? He could see faint pictures now in his head; pictures from the past. Titus had abandoned Dan. He had no need of that erratic, panicked energy. It was no use to him now. The ancient anger that motivated him no longer needed a host. He was strong and focused. And nearby.

Meryn moved further away from the house. He was identifying different centres of memory around him. Up the hill, the child, alone and frightened, his life force leaking away into the ground. A little girl, frightened and angry. He paused. That anger was uncomfortably corrosive on the air. He sensed trouble there. Thoughtfully he moved on, searching for Jess. Nothing. He shook his head, puzzled. He remembered these mountains of old. They held memories as a basin held water, condensed, amplifying, echoing with emotion. Nothing disappeared. Nothing was lost. But here there were patches of opacity. Someone was hiding Jess.

And Eigon. What about Eigon herself? Had she returned to these mountains and if she had what knowledge had she brought with her? He closed his eyes and waited.

Behind him a door opened in the cottage. Aurelia stepped out into the garden and came to stare over the gate, wondering where he had gone. In the starlight she could see him, a black silhouette against the night. He was standing quite still, upright, facing down towards the ancient site of the battlefield. Meryn had changed since she had last met him. He had grown in experience and gravitas. She smiled ruefully. He had power now and an austerity which was slightly forbidding. Strange to think that once she had thought she could fall in love with him. She doubted now if he could love anyone. He was dedicated to his daemons. But if anyone could find Jess it was him. She resisted the urge to call out to him, knowing he must not be interrupted, turned and went back into the cottage. The door closed behind her, leaving him alone. He had not noticed her. Seconds later headlights appeared in the lane; the first police car swept up to the courtyard and stopped. Four men climbed out.

Rhodri stopped, so out of breath he couldn't take another step. He was gasping as he doubled over, trying to collect himself. He had long ago lost sight of Dan and, as he held his breath and listened, he could no longer hear him crashing away through the undergrowth. The woods were silent. He had lost him. He closed his eyes, swearing under his breath. The rage which had overpowered him and given him the energy to come hurtling up the hillside in the dark after him had been so overpowering it had frightened him. He had never felt like that before. He clenched his fists, feeling his heart steadying back to its normal beat and stared round in the dark, straining his ears. Dan couldn't have vanished; he had to be there somewhere. Rhodri knew these woods like the back of his hand; Dan didn't. That gave him the advantage. But he had to use his brain. Now his initial fury was controlled he had to think. He had no torch but moon and starlight would be enough to show him the track and the darker silhouette of the tree trunks on either side of him.

Where would Dan go? Would he try and escape or would he hang around to try and find Jess? Somewhere behind him a twig cracked loudly in the silence. He swung round. He was vulnerable here. If he could see, so could Dan. The bastard might have circled round behind him. Cautiously he moved off the path into the shadows of the trees. He stood with his back to a broad ancient oak, feeling the bark rough and reassuring against his shirt. He rested his head back against the tree and glanced upwards through the branches. The storm had long ago moved on. The sky was clear. Now there wasn't a breath of wind. The night was still; listening. Holding his breath he thought he could hear the distant, muffled roar of the brook as it hurtled down the hillside between the rocks.

Will you play with me?

The voice was clear and high, very close. He felt panic lurch in his throat as he strained his ears towards the sound.

I'm lonely with no one to play with.

He couldn't see anyone. He flattened his hands on either side of him against the tree, gripping the grooves in the bark for reassurance. 'Who's there?' His voice was husky.

Silence.

He could see nothing but the shadows of the trees. A fox barked in the distance and he felt the sweat start out between his shoulder blades. 'Eigon, is that you?'

The quality of the silence changed. She was listening. 'Eigon, sweetheart? Where are you?'

Eigon's gone. She doesn't want to play any more.

He swallowed. My God, he had made contact! He was shredding the tree bark with his nails. 'What's your name, sweetheart?' His heart was pounding in his throat.

No answer.

A whisper of wind fluttered the leaves above his head.

'Where are you, girly? Tell me your name?' He could barely raise his voice. He didn't dare move. 'Can you show yourself? Let me see you.'

Another branch cracked on the path, closer this time. He shifted his head slightly, his eyes scanning the shadows. It was then he heard the low humourless laugh. 'Talking to ghosts, are we?' Dan stepped out onto the track. He was holding a broken branch in front of him like a stave. 'These woods send everyone mad in the end, don't they. Poor Rhodri. You stupid bloody interfering prat!' His voice was full of hatred. 'So, what are we going to do? Fight like Robin Hood and Little John?' He stepped closer, holding the branch out in front of him. It looked sturdy enough to be lethal. Rhodri didn't move. He was eyeing the undergrowth round him, trying to spot something he could use as a weapon himself. Strangely his fear had evaporated. Dan was someone he could deal with.

'What is the matter with you, Dan?' Rhodri tried to keep his voice steady. 'What have any of these people ever done to you, for you to come and wreck their lives like this. What did Will ever do?'

Dan's eyes flickered slightly at the mention of Will's name but otherwise his expression was cold and non-reactive. 'I don't know what you mean. Jess asked for everything she got. She's a tease; she enjoyed every minute of our encounter!' There was a gleam of a cold smile.

Rhodri held himself still. If he rushed at Dan he wouldn't get close with that sharp-ended branch pointing straight at his chest. There was nothing within reach that he could use. All he had for a weapon was his voice. He smiled broadly, putting as much feeling into it as possible. 'Isn't Jess something! Wonderful woman. I'm going to marry her.'

To his surprise he realised that he probably meant it. He registered the flash of cold hatred in Dan's face and saw that at some level he had struck home.

'She's a whore.' Dan spat the words at him.

Rhodri managed to laugh again. 'You would say that, wouldn't you.'

'What do you mean by that?'

The branch was heavy, Rhodri could see the muscles in the other man's arms beginning to flag; the branch lowered a fraction.

'I mean that it sounds as though you have to force women; they never come to you voluntarily do they, Dan? Even your wife, so Steph tells me. You do know the police have been to see her twice now? I get the feeling she is not your greatest fan. Don't expect an alibi there.' He was managing to keep his voice calm, trying to talk him down from whatever manic height he was on. In the distance he could hear the distant sound of an engine, the distinctive batting of rotors. A helicopter. So, the police were already up there. Dan gave no sign that he had heard it. 'So, what are you doing rushing about here, Dan? Are you still chasing Jess?' Rhodri held his breath.

Dan smiled. 'You'd like to know that, wouldn't you. You don't know where she is. She's disappeared and you want to know if I've found her. You want to know if I've killed her.' He sounded almost sleepy.

'It would help to know where she is, but I know you haven't killed her. You haven't got the bottle.' Rhodri held his gaze. 'You took Will by surprise, didn't you? Will was a nice guy. He would never suspect even a lowlife piece of scum like you to jump him. Did you look him in the eye when you killed him, Dan? Or couldn't you bear to think of what a nice decent bloke he was compared to you so you attacked him from behind.' He smiled. 'Ah. I've sussed you there, haven't I. That's exactly what you did.' The helicopter was coming closer.

'You have no proof that I killed Will. The police will never pin that one on me.'

Rhodri shook his head. 'Ah, there you're wrong. Because even that you didn't do efficiently. He lived long enough to write your name in blood on the wall. How corny is that?'

'You're lying again.'

Rhodri shrugged. 'You'll find out soon enough.' He tensed as Dan renewed his grip on the piece of wood and raised it.

'What's your spelling like, Rhodri?' Dan gave a cold grin. 'Shall we find out? All we need is some blood!'

Have you come to play with me?

The voice came from just behind Dan. He froze.

I'm lonely here. Shall we go on playing the game?

A pale shape had appeared, hovering in the clearing. Rhodri could make out the outline of her long hair, her ragged skirt reaching midway down her calf.

'Hello, sweetheart,' he said softly. 'We'd love to play with you, wouldn't we, Dan?'

Dan spun round with a cry of fear. The branch flew out of his hand and without pausing to glance at her he plunged away through the trees. The little girl had gone.

Rhodri breathed again. Pushing himself away from the trunk he ran forward, his anger propelling him towards the undergrowth where Dan had disappeared. Then he stopped, getting a grip on himself with an effort as he stood gazing down the slope where Dan had vanished. There wasn't a sound. No clue which way he had gone. The helicopter had drawn away; it was skirting the base of the hillside. He caught sight of the powerful searchlight sweeping across the distant trees.

A branch cracked behind him. He turned sharply on his heel, eyes narrowed, his heart thumping as he stared round. If it wasn't Dan it had to be the child.

'Well, girly. You sorted him, didn't you? That was very clever of you,' he called out. He was looking at the clearing where the apparition had appeared. Had he really seen her, or was it just the flicker of moonlight through the leaves of the trees, dancing on the path. His fury at Dan was suddenly replaced by a fear of what he had seen. He could feel his skin prickling. He turned round again slowly, his eyes straining into the woodland. 'Are you still there?' he called. Was he addressing Dan or the child? He was being watched, he could sense it. He held his breath. Slowly stepping back from the top of the slope he edged backwards to where Dan had thrown the branch and he picked it up. It was heavy, one end sharpened by the ragged tear where it had been wrenched from the tree. It could have killed him. He stood staring at it as he balanced it in his two hands.

Did you hurt my sister?

The voice seemed closer now. Right beside him. Rhodri blanched, tightening his grip on the piece of wood. 'No, I didn't hurt your sister. That was bad men did that.' He spoke softly, hardly daring to look round. Where was she?

She left us alone. She didn't come back.

'She couldn't come back She wanted to.' He moved his head slightly. Was that her, on the grassy clearing now, deeper in the trees? Just a pale blur, scarcely more than a shadow amongst shadows, moving away.

'God bless, sweetheart,' he murmured.

There was no response.

Then suddenly she was back, almost beside him and he could see every detail. The white bedraggled face, the small neat nose, the large dark eyes and the angry little mouth. 'I've got the lady!' she said clearly. 'And I'm going to make her pay for killing my brother and taking my sister away!'

'What do you mean?' Rhodri reached out towards her, frantically trying to grip the thin air. 'What lady? Do you mean Jess?'

But she had gone.

35

Julius stood on the quay at Portus Dubris, looking round. The journey across Gaul had been fast and more or less without incident and he had obtained a passage easily on one of the swift trading boats which plied in and out of the port of Gesoriacum. Britannia was, as Eigon used to tell him with half-joking mournfulness, wet and cold and windy. But the wind had brought him quickly across the ocean so he could forgive it that. He sought a guide at once and was swiftly ensconced with his young companion, Drusus, by the roaring fire in the first decent inn that could be found, and in front of a hot meal. The port had been like ports everywhere, busy, dirty, noisy. There were decent buildings on the wharf and signs of well-repaired warehouses, good roads and a flourishing market not too far away.

'So, how are we going to know where they've gone?' Drusus looked up from his plate of hot stew. There was a smear of gravy on his chin. Julius grinned at him affectionately and discreetly refrained from mentioning it. He had become very fond of the doctor's precocious teenage son with his unruly dark hair, his infectious grin and his seemingly uncontrollably long limbs. 'I have no idea what we do next.' He shrugged wearily.

'Do you know much about Britannia?' The lad helped himself to another wedge of bread.

Julius gloomily dug a husk of grain from between his teeth. 'Only what Eigon told me. She said it rained a lot.' They both glanced at the doorway. It had opened to allow a party of men in off the street and they could hear the rain pouring down onto the cobbles and streaming down the gutters off the roof. 'She also said it was beautiful and soft and green and full of hills.'

'Not this part of Britannia then,' Drusus deduced practically. 'The man we spoke to on the boat said the hills were in the north and over in the west.' He took another mouthful and chewed thoughtfully. 'How big is Britannia? Do you know?'

Julius gave a wry grin. 'Big enough. There are still huge areas of this land which are not part of the Empire. Wild tribes everywhere.'

'And your lady is a wild tribesman?' The boy gave him a cheeky look.

Julius nodded tolerantly. 'I believe she might be. Although her father was captured, that didn't, I gather, end the opposition of the Silures. If anything they tried harder than ever to defeat us; and further north there are other tribes even fiercer. I feel we should aim for Siluria. I think that is what Eigon would do. Her mother's people came from there and she seems to have loved it. Her father was originally king of the Catuvellauni and the Trinovantes, most of whom are content with the rule of Rome now, though I fear what we are used to hearing in Rome may not be the whole story.' He gave an involuntary shudder.

'So,' Drusus helped himself to yet more stew from the dish near him and added a hefty slurp of fish sauce from the jar on the table, 'we have to find out how to get to Siluria.'

They had to head, it appeared, for Londinium, then towards Calleva of the Atrebates, then towards either Aquae Sulis or to Glevum. But first they had to ride north to Durovernum Cantiacorum. When they asked how long all this would take they were greeted with shrugs and a shaking of heads and indications with outspread hands and counting of fingers that a journey to such outlandish places might take weeks or months or even years. Julius was beginning to feel more and more depressed but luckily for him Drusus was still overwhelmingly excited by this his first real adventure and was full of practical tips on choosing horses and negotiating with the locals, and Julius was good-naturedly happy to let him think he was the only one who could cope with this aspect of such exotic travel. He had long ago worked out that as long as Drusus was fed hugely and regularly the boy would be a tower of strength and good humour.

They negotiated for two good strong horses and headed out onto the road. The ostler who directed them towards the town gate said it was some thirty miles to Durovernum. Of that much he seemed certain and they rode out of the town as the mist began to rise and a thin watery sun began to light the road.

Thirty Roman miles away Eigon leaned against a wall near the gate into the fort. She was swathed in a warm cloak and there was a basket on her arm but she had not moved for a long time now. At first passing men had tried to chat her up; a woman had sworn at her for being a street whore, another had offered her a job but she had ignored them all and eventually they had left her alone. Her eyes were fixed on the gate but in her head she was inside the fort, watching, following, praying for Drusilla and for Commios.

It was several seconds before she noticed the man standing in the shade of the gate, thoughtfully looking her way. His face was in shadow as the weak morning sunlight played across the road and she couldn't see him clearly but she could see the tenseness of his stance, the attention with which he seemed to be studying her. Instinctively she stepped back and half-turned away. Whoever he was she didn't want him to be able to identify her.

Cautiously she turned back, the hood of her cloak pulled tightly around her face. He was still there; still watching.

She turned away and casually walked a few paces, turning down the first road she came to. Hurrying she ran towards the next turning and taking it, doubled back almost at once up a narrow alleyway to come out almost where she had started. The figure had gone. Had he followed her? She glanced over her shoulder warily. There was no sign of him. A cart rattled slowly past her and headed for the main gate into the fortress. It stopped and a guard stepped forward to talk to the driver. The man leaned down. He was waving his arms around. They were both laughing.

Someone touched her arm and she jumped. 'Eigon!' It was Drusilla.

'How did you get out without me seeing you? What happened? Where is Commios?' Eigon clutched at her.

'He's safe,' Drusilla whispered. 'They are going to put him into that cart when it comes out again. It's full of amphorae and they will exchange them for unbroken empties which will go back to the warehouse. You go now. Titus is here; he is putting word round as usual, asking if anyone has seen you and offering a reward. Luckily he's thrown his weight about a bit too much. The men I talked to are quite happy to get one over on him. It will be no skin off their noses and they will be quite a bit richer for it if they do as I want rather than him.' She patted the purse under her cloak and smiled. 'His rewards are becoming more meagre. Either he thinks people are content to do more for less over here, or he is running out of money! You go. Head out of the west gate now, while you can. Follow the road until you come to a villa which lies to the righthand side of the road. I gather it is the first big place you will see – perhaps some three miles on and it acts as a way station. Wait for us there. God bless you!' And she was gone.

Eigon stared after her but there was no time to hesitate. Clutching her cloak round her and with a firm grip on her basket she turned away and headed back down the street to look for the west gate.

Commios caught on quickly. When the guard beckoned, after glancing over his shoulder to make sure no one was observing them, he got up and moved. The man raised a hand to hold him back for one minute while he glanced left and right out of the doorway then he gestured him out into the passage and from there into the outer courtyard. In seconds Commios had hopped up into the wagon, dived for the back, someone had thrown a pile of sacks over him and then a few empty amphorae had been stacked against him for good measure and the two dozy oxen were being turned around with much shouting and cracking of whips. Commios lay still, his heart beating frantically as he listened for a shout, any sound that he had been discovered. None came. The wagon lurched round with a squeaking of anguished wheels and then it was in motion. Glancing upward through a gap between the sacks he saw the great arch above him as the wagon retraced its route out of the fort and down the main street. He was free. He lay still for a long time, not daring to move until a voice yelled at him from the front of the wagon. 'Oi! You! Hop off now, while no one's looking.'

Commios didn't need to be told twice. In seconds he had thrown back the sacks and amidst a sea of rolling amphorae had vaulted over the side of the wagon down into the street.

Drusilla seized his arm and dragged him out of sight. 'That was close. I was sure someone would stick a sword into the wagon to check there was no one hiding. They've done that with one or two loads going in.'

'Wonderful!' Commios took a deep breath, trying to steady himself. 'Where's Eigon?'

'I've sent her on ahead. It was too dangerous for her to wait in the town. Titus seems to have spies everywhere. She's going to wait for us on the road towards Londinium.' She caught his arm. 'Have you still got any money?'

'Not much. They took my purse. They took everything. I had a few coins in another pouch round my neck. They missed that but it won't get us far.' He glanced at her quickly. 'Why?'

'It took all we had to get you out of there,' she said simply. 'We had to outbid Titus.'

Commios muttered something under his breath. 'It's up to us then. We'll have to sing for our supper.' He grinned and linked his arm through hers. 'Come on, let's go and find Eigon and we'll be on our way. After all, it's easier to travel without a load of luggage to weigh us down!'

There was no sign of Eigon at the villa. Drusilla looked round in concern. 'I told her it was the first one on the road. I know I did. I explained where it was. It is exactly where I was told.' She stood staring round in confusion. The villa lay in a slight valley only a short way off the main highway. There was no missing it, and it was obvious that it served in some way as a *hospes*, a stop off point for travellers. Slaves ran at once to see if they required refreshments or to hire horses and they saw one or two pedlars plying their wares around the tables which had been placed in the outhouse near the gate.

Commios sat down. 'She'll be here. God will guide her to us.' He groped in his pouch for a coin and ordered a jug of ale for the two of them. 'We might as well reward ourselves after the fright we've had,' he said with feeling.

They sat there for a long time, but there was still no sign of Eigon as the light began to fail and one by one the other travellers disappeared, leaving them sitting alone by the darkening, windswept road.

Rhodri burst into the house with a shout. 'Where is Meryn?' He found the others sitting anxiously together in the kitchen round the table. There was no sign of any police.

Meryn hauled himself to his feet. 'What's happened?'

'The child. Eigon's sister. She's got Jess!' His face was white and there was a deep scratch across his forehead where he had forced his way through some brambles. 'She appeared up there on the hillside. Dan was there, the bastard. He threatened to kill me, but she turned up and he ran for it. Couldn't face a small child!' He threw himself into a chair. 'I'm not sure he wasn't right. She's vicious. She's not the sweet lost little girl we all thought. She blames her – she blames Eigon – for not going back to look for her and it is terrifying.' He was aware of the others looking at him. Of Meryn's thoughtful calm response. Someone pushed a glass towards him and he grabbed it and drained it. It was whisky. 'Is it possible? Has she hidden Jess somewhere? In another place? Another dimension? Oh Jesus Christ!' He shook his head. 'What are we going to do?' He looked round suddenly. 'Where are the police? Aren't they here?'

'They are here. The whole area has been cordoned off.' Steph sighed. 'We're not supposed to leave the house. They are putting up a helicopter and bringing in the mountain rescue people. I don't think there is anything else we can do.'

Meryn stood up. He put a gentle hand on Rhodri's shoulder. 'Get your breath back. I'm going to step outside for a few minutes then maybe you and I will walk back up the hill if the police don't stop us. Don't worry. We'll find her.'

Outside Meryn stood for a moment, his eyes closed, feeling the air around him, sensing the threads of anger and fear and sorrow weaving backwards and forwards all about him. He frowned. He mustn't let his thoughts wander. Concentrate. Why hadn't he sensed all this? Why couldn't he feel Jess? What if Rhodri was right and she had been taken into another dimension – if that had happened he would have to go after her. He wandered towards the studio. The door was ajar. He pulled it open and walked in, standing still inside. This room was at the epicentre of what was happening. In this place, two thousand years before, a child had been viciously raped; a family had been torn apart, people had been murdered. Another child had come and seen. She had seen the body of her nurse; she had seen the bodies of her sister and her mother, defiled and bloody and when she had called to them she had found that they had gone somewhere she could never reach them. Dead or unconscious, it made no difference to the little girl. Traumatised beyond imagining she had wandered back to look for her little brother and found he too had gone. He had curled up into a tight little ball and his spirit had slipped away. She was alone.

He realised suddenly that Rhodri was standing in the doorway watching him, saying nothing, sensing that the thoughts whirling through Meryn's head should not be interrupted.

'What was her name again, Eigon's little sister?' Meryn asked at last.

'They called her Glads.'

'Good. She needs the dignity of a name. We need to know what happened to her after she saw the massacre that took place here. Give me a few moments, Rhodri.'

Rhodri disappeared from the doorway and Meryn heard his footsteps walking across the yard. The sound died away and he was left with an intense silence. She was listening. He smiled inwardly. This poor damaged child, had she lived to grow up or had she too succumbed on this dreadful hillside or in the god-forsaken valley beneath it?

Godforsaken. He stared down at the floor. Eigon had gone to Rome and come back, if he had understood correctly, a Christian. Perfectly possible. The men who had been given the credit for converting the British Isles to Christianity – Patrick, Columba, Augustine, had all come late to the scene. In an Empire with healthy and swift trade routes ideas had travelled as fast as the speed of the fastest horse. News of the new religion would have been here as fast as it had reached Rome itself. Maybe even sooner by western routes out of the Mediterranean. The legend of Joseph of Arimathaea following the routes of the tin trade with the young Jesus weren't in fact totally improbable.

He shook his head. This was not the time for academic specu-lation. Enough that Eigon had lived in the Rome of Nero at the time of St Peter and St Paul and had returned having met them. Fact. According to Jess.

Where are you, Jess? He sighed.

The footsteps in the courtyard were running this time. Rhodri appeared at the door. 'In case you need to know, the little boy was called Togodumnus after Caratacus's dead brother. Togo for short.' He paused. 'Do you still need to be alone?'

Meryn eyed the big man. He was sensitive in a lot of ways for all his braggadocio, and it was to him that the child had spoken and revealed herself. He shook his head. 'Have you got a torch? Show me where you saw her.'

There was no sign of any police as they headed out of the gate. Rhodri turned off the track after about half a mile. 'I know it was here. I remember this twisted yew tree amongst the others.' He flashed the torch up into the curtains of spiny foliage. 'Then I worked my way through the rhododendrons here and down towards a spring. I could hear it in the distance. Dan took off that way.' He gestured with the torch, sending the beam shafting through the tree branches overhead.

'And the police?' Meryn paused. 'Which way did they go?'

Rhodri shrugged. 'I heard a helicopter but I never saw the others.'

'We'd know if they were still nearby.' Meryn took a few steps further into the undergrowth, then he paused. He could feel it. Suddenly. A wall, ice-cold, forbidding. He glanced back at Rhodri in time to see him shiver. He looked nervous.

'We're getting close, aren't we?' Rhodri whispered.

Meryn nodded. 'Did you speak to her?'

'Yes.'

'What did you say?'

'I tried to be friendly. But she wasn't having any of it. She sounded very hacked off. Accused people of abandoning her; accused Jess.'

'Think of her as an abused child,' Meryn said softly. 'The pain and anger and sense of betrayal have never gone away. They have festered all this time, and like a child she has maybe not fully understood what happened. She doesn't accept that her sister couldn't come back for her.'

'They looked for her. They looked for a long time. Jess told me. The whole legion turned out. She was the king's daughter after all and they wanted as many of the family as possible to take as captives to Rome.'

'So, where did she go? What happened to her?' Meryn said thoughtfully. He looked across at Rhodri. 'Tell me as near as you can when we reach the place you spoke to her.'

Rhodri shrugged. 'Somewhere round here. It all looks much the same.'

Meryn nodded. 'Right. So, did you call her before?'

'No. She just appeared. She was standing behind Dan. I talked to her, and –' he shrugged – 'I think she understood me. She sort of faded away, then she came back suddenly, and this time she was vicious. It was personal. She was threatening. She said she had the lady.'

'And did she say what she was going to do with her?'

'"I'm going to make her pay for killing my brother and taking away my sister," something like that.'

Meryn frowned. 'That is strange. How could Jess be to blame?'

'Did she think she was someone else? Eigon?'

'Call her.' Suddenly Meryn made up his mind. 'She knows we're here. Call her. She has made contact with you, so let's see if she is going to negotiate.'

'Glads?' Rhodri called. He scanned the trees and bushes round them. 'Are you there? We want to help. To try and make this all better in some way. Will you come and talk to us?'

They waited in silence.

'Please, come and tell us how we can make it better.' Rhodri tried again. 'You want this endless game to end, don't you? Let's try and sort it, shall we?'

Rhodri broke off as Meryn put a warning hand on his arm. He nodded in front of them. There was someone there, in the darker shade of one of the ancient oaks. Just the outline of the girl. 'Come on, girly. Please talk to us,' he went on more softly. 'Let us help you.'

Silently Meryn raised his finger to his lips. He stepped forward. 'Greetings, lady. I am trained to walk with the gods. If I can intercede, I will do so.'

She appeared to have moved closer. They could make out her face now, her flaxen hair, her large unhappy eyes. Behind them there was blank despair. 'Who has been looking after you?' Meryn went on. 'Who was it who found you that day when your sister was taken away?'

There was no reply.

'Please, tell me,' Meryn went on gently. 'I want to help you.'

'Ask her where Jess is,' Rhodri murmured.

Meryn frowned. He shook his head. 'Will you talk to me, girly?' He used Rhodri's form of address for her.

Have you come to play with me?

They heard her voice, but her lips hadn't moved.

'Yes, we've come to play with you,' Meryn said gently. 'That's why we're here.'

Where's Eigon?

'She's looking for you. She's been trying so hard to find you. She's been talking to the lady, Jess. Jess has been helping her look for you.' Meryn's whole attention was fixed on the shadowy figure. 'Is Jess there with you, Gwladys?' He gave the name its Welsh intonation.

Jess?

Suddenly the name was all round them in the trees, echoing from hilltop to hilltop, from oak to oak across the valley.

Jess, Jess, JESS!

'God Almighty!' Rhodri looked round, transfixed with fear.

'Where is Jess?' Meryn raised his voice now to match hers. 'I need to see her!' His eyes hadn't left her face.

Jess! Jess has come to play with me! Jess is here, in the woods with me!

'I need to see her, Gwladys!' Meryn was very stern. 'Now.' The wind was rising. Above them the trees were beginning to sway. The leaves were rustling in the darkness.

'Where is she?' Meryn called again. His voice was impressively loud.

The child was fading away.

'Come back. I need you to talk to me!'

But she had gone.

Meryn sighed. 'I couldn't hold her.'

'Is Jess dead?' Rhodri's voice was bleak. 'Is that what she meant?'

'I don't think so.' Meryn gave a sigh. 'I don't sense that she is dead. There is so much going on here, so many different strands, so many stories.'

'What about Titus?'

'I haven't sensed him nearby. Not for a while. I don't know if he is following Dan. Somehow I doubt it. That link has been broken, but that doesn't mean he isn't still around. If he is intent on catching up with Eigon he could well be here somewhere and he may have linked to this child's energy.' He shook his head. 'We're doing no good here, I think we should go back.'

'No! We can't leave! Not yet. We have to look for Jess. Supposing she is lying here somewhere, injured. Maybe she is lapsing in and out of consciousness.' Rhodri was anguished.

'That thought had occurred to me. That could be why she is half in this world and half not.'

'That's what you sense?' Rhodri stared at him aghast.

'I'm not sure what I sense.' Meryn sighed. 'I am getting such mixed signals. Someone is deliberately obscuring the picture. Someone who is trained to do it. An adept, if you like. She is fighting me, hiding what is happening.'

'But you can circumvent that, surely?'

Meryn shrugged. 'I always thought I could. This person is powerful. Very powerful.' He reached out with his hands, his fingers spread as though he was trying to separate the strands of stickiness in the air around them. 'Marcia.' He smiled. 'Just for a second there she let down her guard and I could feel her.' There was a long pause. He had closed his eyes. Rhodri watched anxiously.

'Marcia Maximilla. She's letting me see her now. She thinks she has nothing to fear. She is taunting me with her prowess. She is the best.' He gave a grim smile.

'She's a Roman?' Rhodri whispered the question in awe.

'Oh yes, she's a Roman.' Meryn smiled. 'What a challenge.'

'And does she know where Jess is?'

Meryn was silent for a few seconds. 'As to that, we will have to see.'

The wagon had dropped Eigon at a villa just off the main road as she had been led to expect, but without her realising it, they had followed a road which led south again out of Durovernum, towards Portus Lemanis. Nearby she found a *mansio*, set up for travellers. She waited for the best part of the day and all the following night, huddled in her cloak on one of the benches as she couldn't afford to ask for a bed, and at last she realised that Commios and Drusilla were not going to come. Wearily she stared at the road and wondered what to do. She was fighting off waves of panic as mentally she counted the money left in her purse – hardly any. All she had was the basket, her cloak and a good stout pair of shoes. For a while her mind refused to focus at all. She couldn't contemplate travelling on without her friends or bear to think what might be happening to them. Had they been captured? Should she go back? But what could she do against Titus? Where was he? Was he on her trail or had he temporarily lost track of her?

Perhaps she could negotiate. Perhaps the thought of capturing her would be the lever she could use to bargain for her friends' release. The thought reminded her of Julius and another plan that had gone wrong, in Rome, and her eyes filled with tears. Standing up at last, stiff and hungry and cold, she turned back towards Durovernum. Almost at once someone stopped to give her a lift and it was only then that she realised she was on the wrong road. Taking pity on her the Cantican farmer gave her some bread and cut her a wedge from one of the huge leaf-wrapped cheeses he had brought from the market as they made their way at last in the right direction.

It was late afternoon when she found herself at the meeting place where Commios and Drusilla had waited for her for so long. They had long gone, but they had left a message with one of the slaves at the villa in case she ever caught them up. He recognised her at once from their description and produced a wax tablet with Commios's scrawl. Her heart leaped with joy and relief at the news that they were still free then it plummeted again as she read it. They were going to follow their original plan and make their way westward towards Venta Silurum. Reading it she touched the wax for a moment with a fingertip. The message was signed with the mark of the fish.

They had gone without her. There was no clue as to which road they would follow, which towns they would aim for. The slave looked at her silently, recognising the emotions which chased one another across her face. 'They've abandoned you, eh?' He gave a rueful grin.

She nodded. 'They must have given up hope of ever seeing me again.'

'What will you do?'

She shrugged. 'I must follow them, but I have no money.'

He nodded at the tablet in her hand. 'I've seen that fish sign before.' He glanced up. 'I know someone who can probably help you.'

She looked up at him in astonishment. 'Who is it?'

He glanced over his shoulder to make sure they were not overheard. 'He lives in the woods on the foot of the Downs. Not very far away. I'll get one of the carriers to give you a lift to the milestone where people sometimes leave stuff for him. You will have to follow the trackway from there and he will find you. He's a great man.' He glanced round again. 'I won't tell anyone you were here, but you should make yourself scarce as soon as possible. Your friends said there were soldiers after you.' They had obviously confided in this man, and they too had read the trustworthiness in his face. He saw her appraising glance and grinned. 'Don't worry. I have no love of the Roman army any more than you do! This man will help you. I promise.'

Some two hours later he came to find her in the corner seat where he had suggested she wait. He had brought her a jug of ale and a pie to eat, paid for out of his own tips. 'I've found someone to take you,' he whispered. 'Just as well as someone was here asking for you. A soldier.' He grimaced as she looked up at him in terror. 'Don't worry. I've sent him back the other way.' He winked. 'Wrap your hood round your head and follow me.'

She did as she was bid, allowing him to boost her onto the front of a heavily loaded wagon. The driver didn't even look at her. He offered no conversation. She sat, wrapped in her cloak beside him for what seemed an enormously long time as the wagon lurched and rumbled off the well-made road and onto a trackway which almost at once headed up into the low rolling hills, covered with thick woods.

It was getting dark when he pulled up at last. There was indeed a large milestone beside the track, but it wasn't a Roman stone. She could see the Celtic carvings inscribed on it, and the lines of inscription up the edge which were written in the secret language of the Druids. She slid down over the axle with a smile of thanks at her driver as he pulled some bundles down and began to stack them near the stone. He gave her a slight bow and still without uttering a word pulled himself back onto the draught pole where he sat, his legs swinging. The oxen started again without command and in a frighteningly short time the wagon had lurched into motion and disappeared into the darkness of the trees, leaving her quite alone.

She gazed around nervously. The trees crowded round her on every side. There was no track that she could see in the failing light, and the only sound came from the wind, whispering through the dried autumnal leaves. It was growing cold. Trying to contain her fear she pulled her cloak around her as tightly as possible, drew up her hood against the cold and sat down at the foot of the stone, leaning against it. Presumably this man would come at some point to collect his supplies. All she had to do was wait.

She hadn't realised she had fallen asleep but suddenly her eyes were open and it was full dark. She was staring nervously round trying to make out what had wakened her. She listened intently. Was it a fox or a badger, wild boar? A wolf? She shivered. She pressed herself as closely as possible against the stone, feeling its chill striking through her cloak. Then she heard it again. The low hoot of an owl. She glanced up, straining to see the bird somewhere in the trees above her. It was watching her and it was passing on a message to someone. Slowly she pulled herself to her feet. Perhaps the someone was a Druid.

She never saw him come. At first the silence round her was empty, then she saw him standing quite close to her, leaning on his staff. The owl took off on soundless wings and disappeared into the night.

'I'm sorry. Had I known I had a visitor I would have come sooner.' He spoke softly in the local tongue but she found it was easy to understand. 'My friends have only just told me you were here.' He nodded up towards the branch where the owl had been sitting.

She found herself smiling. Her fear had disappeared. 'I am sorry to arrive unannounced.'

'Come.' He stooped and picked up the bundles. 'We will go back to my house and you can tell me the reason for your visit. You are welcome to my woods.'

She wasn't sure how long they were walking through the trees. There was no track that she could discern, but the journey was easy and he was considerate, threading his way effortlessly through the darkness, pausing from time to time to wait for her if she fell back.

Then suddenly there they were, in a clearing and before her she saw a round house of the kind she remembered so clearly from her childhood. In front of it a fire had been banked up to stay in until he returned and near it there was an oven. Judging by the succulent smells emanating from the heaped up earth he had left something cooking to await his return. She smiled wearily as he turned to her and courteously gestured her towards the log which served as a seat near the fire. In seconds he had kicked away the earth and ashes banking it down and coaxed it into flame with some dry twigs.

He wouldn't let her speak until she was rested and they had eaten. Only then did he allow her to tell him her story. He listened without comment, watching the sparks fly up into the night sky, every now and then climbing to his feet to throw on another log. When at last she fell silent it was a long time before he spoke. She glanced at him. He was a tall man, of considerable age, his face tattooed and scarred. He was, as she had suspected a Druid, and lived in secret in the woods. He shrugged when she asked if he wasn't afraid. Druids had after all been proscribed in Gaul from the days of Julius Caesar and in Britannia since the invasion of Claudius.

'The man at the *mansio* implied you looked kindly on Christians,' Eigon said at last. She bit her lip. She had been hoping she had been directed to a Christian. That was obviously far from the case. 'He recognised the sign of the fish on a message the others had left for me and he thought you might help me.'

Her new friend smiled thoughtfully. 'He was right. I have helped people who follow every god, including the Christ. I have heard much about this Jesus. I see no conflict between what he preaches and my own beliefs. Perhaps while you are my guest you will tell me more about him.' He threw another log on the fire.

Above them in the trees the owl hooted. Eigon smiled. 'She has followed you home.'

He nodded. 'She likes to keep watch over me.'

His name was Gort. When he saw that she could no longer keep her eyes open he showed her into the round house and gave her his own bed. He was, he said, going out for the rest of the night. In the morning they would talk again. For the first time in a long time she felt warm and safe and comfortable. She slept almost at once, lulled by the sound of the wind in the trees and the gentle comments of the owl outside, sounds which grew fainter and died away as the bird followed Gort away from his camp deep into the woods and out of earshot.

She woke next morning to the cheerful crackling of the fire and the smell of new baked bread. As they sat opposite each other eating their breakfast he fixed her with a piercing gaze. 'You didn't tell me you were Caradoc's daughter.'

She froze. 'How did you know?'

'I made enquiries.' He frowned. 'You intend to go back to the land of your father's people or your mother's?'

'My mother's. It is my home.'

'Will they welcome you?'

She shrugged. 'I do not go as a war leader.'

'And they will not accept you as such. So, why are you going there?'

'Jesus's apostle Peter thought I should come home.'

'To teach us about your god?' His eyes sharpened.

'That is always foremost in their minds. They also sent me away to keep me out of trouble.'

'This man Titus?'

She nodded. She had told him everything the night before except that one piece of information about her parentage.

'And you want to find out what happened to your brother and sister?'

She nodded again. 'I can find no peace until I know.'

'You say the Druid Melinus instructed you in Druidic healing.'

She nodded. 'He too felt that serving Christ was a natural part of the Druid way.' She smiled.

He nodded. He was studying her face. 'I feel great power in you, Eigon. I think you underestimate your abilities. I sense that you can do everything you set out to achieve.' He turned away and for a while looked silently into the fire then he glanced back at her. 'If you would like a companion on your travels towards the west, I would be glad to accompany you.'

She stared at him, overwhelmed. 'But you can't just get up and go. You have a home here.'

He smiled. 'My home is with me wherever I go. I bank up the fire; I tell my friends, the birds and animals, to keep an eye on my house for me.' He gestured towards the surrounding trees. 'They will be here when I return.'

'And my friends?' she asked wistfully. 'Commios and Drusilla. What about them?'

'If they are heading for Venta Silurum then you will see them again there.'

'And Titus?'

524

He frowned. 'I fear you will see him again too. He is very close.' He sighed. 'There will be a confrontation, Eigon, but with the help of your god and mine, we will win. He will be banished to outer darkness.'

36

Meryn shivered. Outer darkness. Someone was using powerful words against Titus, but not powerful enough. He leaned thoughtfully against one of the trees, and stood staring into the distance.

'Is it Marcia?' Rhodri whispered.

He shook his head. 'I sense a new player in the game. Marcia has closed herself to me.'

'And Jess?' Rhodri's voice broke as he said her name.

Meryn glanced at him. 'Don't lose hope. She is here somewhere. Not very far away.' He pushed himself away from the tree trunk. Somewhere close by an owl had hooted. He frowned. 'Rhodri, will you go back to the farmhouse now? Wait there for me. I need to be alone again for a while.'

Rhodri nodded. 'If you find anything –'

'You will be the first to hear.'

He waited until the sound of Rhodri's footsteps had faded away then he turned to climb up towards the summit. The rocks there had a feeling of tremendous power about them. It was there that the bones of the little boy, Togo, lay, still undisturbed and unrecognised by anyone but Jess. He walked across to the rocks and laid his hands upon them. The child would have his blessing at least, and his prayers for a safe journey into the underworld.

He felt the crackle of power under his fingertips. This was an ancient place of worship. The prayers of thousands of years were met here. He frowned. He had half-expected to feel that Eigon had come here, that she had blessed the place with her Christian prayers, but there was no Christian feel here. These gods were old gods; and these gods were gods more often invoked in anger. Eigon had not discovered this place; she had not found the remains of her little brother. That was one of the roots of her inability to rest in peace.

So, what about Gwladys? Had she found his body? Did the child have that trauma too to contend with? He waited patiently with eyes closed for the pictures to come. No, she had searched but then she had gone away. Why? Then he saw. Someone else had found her. They had taken her away from the last place she had seen her mother and her brother and sister. That someone had taken her deep into the mountains of the north, into the lands of the Ordovices and there they had held her, sensing the power within her, and they had used her, nurturing her anger and her bitterness to their own ends. He stood very still, his hands on the rocks. These rocks were rooted into the very heart of the land. They acted as a channel to all history, to all dreams, to the old gods and the new. He was feeling his way carefully. Was she the route into this mystery, this child who had been brought to the path of evil? Not Eigon at all, not even Titus, but Gwladys, the youngest daughter of Caradoc.

There was a giggle behind him. He tensed, listening, but he did not turn.

Are you going to play with me?

'What sort of game do you want to play, Gwladys?' He held his hands firmly against the rock, keeping his mind carefully empty.

Glads. I'm called Glads. Eigon called me Glads!

'Then I will call you Glads too. That's much prettier.' He kept his voice low. 'Where is your sister, do you know?'

She went away. She didn't want to play any more.

'But she came back. As soon as she could she came back to look for you. She never forgot you, Glads. She always remembered you in her prayers.' He paused. 'Like the other lady, Jess. She has been trying so hard to help you, Glads. Do you know where she is?'

She wants to play with me!

'And so do I, Glads. But we want to play together. Will you show me where she is?'

Are you going to play with me?

'I am, but I want to find Jess first.' He kept his voice even, resisting the urge to turn round. He sensed she was coming closer. 'What shall we play, Glads?'

His sixth sense served him well. At the last moment he spun round. She was immediately behind him, a tall willowy woman, as transparent as water and in her hand there was a knife. She

527

brought it down as he dodged sideways and it plunged harmlessly into the rock where he had been standing, both rock and knife seeming as soft as butter.

'Enough!' he bellowed at her. 'In the name of whatever gods you hold sacred desist from this nonsense. Do you want to find your family or not?' Somewhat to his surprise she was still standing there. 'Do you know what you have done? You have desecrated the burial place of your little brother!'

There was a terrible silence. He saw a moment of surprise and grief register on her pale flawless face then she was fading. In seconds she had gone.

'Damn!' Now he had lost his chance of getting her to tell him where Jess was, because he was fairly sure she knew.

'OK, Marcia!' He turned back to the rock. 'Let's see if you are as good as you think you are. You have no personal involvement here, am I right?' He was talking out loud, aware at once that somewhere she was listening. 'And I'll bet you would like to see Titus suffer. Did he short change you? Did he despise you even as he sought your advice?' His anger, far from cutting off his clarity seemed to have accentuated it. He could see her now, this seer of Ancient Rome, her bright intelligent eyes alight with amusement. An older woman, secure in her accomplishments, her hair white beneath her veil but her skin as flawless as had been that of the child, Glads. She was watching everything from her eyrie, high in a turret in her townhouse behind the temple of Vesta in Rome. 'Play with him all you like, lady,' he said slowly. 'There is a malignity in these hills which needs to be cleansed. It comes from the blood of battle, and the bloodlust which goes with it; it comes from Titus but it also comes from the emotions of that child, trained in the evil arts and returning to spread her poison and it comes from the man who has inadvertently taken it all in and who even now is wandering round the hills gorging on the energy of it all. Help me, Marcia!' He was staring straight ahead but he wasn't seeing the trees or the stars or the rock on which his palms rested, he was looking straight into the cool all-seeing eyes of this woman of Ancient Rome. He wished, he realised suddenly, that he could know her. He saw the eyes soften and he realised that she had unerringly read the thought.

'Did Titus come here?' He spoke the question in a whisper. 'Did he follow Eigon back to this place? Did she come here to cleanse the evil memories? Did he stand in her way and feed on her sister's hatred?'

'Look!' she whispered back. 'Watch!'

It was spring when Eigon and Gort at last reached Venta Silurum. They had wintered with forest peoples on the roads and track-ways, moving on when the weather relented enough to make the ways passable. They lived as itinerant healers and teachers, earning their bread in each community as they passed, Eigon often singing at the fires of their hosts. They never wanted for food. Hospitality was a sacred duty to Celt and Christian alike. Eigon's feet grew tough in the leather boots she wore. Her face weathered in the ice-cold winds. She was happy, though they heard nothing of Commios or Drusilla. There was no sign of Titus. They did find other Christians here and there, and heard stories that Jesus himself had visited the land of the Durotriges when he was a lad, and that a little church had been set up somewhere there in the vale of apples in the name of his mother, Mary.

The town of the Silures was a Roman outpost, a fort and a market on the far side of the great River Sabrina. It held no mem-ories for Eigon; she sensed nothing from her childhood here and almost at once they set off again, up into the hills in search of Silurian communities who might remember the old king, whose daughter Cerys had married the hero Caradoc and who might know anything about his other daughter Gwladys and his son, Togodumnus.

Gort was watching her as they walked slowly up the trackways and he smiled. 'I see the mountains are talking to you.'

She smiled. 'I have dreamed of them for so long. The soft curves of the hills, the black peaks, the smell of the flowers, the song of the wind in the tall trees.' She paused, leaning on her staff. 'This is a land of poetry.'

He nodded.

'Even the rivers sing.'

He nodded again. He glanced at her, sensing a new lightness about her and his heart sank. There was no escaping the dark days to come. He had prayed to his own gods and to her Lord, but they had answered with a frown. She faced a baptism of fire in this her native land and there was no avoiding it. Slowly he moved on again feeling a new weariness in his bones. Why did she not feel this overwhelming threat? How was it that she could sing?

She followed him, hurrying a little to catch up. 'The end to my quest is coming, isn't it?' She looked across at him. 'I can feel it on the wind and I can see it in your face.'

He raised an eyebrow. 'I was wondering when you would sense it.'

'I sensed it. I just didn't want it to spoil this last bit of our journey. I thought we would be able to stay here in the south near my mother's people, but they no longer remember her, or if they do, they remember only battles and fear and blood.' The word brought a shiver on the wind. 'I have to go back to the place this all started, don't I. To the Valley of the Ravens.'

He nodded.

'And it is there I will meet Titus again.'

This time he shrugged. 'As to what the fates have in store, I cannot tell you.'

They had stopped, facing each other, the wind tugging at their hair, swirling their cloaks around them as the clouds raced eastwards across the mountains throwing great swift moving shadows over the ground. She smiled.

'This time I am a grown woman. I have the protection of my God. I will be expecting him.'

'And you plan to kill him?' Gort held her eyes steadily.

She shook her head. 'The Lord says we should turn the other cheek.'

'And how will that repay the hurt he has caused?'

'I will leave that up to God. I have offered the situation to Him to sort out.' She smiled again. She spent much of her time in meditation every night, surrounded by the warmth of love and comfort that the prayers gave her whether it was outside under the trees, in the sacred groves of her ancestors or in the dark in the houses and shelters where they had hidden from the weather. 'He will tell me what to do when the time comes.'

The time came as the days lengthened and the spring sunshine grew stronger. They followed the river valleys, then they followed the trackways north, heading ever onward towards the place that her father had chosen for his fateful battle with the power of Rome.

The battlefield had long ago returned to grass and shrubs and trees. There was no sign of the burials or the funeral pyres that had marked the place. The palisades of the great hill fort had been torn down, the walls had disappeared and there were sheep grazing on the earth banks and the ramparts. Eigon walked alone out onto the plain and stood still. She could feel it now, the fear, the anguish, the anger, the rage of battle. Closing her eyes she whispered a prayer for the souls of all those who had fallen in this, the Valley of Ravens, then she turned towards the steep hillside which ran to the south and west, the hillside where she and her mother and her nurse and her brother and sister had fled through the darkness to find safety and shelter.

Wordlessly she led the way, feeling by instinct rather than memory the route they should take to find again the ruined byre where they had hidden from the noise and the smell of blood.

When the stone walls were in sight Gort stopped suddenly. He put his hand on her arm and a finger to his lips. There was someone there waiting for them. They heard the click of stone on stone, and the soft whicker of a horse. Cautiously they crept closer.

Titus was sitting on a pile of stones, his arms folded. A naked sword lay next to him, softly cushioned on a bed of moss.

'So, finally you return to your destiny.' He smiled pleasantly at them as they stood side by side on the old stone pathway. 'It has taken you a long time to get here, Eigon, but then the hills are beautiful at this time of year are they not, and it was right that you should enjoy your last days.' As though taking its cue from him a cuckoo began to call from the hillside behind them, the sound echoing out across the valley. He stood up slowly. Eigon flinched backwards. Gort she noticed did not move.

'I have some friends of yours here to greet you.' He smiled again. 'They have been looking for you for a long time. Luckily they asked so often and so insistently for you as they crossed the country that it was easy for me to meet up with them. They have been very pleasant travelling companions.' He gestured behind him towards the wall. 'Sadly they couldn't wait until you actually arrived, but then you wouldn't expect me to allow that, would you?'

Eigon's mouth had gone dry. She glanced towards the wall. The day had suddenly become very cold. 'Commios?' she whispered. 'Drusilla?'

He shrugged. 'I'm sorry. It was very quick.'

Gort caught her arm. 'Don't look.' Taller than her, and standing slightly closer he had already seen the two bodies lying behind the stones. Their arms were bound behind them; they had had their throats cut.

Titus gave a grim smile. 'Strangely I took no pleasure in their end. They were pleasant enough folk. Their mistake was to know you.' He narrowed his eyes. 'You look upset.'

'Was that not the point?' Eigon managed a retort but she had grown numb. The world had receded to this small patch of ruined land, rank with nettles. Somewhere overhead a buzzard called, the lonely yelp echoing across the valley. Almost at once it was answered by the deep croak of a raven. The birds of death had smelled blood.

Gort sighed. He had nothing to defend him but his staff. He leaned forward a little, firming his grip on the good strong wood. It would probably splinter under the slash of a Roman blade, but he would give it a try to protect her. Strangely though he felt she already had protection. An unearthly calm had settled round her; perhaps the wings of angels were forming a fence about her; perhaps the shades of her mother and her father had followed her from Rome. There were other people here with them; in fact the place was crowded. He gave a slight smile and Titus tensed at once.

'You see your imminent death as amusing?'

Gort shook his head slowly. 'I wondered if you could see the other folk here around you. The shades of people you killed; the people you defiled. Those two; they may be dead to your eyes but I can see their spirits standing watching you. He has his arm around her. Was Drusilla in love with Commios, Eigon? They will be together now in the next world.'

Titus had paled. 'Fool! You think you can scare me like that?'

'No, I don't think I can scare you. I think you are beyond emotion of the human variety.' Gort moved slightly, balancing his weight, tightening his grip on the staff. 'The sad part is that your spirit too will roam these hills and yours will spew poison when your throat is cut.'

'And who is going to cut my throat, old man?' Titus seemed amused.

'As to that, I see a queue forming behind you.' Gort returned his smile. He glanced upwards. 'I see the cailleach is here. She, like the raven, warns us of death.'

Eigon followed his gaze. An owl had drifted quietly out of the woodland on silent wings. It settled on the lowest branch of an old ash tree behind Titus and uttered a gentle quavering hoot. He jumped visibly.

'A daylight owl. The harbinger of death.' Gort glanced fondly at the bird. 'As is the man standing behind you, my friend, with his sword drawn.'

Eigon's eyes widened. Titus turned. The lightning stroke of the blade was the last thing he saw.

'Meryn, come quickly!' Rhodri's voice tore Meryn back into the present with a jolt. 'They've found Dan.'

Meryn stood away from the rock, dazed for a moment. He took a deep breath, trying to push away the pictures which flooded his head. 'Where is he? What about Jess?'

Rhodri shook his head. 'There is no sign of her. He's holed up in an old church half a mile from here. The police are there.'

'But he's not armed?'

'They can't be sure of that. They are taking no chances, but he can't escape. What frightens me is what happens if he's hidden Jess somewhere? Supposing he won't tell us where she is?'

'He hasn't got Jess, Rhodri.' Meryn shook his head. 'Remember, it's Glads who has Jess.'

Rhodri stared at him. 'You've spoken to Glads?'

Meryn nodded. 'She's gone for now. I pushed her too hard.' He sighed. 'I have to stay and try to get her back. There is such a confusion here of past and present, so much pain. So much –' He broke off. 'Wait. Marcia is here again. I can hear her voice.'

Marcia Maximilla stared into the dark water of her scrying bowl and smiled. So much chaos; so much anger. How very satisfactory. Then she shook her head. The magician had asked for her help. An attractive man who had seen her beauty and acknowledged it with a slight quickening of his pulse. She liked him instinctively. She swept her palm over the water and watched the ripples settle back into new pictures. The image of Titus was gone. Here was another soul to watch. A seer like herself and a powerful one, a woman who hid inside the body of a child. She peered closer. The sister of the woman Titus had so desired to find. How strange. The one so good. The other so evil. She nodded to herself. One of life's more entertaining conundrums, the duality of good and evil. She glanced at the parchment lying on the table near her. It was an account of the man who had become a god in Judea. Her eye lingered over the sign of a fish at the end of the scroll. She had always thought evil the more amusing path. That was why she had indulged the Emperor so often in his whims. But maybe not any more.

The magician wanted to find the woman, Jess. She leaned forward again, peering into the swirling shadows in the bowl. The seeress had enticed her into a dark ravine, aping the child she had once been, begging her to play a game; then she had lured her back to the house of blood. Jess had followed the sound of the child's voice; already bruised and disorientated she had fallen down some steps and hit her head and she had slept the long sleep which can so easily turn into death. No one would find her there. It was a place hidden from prying eyes, protected by the spirits of the trees which closed their branches over her head and sheltered her from sun and moon, slowly drawing her down into their world.

Suddenly Marcia made up her mind. Closing her eyes she threw out a flood of messages.

'She's here. Somewhere. Behind the studio.' Meryn stood help-lessly looking round. It was all so dark. 'I don't see where. There is a staircase covered in undergrowth.' The others were clustered round him as he stood in the courtyard.

'She's fallen down a staircase?' Steph stared at him.

'A stone staircase leading down. But it's not inside. I can see trees round her.'

'I know!' Suddenly Steph was running past the studio and round the back of the cluster of old sheds and outbuildings behind it. There at the edge of the lawn where the hillside fell away towards the valley there was another stone-built byre. The door had long ago been nailed up. She shone her torch at the wall. 'Down here.'

Someone had forced open the door. It hung drunkenly off its hinges leading into total blackness where the torchlight couldn't reach. The far side of the old building had fallen away, leaving it open to the stars. Inside, a flight of steps led into what had once been a store room deep underground.

'Jess! Jess! I can see her!' Rhodri elbowed Steph out of the way as the beam of torchlight finally found her. 'My God, Jess, are you all right?'

She was lying amongst the roots of the ash tree hidden by a tangle of elder and ancient apple trees. Hurtling down the stairs Rhodri threw himself down and put his arms around her.

'Don't touch her! Don't move her till we see if she's all right!' Steph screamed. She ran after Rhodri. There was a moment's pause as they both looked at her in the torchlight. She was deathly pale, lying, her eyes closed, huddled at the bottom of the stairs. Her skin to Rhodri's touch was very cold.

'Wait. Let me!' Aurelia had hurried after Steph. Pushing the other two aside she knelt beside Jess and picked up her wrist. 'There's a faint pulse.' She laid down Jess's hand and rested her fingers for a moment on her daughter's forehead. 'Jess, sweetheart, can you hear me?'

'Hugo?' Jess's eyelids flickered. 'Mummy?'

'You're safe, Jess. We're going to call an ambulance. Someone bring a rug to keep her warm! Quickly!'

'Rhodri?' Jess's gaze shifted from her mother. Her voice was very weak.

Rhodri was kneeling in the mud and weeds at her other side. He bent and kissed her forehead. 'Thank God you're all right. I was out of my mind with worry.'

Jess smiled. 'Sorry. Where's Hugo?'

'Hugo!' Steph stared down at her. 'Who's Hugo? We had a dog called Hugo but he died years ago.' She was already on her way back up the steps 'Why did you come down here, Jess? It's been boarded up for years.'

'The little girl. I could hear her calling me.' Jess shifted her weight with a groan. Hugo had been there. She was sure of it. But he had gone.

'Don't move!' Rhodri put his hand on her shoulder.

'I'm OK. Nothing broken. I've had long enough to test everything still works.' She managed a grin. 'I can feel all my hands and feet, and I can move my neck and I can see. But my leg is wedged somehow. I can't free it. And I'm so cold.'

She winced as, gently, Rhodri put his arm around her shoulders and held her against him for warmth while Steph ran inside to fetch blankets to keep her warm. She could feel his heart beating steadily under the cotton of his shirt.

Aurelia went with her in the ambulance and Rhodri followed in his car. No one seemed to query his right to be there, nor the fact that it was he who stroked her hair back from her face and held her hand while they waited in the emergency department.

The doctor confirmed that she was hypothermic and bruised and had a badly sprained ankle but there was nothing worse. The hospital kept her in for the night to make sure that her temperature was stabilised and it was Rhodri who went to fetch her next morning.

In the car she kept glancing at him. 'You kissed me yesterday,' she said at last.

He grinned. 'Sorry. Don't know what I was thinking about.'

She smiled. 'It was nice.'

'Really?' He glanced across at her, distracted and the car swerved across the road. She let out a small scream. 'Rhodri!'

'Sorry! Sorry, I just wanted to make sure you were joking.'

'I wasn't joking.'

'Right.' There was a layby just ahead and he pulled in.

'Why are you stopping?'

'To do this.' He gathered her into his arms and kissed her properly. 'How about that? Was that still nice?'

She nodded. 'Very nice.' She pushed him away gently. 'Rhodri, I'm covered in bruises. Sorry. You're hurting me.' She paused as though the words had triggered a memory. 'Dan?' she whispered. 'What happened to Dan?'

'He's been arrested and charged with murder.'

'Murder?' She frowned. 'Who has he murdered?'

Rhodri cursed quietly. She didn't know. He took her hands in his. 'Jess, I'm afraid I have some very sad news, my love. He killed Will.'

She frowned. 'No. No, he can't have. Will is back in London.'

Rhodri shook his head slowly and closing her eyes she put her head back against the seat. Tears ran down her cheeks. 'He didn't deserve that.' She couldn't hold back a sob.

'No. No one deserves something like that.' He sighed. 'Especially not a good man like Will. Dan is safely under lock and key.'

'And Eigon?' She took the tissue he had found for her from a crumpled packet in the glove compartment. 'And Titus?'

He looked at her for a few seconds aching to hold her in his arms, to make everything better for her. But no one could do that. She would have to grieve for Will in her own time.

'I'll drive us home, love. There is a chap there called Meryn Jones. Do you remember, he was on that radio programme about Cartimandua? Well, it turns out your mother knows him quite well; and so does mine come to think of it. He used to live in the hills nearby. He's unbelievable! Truly psychic. He has been sorting everything out. And he will explain.'

Rhodri carried her in from the car and they made her a bed on the sofa. Only when she was comfortable, propped up against a mountain of pillows did they introduce her to Meryn. He sat down beside her with a smile.

'So, the elusive Jess.' He leaned across and shook her hand. 'It is good to meet you at last.' His handshake was firm, reassuring.

'You told them where to look for me,' she said.

'That was a lady called Marcia,' he said with a grave nod. 'I have thanked her for her help.'

'And Eigon? What happened to Eigon?'

'Eigon's story is told, Jess.' He paused. 'I am sure she will speak to you herself, but there is still one last strand to unravel.' His face was grave. 'Her sister.'

'Glads.' Jess shivered. 'What happened to her?'

'That we don't know yet. She was taken away from here by a woman who saw her wandering around near the battlefield. She took Glads with her back to her own tribe in the neighbouring mountains. They taught her some bad stuff. She resented the fact that she thought her family had abandoned her and she let it all fester.' He was studying her face. 'She wanted revenge.'

'So she tried to lure me outside? And it was she who led me to the ravine and then to the steps in the garden?'

He nodded.

'Was she trying to kill me?'

'As to that, I don't know. But she was trying to make mischief.'

They glanced up as Rhodri appeared. He was carrying a tray. 'Whisky for the invalid. And the rest of us!' He was followed by Steph and Aurelia. 'The police just phoned. Dan's been taken back to London but they think he will be declared unfit to plead. He'll

537

be locked up for the rest of his days. You've nothing to fear from him any more.'

Jess gave a wan smile, taking a glass of whisky from him. 'And Titus?'

'I think you'll find Titus has been sorted.' Meryn nodded. 'I'll explain.'

That morning while he was waiting for Rhodri to fetch Jess from the hospital, he had wandered into Steph's studio and sat down at the table. This was where it had all happened – two more murders to add to Titus's toll. He glanced round. Sunlight was filtering in through the windows. The room was pleasantly warm. It felt safe and friendly.

His face had softened into a smile. 'If you're listening, Marcia Maximilla, thank you for all you did.'

She was there. He could sense her. The room was scented suddenly with citrus and warm pine, the smells of a Roman garden. 'One last favour, if you feel you could indulge me?' He smiled. There was no answer but he could tell she was still listening. 'The soul of Titus Marcus Olivinus should not be wandering around loose. In our belief system it would be possible for him to be reborn into another form. To learn some lessons. What do you think?'

Again there was no reply. He left it at that. She would know what to do.

From the wall in the courtyard a small pair of bright black eyes peered out as Meryn made his way back towards the house. He paused. He had a strong feeling he was being watched. He turned and looked back, puzzled. With a squeak the mouse leaped from the wall and fled into the woods. He smiled. Coincidence? Who would ever know.

As Jess lay in her bed that night, staring up at the ceiling Eigon told her the rest of the story. She was drifting into sleep, exhausted, when she saw the woman she had come to know almost as well as she knew herself, standing in the shadows in the corner of her room. Was she awake or was she dreaming? She raised herself on an elbow and smiled uncertainly. 'Eigon?' Eigon was looking towards her, her face indistinct, and yet Jess felt that she could see her. When Eigon began to speak she was speaking directly to Jess.

Titus had stood for a fraction of a second after the sword blade struck him, a look of total astonishment on his face, then he fell forward into the nettles and lay still.

'Julius?' Eigon stared, incredulous, at the man who emerged from the shadow of the ruined wall. 'Julius?' She seemed unable to say anything else.

He smiled. 'The very same.' He scrambled over the loose stones towards her, followed by a dark-haired teenage boy who stood and stared down at Titus, his face white with shock. 'If you're going to be sick, Drusus, do it somewhere else.' Julius grinned at him then he turned back to her. 'He is my bodyguard.' He nodded towards the boy who had managed to regain control of himself. He looked back at Eigon and saw her staring at his face. 'Sorry.' He touched his scar self-consciously. 'Not as pretty as I was.'

She stepped towards him and raised her hand to touch the wound, her fingers lying gently over his for a second. 'Titus did that? That night?'

He nodded.

'We all thought you were dead.'

'I nearly was. I was rescued and brought back from death by a wonderful woman, a doctor!' He smiled. 'This young man is her son. She sent him with me, when she realised I could not be dissuaded from following you, to make sure I kept taking the medicine.' She was still touching his face, as though trying to convince herself that he was real. 'I know one look at me could stampede a herd of wild horses. If you hate me like this, I shall understand. Drusus and I will go back to Rome.'

'No. No, I love you!' Suddenly she was in his arms clinging to him. 'I can't believe you are here; I never thought I would see you again; you saved me; you saved us.' It was a little while before she had remembered Gort. She escaped from Julius's arms and turned to him, catching his hand. 'This man has looked after me and taught me and fed me and followed me across the island of

539

Britannia to keep an eye on me.' She fell silent suddenly with a glance at the wall. 'Commios and Drusilla –'

Gort pulled her back. 'Don't look. There's no point.'

Julius followed his gaze. He stepped over to the wall and looked down. 'No.' He shook his head. 'Dear sweet Lord have mercy on their souls. This man was a monster. No –' As Drusus stepped towards them he caught at the boy's tunic and held him back. 'Don't look. Not now. We will bury them later together. They are in heaven now.' He glanced at Gort. 'You would seem to be a Druid, my friend? Has Eigon not managed to convert you yet to our faith?'

Gort raised an eyebrow. 'Maybe she has persuaded me about one or two things. I've prayed to the Lord Jesus.'

'Like my young friend here,' Julius chuckled, 'you have reservations?'

'I cover my options. He seems to have answered some of our prayers satisfactorily.' He glanced at Eigon with a smile. He was unlacing the cord that held his cloak closed. Taking it off he went over to the wall. 'Do you have a knife?' He took it from Julius and bent to cut the ropes that bound Commios's hands behind him. Then he did the same for Drusilla. He linked their hands gently together, then he covered them with the cloak. 'We will lay them to rest together here.'

They cut the shape of the double grave in the sweet meadow grass behind the byre and the three men began to dig. It took them a long time, but eventually it was ready and they laid the two bodies in one another's arms in the grave and prayed over them. Later Julius and Gort dug another grave for Titus down amongst the trees in a darkly shadowed ravine. The prayers they said for his soul were not sufficient to imprison his restless spirit. It had already gone.

'And Togo and Glads?' Jess murmured. 'Did you look for them?' She could see Eigon still standing there in the corner of the room as she told her story. The folds of her gown were pale shadows in the darkness.

'I didn't know where to start. We asked questions in the hamlets round about. No one knew anything about them. I prayed so hard.' Jess could see her face more clearly now; her eyes were red with weeping. 'I laid flowers for them and I begged the angels to take care of them wherever they were.'

'And then?'

'And then we went away. I couldn't bear to stay.'

'What happened?'

'Julius and I were married. We settled down in a house near a stream on the northern slopes of the Black Mountains not so far from one of the hill forts I had lived in, in the happier times with my mother and father. We built a wall round it, and we taught and prayed there. The people round about came to call it Llan Eigon after me.' She smiled.

'And Gort and Drusus?'

'Drusus went back to his mother in Rome eventually. He sent messages from time to time. Gort stayed for a while too, then he decided to return to the south. He came to see us two or three times over the next few years.'

'And you never had any children?'

She shook her head. 'No.'

'And in the end?'

'Julius died one winter of a fever. He was a great age.' She smiled sadly. 'My dearest love. After that I stayed there. It was my home. Where else was I to go? I was known in the hills around as a healer and an anchorite. Others joined me. They built their little houses inside our walls and in the end we built an oratory so we could pray together. But it was many, many years before the worship of Christ began to spread around the country.'

Rhodri and Jess went to Llanigon a few days later and spent some time in the little churchyard which marked the site of Eigon's home. They walked around the ancient church and the far more ancient walls of the churchyard and laid some flowers in her memory on a pile of moss-covered stones. In the distance they could hear the sound of water from the tumbling stream.

That night she came again to Jess and for the first time Jess saw her as an old lady, the old woman who had lived and loved and worked in the spot beneath the mountains where they had laid the flowers.

'You never found out what happened to Togo and Glads?' Jess asked at last.

'No.'

'Togo lies up there under the rocks. I'm sure it's him. I put flowers on his bones.' Jess felt her own tears soaking into the pillow.

Eigon closed her eyes.

'Do you want us to move him? To bury him perhaps?'

Was that a nod? Jess sat up in bed. 'Do you want them to have a Christian burial?'

They didn't call the coroner to examine those tiny bones. Two weeks after Will was buried in his parents' beloved Cornwall, Megan's cousin from Brecon, an eighty-year-old vicar with clear green eyes and a thatch of white hair and a mind as sharp as a whistle held a funeral service for the little boy who they had brought down the hill with due ceremony, the bones neatly stacked in a small yew wood box. The grave was dug behind the orchard on the hillside at Ty Bran, overlooking the valley, somewhere near the place where in the year of Our Lord 65 Commios and Drusilla, two Christian citizens of Rome, had been buried in one another's arms. He said prayers for them as well. If questions were ever asked about the burial, he said, he would claim senility for his lack of memory about the whole affair. The day was hot and still. There was no sign of the buzzards, or the ravens of Ty Bran. They heaped the grave with flowers.

That left Glads.

Meryn had returned for the ceremony. Afterwards he had wandered outside and he stood staring down the valley as the sun set in a blaze of crimson and gold. Rhodri came out to join him. 'Jess heard Glads calling again this afternoon.'

Meryn nodded. 'She is a troubled soul.'

'Does she sense her brother has been laid to rest?'

'I suspect so.'

'Is there some way of tempering her anger?'

Meryn looked thoughtful. 'It is something that must be done. If these good people are ever going to have any peace in this house and Steph is going to be able to stay here alone without fear, she has to be neutralised.' He folded his arms, watching as the sun sank into the misty distance. 'I have an idea. She of course is not a Christian.' Nor was Meryn. He had watched the funeral that afternoon and added his own prayers in his own way, ever watchful at the perimeter that no stray evil should enter the sacred space of the burial place. None had done so.

He smiled. 'I have a colleague to consult. The studio, I think.'
He went in alone.

They filled the room with flowers and Steph insisted on burning incense there. It smelled very exotic as Meryn let himself into the dusky shadows. Someone had left a candle burning. It was enough to see by.

'Marcia?' He spoke out loud as he had before. 'I know I said I had only one last favour and I asked too much even with that, but I need advice.'

He paused, listening. He could sense no one there. Disappointed, he tried again. 'The soul of Gwladys, daughter of Caradoc, walks the hills filled with misery and hatred. We want her to travel lightly to the land of the ever young, or if she doesn't desire that, to rest in peace with the soul of her brother near her.'

The incense was burning more brightly suddenly; the glowing tip of the stick of lavender and cade brought from Aurelia's home in France flaring as if in a draught. He watched the spiral of smoke curl round the room. The candle flame guttered. Then he heard the voice.

Play with me. Come and play with me. Please.

'You are too old to play now, Glads.' Meryn's voice sounded strangely loud in the shadowy room. 'You lived to be a grown woman and you know now that Eigon and your mother and father did not desert you. They did their best. Your parents mourned for you all their lives. And Eigon came to find you. In the end, after all she had been through, she still came back to try and find you.' He paused, looking round. 'Tell me how I can help you rest in peace, Glads.'

The candle flickered again.

'Eigon brought back a message of peace and love to this valley. She looked for you. She wanted so much to find you. Can you accept that? Can you rest?'

There was a long silence. He could sense her thinking. Then at last she spoke.

Bury my dolly with Togo. I'll go and play with Marcia! The voice was older now. Stronger. *I don't like this valley any more!*

Meryn gave a grim smile. 'Thank you, Marcia Maximilla. I hope she does you credit,' he said quietly. 'And I hope you and I meet one day in the other realms. I owe you one!'

Blowing out the candle he let himself out of the studio and

walked slowly across the yard. Pushing open the door he found the others in the kitchen. Someone had opened a bottle of champagne.

'Ash has passed his exams with flying colours!' Jess planted a kiss onto his cheek. 'One of my most challenging pupils. My ex-boss has just rung to tell me.'

Meryn smiled. He accepted a glass from Aurelia and raised it. 'To absent friends.' They all joined him in the toast. 'And, I hope to the renewal of our old acquaintance,' he glanced at Aurelia. 'I should like to visit your French hideaway if you would permit me, one day? And one more thing,' he glanced at Rhodri with a raised eyebrow, 'to the happy couple.'

Rhodri grinned. 'Hang on a minute! I haven't asked her yet.' He looked round the room in mock despair. 'That's the trouble with having a psychic in the house. They always know what is going to happen next!'

Author's Note

The historical evidence for Eigon's existence is shadowy. We are not even sure who she was or that she existed at all …

I first came across her when my father bought a cottage in the parish of Llanigon some forty years ago. Who, we wanted to know, or what, was Eigon. The church guidebook answered our question. But only sort of. There are two theories. Either HE was a bishop or, SHE was the daughter of the great Welsh hero, Caratacus. Obviously I preferred the second option.

But then came the $64,000 question. If Caratacus had a daughter called Eigon and if she was taken to Rome as a captive as history records, how would she have ended up as the patron saint of an ancient church in the Welsh borders, 300 years before the official conversion of Britain to Christianity? This was the question which inspired this book. My curiosity was further piqued by a splendidly framed engraving of Fuseli's painting of *Caractacus at the Tribunal of Claudius at Rome*, which has hung for years in the hall outside my study. In the picture Caratacus is portrayed as the noble warrior, his fists clenched in iron manacles, his moustaches to the fore, his brow steely. His daughter and his wife and even the Empress Agrippina are depicted as respectively, wilting, fainting, theatrical and buxom. The picture is I have to admit not really to my taste, but for us it is doubly interesting, firstly for its depiction of Eigon and the obviously dramatic story it tells and secondly, because the engraver was my great, great, great grandfather, Andrew Birrell. I had to find out more.

Caratacus the warrior king and opposer of the invading Romans was the son of Cunobelinus (or Cymbeline) king of the Catuvellauni. We know a great deal about his opposition to Rome, his battles, his defeat. I wrote about his capture by Cartimandua in *Daughters of Fire*, but as a character he moved off stage in her story, just as his life was becoming truly fascinating. We know he was taken with his family to Rome, made the famous speech to the Emperor as they stood, facing an almost certainly horrific death and won the Emperor's approbation by the brilliance of his address, whereupon he was pardoned and given a house. (Tacitus quotes his speech at length in his *Annals of Imperial Rome*, written some 50 years after the event, so he might have known the gist of what Caratacus said, but we must bear in mind that the words may, as recorded, owe more to Tacitus's own political views than what was actually said.)

This much is described by the Roman historians. There is however another Caratacus, or Caractacus or Caradoc. Here he is a legendary and mythic hero, the father of many children, the descendant of gods and from the novelist's point of view it is the many interesting gaps and inconsistencies in all the information and misinformation which has come down to us about this period, that pose some of the questions which I have explored. Here we are at the cusp between history and legend and it is from this mixture that I have teased out the single thread of my story.

(I explore more about Caratacus's legend and his possible relations and descendants on my website – fascinating though the subject is, it is not part of this particular novel.)

The questions I asked myself were specific. How and why could Caratacus just disappear from history? Where did he live in Rome? Why did he not immediately plot and plan to return to Britannia and specifically to the mountains of what we now call Wales to continue his fight? Surely so great a hero cannot have been seduced by a Roman retirement plan. The only reasonable explanation that I could come up with was that he died. If so, what happened to the daughter who was taken with him to Rome?

To call Eigon herself shadowy is an understatement; what we know of her is full of mystery and inconsistency. 'Caratacus's daughter' (not mentioned by name by Tacitus and not appearing on the sometimes wild and wonderful lists of Caratacus's children) disappears from history after the great set piece speech in Rome. But then we have her mysterious reappearance as a saint in the foothills of the Black Mountains.

So, more questions: if Eigon existed at all, was she as she is depicted by Elgar in his cantata *Caractacus*, where she is old enough to have a lover, and in the painting by Fuseli, where she is a full-grown woman at the time of her capture? Or was she a child?

The latter would, I thought, make more sense as she was still with her mother on campaign and I decided to make Eigon's mother a 'Welsh' woman. Caratacus was probably married as a young man to someone from his own or a neighbouring tribe to seal a tribal alliance, and if he indeed had other children it was she who would have been their mother. His alliance with the Silures came later in his career as his opposition to Rome pushed him further and further west. So it seemed reasonable to assume that perhaps his leadership of the Silures and his adoption as a legend of Welsh history came through, or was reinforced by, a subsequent marriage alliance with the daughter of their king, whom he later succeeded by dint of his prowess as a military leader. If this supposition is true, then his children by the lady I call Cerys would have been young at the time of the battle and they would have called South Wales home.

Then I wondered where Christianity came in and that at least was obvious. The Rome to which Caratacus and his family were taken was the Rome of St Peter and St Paul; if they survived they would have been there at the time of the Great Fire of Rome and the Christian persecutions under Nero and they would almost certainly have met up with Pomponia Graecina while there; her arrest and the charge that she was following a foreign religion is recorded, again by Tacitus. Some say she had been influenced by Druidry during her time in Britannia; some by the new Christianity. I have covered my options by making her interested in both.

It seemed to me a good guess that Eigon eventually returned to the country of her birth and, if she is remembered here as a saint, then she must have returned as a Christian. In the early Celtic church the term saint meant someone who served God and lived a holy life. The Llan in Llanigon (still spelt Llaneigon in Victorian times) did not imply that this ancient place was originally a parish or even a church. Llan came to mean both those things in later Welsh but in the original meaning the term referred to a small religious community or centre, focused around a particular spiritual person, which would fit in with it being the place where Eigon chose to settle down. She was actually there. In person.

Thus from very slender threads I have woven her story. I can't claim it to be history but I feel I have given a good guess.

That leaves me with one last mystery which Caratacus has

bequeathed us. Where did that last great battle take place? It seems strange, but no one knows for sure. There are many places which claim to be its site. In the end I did not feel qualified to make a choice so I have invented one of my own. My Valley of Ravens does not exist as such! If you are interested in finding out more about some of the possible locations for the battle please look at my website (barbara-erskine.com) where I have listed some of them and posted some of my own photographs.

Researching this book has as with all my books, been a joy. I want to thank Pat Taylor who when I was researching *Daughters of Fire*, introduced me to her beloved Yorkshire and who nobly volunteered to come with me to Rome and helped keep me focused on the places I needed to see on this visit. She also introduced me, while we were there, to her friend Anne Marie Doran Marchetti who gave me wonderful advice about the food, the drink, the way of life and many other aspects of living in the most wonderful city in the world.

Back home very many thanks to Christian Chilton who provided me with information about police procedure. In the end the police presence in the story is mostly off stage, but it is only knowing exactly what they would be doing which allows one accurately to fit them into the action. Thank you too to Raymond and Christine Nickford who saved me from my own ignorance by sending me CDs of Elgar's *Caractacus* of which I had never heard. I have to confess that like Jess I feel it is not altogether my kind of music but it is growing on me!

After editing my books for so many years Rachel Hore has laid aside her blue pencil at least for the time being to write her own wonderful novels. She has been succeeded by Susan Opie who has performed wonders for me as my new editor together with Lucy Ferguson and of course my brilliant agent Carole Blake who have all worked so hard to produce this book. Thank you to them all. And finally I mustn't forget Fiona McIntosh who has been my publicist for many years now and who has made the launch of each of my books so successful and above all so much fun!

www.BarbaraErskine.co.uk
Have you logged in yet?

Visit Barbara's fantastic new website where you will find information about her novels, background, interest in writing and history. Read on for more information about Barbara's ongoing fascination with the supernatural and lose yourself in Barbara's exclusive monthly short stories.

You will also find details about this book, photographs of some of the locations visited by the characters in the story – both in the past and the present day – a bibliography and various items about the historical research involved. Further details on Barbara's upcoming appearances near you and events are also featured here.

Lady of Hay

Jo Clifford, successful journalist, is all set to debunk the idea of past-life regression. But when she submits to a simple hypnotic session, she suddenly finds herself reliving the experiences of Matilda, Lady of Hay, the wife of a baron at the time of King John. Jo's past and present become hopelessly entwined, and a story of secret passion and unspeakable treachery is about to begin again…

978 0 00 725086 8

Kingdom of Shadows

In a childless and unhappy marriage, Clare Royland is rich and beautiful – but lonely. And fuelling her feelings of isolation is a strange, growing fascination with an ancestress from the distant past. Troubled by inexplicable dreams that terrify her, Clare is forced to look back through the centuries for answers.

978 0 00 728866 3

Child of the Phoenix

In 1218 an extraordinary princess is born. Her mystical powers and unquenchable spirit will alter the course of history. Raised by her fiercely Welsh nurse to support the Celtic cause against the predatory English king, Princess Eleyne is taught to worship the old gods, to look into the future and sometimes the past. However, unable to identify time and place in her horrifying visions, she is powerless to avert forthcoming tragedy…

978 0 00 728079 7

Midnight is a Lonely Place

After a broken love affair, biographer Kate Kennedy retires to a remote cottage on the wild Essex coast to work on her new book, until her landlord's daughter uncovers a Roman site nearby and long-buried passions are unleashed. Kate must struggle for her life against earthbound spirits and ancient curses as hate, jealousy, and revenge do battle across the centuries.

978 0 00 728077 3

House of Echoes

Joss Grant is eager to begin a new life when she inherits Belheddon Hall. She brings her husband, Luke, and their small son, Tom, to the dilapidated house, and sets about discovering her family roots in the village. But soon Tom wakes screaming at night. Joss hears echoing voices and senses an invisible presence, watching them from the shadows. Are they spirits from the past? Or is she imagining them?

978 0 00 728078 0

On the Edge of Darkness

Adam Craig is fourteen when, near an isolated Celtic stone in the wild Scottish Highlands, he meets Brid, whose exotic dress and strange attitudes fascinate him. They become friends and, in time, passionate lovers. Brid leads him, unsuspecting, into the sixth century, where she trains as a Druid princess and masters their ancient mysteries and powerful magic...

978 0 00 728865 6

Whispers in the Sand

Recently divorced, Anna decides to retrace a journey her great-grandmother Louisa made in the nineteenth century: a Nile cruise from Luxor to the Valley of the Kings. Anna carries with her two mementoes of Louisa: an ancient Egyptian scent bottle, and the diary of that original voyage, which has lain unread for 100 years, but which contains chilling secrets…

978 0 00 728864 9

Hiding From the Light

The parish of Manningtree and Mistley has a dark history. Matthew Hopkins, Cromwell's Witchfinder General, tortured scores of women there. It's said their spirits haunt the old shop in the High Street. Emma Dickson has given up her career to move to a nearby cottage, but as the feast of Halloween approaches, she is caught up in a struggle that has been raging for generations, as old enemies reach out across the years for their revenge.

978 0 00 728863 2

Daughters of Fire

As the Romans invade Britannia, Princess Cartimandua – destined to be queen of the great tribe of the Brigantes – watches the enemies of her people draw closer. Her world is one of love, conflict, and retribution. In the present day, historian Viv Lloyd Rees has immersed herself in the legends surrounding the Celtic queen. As her obsession grows ever more persistent, the past envelops the present and she finds herself in the greatest danger of her life.

978 0 00 717427 0

What's next?

Tell us the name of an author you love

Barbara Erskine   Go ▶

and we'll find your next great book.